Dick Francis has written forty-one international best-sellers and is widely acclaimed as one of the world's finest thriller writers. His awards include the Crime Writers' Association's Cartier Diamond Dagger for his outstanding contribution to the crime genre, and an honorary Doctorate of Humane Letters from Tufts University of Boston. In 1996 Dick Francis was made a Mystery Writers of America Grand Master for a lifetime's achievement, and in 2000 he received a CBE in the Queen's Birthday Honours list.

Dick Francis Omnibus One

LONGSHOT
STRAIGHT
HIGH STAKES

PAN BOOKS

Longshot first published 1990 by Michael Joseph Ltd
and published by Pan Books in 1991
Straight first published 1989 by Michael Joseph Ltd
and published by Pan Books in 1990
High Stakes first published 1975 by Michael Joseph Ltd
and published by Pan Books in 1997

This combined edition published 1999 by Pan Books
an imprint of Pan Macmillan Ltd
Pan Macmillan, 20 New Wharf Road, London N1 9RR
Basingstoke and Oxford
Associated companies throughout the world
www.panmacmillan.com

ISBN 0 330 39368 5

7 9 8 6

A CIP catalogue record for this book is available from
the British Library.

Phototypeset by Intype London Ltd
Printed and bound in Great Britain by
Mackays of Chatham plc, Chatham, Kent

LONGSHOT

With love to

JOCELYN
MATTHEW
BIANCA
TIMOTHY
WILLIAM

Our grandchildren

and acknowledgements to

The SAS Survival Handbook
by John Wiseman

and

No Need To Die
by Eddic McGee

CHAPTER ONE

I accepted a commission that had been turned down by four other writers, but I was hungry at the time.

Although starving in a garret had seemed a feasible enough plan a year earlier, the present realities of existence under the frozen eaves of a friend's aunt's house in a snowy January were such that without enough income to keep well fed and warm I was a knockover for a risky decision.

My state, of course, was my own fault. I could easily have gone out looking for paid muscular employment. I didn't have to sit shivering in a ski-suit biting the end of a pencil, hunched over a notebook, unsure of myself, of my ability and of the illuminations crashing about my head.

The spartan discomfort was not, either, a self-pitying morass of abject failure, but more the arctic doldrums between the high elation of the recent acceptance of my first novel for publication and the distant date of its launch into literary orbit. This was the downside after the heady receipt of the first advance payment and its division into past debts, present expenses and six months' future rent.

Give it two years, I'd thought, kissing farewell to the security of a salary: if I can't get published in two years I'll admit that the compulsion to write fiction is fools' gold and settle for common sense. Tossing away the pay-cheques had been a fairly desperate step, but I'd tried writing before work and after, in trains and at weekends, and had produced only dust. A stretch of no-excuse solitude, I'd thought, would settle things one way or another. Incipient hypothermia wasn't in any way diminishing the intense happiness of having put my toe into the first crack of the rock face.

I did as it happened know quite a lot about survival in adverse circumstances and the prospect of lean times hadn't worried me. I'd rather looked forward to them as a test of ingenuity. I just hadn't realised that sitting and thinking in itself made one cold. I hadn't known that a busy brain sneakily stole warmth from inactive hands and feet. In every freezing configuration I'd lived through before, I'd been moving.

The letter from Ronnie Curzon came on a particularly cold morning when there was ice like a half-descended curtain over the inside of my friend's aunt's attic window. The window, with its high view over the Thames at Chiswick, over the ebb-tide mud and the wind-sailing seagulls, that window, my delight, had done most, I reckoned, to release invention into words. I'd rigged a chair onto a platform so that I could sit there to write with a long view to the tree-chopped horizon over Kew Gardens. I'd never yet managed an even passable sentence when faced with a blank wall.

'Dear John,' the letter said.
'Care to drop into the office? There's been a suggestion about American rights in your book. You might be interested. I think we might discuss it, anyway.

Yours ever, Ronnie.
Why can't you have a telephone like everyone else?'

American rights! Incredible words.

The day warmed up miraculously. American rights were things that happened to successful authors, not to people struggling in an unfamiliar landscape, afflicted by self-doubts and insecurities, with a need to be told over and over that the book is OK, it's OK, don't worry so much.

'Don't worry,' Ronnie had said heartily, summoning me to his presence after reading the manuscript I'd dumped unheralded on his desk a couple of weeks earlier. 'Don't worry, I'm sure we can find you a publisher. Leave it to me. Let me see what I can do.'

Ronnie Curzon, authors' agent, with his salesman's subtle tongue, had indeed found me a publisher, a house more prestigious than I would have aimed for.

'They have a large list,' Ronnie explained kindly. 'They can afford to take a risk on a few first-timers,

7

though it's all much harder than it used to be.' He sighed. 'The tyrannical bottom line and so on. Still,' he beamed, 'they've asked you to lunch to get acquainted. Look to the bright side.'

I'd grown used to Ronnie's fast swings to pessimism and back. He'd told me in the same breath that I'd sell two thousand copies if I was very lucky indeed, and that a certain lady novelist counted her paperbacks in millions.

'Everything's possible,' he said, encouragingly.

'Including falling flat on one's face?' I asked.

'Don't worry so much.'

On the day of the American rights letter I walked as usual from the friend's aunt's house to Ronnie's office four miles away in Kensington High Street and, as I'd learned a thing or two by that time, I went not precipitously as soon as possible but later in the morning, so as to arrive at noon. Shortly after that hour, I'd discovered, Ronnie tended to offer wine to his visitors and to send out for sandwiches. I hadn't told him much about my reduced domestic arrangements; he was naturally and spontaneously generous.

I misjudged things to the extent that the door of his own room was firmly shut, where normally it stood open.

'He's with another client,' Daisy said.

Daisy smiled easily, an unusual virtue in a receptionist. Big white teeth in a black face. Wild hair. A neat Oxford accent. Going to night school for Italian classes.

'I'll let him know you're here,' she said, lifting her telephone, pressing a button and consulting with her boss.

'He wants you to wait,' she reported, and I nodded and passed some time with patience on one of the two semi-comfortable chairs arranged for the purpose.

Ronnie's suite of offices consisted of a large outer room, partly furnished by the desks of Daisy and her sister Alice, who kept the firm's complicated accounts, and partly by a wall of box-files on shelves and a large central table scattered with published books. Down a passage from the big room lay on one side the doors to three private offices (two housing Ronnie's associates) and on the other the entrance into a windowless store like a library, where from floor to ceiling were ranked copies of all the books that Ronnie and his father before him had nursed to birth.

I spent the time in the outer room looking at a framed corkboard on which were pinned the dust jackets of the crop still in the shops, wondering yet again what my own baby would looked like. First-time authors, it seemed, were allowed little input in the design department.

'Trust the professionals,' Ronnie had said comfortingly. 'After all, they know what will sell books.'

I'd thought cynically that sometimes you'd never guess. All I could do, though, was hope.

Ronnie's door opened and out came his head, his neck and a section of shoulder.

'John? Come along in.'

I went down to his room which contained his desk, his swivelling armchair, two guest chairs, a cupboard and roughly a thousand books.

'Sorry to keep you,' he said.

He was as expansively apologetic as if I'd had a definite appointment and waved me into his office with every appearance of being delighted by my presence. He showed the same manner to everyone. A very successful agent, Ronnie.

He was rounded and enthusiastic. Cuddly was almost the word. Short, with smooth dark hair and soft dry hands, wearing always a business suit over a white shirt and a striped tie. Authors, his presentation seemed to say, could turn up if they pleased in pale blue and red ski-suits and snow-defeating moon-boots, but serious business took place in sober worsted.

'A cold day,' he said, eyeing my clothes forgivingly.

'The slush in the gutters has frozen solid.'

He nodded, only half listening, his eyes on his other client who had remained settled in his chair as if there for the day. It seemed to me that Ronnie was stifling exasperation under a façade of aplomb, a surprising configuration when what he usually showed was unflagging, effortless bonhomie.

'Tremayne,' he was saying jovially to his guest, 'this is John Kendall, a brilliant young author.'

As Ronnie regularly described all his authors as brilliant, even with plentiful evidence to the contrary, I remained unembarrassed.

Tremayne was equally unimpressed. Tremayne, sixty-ish, grey-haired, big and self-assured was clearly not pleased at the interruption.

'We haven't finished our business,' he said ungraciously.

'Time for a glass of wine,' Ronnie suggested, ignoring the complaint. 'For you, Tremayne?'

'Gin and tonic.'

'Ah . . . I meant, white wine or red?'

After a pause, Tremayne said with a show of annoyed resignation, 'Red, then.'

'Tremayne Vickers,' Ronnie said to me non-committally, completing the introduction. 'Red do you, John?'

'Great.'

Ronnie bustled about, moving heaps of books and papers, clearing spaces, producing glasses, bottle and corkscrew and presently pouring with concentration.

'To trade,' he said with a smile, handing me a glass. 'To success,' he said to Vickers.

'Success! What success? All these writers are too big for their boots.'

Ronnie glanced involuntarily at my own boots, which were big enough for anyone.

'It's no use you telling me I'm not offering a decent fee,' Tremayne told him. 'They ought to be glad of the work.' He eyed me briefly and asked me without tact, 'What do you earn in a year?'

11

I smiled as blandly as Ronnie and didn't answer.

'How much do you know about racing?' he demanded.

'Horse racing?' I asked.

'Of course horse racing.'

'Well,' I said. 'Not a lot.'

'Tremayne,' Ronnie protested, 'John isn't your sort of writer.'

'A writer's a writer. Anyone can do it. You tell me I've been wrong looking for a big name. Very well then, find me a smaller name. You said your friend here is brilliant. So how about *him*?'

'Ah,' Ronnie said cautiously. 'Brilliant is just . . . ah . . . a figure of speech. He's inquisitive, capable and impulsive.'

I smiled at my agent with amusement.

'So he's *not* brilliant?' Tremayne asked ironically, and to me he said, 'What have you written, then?'

I answered obligingly, 'Six travel guides and a novel.'

'Travel guides? What sort of travel guides?'

'How to live in the jungle. Or in the Arctic. Or in deserts. That sort of thing.'

'For people who like difficult holidays,' Ronnie said, with all the indulgent irony of those devoted to comfort. 'John used to work for a travel agency which specialises in sending the intrepid out to be stretched.'

'Oh.' Tremayne looked at his wine without enthusiasm and after a while said testily, 'There must be someone who'd leap at the job.'

I said, more to make conversation than out of urgent curiosity, 'What is it that you want written?'

Ronnie made a gesture that seemed to say 'Don't ask', but Tremayne answered straightforwardly.

'An account of my life.'

I blinked. Ronnie's eyebrows rose and fell.

Tremayne said, 'You'd think those race-writing johnnies would be falling over themselves for the honour, but they've all turned me down.' He sounded aggrieved. 'Four of them.'

He recited their names, and such was their eminence that even I, who seldom paid much attention to racing, had heard of them all. I glanced at Ronnie, who showed resignation.

'There must be others,' I said mildly.

'There's some I wouldn't let set foot through my door.' The truculence in Tremayne's voice was one of the reasons, I reflected, why he was having trouble. I lost interest in him, and Ronnie, seeing it, cheered up several notches and suggested sandwiches for lunch.

'I hoped you'd be lunching me at your club,' Tremayne said grouchily, and Ronnie said vaguely 'Work' with a flap of the hand to indicate the papers on his desk. 'I mostly have lunch on the run, these days.'

He went over to the door and put the same section of himself through it as before.

'Daisy?' He called to her along the passage. 'Phone down to the shop for sandwiches, would you? Usual

13

selection. Everyone welcome. Count heads, would you? Three of us here.'

He brought himself in again without more discussion. Tremayne went on looking disgruntled and I drank my wine with gratitude.

It was warm in Ronnie's office. That, too, was a bonus. I took off the jacket of the ski-suit, hung it over a chair back and sat down contentedly in the scarlet sweater I wore underneath. Ronnie winced as usual over the brightness of my clothes but in fact I felt warmer in red, and I never discounted the psychology of colours. Those of my travel-agency friends who dressed in army olive-browns were colonels at heart.

Tremayne went on niggling away at his frustration, not seeming to mind if I learned his business.

'I offered to have them stay,' he complained. 'Can't do fairer than that. They all said the sales wouldn't be worth the work, not at the rate I was offering. Arrogant lot of bastards.' He gloomily drank and made a face over the taste. 'My name alone would sell the book, I told them, and they had the gall to disagree. Ronnie says it's a small market.' He glowered at my agent. 'Ronnie says that he can't get the book commissioned by a publisher without a top-rank writer, and maybe not even then, and that no top-rank writer will touch it without a commission. See where that gets me?'

He seemed to expect an answer, so I shook my head.

'It gets me into what they call vanity publishing. Vanity! Bloody insult. Ronnie says there are companies that will print and bind any book you give them, but *you* have to pay *them*. Then I'd also have to pay someone to write the book. Then I'd also have to sell the book myself, as I would be my own publisher, and Ronnie says there's no way I'd sell enough to cover the costs, let alone make a profit. He says that's why no regular publisher will take the book. Not enough sales. And I ask you, why not? Why not, eh?'

I shook my head again. He seemed to think I should know who he was, that everyone should. I hardly liked to say I'd never heard of him.

He partially enlightened me. 'After all,' he said, 'I've trained getting on for a thousand winners. The Grand National, two Champion Hurdles, a Gold Cup, the Whitbread, you name it. I've seen half a century of racing. There's stories in all of it. Childhood . . . growing up . . . success . . . My life has been *interesting*, dammit.'

Words temporarily failed him, and I thought that everyone's life was interesting to themselves, tragedies and all. Everyone had a story to tell: the trouble lay in the few who wanted to read it, the fewer still who were ready to pay for the privilege.

Ronnie soothingly refilled the glasses and gave us a regretful summary of the state of the book trade, which was in one of its periodical downswings on account of current high interest rates and their adverse effects on mortgage payments.

'It's the people with mortgages who usually buy books,' he said. 'Don't ask me why. For every mortgage

15

there are five people saving into the building societies, and when interest rates are high *their* incomes go up. They've more money to spend, but they just don't seem to buy books with it.'

Tremayne and I looked blank over this piece of sociology, and Ronnie further told us, without noticeably cheering us up, that for a publisher in the modern world turnover was all very well but losses weren't, and that it was getting more and more difficult to get a marginal book accepted.

I felt more grateful than ever that he'd got one particular marginal book accepted, and remembered what the lady from the publisher's had said when she'd taken me for the getting-acquainted lunch.

'Ronnie could sweet-talk the devil. He says we need to catch new authors like you in their early thirties, otherwise we won't have any big names ten years from now. No one knows yet how you'll turn out in ten years. Ronnie says that all salmon are small fry to begin with. So we're not promising you the world, but an opportunity, yes.'

An opportunity was all one could ask, I thought.

Daisy at length appeared in the doorway to say the food had arrived, and we all went along to the big room where the central table had been cleared of books and relaid with plates, knives, napkins and two large platters of healthy-looking sandwiches decorated with a drizzle of cress.

Ronnie's associates emerged from their rooms to join

us, which made seven altogether, including Daisy and her sister, and I managed to eat a lot without, I hoped, it being noticeable. Fillings of beef, ham, cheese, bacon: once-ordinary things that had become luxuries lately. Free lunch, breakfast and dinner. I wished Ronnie would write summoning notes more often.

Tremayne harangued me again over the generic shortcomings of racing writers, holding his glass in one hand and waving a sandwich in the other as he made his indignant points, while I nodded in sympathetic silence and munched away as if listening carefully.

Tremayne made a great outward show of forceful self-confidence, but there was something in his insistence which curiously belied it. It was almost as if he needed the book to be written to prove he had lived; as if photographs and records weren't enough.

'How old are you?' he said abruptly, breaking off in mid flow.

I said with my mouth full, 'Thirty-two.'

'You look younger.'

I didn't know whether 'good' or 'sorry' was appropriate, so I merely smiled and went on eating.

'Could you write a biography?' Again the abruptness.

'I don't know. Never tried.'

'I'd do it myself,' he said belligerently, 'but I haven't got time.'

I nodded understandingly. If there was one biography I didn't want to cut my teeth on, I thought, it was his. Much too difficult.

Ronnie fetched up beside him and wheeled him away, and in between finishing the beef-and-chutney and listening to Daisy's problems with scrambled software I watched Ronnie across the room nodding his head placatingly under Tremayne's barrage of complaints. Eventually, when all that was left on the plates were a few pallidly wilting threads of cress, Ronnie said a firm farewell to Tremayne, who still didn't want to go.

'There's nothing I can usefully offer at the moment,' Ronnie was saying, shaking an unresponsive hand and practically pushing Tremayne doorwards with a friendly clasp on his shoulder. 'But leave it to me. I'll see what I can do. Keep in touch.'

With ill grace Tremayne finally left, and without any hint of relief Ronnie said to me, 'Come along then, John. Sorry to have kept you all this time,' and led the way back to his room.

'Tremayne asked if I'd ever written a biography,' I said, taking my former place on the visitors' side of the desk.

Ronnie gave me a swift glance, settling himself into his own padded dark green leather chair and swivelling gently from side to side as if in indecision. Finally he came to a stop and asked, 'Did he offer you the job?'

'Not exactly.'

'My advice to you would be not to think of it.' He gave me no time to assure him that I wouldn't, and went straight on, 'It's fair to say he's a good racehorse trainer, well known in his own field. It's fair to say he's a better man than you would have guessed today. It's even fair to agree he's had an interesting life. But that isn't enough. It all depends on the writing.' He paused and sighed. 'Tremayne doesn't really believe that. He wants a big name because of the prestige, but you heard him, he thinks anyone can write. He doesn't really know the difference.'

'Will you find him someone?' I asked.

'Not on the terms he's looking for.' Ronnie considered things. 'I suppose I can tell you,' he said, 'as he made an approach to you. He's asking for a writer to stay in his house for at least a month, to go through all his cuttings and records and interview him in depth. None of the top names will do that, they've all got other lives to lead. Then he wants seventy per cent of royalty income which isn't going to amount to much in any case. No top writer is going to work for thirty per cent.'

'Thirty per cent ... including the advance?'

'Right. An advance no bigger than yours, if I could get one at all.'

'That's starvation.'

Ronnie smiled. 'Comparatively few people live by writing alone. I thought you knew that. Anyway,' he leaned forward, dismissing Tremayne and saying more briskly, 'about these American rights ...'

It seemed that a New York literary agent, an occasional associate of Ronnie's, had asked my publishers routinely whether they had anything of interest in the pipeline. They had steered him back to Ronnie. Would I, Ronnie asked, care to have him send a copy of my manuscript to the American agent, who would then, if he thought the book saleable in the American market, try to find it an American publisher.

I managed to keep my mouth shut but was gaping and gasping inside.

'Well?' Ronnie said.

'I . . . er . . . I'd be delighted,' I said.

'Thought you would. Not promising anything, you realise. He's just taking a look.'

'Yes.'

'If you remember, we gave your publisher here only British and Commonwealth rights. That leaves us elbowroom to manoeuvre.' He went on for a while discussing technicalities and possibilities his pendulum way. I was left with a feeling that things might be going to happen but on the other hand probably not. The market was down, everything was difficult, but the publishing machine needed constant fodder and my book might be regarded as a bundle of hay. He would let me know, he said, as soon as he got an opinion back from the New York agent.

'How's the new book coming along?' he asked.

'Slowly.'

He nodded. 'The second one's always difficult. But just keep going.'

'Yes.'

He rose to his feet, looking apologetically at his waiting paperwork, shaking my hand warmly in farewell. I thanked him for the lunch. Any time, he said automatically, his mind already on his next task, and I left him and walked along the passage, stopping at Daisy's desk on the way out.

'You're sending my manuscript to America,' I said, zipping up my jacket and bursting to tell someone, anyone, the good news.

'Yes,' she beamed. 'I posted it last Friday.'

'Did you indeed!'

I went on out to the lift not sure whether to laugh or be vaguely annoyed at Ronnie's asking permission for something he had already done. I wouldn't have minded at all if he'd simply told me he'd sent the book off. It was his job to do the best for me that he could; I would have thought it well within his rights.

I went down two floors and out into the bitter afternoon air thinking of the steps that had led to his door.

Finishing the book had been one thing, finding a publisher another. The six small books I'd previously written, though published and on sale to the public, had all been part of my work for the travel firm who had paid me pretty well for writing them besides sending me to far-flung places to gather the knowledge. The travel firm owned the guides and published them themselves, and they weren't in the market for novels.

I'd taken my precious typescript personally to a small but well-known publisher (looking up the address in the phone book) and had handed it to a pretty girl there who said she would put it in the slush pile and get round to it in due course.

The slush pile, she explained, showing dimples, was what they called the heap of unsolicited manuscripts that dropped through their letter-box day by day. She would read my book while she commuted. I could return for her opinion in three weeks.

Three weeks later, the dimples still in place, she told me my book wasn't really 'their sort of thing', which was mainly 'serious literature', it seemed. She suggested I should take it to an agent, who would know where to place it. She gave me a list of names and addresses.

'Try one of those,' she said. 'I enjoyed the book very much. Good luck with it.'

I tried Ronnie Curzon for no better reason than I'd known where to find his office, as Kensington High Street lay on my direct walk home. Impulse had led to good and bad all my life, but when I felt it strongly, I usually followed it. Ronnie had been good. Opting for poverty had been so-so. Accepting Tremayne's offer was the pits.

CHAPTER TWO

As I walked back to Chiswick from Ronnie's office, I hadn't the slightest intention of ever meeting Tremayne Vickers again. I forgot him. I thought of the present book I was writing: especially of how to get one character down from a runaway, experimental helium-filled balloon with its air pumps out of order. I had doubts about the balloon. Maybe I'd rethink the whole thing. Maybe I'd scrap what I'd done and start again. The character in the balloon was shitting himself with fear. I thought I knew how he felt. The chief unexpected thing I'd learned from writing fiction was fear of getting it wrong.

The book that had been accepted, which was called *Long Way Home*, was about survival in general and in particular about the survival, physical and mental, of a bunch of people isolated by a disaster. Hardly an original theme, but I'd followed the basic advice to write about something I knew, and survival was what I knew best.

In the interest of continuing to survive for another

week or ten days, I stopped at the supermarket nearest to the friend's aunt's house and spent my food allotment on enough provisions for the purpose: bunch of packet soups, loaf of bread, box of spaghetti, box of porridge oats, pint of milk, a cauliflower and some carrots. I would eat the vegetables raw whenever I felt like it, and otherwise enjoy soup with bread in it, soup on spaghetti and porridge with milk. Items like tea, Marmite and salt cropped up occasionally. Crumpets and butter came at scarce intervals when I could no longer resist them. Apart from all that I bought once a month a bottle of vitamin pills to stuff me full of any oddments I might be missing and, dull though it might seem and in spite of frequent hunger, I had stayed in resounding good health all along.

I opened the front door with my latchkey and met the friend's aunt in the hall.

'Hello, dear,' she said. 'Everything all right?'

I told her about Ronnie sending my book to America and her thin face filled with genuine pleasure. She was roughly fifty, divorced, a grandmother, sweet, fair-haired, undemanding and boring. I understood that she regarded the rent I paid her (a fifth of what I had had to fork out for my former flat) as more a bribe to get her to let a stranger into her house than as an essential part of her income. In addition, though, she had agreed I could put milk in her fridge, wash my dishes in her sink, shower in her bathroom and use her washer-drier once a week. I wasn't to make a noise or ask anyone in. We had settled these details amicably. She had installed a coin-in-the-slot electric meter for me, and approved a toaster, a kettle, a tiny table-top cooker and new plugs for a television and a razor.

I'd been introduced to her as 'Aunty' and that's what I called her, and she seemed to regard me as a sort of extension nephew. We had lived for ten months in harmony, our lives adjacent but uninvolved.

'It's very cold . . . are you warm enough up there?' she asked kindly.

'Yes, thank you,' I said. The electric heater ate money. I almost never switched it on.

'These old houses . . . very cold under the roofs.'

'I'm fine,' I said.

She said, 'Good, dear,' amiably, and we nodded to each other, and I went upstairs thinking that I'd lived in the Artic Circle and if I hadn't been able to deal with a cold London attic I would have been ashamed of myself. I wore silk jersey long-sleeved vests and long johns under sweaters and jeans under the ski-suit, and I slept warmly in a sleeping bag designed for the North Pole. It was writing that made me cold.

Up in my eyrie I struggled for a couple of hours to resolve the plight of the helium balloon but ended with only a speculation on nerve pathways. Why didn't terror make one *deaf*, for instance? How did it always beeline to the bowel? My man in the balloon didn't know and was too miserable to care. I thought I'd have to invent a range of mountains dead ahead for him to come to grief on. Then he would merely have the problem of descending from an Everest-approximation with only fingers, toes and resolution. Much easier. I knew a tip or two about that, the first being to look for the longest way down because it would be the least steep. Sharp-faced mountains often had sloping backs.

My attic, once the retreat of the youngest of Aunty's daughters, had a worn pink carpet and cream wallpaper sprigged with pink roses. The resident furniture of bed, chest of drawers, tiny wardrobe, two chairs and a table was overwhelmed by a veritable army of crates, boxes and suitcases containing my collected worldly possessions: clothes, books, household goods and sports equipment, all top quality and in good shape, acquired in carefree bygone affluence. Two pairs of expensive skis stood in their covers in a corner. Wildly extravagant cameras and lenses rested in dark foam beds. I kept in working order a windproof, sandproof, bugproof tent which self-erected in seconds and weighed only three pounds. I checked also climbing gear and a camcorder from time to time. A word processor with a laser printer, which I still used, was wrapped most of the time in sheeting. My helicopter pilot's licence lay in a drawer, automatically expired now since I hadn't flown for a year. A life on hold, I thought. A life suspended.

I thought occasionally that I could eat better if I sold something, but I'd never get back what I'd paid for the skis, for instance, and it seemed stupid to cannibalise things that had given me pleasure. They were mostly the tools of my past trade, anyway, and I might need them again. They were my safety net. The travel firm had said they would take me back once I'd got this foolishness out of my system.

If I'd known I was going to do what I was doing I would have planned and saved a lot more in advance, perhaps: but between the final irresistible impulse and its execution there had been only about six weeks. The vague intention had been around a lot longer; for most of my life.

Helium balloon . . .

The second half of the advance on *Long Way Home* wasn't due until publication day, a whole long year ahead. My small weekly allotted parcels of money wouldn't last that long, and I didn't see how I could live on much less. My rent-in-advance would run out at the end of June. If, I thought, if I could finish this balloon lark by then and if it were accepted and if they paid the same advance as before, then maybe I'd just manage the full two years. Then if the books fell with a dull thud, I'd give up and go back to the easier rigours of the wild.

That night the air temperature over London plummeted still further, and in the morning Aunty's house was frozen solid.

'There's no water,' she said in distress when I went

downstairs. 'The central heating stopped and all the pipes have frozen. I've called the plumber. He says everyone's in the same boat and just to switch everything off. He can't do anything until it thaws, then he'll come to fix any leaks.' She looked at me helplessly. 'I'm very sorry, dear, but I'm going to stay in a hotel until this is over. I'm going to close the house. Can you find somewhere else for a week or two? Of course I'll add the time on to your six months, you won't lose by it, dear.'

Dismay was a small word for what I felt. I helped her close all the stopcocks I could find and made sure she had switched off her water heaters, and in return she let me use her telephone to look for another roof.

I got through to her nephew, who still worked for the travel firm.

'Do you have any more aunts?' I enquired.

'Good God, what have you done with that one?'

I explained. 'Could you lend me six feet of floor to unroll my bedding on?'

'Why don't you gladden the life of your parents on that Caribbean island?'

'Small matter of the fare.'

'You can come for a night or two if you're desperate,' he said. 'But Wanda's moved in with me, and you know how tiny the flat is.'

I also didn't much like Wanda. I thanked him and said I would let him know, and racked my brains for somewhere else.

It was inevitable I should think of Tremayne Vickers.

I phoned Ronnie Curzon and put it to him straight. 'Can you sell me to that racehorse trainer?'

'What?'

'He was offering free board and lodging.'

'Take me through it one step at a time.'

I took him through it and he was all against it.

'Much better to get on with your new book.'

'Mm,' I said. 'The higher a helium balloon rises the thinner the air is and the lower the pressure, so the helium balloon expands, and goes on rising and expanding until it bursts.'

'*What*?'

'It's too cold to invent stories. Do you think I could do what Tremayne wants?'

'You could probably do a workmanlike job.'

'How long would it take?'

'Don't do it,' he said.

'Tell him I'm brilliant after all and can start at once.'

'You're mad.'

'I might as well learn about racing. Why not? I might use it in a book. And I can ride. Tell him that.'

'Impulse will kill you one of these days.'

I should have listened to him, but I didn't.

I was never sure exactly what Ronnie said to Tremayne, but when I phoned again at noon he was mournfully triumphant.

'Tremayne agreed you can write his book. He quite took to you yesterday, it seems.' Pessimism vibrated down the wire. 'He's agreed to guarantee you a writing fee.' Ronnie mentioned a sum which would keep me eating through the summer. 'It's payable in three instalments – a quarter after a month's work, a quarter when he approves the full manuscript, and half on publication. If I can get a regular publisher to take it on, the publisher will pay you, otherwise Tremayne will. He's agreed you should have forty per cent of any royalties after, not thirty. He's agreed to pay your expenses while you research his life. That means if you want to go to interview people who know him he'll pay for your transport. That's quite a good concession, actually. He thinks it's odd that you haven't a car, but I reminded him that people who live in London often don't. He says you can drive one of his. He was pleased you can ride. He says you should take riding clothes with you and also a dinner jacket, as he's to be guest of honour at some dinner or other and he wants you to witness it. I told him you were an expert photographer so he wants you to take your camera.'

Ronnie's absolute and audible lack of enthusiasm for the project might have made me withdraw even then had Aunty not earlier given me a three o'clock deadline for leaving the house.

'When does Tremayne expect me?' I asked Ronnie.

'He seems pathetically pleased that anyone wants to take him on, after the top men turned him down. He says he'd be happy for you to go as soon as you can. Today, even, he said. Will you go today?'

'Yes,' I said.

'He lives in a village called Shellerton, in Berkshire. He says if you can phone to say what train you're catching, someone will meet you at Reading station. Here's the number.' He read it out to me.

'Fine,' I said. 'And Ronnie, thanks very much.'

'Don't thank me. Just . . . well, just write a brilliant chapter or two and I'll try to get the book commissioned on the strength of them. But go on writing fiction. That's where your future is.'

'Do you mean it?'

'Of course, I mean it.' He sounded surprised I should ask. 'For someone who's not afraid of jungles you exhibit the strangest self-confidence deficiency.'

'I know where I am in jungles.'

'Go and catch your train,' he said, and wished me luck.

I caught, instead, a bus, as it was much cheaper, and was met outside the Reading bus station by a shivering young woman in a padded coat and woollen hat who visually checked me over from boots six feet up via ski-suit to dark hair and came to the conclusion that I was, as she put it, the writer.

'You're the writer?' She was positive, used to authority, not unfriendly.

'John Kendall,' I said, nodding.

'I'm Mackie Vickers. That's m, a, c, k, i, e,' she spelled. 'Not Maggie. Your bus is late.'

'The roads are bad,' I said apologetically.

'They're worse in the country.' It was dark and extremely cold. She led the way to a chunky jeep-like vehicle parked not far away and opened the rear door. 'Put your bags in here. You can meet everyone as we go along.'

There were already four people in the vehicle, it seemed, all cold and relieved I had finally turned up. I stowed my belongings and climbed in, sharing the back seat with two dimly seen figures who moved up to give me room. Mackie Vickers positioned herself behind the wheel, started the engine, released the brake and drove out into a stream of cars. A welcome trickle of hot air came out of the heater.

'The writer says his name is John Kendall,' Mackie said to the world in general.

There wasn't much reaction to the introduction.

'You're sitting next to Tremayne's head lad,' she went on, 'and his wife is beside him.'

The shadowy man next to me said, 'Bob Watson.' His wife said nothing.

'In front,' Mackie said, 'next to me, are Fiona and Harry Goodhaven.'

Neither Fiona nor Harry said anything. There was an intense quality in the collective atmosphere that dried up any conversational remark I might have thought of making, and it had little to do with temperature. It was as if the very air were scowling.

Mackie drove for several minutes in continuing silence, concentrating on the slush-lined surface under the yellowish lights of the main road west out of Reading. The traffic was heavy and slow moving, the ill-named rush hour crawling along with flashing scarlet brake lights, a procession of curses.

Eventually Mackie said to me, turning her head over her shoulder as I was sitting directly behind her, 'We're not good company. We've spent all day in court. Tempers are frayed. You'll just have to put up with it.'

'No trouble,' I said.

Trouble was the wrong word to use, it seemed.

As if releasing tension Fiona said loudly, 'I can't *believe* you were so stupid.'

'Give it a rest,' Harry said. He'd already heard it before.

'But you know damned well that Lewis was drunk.'

'That doesn't excuse anything.'

'It *explains* things. You know damned well he was drunk.'

'Everyone *says* he was drunk,' Harry said, sounding heavily reasonable, 'but I don't *know* it, do I? I didn't *see* him drinking too much.'

Bob Watson beside me said 'Liar' on a whispered breath, and Harry didn't hear.

'Nolan is going to *prison*,' Fiona said bitterly. 'Do you realise? *Prison*. All because of you.'

33

'You don't *know* he is,' Harry complained. 'The jury haven't found him guilty yet.'

'But they *will*, won't they? And it will be *your fault*. Dammit, you were under *oath*. All you had to do was say Lewis was drunk. Now the jury thinks he wasn't drunk, so he must be able to remember everything. They think he's lying when he says he can't remember. Christ Almighty, Nolan's whole *defence* was that Lewis can't remember. How could you be so *stupid*?'

Harry didn't answer. The atmosphere if possible worsened, and I felt as if I'd gone into a movie halfway through and couldn't grasp the plot.

Mackie, without contributing any opinions, turned from the Great West Road onto the M4 motorway and made better time westwards along an unlit and uninhabited stretch between snow-covered wooded hills, ice crystals glittering in the headlights.

'*Bob* says Lewis was drunk,' Fiona persisted, 'and he should know, he was serving the drinks.'

'Then maybe the jury will believe Bob.'

'They believed him until you stood there and blew it.'

'They should have had *you* in the witness box,' Harry said defensively, 'then you could have sworn he was paralytic and had to be scraped off the carpet, even if you weren't there.'

Bob Watson said, 'He wasn't paralytic.'

'You keep out of it, Bob,' Harry snapped.

'Sorr-ee,' Bob Watson said, again under his breath.

'All you had to do was swear that Lewis was drunk.'

34

Fiona's voice rose with fury. 'That's *all* the defence called you for. Then you didn't say it. Nolan's lawyer could have killed you.'

Harry said wearily, '*You* didn't have to stand there answering that prosecutor's questions. You heard what he said, how did I know Lewis was drunk? Had I given him a breath test, a blood test, a urine test? On what did I base my judgment? Did I have any clinical experience? You heard him. On and on. How many drinks did I see Lewis take? How did I know what was in the drinks? Had I ever heard of Lewis having black-outs any other time after drinking?'

'That was disallowed,' Mackie said.

'You let that prosecutor tie you in *knots*. You looked absolutely *stupid* . . .' Fiona ran on and on, the rage in her mind unabating.

I began to feel mildly sorry for Harry.

We reached the Chieveley interchange and left the motorway to turn north on the big A34 to Oxford. Mackie had sensibly taken the cleared major roads rather than go over the hills, even though it was further that way, according to the map. I'd looked up the whereabouts of Tremayne's village on the theory that it was a wise man who knew his destination, especially when it was on the Berkshire Downs a mile from nowhere.

Silence had mercifully struck Fiona's tongue by the time Shellerton showed up on a signpost. Mackie slowed, signalled, and cautiously turned off the main road into a very narrow secondary road that was little more than a lane, where snow had been roughly pushed to the sides but still lay in shallow frozen brown ruts over much of the surface. The tyres scrunched on them, cracking the ice. Mist formed quickly on the inside of the windscreen and Mackie rubbed it away impatiently with her glove.

There were no houses beside the lane: it was well over a mile across bare downland, I found later, from the main road to the village. There were also no cars: no one was out driving if they could help it. For all Mackie's care one could sometimes feel the wheels sliding, losing traction for perilous seconds. The engine, engaged in low gear, whined laboriously up a shallow incline.

'It's worse than this morning,' Mackie said, sounding worried. 'This road's a skating rink.'

No one answered her. I was hoping, as I expect they all were, that we would reach the top of the slope without sliding backwards; and we did, only to see that the downside looked just as hazardous, if not more so. Mackie wiped the windscreen again and with extra care took a curve to the right.

Caught by the headlights, stock-still in the middle of the lane, stood a horse. A dark horse buckled into a dark rug, its head raised in alarm. There was the glimmer of sheen on its skin and luminescence in its wide eyes. The moment froze like the landscape.

'*Hell!*' Mackie exclaimed, and slammed her foot on the brake.

The vehicle slid inexorably on the ice and although Mackie released the brakes a moment later it did as much harm as good.

The horse, terrified, tried to plunge out of the lane into the field alongside. Intent on missing him, and at the same time fighting the skid, Mackie miscalculated the curve, the camber and the speed, though to be fair to her it would have taken a stunt driver to come out of there safely.

The jeep slid to the side of the lane, spun its wheels on the snow-covered grass verge, mounted it, ran along and across as if making for the open fields under its own volition and tipped over sideways into an unseen drainage ditch, cracking with noises like pistol shots through a covering sheet of ice.

We'd been going slowly enough for it not to be an instantly lethal crunch, though it was a bang hard enough to rattle one's teeth. The nearside wheels, both front and back, finished four feet lower than road level, the far side of the ditch supporting the length of the roof of the vehicle so that it lay not absolutely flat on its side. I was opening my door, which was half sloping skywards, and hauling myself out more or less before the engine had time to stall.

The downland wind, always on the move, stung my face sharply with a freezing warning. Wind-chill was an unforgiving enemy, deadly to the unwary.

Bob Watson had fallen on top of his wife. I reached down into the car and grasped him, and began to pull him out.

He tried to free himself from my hands, crying 'Ingrid' urgently, and then in horror, 'It's wet . . . she's in water.'

'Come out,' I said peremptorily. 'Then we can both pull her. Come out, you're heavy on her. You'll never get her out like that.'

Some vestige of sense got through to him and he let me yank him out far enough so that he could stretch back in for his wife. I held him and he held her, and between the two of us we brought her out onto the roadway.

The ditch was almost full of muddy freezing water under its coating of ice. Even as we lifted Ingrid out the water deepened fast in the vehicle, and in the front seat Fiona was yelling to Harry to get her out. Harry, I saw in horror, was underneath her and in danger of drowning.

The one headlight which had still been shining suddenly went out.

Mackie hadn't moved to save herself. I pulled open her door and found her dazed and semi-conscious, held in her place by her seat belt.

'Get us out,' Fiona yelled.

Harry, below her, was struggling in water and heaving, whether to save her or himself was impossible to tell. I felt round Mackie until I found the seat-belt clasp, released it, hauled her out bodily and shoved her into Bob Watson's arms.

'Sit her on the verge,' I said. 'Clear the snow off the grass. Hold her. Shield her from the wind.'

'Bob,' Ingrid said piteously, standing helplessly on the road and seeming to think her husband should attend to her alone, 'Bob, I need you. I feel awful.'

Bob glanced at his wife but took Mackie's weight and helped her to sit down. She began moving and moaning and asking what had happened, showing welcome signs of life.

No blood, I thought. Not a drop. Bloody lucky. My eyes became accustomed to the dark.

Fiona, halfway panic-stricken, put her arms up to mine and came out easily into the air, lithe and athletic. I let go of her and leaned in for Harry, who now had his seat belt unfastened and his head above water and had got past the stage of abject fright. He helped himself to climb out and went dripping over to Mackie, showing most concern for her, taking her support from Bob Watson.

Ingrid stood in the road, soaked, thin, frightened, helpless and crying. The wind was piercing, relentless . . . infinitely dangerous. It was easy to underestimate how fast cold could kill.

I said to Bob Watson, 'Take all your wife's clothes off.'

'*What*?'

'Take her wet clothes off or she'll freeze into a block of ice.'

He opened his mouth.

'Start at the top,' I said. 'Take everything off and put my ski jacket on her, quickly. It's warm.' I unzipped it and took it off, folding it together so as to keep the warmth of my body in it as much as possible. The cold bit through my sweater and undershirt as if they were invisible. I was infinitely grateful to be dry.

'I'll help Ingrid,' Fiona said, as Bob still hesitated. 'You don't mean her bra as well?'

'Yes, everything.'

While the two women unbuttoned and tugged I went to the rear of the overturned vehicle and found to my relief that the luggage door would still open. I pushed up my sleeves and literally fished out my two bags and Harry, close behind me, watched the water drip off them with gloom.

'Everything will be wet,' he said defeatedly.

'No.' Waterproof, sandproof, bugproof were the rules I travelled by, even in rural England. I found the aluminium camera case under the water and set it on the road beside the bags.

'Which would you prefer,' I asked Harry, 'bathrobe or dinner jacket?'

He actually laughed.

'Strip off,' I said, 'in case the ice-man cometh. Top half first.'

They had all been dressed for a day in court, not for

trudging about in the open. Even Mackie and Bob Watson, who were dry, hadn't enough on for the circumstances.

Bob Watson took over again with Mackie, and Harry began to struggle out of his sodden overcoat, business suit, shirt and tie, wincing with pain as the cold hit his wet flesh. His singlet was sticking to him. I gave him a hand.

'What did you say your name was?' he said, teeth clenched, shuddering.

'John.'

I handed him a navy blue silk undershirt and long johns, two sweaters, grey trousers and the bathrobe. No one ever dived into clothes faster. My shoes were a size too big, he ironically complained, hopping around and pulling them on over dry socks.

Fiona had changed Ingrid to the waist and was waiting to do the second half. I took off my boots and then my ski-pants, which Fiona put on Ingrid after trying to shield her brief lower nakedness from my eyes, which amazed me. It was hardly the time for fussing. The boots looked enormous, once they were on, and Ingrid was nine inches shorter than my ski-suit.

For myself I brought out a navy blazer and jodphur boots, feeling the ice strike up through wool to my toes.

'My feet are squelching,' Fiona said, eyeing the boots with strong shivers, 'and I'm wet to the neck. Is there anything left?'

'You'd better have these.'

'Well ... I ...' She looked at my bare socks, hesitating.

I thrust the boots and blazer into her hands. My black evening shoes, which were all that remained in the way of footwear, would have fallen off her at every step.

I dug into the bag again for jodphurs, black socks and a sweatshirt. 'These any good to you?' I asked.

She took all the clothes gratefully and hid behind Ingrid to change. I put on my black shoes and the dinner jacket: a lot better than nothing.

When Fiona reappeared, her shivers had grown to shakes. She still had too few layers, even if now dry. The only useful thing still unused in my belongings was the plastic bag which had contained my dinner jacket. I put it over Fiona's head, widening the hole where the hanger usually went, and, if she didn't care to be labelled 'Ace Cleaners' at intervals front and back, at least it stopped the wind a bit and kept some body heat in.

'Well,' Harry said with remarkable cheerfulness, eyeing the dimly seen final results of the motley redistribution, 'thanks to John we should live to see Shellerton. All you lot had better start walking. I'll stay with Mackie and we'll follow when we can.'

'No,' I said. 'How far is it to the village?'

'A mile or so.'

'Then we all start now. We'll carry Mackie. It's too cold, believe me, for hanging about. How about a chair lift?'

So Harry and I sat the semi-conscious Mackie on our linked wrists and draped her arms round our necks, and we set off towards the village with Bob Watson carrying all the wet clothes in one of my bags, Fiona carrying dry things in the other and Ingrid shuffling along in front in the moon-boots with my camera case, lighting the way with the dynamo torch from my basic travel kit.

'Squeeze it.' I showed her how. 'It doesn't have batteries. Shine it on the road, so we can all see.'

'Thank God it isn't snowing,' Harry said: but there were ominous clouds hiding the stars. What little natural light there was was amplified by the whiteness of the snow, the only good thing about it. I was glad it wasn't too far to the village. Mackie wasn't draggingly heavy, but we were walking on ice.

'Doesn't any traffic ever come along this road?' I asked in frustration when we'd gone half a mile and still seen no one.

'There are two other ways into Shellerton,' Harry said. 'God, this wind's the devil. My ears are dropping off.'

My own head also was achingly cold. Mackie and Fiona had woollen hats, Ingrid was warmest in the hood of my ski-suit, Bob Watson wore a cap. Ingrid had my gloves. Harry's hands and mine were going numb under Mackie's bottom. If I'd brought any more socks we could have used them as mitts.

'It's not far now,' Bob said. 'Once we're round the bend you'll see the village.'

He was right. Electricity twinkled not far below us, offering shelter and warmth. Let's not have a power cut, I prayed.

Mackie suddenly awoke to full consciousness on the last stretch and began demanding to know what was happening.

'We skidded into a ditch,' Harry said succinctly.

'The horse! Is the horse all right? Why are you carrying me? Put me down.'

We stopped and set her on her feet, where she swayed and put a hand to the side of her head.

'Did we hit the horse?' she said.

'No,' Harry answered. 'Better let us carry you.'

'What happened to the horse?'

'It buggered off across the Downs. Come on, Mackie, we're literally freezing to death standing here.' Harry swung his arms in my bathrobe, then hugged his body and tried to warm his hands in his armpits. 'Let's get on, for God's sake.'

Mackie refused to let us lift her up again so we began to struggle on towards the village, a shadowy band slipping and sliding downhill, holding on to each other and trying not to fall, cold to the bone. I should have brought the skis, I thought, and it seemed an extraordinarily long time since that morning.

One reason for the dearth of traffic became clear as we reached the first houses; two cars lay impacted across the width of the lane, and certainly nothing was leaving the village that way.

'You'd better all come to our house,' Fiona said in a shaking voice as we edged round the wreck. 'It's nearest.'

No one argued.

We turned into a long village street with no lighting, and passed a garage, darkly shut, and a pub, open.

'How about a quick one?' Harry suggested, half serious.

Fiona said with some of her former asperity, 'I should think you've heard enough about drink for one day. And you're not going anywhere dressed like that except straight home.'

It was too dark to see Harry's expression. No one cared to comment, and presently Ingrid with the torch turned into a driveway which wound round behind some cottages and opened into a snowy expanse in front of a big Georgian-looking house.

Ingrid stopped. Fiona said, 'This way,' and led a still silent procession round to a side door, which she unlocked with a key retrieved from under a stone.

The relief of being out of the wind was like a rebirth. The warmth of the extensive kitchen we filed into was a positive life-giving luxury; and there in the lights I saw my companions clearly for the first time.

CHAPTER THREE

Everyone except Ingrid was visibly trembling, John Kendall included. All the faces were bluish-white, suffering.

'God,' Fiona said, 'that was hell.'

She was older than I'd thought. Forties, not thirties. The Ace Cleaners bag reached nearly to her knees, covering her arms, bordering on the farcical.

'Take this damned thing off me,' she said. 'And don't bloody laugh.'

Harry obligingly pulled the cleaner's plastic bag up and over her head, taking her knitted hat with it, freeing heavy silver-blond hair and transforming her like a *coup de théâtre* from a refugee to an assured, charismatic woman in jodphurs and blue blazer with the turtle-neck sweatshirt showing white at throat and cuffs.

Although she was tall the sleeves were all too long for her; which had been a blessing, it seemed, as she had been able to tuck her hands inside them, using them as gloves. She stared at me across her kitchen, looking with curiosity at the man whose clothes she wore, seeing I supposed a tallish, thinnish, youngish brown-eyed person in jeans, scarlet sweater and incongruous dinner jacket.

I smiled at her and she, aware of the admiration in my expression, swept a reviving glance round her other unexpected guests and went over to the huge red Aga which warmed the whole place, lifting the lid, letting volumes of heat flow out. The bad temper of the journey had disappeared, revealing a sensible, competent woman.

'Hot drinks,' she said decisively. 'Harry, fill the kettle and get some mugs.'

Harry, my height but fair and blue-eyed, complied with the instructions as though thoroughly accustomed to being bidden, and began rootling round also for spoons, instant coffee and sugar. Swaddled in my blue bathrobe he looked ready for bed; and he too was older than I'd thought. He and Fiona were revealed as well off and perhaps rich. The kitchen was large, individual, a combination of technology and sitting-room, and the manner and voices of its owners had the unselfconscious assurance of comfortable social status.

Mackie sat down uncertainly at the big central table, her fingers gingerly feeling her temple.

'I was looking at the horse,' she said. 'Must have hit my head on the window. Is the jeep all right?'

'Shouldn't think so,' Harry said without emotion. 'It's lying in water which will be frozen over again by

47

morning. The door on my side buckled when we hit. Filthy ditch-water just rushed in.'

'Damn,' Mackie said wearily. 'That on top of everything else.'

She huddled into her fawn-coloured padded coat, still deeply shivering, and it was hard to tell what she would look like warm and laughing. All I could see were reddish curls over her forehead followed by closed eyes, pale lips and the rigid muscles of distress.

'Is Perkin home?' Fiona asked her.

'He should be. God, I hope so.'

Fiona, recovering faster than anyone else, perhaps because she was in her own house, went across to a wall telephone and pressed buttons. Perkin, whoever he was, apparently answered and was given a variety of bad news.

'Yes,' Fiona said repeating thing, 'I did say the jeep's in a ditch . . . it's in that hollow just over the top of the hill after you leave the A34 . . . I don't know whose horse, damn it . . . No, we had an *abysmal* day in court. Look, can you get down here and collect everyone? Mackie's all right but she hit her head . . . Bob Watson and his wife are with us . . . Yes, we did pick up the writer, he's here too. Just *come*, Perkin, for God's sake. Stop dithering.' She hung up the receiver with a crash.

Harry poured steaming water onto instant coffee in a row of mugs and then picked up a milk carton in one hand and a bottle of brandy in the other, offering a choice of additives. Everyone except Ingrid chose brandy, and Harry's idea of a decent slug cooled the liquid to drinking point.

Although if we had still been outside the alcohol wouldn't have been such a good idea, the deep trembles in all our bodies abated and faded away. Bob Watson took off his cap and looked suddenly younger, a short stocky man with wiry brown hair and a returning glint of independence. One could still see what he must have looked like as a schoolboy, with rounded cheeks and a natural insolence not far from the surface but controlled enough to keep him out of trouble. He had called Harry a liar, but too quietly for him to hear. That rather summed up Bob Watson, I thought.

Ingrid, swamped in the ski-suit, looked out at the world from a thinly pretty face and sniffed at regular intervals. She sat beside her husband at the table, unspeaking and forever in his shadow.

Standing with his backside propped against the Aga, Harry warmed both hands round his mug and looked at me with the glimmering amusement that, when not under stress from giving evidence, seemed to be his habitual cast of mind.

'Welcome to Berkshire,' he said.

'Thanks a lot.'

'I would have stayed by the jeep and waited for someone to come,' he said.

'I thought someone would,' I agreed.

Mackie said, 'I hope the horse is all right,' as if her mind were stuck in that groove. No one else, it seemed to me, cared an icicle for the survival of the cause of our woes; and I suspected, perhaps unfairly, that Mackie kept on about the horse so as to reinforce in our consciousness that the crash hadn't been her fault.

Warmth gradually returned internally also and everyone looked as if they had come up to room temperature, like wine. Ingrid pushed back the hood of my ski-suit jacket revealing soft mouse-brown hair in need of a brush.

No one had a great wish to talk, and there was something of a return to the pre-crash gloom, so it was a relief when wheels, slammed doors and approaching footsteps announced the arrival of Perkin.

He hadn't come alone. It was Tremayne Vickers who advanced first into the kitchen, his loud voice and large personality galvanising the subdued group drinking coffee.

'Got yourself into a load of shit, have you?' he boomed with a touch of not wholly unfriendly scorn. 'Roads too much for you, eh?'

Mackie went defensively into the horse routine as if she'd merely been rehearsing earlier.

The man who followed Tremayne through the door looked like a smudged carbon copy: same height, same build, same basic features, but none of Tremayne's bullishness. If that was Perkin, I thought, he must be Tremayne's son.

The carbon copy said to Mackie crossly, 'Why didn't

you go round the long way? You ought to have more sense than to take that short cut.'

'It was all right this morning,' Mackie said, 'and I always go that way. It was the horse . . .'

Tremayne's gaze fastened on me. 'So you got here. Good. You've met everyone? My son, Perkin. His wife, Mackie.'

I'd assumed, I realised, that Mackie had been either Tremayne's own wife or perhaps his daughter; hadn't thought of daughter-in-law.

'Why on earth are you wearing a dinner jacket?' Tremayne asked, staring.

'We got wet in the ditch,' Harry said briefly. 'Your friend the writer lent us dry clothes. He issued his dinner jacket to himself. Didn't trust me with it, smart fellow. What I've got on is his bathrobe. Ingrid has his ski-suit. Fiona is his from head to foot.'

Tremayne looked briefly bewildered but decided not to sort things out. Instead he asked Fiona if she'd been hurt in the crash. 'Fiona, my dear . . .'

Fiona, his dear, assured him otherwise. He behaved to her with a hint of roguishness, she to him with easy response. She aroused in all men, I supposed, the desire to flirt.

Perkin belatedly asked Mackie about her head, awkwardly producing anxiety after his ungracious criticism. Mackie gave him a tired understanding smile, and I had a swift impression that she was the one in that marriage who made allowances, who did the looking after, who was the adult to her good-looking husband-child.

'But,' he said, 'I do think you were silly to go down that road.' His reaction to her injury was still to blame her for it, but I wondered if it weren't really a reaction to fright, like a parent clouting a much-loved lost-but-found infant. 'And there was supposed to be a police notice at the turn-off saying it was closed. It's been closed since those cars slid into each other at lunchtime.'

'There wasn't any police notice,' Mackie said.

'Well, there must have been. You just didn't see it.'

'There was no police notice in sight,' Harry said, and we all agreed, we hadn't seen one.

'All the same . . .' Perkin wouldn't leave it.

'Look,' Mackie said, 'if I could go back and do it again then I wouldn't go along there, but it looked all right and I'd come up in the morning, so I just *did*, and that's that.'

'We all saw the *horse*,' Harry said, drawling, and from the dry humour lurking in his voice one could read his private opinion of Perkin's behaviour.

Perkin gave him a confused glance and stopped picking on Mackie.

Tremayne said, 'What's done's done,' as if announcing his life's philosophy, and added that he would 'give the police a ring' when he got home, which would be very soon now.

'About your clothes,' Fiona said to me, 'shall I send them to the cleaners with all our wet things?'

'No, don't bother,' I said. 'I'll come and collect them tomorrow.'

'All right.' She smiled slightly. 'I do realise we have to thank you. Don't think we don't know.'

'Don't know what?' Perkin demanded.

Harry said in his way, 'Fellow saved us from ice-cubery.'

'From *what*?'

Ingrid giggled. Everyone looked at her. 'Sorry,' she whispered, subsiding.

'Quite likely from death,' Mackie said plainly. 'Let's go home.' She stood up, clearly much better for the warmth and the stiffly laced coffee and also, it seemed to me, relieved that her father-in-law hadn't added his weight to her husband's bawling-out. 'Tomorrow,' she added slowly, 'which of us is going back to Reading?'

'Oh, God,' Fiona said. 'For a minute I'd forgotten.'

'Some of us will have to go,' Mackie said, and it was clear that no one wanted to.

After a pause Harry stirred. 'I'll go. I'll take Bob. Fiona doesn't have to go, nor does Ingrid. Mackie . . .' he stopped.

'I'll come with you,' she said. 'I owe him that.'

Fiona said, 'So will I. He's my cousin, after all. He deserves us to support him. Though after what Harry did today I don't know if I can look him in the face.'

'What did Harry do?' Perkin asked.

Fiona shrugged and retreated. 'Mackie can tell you.'
Fiona, it seemed, could attack Harry all she liked herself, but she wasn't throwing him to other wolves. Harry
was no doubt due for further tongue-lashing after we'd
gone, and in fact was glancing at his wife in a mixture
of apprehension and resignation.

'Let's be off,' Tremayne said. 'Come along, Bob.'

'Yes, sir.'

Bob Watson, I remembered, was Tremayne's head
lad. He and Ingrid went over to the door, followed by
Mackie and Perkin. I put down my mug, thanking
Harry for the reviver.

'Come down this time tomorrow to fetch your
clothes,' he said. 'Come for a drink. An ordinary drink,
not an emergency.'

'Thank you. I'd like that.'

He nodded amiably, and Fiona also, and I picked up
my dry clothes-bag and the camera case and followed
Tremayne and the others out again into the snow. The
six of us squeezed into a large Volvo, Tremayne driving,
Perkin sitting beside him, Ingrid sitting on Bob's lap in
the back with Mackie and me. At the end of the village
Tremayne stopped to let Bob and Ingrid get out, Ingrid
giving me a sketchy smile and saying Bob would bring
my suit and boots along in the morning, if that would
be all right. Of course, I said.

They turned away to walk through a garden gate
towards a small shadowy house, and Tremayne started
off again towards open country, grousing that the trial

would take his head lad away for yet another day. Neither Mackie nor Perkin said anything, and I still had no idea what the trial was all about. I didn't know them well enough to ask, I felt.

'Not much of a welcome for you, John, eh?' Tremayne said over his shoulder. 'Did you bring a typewriter?'

'No. A pencil, actually. And a tape recorder.'

'I expect you know what you're doing.' He sounded cheerfully more sure of that than I was. 'We can start in the morning.'

After about a mile of cautious crawling along a surface much like the one we'd come to grief on, he turned in through a pair of imposing gateposts and stopped outside a very large house where many lights showed dimly through curtains. As inhabitants of large houses seldom used their front doors we went into this one also at the side, not directly into the kitchen this time but into a warm carpeted hall leading to doorways in all directions.

Tremayne, saying, 'Bloody cold night,' walked through a doorway to the left, looking back for me to follow. 'Come on in. Make yourself at home. This is the family room, where you'll find newspapers, telephone, drinks, things like that. Help yourself to whatever you want while you're here.'

The big room looked comfortable in a sprawling way, not tidy, not planned. There was a mixture of patterns and colours, a great many photographs, a few poinsettias left over from Christmas and a glowing log fire in a wide stone fireplace.

Tremayne picked up a telephone and briefly told the local force that his jeep was in the ditch in the lane, not to worry, no one had been hurt, he would get it picked up in the morning. Duty done, he went across to the fire and held out his hands to warm them.

'Perkin and Mackie have their own part of the house, but this room is where we all meet,' he said. 'If you want to leave a message for anybody, pin it to that board over there.' He pointed to a chair on which was propped a corkboard much like the one in Ronnie's office. Red drawing pins were stuck into it at random, one of them anchoring a note which in large letters announced briefly, 'BACK FOR GRUB'.

'That's my other son,' Tremayne said, reading the message from a distance. 'He's fifteen. Unmanageable.' He spoke, however, with indulgence. 'I expect you'll soon get the hang of the household.'

'Er . . . *Mrs* Vickers?' I said tentatively.

'Mackie?' He sounded puzzled.

'No . . . Your wife?'

'Oh. Oh, I see. No, my wife took a hike. Can't say I minded. There's just me and Gareth, the boy. I've a daughter, married a Frog, lives outside Paris, has three children, they come here sometimes, turn the place upside down. She's the eldest, then Perkin. Gareth came later.'

He was feeding me the facts without feelings, I

thought. I'd have to change that, if I were to do any good: but maybe it was too soon for feelings. He was glad I was there, but jerky, almost nervous, almost – now we were alone – shy. Now that he had got what he wanted, now that he had secured his writer, a lot of the agitation and anxiety he'd displayed in Ronnie's office seemed to have abated. The Tremayne of today was running on only half-stress.

Mackie, coming into the room, restored him to his confident self. Carrying an ice-bucket, she glanced quickly at her father-in-law as if to assess his mood, to find out if his tolerance in Fiona and Harry's kitchen was still in operation. Reassured in some way she took the ice over to a table bearing a tray of bottles and glasses and began mixing a drink.

She had taken off her padded coat and woolly hat, and was wearing a blue jersey dress over knee-high narrow black boots. Her red-brown hair, cut short, curled neatly on a well-shaped head and she was still pale, without lipstick or vivacity.

The drink she mixed was gin and tonic, which she gave to Tremayne. He nodded his thanks, as for something done often.

'For you?' Mackie said to me. 'John?'

'The coffee was fine,' I said.

She smiled faintly. 'Yes.'

Truth to tell I was hungry, not thirsty. Thanks to no water in the friend's aunt's house, all I had had that day apart from the coffee was some bread and Marmite and two glasses of milk, and even that had been half frozen in its carton. I began to hope that Gareth's return, 'back for grub', was imminent.

Perkin appeared carrying an already full glass of brown liquid that looked like Coca-Cola. He sank into one of the armchairs and began complaining again about the loss of the jeep, not seeing that he was lucky not to have lost his wife.

'The damned thing's insured,' Tremayne said robustly. 'The garage can tow it out of the ditch in the morning and tell us if it can be salvaged. Either way, it's not the end of the world.'

'How will we manage without it?' Perkin grumbled.

'Buy another,' Tremayne said.

This simple solution silenced Perkin and Mackie looked grateful. She sat on a sofa and took her boots off, saying they were damp from snow and her feet were freezing. She massaged her toes and looked across at my black shoes.

'Those shoes of yours are meant for dancing,' she said, 'and not for carrying females across ice. I'm sorry, I really am.'

'*Carrying?*' Tremayne said, eyebrows rising.

'Yes, didn't I tell you? John and Harry carried me for about a mile, I think. I can remember the crash, then I sort of passed out and I woke up just outside the village. I do vaguely remember them carrying me ... it's a bit of a blur ... I was sitting on their wrists... I knew I mustn't fall off... it was like dreaming.'

Perkin stared, first at her, then at me. Not pleased, I thought.

'I'll be damned,' Tremayne said.

I smiled at Mackie and she smiled back, and Perkin very obviously didn't like that. I'd have to be careful, I thought. I was not there to stir family waters but simply to do a job, to stay uninvolved and leave everything as I'd found it.

Thankful for the heat of the fire I shed the dinner jacket, laying it on a chair and feeling less like the decadent remains of an orgy. I wondered how soon I could decently mention food. If it hadn't been for the bus fare I might have bought something sustaining like chocolate. I wondered if I could ask Tremayne to reimburse the bus fare. Frivolous thoughts, mental rubbish.

'Sit down, John,' Tremayne said, waving to an arm-chair. I sat as instructed. 'What happened in court?' he asked Mackie. 'How did it go?'

'It was awful.' She shuddered. 'Nolan looked so... so *vulnerable*. The jury think he's guilty, I'm sure they do. And Harry wouldn't swear after all that Lewis was drunk...' She closed her eyes and sighed deeply. 'I wish to God we'd never had that damned party.'

'What's done is done,' Tremayne said heavily, and I wondered how many times they'd each repeated those regrets.

Tremayne glanced at me and asked Mackie, 'Have

you told John what's going on?' She shook her head and he enlightened me a little. 'We gave a party here last year, in April, to celebrate winning the Grand National with Top Spin Lob. Celebrate! There were a lot of people here, well over a hundred, including of course Fiona and Harry who you met. I train horses for them. And Fiona's cousins were here, Nolan and Lewis. They're brothers. No one knows for sure what happened, but at the end of the party, when most people had gone home, a girl died. Nolan swears it was an accident. Lewis was there . . . he should have been able to settle it one way or the other, but he says he was drunk and can't remember.'

'He *was* drunk,' Mackie protested. 'Bob testified he was drunk. Bob said he served him getting on for a dozen drinks during the evening.'

'Bob Watson acted as barman,' Tremayne told me. 'He always does, at our parties.'

'We'll never have another,' Mackie said.

'Is Nolan being tried for murder?' I asked, into a pause.

'For assault resulting in death,' Tremayne said. 'The prosecution are trying to prove intent, which would make it murder. Nolan's lawyers say the charge means manslaughter but they are pressing hard for involuntary manslaughter, which could be called negligence or plain accident. The case has been dragging on for months. At least tomorrow it will end.'

'He'll appeal,' Perkin said.

'They haven't found him guilty yet,' Mackie protested.

Tremayne told me, 'Mackie and Harry walked together into Mackie and Perkin's sitting-room and found Nolan standing over the girl who was lying on the floor. Lewis was sitting in an armchair. Nolan said he'd put his hands round the girl's neck to give her a shaking, and she just went limp and fell down; and when Mackie and Harry tried to revive her, they found she was dead.'

'The pathologist said in court today that she died from strangulation,' Mackie said, 'but that sometimes it takes very little pressure to kill someone. He said she died of vagal inhibition, which means the vagus nerve stops working, which it apparently can do fairly easily. The vagus nerve keeps the heart beating. The pathologist said it's always dangerous to clasp people suddenly round the neck, even in fun. But there's no doubt Nolan was furious with Olympia – that's the girl – and he had been furious all the evening, and the prosecution produced someone who'd heard him say, "I'll strangle the bitch," so that he had it in his mind to put his hands round her neck . . .' She broke off and sighed again. 'There wouldn't have been a trial at all except for Olympia's father. The pathologist's original report said it could so easily have been an accident that there wasn't going to be a prosecution, but Olympia's father insisted on bringing a private case against Nolan.

He won't let up. He's obsessed. He was sitting there in court glaring at us.'

'If he'd had his way,' Tremayne confirmed, 'Nolan would have been behind bars all this time, not out on bail.'

Mackie nodded. 'The prosecution – and that's Olympia's father talking through his lawyers – wanted Nolan to be remanded in jail tonight, but the judge said no. So Nolan and Lewis have gone back to Lewis's house, and God knows what state they're in after the mauling they got in court. It's Olympia's father who deserves to be strangled for all the trouble he's caused.'

It seemed to me that on the whole it was Nolan who had caused the trouble, but I didn't say so.

'Well,' Tremayne said, shrugging, 'it happened in this house but it doesn't directly concern my family, thank God.'

Mackie looked as if she weren't so sure. 'They are our friends,' she said.

'Hardly even that,' Perkin said, looking my way. 'Fiona and Mackie are friends. That's where it starts. Mackie came to stay with Fiona, and I met her in Fiona's house . . .' he smiled briefly, 'and so, as they say, we were married.'

'And lived happily ever after,' Mackie finished loyally, though I reckoned if she were happy she worked at it. 'We've been married two years now. Two and a half, almost.'

'You won't put all this Nolan business in my book, will you?' Tremayne asked.

'I shouldn't think so,' I said, 'not if you don't want me to.'

'No, I don't. I was saying goodbye to some guests when that girl died. Perkin came to tell me, and I had to deal with it, but I didn't know her, she'd come with Nolan and I'd never met her before. She isn't part of my life.'

'All right,' I said.

Tremayne showed no particular relief, but just nodded. Seen in his own home, standing by his own fire, he was a big-bodied man of substantial presence, long accustomed to taking charge and ruling his kingdom. This was the persona, no doubt, that the book was to be about: the face of control, of worldly wisdom and success.

So be it, I thought. If I were to sing for my supper I'd sing the songs he chose. But meanwhile, *where* was the supper?

'In the morning,' Tremayne said to me, changing the subject and apparently tired of the trial and its tribulations, 'I thought you might come out with me to see my string at morning exercise.'

'I'd like to,' I said.

'Good. I'll wake you at seven. The first lot pulls out at seven-thirty, just before dawn. Of course at present, with this freeze, we can't do any schooling but we've

got an all-weather gallop. You'll see it in the morning.
If it should be snowing hard, we won't go.'

'Right.'

He turned his head to Mackie, 'I suppose you won't
be out for first lot?'

'No, sorry. We'll have to leave early again to get to
Reading.'

He nodded, and to me he said, 'Mackie's my
assistant.'

I glanced at Mackie and then at Perkin.

'That's right,' Tremayne said, reading my thought.
'Perkin doesn't work for me. Mackie does. Perkin never
wanted to be a trainer and he has his own life.
Gareth ... well ... Gareth might take over from me
one day, but he's too young to know what he'll want.
But when Perkin married Mackie he brought me a
damned smart assistant, and it's worked out very well.'

Mackie looked pleased at his audible sincerity and
it seemed the arrangement was to Perkin's liking
also.

'This house is huge,' Tremayne said, 'and as Perkin
and Mackie couldn't afford much of a place of their
own yet we divided it, and they have their private half.
You'll soon get the hang of it.' He finished his drink
and went to pour himself another. 'You can have the
dining-room to work in,' he said to me over his
shoulder. 'Tomorrow I'll show you where to find the
cuttings, video tapes and form books, and you can take

what you like into the dining-room. We'll fix up the
video player there.'

'Fine,' I said. Food in the dining-room would be
better, I thought.

Tremayne said, 'As soon as it thaws I'll take you
racing. You'll soon pick it up.'

'Pick it up?' Perkin repeated, surprised. 'Doesn't he
know about racing?'

'Not a lot,' I said.

Perkin raised ironic eyebrows. 'It's going to be some
book.'

'He's a writer,' Tremayne said, a touch defensively.
'He can learn.'

I nodded to back him up. It was true that I had
learned the habits and ways of life of dwellers in far
places, and didn't doubt I could do the same to the
racing fraternity at home in England. To listen, to see,
to ask, to understand, to check; I would use the same
method that I'd used six times before, and this time
without needing an interpreter. Whether I could
present Tremayne's life and times in a shape others
would enjoy, that was the real, nagging, doubtful
question.

Gareth at long last blew in with a gust of cold air
and, stripping off an eye-dazzling psychedelic padded
jacket, asked his father, 'What's for supper?'

'Anything you like,' Tremayne said, not minding.

'Pizza, then.' His gaze stopped on me. 'Hello, I'm
Gareth.'

Tremayne told him my name and that I would be writing the biography and staying in the house.

'Straight up?' the boy said, his eyes widening. 'Do you want some pizza?'

'Yes, please.'

'Ten minutes,' he said. He turned to Mackie. 'Do you two want some?'

Mackie and Perkin simultaneously shook their heads and murmured that they'd be off to their own quarters, which appeared to be what Gareth and Tremayne expected.

Gareth was perhaps five foot six with a strong echo of his father's self-confidence and a voice still half broken, coming out hoarse and uneven. He gave me an all-over glance as if assessing what he'd got to put up with for the length of my visit and seemed neither depressed nor elated.

'I heard the weather news at Coconut's,' he told his father. 'Today's been the coldest for twenty-five years. Coconut's father's horses have their duvet rugs on under the jute.'

'So have ours,' Tremayne said. 'Did they forecast more snow?'

'No, just cold for a few more days. East winds from Siberia. Have you remembered to send my school fees?'

Tremayne clearly hadn't.

'If you'll just sign the cheque,' his son said, 'I'll give it to them myself. They're getting a bit fussed.'

'The cheque book's in the office,' Tremayne said.

'Right.' Gareth took his Joseph's coat with him out of the door and almost immediately returned. 'I suppose there isn't the faintest chance,' he said to me, 'that you can cook?'

CHAPTER FOUR

In the morning I went downstairs to find the family room dark but lights on in the kitchen.

It wasn't a palatial kitchen like Fiona's but did contain a big table with chairs all round it as well as a solid fuel cooker whose warmth easily defeated the pre-dawn refrigeration. I had been hoping to borrow a coat from Tremayne to go out to watch the horses, but on a chair I found my boots, gloves and ski-suit with a note attached by a safety pin, 'Thanks ever so much.'

Smiling, I unpinned the note and put on the suit and boots and Tremayne, in a padded jacket, cloth cap and yellow scarf came in blowing on his bare hands and generally bringing the arctic indoors.

'Ah, there you are,' he said, puffing. 'Good. Bob Watson brought up your clothes when he came to feed. Ready?'

I nodded.

'I'll just get my gloves.' He checked also that I had gloves. 'It's as cold as I've ever known it. We won't stay out long, the wind's terrible. Come along.'

As we went through the hall I asked him about the feeding.

'Bob Watson comes at six,' he said briefly. 'All horses in training get an early-morning feed. High protein. Keeps them warm. Gives them energy. A thoroughbred on a high-protein diet generates a lot of heat. Just as well in weather like this. You rarely find a bucket of water frozen over in a horse's box, however cold it is outside. Mind you,' he said, 'we do our best to stop draughts round the doors, but you have to give them fresh air. If you don't, if you molly-coddle them too much, you get viruses flourishing.'

As we stepped out into the open, the wind pulled his last words away and sucked the breath out of our lungs and I reckoned we were still dealing with perhaps ten degrees of frost, plus chill factor, the same as the evening before. It wouldn't go on freezing for as long as in 1963, I thought: that had been the coldest winter since 1740.

A short walk took us straight into the stable-yard, dark the night before and dimly seen, now lit comprehensively and bustling with activity.

'Bob Watson,' Tremayne said, 'is no ordinary head lad. He has all sorts of skills, and takes pride in them. Any odd job, carpentering, plumbing, laying concrete, anything to improve the yard and working conditions, he suggests it and mostly does it himself.'

The object of this eulogy came to meet us, noticing I wore the ski-suit, acknowledging my thanks.

'All ready, guv'nor,' he said to Tremayne.

'Good. Bring them out, Bob. Then you'd better be off, if you're going to Reading.'

Bob nodded and gave some sort of signal and from many open doors came figures leading horses; riders in hard helmets, horses in rugs. In the lights and the dark, with plumes of steam swirling as they breathed, with the circling movements and the scrunching of icy gravel underfoot, the great elemental creatures raised in me such a sense of enjoyment and excitement that I felt for the first time truly enthusiastic about what I'd set my hand to. I wished I could paint, but no canvas, and not even film, could catch the feeling of primitive life or the tingle and smell of the frosty yard.

Bob moved through the scene giving a leg-up to each lad and they resolved themselves into a line, perhaps twenty of them, and processed away through a far exit, horses stalking on long strong legs, riders hunched on top, heads bobbing.

'Splendid,' I said to Tremayne, almost sighing.

He glanced at me. 'Horses get to you, don't they?'

'To you too? Still?'

He nodded and said, 'I love them,' as if such a statement were no more than normal, and in the same tone of voice went on, 'As the jeep's in the ditch we'll have to go up to the gallops on the tractor. All right with you?'

'Sure,' I said, and got my introduction to the training of steeplechasers perched high in the cab over chain-wrapped wheels which Tremayne told me had been up to the Downs with his groundsman once already that morning to harrow the tracks and make them safe for the horses to walk on. He drove the tractor himself with the facility of long custom, spending most of his time not looking where he was going but at anything else visible around him.

His house and stables, I discovered, were right on the edge of the grassy uplands so that the horses had merely to cross one public road to be already on a downland track, and the road surface itself had been thinly covered with unidentified muck to make the icy crossing easier.

Tremayne waited until his whole string was safely over before following them at enough distance not to alarm them, then they peeled off to the right while we lumbered onwards and upwards over frozen rutted mud, making for a horizon that slowly defined itself out of shadows as the firmament grew lighter.

Through the wind Tremayne remarked that perfectly still mornings on the long east-west sweep of downland across Berkshire and Wiltshire were as rare as honest beggars. Apart from that the day broke clear and high with a pale grey washed sky that slowly turned blue over the rolling snow-dusted hills. When Tremayne stopped the tractor and the silence and isolation crept into the senses, it was easy to see that this was what it had looked like up here for thousands of years, that this primordial scene before our present eyes had also been there before man.

Tremayne prosaically told me that if we had continued up over the next brow we would have been close to the fences and hurdles of his schooling ground where his horses learned to jump. Today, he said, they would be doing only half-speed gallops on the all-weather track, and he led the way on foot from the tractor across a stretch of powdery snow to a low mound from where we could see a long dark ribbon of ground winding away down the hill and curving out of sight at the bottom.

'They'll come up here towards us,' he said. 'The all-weather surface is wood chips. Am I telling you what you already know?'

'No,' I said. 'Tell me everything.'

He grunted noncommittally and raised a pair of binoculars powerful enough to see into the riders' minds. I looked where he was looking, but it took me much longer to spot the three dark shapes moving over the dark track. They seemed to be taking a long time to come up head-on towards us but the slowness was an illusion merely. Once they drew near and passed us their speed was vivid, stirring, a matter of muscles stretching and hooves thudding urgently on the quiet surface.

Two or three times they all came up in their turn. 'Both of those are Fiona's,' Tremayne said from behind the binoculars, giving me a commentary as a pair of chestnuts scurried past, and, 'The one on the left of this next three is my Grand National winner, Top Spin Lob.'

With interest I watched the pride of the stable go past us and begin to pull up as he reached the prow of the rise, but beside me Tremayne was stiffening in dismay and saying, 'What the hell—?'

I looked back down the hill in the direction of his binoculars but could see only three more horses coming up the track, two in front, one behind. It wasn't until they were almost upon us that I realised that the one at the rear had no rider.

The three horses passed us and began to slow down and Tremayne said 'Shit' with fervour.

'Did the lad fall off?' I asked inanely.

'No doubt he did,' Tremayne said forcefully, watching through his glasses, 'but he's not one of mine.'

'How do you mean?'

'I mean,' Tremayne said, 'that's not my horse. Just look at him. That's not my rug. That horse isn't saddled and has no bridle. Can't you see?'

When I looked, when he'd told me what to look for, then I could see. Tremayne's horses had fawn rugs with horizontal red and blue stripes; rugs which covered the ribs and hindquarters but left the legs free for full movement. The rug of the riderless horse was brownish grey, much thicker, and fastened by straps running under the belly and round in front of the shoulders.

'I suppose you'll think me crazy,' I said to Tremayne, 'but maybe that's the horse that was loose in the lane last night when we crashed. I mean, I saw it for only a split second, really, but it looked like that. Dark, with that sort of rug.'

'Almost every racehorse wears that sort of rug at night in the winter,' Tremayne said. 'I'm not saying you're wrong, though. In a minute, I'll find out.'

He swung his binoculars back to where another couple of his string were putting on their show and calmly watched them before referring again to the stranger.

'They're the last,' he said as they sped past us. 'Now let's see what's what.'

He began to walk up beside the gallop in the direction of the horses and I followed, and we soon came over the brow to where his whole string was circling on snowy grass, steam swelling in clouds from their breath after their exertions. They were silhouetted against the eastern sun, their shapes now black, now gleaming. Brilliant, freezing, moving; unforgettable morning.

Away to the left, apart from the string, the riderless horse made his own white sun-splashed plume, his nervousness apparent, his herding instincts propelling him towards his kin, his wild nature urging flight.

Tremayne reached his horses and spoke to his lads.

'Anyone know whose horse that is?'

They shook their heads.

'Walk on back to the yard then. Go back down the

all-weather track. No one else is using it this morning. Take care crossing the road.'

They nodded and began to form into a line as they had in the stables, walking off in self-generated mist towards the end of the gallop.

Tremayne said to me, 'Go back to the tractor, will you? Don't make any sudden moves. Don't alarm this fellow.' His eyes slid in the direction of the loose horse. 'In the tractor's cab you'll find a rope. Bring it back here. Move slowly when you're coming into sight.'

'Right,' I said.

He nodded briefly and as I turned to go on the errand he reached into a pocket and produced a few horse-feed cubes which he held out to the runaway, speaking to him directly.

'Come on, now, fella. Nice and easy. Come along now, you must be hungry . . .' His voice was calm and cajoling, absolutely without threat.

I walked away without haste and retrieved the rope from the cab, and by the time I cautiously returned over the brow into Tremayne's sight he was standing close to the horse feeding him cubes with his left hand and holding a bunch of mane with his right.

I stopped, then went forward again slowly. The horse quivered, his head turning my way, his alarm transmitting like electricity. With small movements I made a big loop in one end of the supple old rope and tied a running bowline, then went slowly forward holding the rope open, not in a small circle that might frighten the horse more but in a big loop drooping almost to my knees.

Tremayne watched and continued to talk soothingly, feeding horse cubes one by one. I walked cautiously forward suppressing anything that could seem like doubt or anxiety and paused again a step or two away from the horse.

'There's a good fella,' Tremayne said to him, and to me in the same tone, 'If you can put the rope over his head, do it.'

I took the last two paces and without stopping walked alongside the horse on the far side from Tremayne so that the horse's head came as if naturally into and through the dangling loop. Tremayne moved his hand with the horse cubes away from the black muzzle just long enough for the rope to pass, and then still without abruptness I pulled the slack through the bowline until the noose was snug but not tight round the horse's neck.

'Good,' Tremayne said. 'Give me the rope. I'll walk him down to my yard. Can you drive the tractor?'

'Yes.'

'Wait until I'm out of sight at the bottom. We don't want him bolting from fright. I couldn't hold him if he did.'

'Right.'

Tremayne fished a few more cubes out of his pocket and offered them as before but tugged gently on the rope at the same time. Almost as if making up his mind, as if settling for food and captivity, the great creature moved off with him peacefully, and the two of them trailed down to the dark strip of wood chips and plodded towards home.

Food and warmth, I thought. Maybe I had a lot in common with that horse. What had I settled for, but a form of captivity?

I shrugged. What was done was done, as Tremayne would say. I went down to the tractor and in due course drove it back and parked it where it had been before we started out.

In the now sunlit kitchen Tremayne was standing by the table talking crossly into a telephone.

'You'd have thought someone would have noticed by now that they're missing a horse?' He listened a bit, then said, 'Well, I've one here that's surplus to requirements, so let me know.' He put the receiver down with destructive force. 'No one's told the police, would you believe it?'

He took off his coat, scarf and cap and hung them on a single peg, revealing a big diamond-patterned golfing sweater over a boldly checked open-necked shirt. The same eye-clutter as in the family room; same taste.

'Coffee?' he said, going towards the Aga. 'You won't mind getting your own breakfast, will you? Look around, take anything you want.' He slid the heavy kettle on to the hotplate and went along to a refrigerator which disgorged sliced bread, a tub of yellowish spread and a pot of marmalade. 'Toast?' he said, putting two slices in a wire mesh holder which he slid under the second hotplate lid of the cooker. 'There's cornflakes, if you'd rather. Or cook an egg.'

Toast would be fine, I said, and found myself delegated to making sure it didn't burn while he put through two more phone calls, both fairly incomprehensible to my ears.

'Plates,' he said, pointing to a cupboard, and I found those and mugs also and, in a drawer, knives, forks and spoons. 'Hang your jacket in the cloakroom, next door.'

He went on talking; positive, decisive. I hung my jacket, made the coffee and more toast. He put the receiver down with another crash and went out into the hall.

'Dee-Dee,' he shouted. 'Coffee.'

He came back and sat down to eat, waving to me to join him, which I did, and presently in the doorway appeared a slight brown-haired woman who wore jeans and a huge grey sweater reaching to her knees.

'Dee-Dee,' Tremayne said round a mouthful of toast, 'this is John Kendall, my writer.' To me he added, 'Dee-Dee's my secretary.'

I stood up politely and she told me unsmilingly to sit down. My first impression of her as she went across to the Aga to make her own coffee was that she was like a cat, ultra soft-footed, fluid in movement and totally self-contained.

Tremayne watched me watching her and smiled with

amusement. 'You'll get used to Dee-Dee,' he said. 'I couldn't manage without her.'

She took the compliment without acknowledgement and sat half on a chair as if temporarily, as if about to retreat.

'Phone up a few people to see if they've lost a horse,' Tremayne told her. 'If anyone's panicking, he's here. Unhurt. We've given him water and feed. He was out all night on the Downs, it seems. Someone's in for a bollocking.'

Dee-Dee nodded.

'The jeep's in a ditch on the south road to the A34. Skidded last evening with Mackie. No one hurt. Get the garage to fish it out.'

Dee-Dee nodded.

'John, here, will be working in the dining-room. Anything he wants, give it to him. Anything he wants to know, tell him.'

Dee-Dee nodded.

'Get the blacksmith over for two of the string who lost shoes on the gallop this morning. The lads found the shoes, we don't need new ones.'

Dee-Dee nodded.

'If I'm not here when the vet comes, ask him to take a look at Waterbourne after he's cut the colt. She's got some heat in her near-fore fetlock.'

Dee-Dee nodded.

'Check that the haulage people will be on time

delivering the hay. We're running low. Don't take snow for an answer.'

Dee-Dee smiled, which in a triangular way looked feline also, although far from kittenish. I wondered fleetingly about claws.

Tremayne ate his toast and went on giving sporadic instructions which Dee-Dee seemed to have no trouble remembering. When the spate slowed she stood, picked up her mug and said she would finish her coffee in the office while she got on with things.

'Utterly reliable,' Tremayne remarked to her departing back. 'There's always ten damned trainers trying to poach her.' He lowered his voice. 'A shit of an amateur jockey treated her like muck. She's not over it yet. I make allowances. If you find her crying, that's it.'

I was amazed by his compassion and felt I should have recognised earlier how many unexpected layers there were to Tremayne below the loud executive exterior: not just his love of horses, not just his need to be recorded, not even just his disguised delight in Gareth, but other, secret, unrevealed privacies which maybe I would come to in time, and maybe not.

He spent the next half-hour on the telephone both making and receiving calls: it was the time of day, I later discovered, when trainers could most reliably be found at home. Toast eaten, coffee drunk, he reached for a cigarette from a packet on the table and brought a throwaway lighter out of his pocket.

'Do you smoke?' he asked, pushing the pack my way.

'Never started,' I said.

'Good for the nerves,' he commented, inhaling deeply. 'I hope you're not an anti fanatic.'

'I quite like the smell.'

'Good.' He seemed pleased enough. 'We'll get on well.'

He told me that at ten o'clock, by which time the first lot would have been given hay and water and the lads would have had their own breakfasts, he would drive the tractor back to the gallops to watch his second lot work. He said I needn't bother with that: I could set things up in the dining-room, arrange things however I liked working. As all racing was off from frost he could, if I agreed, spend the afternoon telling me about his childhood. When racing began again, he wouldn't have so much time.

'Good idea,' I said.

He nodded. 'Come along, then, and I'll show you where things are.'

We went out into the carpeted hall and he pointed to the doorway opposite.

'That's the family room, as you know. Next to the kitchen . . .' he walked along and opened a closed door, '. . . is my dining-room. We don't use it much. You'll have to turn the heating up, I dare say.'

I looked into the room I was to get to know well; a spacious room with mahogany furniture, swagged crimson curtains, formal cream-and-gold striped walls and a plain dark green carpet. Not Tremayne's own choice, I thought. Much too coordinated.

'That'll be great,' I said obligingly.

'Good.' He closed the door again and looked up the stairs we had climbed to bed the night before. 'We put those stairs in when we divided the house. This passage beside them, this leads to Perkin and Mackie's half. Come along, I'll show you.' He walked along a wide pale-green-carpeted corridor with pictures of horses on both walls and opened double white-painted doors at the end.

'Through here,' he said, 'is the main entrance hall of the house. The oldest part.'

We passed on to a big wood-blocked expanse of polished floor from which two graceful wings of staircase rose to an upper gallery. Under the gallery, between the staircases, was another pair of doors which Tremayne, crossing, opened without flourish, revealing a vista of gold and pale blue furnishings in the same formal style as the dining-room.

'This is the main drawing room,' he said. 'We share it. We hardly use it. We used it last for that damned party . . .' He paused. 'Well, as Mackie said, I don't know when we'll have another.'

A pity, I thought. It looked a house made for parties. Tremayne closed the drawing-room door, and pointed straight across the hall.

'That's the front entrance, and those double doors on the right open into Perkin and Mackie's half. We built a new kitchen for them and another new staircase. We planned it as two separate houses, you see, with this big common section between us.'

'It's great,' I said to please him, but also meaning it.

He nodded. 'It divided quite well. No one needs houses this size these days. Take too much heating.' Indeed, it was cold in the hall. 'Most of this was built about nineteen six. Edwardian. Country house of the Windberry family, don't suppose you've ever heard of them.'

'No,' I agreed.

'My father bought the place for peanuts during the Depression. I've lived here all my life.'

'Was your father a trainer also?' I asked.

Tremayne laughed. 'God, no. He inherited a fortune. Never did a day's work. He liked going racing, so he bought a few jumpers, put them in the stables that hadn't been used since cars replaced the carriages and engaged a trainer for them. When I grew up, I just took over the horses. Built another yard, eventually. I've fifty boxes at present, all full.'

He led the way back through the doors to his own domain and closed them behind us.

'That's more or less all,' he said, 'except for the office.'

Once back in his own hall he veered through the last of the doorways there and I followed him into yet another big room in which Dee-Dee looked lost behind a vast desk.

'This used to be the Windberry's billiards room,' Tremayne said. 'When I was a child, it was our playroom.'

'You had brothers and sisters?'

'One sister,' he said briefly, looking at his watch. 'I'll leave you to Dee-Dee. See you later.'

He went away purposefully, and, after the time it would have taken him to replace coat, cap and scarf, the door out to the yard slammed behind him. He was a natural slammer, I thought; there seemed to be no ingredient of ire.

Dee-Dee said, 'How can I help you?' without any great enthusiasm.

'Don't you approve of the biography project?' I asked.

She blinked. 'I didn't say that.'

'You looked it.'

She fiddled lengthily with some papers, eyes down.

'He's been on about it for months,' she said finally. 'It's important to him. I think . . . if you must know . . . that he should have held out for someone better . . .' She hesitated. 'Better *known*, anyway. He met you one day and the next day you're here, and I think it's too *fast*. I suggested that we should at least run a check on you but he said Ronnie Curzon's word was good enough. So you're here.' She looked up, suddenly fierce. 'He deserves the best,' she said.

'Ah.'

'What do you mean by Ah?'

I didn't answer at once but looked round the jumbo

office, seeing the remains of the classical decorative style overlaid by a host of modern bookshelves, filing cabinets, cupboards, copier, fax, computer, telephones, floor safe, television, tapes by the dozen, cardboard boxes, knee-high stacks of newspapers and another corkboard with red drawing-pinned memos. There was an antique kneehole desk with an outsize leather chair, clearly Tremayne's own territory, and on the floor a splatter of overlapping Persian rugs in haphazard patterns and colours covering most of an old grey carpet. Pictures of horses passing winning posts inhabited the walls alongside a bright row of racing silks hanging on pegs.

I ended the visual tour where I'd begun, on Dee-Dee's face.

'The more you help,' I said, 'the more chance he has.'

She compressed her mouth obstinately. 'That doesn't follow.'

'Then the more you obstruct, the less chance he has.'

She stared at me, her antagonism still clear, while logic made hardly a dent in emotion.

She was about forty, I supposed. Thin but not emaciated, from what one could see via the sweater. Good skin, bobbed straight hair, unremarkable features, pink lipstick, no jewellery, small, strong-looking hands. General air of reserve, of holding back. Perhaps that was habitual; perhaps the work of the shit of an amateur jockey who had treated her like muck.

'How long have you worked here?' I asked, voice neutral, merely enquiring.

'Eight years, about.' Straightforward answer.

'What I chiefly need,' I said, 'are cuttings books.'

She almost smiled. 'There aren't any.'

With dismay I protested, 'There must be. He mentioned cuttings.'

'They're not in books, they're in boxes.' She turned her head, nodding directions. 'In that cupboard over there. Help yourself.'

I went across and opened a white-painted door and inside found stacked on shelves from floor to head height a whole array of uniform white cardboard boxes, all like shirt-boxes but about eight inches deep, all with dates written on their ends in black marker ink.

'I re-boxed all the cuttings three or four years ago,' Dee-Dee said. 'Some of the old boxes were falling to bits. The newspaper is yellow and brittle. You'll see.'

'Can I take them all into the dining-room?'

'Be my guest.'

I loaded up four of the boxes and set off with them, and in a minute found her following me.

'Wait,' she said inside the dining-room door, 'mahogany gets scratched easily.'

She went over to a large sideboard and from a drawer drew out a vast green baize cloth which she draped over the whole expanse of the large oval table.

'You can work on that,' she said.

'Thank you.'

I put down the boxes and went to fetch another load, ferrying them until the whole lot was transferred. Dee-Dee meanwhile went back to her desk and her work, which largely consisted of the telephone. I could hear her still talking on and off while I arranged the boxes of cuttings chronologically and took the lid off the first, realising from the date on its end that it had to go back beyond Tremayne; that he hadn't started training when he was a baby. Tattered yellow pieces of newsprint informed me that Mr Loxley Vickers, of Shellerton House, Berkshire, had bought Triple Subject, a six-year-old gelding, for the record sum for a steeplechaser of twelve hundred guineas. A house, an astonished reporter wrote, could be bought for less.

I looked up, smiling, and found Dee-Dee standing in the doorway, hesitantly hovering.

'I've been talking to Fiona Goodhaven,' she said abruptly.

'How is she?'

'All right. Thanks to you, it seems. Why didn't you tell me about your rescue job?'

'It didn't seem important.'

'Are you mad?'

'Well, it didn't seem important in the context of whether I could or couldn't do justice to Tremayne's biography.'

'God Almighty.' She went away but shortly came back. 'If you turn that thermostat,' she said, pointing, 'it will get warmer in here.'

She whisked away again before I could thank her, but I understood that peace had been declared, or, at the very least, hostilities temporarily suspended.

Tremayne returned in time. I heard him talking forcefully into an office telephone and presently he strode into the dining-room to tell me that someone had finally found they had a horse missing.

'It came over the hill from the next village. They're sending a box to pick it up. How are you doing?'

'Reading about your father.'

'A lunatic. Had an obsession about how things would look in his stomach after he'd eaten them. He used to make his butler put an extra serving of everything he was going to eat into a bucket and stir it round. If my father didn't like the look of it, he wouldn't eat his dinner. Drove the cook mad.'

I laughed. 'What about your mother?'

'She'd fallen off the perch by then. He wasn't so bad when she was alive. He went screwy after.'

'How old were you when she ... er ... fell off the perch?'

'Ten. Same age as Gareth when *his* mother finally hopped it. You might say I know what it's like to be Gareth. Except *his* mother's still alive and he sees her sometimes. I can't remember mine very clearly, to be honest.'

After a moment I said, 'How much can I ask you?'

'Ask anything. If I don't want to answer, I'll say so.'

'Well ... you said your father inherited a fortune. Did he ... er ... leave it to you?'

Tremayne laughed in his throat. 'A fortune seventy or eighty years ago is not a fortune now. But yes, in a way he did. Left me this house. Taught me the principles of landowning which he'd learnt from *his* father but hardly practised. My father spent; my grandfather accumulated. I'm more like my grandfather, though I never knew him. I tell Gareth sometimes that we can't afford things even if we can. I don't want him to turn out a spender.'

'What about Perkin?'

'Perkin?' For a second Tremayne looked blank. 'Perkin has no money sense at all. Lives in a world of his own. It's no use talking to Perkin about money.'

'What does he do,' I asked, 'in his world?'

Tremayne looked as if his elder son's motivations were a mystery, but somewhere also I sensed a sort of exasperated pride.

'He makes furniture,' he said. 'Designs it. Makes it himself, piece by piece. Chests, tables, screens, anything. Two hundred years from now they will be valuable antiques. That's Perkin's money sense for you.' He sighed. 'Best thing he ever did was marry a smart girl like Mackie. She sells his pieces, makes sure he makes a profit. He used to sell things sometimes for less than they cost to make. Absolutely hopeless.'

'As long as he's happy.'

Tremayne made no comment on his son's state of happiness but asked about my tape recorder.

'Didn't it get wet last night? Won't it be ruined?'

'No. I keep everything in waterproof bags. Sort of habit.'

'Jungles and deserts?' he asked, remembering.

'Mm.'

'Then you go and fetch it, and we'll start. And I'll move the office television in here with the video player so you can watch the races I've won. And if you want any lunch,' he added as an afterthought, 'I nearly always have beef sandwiches; buy them by the fifty, ready-made from the supermarket, and put them in the freezer.'

We both ate mostly-thawed uninteresting beef sandwiches in due course and I thought that even if Tremayne's housekeeping were slightly eccentric, at least he hadn't stirred his food up first in a bucket.

CHAPTER FIVE

At about six-thirty that day I walked down to Shellerton to collect my clothes from the Goodhavens, Fiona
and Harry. Darkness had fallen but it seemed to me
that the air temperature hadn't, and there was less
energy in the wind than in the morning.

I had by that time taped three hours' worth of Tremayne's extraordinary childhood and walked round
with him to inspect his horses at evening stables. At
every one of the fifty doors he had stopped to check
on the inmate's welfare, discussing it briefly with the
lad and dispensing carrots to enquiring muzzles with
little pats and murmurs of affection.

In between times as we moved along the rows he
explained that the horses would now be rugged up
against the frost in wool blankets and duvets, then
covered with jute rugs (like sacking) securely buckled
on. They would be given their main feed of the day
and be shut up for the night to remain undisturbed
until morning.

'One of us walks round last thing at night,' he said,

'Bob or Mackie or I, to make sure they're all right. Not kicking their boxes and so on. If they're quiet they're all right, and I don't disturb them.'

Like fifty children, I thought, tucked up in bed.

I'd asked him how many lads he had. Twenty-one, he said, plus Bob Watson, who was worth six, and the travelling head lad and a box driver and a groundsman. With Mackie and Dee-Dee, twenty-seven full-time employees. The economics of training racehorses, he remarked, put the book trade's problems in the shade.

When I reminded him that I was going down to Fiona and Harry's to fetch my belongings he offered me his car.

'I quite like walking,' I said.

'Good God.'

'I'll cook when I get back.'

'You don't have to,' he protested. 'Don't let Gareth talk you into it.'

'I said I would, though.'

'I don't care much what I eat.'

I grinned. 'Maybe that will be just as well. I'll be back soon after Gareth, I expect.'

I'd discovered that the younger son rode his bicycle each morning to the house of his friend Coconut, from where both of them were driven to and from a town ten miles away, as day boys in a mainly boarding school. The hours were long, as always with that type of school: Gareth was never home much before seven, often later. His notice 'BACK FOR GRUB' seemed to be a fixture. He removed it, Tremayne said, only when he knew in the morning that he would be out until bedtime. Then he would leave another message instead, to say where he was going.

'Organised,' I commented.

'Always has been.'

I reached the main street of Shellerton and tramped along to the Goodhavens' house, passing three or four cars in their driveway and walking round to the kitchen door to ring the bell.

After an interval the door was opened by Harry whose expression changed from inhospitable to welcoming by visible degrees.

'Oh, hello, come in. Forgot about you. Fact is, we've had another lousy day in Reading. But home without crashing, best you can say.'

I stepped into the house and he closed the door behind us, at the same time putting a restraining hand on my arm.

'Let me tell you first,' he said. 'Nolan and Lewis are both here. Nolan got convicted of manslaughter. Six months' jail suspended for two years. He won't go behind bars but no one's happy.'

'I don't need to stay,' I said. 'Don't want to intrude.'

'Do me a favour, dilute the atmosphere.'

'If it's like that . . .'

He nodded, removed his hand and walked me through the kitchen into a warm red hallway and on into a pink-and-green chintzy sitting-room beyond.

Fiona, turning her silver-blond head said, 'Who was it?' and saw me following Harry. 'Oh, good heavens, I'd forgotten.' She came over, holding out a hand, which I shook, an odd formality after our previous meeting.

'These are my cousins,' she said. 'Nolan and Lewis Everard.' She gave me a wide don't-say-anything stare, so I didn't. 'A friend of Tremayne's,' she said to them briefly. 'John Kendall.'

Mackie, sitting exhaustedly in an armchair, waggled acknowledging fingers. Everyone else was standing and holding a glass. Harry pressed a pale gold drink into my hand and left me to discover for myself what lay under the floating ice. Whisky, I found, tasting it.

I had had no mental picture of either Nolan or Lewis but their appearance all the same was a surprise. They were both short, Nolan handsome and hard, Lewis swollen and soft. Late thirties, both of them. Dark hair, dark eyes, dark jaws. I supposed I had perhaps expected them to be like Harry in character if not in appearance, but it was immediately clear that they weren't. In place of Harry's amused urbanity, Nolan's aristocratic-sounding speech was essentially violent and consisted of fifty per cent obscenity. The gist of his first sentence was that he wasn't in the mood for guests.

Neither Fiona nor Harry showed embarrassment, only weary tolerance. If Nolan had spoken like that in court, I thought, it was no wonder he'd been found guilty. One could quite easily imagine him throttling a nymph.

Harry said calmly, 'John is writing Tremayne's biography. He knows about the trial and the Top Spin Lob party. He's a friend of ours, and he stays.'

Nolan gave Harry a combative stare which Harry returned with blandness.

'Anyone can know about the trial,' Mackie said. 'It was in all the papers this morning, after all.'

Harry nodded. 'To be continued in reel two.'

'It's not an expletive joke,' Lewis said. 'They took photos of us when we were leaving.' His peevish voice was like his brother's though a shade higher in pitch and, as I progressively discovered, instead of truly offensive obscene words he had a habit of using euphemisms like 'expletive', 'bleep' and 'deleted'. In Harry's mouth it might have been funny; in Lewis's it seemed a form of cowardice.

'Gird up such loins as you have,' Harry told him peaceably. 'The public won't remember by next week.'

Nolan said between four-letter words that everyone that mattered would remember, including the Jockey Club.

'I doubt if they'll actually warn you off,' Harry said. 'It wasn't as if you hadn't paid your bookmaker.'

'Harry!' Fiona said sharply.

'Sorry, m'dear,' murmured her husband, though his lids half veiled his eyes like blinds drawn over his true feelings.

Tremayne and I had each read two accounts of the previous day's proceedings while dealing with the sandwiches, one in a racing paper, another in a tabloid. Tremayne's comments had been grunts of disapproval, while I had learned a few facts left out by the Vickers family the evening before.

Fiona's cousin Nolan, for starters, was an amateur jockey ('well-known', in both papers) who often raced on Fiona's horses, trained by Tremayne Vickers. Nolan Everard had once briefly been engaged to Magdalene Mackenzie (Mackie) who had subsequently married Perkin Vickers, Tremayne's son. 'Sources' had insisted that the three families, Vickers, Goodhavens and Everards were on friendly terms. The prosecution, not disputing this, had suggested that indeed they had all closed ranks to shield Nolan from his just deserts.

A demure photograph of Olympia (provided by her father) showed a fair-haired schoolgirl, immature, an innocent victim. No one seemed to have explained why Nolan had said he would strangle the bitch, and now that I'd heard him talk I was certain those had not been his only words.

'The question really is,' Fiona said, 'not whether the Jockey Club will warn him off racecourses altogether, because I'm sure they won't – they let real villains go racing – but whether they'll stop him riding as an amateur.'

Harry said, as if sympathetically, to Nolan, 'It's rather put paid to your ambitions to be made a *member* of the Jockey Club, though, hasn't it, old lad?'

Nolan looked blackly furious and remarked with

venom that Harry hadn't helped the case by not swearing to hell and back that Lewis had been comprehensively pissed.

Harry didn't reply except to shrug gently and refill Lewis's glass, which was unquestionably comprehensively empty.

If one made every possible allowance for Nolan, I thought; if one counted the long character-withering ordeal of waiting to know if he were going to prison; if one threw in the stress of having undoubtedly killed a young woman, even by accident; if one added the humiliations he would forever face because of his conviction; if one granted all that, he was still unattractively, viciously ungrateful.

His family and friends had done their best for him. I thought it highly likely that Lewis had in fact perjured himself and that Harry had also, very nearly, in the matter of the alcoholic blackout. Harry had at the last minute shrunk from either a positive opinion or from an outright lie, and I'd have put my money on the second. They had all gone again to court to support Nolan when they would much rather have stayed away.

'I still think you ought to appeal,' Lewis said.

Nolan's pornographic reply was to the effect that his lawyer had advised him not to push his luck, as Lewis very well knew.

'Bleep the lawyer,' Lewis said.

'Appeal courts can *increase* sentences, I believe,'

Fiona said warningly. 'They might cancel the suspension. Doesn't bear thinking about.'

'Olympia's father was incandescent afterwards,' Mackie said gloomily, nodding. 'He wanted Nolan put away for life. Life for a life, that's what he was shouting.'

'You can't just appeal against a sentence because you don't happen to like it,' Harry pointed out. 'There has to be some point of law that was conducted wrongly at the trial.'

Lewis said obstinately, 'If Nolan doesn't appeal it's as good as admitting he's expletive guilty as charged.'

There was a sharp silence all round. They all did think him guilty, though maybe to different degrees. Don't push your luck seemed good pragmatic advice.

I looked speculatively at Mackie, wondering about her sometime engagement to Nolan. She showed nothing for him now but concerned friendship: no lingering love and no hard feelings. Nolan showed nothing but concern for himself.

Fiona said to me, 'Stay to dinner?' and Harry said, 'Do,' but I shook my head.

'I promised to cook for Gareth and Tremayne.'

'Good God,' Harry said.

Fiona said, 'That'll make a change from pizza! They have pizza nine nights out of ten. Gareth just puts one in the microwave, regular as clockwork.'

Mackie put down her glass and stood up tiredly. 'I

think I'll go too. Perkin will be waiting to hear the news.'

Nolan remarked tartly between 'f's that if Perkin had bothered to put in an appearance at Reading he would know the news already.

'He wasn't needed,' Harry said mildly.

'Olympia died in his half of the house,' Lewis said. 'You'd have thought he'd have taken an interest.'

Nolan remembered with below-the-waist indelicacies that Tremayne hadn't supported him either.

'They were both busy,' Mackie said gamely. 'They both work, you know.'

'Meaning we don't?' Lewis asked waspishly.

Mackie sighed. 'Meaning whatever you like.' To me she said, 'Did you come in Tremayne's car?'

'No, walked.'

'Oh! Then . . . do you want a lift home?'

I thanked her and accepted and Harry came with us to see us off.

'Here are your clothes in your bag,' he said, handing it to me. 'Can't thank you enough, you know.'

'Any time.'

'God forbid.'

Harry and I looked at each other briefly in the sort of appreciation that's the beginning of friendship, and I wondered whether he, of all of them, would have been least sorry to see Nolan in the cells.

'He's not always like that,' Mackie said as she steered

out of the drive. 'Nolan, I mean. He can be enormously good fun. Or rather, he used to be, before all this.'

'I read in today's paper that you were once engaged to him.'

She half laughed. 'Yes, I was. For about three months, five years ago.'

'What happened?'

'We met in February at a Hunt Ball. I knew who he was. Fiona's cousin, the amateur jockey. I'd been brought up in eventing. Had ponies before I could walk. I told him I sometimes went to stay with Fiona. Small world, he said. We spent the whole evening together and . . . well . . . the whole night. It was sudden, like lightning. Don't tell Perkin. Why does one tell total strangers things one never tells anyone else? Sorry, forget it.'

'Mm,' I said. 'What happened when you woke up?'

'It was like a roller-coaster. We spent all our time together. After two weeks he asked me to marry him and I said yes. Blissful. My feet never touched the ground. I went to the races to watch him . . . he was spell-binding. Kept winning, saying I'd brought him luck.' She stopped, but she was smiling.

'Then what?'

'Then the jumping season finished. We began planning the wedding . . . I don't know. Maybe we just got to know each other. I can't say which day I realised it was a mistake. He was getting irritable. Flashes of rage, really. I just said one day, "It won't work, will it?" and he said, "No," so we fell into each other's arms and had a few tears and I gave him his ring back.'

'You were lucky,' I commented.

'Yes. How do you mean?'

'To come out of it without a fighting marriage and a spiteful divorce.'

'You're so right.' She turned into Tremayne's drive and came to a halt. 'We've been friends ever since, but Perkin has always been uncomfortable with him. See, Nolan is brilliant and brave on horses and Perkin doesn't ride all that well. We don't talk about horses much, when we're alone. It's restful, actually. I tell Perkin he ought to be grateful to Nolan that I was free for *him*, but I suppose he can't help how he feels.'

She sighed, unbuckled her seat belt and stood up out of the car.

'Look,' she said, 'I like you, but Perkin does tend to be jealous.'

'I'll ignore you,' I promised.

She smiled vividly. 'A touch of old-fashioned formality should do the trick.' She began to turn away, and then stopped. 'I'm going in through our own entrance, Perkin's and mine. I'll see how he's doing. See if he's stopped work. We'll probably be along for a drink. We often do, at this time of day.'

'OK.'

She nodded and walked off, and I went round and into Tremayne's side of the house as if I'd lived there for ever. Yesterday morning, I thought incredulously, I awoke to Aunty's freeze.

Tremayne in the family room had lit the log fire and poured his gin and tonic and, standing within heating range of the flames, he listened with disillusion to the outcome of Nolan's trial.

'Guilty but unpunished,' he observed. 'New-fangled escape clause.'

'Should the guilty always be punished?'

He looked at me broodingly. 'Is that a character assessment question?'

'I guess so.'

'It's unanswerable, anyway. The answer is, I don't know.' He turned and with a foot pushed a log further into the fire. 'Help yourself to a drink.'

'Thanks. Mackie said they might be along.'

Tremayne nodded, taking it for granted, and in fact she and Perkin came through from the central hall while I was dithering between the available choices of whisky or gin, neither of which I much liked. Perkin solved the liquid question for himself by detouring into the kitchen and reappearing with a glass of Coke.

'What do you actually *like*?' Mackie asked, seeing my hesitation as she poured tonic into gin for herself.

'Wine, I suppose. Red for preference.'

'There will be some in the office. Tremayne keeps it for owners, when they come to see their horses. I'll get it.'

She went without haste and returned with a Bordeaux-shaped bottle and a sensible corkscrew, both of which she handed over.

Tremayne said, as I liberated the Château Kirwan, 'Is that stuff any good?'

'Very,' I said, smelling the healthy cork.

'It's all grape-juice as far as I'm concerned. If you like the stuff, put it on the shopping list.'

'The shopping list,' Mackie explained, 'is a running affair pinned to the kitchen corkboard. Whoever does the shopping takes the list with him. Or her.'

Perkin, slouching in an armchair, said I might as well get used to the idea of doing the shopping myself, particularly if I liked eating.

'Tremayne takes Gareth to the supermarket sometimes,' he said, 'and that's about it. Or Dee-Dee goes, if there's no milk for the coffee three days running.' He looked from me to Mackie. 'I used to think it quite normal until I married a sensible housekeeper.'

Perkin, I thought, as he reaped a smile from his wife, was a great deal more relaxed than on the evening before, though the faint hostility he'd shown towards me was still there. Tremayne asked him his opinion of the verdict on Nolan and Perkin consulted his glass lengthily as if seeking illumination.

'I suppose,' he said finally, 'that I'm glad he isn't in jail.'

It was a pretty ambiguous statement after so much thought, but Mackie looked pleasantly relieved. Only she of the three, it was clear, cared much for Nolan the man. To father and son, having Nolan in jail would have been an inconvenience and an embarrassment which they were happy to avoid.

Looking at the two of them, the differences were as powerful as the likenesses. If one discounted Tremayne's hair, which was grey where Perkin's was brown, and the thickness in Tremayne's neck and body that had come with age, then physically they were of one cloth; but where Tremayne radiated strength, Perkin was soggy; where Tremayne was a leader, Perkin retreated. Tremayne's love was for living horses, Perkin's was for passive wood.

It came as a shock to me to wonder if Tremayne wanted his own achievements written in an inheritable book because Perkin's work would be valuable in two hundred years. Wondered if the strong father felt he had to equal his weaker son. I dismissed the idea as altogether too subtle and as anyway tactless in an employed biographer.

Gareth came home with his usual air of a life lived on the run and eyed me with disapproval as I sat in an armchair drinking wine.

'I thought you said—' he began, and stopped, shrugging, an onset of good manners vying with disappointment.

'I will,' I said.

'Oh, really? Now?'

I nodded.

'Good. Come on, then, I'll show you the freezers.'

'Let him alone,' Mackie said mildly. 'Let him finish his drink.'

Perkin reacted to this harmless remark with irritation. 'As he said he'd cook, let him do it.'

'Of course,' I said cheerfully, getting up. I glanced at Tremayne. 'All right with you?'

'You're all right with me until further notice,' he said, and Perkin didn't like that testimony of approval either, but Gareth did.

'You're home and dry with Dad,' he told me happily, steering me through the kitchen. 'What did you do to him?'

'Nothing.'

'What did you do to me?' he asked himself comically, and answered himself, 'Nothing. I guess that's it. You don't have to do anything, it's just the way you are. The freezers are through here, in the utility room. If you go straight on through the utility room you get to the garage. Through that door there.' He pointed ahead to a heavy-looking door furnished with business-like bolts. 'I keep my bike through there.'

There were two freezers, both upright, both with incredible contents.

'This one,' Gareth said, opening the door, 'is what Dad calls the peezer freezer.'

'Or the pizza frizza?' I suggested.

'Yes, that too.'

It was stacked with pizzas and nothing else, though only half full.

'We eat our way down to the bottom,' Gareth said reasonably, 'then fill up again every two or three months.'

'Sensible,' I commented.

'Most people think we're mad.'

He shut the freezer and opened the other, which proved to contain four packs of beef sandwiches, fifty to a pack. There were also about ten sliced loaves (for toast, Gareth explained), one large turkey (someone gave it to Tremayne for Christmas), pints galore of chocolate ripple ice-cream (Gareth liked it) and a whole lot of bags of ice-cubes for gins and tonic.

Was it for this, I surmised wildly, that I'd sold my soul?

'Well,' I said in amusement, 'what do we have in the larder?'

'What larder?'

'Cupboards, then.'

'You'd better look,' Gareth said, closing the second freezer's door. 'What are you going to make?'

I hadn't the faintest idea; but what Tremayne, Gareth and I ate not very much later was a hot pie made of beef extracted from twenty defrosted sandwiches and chopped small, then mixed with undiluted condensed mushroom soup (a find) and topped with an inch-thick layer of sandwich breadcrumbs fried crisp.

Gareth watched the simple cooking with fascination and I found myself telling him about the techniques I'd been taught of how to live off the countryside without benefit of shops.

'Fried worms aren't bad,' I said.

'You're kidding me.'

'They're packed with protein. Birds thrive on them. And what's so different from eating snails?'

'Could you really live off the land? You yourself?'

'Yes, sure,' I said. 'But you can die of malnutrition eating just rabbits.'

'How do you *know* these things?'

'It's my business, really. My trade.' I told him about the six travel guides. 'The company used to send me to all those places to set up holiday expeditions for real rugged types. I had to learn how to get them out of all sorts of local trouble, especially if they struck disasters like losing all their equipment in raging torrents. I wrote the books and the customers weren't allowed to set off without them. Mind you, I always thought the book on how to survive would have been lost in the raging torrent with everything else, but maybe they would remember some of it, you never know.'

Gareth, helping make breadcrumbs in a blender, said a shade wistfully, 'How did you ever start on something like that?'

'My father was a camping nut. A naturalist. He worked in a bank, really, and still does, but every spare second he would head for the wilds, dragging me and my mother along. Actually I took it for granted, as just a fact of life. Then after college I found it was all pretty useful in the travel trade. So bingo.'

'Does he still go camping? Your father, I mean?'

'No. My mother got arthritis and refused to go any more, and he didn't have much fun without her. He's worked in a bank in the Cayman Islands for three or four years now. It's good for my mother's health.'

Gareth asked simply, 'Where are the Cayman Islands?'

'In the Caribbean, south of Cuba, west of Jamaica.'

'What do you want me to do with these bread-crumbs?'

'Put them in the frying pan.'

'Have *you* ever been to the Cayman Islands?'

'Yes,' I said, 'I went for Christmas. They sent me the fare as a present.'

'You are *lucky*,' Gareth said.

I paused from cutting up the beef. 'Yes,' I agreed, thinking about it. 'Yes, I am. And grateful. And you've got a good father, too.'

He seemed extraordinarily pleased that I should say so, but it seemed to me, unconventional housekeeping or not, that Tremayne was making a good job of his younger son.

Notwithstanding Tremayne's professed lack of interest in food he clearly enjoyed the pie, which three healthy appetites polished off to the last fried crumb. I got promoted instantly to resident chef, which suited me fine. Tomorrow I could do the shopping, Tremayne said, and without ado pulled out his wallet and gave me enough to feed the three of us for a month, though he said it was for a week. I protested it was too much and he kindly told me I had no idea how much things cost. I thought wryly that I knew how much things cost to the last anxious penny, but there was no point in arguing. I stowed the money away and asked them what they didn't like.

'Broccoli,' Gareth said instantly. 'Yuk.'

'Lettuce,' said Tremayne.

Gareth told his father about fried worms and asked me if I had any of the travel guides with me.

'No, sorry, I didn't think of bringing them.'

'Couldn't we possibly get some? I mean, I'd buy them with my pocket money. I'd like to keep them. Are they in the shops?'

'Sometimes, but I could ask the travel company to send a set,' I suggested.

'Yes, do that,' Tremayne said, 'and I'll pay for them. We'd all like to look at them, I expect.'

'But Dad . . .' Gareth protested.

'All right,' Tremayne said, 'get two sets.'

I began to appreciate Tremayne's simple way of solving problems and in the morning, after I'd driven him on the tractor up to the Downs to see the horses exercise, and after orange juice, coffee and toast, I phoned my friend in the travel agency and asked him to organise the books.

'Today?' he said, and I said, 'Yes, please,' and he said

he would Red-Star-parcel them by train, if I liked. I consulted Tremayne who thought it a good idea and told me to get them sent to Didcot station where I could go to pick them up when I went in to do the shopping.

'Fair enough,' the friend said. 'You'll get them this afternoon.'

'My love to your aunt,' I said, 'and thanks.'

'She'll swoon.' He laughed. 'See you.'

Tremayne began reading the day's papers, both of which carried the results of the trial. Neither paper took any particular stance either for or against Nolan, though both quoted Olympia's father at length. He came over as a sad, obsessed man whose natural grief had turned to self-destructive anger and one could feel sorry for him on many counts. Tremayne read and grunted and passed no opinion.

The day slowly drifted into a repetition of the one before. Dee-Dee came into the kitchen for coffee and instructions and when Tremayne had gone out again with his second lot of horses I returned to the boxes of clippings in the dining-room.

I decided to reverse yesterday's order; to start at the most recent clippings and work backwards.

It was Dee-Dee, I had discovered, who cut the sections out of the newspapers and magazines, and certainly she had been more zealous than whoever had done it before her, as the boxes for the last eight years were much fuller.

I laid aside the current box as it was still almost empty and worked through from January to December of the previous year, which had been a good one for Tremayne, embracing not only his Grand National win with Top Spin Lob but many other successes important enough to get the racing hacks excited. Tremayne's face smiled steadily from clipping after clipping including, inappropriately, those dealing with the death of the girl, Olympia.

Drawn irresistibly, I read a whole batch of accounts of that death from a good many different papers, the number of them suggesting that someone had gone out and bought an armful of everything available. In total, they told me not much more than I already knew, except that Olympia was twice described as a 'jockette', a word I somehow found repulsive. It appeared that she had ridden in several ladies' races at point-to-point meetings which one paper, to help the ignorant, described as 'the days the hunting classes stop chasing the fox and chase each other instead'. Olympia the jockette had been twenty-three, had come from a 'secure suburban background' and had worked as an instructor in a riding-school in Surrey. Her parents, not surprisingly, were said to be 'distraught'.

Dee-Dee came into the dining-room offering more coffee and saw what I was reading.

'That Olympia was a sex-pot bimbo,' she remarked flatly. 'I was there at the party and you could practically smell it. Secure little suburban riding instructor, my foot.'

'Really?'

'Her father made her out to be a sweet innocent little saint. Perhaps he even believes it. Nolan never said any different because it wouldn't have helped him, so no one told the truth.'

'What was the truth?'

'She had no underclothes on,' Dee-Dee said calmly. 'She wore only a long scarlet strapless dress slit halfway up her thigh. You ask Mackie. She knows, she tried to revive her.'

'Er . . . quite a lot of women don't wear underclothes,' I said.

'Is that a fact?' She gave me an ironic look.

'My blushing days are over.'

'Well, do you or don't you want any coffee?'

'Yes, please.'

She went out to the kitchen and I continued reading clippings, progressing from 'no action on the death at Shellerton House' to 'Olympia's father brings private prosecution' and 'Magistrates refer Nolan Everard case to Crown Court'. A *sub judice* silence then descended and the clippings stopped.

It was after a bunch of end-of-jumping-season statistics that I came across an oddity from a Reading paper published on a Friday in June.

'Girl groom missing', read the headline, and there

was an accompanying photo of Tremayne, still looking cheerful.

> Angela Brickell, 17, employed as a 'lad' by prominent racehorse trainer Tremayne Vickers, failed to turn up for work on Tuesday afternoon and hasn't been seen in the stables since. Vickers says lads leave without notice all too often, but he is puzzled that she didn't ask for pay due to her. Anyone knowing Angela Brickell's whereabouts is asked to get in touch with the police.

Angela Brickell's parents, like Olympia's, were reported to be 'distraught'.

CHAPTER SIX

By the following week, Angela Brickell's disappearance had been taken up by the national dailies who all mentioned the death of Olympia at Shellerton two months earlier but drew no significant conclusions.

Angela, I learned, lived in a stable hostel with five other girls who described her as 'moody'. An indistinct photograph of her showed the face of a child, not a young woman, and pleas to 'Find This Girl' could realistically never have been successful if they depended on recognising her from her likeness in newsprint.

There was no account, in fact, of her having been found, and after a week or so the clippings about her stopped.

There were no cuttings at all for July, when it seemed the jump racing fraternity took a holiday, but they began again with various accounts of the opening of the new season in Devon in August. 'Vickers' Victories Continue!'

Nolan had ridden a winner on one of Fiona's horses:

'the well-known amateur now out on bail facing charges of assault resulting in death . . .'

In early September Nolan had hit the news again, this time in giving evidence at a Jockey Club enquiry in defence of Tremayne, who stood accused of doping one of his horses.

With popping eyes, since Tremayne to me even on such short acquaintance seemed the last person to put his whole way of life in jeopardy for so trivial a reason, I read that one of his horses had tested positive to traces of the stimulants theobromine and caffeine, prohibited substances.

The horse in question had won an amateurs' race back in May. Belonging to Fiona, it had been ridden by Nolan, who said he had no idea how the drugs had been administered. He had himself been in charge of the horse that day since Tremayne hadn't attended the meeting. Tremayne had sent the animal in the care of his head travelling lad and a groom, and neither the head lad nor Tremayne knew how the drugs had been administered. Mrs Fiona Goodhaven could offer no explanation either, though she and her husband had attended and watched the race.

The Jockey Club's verdict at the end of the day had been that there was no way of determining who had given the drugs or how, since they couldn't any longer question the groom who had been in charge of the horse as she, Angela Brickell, could not be found.

Angela Brickell. Good grief, I thought.

Tremayne had nevertheless been adjudged guilty as charged and had been fined fifteen hundred pounds. A slapped wrist, it seemed.

Upon leaving the enquiry Tremayne had shrugged and said, 'These things happen.'

The drug theobromine, along with caffeine, commented the reporter, could commonly be found in chocolate. Well, well, I thought. Never a dull moment in the racing industry.

The rest of the year seemed an anti-climax after that, though there had been a whole procession of notable wins. 'The Stable in Form' and 'More Vim to Vickers' and 'Loadsa Vicktories', according to which paper or magazine one read.

I finished the year and was simply sitting and thinking when Tremayne breezed in with downland air still cool on his coat.

'How are you doing?' he said.

I pointed to the pile of clippings out of their box. 'I was reading about last year. All those winners.'

He beamed. 'Couldn't put a foot wrong. Amazing. Sometimes things just go right. Other years, you get the virus, horses break down, owners die, you have a ghastly time. All the luck of the game.'

'Did Angela Brickell ever turn up?' I asked.

'Who? Oh, her. No, silly little bitch, God knows where she made off to. Every last person in the racing world knows you mustn't give chocolate to horses in training. Pity really, most of them love it. Everybody also knows a Mars Bar here or there isn't going to make a horse win a race, but there you are, by the rules chocolate's a stimulant, so bad luck.'

'Would the girl have got into trouble if she'd stayed?'

He laughed. 'From me, yes. I'd have sacked her, but she'd gone before I heard the horse had tested positive. It was a routine test; they test most winners.' He paused and sat down on a chair across the table from me, staring thoughtfully at a heap of clippings. 'It could have been anyone, you know. Anyone here in the yard. Or Nolan himself, though God knows why he should. Anyway,' he shrugged, 'it often happens because the testing techniques are now so highly developed. They don't automatically warn off trainers any more, thank God, when odd things turn up in the analysis. It has to be gross, has to be beyond interpretation as an accident. But it's still a risk every trainer runs. Risk of crooks. Risk of plain malice. You take what precautions you can and pray.'

'I'll put that in the book, if you like.'

He looked at me assessingly. 'I got me a good writer after all, didn't I?'

I shook my head. 'You got one who'll do his best.'

He smiled with what looked like satisfaction and after lunch (beef sandwiches) we got down to work again on taping his early life with his eccentric father. Tremayne seemed to have soared unharmed over such psychological trifles as being rented out in Leicestershire as a harness and tack cleaner to a fox-hunting family and a year later as stable boy to a polo player in Argentina.

'But that was child abuse,' I protested.

Tremayne chuckled unconcernedly. 'I didn't get buggered, if that's what you mean. My father hired me out, picked up all I earned and gave me a crack or two with his cane when I said it wasn't fair. Well, it wasn't fair. He told me that that was a valuable lesson, to learn that things weren't fair. Never expect fairness. I'm telling you what he told me, but you're lucky, I won't beat it into you.'

'Will you pay me?'

He laughed deeply. 'You've got Ronnie Curzon looking after that.' His amusement continued. 'Did your father ever beat you?'

'No, he didn't believe in it.'

'Nor do I, by God. I've never beaten Perkin, nor Gareth. Couldn't. I remember what it felt like. But then, see, he did take me with him to Argentina and all round the world. I saw a lot of things most English boys don't. I missed a lot of school. He was mad, no doubt, but he gave me a priceless education and I wouldn't change anything.'

'You had a pretty tough mind,' I said.

'Sure.' He nodded. 'You need it in this life.'

You might need it, I reflected, but tough minds weren't regulation issue. Many children would have disintegrated where Tremayne had learned and thrived.

I tended to feel at home with stoicism and, increasingly, with Tremayne.

About mid-afternoon, when we stopped taping, he lent me his Volvo to go to Didcot to fetch the parcel of books from the station and to do the household shopping, advising me not to slide into any ditches if I could help it. The roads, however, were marginally better and the air not so brutally cold, though the forecasters still spoke of more days' frost. I shopped with luxurious abandon for food and picked up the books, getting back to Shellerton while Tremayne was still out in his yard at evening stables.

He came into the house with Mackie, both of them stamping their feet and blowing onto their fingers as they discussed the state of the horses.

'You'd better ride Selkirk in the morning,' Tremayne said to her. 'He's a bit too fresh these days for his lad.'

'Right.'

'And I forgot to tell Bob to get the lads to put two rugs on their mounts if they're doing only trotting exercise.'

'I'll remind him.'

'Good.'

He saw me in the kitchen as I was finishing stowing the stores and asked if the books had arrived. They had, I said.

'Great. Bring them into the family room. Come on, Mackie, gin and tonic.'

The big logs in the family room fireplace never

entirely went cold; Tremayne kicked the embers smartly together, adding a few small sticks and a fresh chunk of beech to renew the blaze. The evening developed as twice before, Perkin arriving as if on cue and collecting his Coke.

With flattering eagerness Tremayne opened the package of books and handed some of them to Mackie and Perkin. So familiar to me, they seemed to surprise the others, though I wasn't sure why.

Slightly larger than paperbacks, they were more the size of video tapes and had white shiny hard covers with the title in various bright black-edged colours: *Return Safe from the Jungle* in green, *Return Safe from the Desert* in orange, *Return Safe from the Sea* in blue, *Return Safe from the Ice* in purple, *Return Safe from Safari* in red, *Return Safe from the Wilderness* in a hot rusty brown.

'I'll be damned,' Tremayne said. 'Real books.'

'What did you expect?' I asked.

'Well ... pamphlets, I suppose. Thin paperbacks, perhaps.'

'The travel agency wanted them glossy,' I explained, 'and also useful.'

'They must have taken a lot of work,' Mackie observed, turning the pages of *Ice* and looking at illustrations.

'There's a good deal of repetition in them, to be honest,' I said. 'I mean, quite a lot of survival techniques are the same wherever you find yourself.'

'Such as what?' Perkin asked, faintly belligerent as usual.

'Lighting fires, finding water, making a shelter. Things like that.'

'The books are fascinating,' Mackie said, now looking at *Sea*, 'but how often do people get marooned on desert islands these days?'

I smiled. 'Not often. It's just the *idea* of survival that people like. There are schools where people on holiday go for survival courses. Actually the most lethal place to be is up a British mountainside in the wrong clothes in a cold mist. A fair number of people each year don't survive *that*.'

'Could you?' Perkin asked.

'Yes, but I wouldn't be up there in the wrong clothes in the first place.'

'Survival begins before you set out,' Tremayne said, reading the first page of *Jungle*: he looked up, amused, quoting, ' "Survival is a frame of mind." '

'Yes.'

'I have it,' he said.

'Indeed you do.'

All three of them went on reading the books with obvious interest, dipping into the various sections at random, flicking over pages and stopping to read more: vindicating, I thought, the travel agency's contention that the back-to-nature essentials of staying alive held irresistible attractions for ultra-cosseted sophisticates, just as long as they never had to put them into practice in bitter earnest.

Gareth erupted into the peaceful scene like a rehearsing poltergeist.

'What are you all so busy with?' he demanded, and then spotted the books, 'Boy, oh *boy*. They've come!'

He grabbed up *Return from the Wilderness* and plunged in, and I sat drinking wine and wondering if I would ever see four people reading *Long Way Home*.

'This is pretty earthy stuff,' Mackie said after a while, laying her book down. 'Skinning and de-gutting animals, ugh.'

'You'd do it if you were starving,' Tremayne told her.

'I'd do it *for* you,' Gareth said.

'So would I,' said Perkin.

'Then I'll arrange not to get stranded anywhere without you both.' She was teasing, affectionate. 'And I'll stay in camp and grind the corn.' She put a hand to her mouth in mock dismay. 'Dear heaven, may feminists forgive me.'

'It's pretty boring about all these jabs,' Gareth complained, not being interested in gender typing.

' "Better the jabs than the diseases", it says here,' Tremayne said.

'Oh well, then.'

'And you've had tetanus jabs already.'

'I guess so,' Gareth agreed. He looked at me. 'Have you had all these jabs?'

'Afraid so.'

'Tetanus?'

'Especially.'

'There's an awful lot about first aid,' he said, turning pages. ' "How to stop wounds bleeding ... pressure points," A whole map of arteries. "How to deal with poisons ... swallow *charcoal*"!' He looked up. 'Do you mean it?'

'Sure,' I said. 'Scrape it into water and drink it. The carbon helps take some sorts of poison harmlessly through the gut, if you're lucky.'

'Good God,' Tremayne said.

His younger son went on reading. 'It says here you can drink urine if you distil it.'

'Gareth!' Mackie said, disgusted.

'Well, that's what it says. "Urine is sterile and cannot cause diseases. Boil it and condense the steam which will then be pure distilled water, perfectly safe to drink." '

'John, really!' Mackie protested.

'It's true,' I said, smiling. 'Lack of water is a terrible killer. If you've a fire but no water, you now know what to do.'

'I couldn't.'

'Survival is a frame of mind,' Tremayne repeated. 'You never know what you can do until you have to.'

Perkin asked me, 'Have you ever drunk it?'

'Distilled water?'

'You know what I mean.'

I nodded. 'Yes, I have. To test it for the books. And

I've distilled all sorts of other things too. Filthy jungle water. Wet mud. Sea water, particularly. If the starter liquid is watery and not fermenting, the steam is pure H_2O. And when sea water boils dry you have salt left, which is useful.'

'What if the starter liquid *is* fermenting?' Gareth asked.

'The steam is alcohol.'

'Oh yes, I'm supposed to have learned that in school.'

'Gin and tonic in the wilderness?' Tremayne suggested.

I said with enjoyment, 'I could certainly get you *drunk* in the wilderness, but actual gin would depend on juniper bushes, and tonic on chinchona trees for quinine, and I don't think they'd both grow in the same place, but you never know.' I paused. 'Ice cubes might be a problem in the rain forest.'

Tremayne laughed deep in his chest. 'Did you ever rely on all this stuff to save your life?'

'Not entirely,' I said. 'I lived by these techniques for weeks at a time, but someone always knew roughly where I was. I had escape routes. I was basically testing what was practicable and possible and sensible in each area where the agency wanted to set up adventure holidays. I've never had to survive after a plane crash in the mountains, for instance.'

There had been a plane crash in the Andes in 1972 when people had eaten other people in order to stay alive. I didn't think I would tell Mackie, though.

'But,' she said, 'did things ever go wrong?'

'Sometimes.'

'Like what? Do say.'

'Well . . . like insect bites and eating things that disagreed with me.'

They all looked as if these were everyday affairs, but I'd been too ill a couple of times to care to remember.

I said with equal truth but more drama, 'A bear smashed up my camp in Canada once and hung around it for days. I couldn't reach anything I needed. It was a shade fraught there for a bit.'

'Do you mean it?' Gareth was open-mouthed.

'Nothing happened,' I said. 'The bear went away.'

'Weren't you afraid he would come back?'

'I packed up and moved somewhere else.'

'Wow,' Gareth said.

'Bears eat people,' his brother told him repressively. 'Don't get any ideas about copying John.'

Tremayne looked at his sons mildly. 'Have either of you ever heard of vicarious enjoyment?'

'No,' Gareth said. 'What is it?'

'Dreaming,' Mackie suggested.

Perkin said, 'Someone else does the suffering for you.'

'Let Gareth dream,' Tremayne said, nodding. 'It's natural. I don't suppose for one moment he'll go chasing bears.'

'Boys do stupid things, Gareth included.'

'Hey,' his brother protested. 'Who's talking? Who climbed on to the roof and couldn't get down?'

'Shut your face,' Perkin said.

'Do give it a rest, you two,' Mackie said wearily. 'Why do you always quarrel?'

'We're nothing compared with Lewis and Nolan,' Perkin said. 'They can get really vicious.'

Mackie said reflectively, 'They haven't quarrelled since Olympia died.'

'Not in front of us,' her husband agreed, 'but you don't know what they've said in private.'

Diffidently, because it wasn't really my business, I asked, 'Why do they quarrel?'

'Why does anyone?' Tremayne said. 'But those two envy each other. You met them last night, didn't you? Nolan has the looks and the dash, Lewis is a drunk with brains. Nolan has courage and is thick, Lewis is a physical disaster but when he's sober he's a whiz at making money. Nolan is a crack shot, Lewis misses every pheasant he aims at. Lewis would like to be the glamorous amateur jockey and Nolan would like to be upwardly disgustingly rich. Neither will ever manage it, but that doesn't stop the envy.'

'You're too hard on them,' Mackie murmured.

'But you know I'm right.'

She didn't deny it, but said, 'Perhaps the Olympia business has drawn them together.'

'You're a sweet young woman,' Tremayne told her. 'You see good in everyone.'

Perkin said, 'Hands off my wife,' in what might or might not have been a joke. Tremayne chose to take it lightly, and I thought he must be well used to his son's acute possessiveness.

He turned from Perkin to me and with a swift change of subject said, 'How well do you ride?'

'Er . . .' I said, 'I haven't ridden a racehorse.'

'What then?'

'Hacks, dude ranch horses, pony trekking, arab horses in the desert.'

'Hm.' He pondered. 'Care to ride my hack with the string in the morning? Let's see what you can do.'

'OK.' I must have sounded half-hearted, because he pounced on it.

'Don't you want to?' he demanded.

'Yes, please.'

'Right, then,' he nodded. 'Mackie, tell Bob to have Touchy saddled up for John, if you're out in the yard before me.'

'Right.'

'Touchy won the Cheltenham Gold Cup,' Gareth told me.

'Oh, did he?' Some hack.

'Don't worry,' Mackie said, smiling, 'he's fifteen now and almost a gentleman.'

'Dumps people regularly on Fridays,' Gareth said.

*

127

With apprehension, I went out into the yard on the following morning, Friday, in jodhpurs, boots, ski-jacket and gloves. I hadn't sat on a horse of any sort for almost two years and, whatever Mackie might say, my idea of a nice quiet return to the saddle wasn't a star steeplechaser, pensioned or not.

Touchy was big with bulging muscles; he would have to be, I supposed, to carry Tremayne's weight. Bob Watson gave me a grin, a helmet and a leg-up, and it seemed a fair way down to the ground.

Oh well, I thought. Enjoy it. I'd said I could ride: time to try and prove it. Tremayne, watching me appraisingly with his head on one side, told me to take my place behind Mackie who would be leading the string. He himself would be driving the tractor. I could take Touchy up the all-weather gallop at a fast canter when everyone else had worked.

'All right,' I said.

He smiled faintly and walked away and I collected the reins and a few thoughts and tried not to make a fool of myself.

Bob Watson appeared again at my elbow.

'Get him anchored when you set off up the gallop,' he said, 'or he'll pull your arms out.'

'Thanks,' I said, but he had already moved on.

'All out,' he was saying, and out they all came from the boxes, circling in the lights, breathing plumes, moving in circles as Bob threw the lads up, all as before, only now I was part of it, now on the canvas in the

picture, as if alive in a Munnings painting, extraordinary.

I followed Mackie out of the yard and across the
road and on to the downland track, and found that
Touchy knew what to do from long experience but
would respond better to pressure with the calf rather
than to strong pulls on his tough old mouth.

Mackie looked back a few times as if to make sure
I hadn't evaporated and watched while I circled with
the others as it grew light and we waited for Tremayne
to reach the top of the hill.

Drifting alongside, she asked, 'Where did you learn
to ride?'

'Mexico,' I said.

'You were taught by a Spaniard!'

'Yes, I was.'

'And he had you riding with your arms folded?'

'Yes, how do you know?'

'I thought so. Well, tuck your elbows in on old
Touchy.'

'Thanks.'

She smiled and went off to arrange the order in
which the string should exercise up the gallop.

Snow still lay thinly over everything and it was
another clear morning, stingingly, beautifully cold. January dawn on the Downs; once felt, never forgotten.

Bit by bit the string set off up the wood-chippings
track until only Mackie and I were left.

'I'll go with you on your right,' she said, coming up behind me. 'Then Tremayne can see how you ride.'

'Thanks very much,' I said ironically.

'You'll do fine.'

She swayed suddenly in the saddle and I put out a hand to steady her.

'Are you OK?' I asked anxiously. 'You should have rested more after that bang on the head.' She was pale. Huge-eyed. Alarming.

'No... I...' She took an unsteady breath. 'I just felt... oh... oh...'

She swayed again and looked near to fainting. I leaned across and put my right arm round her waist, holding her tight to prevent her falling. Her weight sagged against me limply until I was supporting her entirely, and since she had an arm through her reins her horse was held close to mine, their heads almost touching.

I took hold of her reins in my left hand and simply held her tight with my right, and her horse moved his rump sideways away from me until she slid off out of her saddle altogether and finished half lying across my knee and Touchy's withers, held only by my grasp.

I couldn't let her fall and I couldn't dismount without dropping her, so with both hands I pulled and heaved her up onto Touchy until she was half sitting and half lying across the front of my saddle, held in my arms. Touchy didn't much like it and Mackie's horse had backed away sharply to the length of his reins and was on the edge of bolting, and I began to wonder if I should just let him go free in spite of the icy dangers everywhere lurking. I might then manage to walk Touchy back to the stable with his double cargo and we might yet not have a worse disaster than Mackie's unconsciousness. The urgency of getting help for her made more things possible than I could have thought.

Touchy got an unmistakable signal from my leg and obediently turned towards home. I decided I would hold on to Mackie's horse as long as it would come too, and as if by magic he got the going-home message and decided not to object any further.

We had gone perhaps three paces in this fashion when Mackie woke up and came to full consciousness as if a light had been switched on.

'What happened . . .?'

'You fainted. Fell this way.'

'I can't have done.' But she could see that she must have. 'Let me down,' she said. 'I feel awfully sick.'

'Can you stand?' I asked worriedly. 'Let me take you home like this.'

'No.' She rolled against me onto her stomach and slid down slowly until her feet were on the ground. 'What a stupid thing to do,' she said. 'I'm all right now, I am really. Give me my reins.'

'Mackie . . .'

She turned away from me suddenly and vomited convulsively onto the snow.

I hopped down off Touchy with the reins of both horses held fast and tried to help her.

'God,' she said weakly, searching for a tissue, 'must have eaten something.'

'Not my cooking.'

'No.' She found the tissue and smiled a fraction. She and Perkin hadn't stayed for the previous evening's grilled chicken. 'I haven't felt well for days.'

'Concussion,' I said.

'No, even before that. Tension over the trial, I suppose.' She took a few deep breaths and blew her nose. 'I feel perfectly all right now. I don't understand it.'

She was looking at me in puzzlement and I quite clearly saw the thought float into her head and transfigure her face into wonderment and hope . . . and joy.

'Oh!' she said ecstatically. 'Do you think . . . I mean, I've been feeling sick every morning this week . . . and after two years of trying I'd stopped expecting anything to happen, and anyway, I didn't know it could make you feel so ill right at the beginning . . . I mean, I didn't even *suspect* . . . I'm always wildly irregular.' She stopped and laughed. 'Don't tell Tremayne. Don't tell Perkin. I'll wait a bit first, to make sure. But I *am* sure. It explains all sorts of odd things that have happened this last week. Like my nipples itching. My hormones must be rioting. I can't believe it. I think I'll burst.'

I thought that I had never before seen such pure uncomplicated happiness in anyone, and was tremendously glad for her.

'What a revelation!' she said. 'Like an angel announcing it . . . if that's not blasphemous.'

'Don't hope too much,' I said cautiously.

'Don't be silly. I *know*.' She seemed to wake suddenly to our whereabouts. 'Tremayne will be going mad because we haven't appeared.'

'I'll ride up and tell him you're not well and have gone home.'

'No, definitely not. I *am* well. I've never felt better in my whole life. I am gloriously and immensely well. Give me a leg-up.'

I told her she needed to rest but she obstinately refused, and in the end I bowed to her judgment and lifted her lightly into the saddle, scrambling up myself onto Touchy's broad back. She shook up her reins as if nothing had happened and set off up the wood chippings at a medium canter, glancing back for me to follow. I joined her expecting to go the whole way at that conservative pace but she quickened immediately I reached her and I could hardly hang back and say hold on a minute, I haven't done this in a while and could easily fall off. Instead, I tucked in my elbows as instructed and relied on luck.

Towards the end Mackie kicked her horse into a frank gallop and it was at that speed that we both passed Tremayne. I was peripherally aware of him standing four-square on the small observation mound, though all my direct attention was acutely focused on balance, grip and what lay ahead between Touchy's ears.

Touchy, I thanked heaven, slowed when Mackie slowed and brought himself to a good-natured halt without dumping his rider, Friday or not. I was breathless and also exhilarated and thought I could easily get hooked on Touchy after a fix or two more like that.

'Where the hell did you get to?' Tremayne enquired of me, joining us and the rest of the string. 'I thought you'd chickened out,'

'We were just talking,' Mackie said.

Tremayne looked at her now glowing face and probably drew the wrong conclusion but made no further comment. He told everyone to walk back down the gallop and dismount and lead them the last part of the way, as usual.

Mackie, taking her place at the head, asked me to ride at the back, to make sure everyone returned safely, which I did. Tremayne's tractor followed slowly, at a distance.

He came stamping into the kitchen where I was fishing out orange juice and without preamble demanded, 'What were you and Mackie talking about?'

'She'll tell you,' I said, smiling.

He said belligerently, 'Mackie's off limits.'

I put down the orange juice and straightened, not knowing quite what to say.

'If you mean do I fancy Mackie,' I said, 'then yes, she's a great girl. But off limits is right. We were not flirting, chatting up, or whatever else you care to call it. *Not.*'

After a grudging minute he said, 'All right then,' and I thought that in his way he was as possessive of Mackie as Perkin was.

A short while later, munching the toast I'd made for him, he seemed to have forgotten it.

'You can ride out every morning,' he said, 'if you'd like.'

He could see I was pleased. I said, 'I'd like it very much.'

'Settled, then.'

The day passed in the way that had become routine: clippings, beef sandwiches, taping, evening drinks, Gareth home, cook the dinner. Dee-Dee's distrust of me had vanished; Perkin's hadn't. Tremayne seemed to have accepted my assurance of the morning, and Mackie smiled into her plain tonic and carefully avoided my eyes for fear of revealing that a secret lay between us.

On Saturday morning I rode Touchy again but Mackie didn't materialise, having phoned Tremayne to say she wasn't well. She and Perkin appeared in the kitchen during breakfast, he with an arm round her shoulders in a supremely proprietary way.

'We've something to tell you,' Perkin said to Tremayne.

'Oh, yes?' Tremayne was busy with some papers.

'Yes. Do pay attention. We're having a baby.'

'We think so,' Mackie said.

Tremayne paid attention abruptly and was clearly profoundly delighted. Not an over-demonstrative man he didn't leap up to embrace them but literally purred in his throat like a cat and beat the table with his fist. Son and daughter-in-law had no difficulty in reading the signals and looked smugly pleased with themselves, sitting down, drinking coffee and working out that the birth would occur in September, but they weren't quite sure of the date.

Mackie gave me a shy smile which Perkin forgave. Each of them looked more in love with the other, more relaxed, as if the earlier failure to conceive had caused tension between them, now relieved.

After that excitement I laboured all morning again on the clippings, unsustained by cups from Dee-Dee, who didn't work on Saturdays. Gareth went to Saturday morning school and pinned a second message on the corkboard – 'FOOTBALL MATCH PM' – leaving 'BACK FOR GRUB' in place.

Tremayne, cursing the persistent absence of racing even on television, taped the saga of his younger life up to the time he accompanied his father to a brothel.

'My father wouldn't have anybody but the madam and she said she'd retired long ago but she accommodated him in the end. Couldn't resist him, the mad old charmer.'

In the evening I fed the three of us on lamb chops, peas and potatoes in their skins and on Sunday morning Fiona and Harry came to the stables to see her horses and drink with Tremayne afterwards in the family room. Nolan came with them, but not Lewis. An aunt of Harry's, another Mrs Goodhaven, tagged quietly along. Mackie, Perkin and Gareth congregated as if for a normal ritual.

Mackie couldn't keep her good news to herself and Fiona and Harry hugged her while Perkin looked important and Nolan gave half-hearted congratulations. Tremayne opened champagne.

At about that time, ten miles away in lonely woodland, a gamekeeper came across what was left of Angela Brickell.

CHAPTER SEVEN

The discovery made no impact on Shellerton on that Sunday because at first no one knew whose bones lay among the dead brambles and the dormant oaks.

The gamekeeper went home to his Sunday lunch and telephoned the local police after he'd eaten, feeling that as the bones were old it wouldn't matter if they waited one hour longer.

In Tremayne's house, when the toasts to the future Vickers had been drunk, Gareth showed Fiona a couple of the travel guides and Fiona in astonishment showed Harry. Nolan picked up *Safari* as if absent-mindedly and said that no one but a bloody fool would go hunting tigers in Africa.

'There aren't any tigers in Africa,' Gareth said.

'That's right. He'd be a bloody fool.'

'Oh . . . it's a joke,' Gareth said, obviously feeling that it was he who'd been made a fool of. 'Very funny.'

Nolan, though the shortest man there, physically

dominated the room, eclipsing even Tremayne. His strong animal vigour and powerful saturnine features seemed to charge the very air with static, as if his presence alone could generate sparks. One could see how Mackie had been struck by lightning. One could see how Olympia might have died by violent accident. One's reactions to Nolan had little to do with reason, all with instinct.

Harry's aunt was looking into *Ice* in a faintly superior way as if confronted with a manifestation of the lower orders.

'How frightfully *rugged*,' she said, her voice as languid as Harry's but without the God-given amusement.

'Er,' Harry said to me. 'I didn't introduce you properly. I must present you to my aunt, Erica Goodhaven. She's a writer.'

There was a subterranean flood of mischief in his eyes. Fiona glanced at me with a hint of a smile and I thought both of them looked as though I were about to be thrown to the lions for their entertainment. Anticipation of enjoyment, loud and clear.

'Erica,' Harry said, 'John wrote these books.'

'And a novel,' Tremayne said defensively, coming to an aid I didn't realise I needed. 'It's going to be published. And he's writing my biography.'

'A *novel*,' Harry's aunt said, in the same way as before.

'Going to be published. How *interesting*. I, also, write novels. Under my unmarried name, Erica Upton.'

Thrown to a literary lion, I perceived. A real one, a lioness. Erica Upton's five-star prize-winning reputation was for erudition, elegant syntax, esoteric backgrounds, elegiac characters and a profound understanding of incest.

'Your aunt?' I said to Harry.

'By marriage.'

Tremayne refilled my glass with champagne as if I would need it and muttered under his breath, 'She'll eat you.'

From across the room she did look faintly predatory at that moment, though was otherwise a slender, intense-looking, grey-haired woman in a grey wool dress with flat shoes and no jewellery. A quintessential aunt, I thought; except that most people's aunts weren't Erica Upton.

'What is your novel *about?*' she enquired of me. Her voice was patronising but I didn't mind that: she was entitled to it.

The others all waited with her to hear my answer. Incredible, I thought, that nine people in one room weren't carrying on noisy separate conversations, as usually happened.

'It's about survival,' I said politely.

Everyone listened. Everyone always listened to Erica Upton.

'What sort of survival?' she asked. 'Medical? Economic? Creative?'

'It's about some travellers cut off by an earthquake. About how they coped. It's called *Long Way Home*.'

'How *quaint*,' she said.

She wasn't intending to be outright offensive, I thought. She seemed merely to know that her own work was on a summit I would never reach, and in that she was right. All the same I felt again the mild recklessness that I had on Touchy: even if I lacked confidence, relax and have a go.

'My agent says,' I said neutrally, 'that *Long Way Home* is really about the spiritual consequences of deprivation and fear.'

She knew a gauntlet when she heard one. I saw the stiffening in her body and suspected it in her mind.

She said, 'You are too young to write with authority of spiritual consequences. Too young for your soul to have been tempered. Too young to have learned the intensity of understanding that comes only through deep adversity.'

Was that true, I wondered? How old was old enough?

I said, 'Shouldn't contentment be allowed its insights?'

'It has none. Insight grows best on stony ground. Unless you have suffered or are poor or can tap into melancholy, you have defective perception.'

I rolled with that one. Sought for a response.

'I *am* poor,' I said. 'Well, fairly. Poor enough to perceive that poverty is the enemy of moral strength.'

She peered at me as if measuring a prey for the pounce.

'You are a lightweight person,' she said, 'if you have no conception of the moral strength of redemption and atonement in penury.'

I swallowed. 'I don't seek sainthood. I seek insight through a combination of imagination and common sense.'

'You are not a serious writer.' A dire accusation; her worst.

'I write to entertain,' I said.

'I,' she said simply, 'write to enlighten.'

I could find no possible answer. I said wryly, with a bow, 'I am defeated.'

She laughed with pleasure, her muscles loosening. The lion had devoured the sacrifice and all was well. She turned away to begin talking to Fiona, and Harry made his way to my side, watching me dispatch my champagne with a gulp.

'You didn't do too badly,' he said. 'Nice brisk duel.'

'She ran me through.'

'Oh yes. Never mind. Good sport, though.'

'You set it up.'

He grinned. 'She phoned this morning. She comes occasionally for lunch, so I told her to beetle over. Couldn't resist it.'

'What a pal.'

'Be honest. You enjoyed it.'

I sighed. 'She outguns me by far.'

'She's more than twice your age.'

'That makes it worse.'

'Seriously,' he said, as if he thought my ego needed patching, 'these survival guides are pretty good. Do you mind if we take a few of them home?'

'They're Tremayne's and Gareth's, really.'

'I'll ask them then.' He looked at me shrewdly. 'Nothing wrong with your courage, is there?'

'How do you mean?'

'You took her on. You didn't have to.'

I half laughed. 'My agent calls it impulsive behaviour. He says it will kill me, one day.'

'You're older than you look,' he said cryptically, and went off to talk to Tremayne.

Mackie, her drink all but untouched, took his place as kind blotter of bleeding feelings.

'It's not fair of her to call you lightweight,' she said. 'Harry shouldn't have brought her. I know she's highly revered but she can make people cry. I've seen her do it.'

'My eyes are dry,' I said. 'Are you drinking that champagne?'

'I'd better not, I suppose.'

'Care to give it to the walking wounded?'

She smiled her brilliant smile and we exchanged glasses.

'Actually,' she said, 'I didn't understand all Erica was saying.'

'She was saying she's cleverer than me.'

'I.'

'I,' I agreed.

'I'll bet she can't catch people who're fainting off horses.'

Mackie was, as Tremayne had said, a sweet young woman.

Angela Brickell's remains lay on the Quillersedge Estate at the western edge of the Chilterns.

The Quillersedge gamekeeper arranged on the telephone for the local police to collect him from his cottage on the estate and drive as near to the bones as possible on the estate's private roads. From there, everyone would have to go through the woods on foot.

The few policemen on duty on Sunday afternoon thought of cold wet undergrowth and shivered.

In Tremayne's house, the informal party lingered cheerfully. Fiona and Mackie sat on a sofa, silver-blond head beside dark red-brown, talking about Mackie's baby. Nolan discussed with Tremayne the horses Nolan hoped still to be riding when racing resumed. Gareth handed round potato crisps while eating most of them himself and Perkin read aloud how to return safely from getting lost.

' "Go downhill, not up," ' he read. ' "People live in valleys. Follow streams in their flow direction. People live beside rivers." I can't imagine I'll ever need this advice. I steer clear of jungles.'

'You could need it in the Lake District,' I said mildly.

'I don't like walking, period.'

Harry said, 'John, Erica wants to know why you've ignored mountain climbing in your guides.'

'Never got round to it,' I said, 'and there are dozens of mountain climbing books already.'

Erica, the sparkle of victory still in her eyes, asked who was publishing my novel. When I told her she raised her eyebrows thoughtfully and made no disparaging remarks.

'Good publishers, aren't they?' Harry asked, his lips twitching.

'Reputable,' she allowed.

Fiona, getting to her feet, began to say goodbyes, chiefly with kisses. Gareth ducked his but she stopped beside me and put her cheek on mine.

'How long are you staying?' she asked.

Tremayne answered for me forthrightly. 'Three more weeks. Then we'll see.'

'We'll fix a dinner,' Fiona said. 'Come along, Nolan. Ready, Erica? Love you, Mackie, take care of yourself.'

When they'd gone Mackie and Perkin floated off home on cloud nine, and Tremayne and I went round collecting glasses and stacking them in the dishwasher.

Gareth said, 'If we can have beef sandwich pie again, I'll make it for lunch.'

*

145

At about the time we finally ate the pie, two policemen and the gamekeeper reached the pathetic collection of bones and set nemesis in motion. They tied ropes to trees to ring and isolate the area and radioed for more instructions. Slowly the information percolated upwards until it reached Detective Chief Inspector Doone, Thames Valley Police, who was sleeping off his Yorkshire pudding.

He decided, as daylight would die within the hour, that first thing in the morning he would assemble and take a pathologist for an on-site examination and a photographer for the record. He believed the bones would prove to belong to one of the hundreds of teenagers who had infested his patch with all-night parties the summer before. Three others had died on him from drugs.

In Tremayne's house Gareth and I went up to my bedroom because he wanted to see the survival kit that he knew I'd brought with me.

'Is it just like the ones in the books?' he asked as I brought out a black waterproof pouch that one could wear round one's waist.

'No, not entirely.' I paused. 'I have three survival kits at present. One small one for taking with me all the time. This one here for longer walks and difficult areas. And one that I didn't bring, which is full camping survival gear for going out into the wilds. That's a back-pack on a frame.'

'I wish I could see it,' Gareth said wistfully.

'Well, one day, you never know.'

'I'll hold you to it.'

'I'll show you the smallest kit first,' I said, 'but you'll have to run down and get it. It's in my ski-suit jacket pocket in the cloakroom.'

He went willingly but presently returned doubtfully with a flat tin, smaller than a paperback book, held shut with black insulating tape.

'Is that it?' he said.

I nodded. 'Open it carefully.'

He did as I said, laying out the contents on the white counterpane on the bed and reciting them aloud.

'Two matchbooks, a bit of candle, a little coil of thin wire, a piece of jagged wire, some fishhooks, a small pencil and piece of paper, needles and thread, two sticking plasters and a plastic bag folded up small and held by a paperclip.' He looked disappointed. 'You couldn't do much with those.'

'Just light a fire, cut wood, catch food, collect water, make a map and sew up wounds. That jagged wire is a flexible saw.'

His mouth opened.

'Then I always carry two things on my belt.' I unstrapped it and showed it to him. 'The belt itself has a zipped pocket all along the inside where you can keep money. What's in there at the moment is your father's. I don't often carry a wallet. Those other things on the belt, one is a knife, one is a multi-purpose survival tool.'

'Can I look?'

'Yes, sure.'

The knife, in a black canvas sheath with a flap fastened by Velcro, was a strong folding knife with a cunningly serrated blade, very sharp indeed, nine inches overall when open, only five when closed. Gareth opened it until it locked with a snap and stood looking at it in surprise.

'That's some knife,' he said. 'Were you wearing it while we were having drinks?'

'All the time. It weighs only four and a half ounces, about one eighth of a kilo. Weight's important too, don't forget. Always travel as light as you can if you have to carry everything.'

He opened the other object slotted onto the belt, a small leather case about three inches by two and a half, which contained a flat metal rectangular object a shade smaller in dimension: total weight altogether, three and a half ounces.

'What's this?' he asked, taking it out onto his hand. 'I've never seen anything like this.'

'I carry that instead of an ordinary penknife. It has a blade slotted in one side and scissors in the other. That little round thing is a magnifying glass for starting fires if there's any sun. With those other odd-shaped edges you can make holes in a tin of food, open crown cork bottles, screw in screws, file your nails and sharpen knives. The sides have inches and centimetres marked like a ruler, and the back of it all is polished like a mirror for signalling.'

'Wow.' He turned it over and looked at his own face. 'It's really brill.'

He began to pack all the small things back into the flat tin and remarked that fishhooks wouldn't be much good away from rivers.

'You can catch birds on fishhooks. They take bait like fish.'

He stared at me. 'Have you eaten birds?'

'Chickens are birds.'

'Well, ordinary birds?'

'Pigeons? Four and twenty blackbirds? You eat anything if you're hungry enough. All our ancestors lived on whatever they could get hold of. It was normal, once.'

Normal for him was a freezer full of pizzas. He had no idea what it was like to be primevally alone with nature, and it was unlikely he would ever find out, for all his present interest.

I'd spent a month once on an island without any kit or anything modern at all, knowing only that there was water and that I would be collected at the end, and even with those certainties and all the craft I'd ever learned, I'd had a hard job lasting out; and it was then that I'd discovered for myself that survival was a matter of mind rather than body.

The travel agency, on my urgent advice, had decided against offering holidays of that sort.

'What about a group?' they said. 'Not one alone.'

'A group eats more,' I pointed out. 'The tensions are terrible. You'd have a murder.'

'All right. Full camping kit then, with essential stores and radios.'

'And choose the leader before they set out.'

Even so, few of the 'marooned' holidays had passed off without trouble, and in the end the agency had abandoned them.

Gareth replaced the coil of fine wire in the tin and said, 'I suppose this wire is for all the traps in the books?'

'Only the simplest ones.'

'Some of the traps are really sneaky.'

'I'm afraid so.'

'There you are, a harmless rabbit, hopping along about your business and you don't see the wire hidden in dead leaves and you trip over it and suddenly pow! you're all tied up in a net or squashed under logs. Have you done all that?'

'Yes, lots of times.'

'I like the idea of the bow and arrows better,' he said.

'Yes, well, I put in the instructions of how to make them effectively because our ancestors had them, but it's not easy to hit anything if it's moving. Impossible, if it's small. It's not the same as using a custom-made bow shooting metal arrows at a nice round stationary target, like in archery competitions. I've always preferred traps.'

'Didn't you ever hit *anything* with a bow and arrow?'

I smiled. 'I shot an apple off a tree in our garden once when I was small because I was only allowed to eat windfalls, and there weren't any. Bad luck that my mother was looking out of the window.'

'Mothers!'

'Tremayne says you see yours sometimes.'

'Yes, I do.' He glanced up at me quickly and down again. 'Did Dad tell you my mother isn't Perkin's mother?'

'No,' I said slowly. 'I guess we haven't come to that bit yet.'

'Perkin and Jane's mother died yonks ago. Jane's my sister – well, half-sister really. She's married to a French trainer and they live in Chantilly, which is a sort of French Newmarket. It's good fun, staying with Jane. I go summers. Couple of weeks.'

'Do you speak French?'

He grinned. 'Some. I always seem to come home just when I'm getting the hang of it. What about you?'

'French a bit, but Spanish more, only I'm rusty in both now too.'

He nodded and fiddled for a bit putting the insulating tape back on the tin.

I watched him, and in the end he said, 'My mother's

on television quite a lot. That's where Dad means I see.'

'Television? Is she an actress?'

'No. She cooks. She does one of those afternoon programmes sometimes.'

'A *cook*?' I could hardly believe it. 'But your father doesn't care about food.'

'Yeah, that's what he says, but he's been eating what you've made, hasn't he? But I think she used to drive him barmy always inventing weird fancy things he didn't like. I didn't care that much except that I never got what I liked either, so when she left us we sort of relapsed into what we *did* like, and we stayed like that. Only recently I've been wishing I could make custard and I tried but I burned the milk and it tasted awful. Did you know you could burn milk? So, anyway, she's married to someone else now. I don't like him though. I don't bother with them much.'

He sounded as if he'd said all he wanted to on the subject and seemed relieved to go back to simple things like staying alive, asking to see inside kit number two, the black pouch.

'You're not bored?' I said.

'Can't wait.'

I handed it to him and let him open its three zipped and Velcroed pockets, to lay the contents again on the bed. Although the pouch itself was waterproof, almost every item inside it was further wrapped separately in a small plastic bag, fastened with a twist tie; safe from sand and insects. Gareth undid and emptied some of the bags and frowned over the contents.

'Explain what they are,' he said. 'I mean, twenty matchbooks are for lighting fires, right, so what are the cotton wool balls doing with them?'

'They burn well. They set fire to dry leaves.'

'Oh. The candle is for light, right?'

'And to help light fires. And wax is useful for a lot of things.'

'What's this?' He pointed to a short fat spool of thin yellow thread.

'That's kevlar fibre. It's a sort of plastic, strong as steel. Six hundred yards of it. You can make nets of it, tie anything, fish with it, twist it into fine unbreakable rope. I didn't come across it in time to put in the books.'

'And this? This little jar of whitish liquid packed with the sawn-off paintbrush?'

I smiled. 'That's in the *Wilderness* book. It's luminous paint.'

He stared.

'Well,' I said reasonably, 'if you have a camp and you want to leave it to go and look for food or firewood, you want to be able to find your way back again, don't you? Essential. So as you go, you paint a slash of this on a tree trunk or a rock, always making sure you can see one slash from another, and then you can find your way back even in the dark.'

'Cool,' he said.

'That little oblong metal thing with the handle,' I

said, 'that's a powerful magnet. Useful but not essential. Good for retrieving fishhooks if you lose them in the water. You tie the magnet on a string and dangle it. Fishhooks are precious.'

He held up a small, cylindrical transparent plastic container, one of about six in the pouch. 'More fishhooks in here,' he said. 'Isn't that what films come in? I thought they were black.'

'Fuji films come in these clear cases. As you can see what's inside, I use them all the time. They weigh nothing. They shut tight. They're everything-proof. Perfect. These other cases contain more fishhooks, needles and thread, safety-pins, aspirins, water purifying tables, things like that.'

'What's this knobbly-looking object? Oh, it's a telescope!' He laughed and weighed it in his hand.

'Two ounces,' I said, 'but eight by twenty magnification.'

He passed over as mundane a torch that was also a ball-point pen, the light in the tip for writing, and wasn't enthralled by a whistle, a Post-it pad, or a thick folded wad of aluminium foil. ('For wrapping food to cook in the embers,' I said.) What really fascinated him was a tiny blow-torch which shot out a fierce blue flame hot enough to melt solder.

'Cool,' he said again. 'That's really *ace*.'

'Infallible for lighting fires,' I said, 'as long as the butane lasts.'

'You said in the books that fire comes first.'

I nodded. 'A fire makes you feel better. Less alone. And you need fire for boiling river water to make it OK to drink, and for cooking, of course. And signalling where you are, if people are looking for you.'

'And to keep warm.'

'That too.'

Gareth, had come to the last thing, a pair of leather gloves, which he thought were sissy.

'They give your hands almost double grip,' I said. 'They save you from cuts and scratches. And apart from that they're invaluable for collecting stinging nettles.'

'I'd hate to collect stinging nettles.'

'No, you wouldn't. If you boil the leaves they're not bad to eat, but the best things are the stalks. Incredibly stringy. You can thrash them until they're supple enough for lashing branches together, for making shelters and also racks to keep things off the ground away from damp and animals.'

'You know so much,' he said.

'I went camping in my cradle. Literally.'

He methodically packed everything back as he'd found it and asked what it weighed altogether.

'About two pounds. Less than a kilo.'

A thought struck him. 'You haven't got a compass!'

'It's not in there,' I agreed. I opened a drawer in the chest of drawers and found it for him: a slim liquid-filled compass set in a clear oblong of plastic which had inch and centimetre measures along the sides. I showed him how it aligned with maps and made setting a course

155

relatively easy, and told him I always carried it in my shirt pocket to have it handy.

'But it was in the drawer,' he objected.

'I'm not likely to get lost in Shellerton.'

'You could up on the Downs,' he said seriously.

I doubted it, but said I would carry it to please him, which earned the sideways look it deserved.

Putting everything on top of the chest of drawers I reflected how little time I'd spent in that room amid the mismatched furniture and faded fabrics. I hadn't once felt like retreating to be alone there, though for one pretty accustomed to solitude it was odd to find myself living in the lives of all these people, as if I'd stepped into a play that was already in progress and been given a walk-on part in the action. I would spend another three weeks there and exit, and the play would go on without me as if I hadn't been onstage at all. Meanwhile, I felt drawn in and interested and unwilling to miss any scene.

'This room used to be Perkin's,' Gareth observed, as if catching a swirl of my thought. 'He took all his own stuff with him when they divided the house. It used to be terrif in here.' He shrugged. 'You want to see my room?'

'I'd love to.'

He nodded and led the way. He and I shared the bathroom which lay between us, and along the hallway lay Tremayne's suite into which he was liable to vanish with a brisk slam of the door.

Gareth's room was all pre-adolescent. He slept on a platform with a pull-out desk below and there were a good many white space-age fitments liberally plastered with posters of pop stars and sportsmen. Prized objects filled shelves. Clothes adorned the floor.

I murmured something encouraging but he swept his lair with a disparaging scrutiny and said he was going to do the whole thing over, Dad willing, in the summer.

'Dad got this room done for me after Mum left, and it was top ace at the time. Guess I'm getting too old for it now.'

'Life's like that,' I said.

'Always?'

'It looks like it.'

He nodded as if he'd already discovered that changes were inevitable and not always bad, and in undemanding accord we shut the door on his passing phase and went down to the family room, where we found Tremayne asleep.

Gareth retreated without disturbing him and beckoned me to follow him through to the central hall. There he walked across and knocked briefly on Mackie and Perkin's door, which after an interval was opened slowly by Perkin.

'Can we come in for five mins?' Gareth said. 'Dad's asleep in his chair. You know what he's like if I wake him.'

Perkin yawned and opened his door wide though without excessive willingness, particularly on my account. He led the way into his sitting-room where it was clear he and Mackie had been spending a lazy afternoon reading the Sunday newspapers.

Mackie started to get up when she saw me and then relaxed again as if to say I was now family, not a visitor, and could fend for myself. Perkin told Gareth there was Coke in the fridge if he wanted some. Gareth didn't.

I remembered with a small jerk that it was in this room, Perkin and Mackie's sitting-room, that Olympia had died. I couldn't help but glance around wondering just where it had happened; where Mackie and Harry had found Nolan standing over the girl without under-clothes in a scarlet dress, with Lewis – drunk or not – in a chair.

There was nothing left of that violent scene now in the pleasant big room, no residual shudder in the comfortable atmosphere, no regrets or grief. The trial was over, Nolan was free, Olympia was ashes.

Gareth, unconcerned, asked Perkin, 'Can I show John your workroom?'

'Don't touch anything. I mean *anything*.'

'Cross my heart.'

With me still obediently in tow he crossed Perkin and Mackie's inner hall and opened a door which led into a completely different world, one incredibly fra-grant with the scent of untreated wood.

The room where Perkin created his future antiques was of generous size, like all the rooms in the entire big house, but also no larger than the others. It was extremely tidy, which in a way I wouldn't have expected, with a polished wood-block floor swept spotless, not a shaving or speck of sawdust in sight.

When I commented on it Gareth said it was always like that. Perkin would use one tool at a time and put it away before he used another. Chisels, spokeshaves, things like that.

'Dead methodical,' Gareth said. 'Very fussy.'

There was surprisingly a gas cooker standing against one wall. 'He heats glue on that,' Gareth said, seeing me looking, 'and other sorts of muck like linseed oil.' He pointed across the room. 'That's his lathe, that's his saw-bench, that's his sanding machine. I haven't seen him working much. He doesn't like people watching him, says it interferes with the feeling for what he's doing.'

Gareth's voice held disbelief, but I thought if I had to write with people watching I'd get nothing worthwhile done either.

'What's he making at the moment?' I asked.

'Don't know.'

He swanned round the room looking at sheets of veneer stacked against a wall and at little orderly piles of square-cut lengths from exotic black to golden walnut. 'He makes legs with those,' Gareth said, pointing.

He stopped by a long solid worktop like a butcher's

block and said to me over his shoulder, 'I should think he's just started on this.'

I went across to look and saw a pencil drawing of a display cabinet of sharply spare and unusual lines, a piece designed to draw the eye to its contents, not itself.

The drawing was held down by two blocks of wood, one, I thought, cherry, the other bleached oak, though I was better at living trees than dead.

'He often slats one sort of wood into the other,' Gareth said. 'Makes a sort of stripe. His things don't actually look bad. People buy them all the time.'

'I'm not surprised,' I said.

'Aren't you?' He seemed pleased, as if he'd been afraid I wouldn't be impressed, but I was, considerably.

As we turned to leave I said, 'Was it in their sitting-room that that poor girl died?'

'Gruesome,' Gareth said, nodding. 'I didn't see her. Perkin did, though. He went in just after Mackie and Harry and found it all happening. And, I mean, disgusting ... there was a mess on the carpet where she'd been lying and by the time they were allowed to clean it up, they couldn't. So they got a new carpet from insurance but Perkin acts as if the mess is still there and he's moved a sofa to cover the place. Bonkers, I think.'

I thought I might easily have done the same. Whoever would want to walk every day over a deathbed? We went back to the sitting-room and one could see, if one knew, just which of the three chintz-covered sofas wasn't in a logical place.

We stayed only a short while before returning to the family room where Tremayne was safely awake and yawning, getting ready to walk round his yard at evening stables. He invited me to go with him, which I did with pleasure, and afterwards I made cauliflower cheese for supper which Tremayne ate without a tremor.

When he went out at bedtime for a last look round, he came back blowing on his hands cheerfully and smiling broadly.

'It's thawing,' he said. 'Everything's dripping. Thank God.'

The world indeed turned from white to green during the night, bringing renewed life to Shellerton and racing.

Out in the melting woodlands, Angela Brickell spent her last night in the quiet undergrowth among the small scavenging creatures that had blessedly cleaned her bones. She was without odour and without horror, weather-scrubbed, long gone into everlasting peace.

CHAPTER EIGHT

Tremayne promoted me from Touchy to a still actively racing steeplechaser that Monday morning, a nine-year-old gelding called Drifter. I was also permitted to do a regular working gallop and by great good fortune didn't fall off. Neither Tremayne nor Mackie made any comment on my competence or lack of it, only on the state of fitness of the horse. They were taking me for granted, I realised, and was flattered and glad of it.

When we returned from the newly greenish-brownish Downs there was a strange car in the yard and a strange man drinking coffee in the kitchen; but strange to me only. Familiar to everyone else.

He was young, short, thin, angular and bold, wearing self-assurance as an outer garment. He was, I soon found, almost as foul-mouthed as Nolan but, unlike him, funny.

'Hello, Sam,' Tremayne said. 'Ready for work?'

'Too sodding right. I'm as stiff as a frigging virgin.'

I wondered idly how many virgins he had personally

introduced to frigging: there was something about him that suggested it.

Tremayne said to me, 'This is Sam Yaeger, our jockey.' To Sam Yaeger he explained my presence and said I'd been riding out.

Sam Yaeger nodded to me, visibly assessing what threat or benefit I might represent to him, running a glance over my jodhpurs and measuring my height. I imagined that because of my six feet alone he might put away fears that I could annex any of his racing territory.

He himself wore jodhpurs also, along with a brilliant yellow sweatshirt. A multi-coloured anorak, twin of Gareth's, hung over the back of his chair, and he had brought his own helmet, bright turquoise, with YAEGER painted large in red on the front. Nothing shy or retiring about Sam.

Dee-Dee, appearing for her coffee, brightened by fifty watts at the sight of him.

'Morning, Lover-boy,' she said.

Lover-boy made a stab at pinching her bottom as she passed behind him, which she seemed not to mind. Well, well, well, I thought, there was a veritable pussy-cat lurking somewhere inside that self-contained, touch-me-not secretarial exterior. She made her coffee and sat at the table beside the jockey, not overtly flirting but very aware of him.

I made the toast, which had become my accepted

job, and put out the juice, butter, marmalade and so on. Sam Yaeger watched with comically raised eyebrows.

'Didn't Tremayne say you were a writer?' he asked.

'Most of the time. Want some toast?'

'One piece, light brown. You don't look like a sodding writer.'

'So many people aren't.'

'Aren't what?'

'What they look like,' I said. 'Sodding or not.'

'What do I look like?' he demanded, but with, I thought, genuine curiosity.

'Like someone who won the Grand National among eighty-nine other races last year and finished third on the jockeys' list.'

'You've been peeking,' he said, surprised.

'I'll be interviewing you soon for your views on your boss as a trainer.'

Tremayne said with mock severity, 'And they'd better be respectful.'

'They bloody well would be, wouldn't they?'

'If you have any sense,' Tremayne agreed, nodding.

I dealt out the toast and made some more. Sam's extremely physical presence dominated breakfast throughout and I wondered briefly how he got on with Nolan, the dark side of the same coin.

I asked Dee-Dee that question after Sam and Tremayne had gone out with the second lot; asked her in the office while I checked some facts in old form books.

'Get on?' she repeated ironically. 'No, they do not.'

She paused, considered whether to tell me more, shrugged and continued. 'Sam doesn't like Nolan riding so many of the stable's horses. Nolan rides most of Fiona's runners, he accepts that, but Tremayne runs more horses in amateur races than most trainers do. Wins more, too, of course. The owners who bet, they like it, because whatever else you can say about Nolan, no one denies he's a brilliant jockey. He's been top of the amateurs' list for years.'

'Why doesn't he turn professional?' I asked.

'The very idea of that scares Sam rigid,' Dee-Dee said calmly, 'but I don't think it will happen. Especially not now, since the conviction. Nolan prefers his amateur status, anyway. He thinks of Sam as blue collar to his white. That's why . . .' she stopped abruptly as if blocking a revelation that was already on its way from brain to mouth, stopped so sharply that I was immediately interested, but without showing it asked, 'Why what?'

She shook her head. 'It's not fair to them.'

'Do go on,' I said, not pressing too much. 'I won't repeat it to anyone.'

'It wouldn't help you with the book,' she said.

'It might help me to understand the way the stable works and where its success comes from, besides Tremayne's skill. It might come partly, for instance, from rivalry between two jockeys each of whom wants to prove himself better than the other.'

She gazed at me. 'You have a twisty mind. I'd never

have thought of that.' She paused for decision and I simply waited. 'It isn't just riding,' she said finally. 'It's women.'

'*Women*?'

'They're rivals there, too. The night Nolan – I mean, the night Olympia died . . .'

They all said, I'd noticed, 'when Olympia died', and never 'when Nolan killed Olympia', though Dee-Dee had just come close.

'Sam set out to seduce Olympia,' Dee-Dee said, as if it were only to be expected. 'Nolan brought her to the party and of course Sam made a bee-line for her.' Somewhere in her calm voice was indulgence for Sam Yaeger, censure for Nolan, never mind that Nolan seemed to be the loser.

'Did Sam . . . er . . . know Olympia?'

'Never set eyes on her before. None of us knew her. Nolan had been keeping her to himself. Anyway, he brought her that night and she took one look at Sam and *giggled*. I know, I was there. Sam has that effect on females.' She raised her eyebrows. 'Don't say it. I respond to him too. Can't help it. He's fun.'

'I can see that,' I said.

'Can you? Olympia did. Putty in his hands which of course were all over her the minute Nolan went to fetch her a drink. When he came back, she'd gone off with Sam. Like I told you, she had on a low-cut long scarlet dress slit up the thigh . . . next best thing to a written invitation. Nolan seemed to think that Sam and

Olympia would have headed for the stables and he went looking for them there, but without results.'

She stopped again as if doubting the wisdom of telling me these things, but it seemed harder for her to stop than to start.

'Nolan came back into the house cursing and swearing and telling me he would strangle the . . . er . . . bitch because, you see, I think he blamed *her*, not Sam, for making him feel a fool. Him, Nolan, the white-collar amateur. He wasn't going to make it public and he shut up pretty soon, though he went on being angry. So, anyway, there you are, that's really what happened.'

'Which no one,' I said slowly, 'brought up at the trial.'

'Of course not. I mean, not many people knew, and it gave Nolan a *motive*.'

'Yes, it did.'

'But he didn't mean to kill her. Everyone knows that. If he'd attacked and killed *Sam*, it would have been a different matter.'

I said, frowning, 'It wasn't you, though, who said at the trial they'd heard him say he would strangle the bitch.'

'No, of course not. Some other people heard him before he reached me, and they didn't know *why* he was saying it. It didn't seem important at that time. Of course, no one ever asked me if *I* knew why he'd said it, so no one found out.'

'But the prosecution must have asked *Nolan* why he said it?'

'Yes, sure, but he said it was because he couldn't find her, nothing else. Extravagant language but not a threat.'

I sighed. 'And *Sam* wasn't for saying why, as it would further torpedo his shaky reputation?'

'Yes. And anyway he didn't believe Nolan meant to kill her. He told me that. He said it wasn't the first time he and Nolan had bedded the same girl, and sometimes Nolan had pinched one of his, and it was a bit of a lark on the whole, not a killing matter.'

'More a lark to Sam than to Nolan,' I suggested.

'Probably.' She shook herself. 'I'm getting no work done.'

'You've done some of mine.'

'Don't put it in the book,' she insisted, alarmed.

'I promise I won't,' I said.

I retired to the dining-room and, since the shape of Tremayne's passage through life was becoming more and more clear, I began to map out the book into sections, giving each a tentative title with subheadings. I still hadn't put an actual sentence on paper and was feeling tyrannised by all the blank pages lying ahead. I'd heard of writers who leaped to their typewriters as to a lover. There were days when I'd do any chore I could think of rather than pick up a pencil, and it was never easy, ever, to dig words and ideas from my brain. Half the time I couldn't believe I'd chosen this occupation; half of the time I longed for the easier solitude under the stars.

I scribbled 'Find something you like doing and spend your life doing it' at the end of the outline plan and decided it was enough for one day. If tomorrow it looked all right, maybe I'd let it stand, and go on.

Out in the woodland Detective Chief Inspector Doone looked morosely at Angela Brickell's jumbled bones while the pathologist told him they were those of a young female, dead probably less than a year.

The photographer took photographs. The game-keeper marked the spot on a large-scale map. The pathologist said it was impossible to determine the cause of death without a detailed autopsy, and very likely not even then.

With sketchy reverence for whoever they had been, the skull and other bones were packed into a coffin-shaped box, carried to a van, and driven to the mortuary.

Detective Chief Inspector Doone, seeing there was no point in looking for tyre tracks, footprints or ciga-rette ends, set two constables to searching the under-growth for clothes, shoes, or anything not rotted by time; and it was in this way that under a blanket of dead leaves they came across some wet filthy jeans, a small-sized bra, a pair of panties and a T-shirt with the remains of a pattern on the front.

Detective Chief Inspector Doone watched his men pack these sad remnants into a plastic bag and reflected that none of the clothes had been on or even near the bones.

The girl, he reckoned, had been naked when she died.

He sighed deeply. He didn't like these sorts of cases. He had daughters of his own.

Tremayne came back from the second lot in a good mood, whistling between his teeth. He wheeled straight into the office, fired off a fresh barrage of instructions to Dee-Dee and made several rapid phone calls himself. Then he came into the dining-room to let me know the state of play and to ask a favour or two, taking it (correctly) for granted that I would oblige.

The ditched jeep had gone to the big scrap heap in the sky: a replacement had been found in Newbury, a not new but serviceable Land Rover. If I would go to Newbury in the Volvo with Tremayne, I could drive the substitute home to Shellerton.

'Of course,' I said.

The racing industry was scrambling back into action, with Windsor racecourse promising to be operational on Wednesday. Tremayne had horses entered, four of which he proposed to run. He would like me to come with him, he said, to see what his job entailed.

'Love to,' I said.

He wished to go out for the evening to play poker

with friends, and he'd be back late: would I stay in for Gareth?

'Sure,' I said.

'He's old enough to be safe on his own, but . . . well . . .'

'Company,' I said. 'Someone around.'

He nodded.

'You're welcome,' I said.

'Dee-Dee thinks we take advantage of you,' he said bluntly. 'Do we?'

'No.' I was surprised. 'I like what I'm doing.'

'Cooking, baby-sitting, spare chauffeur, spare lad?'

'Sure.'

'You have the right to say no,' he said uncertainly.

'I'll tell you soon enough if I'm affronted. As for now, I'd rather be part of things, and useful. OK?'

He nodded.

'And,' I said, 'this way I get to know you better for the book.'

For the first time he looked faintly apprehensive, as if perhaps after all he didn't want his whole self publicly laid bare; but I would respect any secrecies I learned, I thought again, if he didn't want them told. This was not an investigate blast-the-lid-off exercise; this was to be the equivalent of a commissioned portrait, an affirmation of life. It might be fair to include a wart or two, but not to put every last blemish under magnification.

The day went ahead as planned and, in addition, in the Volvo on the way to Newbury, Tremayne galloped through his late adolescence and his introduction (by his father, naturally) to high-stakes gambling. His father's advice, he said, was always to wager more than one could afford, otherwise one would get no thrill and feel no despair.

'He was right, of course,' Tremayne said, 'but I'm more prudent. I play poker, I back horses, I bet a little, win a little, lose a little, it doesn't flutter my pulse. I've owners who go white and shake at the races. They look on the point of dying, they stand to lose or win so much. My father would have understood it. I don't.'

'All your life's a gamble,' I said.

He looked blank for a moment. 'You mean training racehorses? True enough, I get thrills like Top Spin Lob, and true enough, great slabs of despair. You might say I wager my heartstrings, but not much cash.'

I wrote it down. Tremayne, driving conservatively, slanted a glance at my notebook and seemed pleased to be quoted. The man himself, I thought with a stirring of satisfaction, was going to speak clearly from the pages, coming alive with little help from me.

In the evening, after Tremayne had departed to his card game, Gareth asked me to teach him to cook.

I was nonplussed. 'It's easy,' I said.

'How did you learn?'

'I don't know. Maybe from watching my mother.' I looked at his face. 'Sorry, I forgot.'

'My mother makes it all difficult, not easy. And she would never let me watch her at home. She said I got under her feet.'

My own mother, I reflected, had always let me clean out raw cake mixture with my finger: had always liked to talk to me while things bubbled.

'Well,' I said, 'what do you want to eat?'

We went into the kitchen where Gareth tentatively asked for 'real' shepherd's pie, 'not that stuff in supermarket boxes that tastes of cardboard and wouldn't feed a pygmy'.

'Real, easy shepherd's pie,' I assented. 'First of all, catch your shepherd.'

He grinned and watched me assemble some minced beef, an onion, gravy powder and a jar of dried herbs.

'The gravy powder's sort of cheating,' I said. 'Your mother would be horrified, but it thickens the meat and tastes good.'

I dissolved some powder into a little water, added it to the beef, chopped the onion finely, added that, sprinkled some herbs, stirred it all around in a saucepan, put the lid on and set it to cook on a low heat.

'Next thing to decide,' I said, 'is real potatoes or dried potato granules. How are you with peeling potatoes? No? Granules then?'

He nodded.

'Follow the directions,' I said, giving him the packet.

' "Heat eight fluid ounces of water and four fluid

ounces of milk",' he said, reading. He looked up, 'Hey, I was going to ask you . . . You know you said to boil river water before you drink it? Well, what *in*?'

I smiled. 'Best thing is a Coca-Cola can. You can usually find an empty one lying about, the litter habits of this nation being what they are. You want to just shake it up with water to wash it out a few times in case there are any spiders or anything inside, but Coke cans are pretty clean.'

'Ace,' he said emphatically. 'Well, for the potatoes we need some butter and salt . . . Will you write down all you bought last week, so I can get them again and cook when you're gone?'

'Sure thing.'

'I wouldn't mind if you stayed.'

Loneliness was an ache in his voice. I said, 'I'll be here another three weeks.' I paused. 'Would you like, say perhaps next Sunday if it's a decent day, to come out with me into some fields and perhaps some woods? I could show you a few things in the books . . . how to do them in real life.'

His face shone: my own reward.

'Could I bring Coconut?'

'Absolutely.'

'Mega cool.'

He whipped the potato granules happily into the hot liquid and we piled the fluffy result onto the cooked meat mixture in a round pie dish. Put it under the grill to brown the top. Ate the results with mutual fulfilment and cleared everything away afterwards.

'Can we take the survival kit?' he asked.

'Of course.'

'And light a fire?'

'Perhaps on your own land, if your father will let us. You can't just light fires anywhere in England. Or anyway, you shouldn't, unless it's an emergency. People do, actually, but you're supposed to get the landowner's permission first.'

'He's sure to let us.'

'Yes. I'd think so.'

'I really can't wait,' he said.

On Tuesday morning the pathologist made his report to Detective Chief Inspector Doone.

'The bones are those of a young adult female, probably five foot four or five; possible age, twenty. Could be a year or two younger or older, but not much. There was a small remaining patch of scalp, with a few hairs still adhering: the hairs are medium brown, four inches long, can't tell what length her hair was overall.'

'How long since she died?' Doone asked.

'I'd say last summer.'

'And cause of death? Drugs? Exposure?'

'As to drugs, we'll have to analyse the hairs, see what we can find. But no, you've got a problem here.'

Doone sighed. 'What problem?'

'Her hyoid bone is fractured.'

Depression settled on Doone. 'You're sure?'

'Positive. She was strangled.'

At Shellerton, Tuesday passed uneventfully with riding out, breakfast, clippings, lunch, taping, evening drinks and dinner.

In the morning I came across Dee-Dee weeping quietly into her typewriter and offered a tissue.

'It's nothing,' she said, sniffing.

'Care to unbutton?'

'I don't know why I tell you things.'

'I listen.'

She blew her nose and gave me a brief apologetic look.

'I'm old enough to know better. I'm thirty-six.' She gave her age almost in desperation, as if the figure itself were a disaster.

'Tremayne told me you'd had a disappointment in the love department,' I said hesitatingly. 'He didn't exactly say who.'

'Disappointment! Huh!' She sniffed hard. 'I loved the beast. I mean, I even ironed his shirts for him. We were lovers for ages and he dumped me from one minute to the next. And now Mackie's having a *baby*.' Her eyes filled with tears again, and I saw it was the raw ache for motherhood, that fierce instinct which could cause such unassuageable pain, that grieved her at least as much as the loss of the man.

'Do you know what?' Dee-Dee said with misery. 'That louse didn't want a child until after we were married. *After*. He never meant to marry me, I know it now, but I waited for his sake . . . and I wasted . . . *three years* . . .' She gulped, a sob escaping. 'I'll tell you, I'll take *anyone* now. I don't need a wedding ring. I want a *child*.'

Her voice died in a forlorn pining wail, a keen of mourning. With a hunger that strong she could make dreadful decisions, but who could tell which would be better for her to be in the end, reckless or barren? Either way, there would be regrets.

She dried her eyes, blew her nose again and shook herself as if straightening her emotions by force, and when I next looked in on her she was typing away collectedly in her usual self-contained manner as if our conversation had never taken place.

On Tuesday afternoon Detective Chief Inspector Doone sent his men to search the whole area where the bones had been discovered. Chiefly, he told them, they were to look for shoes. Also for anything else man-made. They could use metal detectors. They should look under dead leaves. They were to mark on the map where each artefact was found, and also tag the artefact, being careful not to destroy evidence.

This was now a murder investigation, he reminded them.

On Wednesday morning when we came in from first lot Sam Yaeger was again in the kitchen.

This time he came not in his car but with a borrowed pick-up truck in which he proposed to collect some Burma teak that Perkin had acquired for him at trade discount.

'Sam has a boat,' Tremayne told me dryly. 'An old wreck that he's slowly turning into a palace fit for a harem.'

Sam Yaeger grinned cheerfully and made no denials. 'It's already sold, or as good as,' he told me. 'Every jockey's got to have an eye to the sodding future. I buy clapped out antique boats and make them better than new. I sold the last one to one of those effing newspaper moguls. They'll pay the earth for good stuff. No fibre-glass crap.'

Life was full of surprises, I thought.

'Where do you keep the boat?' I asked, making toast.

'Maidenhead. On the Thames. I bought a bankrupt boatyard there a while back. It looks a right shambles but a bit of dilapidation's a good thing. Sodding thieves think there's nothing worth stealing. Better than a Rottweiler, is a bit of squalor.'

'So I suppose,' Tremayne said, 'that you're taking the wood to the boatyard on your way to the races.'

Sam looked at me in mock amazement. 'Don't know how he works these things out, do you?'

'That'll do, Sam,' Tremayne said, and one could see just where he drew the line between what he would take from Sam Yaeger, and what not. He began to discuss the horses he would be running at Windsor races that afternoon, telling Sam that 'Bluecheesecake is better, not worse, for the lay off,' and 'Give Just The Thing an easy if you feel her wavering. I don't want her ruined while she's still green.'

'Right,' Sam said, concentrating. 'What about Cashless? Do I ride him in front again?'

'What do you think?'

'He likes it better. He just got beat by faster horses, last time.'

'Go off in front, then.'

'Right.'

'Nolan rides Telebiddy in the amateur race,' Tremayne said. 'Unless the Jockey Club puts a stop to it.'

Sam scowled but spoke no evil. Tremayne told him what he would be riding on the morrow at Towcester and said he'd have no runners at all on Friday.

'Saturday, I'm sending five or six to Chepstow. You'll go there. So will I. With luck, Nolan rides Fiona's horse in the Wilfred Johnstone Hunter Chase at Sandown. Maybe Mackie will go to Sandown; we'll have to see.'

Dee-Dee came in composedly for her coffee and as before sat next to Sam. Sam might be a constant seducer, I thought, looking at them, but he wouldn't want to leave a trail of paternity problems. Dee-Dee might get him into bed but not into fatherhood. Bad luck, try again.

Tremayne gave Dee-Dee instructions about engaging transport for Saturday, which she memorized as usual.

'Remember to phone through the entries for Folkestone and Wolverhampton. I'll decide on the Newbury entries this morning before I go to Windsor.'

Dee-Dee nodded.

'Pack the colours for Windsor.'

Dee-Dee nodded.

'Phone the saddler about collecting those exercise sheets for repair.'

Dee-Dee nodded.

'Right then. That's about it.' He turned to me. 'We'll leave for Windsor at twelve-thirty.'

'Fine,' I said.

He went up to the Downs to watch the second lot, driving the newly acquired Land Rover. Sam Yaeger took the pick-up round to Perkin's half of the house and loaded up his teak. Dee-Dee took her coffee into the office and I made a determined attempt to sort each year's clippings into order of significance, the most newsworthy on top.

At about that time, Detective Chief Inspector Doone went into the formerly unused office that had been dubbed 'Incident Room' for the bones investigation and laid out on a trestle table the bits and pieces that his men had gleaned from the woodland.

There were the clothes found originally, now drying out in the centrally-heated air. There was also a pair of well-worn and misshapen trainers, still sodden, which might once have been white.

Apart from those, there were four old, empty and dirty soft drink cans, a heavily rusted toy fire-engine, a pair of broken sunglasses, a puckered leather belt with split stitches, a gin bottle, a blue plastic comb uncorrupted by time, a well-chewed rubber ball, a gold-plated ball-point pen, a pink lipstick, chocolate bar wrappers, a pitted garden spade and a broken dog collar.

Detective Chief Inspector Doone walked broodingly round the table staring at the haul from all angles.

'Speak to me, girl,' he said. 'Tell me who you are.'

The clothes and the shoes made no answer.

He called in his men and told them to go back to the woods and widen the search, and he himself, as he had the day before, went through the lists of missing persons, trying to make a match.

He knew it was possible the young woman had been a far stranger to the area but thought it more likely that she was within fifty miles of her home. They usually were, these victims. He decided automatically to beam in on the locally lost.

He had a list of twelve persistent adolescent runaways: all possibles. A list of four defaulters from youth custody. A short list of two missing prostitutes. A list of six missing for 'various reasons'.

One of those was Angela Brickell. The reason given was: 'Probably doped a racehorse in her charge. Skipped out.'

Doone's attention passed over her and fastened thoughtfully on the wayward daughter of a politician. Reason for being missing: 'Mixed with bad crowd. Unmanageable.'

It might do his stalled career a bit of good, Doone reckoned, if it turned out to be *her*.

CHAPTER NINE

Tremayne told me that the only place that he couldn't take me on Windsor racecourse was into the Holy of Holies, the weighing room. Everywhere else, he said, I should stay by his side. He wouldn't forever be looking back to make sure I was with him: I was to provide my own glue.

Accordingly I followed him doggedly, at times at a run. Where he paused briefly to talk to other people he introduced me as a friend, John Kendall, not as Boswell. He left me to sort out for myself the information bombarding me from all sides, rarely offering explanations, and I could see that explanations would have been a burden for him when he was so busy. His four runners, as it happened, were in four consecutive races. He took me for a quick sandwich and a drink soon after our arrival on the racecourse and from then on began a darting progress: into the weighing room to fetch his jockey's saddle and weight cloth containing the correct amount of lead; off at a trot to the saddling boxes to do up the girths himself and straighten the tack to send the horse out looking good; into the parade ring to join the owners and give last-minute orders to the jockey; off up to the stands to watch the horse run; down again to the unsaddling areas, hoping to greet a winner, otherwise to listen to the why-not story from the jockey, and then off to the weighing room to pick up another saddle and weight cloth to start all over again.

Nolan was there, anxiously asking if Tremayne had received any thumbs-down from the Jockey Club.

'No,' Tremayne said. 'Have you?'

'Not an effing peep.'

'You ride, then,' Tremayne said. 'And don't ask questions. Don't invite a no. They'll tell you quickly enough if they want you off. Apply your mind to winning. Telebiddy's owners are here with their betting money burning holes in their pockets, so deliver the goods, eh?'

'Tell them I want a better effing present than last time.'

'Win the race first,' Tremayne said.

He made one of his dives into the weighing room, leaving me outside with Nolan who had come dressed to stifle criticism. All the same he complained to me bitterly that the effing media had snapped him coming through the main gate and he could do without their sodding attentions, the obscene so and sos.

The filth of Nolan's language tended to wash over one, I found: the brain tended finally to filter it out.

Much the same could be said about Sam Yaeger who slouched up beside us and annoyed Nolan by patting him on the back. Sam, too, was transformed by tidiness and I gradually observed that several of the jockeys arrived and departed from the racecourse dressed for the boardroom. Their working clothes might be pink, purple and the stuff of fantasy but they were saying they were businessmen first.

The physical impact of each of Nolan and Sam was diluted and dissipated by the open air that incidentally was still as cold as their relationship.

'Go easy on Bluecheesecake,' Nolan said. 'I don't want him effing loused up before the Kim Muir at Cheltenham.'

Sam answered, 'I'm not nannying any sodding amateur.'

'The Kim Muir is his main effing target.'

'Eff his sodding target.'

Did anyone ever grow up, I wondered. The school playground had a lot to answer for.

Away from each other, as I discovered during the afternoon, they were assured, sensible and supremely expert.

Sam made no concessions on Bluecheesecake. Through a spare pair of Tremayne's binoculars I watched his gold cap from start to finish, seeing the smooth pattern of his progress along the rails, staying in third or fourth place while others surged forward and fell back on his outside.

185

The steeplechase course at Windsor proved to be a winding figure-of-eight, which meant that tactics were important. At times one saw the runners from head-on; difficult to tell who was actually in front. Coming round the last of several bends Bluecheesecake made a mess of one head-on-view fence, his nose going down to the ground, Sam's back wholly visible from shoulders down to bottom up. Tremayne beside me let go of a Nolan-strength curse, but both horse and jockey righted themselves miraculously without falling and lost, Sam said afterwards, no more than three or four lengths.

Perhaps because of having to make up for those lengths in limited time before the winning post, Sam, having given his mount precious extra seconds for recovery of balance, rode over the last two fences with what even I could see was total disregard for his own safety and pressed Bluecheesecake unceremoniously for every ounce of effort.

Tremayne put down his glasses and watched the rocketing finish almost impassively, giving no more than a satisfied grunt when in the last few strides Bluecheese-cake's nose showed decisively in front.

Before the cheers had died, Tremayne had set off at a run to the winners' enclosure with me in pursuit, and after he'd received his due congratulations, inspected his excited, sweating, breathless charge for cuts and damage (none), and talked briefly to the press he followed Sam into the weighing room to fetch the saddle again for Just The Thing.

When he came out he was escorted by Nolan who fell into step beside him complaining ferociously that Sam had given Bluecheesecake a viciously hard race and spoiled his, Nolan's, chances at Cheltenham.

'Cheltenham is six weeks off,' Tremayne said calmly. 'Plenty of time.'

Nolan repeated his gripe.

Tremayne said with amazing patience, 'Sam did exactly right. Go and do the same with Telebiddy.'

Nolan stalked away still looking more furious than was sensible in his position and Tremayne allowed himself a sigh but no comment. He took a lot more from Nolan, I reflected, than he would allow from Sam, even though it seemed to me that he liked Sam better. A lot of things were involved there: status, accent, connections; all the signal flags of class.

Sam rode Just The Thing in the next event, a hurdle race, with inconspicuous gallantry, providing the green mare with a clear view of the jumps and urging her on at the end to give her a good idea of what was expected. She finished a respectable third to Tremayne's almost tangible pleasure: and it was fascinating to me to have heard the plans beforehand and see them put into exact effect.

While Tremayne was on his way from weighing room to saddling boxes for Telebiddy in the next race he handed me an envelope and asked me to put the contents for him on the Tote; Telebiddy, all to win.

'I don't like people to see me bet,' he said, 'because

for one thing it shows them I'm pretty confident, so they put their money on too and it shortens the odds. I usually bet by phone with a bookmaker, but today I wanted to judge the state of the ground first. It can be treacherous, after snow. You don't mind, do you?'

'Not at all.'

He nodded and hurried off, and I made my way to the Tote windows and disposed of enough to keep me in food for a year. Small, as in Tremayne's 'small bet', was a relative term, I saw.

I joined him in the parade ring and asked if he wanted the tickets.

'No. If he wins, collect for me, will you?'

'OK.'

Nolan was talking to the owners, exercising his best charm and moderating his language. In jockey's clothes he still looked chunky, strong and powerfully arrogant, but the swagger seemed to stop the moment he sat on the horse. Then professionalism took over and he was concentrated, quiet and neat in the saddle.

I tagged along behind Tremayne and the owners and, from the stands, watched Nolan give a display of razor-sharp competence that made most of the other amateurs look like Sunday drivers.

He saved countable seconds over the fences, his mount gaining lengths by always seeming to take off at the right spot. Judgment, not luck. The courage that Mackie loved was still there, unmistakable.

The owners, mother and daughter, were tremblers.

They weren't entirely white and near to dying, but from what they said the betting money was out of their pockets and on the horse in a big way and there was a good deal of lip- and knuckle-biting from off to finish

Nolan, as if determined to outride Sam Yaeger, hurled himself over the last three fences and won by ten lengths pulling up. Tremayne let out a deep breath and the owners hugged each other, hugged Tremayne and stopped shaking.

'You could give Nolan a good cash present for that,' Tremayne said bluntly.

The owners thought Nolan would be embarrassed if they gave him such a present.

'Give it to me, to give to him. No embarrassment.'

The owners said they'd better run down and lead in their winner, which they did.

'Stingy cats,' Tremayne said in my ear as we watched them fuss over the horse and have their picture taken.

'Won't they really give Nolan anything?' I asked.

'It's against the rules, and they know it. Amateurs aren't supposed to be given money for winning. Nolan will have backed the horse anyway, he always does with a hot chance like this. And I get one hundred per cent commitment from my jockey.' His voice was dry with humour. 'I often think the Jockey Club has it wrong, not letting professional jockeys bet on their own mounts.'

He returned to the weighing room to fetch Sam's saddle and weight cloth for Cashless, and I went off to the Tote and collected his Telebiddy winnings, which approximately equalled his stake. Nolan, it appeared, had been riding the hot favourite.

When I commented on it to Tremayne in the parade ring as we watched Cashless being led round, he told me that Nolan's presence on any horse shortened its odds, and Telebiddy had won twice for him already this season. It was a wonder, Tremayne said, that the Tote had paid evens: he'd expected less of a return. I would do him a favour, he added, if I would give him his winnings on the way home, not in public, so I walked around with a small fortune I had no hope of repaying if I lost it, keeping it clutched in my left-hand trouser pocket.

We went up to the stands for the race and watched Cashless set off in front as expected, a position he easily held until right where it mattered, the last fifty yards. Then three jockeys who had been waiting behind him stepped on the accelerator, and although Cashless didn't in any way give up, the three others passed him.

Tremayne shrugged. 'Too bad.'

'Will you run him in front again next time?' I asked, as we went down off the stands.

'I expect so. We've tried keeping him back and he runs worse. He's one-paced in a finish, that's his trouble. He's game enough, but it's hard to find races he can win.'

We reached the parade ring where the unsuccessful runners were being unsaddled. Sam, looping girths over his arm, gave Tremayne a rueful smile and said Cashless had done his best.

'I saw,' Tremayne agreed. 'Can't be helped.' We watched Sam walk off towards the weighing room and Tremayne remarked thoughtfully that he might try Cashless in an amateur race, and see what Nolan could do.

'Do you play them off against each other on purpose?' I asked.

Tremayne gave me a flickering glance. 'I do the best for my owners,' he said. 'Like a drink?'

It appeared he had arranged to meet the owners of Telebiddy in the Club bar and when we arrived they were already celebrating with a bottle of champagne. Nolan, too, was there, being incredibly nice to them but without financial results.

When the two women had left in a state of euphoria, Nolan asked belligerently whether Tremayne had told them to give him a present.

'I suggested it,' Tremayne said calmly, 'but you'll be lucky. Better settle for what you took from the bookmakers yourself.'

'Damn little,' Nolan said, or words to that effect, 'and the bloodsucking lawyers will get the lot.' He shouldered his way out of the bar in self-righteous outrage, which seemed to be his uppermost state of mind oftener than not.

With non-commital half-lowered eyelids Tremayne watched him go, then transferred his gaze to me.

'Well,' he asked, 'what have you learned?'

'What you intended me to, I expect.'

He smiled. 'And a bit more than I intended. I've noticed you do that all the time.' With a contented sigh he put down his empty glass. 'Two winners,' he said. 'A better than average day at the races. Let's go home.'

At about the same time we were driving home with Tremayne's winnings safely stowed in his own pockets, not mine, Detective Chief Inspector Doone was poring over the increased pickings from the woodland.

The Detective Chief Inspector could be said to be purring. Among some insignificant long-rusted detritus lay the star of the whole collection, a woman's handbag. Total satisfaction had been denied him, as the prize had been torn open on one side, probably by a dog, whose toothmarks still showed, so that most of the contents had been lost. All the same, he was left with a shoulder strap, a corroded buckle and at least half of a brown plastic school-style bag which still held, in an intact inner zipped pocket, a small mirror and a folded photograph frame.

With careful movements Doone opened the frame and found inside, water-stained along one edge but otherwise sharply clear, a coloured snapshot of a man standing beside a horse.

Disappointed that there was still no easy identification of the handbag's past owner, Doone took a telephone call from the pathologist.

'You were asking about the teeth,' the pathologist said. 'The dental records you gave me are definitely not those of our bones. Our girl had good teeth. One or two missing, but no fillings. Sorry.'

Doone's disappointment deepened. The politician's daughter had just been ruled out. He mentally reviewed his list again, skipped the prostitutes and provisionally paused on Angela Brickell, stable lad. Angela Brickell . . . horse.

The bombshell burst on Shellerton on Thursday.

Tremayne was upstairs showering and dressing before going to Towcester races when the doorbell rang. Dee-Dee went to answer it and presently came into the dining-room looking mystified.

'It's two men,' she said. 'They say they're policemen. They flashed some sort of identity cards, but they won't say what they want. I've put them in the family room until Tremayne comes down. Go and keep an eye on them, would you mind?'

'Sure,' I said, already on the move.

'Thanks,' she said, returning to the office. 'Whatever they want it looks boring.'

I could see why she thought so. The two men might have invented the word grey, so characterless did they appear at first sight. Ultimate plain clothes, I thought.

'Can I help you?' I said.

'Are you Tremayne Vickers?' one of them asked.

'No. He'll be down soon. Can I help?'

'No, thank you, sir. Can you fetch him?'

'He's in the shower.'

The policeman raised his eyebrows. Trainers, however, didn't shower before morning exercise, they showered after, before going racing. That was Tremayne's habit, anyway. Dee-Dee had told me.

'He's been up since six,' I said.

The policeman's eyes widened, as if I'd read his mind.

'I am Detective Chief Inspector Doone, Thames Valley Police,' he said. 'This is Detective Constable Rich.'

'How do you do,' I said politely. 'I'm John Kendall. Would you care to sit down?'

They perched gingerly on chairs and said no to an offer of coffee.

'Will he be long, sir?' Doone asked. 'We must see him soon.'

'No, not long.'

Doone, on further inspection, appeared to be about fifty, with grey-dusted light brown hair and a heavy medium-brown moustache. He had light brown eyes, big bony hands and, as we all slowly discovered, a habit of talking a lot in a light Berkshire accent.

This chattiness wasn't at all apparent in the first ten minutes before Tremayne came downstairs buttoning the blue and white striped cuffs of his shirt and carrying his jacket gripped between forearm and chest

'Hello,' he said, 'who's this?'

Dee-Dee appeared behind him, apparently to tell him, but Doone introduced himself before either she or I could do so.

'Police?' Tremayne said, unworried. 'What about?'

'We'd like to speak to you alone, sir.'

'What? Oh, very well.'

He asked me with his eyes to leave with Dee-Dee, shutting the door behind us. I returned to the dining-room but presently heard the family room door open and Tremayne's voice calling.

'John, come back here, would you?'

I went back. Doone was protesting about my presence, saying it was unnecessary and inadvisable.

Tremayne said stubbornly, 'I want him to hear it. Will you repeat what you said?'

Doone shrugged. 'I came to inform Mr Vickers that some remains have been found which may prove to be those of a young woman who was once employed here.'

'Angela Brickell,' Tremayne said resignedly.

'Oh.'

'What does "Oh" mean, sir?' Doone enquired sharply.

'It means just oh,' I said. 'Poor girl. Everyone thought she'd just done a bunk.'

'They have a photograph,' Tremayne said. 'They're trying to identify the man.' He turned to Doone. 'Show

195

it to him.' He nodded in my direction. 'Don't take my word for it.'

Unwillingly Doone handed me a photograph enclosed in a plastic holder.

'Do you know this man, sir?' he asked.

I glanced at Tremayne who was not looking concerned.

'You may as well tell him,' he said.

'Harry Goodhaven?'

Tremayne nodded. 'That's Fiona's horse, Chickweed, the one they said was doped.'

'How can you recognise a horse?' Doone asked.

Tremayne stared at him. 'Horses have faces, like people. I'd know Chickweed anywhere. He's still here, out in the yard.'

'Who is this man, this Harry Goodhaven?' Doone demanded.

'The husband of the owner of the horse.'

'Why would Angela Brickell be carrying his photograph?'

'She wasn't,' Tremayne said. 'Well, I suppose she was, but it was the *horse*'s photograph she was carrying. She looked after it.'

Doone looked completely unconvinced.

'To a lad,' I said, 'the horses they look after are like children. They love them. They defend them. It makes sense that she carried Chickweed's picture.'

Tremayne glanced at me with half-stifled surprise, but I'd been listening to the lads for a week.

'What John says,' Tremayne nodded, 'is absolutely true.'

The attendant policeman, Constable Rich, was all the time taking notes, though not at high speed: not shorthand.

Doone said, 'Sir, can you give me the address of this Harry Goodhaven?'

With slight irritation Tremayne answered, 'This Harry Goodhaven, as you call him, is Mr Henry Goodhaven who owns the Manor House, Shellerton.'

Doone very nearly said 'Oh' in his turn, and made a visible readjustment in his mind.

'I'm already running late,' Tremayne said, making moves to leave.

'But sir . . .'

'Stay as long as you like,' Tremayne said, going. 'Talk to John, talk to my secretary, talk to whoever you want.'

'I don't think you understand, sir,' Doone said with a touch of desperation. 'Angela Brickell was *strangled*.'

'*What?*' Tremayne stopped dead, stunned. 'I thought you said . . .'

'I said we'd found some remains. Now that you've recognised the . . . er . . . horse, sir, we're pretty sure of her identity. Everything else fits; height, age, possible time of death. And, sir . . .' he hesitated briefly as if to summon courage, 'only last week, sir, we had a Crown Court case about another young woman who was strangled . . . strangled here in this house.'

There was silence.

Tremayne said finally, 'There can't be any connection. The death that occurred in this house was an accident, whatever the jury thought.'

Doone said doggedly, 'Did Mr Nolan Everard have any connections with Angela Brickell?'

'Yes, of course he did. He rides Chickweed, the horse in that photograph. He saw Angela Brickell quite often in the course of her work.' He paused for thought. 'Where did you say her . . . remains . . . were found?'

'I don't think I said, sir.'

'Well, where?'

Doone said, 'All in good time, sir,' a shade uncomfortably, and it occurred to me that he was hoping someone would *know*, and anyone who knew would very likely have strangled her.

'Poor girl,' Tremayne said. 'But all the same, Chief Inspector, I do now have to go to the races. Stay as long as you like, ask whatever you want. John here will explain to my assistant and head lad. John, tell Mackie and Bob what's happened, will you? Phone the car if you need me. Right, I'm off.'

He continued purposefully and at good speed on his way and one could see and hear the Volvo start up and depart. In some bemusement Doone watched him go: his first taste of the difficulty of deflecting Tremayne from a chosen course.

'Well, Chief Inspector,' I said neutrally, 'where do you want to begin?'

'Your name, sir?'

I gave it. He was a good deal more confident with me, I noticed: I didn't have a personality that over-shadowed his own.

'And your ... er ... position here?'

'I'm writing a history of the stables.'

He seemed vaguely surprised that someone should be engaged on such an enterprise and said lamely, 'Very interesting, I'm sure.'

'Yes, indeed.'

'And ... er ... did you know the deceased?'

'Angela Brickell? No, I didn't. She vanished last summer, I believe, and I've been here only a short time, roughly ten days.'

'But you knew about her, sir,' he said shrewdly.

'Let me show you how I knew,' I said. 'Come and look.'

I led him into the dining-room and showed him the piles of clippings, explaining they were the raw materials of my future book.

'This is my workroom,' I said. 'Somewhere in *that* pile of cuttings,' I pointed, 'is an account of Angela Brickell's disappearance. That's how I know about her, and that's all I know. No one has mentioned her outside of this room since I've been here.'

He looked through the past year's cuttings and found the pieces about the girl. He nodded a few times and laid them back carefully where he'd found them, and seemed reassured about me personally. I got the first hint of the garrulity to come.

'Well, sir,' he said, relaxing, 'you can start introducing me to all the people here and explain why I'm asking questions and, as I've found on other cases when only remains are found that people tend to think the worst and imagine all sorts of horrors so that it makes them feel sick and wastes a good deal of time altogether, I'll tell you, sir, and you can pass it on, that what was found was *bones*, sir, quite clean and no smell, nothing horrible, you can assure people of that.'

'Thank you,' I said, a shade numbly.

'Animals and insects had cleaned her, you see.'

'Don't you think that fact alone will make people feel sick?'

'Then don't stress it, sir.'

'No.'

'We have her clothes and shoes and her handbag and lipstick back at the police station... they were scattered around her and I've had my men searching...' He stopped, not telling me then where the search had occurred; except that if she'd been scavenged it had to have been out of doors. Which for a stable girl, in a way, made sense.

'And if you don't mind, sir, will you please just tell everyone she's been found, not that she was strangled.'

'How do you know that she was strangled, if there's nothing much left?'

'The hyoid bone, sir. In the throat. Fractured. Only

a direct blow or manual pressure does that. Fingers usually, from behind.'

'Oh, I see. All right, I'll leave it to you. We'd better start with Mr Vickers' secretary, Dee-Dee.'

I steered him into the office and introduced him. Detective Constable Rich followed everywhere like a shadow, a non-speaking taker of notes. I explained to Dee-Dee that Angela Brickell had probably been found.

'Oh good,' she said spontaneously, and then, seeing it wasn't good at all, 'Oh dear.'

Doone asked to use the telephone, Dee-Dee at once assenting. Doone called his people back at base.

'Mr Vickers identified the horse as one that Angela Brickell tended in his stable, and the man as the owner of the horse, or rather the owner's husband. I'd say it's fairly sure we have Angela Brickell in the mortuary. Can you arrange to send round a WPC to her parents? They live out Wokingham way. The address is in my office. Do it pronto. We don't want anyone from Shellerton upsetting them first. Break it to them kindly, see? Ask if they could recognise any clothes of hers, or handbag. Ask Mollie to go to them, if she's on duty. She makes it more bearable for people. She mops up their grief. Get Mollie. Tell her to take another constable with her, if she wants.'

He listened for a moment or two and put down the receiver.

'The poor lass has been dead six months or more,' he said to Dee-Dee. 'All that's left is sweet clean bones.'

Dee-Dee looked as if that thought were sick-making enough, but I could see that Doone's rough humanity would comfort in the end. He was like a stubby-fingered surgeon, I thought: delicate in his handiwork against the odds.

He asked Dee-Dee if she knew of any reason for Angela Brickell's disappearance. Had the girl been unhappy? Having rows with a boyfriend?

'I've no idea. We didn't find out until after she'd gone that she must have given chocolate to Chickweed. Stupid thing to do.'

Doone looked lost. I explained about the theobromine. 'That's in those clippings, too,' I said.

'We found some chocolate bar wrappers with the lass,' Doone said. 'No chocolate. Is that what was meant in our notes by "possibly doped horse in her charge"?'

'Spot on,' I said.

'Chocolate!' he said disgustedly. 'Not worth dying for.'

I said, enlightened, 'Were you looking for a big conspiracy? A doping ring?'

'Have to consider everything.'

Dee-Dee said positively, 'Angela Brickell wouldn't have been in a doping ring. You don't know what you're talking about.'

Doone didn't pursue it but said he'd like to talk to the rest of the stable staff, asking Dee-Dee meanwhile not to break the news to anyone else as he would prefer to do it himself. Also he didn't want anyone springing the tragedy prematurely onto the poor parents.

'Surely I can tell Fiona,' she protested.

'Who's Fiona?' He frowned, perhaps trying to remember.

'Fiona Goodhaven, who owns Chickweed.'

'Oh, yes. Well, not her either. *Especially* not her. I like to get people's first thoughts, first impressions, not hear what they think after they've spent hours discussing something with all their friends. First thoughts are clearer and more valuable, I've found.'

He said it with more persuasion than command, with the result that Dee-Dee agreed to stay off the grapevine. She didn't ask how the girl had died. If she realised Doone's remarks best fitted a murder scenario, she didn't say so. Perhaps she simply shied away from having to know.

Doone asked to be taken out to the stables. On the way I asked him to remember, if he met Mackie, Tremayne's daughter-in-law and assistant trainer, that she was newly pregnant.

He gave me a sharp glance.

'You're considerate,' I said mildly. 'I thought you might want to modify the shocks.'

He looked disconcerted but made no promise either way and, as it happened, by the time we reached the yard, Mackie had gone home and Bob Watson was alone there, beavering away with saw, hammer and nails, making a new saddle-horse to hold the saddles in the tack room. We found him outside the tack-room door, not too pleased to be interrupted.

I introduced Bob to Doone, Doone to Bob. Doone told him that some human remains discovered by chance were thought to be those of Angela Brickell.

'No!' Bob said. 'Straight up? Poor little bitch. What did she do, fall down a quarry?' He looked absent-mindedly at a piece of wood he held as if he'd temporarily forgotten its purpose.

'Why should you say that, sir?' Doone asked attentively.

'Manner of speaking,' Bob said, shrugging. 'I always thought she'd just scarpered. The guv'nor swore she'd given Chickweed chocolate, but I reckon she didn't. I mean, we all know you mustn't. Anyway, who found her? Where did she go?'

'She was found by chance,' Doone said again. 'Was she unhappy over a boyfriend?'

'Not that I know of. But there's twenty lads and girls here, and they come and go all the time. Truth to tell, I can't remember much about her, except she was sexy. Ask Mrs Goodhaven, she was always kind to her. Ask the other girls here, some of them lived in a hostel with her. Why did you want to know about a boyfriend? She didn't take a high jump, did she? Is that what she did?'

Doone didn't say yes or no, and I understood what he'd meant by preferring to listen to unadulterated first thoughts, to the first pictures and conclusions that minds leaped to when questioned.

He talked to Bob for a while longer but as far as I could see learned nothing much.

'You want to see Mackie,' Bob said in the end. 'That's young Mrs Vickers. The girls tell her things they'd never tell me.'

Doone nodded and I led him and the ubiquitous Rich round the house to Mackie and Perkin's entrance, ringing the bell. It was Perkin himself who came to the door, appearing in khaki overalls, looking wholly artisan and smelling, fascinatingly, of wood and linseed oil.

'Hello,' he said, surprised to see me. 'Mackie's in the shower.'

Doone took it in his stride this time, introducing himself formerly.

'I came to let Mrs Vickers know that Angela Brickell's been found,' he said.

'Who?' Perkin said blankly. 'I didn't know anyone was lost. I don't know any Angela . . . Angela who did you say?'

Doone patiently explained she'd been lost for seven or more months. Angela Brickell.

'Good Lord. Really? Who is she?' A thought struck him. 'I say, is she the stable girl who buggered off sometime last year? I remember a bit of a fuss.'

'That's the one.'

'Good then, my wife will be glad she's found. I'll give her the message.'

He made as if to close the door but Doone said he would like to see Mrs Vickers himself.

'Oh? All right. You'd better come in and wait. John? Come in?'

'Thanks,' I said.

He led the way into a kitchen-dining room where I hadn't been before and offered us rattan armchairs round a table made of a circular slab of glass resting on three gothic plaster pillars. The curtains and chair covers were bright turquoise overprinted with blowsy grey, black and white flowers, and all the kitchen fitments were faced with grey-white streaked Formica; thoroughly modern.

Perkin watched my surprise with irony and said, 'Mackie chose everything in a revolt against good taste.'

'It's happy,' I said. 'Light-hearted.'

The remark seemed somehow to disturb him, but Mackie herself arrived with damp hair at that point looking refreshed and pleased with life. Her reaction to Doone's first cautious words was the same as everyone else's. 'Great. Where is she?'

The gradual realisation of the true facts drained the contentment and the colour from her face. She listened to his questions and answered them, and faced the implications squarely.

'You're telling us, aren't you,' she said flatly, 'that either she killed herself ... or somebody killed her?'

'I didn't say that, madam.'

'As good as.' She sighed desolately. 'All these ques-

tions about doping rings . . . and boyfriends. Oh God.'
She closed her eyes briefly, then opened them to look
at Doone and me.

'We've just had months and months of trouble and
anxiety over Olympia and Nolan, we've had the TV
people and reporters in droves, driving us mad with
their questions, we're only just beginning to feel free
of it all . . . and I can't bear it . . . I can't bear it . . . it's
starting all over again.'

CHAPTER TEN

I borrowed the Land Rover and at Doone's request led him down to the village and into Harry and Fiona's drive. I was surprised that he still wanted me with him and said so, and he explained a little solemnly that he found people felt less *threatened* by a police officer if he turned up with someone they knew.

'Don't you want them to feel threatened?' I asked. 'Many police seem to like it that way.'

'I'm not many policemen.' He seemed uninsulted. 'I work in my own way, sir, and if sometimes it's not how my colleagues work then I get my results all the same and it's results that count in the end. It may not be the best way to the highest promotion,' he smiled briefly, 'but I do tend to solve things, I assure you.'

'I don't doubt it, Chief Inspector,' I said.

'I have three daughters,' he said, sighing, 'and I don't like cases like this one.'

We were standing in the drive looking at the noble façade of a fine Georgian manor.

'Never make assumptions,' he said absent-mindedly,

as if giving me advice. 'You know the two most pathetic words a policeman can utter when his case falls apart around him?'

I shook my head.

'I assumed,' he said.

'I'll remember.'

He looked at me calmly in his unthreatening way and said it was time to trouble the Goodhavens.

As it happened, only Fiona was there, coming to the kitchen door in a dark blue tailored suit with a white silk blouse, gold chains, high-heeled black shoes and an air of rush. She smiled apologetically when she saw me.

'John,' she said. 'What can I do for you? I'm going out to lunch. Can you make it quick?'

'Er . . .' I said, 'this is Detective Chief Inspector Doone, Thames Valley Police. And Constable Rich.'

'Policemen?' she asked, puzzled, and then in terrible flooding anxiety, 'Nothing's happened to Harry?'

'No, no. Nothing. It's not about Harry. Well, not exactly. It's about Angela Brickell. They've found her.'

'Angela . . .? Oh yes. Well, I'm glad. Where did she go?'

Doone was very adroit, I thought, at letting silence itself break the bad news.

'Oh my dear,' Fiona said, after a few quiet revelationary seconds, 'is she dead?'

'Yes, I'm afraid so, madam.' Doone nodded. 'I need to ask you a few questions.'

'Oh, but . . .' She looked at her watch. 'Can't it wait? It's not just a lunch, I'm the guest of honour.'

We were still standing on the doorstep. Doone without arguing produced the photograph and asked Fiona to identify the man, if she could.

'Of course. It's Harry, my husband. And that's my horse, Chickweed. Where did you get this?'

'From the young woman's handbag.'

Fiona's face was full of kindness and regret. 'She loved Chickweed,' she said.

'Perhaps I could come back when your husband's at home?' Doone suggested.

Fiona was relieved. 'Oh, yes, do that. After five tonight or tomorrow morning. He'll be here until about . . . um . . . eleven, I should think, tomorrow. Bye, John.'

She hurried back into the house, leaving the door open, and presently, from beside our own cars, we saw her come out, lock the back door, hide the key under the stone (Tut, tut, Doone said disapprovingly) and drive away in a neat BMW, her blond hair shining, cheerful hand waving goodbye.

'If you had to describe her in one word,' Doone said to me, 'what would it be?'

'Staunch,' I said.

'That was quick.'

'That's what she is. Steadfast, I'd say.'

'Have you known her long?'

'Ten days, like the others.'

'Mm.' He pondered. 'I won't have ten days, not living in their community, like you do. I might ask you again what people here are really like. People sometimes don't act natural when they're with policemen.'

'Fiona did. Surely everyone did who you've met this morning?'

'Oh yes. But there's some I haven't met. And there are loyalties . . . I read the transcript of part of that trial before I came here. Loyalty is strong here, wouldn't you agree? Staunch, steadfast loyalty, wouldn't you say?'

Doone might look grey, I thought, and his chatty almost sing-song Berkshire voice might be disarming, but there was a cunningly intelligent observer behind the waffle, and I did suddenly believe, as I hadn't entirely before, that usually he solved his cases.

He said he would like to speak to all the other stable girls before they heard the news from anyone else, and also the men, but the women first.

I took Doone and Rich to the house in the village which I knew the girls called their hostel, though I'd never been in it. It was a small modern house in a cul-de-sac, bought cheaply before it was built, Tremayne had told me, and appreciating nicely with the years. I explained to Doone that I didn't know all the girls' names: I saw them only at morning exercise and sometimes at evening stables.

'Fair enough,' he said, 'but they'll all know *you*. You can tell them I'm not an ogre.'

I wasn't any longer so sure about that but I did what

211

he asked. He sat paternally on a flower-patterned sofa in the sitting-room, at home among the clutter of pot plants, satin cushions, fashion magazines and endless photographs of horses, and told them without drama that it looked possible Angela Brickell had died the day she hadn't returned for evening stables. They had found her clothes, her handbag and her bones, he said, and naturally they were having to look into it. He asked the by now familiar questions: did they think Angela had been deeply involved in doping horses, and did they know if she'd had rows with her boyfriend.

Only four of the six girls had been employed at the yard in Angela's time, they said. She definitely hadn't been doping horses; they found the idea funny. She wasn't bright enough, one of them said unflatteringly. She hadn't been their close friend. She was moody and secretive, they all agreed, but they didn't know of any one steady boyfriend. They thought Sam had probably had her, but no one should read much in that. Who was Sam? Sam Yaeger, the stable jockey, who rode more than the horses.

There were a few self-conscious giggles. Doone, father of three daughters, interpreted the giggles correctly and looked disillusioned.

'Did Angela and Sam Yaeger quarrel?'

'You don't quarrel with Sam Yaeger,' the brightest of them said boldly. 'You go to bed with him. Or in the hay.'

Gales of giggles.

They were all in their teens, I thought. Light-framed, hopeful, knowing.

The bold girl said, 'But no one takes Sam seriously. It's just a bit of fun. He makes a joke of it. If you don't want to, you just say no. Most of us say no. He'd never try to force anyone.'

The others looked shocked at the idea. 'It's casual with him, like.'

I wondered if Doone were thinking that maybe with Angela it hadn't been casual after all.

The bold girl, whose name was Tansy, asked when they'd found the poor little bitch.

'When?' Doone considered briefly. 'Someone noticed her last Sunday morning. Mind you, he wasn't in a great hurry to do anything because he could see she'd been lying there peacefully a long time, but then he phoned us and the message reached me late Sunday afternoon while I was sleeping off my wife's Yorkshire pudding – great grub, that is – so Monday I went to see the lass and we started trying to find out who she was, because we have lists of missing people, runaways mostly, you see? Then yesterday we found her handbag, and it had this photo in it, so I came over this morning to check if she was the missing stable girl on our missing persons list. So I should think you could say we really found her this morning.'

His voice had lulled them into accepting him on friendly terms and they willingly looked at the photograph he passed around.

'That's Chickweed,' they said, nodding.

'You're sure you can tell one horse from another?'

'Of course you can,' they said, 'when you see them every day.'

'And the man?'

'Mr Goodhaven.'

Doone thanked them and tucked the photo away again. Rich took slow notes, none of the girls paying him any attention.

Doone asked if by any chance Angela Brickell had owned a dog. The girls, mystified, said no. Why would he think so? They'd found a dog's collar near her, he explained, and a well-chewed ball. None of them had a dog, Tansy said.

Doone rose to go and told them if anything occurred to them, to send him a message.

'What sort of thing?' they asked.

'Well now,' he said kindly. 'We know she's dead, but we want to know how and why. It's best to know. If you were found dead one day, you'd want people to know what happened, wouldn't you?'

Yes, they nodded, they would.

'Where did she go?' Tansy asked.

Doone as near as dammit patted her head, but not quite. I thought that that would have undone all his good fatherly work. Willing they might be, but feminists all, too smart to be patronised.

'We have to do more tests first, miss,' he said obscurely. 'But soon we hope to make a statement.'

214

They all accepted that easily enough and we said our goodbyes, travelling back through the village to a bungalow nearer Bob Watson's house, where the unmarried lads lived.

The living-room in the lads' hostel, in sharp contrast to the girls', was plantless, without cushions and was grubbily scattered with newspapers, empty beer cans, pornography, dirty plates and muddy boots. Only the televisions and video players in both places looked the same.

The lads all knew that Angela Brickell had been found dead as one of them had learned it from Bob Watson. None of them seemed to care about her personally (exactly like the girls) and they too had no information and few opinions about her.

'She rode all right,' one of them said, shrugging.

'She was a bit of a hot pants,' said another.

They identified Chickweed's picture immediately and one of them asked if he could have the photo when the police had done with it.

'Why?' Doone asked.

'Because I look after the old bugger now, that's why. Wouldn't mind having a snap of him.'

'Better take another one,' Doone advised him. 'By rights this belongs to the lass's parents.'

'Well,' he later demanded of me, after we'd left. 'What do you think?'

'It's *your* job to think,' I protested.

He half smiled. 'There's a long way to go yet. If you

think of anything, you tell me. I'll listen to everything anyone wants to say. I'm not proud. I don't mind the public telling me the answers. Make sure everyone knows that, will you?'

'Yes,' I said.

The telephone in Shellerton House began ringing that afternoon in a clamour that lasted for days. However reticent Doone had been, the news had spread at once like a bush fire through the village that *another* young woman connected with Tremayne Vickers' house and stables had been found dead. Newspapers, quickly informed, brusquely demanded to be told where, when and why. Dee-Dee repeated and repeated that she didn't know until she was almost in tears. I took over from her after a while and dispensed enormous courtesy and goodwill but no facts, of which, at the time anyway, I knew very few.

I worked on the book and answered the phone most of Friday and didn't see Doone at all, but on Saturday I learned that he had spent the day before scattering fear and consternation.

Tremayne had asked if I would prefer to go to Sandown with Fiona, Harry and Mackie, saying he thought I might find it more illuminating: he himself would be saddling five runners at Chepstow and dealing with two lots of demanding owners besides. 'To be frank, you'd be under my feet. Go and carry things for Mackie.'

With old fashioned views, which Mackie herself tolerated with affection, he persisted in thinking pregnant women fragile. I wondered if Tremayne understood how little Perkin would like my carrying things for Mackie and determined to be discreet.

'Fiona and Harry are taking Mackie,' Tremayne said, almost as if the same thought had occurred to him. I'll check that they'll take you too, though it's a certainty if they have room.'

They had room. They collected Mackie and me at the appointed time and they were very disturbed indeed.

Harry was driving. Fiona twisted round in the front seat to speak to Mackie and me directly and with deep lines of worry told us that Doone had paid two visits to them the day before, the first apparently friendly and the second menacing in the extreme.

'He seemed all right in the morning,' Fiona said. 'Chatty and easy-going. Then he came back in the evening . . .' She shivered violently, although it was warm in the car, '. . . and he more or less accused Harry of strangling that bloody girl.'

'*What?*' Mackie said. 'That's ridiculous.'

'Doone doesn't think so,' Harry said gloomily. 'He says she was definitely strangled. And did he show you that photo of me with Chickweed?'

Mackie and I both said yes.

'Well, it seems he got it enlarged. I mean, blown up really big. He said he wanted to see me alone, without Fiona, and he showed me the enlargement which was just of me, not the horse. He asked me to confirm that I was wearing my own sunglasses in the photo. I said of course I was. Then he asked me if I was wearing my own belt, and I said of course. He asked me to look carefully at the buckle. I said I wouldn't be wearing anyone else's things. Then he asked me if the pen clipped onto the racecard I was holding in the photo was mine also . . . and I got a bit shirty and demanded to know what it was all about.' He stopped for a moment, and then in depression went on. 'You won't believe it . . . but they found my sunglasses and my belt and my gold pen lying with that girl, wherever she was, and Doone won't *tell* us where for some God-silly reason. I don't know how the hell those things got there. I told Doone I hadn't seen any of them for ages and he said he believed it. He thought they'd been with Angela Brickell all these months . . . that I'd dropped them when I was with her.'

He stopped again, abruptly, and at that point added no more.

Fiona, in a strong mixture of indignation and alarm, said, 'Doone demanded to know precisely where Harry had been on the day that girl went missing and also he said he might want to take Harry's *fingerprints*.'

'He thinks I killed her,' Harry said. 'It's obvious he does.'

'It's ridiculous,' Mackie repeated. 'He doesn't know you.'

'Where *were* you on that day?' I asked. 'I mean, you might have a perfect alibi.'

'I might have,' he said, 'but I don't know where I was. Could you say for certain what you were doing on the Tuesday afternoon of the second week of June last year?'

'Not for sure,' I said.

'If it had been the *third* week,' Harry said, 'we'd have been at Ascot races. Royal Ascot. Tarted up in top hats and things.'

'We keep a big appointments diary,' Fiona said fiercely. 'I dug up last year's. There's nothing listed at all on that second Tuesday. Neither of us can remember what we were doing.'

'No work?' I suggested. 'No meetings?'

Harry and Fiona simultaneously said no. Fiona was on a couple of committees for good causes, but there'd been no meetings that day. Harry, whose personal fortune seemed to equal Fiona's in robust good health, had in the past negotiated the brilliant sale of an inherited tyre-making company (so Tremayne had told me) and now passed his time lucratively as occasional consultant to other private firms looking for a golden corporate whale to swallow them. He couldn't remember any consultations for most of June.

'We went to see Nolan ride Chickweed at Uttoxeter near the end of May,' Fiona said worriedly. 'Angela was there looking after the horse. That was the day someone fed him theobromine and caffeine, and if she didn't give Chickweed chocolate herself then she must have let someone else do it. Sheer negligence, probably. Anyway, Chickweed won and Angela went back to Shellerton with him and we saw her a few days later and gave her an extra present, as we were so pleased with the way she looked after the horse. I mean, a horse's success is always partly due to whoever cares for it and grooms it. And I can't remember seeing the wretched girl again after that.'

'Nor can I,' Harry said.

They went over and over the same old ground all the way to Sandown and it was clear they had spoken of little else since Doone's devastating identification of Harry's belongings.

'Someone must have put those things there to incriminate Harry,' Mackie said unhappily.

Fiona agreed with her, but it appeared that Doone didn't.

Harry said, 'Doone believes it was an unpremeditated murder. I asked him why and he just said that most murders were unpremeditated. Useless. He said people who commit unpremeditated murder often drop things from extreme agitation and don't know they've dropped them. I said I couldn't even remember ever talking to the girl except in the company of my wife and he simply stared at me, not believing me. I'll tell you, pals, it was unnerving.'

'Awful,' Mackie said vehemently. '*Wicked.*'

Harry, trying to sound balanced, was clearly horribly

disconcerted and was driving without concentration, braking and accelerating jerkily. Fiona said they had thought of not going to Sandown as they weren't in a fun-day mood, but they had agreed not to let Doone's suspicions ruin everything. Doone's suspicions were nevertheless conspicuously wrecking their equilibrium and it was a subdued little group that stood in the parade ring watching Fiona's tough hunter, the famous Chickweed, walk round before the Wilfred Johnstone Hunter Chase.

No one, one hoped, had given him chocolate.

Fiona had told Nolan about Doone's accusations. Nolan told Harry that now he, Harry, knew what it was like to have a charge of murder hanging over him he would in retrospect have more sympathy for him, Nolan. Harry didn't like it. With only vestiges of friendliness he protested that he, Harry, had not been found with a dead girl at his feet.

'As good as, by the sound of things,' Nolan said, rattled.

'Nolan!' Fiona wasn't amused. 'Everyone, stop talking about it. Nolan, put your mind on the race. Harry, not another word about that *bloody* girl. Everything will be sorted out. We'll just have to be patient.'

Harry gave her a fond but rueful glance and, over her shoulder, caught my eye. There was something more in his expression, I thought, and after a moment identified it as fear: maybe faint, but definitely present. Harry and fear hadn't, until then, gone together in my mind, particularly not since his controlled behaviour in a frozen ditch.

Mackie, *in loco* Tremayne, saw Nolan into the saddle and the four of us walked towards the stands to see the race. With Mackie and Fiona in front, Harry fell into step beside me.

'I want to tell you something,' he said, 'but not Fiona.'

'Fire away.'

He looked quickly around him, checking no one could hear.

'Doone said ... Christ ... he said the girl had no clothes on when she died.'

'God, Harry.' I felt my mouth still open, and closed it consciously.

'I don't know what to do,' he said.

'Absolutely nothing.'

'Doone asked what I was doing there with my belt off.'

The shock still trembled in his voice.

'The innocent aren't found guilty,' I protested.

He said miserably, 'Oh, yes, they are. You know they are.'

'But not on such flimsy evidence.'

'I haven't been able to tell Fiona. I mean, we've always been fine together, but she might start *wondering* ... I don't honestly know how I'd bear that.'

We reached the stands and went up to watch, Harry falling silent in his torturing troubles amid the raucous calls of bookmakers and the enfolding hubbub of the gathering crowd. The runners cantered past on their way to the starting gate, Nolan looking professional as usual on the muscly chestnut that Fiona had ridden all autumn out hunting. Chickweed, Mackie had told me, was Fiona's especial pet: her friend as much as her property. Chickweed, circling and lining up, running in the first hunter chase of the spring season, was going to win three or four times before June, Tremayne hoped.

We were joined at that point by pudgy unfit Lewis, who panted that he had only just arrived in time and asked if the Jockey Club had said anything about Nolan going on riding.

'Not a word,' Fiona said. 'Fingers crossed.'

'If they were going to stop him,' Lewis opined judiciously, taking deep breaths, 'they'd surely have let him know by today, so perhaps the expletive sod's got away with it.'

'Brotherly love,' Fiona remarked ironically.

'He owes me,' Lewis said darkly and with such growling intensity that all of us, I thought, recognised the nature of the debt, even if some hadn't wanted to believe it earlier.

'And will you collect?' Harry asked, his sarcasm showing.

'No thanks to you,' Lewis replied sharply

'Perjury's not my best act.'

Lewis smiled like a snake, all fangs.

'I,' he said, 'am the best bleep bleep actor of you all.'

Fiona starkly faced the certainty that Lewis had not

after all been too drunk to see straight when Olympia died. Mackie's clear face was pinched with dismay. Harry, who had known all along, would have shrugged off Lewis's admission philosophically were it not for his own ominous future.

'What would you have me do?' Lewis demanded, seeing the general disapproval. 'Say he called her every filthy name in the book and shook her by the neck until her eyes popped out?'

'Lewis!' Fiona exclaimed, not believing him. 'Shut up.'

Lewis gave me a mediumly hostile glance and wanted to know why I was always hanging around. No one answered him, me included.

Fiona said, 'They're off' a split second before the official announcement and concentrated through her raceglasses.

'I asked you an expletive question,' Lewis said to me brusquely.

'You know why,' I replied, watching the race.

'Tremayne isn't here,' he objected.

'He sent me to see Sandown.'

Chickweed was easy to spot, I discovered, with the white blaze down his chestnut face that so clearly distinguished him in the photograph nodding away on the rails at every galloping step. The overall pace seemed slower to me than the other races I'd watched, the jumping more deliberate; but it wasn't, as Tremayne had warned me, an easy track even for the sport's top performers, and for hunters a searching test. 'Watch them jump the seven fences down the far side,' he'd said. 'If a horse meets the first one right, the others come in his stride. Miss the first, get it wrong, legs in a tangle, you might as well forget the whole race. Nolan is an artist at meeting that first fence right.'

I watched particularly. Chickweed flew the first fence and all the next six down the far side, gaining effortless lengths. 'There's nothing like the hunting field for teaching a horse to jump,' Tremayne had said. 'The trouble is, hunters aren't necessarily fast. Chickweed is, though. So was Oxo who won the Grand National years back.'

Chickweed repeated the feat on the second circuit and then, a length in front of his nearest pursuer, swept round the long bend at the bottom end of the course and straightened himself for the third fence from home – the Pond fence, so called because the small hollow beside it had once been wet, though now held mostly reeds and bushes.

'Oh, come on,' Fiona said explosively, the tension too much. 'Chicky Chickweed ... jump it.'

Chicky Chickweed rose to it as if he'd heard her, his white blaze showing straight on us before he veered right towards the second last fence and the uphill pull to home.

'A lot of races are lost on the hill,' Tremayne had told me. 'It's where stamina counts, where you need the reserves. Any horse that has enough left to accelerate there is going to win. Same at Cheltenham. A race at either place can change dramatically after the last fence. Tired horses just fade away, even if they're in the lead.'

Chickweed made short work of the second last fence but didn't shake off his pursuer.

'I can't bear it,' Fiona said.

Mackie put down her raceglasses to watch the finish, anxiety digging lines on her forehead.

It was only a race, I thought. What did it matter? I answered my own question astringently: I'd written a novel, what did it matter if it won or lost on its own terms? It mattered because I cared, because it was where I'd invested all thought, all effort. It mattered to Tremayne and Mackie the same way. Only a race . . . but also their skill laid on the line.

Chickweed's pursuer closed the gap coming to the last fence.

'Oh, no,' Fiona groaned, lowering her own glasses. 'Oh, Nolan, come on.'

Chickweed made a spectacular leap, leaving unnecessary space between himself and the birch, wasting precious time in the air. His pursuer, jumping lower in a flatter trajectory, landed first and was fastest away.

'*Damn*,' Harry said.

Fiona was silent, beginning to accept defeat.

Nolan had no such thoughts. Nolan, aggressive instincts in full flood, was crouching like a demon over Chickweed's withers delivering the message that losing was unacceptable. Nolan's whip rose and fell twice, his arm swinging hard. Chickweed, as if galvanised, reversed his decision to slow down now that he'd been passed and took up the struggle again. The jockey and horse in front, judging the battle won, eased up fractionally too soon. Chickweed caught them napping a stride from the winning post and put his head in front just where it mattered, the crowd cheering for him, the favourite, the fighter who never gave up.

It was Nolan, I saw, who had won that race. Nolan himself, not the horse. Nolan's ability, Nolan's character acting on Chickweed's. Through Nolan I began to understand how much more there was to riding races than fearlessness and being able to stay in the saddle. More than tactics, more than experience, more than ambition. Winning races, like survival, began in the mind.

Fiona, triumphant where all had looked lost, breathless and shiny-eyed, hurried ahead with Mackie to meet the returning warriors. Lewis, Harry and I pressed along in their wake.

'Nolan's a genius,' Harry was saying.

'The other expletive jockey threw it away,' Lewis had it.

Never assume, I thought, thinking of Doone. Never assume you've won until you hold the prize in your hand.

Doone *was* assuming things, I thought. Not taking his own advice. Or so it seemed.

We all went for a celebratory drink, though in Mackie's case it was ginger ale. Harry ordered the obligatory bubbles, his heart in his boots. Nolan was as high as Fiona, Lewis a grudging applauder. I, I supposed, an observer, still on the outside looking in. Six of us in a racecourse bar smiling in unison while the cobweb ghosts of two young women set traps for the flies.

We arrived back at Shellerton before Tremayne returned from Chepstow. Fiona dropped Mackie off at her side of the house and I walked round to Tremayne's, unlocking the door with the key he'd given me and switching on lights.

There was a message from Gareth on the family room corkboard: 'GONE TO MOVIE BACK FOR GRUB.' Smiling, I kicked the hot logs together and blew some kindling sticks to life with the bellows to revive the fire and poured some wine and felt at home.

A knock on the back door drew me from comfort to see who it was, and I didn't at first recognise the young woman looking at me with a shy enquiring smile. She was pretty in a small way, brown haired, self-effacing . . . Bob Watson's wife, Ingrid.

'Come in,' I said warmly, relieved to have identified her. 'But I'm the only one home.'

'I thought maybe Mackie. Mrs Vickers . . .'

'She's round in her own house.'

'Oh. Well . . .' She came over the threshold tentatively and I encouraged her into the family room where she stood nervously and wouldn't sit down

'Bob doesn't know I'm here,' she said anxiously.

'Never mind. Have a drink?'

'Oh no. Better not.'

She seemed to be screwing herself up to something, and out it all finally came in a rush.

'You were ever so kind to me that night. Bob reckons you saved me from frostbite at the least . . . and pneumonia, he said. Giving me your own clothes. I'll never forget it. Never.'

'You looked so cold,' I said. 'Are you sure you won't sit down?'

'I was *hurting* with cold.' She again ignored the chair suggestion. 'I knew you'd come back just now . . . I saw Mrs Goodhaven's car come up the road . . . I came to talk to you, really. I've got to tell someone, I think, and you're . . . well . . . easiest.'

'Go on then. Talk. I'm listening.'

She said in a small burst, unexpectedly, 'Angela Brickell was a Roman Catholic, like I am.'

'Was she?' The news meant very little.

Ingrid nodded. 'It said on the local radio news tonight that Angela's body was found last Saturday by a gamekeeper on the Quillersedge Estate There was quite a bit about her on the news, about how the police were proceeding with their enquiries and all that. And it said foul play was suspected. They're such stupid words, foul play. Why didn't they just say someone probably did her in? Anyway, after she'd vanished last year Mrs Vickers asked me to clear all her things out of the hostel and send them to her parents, and I did.'

She stopped, staring searchingly at my face for understanding.

'What,' I asked, feeling the way, 'did you find in her belongings? Something that worries you ... because she's dead?'

Ingrid's face showed relief at being invited to tell me.

'I threw it away,' she said. 'It was a do-it-yourself home kit for a pregnancy test. She'd used it. All I found was the empty box.'

CHAPTER ELEVEN

Tremayne came home and frightened Ingrid away like Miss Muffet and the spider.

'What did she want?' he asked, watching her scuttling exit. 'She always seems scared of me. She's a real mouse.'

'She came to tell me something she thinks should be known,' I said reflectively. 'I suppose she thought I could do the telling, in her place.'

'Typical,' Tremayne said. 'What was it?'

'Angela Brickell was perhaps pregnant'.

'What?' He stared at me blankly. '*Pregnant?*'

I explained about the used test. 'You don't buy or use one of those tests unless you have good reason to.'

He said thoughtfully. 'No, I suppose not.'

'So,' I said, 'there are about twenty lusty males connected with this stable and dozens more in Shellerton and throughout the racing industry; and even if she *were* pregnant – and from what Doone said about bones I don't see how they can tell yes or no, even if she were – it still might have nothing to do with her death.'

231

'But it might.'

'She was a Roman Catholic, Ingrid says.'

'What's that got to do with it?'

'They're against abortion.'

He stared into space.

I said, 'Harry's in trouble. Have you heard?'

'No, what trouble?'

I told him about Doone's accusations, and also about Chickweed's way of winning and about Lewis's more or less explicit admission of perjury. Tremayne poured himself a gin and tonic of suitably gargantuan proportions and told me in his turn that he'd had a rotten day at Chepstow. 'One of my runners broke down and another went crashing down arse over tip at the last fence with the race in his pocket. Sam dislocated his thumb, which swelled like a balloon, and although he's OK he won't realistically be fit again until Tuesday, which means I have to scratch around for a replacement for Monday. And one lot of owners groused and groaned until I could have knocked their heads together and all I can do is be nice to them and sometimes it all drives me up the bloody wall, to tell you the truth.'

He flopped his weight into an armchair, stretched out his legs and rested his gaze on his toecaps, thinking things over.

'Are you going to tell Doone about the pregnancy test?' he asked finally.

'I suppose so. It's on Ingrid's conscience. If I don't pass on what she's said, she'll find another mouthpiece.'

He sighed. 'It won't do Harry much good.'

'Nor harm.'

'It's a motive. Juries believe in motives.'

I grunted. 'Harry won't come to trial.'

'Nolan did. And a good motive would have jailed him, you can't say it wouldn't.'

'The pregnancy test is a non-starter,' I said. 'Ingrid threw the empty box away; there's no proof it really existed; there's no saying if Angela used it or when; there's no certainty about the result; there's no knowing who she'd been sleeping with.'

'You should have been a lawyer.'

Mackie and Perkin came through for their usual drink and news-exchange and even Chickweed's win couldn't disperse the general gloom.

'Angela pregnant?' Mackie shook her head, almost bewildered. 'She didn't say anything about it.'

'She might have done, given time,' Tremayne said, 'if the test was positive.'

'Damned careless of her,' Perkin said. 'That bloody girl's nothing but trouble. It's all upsetting Mackie just when she should be feeling relaxed and happy, and I don't like it.'

Mackie stretched out a hand and squeezed her husband's in gratitude, the underlying joy resurfacing, as persistent as pregnancy itself. Perhaps Angela Brickell too, I speculated, had been delighted to be needing her test. Who could tell?

Gareth gusted in full of plans for an expedition I'd forgotten about, a fact he unerringly read on my face.

'But you said you would teach us things, and we could light a fire.' His voice rose high with disappointment.

'Um,' I said. 'Ask your father.'

Tremayne listened to Gareth's request for a patch of land for a camp fire and raised his eyebrows my way.

'Do you really want to bother with all this?'

'Actually, I suggested it, in a rash moment.'

Gareth nodded vigorously. 'Coconut's coming at ten.'

Mackie said, 'Fiona asked us to go down in the morning to toast Chickweed and cheer Harry up.'

'But John *promised*,' Gareth said anxiously.

Mackie smiled at him indulgently. 'I'll make John's excuses.'

Sunday morning crept in greyly on a near-freezing drizzle, enough to test the spirits of all would-be survivors. Tremayne, drinking coffee in the kitchen with the lights on at nine-thirty, suggested scrubbing the whole idea. His son would vehemently have none of it. They compromised on a promise from me to bring everyone home at the first sneeze, and Coconut arrived on his bicycle in brilliant yellow oilskins with a grin to match.

It was easy to see how he'd got his name. He stood in the kitchen dripping and pulled off a sou'wester to reveal a wiry tuft of light brown hair sticking straight up from the top of his head. (It would never lie down properly, Gareth later explained.)

Coconut was nearly fifteen. Below the top-knot he had bright intelligent eyes, a big nose and a sloppy loose-lipped mouth, as if his face hadn't yet synthesised with his emerging character. Give him a year, I thought, maybe two, then the shell would firm to define the man.

'There's a bit of wasteland at the top of the apple orchard,' Tremayne said. 'You can have that.'

'But, Dad . . .' Gareth began, raising objections.

'It sounds fine,' I said firmly. 'Survivors can't choose.'

Tremayne looked at me and then at Gareth thoughtfully and nodded as if to confirm a private thought.

'But February's a bad month for food,' I said, 'and I suppose we'd better not steal a pheasant, so we'll cheat a bit and take some bacon with us. Bring gloves and a penknife each. We'll go in ten minutes.'

The boys scurried to collect waterproofs for Gareth, and Tremayne asked what exactly I planned to do with them.

'Build a shelter,' I said. 'Light a fire, gather some lunch and cook it. That'll be enough, I should think. Everything takes forever when you start with nothing.'

'Teach them they're lucky.'

'Mm.'

235

He came to the door to see off the intrepid expedition, all of us unequipped except for the survival kit (with added bacon) that I wore round my waist and the penknives in their pockets. The cold drizzle fell relentlessly but no one seemed to mind. I waved briefly to Tremayne and went where Gareth led; which was through a gate in a wall, through a patch of long-deserted garden, through another gate and up a slow gradient through about fifty bare-branched apple trees, fetching up on a small bedraggled plateau roughly fenced with ruined dry-stone walling on one side and a few trees in the remains of a hawthorn hedge full of gaps round the rest. Beyond that untidy boundary lay neat prosperous open acres of winter ploughing, the domain of the farmer next door.

Gareth looked at our terrain disgustedly and even Coconut was dismayed, but I thought Tremayne had chosen pretty well, on the whole. Whatever we did, we couldn't make things worse.

'First of all,' I said, 'we build a shelter for the fire.'

'Nothing will burn in this rain,' Gareth said critically.

'Perhaps we'd better go back indoors, then.'

They stared in faint shock.

'No,' Gareth said.

'Right.' I brought the basic survival tin out of my pocket and gave him the coil of flexible saw. 'We passed at least four dead apple trees on the way up here. Slide a couple of sticks through the loops at the ends of this saw, and you and Coconut go and cut down one of those dead trees and bring it up here. Cut it as near the ground as you can manage.'

It took them roughly three seconds to bounce off with renewed enthusiasm, and I wandered round the decrepit piece of what Tremayne had truly described as wasteland, seeing everywhere possibilities of a satisfactory camp. The whole place, for instance, was pale brown with the dead stalks of last year's unmown grass; an absolute gift.

By the time the boys returned, puffing, red-faced and dragging the results of their exertions, I'd wrenched out a few rusty old metal fence posts, cut a lot of living hawthorn switches from the hedge and harvested a pile of the dead grass stalks from a patch near the last row of apple trees. We made a short trip down to the deserted garden to reap a patch of old stinging nettles for bindings, and about an hour after setting off were admiring a free-standing four-foot-square shelter made of a metal frame with a slightly sloping roof of closely latticed hawthorn switches thickly thatched on top with endless piled-on bundles of dried grass. While we watched, the drizzle trickled down the top layer of brownish stalks and dripped off to one side, leaving a small rain-free area underneath.

After that, by themselves, the boys made a simple square frame lashed with thickly criss-crossed hawthorn which we could lean against any one side of the fire shelter to prevent the rain from blowing straight in.

Gareth understood without being told and explained it to Coconut matter-of-factly.

'OK,' I said. 'Next, we find some flat dry stones from that broken-down wall to make a floor for the fire. Don't bring very wet stones, they can explode when they get hot. Then we go around looking for anything very small and dry that will burn. Dead leaves. Bits of fluff caught on fences. Anything inside that wrecked old greenhouse in the garden. When you find something, keep it dry in your pockets. When we've got enough tinder, we'll feather some kindling sticks. We also need enough dry wood, if you can find any. And bring any old cowpats you come across: they burn like peat.'

After another hour's labour we had stacked under the fire shelter the remains of an old cucumber frame from the greenhouse and enough dry tinder to take kindly to a flame. Then, working with my hands under the shelter, I showed them how to strip the bark off a wet stick and make shallow lengthwise cuts in the dry dead wood underneath so that fine shavings curled outwards and the stick looked feathered all over. They each made one with their knives: Gareth quick and neat, Coconut all thumbs.

Finally with a match, a piece of candle, the tinder of dead leaves and flower heads, the feather kindling sticks, the cucumber frame and a good deal of luck (but no cowpats) a bright little fire burned healthily against the drizzly odds and Gareth and Coconut looked as if the sun had risen where they didn't expect it

The smoke curled up and out over the edges of the thatched roofing. I remarked that if we'd had to live there for months we could hang spare meat and fish under the roof to smoke it. Apple wood made sweet smoke. Oak would smoke some meats better.

'We couldn't live out here for months.' Coconut couldn't imagine it.

'It wasn't always sunny in Sherwood Forest,' I said.

We snapped all the smaller twigs off the felled apple tree and added them gradually to the blaze, then made the beginnings of a human-sized shelter by wedging the dead tree as a roof and rear wall between two live trees, bringing more hawthorn to weave through the branches, heaping onto the top and rear surface any boughs, dead plants and turves we could cut and thickly laying a floor below of grass stalks, the nearest thing to straw. Apart from a few drips, we were out of the rain.

Lunch, when we finally ate it after a long forage, consisted mainly of finds from the old garden: some tubers of wild parsley, comfrey and Jerusalem artichoke, a handful of very small Brussels sprouts (ugh, Gareth said) and a rather bitter green leaf salad of plantain, dock and dandelion (double ugh). Never eat poisonous buttercups, I said, be grateful for dandelions. Coconut flatly refused to contemplate worms, the only things plentiful. Both boys fell on the bacon, threaded and grilled on sharpened peeled sticks, and such was their hunger that they afterwards chewed for ages on strips of the inner sweet bark of a young birch tree that was struggling away in the hedge. Birch bark was good nourishing food, I said. Gareth said they would take my word for it.

We drank rather scummy rainwater found in an old watering can and boiled in a Coke can Gareth collected from the Shellerton House dustbin. They declined my offer to make coffee from roast dandelion root. Next time they went camping they would take tea bags, they said.

We were sitting in the shelter, the fire burning red with embers on its stone base a few feet away, the drizzle almost a permanence, the odd foods eaten, the end of the experiment not far ahead.

'How about staying out here all night?' I asked.

They both looked horrified.

'You'd survive,' I said, 'with shelter and a fire.'

'It would be miserable,' Gareth said. 'It's freezing cold.'

'Yes.'

There was a pause, then Gareth added, 'Survival isn't really much fun, is it?'

'Often not,' I agreed. 'Just a matter of life or death.'

'If we were outlaws in Sherwood Forest,' he said, 'the Sheriff's men would be hunting us.'

'Nasty.'

Coconut involuntarily looked around for enemies, shivering at the thought.

'We can't stay out all night. We have to go to school tomorrow,' he said.

The relief on both their faces was comical, and I thought that perhaps for a second or two they'd had a vision of a much older, more brutal world where every tomorrow was a struggle, where hunger and cold were normal and danger ever present and cruel. A primitive world, far back from Robin Hood, back from the Druids who'd walked the ancient Berkshire Downs, back where laws hadn't been invented or rights thought of, back before organisation, before tribes, before ritual, before duty. Back where the strong ate and the weak died, the bedrock and everlasting design of nature.

When a dark shade of iron seeped into the slate-grey light, we pulled the fire to pieces and dowsed the hot ends in wet grass. Then we stacked the remaining pile of apple wood neatly under the fire's roofing and started for home, carrying as little as we'd brought.

Gareth looked back at the intertwined tree shelter and the dead fireplace and seemed for a moment wistful, but it was with leaps and whoops that he and Coconut ran down from there to re-embrace the familiar constraints of civilisation.

'God,' Gareth said, barging in through the back door, 'lead me to a pizza. To two pizzas, maybe three.'

Laughing, I peeled off my long-suffering ski-suit and

left them to it in the kitchen, heading myself for warmth in the family room; and there I found a whole bunch of depressed souls sprawling in armchairs contemplating a different sort of disastrous tomorrow where food was no problem but danger abounded.

Harry, Fiona, Nolan, Lewis, Perkin, Mackie and Tremayne, all silent, as if everything useful had been said already. Tight-knit, interlocked, they looked at me vaguely, at the stranger within their gates, the unexpected character in their play.

'Ah . . . John,' Tremayne said, stirring, remembering, 'are both boys still living?'

'More or less.'

I poured myself some wine and sat on an unoccupied footstool, feeling the oppression of their collective thoughts and guessing that they all now knew everything I did, and perhaps more.

'If Harry didn't do it, who did?' It was Lewis's question, which got no specific reply, as if it had been asked over and over before.

'Doone will find out,' I murmured.

Fiona said indignantly, 'He's not trying. He's not looking beyond Harry. It's disgraceful.'

Proof that Doone was still casting about, however, arrived noisily at that point in the shape of Sam Yaeger, who hooted his horn outside as a preliminary and swept into the house in a high state of indignation.

'Tremayne!' he said in the doorway, and then stopped

abruptly at the sight of the gathered clan. 'Oh. You're all here.'

'You're supposed to be resting,' Tremayne said repressively.

'To hell with bloody resting. There I was, quietly nursing my bruises according to orders, when this Policeman Plod turns up on my doorstep. Sunday afternoon! Doesn't the bugger ever sleep? And d'you know what little gem he tossed at me? Your bloody stable girls told him I'd had a bit of how's-your-father with Angela effing Brickell.'

The brief silence which greeted this announcement wasn't exactly packed with disbelief.

'Well, did you?' Tremayne asked.

'That's not the point. The point is that it wasn't any Tuesday last June. So this Doone fellow asks me what I was doing that day, as if I could remember. Working on my boat, I expect. He asked if I logged the hours I worked on it. Is this man for real? I said I hadn't a bloody clue what I was doing, maybe it was a couple of willing maidens, and he has no sense of humour, it's in a permanent state of collapse, he said it wasn't a joking matter.'

'He has three daughters,' I said. 'It worries him.'

'I can't help his effing hang-ups,' Sam said. 'He said he had to check every possibility, so I told him he'd have a long job considering old Angie's opportunities, not to mention willingness.' He paused. 'She was even making goo-goo eyes at Bob Watson at one time.'

'She wouldn't have got past Ingrid,' Mackie said. 'Ingrid looks meek and mild but you should see her angry. She keeps Bob in her sight. She doesn't trust any girl in the yard. I doubt if Angela got anywhere with Bob.'

'You never know,' Sam said darkly. 'Can I have a drink? Coke?'

'In the fridge in the kitchen,' Perkin said, not stirring to fetch it.

Sam nodded, went out and came back carrying a glass, followed by Gareth and Coconut busily stoking their furnaces with pizza wedges.

Tremayne raised his eyebrows at the food.

'We're starving,' explained his younger son. 'We ate *roots*, and birch bark and dandelion leaves, and no one in their right mind would live in Sherwood Forest being chased by the Sheriff.'

Sam looked bewildered. 'What *are* you on about?' he demanded.

'Survival,' Gareth said. He marched over to a table, picked up *Return Safe from the Wilderness* and thrust it into Sam's hands. 'John wrote it,' he said, 'and five other books like it. So we built a shelter and made a fire and cooked roots and boiled water to drink . . .'

'What about Sherwood Forest?' Harry drawled, smiling but looking strained notwithstanding.

Coconut explained, 'We might be cold and hungry but there weren't any enemies lurking behind the apple trees.'

'Er . . .' Sam said.

Tremayne, amused, enlightened everyone about our day.

'Tell you what,' Gareth said thoughtfully, 'it makes you realise how lucky you are to have a bed and a pizza to come home to.'

Tremayne looked at me from under lowered lids, his mouth curving with contentment. 'Teach them they're lucky,' he'd said.

'Next time,' Coconut enquired, 'why don't we make some bows and arrows?'

'What for?' asked Perkin.

'To shoot the Sheriff's men, of course.'

'You'd wind up hanged in Nottingham,' Tremayne said. 'Better stick to dandelion leaves.' He looked at me. 'Is there going to be a next time?'

Before I could answer, Gareth said 'Yes.' He paused. 'Well, it wasn't all a laugh a minute, but we did *do* something. I could do it again. I could live out in the cold and the rain . . . I feel good about it, that's all.'

'Well done!' Fiona exclaimed sincerely. 'Gareth you're a great boy.'

It embarrassed him, of course, but I agreed with her.

'How about it?' Tremayne asked me.

'Next Sunday,' I said, 'we could go out again, do something else.'

'Do what?' Gareth demanded.

'Don't know yet.'

The vague promise seemed enough for both boys

who drifted back to the kitchen for further supplies, and Sam, leafing through the book, remarked that some of my more ingenious traps looked as if they would kill actual people, not only big animals like deer.

'Eating venison in Sherwood Forest was a hanging matter too,' Harry observed.

I said, agreeing with Sam, 'Some traps aren't safe to set unless you know you're alone.'

'If Gareth's confident after one day,' Nolan said to me without much friendliness from the depths of an armchair, 'what does that make you? Superman?'

'Humble,' I said, with irony.

'How very goody-goody,' he said sarcastically, with added obscenities. 'I'd like to see you ride in a steeplechase.'

'So would I,' Tremayne said heartily, taking the sneering words at face value. 'We might apply for a permit for you, John.'

No one took him seriously. Nolan took offence. He didn't like even a semi-humorous suggestion that anyone else should muscle in on his territory.

Monday found Dee-Dee in tears over Angela Brickell's pregnancy test. Not tears of sympathy, it seemed, but of envy.

Monday also found Doone on our doorstep, wanting to check up on the dates which Chickweed had won and Harry had been there to watch.

'Mr Goodhaven?' Tremayne echoed. 'It's Mrs Goodhaven's horse.'

'Yes, sir, but it was Mr Goodhaven's photo the dead lass was carrying.'

'It was the *horse*'s photo,' Tremayne protested. 'I told you before.'

'Yes, sir,' Doone agreed blandly. 'Now, about those dates...'

In suppressed fury, Tremayne sorted the way through the form book and his memory, saying finally that there had been no occasion that he could think of when Harry had been at the races without Fiona.

'How about the fourth Saturday in April?' Doone asked slyly.

'The what?' Tremayne looked it up again. 'What about it?'

'Your travelling head lad thinks Mrs Goodhaven had flu that day. He remembers her saying later at Stratford, when the horse won but failed the dope test later, that she was glad to be there, having missed his last win at Uttoxeter.'

Tremayne absorbed the information in silence.

'If Mr Goodhaven went alone to Uttoxeter,' Doone insinuated, 'and Mrs Goodhaven was at home tucked up in bed feeling ill...'

'You really don't know what you're talking about,' Tremayne interrupted. 'Angela Brickell was in charge of a *horse*. She couldn't just go off and leave it. And she came back here with it in the horse-box. I'd have

247

known if she hadn't, and I'd have sacked her for negligence.'

'But I understood from your travelling head lad, sir,' Doone said with sing-song deadliness, 'that they had to wait for Angela Brickell that day at Uttoxeter because when they were all ready to go home she couldn't be found. She *did* leave her horse unattended, sir. Your travelling head lad decided to wait another half-hour for her, and she turned up just in time, and wouldn't say where she'd been.'

Tremayne said blankly, 'I don't remember any of this.'

'No doubt they didn't trouble you, sir. After all, no harm had been done . . . had it?'

Doone left one of his silences hovering, in which it was quite easy to imagine the specific harm that could have been done by Harry.

'There's no privacy for anything odd on racecourses,' Tremayne said, betraying the path his own thoughts had taken. 'I don't believe a word of what you're hinting.'

'Angela Brickell died about six weeks after that,' Doone said, 'by which time she'd have used a pregnancy test.'

'Stop it,' Tremayne said. 'This is supposition of the vilest kind, aimed at a good intelligent man who loves his wife.'

'Good intelligent men who love their wives, sir, aren't immune to sudden passions.'

'You've got it wrong,' Tremayne said doggedly.

Doone rested a glance on him for a long time and then transferred it to me.

'What do you think, sir?' he said.

'I don't think Mr Goodhaven did anything.'

'Based on your ten days' knowledge of him?'

'Twelve days now. Yes.'

He ruminated, then asked me slowly, 'Do you yourself have any feelings as to who killed the lassie? I ask about feeling, sir, because if it were solid knowledge you would have given it to me, wouldn't you?'

'Yes, I would. And no, I have no feeling, no intuition, unless it is that it was someone unconcerned with this stable.'

'She worked here,' he said flatly. 'Most murders are close to home.' He gave me a long assessing look. 'Your loyalties, sir,' he said, 'are being sucked into this group, and I'm sorry about that. You're the only man here who couldn't have had any hand in the lassie's death, and I'll listen to you and be glad to, but only if you go on seeing straight, do you get me?'

'I get you,' I said, surprised.

'Have you asked Mr Goodhaven about the day he went racing without his wife?' Tremayne demanded.

Doone nodded. 'He denies anything improper took place. But then, he would.'

'I don't want to hear any more of this,' Tremayne announced. 'You're inventing a load of rubbish.'

'Mr Goodhaven's belongings were found with the

lassie,' Doone said without heat, 'and she carried his photograph, and that's not rubbish.'

In the silence after this sombre reminder he took his quiet leave and Tremayne, very troubled, said he would go down to the Goodhavens' house to give them support.

Fiona however telephoned while he was on his way, and I answered the call because Dee-Dee had already gone home, feeling unwell.

'John!' she exclaimed. 'Where's Tremayne?'

'On his way down to you.'

'Oh. Good. I can't tell you how awful this is. Doone thinks . . . he says . . .'

'He's been here,' I said. 'He told us.'

'He's like a bulldog.' Her voice shook with distress. 'Harry's strong, but this . . . this *barrage* is wearing him down.'

'He's desperately afraid you'll doubt him,' I said.

'What?' She sounded overthrown. 'I don't, for a minute.'

'Then tell him.'

'Yes, I will.' She paused briefly. 'Who did it, John?'

'I don't know.'

'But you'll see. You'll see what we're too close to see. Tremayne says you understand things without being told, more than most people do. Harry says it comes of all those qualities his Aunt Erica wouldn't allow you, insight through imagination and all that.'

They'd been discussing me; odd feeling.

I said, 'You might not want to know.'

'Oh.' It was a cry of admission, of revelation.
'John . . . save us all.'

She put the phone down without waiting for a
response to her extraordinary plea, and I wondered
seriously what they expected of me, what they saw me
to be: the stranger in their midst who would solve all
problems as in old-fashioned Westerns, or an eminently
ordinary middling writer who was there by accident
and would listen to everyone but in the end be ineffec-
tual. Given a choice, I would without question have
opted for the latter.

By Tuesday the press had been drenched with leaks
from all quarters. Trial by public opinion was in full
swing, the libel laws studiously skirted by a profligate
scattering of the word 'alleged' but the underlying
meaning plain: Harry Goodhaven had allegedly bedded
a stable girl, got her pregnant, and throttled her to
save his marriage to a 'wealthy heiress', without whose
money he would be penniless.

Wednesday's papers, from Harry's point of view,
were even worse, akin to the public pillory.

He phoned me soon after lunch.

'Did you see the bloody tabloids?'

'Yes,' I said.

'If I come and pick you up, will you just come out
driving with me?'

'Sure.'

'Fine. Ten minutes.'

Without any twinges of conscience I laid aside my notes on Tremayne's mid-career. With two weeks already gone of my four-week allocation, I was feeling fairly well prepared to get going on the page, but as usual any good reason for postponing it was welcome.

Harry came in his BMW, twin of Fiona's, and I climbed in beside him, seeing more new lines of strain in his face and also rigidity in his neck muscles and fingers. His fair hair looked almost grey, the blue eyes altogether without humour, the social patina wearing thin.

'John, good of you,' he said. 'Life's bloody.'

'I'll tell you one thing,' I tried a shot at comfort, 'Doone knows there's something wrong with his case, otherwise he would have arrested you already.' I settled into the seat beside him, fastening the belt.

He glanced my way as he put the car into gear and started forward. 'Do you think so? He keeps coming back. He's on our doorstep every day. Every day, a new pin-prick, a new awkward bloody circumstance. He's building a cage round me, bar by bar.'

'He's trying to break your nerve,' I said, guessing. 'Once he'd arrested and charged you, the papers would have to leave you alone. He's letting them have a field day, waiting for someone to remember something and waiting for you to crack and incriminate yourself. I shouldn't think he's tried to stop any of the leaks since the press found out where the girl was lying and he had to make an official statement. Maybe he's even organised a leak or two himself; I wouldn't put it past him.'

Harry turned the nose of the car towards Reading to travel by the hilly route that would take us through the Quillersedge Estate. I wondered why he'd gone that way but I didn't directly ask him.

'Yesterday,' he said bitterly, 'Doone asked me what Angela Brickell had been wearing. It's been in all the papers. He asked me if she'd undressed willingly. I could have strangled him... Oh God, what am I saying?'

'Shall I drive?' I asked.

'What? Oh yes, we nearly hit that post... I didn't see it. No, I'm all right. Really I am. Fiona says not to let him rattle me, she's being splendid, absolutely marvellous, but he *does* rattle me, I can't help it. He tosses out these lethal questions as if they were harmless afterthoughts... "Did she undress willingly?" How can I answer? I wasn't there.'

'That's the answer.'

'He doesn't believe me.'

'He isn't sure,' I said. 'Something's bothering him.'

'I wish it would bother him into an early grave.'

'His successor might be worse. Might prefer a conviction to the truth. Doone does at least seek the truth.'

'You can't mean you like him!' The idea was an enormity.

'Be grateful to him. Be glad you're still free.' I paused. 'Why are we going this way?'

The question surprised him. 'To get to where we're going, of course.'

'So we're not just out for a drive?'

'Well, no.'

'All around you,' I said, 'is the Quillersedge Estate.'

'I suppose so,' he said vaguely. Then: 'Dear God, we go along this road all the time. I mean, everyone in Shellerton goes to Reading this way unless it's snowing.'

A long stretch of the road was bordered on each side by mixed woodland, dripping now with yesterday's rain and looking bare-branched and bedraggled in the scrag end of winter. Part of the woodland was thinned and tamed and fenced neatly with posts and wire, policed with 'no trespassing' notices; part was wild and open to anyone caring to push through the tangle of trees, saplings and their assorted undergrowth. Five yards into that, I thought, and one would be invisible from the road. Only the strongly motivated, though, would try to go through it: it was no easy afternoon stroll.

'Anyway,' Harry said, 'the Quillersedge Estate goes on for miles. This is just the western end of it. The place where they found Angela was much nearer Bucklebury.'

'How do you know?'

'Dammit, it was in the papers. Are *you* doubting me now?' He was angered and disconcerted by my question, then shook his head in resignation. 'That was a

Doone question. How do I know? Because the Reading papers printed a map, that's how. The gamekeeper put his X on the spot.'

'I don't doubt you,' I said. 'If I doubted you I would doubt my own judgement too, and in your case I don't.'

'I suppose that's a vote of confidence.'

'Yes.'

We drove a fair way along the roads and through villages unknown to me, going across country to heaven knew where. Harry, however, knew where, and turned down a mostly uninhabited lane, through some broken gateposts into a rutted drive; this led to a large sagging barn, an extensive dump of tangled metal and wood and a smaller barn to one side. Beyond this unprepossessing mess lay a wide expanse of muddy grey water sliding sluggishly by with dark wooded hills on the far side.

'Where are we?' I asked, as the car rolled to a stop, the only bright new thing in the general dilapidation.

'That's the Thames,' Harry said. 'Almost breaking its banks, by the look of things, after all that rain and melted snow. This is Sam's boatyard, where we are now.'

'*This?*' I remembered what Sam had said about useful squalor. it had been an understatement.

'He keeps it this way on purpose,' Harry confirmed. 'We all came here for a huge barbecue party he gave to celebrate being champion jockey...eighteen months ago, I suppose. It looked different that night.

One of the best parties we've been to . . .' His voice tailed off, as if his thoughts had moved away from what his mouth was saying; and there was sweat on his forehead.

'What's making you nervous?' I asked.

'Nothing.' It was clearly a lie. 'Come with me,' he said jerkily. 'I want someone with me.'

'All right. Where are we going?'

'Into the boathouse.' He pointed to the smaller of the barns. 'That big place on the left is Sam's workshop and dock where he works on his boats. The boathouse isn't used much, I don't think, though Sam made it into a grotto the night of the party. I'm going to meet someone there.' He looked at his watch. 'I'm a bit early. Don't suppose it will matter.'

'Who are you going to meet?'

'Someone,' he said, and got out of the car. 'I don't know who. Look,' he went on, as I followed him, 'someone's going to tell me something which may clear me with Doone. I just . . . . I wanted *support* . . . a witness, even. I suppose you think that's stupid.'

'No.'

'Come on, then.'

'I'll come, but don't put too much hope on anyone keeping the appointment. People can be pretty spiteful, and you've had a rotten press.'

'You think it's a hoax?' The idea bothered him, but he'd obviously considered it.

'How was the meeting arranged?'

'On the telephone,' he said. 'This morning. I didn't know the voice. Don't even know if it was a man or woman. It was low. Sort of careful, I suppose, looking back.'

'Why here,' I asked, 'of all places?'

He frowned. 'I've no idea. But I can't afford not to listen, if it's something which will clear me. I can't, can I?'

'I guess not.'

'I don't really like it either,' he confessed. 'That's why I wanted company.'

'All right,' I shrugged. 'Let's wait and see.'

With relief he smiled wanly and led the way across some rough ground of stones and gnarled old weeds, joining a path of sorts that ran from the big barn to the boathouse and following that to our destination.

Close to, the boathouse was if anything less attractive than from a distance, though there were carved broken eaves that had once been decorative in an Edwardian way and could have been again, given the will. The construction was mostly of weathered old brick, the long side walls going down to the water's edge, the whole built on and into the river's sloping bank.

True to Sam's philosophy the ramshackle wooden door had no latch, let alone a padlock, and pushed inwards, opening at a touch.

Windows in the walls gave plenty of light, but inside all one could see was a bare wooden floor stretching to double glass doors leading to a railed balcony over-hanging the swollen river.

'Don't boathouses have water in them?' I enquired mildly.

'The water's underneath,' Harry said. 'This room was for entertaining. There's another door down by the edge of the river for going into the boat dock. That's where the grotto was. Sam had just put coloured lights all round and some actually in the water . . . it looked terrific. There was a bar up here in this room. Fiona and I went out onto the balcony with our drinks and looked at the sky full of stars. It was a warm night. Everything perfect.' He sighed. 'Perkin and Mackie were with us, smooching away in newly-wedded bliss. It all seems so long ago, when everyone was happy, everything simple. Nothing could go wrong . . . Then Tremayne had a spectacular year and to crown it Top Spin Lob won the National . . . and since then not much has gone right.'

'Did Sam invite Nolan to his party?'

Harry smiled briefly. 'Sam felt good. He asked Dee-Dee, Bob Watson, the lads, everyone. Must have been a hundred and fifty people. Even Angela . . .' He stopped and looked at his watch. 'It's just about time.'

He turned and took a step towards the far-end balcony, the ancient floorboards creaking underfoot.

There was a white envelope lying on the floor about halfway to the balcony and, saying perhaps it was a message, he went towards it and bent to pick it up, and with a fearsome crack a whole section of the floor gave way under his weight and shot him, shouting, into the dock beneath.

CHAPTER TWELVE

It happened so fast and so drastically that I nearly slid after him, managing only instinctively to pivot on one foot and throw myself headlong back onto the boards still remaining solid behind the hole.

Harry, I thought ridiculously, was dead unlucky with cold dirty water. I wriggled until I could peer over the edge into the wet depths below and I couldn't see him at all.

Shit, I thought, peeling off my jacket. Come up for God's sake, Harry, so I can pull you out.

No sign of him. Nothing. I yelled to him. No reply.

I kicked off my boots and swung down below, holding on to a bared crossbeam that creaked with threat, swinging from one hand while I tried to see Harry and not land on top of him.

All that was visible was brownish opaque muddy water. No time for anything except getting him out. I let go of the beam and dropped with bent legs so as to splash down softly and felt the breath rush out of my lungs from the iciness of the river. Letting the water buoy up my weight I stretched my feet down to touch bottom and found the water came up to my ears; took a deep breath, put the rest of my head under and reached around for Harry, unable to see him, unable with open eyes to see anything at all.

He had to be there. Time was short. I stood up for a gasp of air, ducked down again, searching with fingers, with feet, with urgency turning to appalling alarm. I could feel things, pieces of metal, sharp spiky things, nothing living.

Another gasp of air. I looked for bubbles rising, hoping to find him that way, and saw not bubbles but a red stain in the water a short way off, a swirl of colour against drab.

At least I'd found him. I dived towards the scarlet streaks and touched him at once, but there was no movement in him, and when I tried to pull him to the surface, I couldn't.

Shit . . . Shit . . . Stupid word kept repeating in my brain. I felt and slid my arms under Harry's and with my feet slipping on the muddy bottom yanked him upwards as fiercely as I could and found him still stuck and yanked again twice more with increasing desperation until finally whatever had been holding him released its grasp and he came shooting to the surface, only to begin falling sluggishly back again as a dead weight.

With my own nose barely above water I held him with his head just higher than mine, but he still wasn't breathing. I laced my arms round his back, under his own arms, letting his face fall on mine, and in that awkward position I blew my own breath into him, not in the accepted way with him lying flat with most things in control, but into his open nostrils, into his flaccid mouth, into either or both at once, as fast as I could, trying to pump his chest in unison, to do what his own intercostal muscles had stopped doing, pulling his ribcage open for air to flow in.

They tell you to go on with artificial respiration for ever, for long after you've given up hope. Go on and on, I'd been told. Don't give up. Don't ever give up.

He was heavy in spite of the buoyancy from the water. My feet went numb down on the mud. I blew my breath into him rhythmically, faster than normal breathing, squeezing him, telling him, ordering him in my mind to take charge of himself, come back, come back . . . Harry, come back . . .

I grieved for him, for Fiona, for all of them, but most for Harry. That humour, that humanity; they couldn't be lost. I gave him my breath until I was dizzy myself and I still wouldn't accept it was all useless, that I might as well stop.

I felt the jolt in his chest as I hugged it in rhythm against mine and for a second couldn't believe it, but then he heaved again in my arms and coughed in my face and a mouthful of dirty water shot out in a spout and he began coughing in earnest and choking and gasping for air . . . gasping, gulping air down, wheezing in his throat, whooping like whooping cough, struggling to fill his functioning lungs.

He couldn't have been unconscious for long, looking back, but it seemed an eternity at the time. With coughing, he opened his eyes and began groaning which was at least some sign of progress, and I started looking about to see how we were going to get out of what appeared to be uncomfortably like a prison.

Another door, Harry had said, down by the river's edge: and in fact, when I looked I could see it, a once-painted slab of wood set in brickwork, its bottom edge barely six inches above the water.

Across the whole end of the building, stretching from the ceiling down into the river, was a curtain of linked metal like thick over-sized chicken wire, presumably originally installed to keep thieves away from any boat in the dock. Beyond it flowed the heavy mainstream, with small eddies curling along and through the wire on the surface.

The dock itself, I well understood, was deeper than usual because of the height of the river. The door was still six inches above it, though . . . it didn't make sense to build a door high if the water was usually lower . . . not unless there was a step somewhere . . . a step or walkway even, for the loading and unloading of boats . . .

Taking Harry gingerly with me I moved to the left, towards the wall, and with great relief found that there was indeed a walkway there at about the height of my

263

waist. I lifted Harry until he was sitting on the walkway and then, still gripping him tightly, wriggled up beside him so that we were both sitting there with our heads wholly above water, which may not sound a great advance but which was probably the difference between life and death.

Harry was semi-conscious, confused and bleeding. The only good thing about the extreme cold of the water, I thought, was that whatever the damage, the blood loss was being minimised. Apart from that, the sooner we were out of there, the better.

The hole through which Harry had fallen was in the centre of the ceiling. If I stood up on the walkway, I thought, I could probably stretch up and touch the ceiling, but wouldn't be able to reach the hole. Might try jumping . . . might pull more of the floor down. It didn't look promising. There seemed to be part of a beam missing in the area. Rotted through, no doubt.

Meanwhile I had to get Harry well propped so that he wouldn't fall forward and drown after all, and to do that I reckoned we needed to be in the corner. I tugged him gently along the walkway, which was made of planks, I discovered, with short mooring posts sticking up at intervals, needing me to lift his legs over one at a time. Still, we reached the end in a while, and I stood up and tugged him back until he was sitting wedged in the corner, supported by the rear and side walls.

He had stopped coughing, but still looked dazed. The blood streaking scarlet was from one of his legs, now stretched out straight before him but still not in view on account of the clouded water. I was debating whether to try to stop the bleeding first or to leave him in his uncertain state while I found a way out, trusting he wouldn't totally pass out, when I heard the main door creak open directly above our heads; the way Harry and I had come in.

My first natural impulse was to shout, to get help from whoever had come: and between intention and voice a whole stream of thoughts suddenly intruded and left me silent, open-mouthed to call out but unsure of the wisdom.

Thoughts. Harry had come to this place to meet someone. He didn't know who. He'd been given a meeting place he knew of. He'd gone there trustingly. He'd walked into the boathouse and tried to pick up an envelope and the floor had given way beneath him and a piece of beam was missing; and if I hadn't been there with him he would certainly have drowned in the dock, impaled on something lurking beneath the surface.

Part of my later training had been at the hands of an ex-SAS instructor whose absolute priority for survival was evading the enemy; and with doubt but also awareness of danger I guessed at an enemy above our heads, not a saviour. I waited for exclamations of horror from above, for someone to call Harry's name in alarm, for some natural, innocent reaction to the floor's collapse.

Instead there was silence. Then the creak of a step or two, then the sound of the door being quietly closed. Eerie.

All sounds from outside were muffled because of the dock being partly below ground level, set into the slope of the bank, but in a short while I heard the sound of a car door slamming and after that the noise of an engine starting up and being driven away.

Harry suddenly said, 'Bloody hell.' A couple of sweet words. Then he said, 'What the hell's happening?' and then, 'God, my leg hurts.'

'We came through the boathouse floor.' I pointed to the hole. 'The floorboards gave way. You landed on something that pierced your leg.'

'I'm f . . . freezing.'

'Yes, I know. Are you awake enough to sit here on your own for a bit?'

'John, for God's sake . . .'

'Not long,' I said hastily. 'I'll not leave you long.'

As I stood on the walkway, the water level reached above my knees, and I waded along beside the wall in the direction of the lower door and the river. There were indeed steps by the door, three steps and a flat landing along below the door itself. I went up the steps until the water barely covered my ankles and tried the doorlatch.

This time, no easy exit. The door was solid as rock.

On the walls beside the door there was a row of three electric switches. I pressed them all without any results from the electric light bulbs along the ceiling. There was also a control box with cables leading to the top of the metal curtain: I opened the box and pressed the red button and the green button to be found inside there but, again, nothing changed in the boathouse.

The arrangement for raising the curtain was a matter of gear wheels designed to turn a rod to wind the metal mesh up onto it like a blind. The sides of the curtain were held in tracks to help it run smoothly. Without electricity, however, it wasn't going to oblige. On the other hand, because of its construction, the whole barrier had to be reasonably light in weight.

'Harry?' I called.

'God, John . . .' His voice sounded weak and strained.

'Sit there and don't worry. I'll come back.'

'Where . . . are you going?' There was fear in his voice but also control.

'Out.'

'Well . . . hurry.'

'Yes.'

I slipped back into the water and swam a couple of strokes to the curtain. Tried standing up, but the water was much deeper there. Hung onto the wire feeling the tug of the eddies from the river.

With luck, with extreme luck, the curtain wouldn't go all the way down to the river's bed. It had no practical need to reach down further than the drought level of the river which had to leave a gap of at least two or three feet. From the weight point of view, a gap was sensible.

Simple.

I took a breath and pulled myself hand over hand down the curtain, seeking to find the bottom of it with my feet: and there was indeed a gap between the bottom edge of the curtain and the mud, but only a matter of inches, and there was clutter down there, unidentifiable, pressing against the barrier, trying to get past it.

I came up for air.

'Harry?'

'Yes.'

'There's a space under the metal curtain. I'm going out into the river and I'll be back for you very soon.'

'All right.' More control this time: less fear.

Deep breath. Dived, pulling myself down the wire. Came to the end of it, felt the mud below. The bottom edge of the curtain was a matter of free links, not a connecting bar. The links could be raised, but only singly, not all together.

Go under it, I told myself. The temptation to return safely back up where I'd come from was enormous. Go *under* . . .

I swung down at the bottom, deciding to go head first, face up, curling my back down into the soft river bed, praying . . . *praying* that the links wouldn't catch on my clothes . . . in my knitted sweater . . . should have stripped . . . head under, metal laying on my face, push the links up with hands, full strength, take care, don't rush, don't snag clothes, get free of the jumble of things on the mud around me, hold onto the wire outside, don't let go, the current in the river was appreciable, tugging, keep straight, *hang on*, shoulders through, raise the links, back through, bottom through, legs . . . links . . . short of breath . . . lungs hurting . . . careful, careful . . . unknown things round my ankles, hampering . . . *had* to breathe soon . . . feet catching . . . feet . . . *through*.

The river immediately floated my free legs away as if it would have them, and I had to grab the wire fiercely to avoid going with the current. But I was through and not stuck in the dreadful clutch of metal links, not grasped by debris, not drowning without any chance of rescue.

I came up into the air gasping deeply, panting, aching lungs swelling, feeling a rush of suppressed terror, clinging onto the curtain in a shaky state.

'Harry?' I called.

The dock looked dark beyond the curtain and I couldn't see him, but he could indeed see me.

'Oh John . . .' His relief was beyond measure. 'Thank God.'

'Not long now,' I said, and heard the strain in my own voice too.

I edged along the curtain in the upstream direction of the shut door and by hauling my way up the links at the side managed to scramble round the boathouse wall and up out of the water to roll at last onto the grassy bank. Bitterly cold, shivering violently from several causes, but *out*.

I stood up with knees that felt like buckling and tried to open the door into the dock; and it was as immovable from outside as in. It had a mortise lock, a simple keyhole and no key.

Perhaps the best thing to do, I thought despairingly, was to find a telephone and get professional help: the fire brigade and an ambulance. If I couldn't find a telephone in Sam's big workshop I could drive Harry's car to the nearest house . . .

Big snag.

Harry's car had gone.

My mind started playing the shit tape monotonously.

Before I did anything, I thought, I needed to put on my boots. Went into the boathouse through the top door.

Another big snag.

No boots.

No ski-jacket either.

Harry's voice came from below, distant and wavery, 'Is anyone there?'

'It's me, John,' I shouted. 'Just hold on.'

No reply. He was weaker, perhaps. Better hurry.

There was now no doubt about murderous intention on someone's part and the certainty made me perversely angry, stimulating renewed strength and a good deal of bloody-mindedness. I ran along the stony path to Sam's large shed in my socks and hardly felt the discomfort, and found to my relief that I could get inside easily enough – no lock on the door.

The space inside looked as much like a junkyard as the space outside. The centre, I saw briefly, was occupied by a large boat on blocks, its superstructure covered with lightweight grey plastic sheeting.

I spent a little precious time searching for a telephone, but couldn't find one. There was no office, no place partitioned off or locked. Probably Sam kept good tools somewhere, but he'd hidden them away.

All around lay old and rusting tools and equipment, but among the junk I found almost at once two perfect aids: a tyre lever and a heavy mallet for driving in mooring pegs.

With those I returned at speed to the boathouse and attacked the lower door, first hammering the toe of the tyre lever into a non-existent crack between the wooden door frame and the surrounding brickwork at a level just below the keyhole, then bashing the far end of that iron to put heavy leverage against the door frame, then wrenching out the lever and repeating the whole process above the lock, this time with fury.

The old wood of the door frame gave up the struggle and splintered, freeing the tongue of the lock, and without much more trouble I pulled the door open towards me, swinging it wide. I left the tyre lever and mallet on the grass and stepped down into the boathouse, the shocking chill of the water again a teeth-gritter.

At least, I thought grimly, it was a calm day. No wind-chill to speak of, to polish us off.

I waded along to Harry who was sagging back against the corner, his head lolling only just above the surface.

'Come on,' I said urgently. 'Harry, wake up.'

He looked at me apathetically through a mist of weakness and pain and one could see he'd been in that water a lot too long. Apathy, like cold, was a killer. I bent down and turned him until I had my hands under his arms, his back towards me, and I floated him along in the water to the steps and there strained to pull him up them and out onto the grass.

'My leg,' he said, moaning.

'God, Harry, what do you weigh?' I asked, lugging.

'None of your bloody business,' he mumbled.

I half laughed, relieved. If he could say that, for all his suffering, he wasn't in a dying frame of mind. It gave me enough impetus to finish the exit, though I dare say he, like me, felt only marginally warmer for being on land.

His leg seemed to have stopped bleeding, or very nearly, and he couldn't have severed an artery or he'd have bled to death by now, but all the same there had to be a pretty serious wound under the cloth of his trousers and the faster I could get him to a doctor the better.

As far as I remembered from our arrival, the boatyard lay down a lane with no houses nearby: I'd have a fair run in my socks to find help.

On the other hand, among the general clutter, only a few feet off, I could see the upturned keel of an old clinker-built rowing boat. Small. Maybe six feet overall. A one-man job, big enough for two. If it weren't full of holes . . .

Leaving Harry briefly I went to the dinghy and heaved it over right side up. Apart from needing varnish and loving care it looked seaworthy, but naturally there were no rowlocks and no oars.

Never mind. Any piece of pole would do. Plenty lying about. I picked up a likely length and laid it in the boat.

The dinghy had a short rope tied to its bow: a painter.

'Harry, can you hop?' I asked him.

'Don't know.'

'Come on. Try. Let's get you into the boat.'

'Into the *boat*?'

'Yes. Someone's taken your car.'

He looked bewildered, but the whole afternoon must have seemed so unbelievable to him that hopping into a boat would seem to be all of a piece. In any case, he made feeble efforts to help me get him to his left foot, and with my almost total support he made the few hops to reach the boat, though I could see it hurt him sorely. I helped him sit down on the one centre thwart and arranged his legs as comfortably as possible, Harry cursing and wincing by turns.

'Hang on tight to the sides,' I said. 'Tight.'

'Yes.'

He didn't move, so I pulled his hands out and positioned them on the boat's edges.

'Grip,' I said fiercely.

'Fine.' His voice was vague, but his hands tightened.

I tugged and lugged the dinghy until it was sliding backwards down the bank, and then held on to the painter, digging my heels in, leaning back to prevent too fast and splashy a launch. At the last minute, when the stern hit the swollen water and the dinghy's progress flattened out, I jumped in myself and simply hoped against all reasonable hope that we wouldn't sink at once.

We didn't. The current took the dinghy immediately and started it on its way downstream, and I edged past Harry into the stern space behind him and retrieved my piece of pole.

'What's that?' Harry asked weakly, trying to make sense of things.

'Rudder.'

'Oh.'

I made a crook of my left elbow on the back of the boat and laid the pole across it, the shorter end in my right hand, the longer end trailing behind in the water. The steering was rudimentary, but enough to keep us travelling bow-first downstream.

Downstream was always the way to people . . . Bits of

the guide books floated familiarly to the surface. *Some of your traps are horrific.*

Some of the traps described how to arrange for the prey to fall through seemingly firm ground into a pit full of spikes beneath.

Everyone had read the guides.

'John?' Harry said. 'Where are we going?'

'Maidenhead, possibly. I'm not quite sure.'

'I'm bloody cold.'

There was some water in the boat now, sloshing about under our feet.

Shit.

Nowhere on the Thames was far from civilisation, not even Sam's boatyard. The wide river narrowed abruptly with a notice on our left saying DANGER in huge letters, and smaller notice saying LOCK with an arrow to the right.

I steered the dinghy powerfully to the right. DANGER led to a weir. A lock would do just fine. Locks had keepers.

At about then I took note that there weren't in fact any other boats moving on the river and I remembered that often the locks closed for maintenance in winter and maybe the lock-keeper would have gone shopping ...

Never mind. There were houses in sight on the right.

They proved to be summer cottages, all closed.

We floated on as if in a timeless limbo. The water in the bottom of the boat grew deeper. The current away from the mainstream, was much weaker. The lock cut seemed to last for ever, narrowing though, with high dark trees on the left; finally, blessedly, on the right, there were moorings for boats wanting passage through the lock to the lower level of the river below. No boats there, of course. No helping hands. Never mind.

I took the dinghy as far as we could go, right up near to the lock gates. Tied the painter to a mooring post and stepped up out of the boat.

'Won't be long,' I told Harry.

He nodded merely. It was all too much.

I climbed the steps up onto the lock and knocked on the door of the lock-keeper's house, and through great good fortune found him at home. A lean man: kind eyes.

'Fell in the river, did you?' he asked cheerfully, observing my soaked state. 'Want to use the phone?'

CHAPTER THIRTEEN

I went with Harry in the ambulance to Maidenhead hospital, both of us swathed in blankets, Harry also in a foil-lined padded wrap used for hypothermia cases; and from then on it was a matter of phoning and reassuring Fiona and waiting to see the extent of Harry's injuries, which proved to be a pierced calf, entry and exit wounds both clean and clotted, with no dreadful damage in between.

While Fiona was still on her way the medics stuffed Harry full of antibiotics and other palliatives and put stitches where they were needed, and by the time she'd wept briefly in my arms he was warm and responding nicely in the recovery room somewhere.

'But why,' she asked, half cross, half mystified, 'did he go to Sam's boatyard in the first place?' Like a mother scolding her lost child, I thought, after he's come back safe: just like Perkin with Mackie.

'He'll tell you about it,' I said. 'They say he's doing fine.'

'You're damp!' She disengaged herself and held me at arm's length. 'Did you fall through the floor too?'

'Sort of.' The hospital's central heating had been doing a fine job of drying everything on me and I felt like one of those old-fashioned clothes-horses, steaming slightly in warm air. Still no shoes or boots; couldn't be helped.

Fiona looked at my feet dubiously.

'I was going to ask you to drive Harry's car home,' she said, 'but I suppose you can't.'

I explained that Harry's car had already been driven away.

'Where is it, then?' she asked, bewildered. 'Who took it?'

'Maybe Doone will find out.'

'That man!' She shivered. 'I hate him.'

Before I could comment, a nurse came to fetch her to see Harry, and she went anxiously, calling over her shoulder for me to wait for her; and when she returned half a hour later she looked dazed.

'Harry's sleepy,' she said. 'He kept waking up and telling me silly things . . . How could he possibly get to this hospital in a *boat*?'

'I'll tell you on the way home. Would you like me to drive?'

'But . . .'

'It's quite easy with bare feet. I'll take off my socks.'

She unlocked the car herself and handed me the keys without comment. We arranged ourselves in the seats and as we headed for Shellerton in the early dark I told her calmly, incompletely and without terrors, the gist of what had befallen us in Sam's boatyard.

She listened with a frown, adding her own worry.

'Turn right here,' she said once, automatically, and another time, 'Sorry, we should have turned left there, we'll have to go back,' and finally, 'Go straight to Shellerton House. I'll drive home from there. I'm all right, really. It's just so upsetting. It made me shaky, seeing Harry dopey like that, pumped full of drugs.'

'I know.'

I pulled up outside Tremayne's house and while I put on my socks again she said she would come in for a while for company, 'to cure the trembles'.

Tremayne, Mackie and Perkin were all in the family room for the usual evening drinks. Tremayne made more than his usual fuss over Fiona, sensing some sort of turmoil, telling her comfortably that Mackie had just come back from Ascot races where he'd sent a runner for the apprentice race which had proved a total waste of time.

The note I'd left for Tremayne, 'GONE OUT WITH HARRY, BACK FOR GRUB', was still pinned to the corkboard. He took my arrival with Fiona as not needing comment.

'I think someone tried to kill Harry,' Fiona said starkly, cutting abruptly through Tremayne's continuing Ascot chat.

'What?'

There was an instant silence and general shock on all the faces, including Fiona's own.

'He went to Sam's boatyard and fell through some floorboards and was nearly drowned . . .' She told it to them much as I'd told her myself. 'If John hadn't been with him to help . . .'

Tremayne said robustly, 'My dearest girl, it must have been the most dreadful accident. Whoever would want to kill Harry?'

'No one,' Perkin said, his voice an echo of Tremayne's. 'I mean, what for?'

'Harry's a dear,' Mackie said, nodding.

'You'd never think so to read the papers recently,' Fiona pointed out, lines creasing her forehead. 'People can be incredibly vicious. Even people in the village. I went into the shop this morning and everyone stopped talking and stared at me. People I've known for years. I told Harry and he was furious, but what can we do? And now this . . .'

'Did Harry say someone tried to kill him?' Perkin asked.

Fiona shook her head. 'Harry was too dopey.'

'Does John think so?'

Fiona glanced at me. 'John didn't actually say so. It's what I think myself. What I'm afraid of. It scares me to think of it.'

'Then don't, darling,' Mackie put an arm round her and kissed her cheek. 'It's a frightening thing to have happened, but Harry *is* all right.'

'But someone stole his car,' Fiona said, hollow-eyed.

'Perhaps he left the key in the ignition,' Tremayne guessed, 'and a passer-by saw an opportunity.'

Fiona agreed unwillingly. 'Yes, he would have left his keys. He trusts people. I've told him over and over again that you simply *can't* these days.'

They all spent time reassuring Fiona until the worst of the worry unwound from her body and I watched the movement of her silver-blond hair in the soft lights and made no attempt to throw doubts because it would have achieved nothing good.

With Doone, early the next afternoon, it was a different matter. He'd had my bald account of events over the telephone in the morning, his first knowledge of what had happened. Now he came into the dining-room where I was working and sat down opposite me at the table.

'I hear you're a proper little hero,' he said dryly.

'Oh, really, who says so?'

'Mr Goodhaven.'

I stared back blandly with the same expression that he was trying on me. The morning's bulletin on Harry had been good, the prognosis excellent, his memory of events reportedly clarifying fast.

'Accident or attempted murder?' Doone asked, apparently seeking a considered answer.

I gave him one. 'The latter, I'd say. Have you found his car?'

'Not yet.' He frowned at me with a long look in which I read nothing. 'Where would you search for it?' he asked.

After a pause I said, 'At the top of a cliff.'

He blinked.

'Don't you think so?' I said.

'Beachy Head? Dover?' he suggested. 'A long drive to the sea.'

'Maybe a metaphorical cliff,' I said.

'Go on, then.'

'Is it usual,' I asked, 'for policemen to ask for theories from the general public?'

'I told you before, I like to hear them. I don't always agree, but sometimes I do.'

'Fair enough. Then what would you have thought if Harry Goodhaven had disappeared for ever yesterday afternoon and you'd found his car later by a cliff, real or metaphorical?'

'Suicide,' he said promptly. 'An admission of guilt.'

'End of investigation? Books closed?'

He stared at me sombrely. 'Perhaps. But unless we eventually found a body, there would also be the possibility of simple flight. We would alert Australia . . . look for him round the world. The books would remain open.'

'But you wouldn't investigate anyone else, because you would definitely consider him guilty.'

'The evidence points to it. His flight or suicide would confirm it.'

'But something about that evidence bothers you.'

I was beginning to learn about his expressions, or lack of them. The very stillness of his muscles meant that I'd touched something he'd thought hidden.

'Why do you say so?' he asked eventually.

'Because you've made no arrest.'

'That simple.'

'Without your knowledge, I can only guess.'

'Guess away,' he invited.

'Then I'd say perhaps Harry's sunglasses and pen and belt were with Angela Brickell because she took them there herself.'

'Go on,' he said neutrally. It wasn't, I saw, a new idea to him.

'Didn't you say her handbag had been torn open, the contents gone except for the photo in a zipped pocket?'

'I did say so, yes.'

'And you found chocolate wrappings lying about?'

'Yes.'

'And traces of dogs?'

'Yes.'

'And any dog worth his salt would bite open a handbag to get to the chocolate?'

'It's possible.' He made a decision and a big admission. 'There were toothmarks on the handbag.'

'Suppose then,' I said, 'that she did in fact have a

thing about Harry. He's a kind and attractive man. Suppose she did carry his photo with the horse, not Fiona's, who's the owner after all. Suppose she'd managed to acquire personal things of Harry's, his sunglasses, a pen, even a belt, and wore them or carried them with her, as young people do. They'd only be evidence of her crush on Harry, not of his presence at her death.'

'I considered all that, yes.'

'Suppose someone couldn't understand why you didn't arrest Harry, particularly in view of all the hounding in the papers, and decided to remove any doubts you might be showing?'

He sat for a while without speaking, apparently debating how many of his thoughts to share. Not many more, it transpired.

'Whoever took Harry's car,' I said, 'removed my jacket and boots as well. I took them off before I went through the floor into the dock.'

'Why didn't you tell me that?' He seemed put out, severe.

'I'm telling you now.' I paused. 'I would think that whoever took those things is very worried indeed now to find that I was with Harry and that he is alive. I'd say there wasn't supposed to be any reason to think Harry had gone to Sam's boatyard. No one would ever have looked for him there. I'd say it was an attempt to confirm Harry's guilt that went disastrously wrong, leaving you with bristling new doubts and a whole lot more to investigate.'

He said formally, 'I would like you to be present at the boatyard tomorrow morning.'

'What do you think of the place?' I asked.

'I've taken statements from Mr and Mrs Goodhaven and others,' he said stiffly. 'I haven't been to the boatyard yet. It has, however, been cordoned off. Mr Yaeger is meeting me there tomorrow at nine a.m. I would have preferred this afternoon but it seems he is riding in three races at Wincanton.'

I nodded. Tremayne had gone there, also Nolan. Another clash of the Titans.

'You know,' Doone said slowly, 'I had indeed started to question others besides Mr Goodhaven.'

I nodded. 'Sam Yaeger for one. He told us. Everyone knew you'd begin casting wider.'

'The lass had been indiscriminate,' he said regretfully.

Tremayne lent me his Volvo to go to the boatyard in the morning, reminding me before I set off that it was the day of the awards dinner at which he was to be honoured.

I'd seen the invitation pinned up prominently by Dee-Dee in the office: most of the racing world, it seemed, would be there to applaud. For Tremayne, though he had a few self-deprecating jokes about it, the event gave proof of the substance of his life, much like the biography.

Sam and Doone were already in the boatyard by the time I'd found my way there, neither of them radiating joy, Sam's multicoloured jacket only emphasising the personality clash with grey plain clothes. They'd been waiting for me, it seemed, in a mutual absence of civility.

'Right, sir,' Doone said, as I stood up out of the car, 'we've done nothing here so far. Moved nothing. Please take us through your actions of Wednesday afternoon.'

Sam said crossly, 'Asking for sodding trouble, coming here.'

'As it turned out,' Doone said placidly. 'Go on, Mr Kendall.'

'Harry said he was due to meet someone in the boathouse, so we went over there.' I walked where we'd gone, the others following. 'We opened this main door. It wasn't locked.'

'Never is,' Sam said.

I pushed open the door and we looked at the hole in the floor.

'We walked in,' I said. 'Just talking.'

'What about?' Doone asked.

'About a great party Sam gave here once. Harry was saying there had been a bar here in the boathouse and a grotto below. He began to walk down to the windows and saw an envelope on the floor and when he bent to pick it up, the floor creaked and gave way.'

Sam looked blank.

'Is that likely?' Doone asked him. 'How long ago was the floor solid enough to hold a party on it?'

'A year last July,' Sam said flatly.

'Quick bit of rot,' Doone commented, in his sing-song voice.

Sam made no answer, in itself remarkable.

'Anyway,' I said, 'I took off my boots and jacket and left them up here and I dropped into the water, because Harry hadn't come up for air, like I told you.'

'Yes,' Doone said.

'You can see better from the lower door,' I remarked, turning to go down the path. 'This door down here leads into the dock.'

Sam disgustedly fingered the splintered door frame.

'Did you sodding do this?' he demanded. 'It wasn't locked.'

'It was,' I said. 'With no key in sight.'

'The key was in the keyhole on the inside.'

'Absolutely not,' I said.

Sam pulled the door open and we looked into the scene that was all too familiar to my eyes; an expanse of muddy water, the hole in the ceiling overhead and the curtain of iron mesh across the exit to the river; a dock big enough for a moderate-sized cabin cruiser or three or four smaller boats. The water smelled dankly of mud and winter, which I hadn't seemed to notice when I'd been in it.

'There's a sort of walkway along this right-hand wall,'

I told Doone. 'You can't see it now because of the floodwater.'

Sam nodded. 'A mooring dock, with bollards.'

'If you care to walk along there,' I suggested, dead-pan, 'I'll show you an interesting fact about that hole.'

They both stared at the water with reluctance stamped all over their faces, then Sam's cleared as he thought of a more palatable solution.

'We'll go and look in a boat.'

'How about the curtain?'

'Roll it up, of course.'

'Now, wait,' Doone said. 'The boat can wait. Mr Kendall, you came through the hole, found Mr Good-haven and brought him to the surface. You sat him on the dock, then dived out under the curtain and climbed onto the bank. Is that right?'

'Yes, except that while I was pulling Harry along to that far corner to give him better support, someone opened the main door above our heads, like I told you, and then went away without saying anything, and I heard a car drive off, which might have been Harry's.'

'Did you hear any car *arriving*?' Doone asked.

'No.'

'Why didn't you call out for help?'

'Harry had been enticed here ... It all felt like a trap. People who set traps come back to see what they've caught.'

Doone gave me another of his assessments.

Sam said, frowning, 'You can't have dived out under the curtain, it goes right down to the river bed.'

'I sort of slithered under it.'

'You took a sodding risk.'

'So do you,' I said equably, 'most days of the week. And I didn't have much choice. If I hadn't found a way out we'd both eventually have died of cold or drowning, or both. Certainly by now. Most likely Wednesday night.'

After a short thoughtful silence Doone said, 'You're out on the bank. What next?'

'I saw the car had gone. I went to collect my boots and jacket, but they'd gone too. I called to Harry to reassure him, then I went out to that big shed to find a telephone, but I couldn't.'

Sam shook his head. 'There isn't one. When I'm here I use the portable phone from my car.'

'I couldn't find any decent tools, either.'

Sam smiled. 'I hide them.'

'So I used a rusty tyre lever and a mallet, and I'm sorry about your woodwork.'

Sam shrugged.

'Then what?' Doone asked.

'Then I got Harry out here and put him in a dinghy and we . . er . . . floated down to the lock.'

'My sodding dinghy!' Sam exclaimed, looking at the imitation scrapyard. 'It's gone!'

'I'm sure it's safe down at the lock,' I said. 'I told the lock-keeper it was yours. He said he'd look after it.'

'It'll sink,' Sam said. 'It leaks.'

'It's out on the bank.'

'You'll never make a writer,' he said.

'Why not?'

'Too sodding sensible.'

He read my amusement and gave me a twisted grin.

I said, 'What happens to the rubbish lying in the dock when you roll up the curtain?'

'Sodding hell!'

'What are you talking about?' Doone asked us.

'The bed of this dock is mud, and it slopes downwards towards the river,' I said. 'When the curtain's rolled up, there's nothing to stop things drifting out by gravity into the river and being moved downstream by the current. Bodies often float to the surface, but you of all people must know that those who drown in the Thames can disappear altogether and are probably taken by undercurrents down through London and out to sea.' Sometimes from my high Chiswick window I'd thought about horrors down below the surface, out of sight. Like hidden motives, running deadly, running deep.

'Everyone in the Thames Valley knows they disappear,' Doone nodded. 'We lose a few holidaymakers every year. Very upsetting.'

'Harry's leg was impaled on something,' I said mildly. 'He was stuck underwater. He'd have been dead in a very few minutes. Next time Sam rolled the curtain up, Harry would have drifted quietly out of there, I should think, and no one would ever have known he'd been here. If his body were found anywhere downstream, well then, it could be suicide. If it wasn't found, then he'd escaped justice.' I paused, and asked Sam directly, 'How soon would you have rolled up the curtain?'

He answered at once. 'Whenever I'd found the hole in the floor. I'd have gone to take a look from beneath. Like we're going to now. But I hardly ever come over here. Only in summer.' He gave Doone a sly look. 'In the summer I bring a mattress.'

'And Angela Brickell?' Doone asked.

Sam, silenced, stood with his mouth open. A bull's-eye, I thought, for the Detective Chief Inspector.

I asked Sam, 'What's under the water in the dock?'

'Huh?'

'What did Harry get stuck on?'

He brought his mind back from Angela Brickell and said vaguely, 'Haven't a clue.'

'If you raise the curtain,' I said, 'we may never know.'

'Ah,' Doone stared judiciously at Sam, all three of us still clustered round the open door. 'It's a matter for grappling irons, then. Can we get a light inside there?'

'The main switch for here is over in the shed,' Sam said as if automatically, his mind's attention elsewhere. 'There's nothing in the dock except maybe a couple of beer cans and a radio some clumsy bimbo dropped when she was teetering out of a punt in high heels. I ask you . . .'

'Harry wasn't impaled on a radio,' I said.

Sam turned away abruptly and walked along the path to his workshop. Doone made as if to go after him, then stopped indecisively and came back.

'This could have been an accident, sir,' he said uneasily.

I nodded. 'A good trap never looks like one.'

'Are you quoting someone?'

'Yes. Me. I've written a good deal about traps. How to set them. How to catch game. The books are lying about all over the place in Shellerton. Everyone's dipped into them. Follow the instructions and kill your man.'

'You're not joking by any chance, are you, sir?'

I said regretfully, 'No, I'm not.'

'I'll have to see those books.'

'Yes.'

Sam came back frowning and, stretching inside without stepping into the water, pressed the three switches that had been unresponsive two days earlier. The lights in the ceiling came on without fuss and illuminated the ancient brick walls and the weathered old grey beams which crossed from side to side, holding up the planks of the floor above: holding up the planks, except where the hole was.

Doone looked in briefly and made some remark about returning with assistance. Sam looked longer and said to me challengingly, 'Well?'

'There's a bit of beam missing,' I said, 'isn't there?'

He nodded unwillingly. 'Looks like it. But I didn't know about it. How could I?'

Doone, in his quiet way a pouncer, said meaningfully, 'You yourself, sir, have all the knowledge and the tools for tampering with your boathouse.'

'I didn't.' Sam's response was belligerence, not fear. 'Everyone knows this place. Everyone's been here. Everyone could cut out a beam that small, it's child's play.'

'Who, precisely?' Doone asked. 'Besides you?'

'Well ... anybody. Perkin! He could. Nolan ... I mean, most people can use a saw, can't they? Can't you?'

Doone's expression assented but he said merely, 'I'll take another look upstairs now, if you please, sir.'

We went in gingerly but as far as one could tell the floor was solid except for the one strip over the missing bit of beam. The floorboards themselves were grey with age, and dusty, but not worm-eaten, not rotten.

Sam said, 'The floorboards aren't nailed down much. Just here and there. They fit tightly most of the time because of the damp, but when we have a hot dry summer they shrink and you can lift them up easily. You can check the beams for rot.'

'Why are they like that?' Doone asked.

'Ask the people who built it,' Sam said, shrugging. 'It was like this when I bought it. The last time I took the floorboards up was for the party, installing coloured spotlights and strobes in the ceiling underneath.'

293

'Who knew you took the floorboards up?' Doone asked.

Sam looked at him as if he were retarded. 'How do I know?' he demanded. 'Everyone who asked how I'd done the lighting. I told them.'

I went down on my knees and edged towards the hole.

'Don't do that,' Doone exclaimed.

'Just having a look.'

The way the floorboards had been laid, I saw, had meant that the doctored beam had been a main load-bearer. Several of the planks, including those that had given way under Harry's weight, had without that beam's support simply been hanging out in space, resting like a seesaw over the previous beam but otherwise supported only by the tight fit of each plank against the next. The floorboards hadn't snapped, as I'd originally thought; they'd gone down into the dock with Harry.

I tested a few planks carefully with the weight of my hand, then retreated and stood up on safer ground.

'Well?' Doone said.

'It's still lethal just each side of the hole.'

'Right.' He turned to Sam. 'I'll have to know, sir, when this tampering could have been carried out.'

Sam looked as if he'd had too much of the whole thing. With exasperation, he said, 'Since when? Since Christmas?'

Doone said stolidly. 'Since ten days ago.'

Sam briefly gave it some thought. 'A week last Wednesday I dropped off a load of wood here on my way to Windsor races. Thursday I raced at Towcester. Friday I spent some time here, half a day. Saturday I raced at Chepstow and had a fall and couldn't ride again until Tuesday. So Sunday I was nursing myself until you came knocking on my door, and Monday I spent here, pottering about. Tuesday I was back racing at Warwick. Wednesday I went to Ascot, yesterday Wincanton, today Newbury . . .' He paused. 'I've never been here at night.'

'What races did you ride in on Wednesday afternoon?' Doone asked. 'At Ascot.'

'What races?'

'Yes.'

'The two-mile hurdle, the novice hurdle, novice chase.'

I gathered from Doone's face that it wasn't the type of answer he'd expected, but he pulled out a notebook and wrote down the reply as given, checking that he'd got it right.

Sam, upon whom understanding had dawned, said, 'I wasn't here driving Harry's sodding car away, if that's what you're thinking.'

'I'll need to ascertain a good many people's where-abouts on Wednesday afternoon,' Doone said placidly in a flourish of jargon. 'But as for now, sir, we can proceed with our investigations without taking any more of the time of either of you two gentlemen, for the present.'

'Class dismissed?' Sam said with irony.

Doone, unruffled, said we would be hearing from him later.

Sam came with me to where I'd parked Tremayne's car on stone-strewn grass. The natural jauntiness remained in his step but there was less confidence in his thoughts, it seemed.

'I like Harry,' he said, as we reached the Volvo.

'So do I.'

'Do you think I set that trap?'

'You certainly could have.'

'Sure,' he said. 'Dead easy. But I didn't.'

He looked up into my face, partly anxious, partly still full of his usual machismo.

'Unless you killed Angela Brickell,' I said, 'you wouldn't have tried to kill Harry. Wouldn't make sense.'

'I didn't do the silly little bimbo any harm.' He shook his head as if to free her from his memory. 'She was too intense for me, if you want to know. I like a bit of a giggle, not remorse and tears afterwards. Old Angie took everything seriously, always going on about mortal sin, and I got sodding tired of it, and of her, tell the truth. She wanted me to marry her!' His voice was full of the enormity of such a thought. 'I told her I'd got my sights set on a high-born heiress and she damned near scratched my eyes out. A bit of a hell-cat, she could be, old Angie. And hungry for it! I mean, she'd whip her clothes off before you'd finished the question.'

I listened with fascination to this insider viewpoint,

and the moody Miss Brickell suddenly became a real person; not a pathetic collection of dry bones, but a mixed-up pulsating young woman full of strong urges and stronger guilts who'd piled on too much pressure, loaded her need of penitence and her heavy desires and perhaps finally her pregnancy onto someone who couldn't bear it all, and who'd seen a violent way to escape her.

Someone, I thought with illumination, who knew how easily Olympia had died from hands round the neck.

Angela Brickell had to have invited her own death. Doone, I supposed, had known that all along.

'What are you thinking?' Sam asked, uncertainly for him.

'What did she look like?' I said.

'Angie?'

'Mm.'

'Not bad,' he said. 'Brown hair. Thin figure, small tits, round bottom. She agonised about having breast implants. I told her to forget bloody implants, what would her babies think? That turned on the taps, I'll tell you. She bawled for ages. She wasn't much fun, old Angie, but effing good on a mattress.'

What an epitaph, I thought. Chisel it in stone.

Sam looked out over the flooding river and breathed in the damp smell of the morning as if testing wine for bouquet, and I thought that he lived through his senses to a much greater degree than I did and was intensely alive in his direct approach to sex and his disregard of danger.

He said cheerfully, as if shaking off murder as a passing inconvenience, 'Are you going to this do of Tremayne's tonight?'

'Yes. Are you?'

He grinned. 'Are you kidding? I'd be shot if I wasn't there to cheer. And anyway,' he shrugged as if to disclaim sentiment, 'the old bugger deserves it. He's not all bad, you know.'

'I'll see you there, then,' I said, agreeing with him.

'If I don't break my neck.' It was flippantly said, but an insurance against fate, like crossed fingers. 'I'd better tell this sodding policeman where the main electric switch is. I've got it rigged so no one can find it but me, as I don't want people being able to walk in here after dark and turn the lights on. Inviting vandalism, that is. When the force have finished here, they can turn the electric off.'

He bounced off towards Doone, who was writing in his notebook, and they were walking together to the big boatshed as I drove away.

Even after having done the week's shopping en route, I was back at Shellerton House as promised in good time for Tremayne to drive his Volvo to Newbury races. He had sent three runners off in the horse-box and was taking Mackie to assist, leaving me to my slowly growing first chapter in the dining-room.

When they'd gone Dee-Dee came in, as she often did now, to drink coffee over the sorted clippings.

I said, 'I hope Tremayne won't mind my taking all these with me when I go home.'

'Home . . .' Dee-Dee smiled. 'He doesn't want you to go home, didn't you know? He wants you to write the whole book here. Any day now he'll probably make you an offer you can't refuse.'

'I came for a month. That's what he said.'

'He didn't know you then.' She took a few mouthfuls of coffee. 'He wants you for Gareth, I think.'

That made sense, I thought; and I wasn't sure which I would choose, to go or to stay, if Dee-Dee was right.

When she'd returned to the office I tried to get on with the writing but couldn't concentrate. The trap in Sam's boathouse kept intruding and so did Angela Brickell; the cold threat of khaki water that could rush into aching lungs to bring oblivion and the earthy girl who'd been claimed back by the earth, eaten clean by earth creatures, become earth-digested dirt.

Under the day-to-day surface of ordinary life in Shellerton the fish of murder swam like a shark, silent, unknown, growing new teeth. I hoped Doone would net him soon, but I hadn't much faith.

Fiona telephoned during the afternoon to say that she'd brought Harry home and he wanted to see me, so with a sigh but little reluctance I abandoned the empty page and walked down to the village.

Fiona hugged me as a long-lost brother and said Harry still couldn't be quite clear in his mind as he was saying now that he remembered drowning. However could one remember drowning?

'Quite hard to forget, I should think.'

'But he didn't drown!'

'He came close.'

She led me into the pink-and-green chintzy sitting-room where Harry, pale with blue shadows below the eyes, sat in an armchair with his bandaged leg elevated on a large upholstered footstool.

'Hello,' he said, raising a phantom smile. 'Do you know a cure for nightmares?'

'I have them awake,' I said.

'Dear God.' He swallowed. 'What's true, and what isn't?'

'What you remember is true.'

'Drowning?'

'Mm.'

'So I'm not mad.'

'No. Lucky.'

'I told you,' he said to Fiona. 'I tried not to breathe, but in the end I just did. I didn't mean to. Couldn't help it.'

'No one can,' I said.

'Sit down,' Fiona said to me, kissing Harry's head. 'What's lucky is that Harry had the sense to take you with him. And what's more, everyone's apologising all over the place except for one vile journalist who says It's possible a misguided vigilante thought getting rid of Harry the only path to real justice, and I want Harry to sue him, it's truly vicious.'

'I can't be bothered,' Harry said in his easy-going way. 'Doone was quite nice to me! That's enough.'

'How's the leg?' I asked.

'Lousy. Weighs a couple of tons. Still, no gangrene as yet.'

He meant it as a joke but Fiona looked alarmed.

'Darling,' he said placatingly, 'I'm bloated with anti-biotics, punctured with tetanus jabs and immunised against cholera, yellow-spotted mountain fever and ath-lete's foot. I have it on good authority that I'm likely to live. How about a stiff whisky?'

'No. It'll curdle the drugs.'

'For John, then.'

I shook my head.

'Take Cinderella to the ball,' he said.

'What?'

'Fiona to Tremayne's party. You're going, aren't you?'

I nodded.

'I'm not leaving you,' Fiona protested.

'Of course you are, love. It wouldn't be the same for Tremayne if you weren't there. He dotes on you. John can take you. And,' his eyes brightened mischievously with reawakening energy, 'I know who'd love to use my ticket.'

'Who?' his wife demanded.

'Erica. My sainted aunt.'

CHAPTER FOURTEEN

The Lifetime Award to Tremayne was the work of a taken-over, revitalised hotel chain aiming to crash the racing scene with sponsorship in a big way. They, Castle Houses, had put up the prize for a steeplechase and had also taken over a prestigious handicap hurdle race already in the programme for Saturday.

The cash on offer for the hurdle race had stretched the racing world's eyes wide and excited owners into twisting their trainers' arms so that the entries had been phenomenal (Dee-Dee said). The field would be the maximum allowed on the course for safety and several lightweights had had to be balloted out.

As a preliminary to their blockbuster, Castle Houses had arranged the awards dinner and subsidized the tickets so that more or less everyone could afford them. The dinner was being held on the racecourse, in the grandstand with its almost limitless capacity; and the whole affair, Mackie had told me, was frankly only a giant advertisement, but everyone might as well enjoy it.

Before we went we met in the family room, Tremayne pretending nonchalance and looking unexpectedly sophisticated in his dinner jacket: grey hair smooth in wings, strong features composed, bulky body slimmed by ample expert tailoring. Perkin's jacket by contrast looked a shade too small for him and in hugging his incipient curves diminished the difference between the sizes of father and son.

Gareth's appearance surprised everyone, especially Tremayne: he made a bravado entrance to cover shyness in a dinner jacket no one knew he had, and he looked neat, personable and much older than fifteen.

'Where did you get that?' his father asked, marvelling.

'Picked it off a raspberry bush.' He smiled widely. 'Well, actually, Sam said I was the same height as him now and he happened to have two. So he's lent it to me. OK?'

'It's great,' Mackie said warmly, herself shapely in a shimmering black dress edged with velvet. 'And John's jacket, I see, survived the plunge into the ditch.'

The ditch seemed a long time ago: two weeks and three days back to the lonely silent abandoned struggle in the attic, to the life that seemed now to be the dream, with Shellerton the reality. Shellerton the brightly-lit stage; Chiswick the darkened amphitheatre where one sat watching from the gods.

'Don't get plastered tonight, John,' Tremayne said. 'I've a job for you in the morning.'

'Do you know how to avoid a hangover for ever?' Gareth asked me.

'How?' I said.

'Stay drunk.'

'Thanks a lot,' I said, laughing.

Tremayne, happy with life, said, 'You feel confident riding Drifter now, don't you?'

'More or less,' I agreed.

'Tomorrow you can ride Fringe. I own a half-share in him. He's that five-year-old in the corner box. You can school him over hurdles.'

I must have looked as astonished as I felt. I glanced at Mackie, saw her smiling, and knew she and Tremayne must have discussed it.

'Second lot,' Tremayne said. 'Ride Drifter first lot as usual.'

'If you think so,' I said a shade weakly.

'If you stay here a bit longer,' Tremayne said, 'and if you ride schooling satisfactorily, I don't see why you shouldn't eventually have a mount in an amateur race, if you put your mind to it.'

'*Cool*,' Gareth said fervently.

'I shouldn't think he wants to,' Perkin remarked as I hadn't answered in a rush. 'You can't make him.'

An offer I couldn't refuse, Dee-Dee had said; and I'd thought only of money. Instead, he was holding out like a carrot a heart-stopping headlong plunge into a new dimension of existence.

'Say you will,' Gareth begged.

Here goes impulse again, I thought. To hell with the helium balloon, it could wait a bit longer.

'I will.' I looked at Tremayne. 'Thank you.'

He nodded, beaming and satisfied, saying, 'We'll apply for your permit next week.'

We all loaded into the Volvo and went down to Shellerton Manor where everyone trooped in to see Harry. Tired but cheerful he held court from his chair and accepted Mackie's heartfelt kiss with appreciative good humour.

'I'm so glad you're alive,' she said, with a suspicion of tears, and he stroked her arm and said lightly that he was too, on the whole.

'What did it feel like?' Perkin said curiously, glancing at the bandaged leg.

'It happened too fast to feel much,' Harry said, smiling lopsidedly. 'If John hadn't been there I'd have died without knowing it, I dare say.'

'Don't!' Fiona exclaimed. 'I can't bear even to think of it. Tremayne, off you go or you'll be late. John and I will pick up Erica and see you soon.' She swept them out, following them, fearing perhaps that they would add to Harry's fatigue; and he and I looked at each other across the suddenly empty room in a shared fundamental awareness.

'Do you know who did it?' he asked, weariness and perhaps despair returning, stress visible.

I shook my head.

'Couldn't be someone I know.' He meant that he didn't want it to be. 'They meant to *kill* me, dammit.'

'Dreary thought.'

'I don't want to guess, I try not to. It's pretty awful to know someone hates me enough . . .' He swallowed. 'That hurts more than my leg.'

'Yes.' I hesitated. 'It was maybe not hate. More like a move in a chess game. And it went wrong, don't forget. The strong presumption of guilt has changed to a stronger presumption of innocence. Entirely and diametrically the wrong result. That can't be bad.'

'I'll hang onto that.'

I nodded. 'Better than a funeral.'

'Anything is.' He dredged up a smile. 'I've got a neighbour coming in to be with me tonight while you're all out. I feel a bit of a coward.'

'Rubbish. Bodyguards make good sense.'

'Do you want a permanent job?'

Fiona returned, pulling on a fluffy white wrap over her red silk dress, saying she really didn't want to go to the dinner and being persuaded again by her husband. He would be fine, he said, his friend would be there in a moment and goodbye, have a good time, give Tremayne the evening of his life.

Fiona drove her own car, the twin of Harry's (still lost), and settled Erica Upton in the front beside her when we collected her on a westerly detour. The five-star novelist gave me an unfathomable glimmer when I closed the car door for her and remarked that she'd

307

had a long chat with Harry that afternoon on the telephone.

'He told me to lay off, as you'd saved his life,' she announced badly. 'A proper spoilsport.'

I said in amusement, 'I don't suppose you'll obey him.'

I heard the beginning of a chuckle from the front seat, quickly stifled. The battle lines, it seemed, had already been drawn. Hostilities however were in abeyance during arrival at the racecourse, disrobing, hair-tidying and first drinks. Half the racing world seemed to have embraced the occasion, for which after the last race that afternoon there had been much speedy unrolling of glittering black and silver ceiling-to-floor curtaining, transforming the workaday interior of the grandstand into something ephemerally magnificent.

'Theatrical,' Erica said disapprovingly of the décor, and so it was, but none the worse for that. It lifted the spirits, caused conversation, got the party going. Background music made a change from bookies' cries. Fiona looked at the seating plan and said to meet at table six. People came and surrounded her and Erica, and I drifted away from them and around, seeing a few people I knew by sight and hundreds I didn't. Like being at a gravediggers' convention, I thought, when one had marked out one's first plot.

My thoughts ran too much on death.

Bob Watson was there, dapper in a dark grey suit, with Ingrid shyly pretty in pale blue.

'Couldn't let down the guv'nor,' Bob said cheerfully. 'Anyway, he gave us the tickets.'

'Jolly good,' I said inanely.

'You're riding Fringe tomorrow,' he said, halfway between announcement and question. 'Schooling. The guv'nor just told me.'

'Yes.'

'Fringe will look after you,' he said inscrutably, looking around. 'Done this place up like an Egyptian brothel, haven't they?'

'I don't really know.'

'Oh, very funny.'

Ingrid giggled. Bob quelled her with a look, but I noticed slightly later and indeed all evening that she stuck very closely to his side; this could have been interpreted as her own insecurity if I hadn't remembered Mackie saying that meek little Ingrid never gave Bob much chance to stray with the likes of Angela Brickell and God help him if he did.

Sam Yaeger, ever an exhibitionist, had come in a white dinner jacket, having lent Gareth his black. He also had a frilled white shirt, a black shoestring tie and a definite air of strain under the confident exterior. Doone, it appeared, had more or less accused him straight out of sabotaging his own boathouse.

'He says I had the tools, the knowledge, the opportunity and the location, and he looked up those races I rode at Ascot and worked out that I could have had time between the first two and the last to drive to

Maidenhead and remove Harry's car. I asked why should I bother to do that when presumably if I had set the trap I would expect Harry's car still to be there *after* the races, and he just wrote down my answer as if I'd made a confession.'

'He's persistent.'

'He listens to you,' Sam said. 'We've all noticed. Can't you tell him I didn't sodding do it?'

'I could try.'

'And he whistled up his cohorts after you'd gone,' Sam complained, 'and they came with wet-suits and grappling irons and a heavy magnet and dredged up a lot of muck from the dock. An old broken bicycle frame, some rusted railings, an old disintegrating metal gate ... it had all been lying here and there on the property. They clammed up after a bit and wouldn't show me everything, but he thinks I put it all in the water hoping Harry would get tangled in it.'

'Which he did.'

'So I'm asking you, how come *you* didn't get spiked when you went down there after him?'

'I learned how to jump into shallow water very young. So I didn't go down far. Put my feet down cautiously after I was floating.'

He stared. 'How the sod do you do that?'

'Jump shallow? The second your feet touch the water you raise your knees and crumple into a ball. The water itself acts as a brake. You must have done it

310

yourself some time or other. And I had the air in my clothes to hold me up, don't forget.'

'Doone asked me if I'd left your jacket and boots in Harry's car. Tricky bastard. I know now how Harry's been feeling. You get that flatfoot looking to tie you in knots and it's like being squeezed by coils and coils of a sodding boa constrictor. Everything you say, he takes it in the wrong way. And he looks so damned harmless. He got me so riled I lost a race this afternoon I should have won. Don't say I said that. I don't bloody know why we all tell you things. You don't belong here.'

'Perhaps that's why.'

'Yeah, perhaps.'

He seemed to have let out sufficient steam and resentment for the moment and turned to flirt obligingly with a middle-aged woman who touched his arm in pleased anticipation. Owners, Tremayne had said, either loved or hated Sam's manner: the women loved it; the men put up with it in exchange for winners.

Nolan, glowering routinely at Sam from a few feet away, switched his ill-humour to me.

'I don't want you treading on my effing toes,' he said forcefully. 'Why don't you clear off out of Shellerton?'

'I will in a while.'

'I told Tremayne there'll be trouble if he gives you any of my rides.'

'Ah.'

'He has the effing gall to say I suggested it myself and he knows bloody well I was taking the piss.' He

311

glared at me. 'I don't understand what Fiona sees in you. I told her you're just a bag of shit with a pretty face who needs his arse kicked. You keep away from her horses, understand?'

I understand that he like everyone else was suffering from the atmospheric blight cast by Angela Brickell; he perhaps most because the strain of his own trial and conviction was so recent. There was no way I was ever going to ride as well as he did and he surely knew it. Fiona would never jock him off, in racing's descriptive phrase.

He stomped away, his place almost immediately taken by his brother, who gave me a malicious imitation of a smile and said, 'Nolan doesn't expletive like you, dear heart.'

'You don't say.'

Lewis was sober, so far. Also unaccompanied, like Nolan, though Harry had mentioned at one time that Lewis was married: his reclusive wife preferred to stay at home to avoid the fuss and fracas of Lewis drunk.

'Nolan likes to be the centre of attention and you've usurped his pinnacle,' Lewis said.

'Rubbish.'

'Fiona and Mackie look to you, now, not to him. And as for Tremayne, as for Gareth . . .' He gave me a sly leer. 'Don't put your neck within my brother's reach.'

'Lewis!' His lack of fraternal feeling shocked me more than his suggestion. 'You stuck *your* neck out for him, anyway.'

312

'Sometimes I hate him,' he said with undoubted truth, and wheeled away as if he had said enough.

Glasses in hand, the chattering groups mixed and mingled, broke and re formed, greeted each other with glad cries as if they hadn't seen each other for years, not just that afternoon. Tremayne, large smile a permanence, received genuinely warm congratulations with believable modesty and Gareth, appearing eel-like at my elbow, said with gratification, 'He deserves it, doesn't he?'

'He does.'

'It makes you think a bit.'

'What about?'

'I mean, he's just Dad.' He struggled to get it right. 'Everyone's two people, aren't they?'

I said with interest, 'That's profound.'

'Get away.' He felt awkward at the compliment. 'I'm glad for him, anyway.'

He snaked off again and within minutes the throng began moving towards dinner, dividing into ten to a table, lowering bottoms onto inadequate chairs, fingering menus, peering at the print through candlelight, scanning their allotted neighbours. At table number six I found myself placed between Mackie and Erica Upton, who were already seated.

Erica was inevitable, I supposed, though I suspected Fiona had switched a few place cards before I reached there: a certain bland innocence gave her away.

'I did ask to sit next to you,' Erica remarked, as if

reading my thoughts as I sat down, 'once I knew you'd be here.'

'Er ... why?'

'Do you have so little self-confidence?'

'It depends who I'm with.'

'And by yourself?'

'In a desert, plenty. With pencil and paper, little.'

'Quite right.'

'And you?' I asked.

'I don't answer that sort of question.'

I listened to the starch in her voice, observed it in the straightness of her backbone, recognised the ramrod will that made no concessions to hardship.

'I could take you across a desert,' I said.

She gave me a long piercing inspection. 'I hope that's not an accolade.'

'An assessment,' I said.

'You've found your courage since I met you last.'

She had a way of leaving one without an answer. She turned away, satisfied, to talk to Nolan on her other side, and I, abandoned, found Mackie on my right smiling with enjoyment.

'She's met her match,' she said.

I shook my head regretfully. 'If I could write like her ... or ride like Sam or Nolan ... if I could do *anything* that well, I'd be happy.'

Her smile sweetened. 'Try cooking.'

'Dammit ...'

She laughed. 'I hear the power of your banana flambées made Gareth oversleep.'

Perkin, on her other side, murmured something to get her attention and for a while I watched Tremayne make the best of our table having been graced by the sponsor's wife, a gushing froth of a lady in unbecoming lemon. He would clearly have preferred to be talking to Fiona on his other side, but the award was having to be paid for with politeness. He glanced across the table, saw me smiling, interpreted my thought and gave me a slow ironic blink.

He soldiered manfully through the salmon soufflé and the beef Wellington while Lewis on the lady's other side put away a tumbler full of vodka poured from a half-bottle in his pocket. Fiona watched him with a frown: Lewis's drinking, even to my eyes, was increasingly without shame. Almost as if, having proclaimed himself paralytic in court, he was setting about proving it over and over again.

Glumly fidgeting between Lewis and Perkin, Gareth ate everything fast and looked bored. Perkin with brotherly bossiness told him to stop kicking the table leg and Gareth uncharacteristically sulked. Mackie made a placatory remark and Perkin snapped at her too.

She turned her head my way and with a frown asked, 'What's wrong with everyone?'

'Tension.'

'Because of Harry?' She nodded to herself. 'We all

315

pretend, but no one can help *wondering* . . . This time it's much worse. Last time at least we knew how Olympia died. Angela Brickell's on everyone's nerves. Nothing feels safe any more.'

'You're safe,' I said. 'You and Perkin. Think about the baby.'

Her face cleared as if automatically: the thought of the baby could diminish to trivia the grimmest forebodings.

Perkin on her other side was saying contritely, 'Sorry, darling, sorry,' and she turned to him with ever-ready forgiveness, the adult of the pair. I wondered fleetingly if Perkin, as a father, would be jealous of his child.

Dinner wound to a close: speeches began. Cultured gents, identified for me by Mackie as being the Himalayan peaks of the Jockey Club, paid compliments to Tremayne from an adjacent table and bowed low to the sponsor. He, the lemon lady's husband, eulogised Tremayne, who winced only slightly over Top Spin Lob being slurred to Topsy Blob, and a minion in the livery of Castle Houses brought forth a tray bearing the award itself, a silver bowl rimmed by a circle of small galloping horses, an award actually worthy of the occasion.

Tremayne was pink with gratification. He accepted the bowl. Everyone cheered. Photos flashed. Tremayne made a brief speech of all-round thanks: thanks to the sponsors, to his friends, his staff, his jockeys, to racing itself. He sat down, overcome. Everyone cheered him again and clapped loudly. I began to wonder how many of them would buy Tremayne's book. I wondered whether after that night Tremayne would need the book written.

'Wasn't that great?' Mackie exclaimed, glowing.

'Yes, indeed.'

The background music became dance music. People moved about, flocking round Tremayne, patting his back. Perkin took Mackie to shuffle on the square of dance floor adjoining the table. Nolan took Fiona, Lewis got drunker, Gareth vanished, the sponsor retrieved his lady: Erica and I sat alone.

'Do you dance?' I asked.

'No.' She looked out at the still-alive party. 'The Duchess of Richmond's Ball,' she said.

'Do you expect Waterloo tomorrow?'

'Sometime soon. Who is Napoleon?'

'The enemy?'

'Of course.'

'I don't know,' I said.

'Use your brains. What about insight through imagination?'

'I thought you didn't believe in it.'

'For this purpose, I do. Someone tried to kill Harry. That's extremely disturbing. What's disturbing about it?'

It seemed she expected an answer, so I gave it. 'It was premeditated. Angela Brickell's death may or may not have been, but the attack on Harry was vastly thought out.'

She seemed minutely to relax.

'My God!' I said, stunned.

'What? What have you thought of?' She was alert again, and intent.

'I'll have to talk to Doone.'

'Do you know who did it?' she demanded.

'No, but I know what he knew.' I frowned. 'Everyone knows it.'

'What? Do explain.'

I looked at her vaguely, thinking.

'I don't believe it's very important,' I said in the end.

'Then what is it?' she insisted.

'Wood floats.'

She looked bemused. 'Well, of course it does.'

'The floorboards that went down to the water with Harry, they stayed under. They didn't float.'

'Why not?'

'Have to find out,' I said. 'Doone can find out.'

'What does it matter?'

'Well,' I said, 'no one could be absolutely certain that Harry would be spiked and drown immediately. So suppose he's alive and swimming about. He's been in that place before, at Sam's party, and he knows there's a mooring dock along one wall. He knows there's a door and he had daylight and can see the river through the metal curtain. So how does he get out?'

She shook her head. 'Tell me.'

'The door opens outwards. If you're inside, and you're standing in only six inches of water, not six feet, and you've got three or four floorboards floating about, you use one of them as a ram to break the lock or batter the door down. You're big and strong like Harry and also wet, cold, desperate and angry. How long does it take you to break out?'

'I suppose not long.'

'When Napoleon came to the boathouse,' I said, 'there wasn't any sound of Harry battering his way out. In fact,' I frowned, 'there's no saying how long the enemy had been there, waiting. He might have been hiding . . . heard Harry's car arrive.'

Erica said, 'When your book's published, send me a copy.'

I looked at her open-mouthed.

'Then I can tell you the difference between invention and insight.'

'You know how to pierce,' I said, wincing.

She began to say something else but never completed it. Instead our heads turned in unison towards the dancers, among whom battle seemed already to have started. There was a crash and a scream and bizarrely against the unrelentingly cheerful music two figures could be seen fighting.

Sam . . . and Nolan.

Sam had blood on his white jacket and down the white ruffles. Nolan's shirt was ripped open, showing a lot of hairy chest. They were both reeling about exchanging swinging blows not ten feet from table six and I stood up automatically, more in defence than interference.

Perkin tried to pull them apart and got smartly knocked down by Nolan, quick and tough with his fists as with his riding. I stepped without thinking onto the polished square and tried words instead.

'You stupid fools,' I said: not the most inventive sentence ever.

Nolan took his attention off Sam for a split second, lashed out expertly at my face and whirled back to his prime target in time to parry Sam's wildly lunging arm and kick him purposefully between the legs. Sam's head came forward. Nolan's fist began a descent onto the back of Sam's vulnerable neck.

With instinct more than thought, I barged into Nolan bodily, pushing him off line. He turned a face of mean-eyed fury in my direction and easily transferred his hatred.

I was vaguely aware that the dance floor had cleared like morning mist and also acutely conscious that Nolan knew volumes more about bare-knuckle fisticuffs than I did.

Racing people were extraordinary, I thought. Far from piling into Nolan in a preventative heap, they formed an instant ring around us and, as the band came to a straggling sharp-flat unscheduled halt, Lewis's drunken aristocratic voice could be heard drawling, 'Five to four the field.'

Everyone laughed. Everyone except Nolan. I

doubted if he'd heard. He was high on the flooding wave from the bursting dam of his dark nature, all the anxiety, guilt, hate and repressions sweeping out in a reckless torrent, no longer containable.

In a straight fight I wasn't going to beat him. All I would be was a punchbag for his escaping fury, the entity he saw as a new unbearable threat to his dominance in Tremayne's stable; the interloper, usurper, legitimate target.

I turned my back on him and took a step or two away. All I knew about fighting was ruse and trickery. I could see from the onlooking faces that he was coming for me and at what speed, and when I felt the air behind me move and heard the brush of his clothes I went down fast on one knee and whirled and punched upwards hard into the bottom of his advancing rib cage and then shifted my weight into his body and upwards so as to lift him wholesale off the floor, and before he'd got that sorted out I had one of his wrists in my hand and he ended up on his feet with me behind him, his arm in a nice painful lock and my mouth by his ear.

'You stupid shit,' I said intensely. 'The Jockey Club are here. Don't you care about your permit?'

For answer, he kicked back and caught me on a shin.

'Then I'll ride all your horses,' I said unwisely.

I gave him a hard releasing shove in the general direction of Sam, Perkin and an open-mouthed Gareth and at last watched a dozen restraining hands clutch and keep him from destroying himself entirely, but he struggled against them and turned his vindictive face my way and shouted in still exploding rage, '*I'll kill you.*'

I stood unmoving and listened to those words, and thought of Harry.

CHAPTER FIFTEEN

I apologized to Tremayne.

'Nolan started it,' Mackie said.

She peered anxiously at the reddening bruise on Perkin's cheek, a twin to one on mine.

Perkin sat in angry confusion at table six while the racing crowd, entertaining skirmish over, drifted away and got the band re-started.

Nolan was nowhere in sight. Sam took off his stained jacket, wiped his bloody nose, sucked his knuckles and began making jokes as a form of released tension.

'I bumped into him, that's all I did,' he proclaimed with tragicomic gestures. 'Well, say I then took Fiona off him and maybe I told him to go find himself another filly and the next thing was he got a pincer-hold on my ear and was bopping me one on the nose and there I was bleeding fit to fill the Frenchy furrows so naturally I gave him one back.'

He collected an appreciative audience which definitely didn't include Tremayne. The shambles at the end of his splendid evening was aggravating him sorely and he propelled Fiona into a seat at the table with some of the disgruntled force he'd shown in Ronnie Curzon's office.

Fiona said anxiously, 'But, Tremayne, Sam meant it as a joke.'

'He should have had more sense,' Tremayne's voice was rough. Gareth, next to Perkin, looked at his father with apprehension, knowing the portents.

'Nolan's been through a lot,' Fiona said excusingly.

'Nolan's a violent man,' Tremayne stated with fierce irritation. 'You don't go poking a stick at a rattlesnake if you don't want to get bitten.'

'Tremayne!' She was alarmed at his brusqueness, which he immediately softened.

'My dear girl, I know he's your cousin. I know he's been through a lot, I know you're fond of him, but he and Sam shouldn't be in the same room together just now.' He looked from her to me. 'Are you all right?'

'Yes.'

'John was splendid!' Mackie explained, and Perkin scowled.

Erica grinned at me like a witch, saying, 'You're much too physical for the literati.'

'Let's go home,' Tremayne said abruptly. He stood, kissed Fiona, picked up the box containing his silver bowl and waited for obedience from his sons, his daughter-in-law and his prospective biographer. We stood. We followed him meekly. He made a stately, somewhat forbidding exit, his displeasure plainly visible to all around, his mien daring unkind souls to snigger.

No one did. Tremayne was held in genuine respect and I saw more sympathy than smirks: yet he in many respects was the stoker of the ill-feeling between his warring jockeys, and putting me among them wasn't a recipe for a cease-fire.

'Perhaps I'd better not ride schooling in the morning,' I suggested, as we reached the gate to the car park.

'Are you scared?' he demanded, stopping dead.

I stopped beside him as the other three went on ahead.

'Nolan and Sam don't like it, that's all,' I said.

'You bloody well ride. I'll get you that permit. I'll tame Nolan by threats. Understand?'

I nodded.

He stared at me intently. 'Is that why Nolan said he would kill you? Besides your making a public fool of him?'

'I think so.'

'Do you want to ride in a race or two, or don't you?'

'I do.'

'School Fringe tomorrow, then. And as for now, you'd better go back with Fiona. Make sure she gets home safe. Harry won't want Nolan pestering her and he's quite capable of it.'

'Right.'

He nodded strongly and went on towards his Volvo, and I returned to find Fiona arguing with Nolan in the entrance hall. She and Erica beside her saw me with relief, Nolan with fresh fury.

'I was afraid you'd gone,' Fiona said.

'Thank Tremayne.'

Nolan said angrily, 'Why is this bag of slime always hanging about?'

He made no move, though, to attack me.

'Harry asked him to see me home,' Fiona said placatingly. 'Get some rest, Nolan, or you won't be fit for Groundsel tomorrow.'

He heard, as I did, the faint threat in the cousinly concern, and at least it gave him an excuse for a face-saving exit. Fiona watched his retreating back with a regret neither Erica nor I shared.

I rode Drifter with the first lot in the morning and crashed off on to the wood chippings halfway up the gallop.

Tremayne showed a modicum of anxiety but no sympathy, and the anxiety was for the horse. He sent a lad after it to try to catch it and with disgust watched me limp towards him rubbing a bruised thigh.

'Concentrate,' he said. 'What the hell do you think you were doing?'

'He swerved.'

'You weren't keeping him straight. Don't make excuses, you weren't concentrating.'

The lad caught Drifter and brought him to join us.

'Get up,' Tremayne said to me testily.

I wriggled back into the saddle. I supposed he was right about not concentrating: a touch of the morning afters.

They'd all gone to bed the night before when I'd returned from a last noggin with Harry. I'd walked up from the village under a brilliantly starry sky, breathing cold shafts of early-morning air, thinking of murder. Sleep had come slowly with anxiety dreams. I felt unsettled, not refreshed.

I rode Drifter back with the rest of the string and went in to breakfast, half expecting to be told I wouldn't be allowed to ride Fringe. Tremayne's own mood appeared to be a deepening depression over the evening's finale, and I was sorry because he deserved to look back with enjoyment.

He was reading a newspaper when I went in, and scowling heavily.

'How did they get hold of this so damned fast?'

'What?'

'This.' He pushed the opened paper violently across the table and I read that a brace of brawling jockeys had climaxed the prestigious award dinner with a bloody punch-up. Ex-champion Yaeger and amateur champion Nolan Everard (recently convicted of manslaughter) had been restrained by friends. Tremayne Vickers had said 'no comment'. The sponsor was furious. The Jockey Club were 'looking into it'. End of story.

'It's rubbish,' Tremayne snorted. 'I never said "no comment". No one asked me for any comment. The sponsor had left by the time it happened, so how can he be furious? So had the Jockey Club members. They went after the speeches. I talked to some of them as they were leaving. They congratulated me. Huh!'

'The fuss will die down,' I assured him.

'Makes me look a bloody fool.'

'Make a joke of it,' I suggested.

He stared. 'I don't feel like joking.'

'No one does.'

'It's this business about Harry, isn't it? Upsets everyone. Bloody Angela Brickell.'

I made the toast.

He said, 'Are you fit enough to ride Fringe?'

'If you'll let me.'

He studied me, some of his ill-feeling fading. 'Concentrate, then.'

'Yes.'

'Look,' he said a touch awkwardly, 'I don't mean to take my bad temper out on you. If you hadn't been here we'd all be in a far worse pickle. Best thing I ever did, getting you to come.'

In surprise, I searched for words to thank him but was forestalled by the telephone ringing. Tremayne picked up the receiver and grunted, 'Hello?', not all his vexation yet dissipated.

His face changed miraculously to a smile. 'Hello, Ronnie. Calling to find out how the book's going? Your boy's been working on it. What? Yes, he's here. Hold on.' He passed me the receiver, saying unnecessarily, 'It's Ronnie Curzon.'

'Hello, Ronnie,' I said.

'How's it going?'

'I'm riding a good deal.'

'Keep your mind on the pages. I've got news for you.'

'Good or bad?'

'My colleague in America phoned yesterday evening about your book.'

'Oh.' I felt apprehensive. 'What did he say?'

'He says he likes *Long Way Home* very much indeed. He will gladly take it on, and he is certain he can place it with a good publisher.'

'Ronnie!' I swallowed, unable to get my breath. 'Are you sure?'

'Of course, I'm sure. I always told you it was all right. Your English publisher is very enthusiastic. She told my American colleague the book is fine and he agrees. What more do you want?'

'Oh . . .'

'Come down from the ceiling. A first novel by an unknown British writer isn't going to be given a huge advance.' He mentioned a sum which would pay my rent until I'd finished the helium balloon and leave some over for sandwiches. 'If the book takes off like they hope it will, you'll get royalties.' He paused. 'Are you still there?'

'Sort of.'

He laughed. 'It's all beginning. I have faith in you.'

Ridiculously, I felt like crying. Blinked a few times instead and told him in a croaky voice that I'd met Erica Upton twice and had sat next to her at dinner.

'She'll destroy you!' he said, horrified.

'I don't think so. She wants a copy of the book when it's published.'

'She'll tear it apart. She likes making mincemeat of new writers.' He sounded despairing. 'She does hatchet jobs, not reviews.'

'I'll have to risk it.'

'Let me talk to Tremayne.'

'OK, and Ronnie . . . thanks.'

'Yes, yes . . .'

I handed back the receiver and heard Ronnie being agitated on the other end.

'Hold on,' Tremayne said, 'she likes him.'

I distinctly heard Ronnie's disbelieving '*What?*'

'Also she's very fond of her nephew, Harry, and on Wednesday John saved Harry's life. I grant you she may write him a critical review, but she won't demolish him.' Tremayne listened a bit and talked a bit and then gave me the receiver again.

'All right,' Ronnie said more calmly, 'any chance you get, save her life too.'

I laughed, and with a sigh he disconnected.

'What happened?' Tremayne asked. 'What did he tell you?'

'I'm going to be published in America. Well ... probably.'

'Congratulations.' He beamed, pleased for me, his glooms lifting. 'But that won't change things, will it? I mean here, between us. You will still write my book, won't you?'

I saw his anxiety begin to surface and promptly allayed it.

'I will write it. I'll do the very best I can and just hope it does you justice. And will you excuse me if I run and jump and do handsprings? I'm bursting ... Ronnie said it's all beginning. I don't know that I can bear it.' I looked at him. 'Did you feel like this when Top Spin Lob won the National?'

'I was high for days. Kept smiling. Topsy Blob, I ask you!' He stood up. 'Back to business. You'll come up with me in the Land Rover. Fringe's lad can ride him up, then change with you.'

'Right.'

Ronnie's news, I found, had given me a good deal more confidence in Fringe than I had had on Drifter, illogical though it might be.

It's all beginning ...

Concentrate.

Fringe was younger, whippier and less predictable than Drifter: rock music in place of classical. I gathered the reins and lengthened the stirrup leathers a couple of holes while Fringe made prancing movements, getting used to his new and heavier rider.

'Take him down below the three flights of hurdles,' Tremayne said, 'then bring him up over them at a useful pace. You're not actually racing. Just a good half-speed gallop. Bob Watson will be with you for company. Fringe jumps well enough but he likes guidance. He'll waver if you don't tell him when to take off. Don't forget, it's you that's schooling the horse, not the other way round. All ready?'

I nodded.

'Off you go, then.'

He seemed unconcerned at letting me loose on his half-share investment and I tried telling myself that ahead lay merely a quick pop over three undemanding obstacles, not the first searching test of my chances of racing. I'd ridden over many jumps before, but never on a racehorse, never fast, never caring so much about the outcome. Almost without being aware of it I'd progressed from the hesitancy of my first few days there to a strong positive desire to go down to the starting gate: any starting gate, anywhere. I had to admit that I envied Sam and Nolan.

Bob was circling on his own horse, waiting for me. Both his horse and Fringe, aware they would be jumping, were stimulated and keen.

'Guv'nor says you're to set off on the side nearest him,' Bob said briefly. 'He wants to see what you're doing.'

I nodded, slightly dry-mouthed. Bob expertly trotted his mount into position, gave me a raised-eye query about readiness and kicked forward into an accelerating gallop. Fringe took up his position alongside with familiarity and eagerness, an athlete doing what he'd been bred for, and enjoyed.

First hurdle ahead. Judge the distance . . . give Fringe the message to shorten his stride . . . I gave it to him too successfully, he put in a quick one, got too near the hurdle, hopped over it nearly at a standstill, lost lengths on Bob.

Damn, I thought. *Damn.*

Second hurdle, managed it a bit better, gave him the signal three strides from the jump, felt him lift off at the right time, felt his assurance flow back and his faith in me revive, even if provisionally.

Third hurdle, I left him too much to his own devices as the distance was awkward. I couldn't make up my own mind whether to get him to lengthen or shorten and in consequence I didn't make his mind up to do either and we floundered over it untidily, his hooves rapping the wooden frames, my weight too far forward . . . a mess.

We pulled up at the end of the schooling stretch and trotted back to where Tremayne stood with his binoculars. I didn't look at Bob; didn't want to see his disapproval, all too wretchedly aware that I hadn't done very well.

Tremayne with pursed lips offered no direct opinion. Instead he said, 'Second pop, Bob. Off you go,' and I gathered we were to go back to the beginning and start again.

I seemed to have more time to get things together the second time and Fringe stayed beside Bob fairly smoothly to the end. I felt exalted and released and newly alive in myself, but also I'd watched Sam Yaeger in a schooling session one morning and knew the difference.

Tremayne said nothing until we were driving back to the stable and then all he did was ask me if I were happy with what I'd done. Happy beyond expression in one way, I thought, but not in another. I knew for certain I wanted to race. Knew I had elementary skill.

'I'll learn,' I said grimly, and he didn't answer.

When we reached the house, however, he rummaged about in the office for a while complaining that he could never find anything on Dee-Dee's days off and eventually brought a paper into the dining-room, plonked it on the table and instructed me to sign.

It was, I saw, an application for a permit to race as an amateur jockey. I signed it without speaking, incredibly delighted, grinning like a maniac.

Tremayne grunted and bore the document away, coming back presently to say I should stop working and go with him to Newbury races, if I didn't mind. Also Mackie would be coming with us and we'd be picking up Fiona.

'And frankly,' he said, coming to the essence of the

matter, 'those two don't want to go without you, and Harry wants you to be there and . . . well . . . so do I.'

'All right,' I said.

'Good.'

He departed again and, after a moment's thought, I went into the office to put through a call to Doone's police station. He was off duty, I was told. I could leave my name and a message.

I left my name.

'Ask him,' I said, 'why the floorboards in the boathouse didn't float.'

'Er . . . would you repeat that, sir?'

I repeated it and got it read back with scepticism.

'That's right,' I confirmed, amused. 'Don't forget it.'

We went to the races and watched Nolan ride Fiona's horse Groundsel and get beaten by a length into second place, and we watched Sam ride two of Tremayne's runners unprofitably and then win for another trainer.

'There's always another day,' Tremayne said philosophically.

Fiona told us on the way to the races that the police had phoned Harry to say they'd found his car in the station car park at Reading.

'They said it looks OK but they've towed it off somewhere to search for clues. I never knew people really said "search for clues", but that's what they said.'

'They talk like their notebooks,' Tremayne nodded. From Reading station one could set off round the world. Metaphorical cliff, I thought. A guilty disappearance had been the intended scenario, not a presumption of suicide. Unless of course the car had been moved again after Harry had made his unscheduled reappearance.

The racecourse was naturally buzzing with accounts of the row at Tremayne's dinner, most of the stories inflamed and inaccurate because of the embroidery by the press. Tremayne bore the jokes with reasonable fortitude, cheered by the absence of enquiry or even remarks from the Jockey Club, not even strictures about 'bringing racing into disrepute' which I'd learned was the yardstick for in-house punishment.

By osmosis of information, both Sam and Nolan knew details of Fringe's schooling. Sam said, 'You'll be taking my sodding job next,' without meaning it in the least, and Nolan, bitter-eyed and cursing, saw Tremayne's warning glare and subsided with festering rancour.

'How on earth do they know?' I asked, mystified.

'Sam phoned Bob to find out,' Tremayne said succinctly. 'Bob told him you did all right. Sam couldn't wait to tell Nolan. I heard him doing it. Bloody pair of fools.'

All afternoon Fiona kept me close by her side, looking around for me any time I fell a step behind. She tried unsuccessfully to hide what she described as 'preposterous fear', and I understood that her fear had no focus and no logic, but was becoming a state of mind. Tremayne, sensing it also, fussed over her even more than usual and Fiona herself made visible efforts to act normally and as she said 'be sensible'.

Whenever Mackie wasn't actively helping Tremayne she stayed close also to Fiona, and although I tried I couldn't dislodge the underlying anxiety in their eyes. Silver-blond and red-head, they clung to each other occasionally as long-time friends, and spoke to Nolan, cousin of one, ex-fiancé of the other, with an odd mixture of dread, exasperation and compassion.

Nolan was disconcerted by having lost on Groundsel though I couldn't see that he'd done anything wrong. Tremayne didn't blame him, still less Fiona, but the non-success intensified if possible his ill-will towards me. I was truly disconcerted myself to have acquired so violent an enemy without meaning to and could see no resolution short of full retreat; and the trouble was that since that morning's schooling any inclination to retreat had totally vanished.

I looked back constantly to the morning with huge inward joy; to Ronnie's phone call, to the revelation over hurdles. Doors opening all over the place. All beginning.

The afternoon ending, we took Fiona home and went on to Shellerton House where Perkin came through for drinks, Tremayne went out to see the horses and Gareth returned from a football match. An evening like most others in that house, but to me the first of a changed life.

*

The next day, Sunday, Gareth held me to my promise to take him and Coconut out on another survival trip.

The weather was much better; sunny but cold still with a trace of breeze, a good day for walking. I suggested seven miles out, seven miles back; Gareth with horror suggested two. We compromised on borrowing the Land Rover for positioning, followed by walking as far as their enthusiasm took them.

'Where are you going?' Tremayne asked.

'Along the road over the hills towards Reading,' I said. 'There's some great woodland there, unfenced, no signs saying "keep out".'

Tremayne nodded. 'I know where you mean. It's all part of the Quillersedge Estate. They only try to keep people out just before Christmas, to stop them stealing the fir trees.'

'We'd better not light a fire there,' I said, 'so we'll take our food and water with us.'

Gareth looked relieved. 'No fried worms.'

'No, but it will be survival food. Things you could pick or catch.'

'OK,' he said with his father's brand of practical acceptance. 'How about chocolate instead of dandelion leaves?'

I agreed to the chocolate. The day had to be bearable. We set off at ten, collected Coconut and bowled along to the woods.

There were parking places all along that road, not planned, official, tarmacked areas but small inlets of

338

beaten earth formed by the waiting cars of many walkers. I pulled into one of them, put on the handbrake and, when the boys were out, locked the doors.

Gareth wore of course his psychedelic jacket. Coconut's yellow oilskins had been superseded by an equally blinding anorak and I, in the regrettable absence of my ski-suit jacket, looked camouflaged against the trees in stone-washed jeans and a roomy olive-drab Barbour borrowed from Tremayne.

'Right,' I said, smiling, as they slid the straps of bright blue nylon knapsacks over their shoulders, 'we'll take a walk into the Berkshire wilderness. Everyone fit?'

They said they were, so we stepped straight into the tangled maze of alder, hazel, birch, oak, pine, fir and laurel and picked out steps over dried grass, scratchy brambles and the leafless knee-high branching shoots of the wood's next generation. None of this had been cleared or replanted; it was scrub woodland as nature had made it, the real thing as far as the boys were concerned.

I encouraged them to lead but kept them going towards the sun by suggesting detours round the obstructing patches, and I identified the trees for them, trying to make it interesting.

'We're not eating the bark again, are we?' Coconut said, saying ugh to a birch tree.

'Not today. Here is a hazel. There might still be some nuts lying round it.'

They found two. Squirrels had been there first.

We went about a mile before they tired of the effort involved, and I didn't mean to go much further in any case because according to the map I had in my pocket we were by then in about the centre of the western spur of the Quillersedge woods. We'd come gently up and down hill, but not much further on the ground fell away abruptly, according to the map's contour lines, with too hard a climb on the return.

Gareth stopped in one of the occasional small clearings and mentioned food hopefully.

'Sure,' I said. 'We can make some reasonable seats with dead twigs to keep our bottoms off the damp ground, if you like. No need today for a shelter.'

They made flat piles of twigs, finishing them off with evergreen, then emptied their rucksacks and spread the blue nylon on top. We all sat fairly comfortably and ate things I'd bought for the occasion.

'Smoked trout!' Gareth exclaimed. 'That's an advance on roots.'

'You could catch trout and smoke them if you had to,' I said. 'The easiest way to catch them is with a three-pronged spear, but don't tell that to fishermen.'

'How do you smoke them?'

'Make a fire with lots of hot embers. Cover the embers thickly with green fresh leaves: they'll burn slowly with billows of smoke. Make a latticed frame to go over the fire and put the trout on it or otherwise hang them over the smoke, and if possible cover it all with branches or more leaves to keep the smoke inside.

The best leaves for smoking are things like oak or beech. The smell of the smoke will go into the fish to some extent, so don't use anything you don't like the smell of. Don't use holly or yew, they're poisonous. You can smoke practically anything. Strips of meat. Bits of chicken.'

'Smoked salmon!' Coconut said. 'Why not?'

'First catch your salmon,' said Gareth dryly.

He had brought a camera and he took photos of everything possible; the seats, the food, ourselves.

'I want to remember these days when I'm old like Dad,' Gareth said. 'Dad wishes he'd had a camera when he went round the world with his father.'

'Does he?' I asked.

He nodded. 'He told me when he gave me this one.'

We ate the trout with unleavened bread and healthy appetites and afterwards filled up with mixed dried fruit and pre-roasted chestnuts and almonds. The boys declared it a feast compared with the week before and polished off their chocolate as a bonus.

Gareth said casually, 'Was it in a place like this that someone killed Angela Brickell?'

'Well . . . I should think so. But five miles or so from here,' I said.

'And it was summer,' he commented. 'Warm. Leaves on the trees.'

'Mm.' Imaginative of him, I thought.

'She wanted to kiss me,' he said with a squirm.

Both Coconut and I looked at him in astonishment.

'I'm not as ugly as all that,' he said, offended.

'You're not ugly,' I assured him positively, 'but you're young.'

'She said I was growing up.' He looked embarrassed, as did Coconut.

'When did she say that?' I asked mildly.

'In the Easter holidays, last year. She was always out there in the yard. Always looking at me. I told Dad about it, but he didn't listen. It was Grand National time and he couldn't think of anything but Top Spin Lob.' He swallowed. 'Then she went away and I was really glad. I didn't like going out into the yard when she was there.' He looked at me anxiously. 'I suppose it's wrong to be glad someone's dead.'

'Is glad what you feel?'

He thought about it.

'Relieved,' he said finally. 'I was afraid of her.' He looked ashamed. 'I used to think about her, though. Couldn't help it.'

'It won't be the last time someone makes a pass at you,' I said prosaically. 'Next time, don't feel guilty.'

Easier said than done, I supposed. Shame and guilt tormented the innocent more than the wicked.

Gareth seemed liberated by having put his feelings into words and he and Coconut jumped up and ran around, throwing mock punches at each other, swinging on tree branches, getting rid of bashfulness with shouts and action and shows of strength. I supposed I'd been like that too, but I couldn't remember.

'Right,' I said, as they subsided onto the seats and panted while I packed away our food wrappings (which would have started a dinky fire). 'Which way to the Land Rover?'

'That way,' said Gareth immediately, pointing east.

'That way,' Coconut said, pointing west.

'Which way is north?' I asked.

They both got it instinctively wrong, but then worked it out roughly by the sun, and I showed them how to use a watch as a compass, which Gareth half remembered, having learned before.

'Something to do with pointing the hands at the sun,' he guessed.

I nodded. 'Point the hour hand at the sun, then halfway between the hand and twelve o'clock is the north-south line.'

'Not in Australia,' Gareth said.

'We're not in Australia,' Coconut objected. He looked at his watch and around him. 'That way is north,' he said, pointing. 'But which way is the Land Rover?'

'If you go north you'll come to the road,' I said.

'What do you mean "you"?' Gareth demanded. 'You're coming too. You've got to guide us.'

'I thought,' I said, 'that it would be more fun for you to find your own way back. And,' I went on as he tried to interrupt, 'so as you don't get lost if the sun goes in, you can paint the trees as you go with luminous paint. Then you can always come back to me.'

'*Cool*,' he said, entranced.

343

'What?' Coconut wanted to know.

Gareth told him about finding one's way back to places by blazing the trail.

'I'll follow you,' I said, 'but you won't see me. If you go really badly wrong, I'll tell you. Otherwise, survival's up to you.'

'Ace,' Gareth said happily.

I unzipped the pouch round my waist and gave him the small jar of paint and the sawn-off paintbrush.

'Don't forget to paint so you can see the splash from both directions, coming and going, and don't get out of sight of your last splash.'

'OK.'

'Wait for me when you hit the road.'

'Yes.'

'And take the whistle.' I held it out to him from the pouch. 'It's just a back-up in case you get stuck. If you're in trouble, blow it, and I'll come at once.'

'It's only a mile,' he protested, slightly hurt, not taking it.

'What do I say to your father if I mislay you?'

He grinned in sympathy, giving way, and put the best of all insurances in his pocket.

'Let's go back the way we came,' Coconut said to Gareth.

'Easy!' Gareth agreed.

I watched them decide on the wrong place and paint the first mark carefully round a sapling's trunk. They might just possibly have been able to find the morning's path if they'd been starting again from the road, but tracking backwards was incredibly difficult. All the identifiable marks of our passage, like broken twigs and flattened grass, pointed forward into the wood, not out of it.

They consulted their watches and moved north through the trees, looking back and painting as they went. They waved once and I waved back, and for some time I could see the bright jackets in the dappled shade of the afternoon sun. Then, when they had gone, I began to slowly follow their splashes.

I could go much faster than they could. When I saw them again I dropped down on one knee, knowing that even though they were constantly looking back they wouldn't see me at that low level, in my nature-coloured clothes.

Besides the map I'd brought along my faithful compass, and by its reckoning checked the boys' direction all the time. They wandered off to the north-east a bit but not badly enough to get really lost, and after a while made a correction to drift back to north.

The pale cream splashes were easy to spot, never far apart. Gareth had intelligently chosen smooth-barked saplings all the way and all the marks were at the same height, at about waist level, where painting came to him most naturally, it seemed.

I kept the boys in sight intermittently all the way. They were talking to each other loudly as if to keep lurking wood-spirits at bay, and I did vividly remember that teenage spooky feeling of being alone in wild woodland and at the mercy of supernatural eyes. Even in sunshine one could be nervous. At night a couple of times at fifteen I'd been terrified.

On that day, as I slowly followed the trail, I simply felt at home and at peace. There were birds singing, though not yet many, and apart from the boys' voices the quiet was as old and deep as the land. The woods still waited the stirring of spring, lying chilly and patient with sleeping buds and butterflies in cocoons. The smells of autumn, of compost and rot, still faintly lingered into the winter thaw, only the pines and firs remaining fragrant if one brushed them. Pine resin, collected by tapping, dried to lumps that made brilliant firelighters.

It was a slow-going mile, but towards the end one could hear occasional cars along the road ahead and Gareth and Coconut with whoops crashed through the last few yards, again, as the week before, relieved to be back in the space age.

I speeded up and stepped out behind them, much to Gareth's surprise.

'We thought you were miles back,' he exclaimed.

'You laid an excellent trail.'

'The paint's nearly finished.' He held it up to show me and the jar slipped out of his hand, rolling the remains of its contents onto the earth. 'Hey, sorry,' he said. 'But there wasn't much left.'

'Doesn't matter.' I picked up the jar which was slippery on the outside from dripped paint and, screwing its lid on, dropped it with the brush into a plastic bag before stowing it again in my pouch.

'Can we get some more?' Coconut asked.

'Sure. No problem. Ready to go home?'

The boys, both pumped up by their achievement, ran and jumped all along the road to the Land Rover that we found round the next bend, and rode back in euphoric good spirits.

'Terrific,' Gareth told Tremayne, bursting into the family room after we'd dropped Coconut and returned to Shellerton. 'Fantastic.'

Whether they wanted to or not, Tremayne, Mackie and Perkin received a minute-by-minute account of the whole day with the sole exception of the discussion about Angela Brickell. Tremayne listened with veiled approval, Mackie with active interest, Perkin with boredom.

'It's a real wilderness,' Gareth said. 'You can't hear *anything*. And I took lashings of photos—' He stopped, suddenly frowning. 'Hold on a minute.'

He sped out of the room and came back with his blue knapsack, searching the contents worriedly.

'My camera's not here!'

'The one I gave you for Christmas?' Tremayne asked, not over-pleased.

'Perhaps Coconut's got it,' Perkin suggested languidly.

'Thanks.' Gareth leaped to the telephone in hopes

that were all too soon dashed. 'He says he didn't see it after lunchtime.' He looked horrified. 'We'll have to go back at once.'

'No, you certainly won't,' Tremayne said positively. 'It sounds a long way and it'll be getting dark soon.'

'But it's *luminous* paint,' Gareth begged. 'That's the whole point, you can see it in the dark.'

'No,' said his father.

Gareth turned to me. 'Can't we go back?'

I shook my head. 'Your father's right. We could get lost in those woods at night, paint or no paint. You've only got to miss one mark and you'd be out there till morning.'

'*You* wouldn't get lost.'

'I might,' I said. 'We're not going.'

'Did you drop it on the path back?' Mackie asked sympathetically.

'No ...' He thought about it. 'I must have left it where we had lunch. I hung it on a branch to keep it from getting damp. I just forgot it.'

He was upset enough for me to say, 'I'll get it tomorrow afternoon.'

'Will you?' Disaster swung back to hope. 'Oh, *great*.'

Tremayne said doubtfully, 'Will you find one little camera hanging in all those square miles of nothing?'

'Of course he will,' Gareth told him confidently. 'I told you, we left a *trail*. And oh!' He thought of something. 'Isn't it lucky I dropped all the paint, because now you can see where the trail starts, because we didn't paint any trees once we could see the road.'

'Do explain,' Mackie said.

Gareth explained.

'Will you really find the trail?' Mackie asked me, shaking her head.

'As long as someone hasn't parked on the patch of paint and taken it all away on their tyres.'

'Oh, no,' Gareth said, anguished.

'Don't worry,' I told him. 'I'll find your camera if it's still in the clearing.'

'It is. I'm sure. I remember hanging it up.'

'All right then,' Tremayne said. 'Let's talk about something else.'

'Grub?' Gareth asked hopefully. 'Pizza?'

CHAPTER SIXTEEN

On Monday morning, first lot, I was back on Drifter.

'He's entered in a race at Worcester the day after tomorrow,' Tremayne said, as we walked out to the yard at seven in the half-dawn. 'Today's his last training gallop before that, so don't fall off again. The vet's been here already this morning to test his blood.'

Tremayne's vet took small blood samples of all the stable's runners prior to their last training gallop before they raced, the resulting detailed analysis being able to reveal a whole host of things from a raised lymphocyte count to excreted enzymes due to muscle damage. If there were too many contra-indications in the blood the vet would advise Tremayne that the horse was unlikely to run well or win. Tremayne said the process saved the owners from wasting money on fruitless horsebox expenses and jockey fees and also saved himself a lot of inexplicable and worrying disappointments.

'Are you going to Worcester yourself?' I asked.

'Probably. Might send Mackie. Why?'

'Er . . . I wondered if I could go to see Drifter race.'

He turned his head to stare at me as if he couldn't at once comprehend my interest, but then, understanding, said of course I could go if I wanted to.

'Thanks.'

'You can gallop Fringe this morning, second lot.'

'Thanks again.'

'And thanks to you for giving Gareth such a good day yesterday.'

'I enjoyed it.'

We reached the yard and stood watching the last preparations as usual.

'That's a good camera,' Tremayne said regretfully. 'Stupid boy.'

'I'll get it back.'

'Along his precious trail?' He was doubtful.

'Maybe. But I had a map and a compass with me yesterday. I know pretty well where we went.'

He smiled, shaking his head. 'You're the most competent person. Like Fiona says, you put calamities right.'

'It's not always possible.'

'Give Drifter a good gallop.'

We went up to the Downs and at least I stayed in the saddle, and felt indeed a new sense of being at home there, of being at ease. The strange and difficult was becoming second nature in the way that it had when I'd learned to fly. Racehorses, helicopters; both needed hands responsive to messages reaching them, and both would usually go where you wanted if you sent the right messages back.

Drifter flowed up the gallop in a smooth fast rhythm and Tremayne said he would have a good chance at Worcester if his blood was right.

When I'd left the horse in the yard and gone in for breakfast I found both Mackie and Sam Yaeger sitting at the table with Tremayne, all of them discussing that day's racing at Nottingham. The horse that Tremayne had been going to run had gone lame, and another of Sam's rides had been withdrawn because its owner's wife had died.

'I've only got a no-hoper left,' Sam complained. 'It's not bloody worthwhile going. Reckon I'll catch flu and work on the boat.' He telephoned forthwith, made hoarse-voiced excuses and received undeserved sympathy. He grinned at me, putting down the receiver. 'Where's the toast, then?'

'Coming.'

'I hear you played Cowboys and Indians all over Berkshire with Gareth and Coconut yesterday.'

'News travels,' I said resignedly.

'I told him,' Mackie said, smiling. 'Any objections?'

I shook my head and asked her how she was feeling. She'd stopped riding out with the first lot because of nausea on waking, and Tremayne, far from minding, continually urged her to rest more.

'I feel sick,' she said to my enquiry. 'Thank goodness.'

'Lie down, my dear girl,' Tremayne said.

'You all fuss too much.'

Sam said to me, 'Doone spent all Saturday afternoon at the boatyard.'

'I thought he was off duty.'

'He got a message from you, it seems.'

'Mm. I did send one.'

'What message?' Tremayne asked.

'I don't know,' Sam answered. 'Doone phoned me yesterday to say he'd been to the boatyard and taken away some objects for which he would give me a receipt.'

'What objects?' asked Tremayne.

'He wouldn't say.' Sam looked at me. 'Do you know what they were? You steered him to them, it seems. He sounded quite excited.'

'What was the message?' Mackie asked me.

'Um . . .' I said. 'I asked him why the floorboards didn't float.'

Tremayne and Mackie appeared mystified but Sam immediately understood and looked thunderstruck.

'Bloody hell, how did you think of it?'

'Don't know,' I said. 'It just came.'

'Do explain,' Mackie begged.

I told her what I'd told Erica at Tremayne's dinner, and said it might not lead to anything helpful.

'But it certainly might,' Mackie said.

Sam said to me thoughtfully, 'If you hadn't stopped me, I'd have rolled up the curtain so as to go into the dock in a boat, and all that stuff under the water would have slithered away into the river and no one would have been any the wiser.'

'Fiona's sure John will find out, before Doone does, who set that trap for Harry,' Mackie said.

I shook my head. 'I don't know who it was. Wish I did.'

'Matter of time,' Tremayne said confidently. He looked at his watch. 'Talking of time, second lot.' He stood up. 'Sam, I want a trial of that new horse Roydale against Fringe. You ride Roydale, John's on Fringe.'

'OK,' Sam said easily.

'John,' Tremayne turned to me, 'don't try to beat Sam as if it were a race. This is a fact-finder. I want you to see which has most natural speed. Go as fast as you can but if you feel Fringe falter don't press him, just ease back.'

'Right.'

'Mackie, talk to Dee-Dee or something. I'm not taking you up there to vomit in the Land Rover.'

'Oh, Tremayne, as if I would.'

'Not risking it,' he said gruffly. 'Don't want you bouncing about on those ruts.'

'I'm not an invalid,' she protested, but she might as well have argued with a rock. He determinedly left her behind and drove Sam and me up to the gallops.

On the way, Sam said to me dryly, 'Nolan usually rides any trials. He'll be furious.'

'Thanks a lot.'

Tremayne said repressively, 'I've told Nolan he won't be riding work here again until he cools off.'

Sam raised his eyebrows comically. 'Do you want John shot? Nolan's a whiz with a gun.'

'Don't talk nonsense,' Tremayne said a shade uneasily, and bumped the Land Rover across the ruts of the track and onto the smooth upland grass before drawing to a halt. 'Keep your mind on Roydale. He belongs to a new owner. I want your best judgment. His form's not brilliant, but nor is the trainer he's come from. I want to know where we're at.'

'Sure,' Sam said.

'Stay upsides Fringe as long as you can.'

Sam nodded. We took Roydale and Fringe from the lads and, when Tremayne had driven off and positioned himself on his hillock, we started together up the all-weather gallop, going the fastest I'd ever been. Fringe, flat out at racing pace, had a wildness about him I couldn't really control and I guessed it was that quality which won him races. Whenever Roydale put his nose in front, Fringe found a bit extra, but it seemed there wasn't much between them, and with the end of the wood chippings in sight the contest was still undecided. I saw Sam sit up and ease the pressure, and copied him immediately, none too soon for my taxed muscles and speed-starved lungs. I finished literally breathless but Sam pulled up nonchalantly and trotted back to Tremayne for a report in full voice.

'He's a green bugger,' he announced. 'He has a

mouth like elephant skin. He shies at his own shadow and he's as stubborn as a pig. Apart from that, he's fast, as you saw.'

Tremayne listened impassively. 'Courage?'

'Can't tell till he's on a racecourse.'

'I'll enter him for Saturday. We may as well find out. Perhaps you'd better give him a pop over hurdles tomorrow.'

'OK.'

We handed the horses back to their respective lads and went down the hill again with Tremayne and found Doone waiting for us, sitting in his car.

'That man gives me the sodding creeps,' Sam said as we disembarked.

The greyly persistent Detective Chief Inspector emerged like a turtle from his shell when he saw us arrive, and he'd come alone for once: no silent note-taker in his shadow.

'Which of us do you want?' Tremayne enquired bullishly.

'Well, sir.' The sing-song voice took all overt menace away, yet there was still a suggestion that collars might be felt at any minute. 'All of you, sir, if you don't mind.'

Just the same if we did mind, he meant.

'You'd better come in, then,' Tremayne offered, shrugging.

Doone followed us into the kitchen, removed a grey tweed overcoat and sat by the table in his much-lived-in grey suit. He felt comfortable in kitchens, I thought.

Tremayne vaguely suggested coffee, and I made a mug of instant for us each.

Mackie came through from having breakfasted with Perkin saying she wanted to know how the trial had gone. She wasn't surprised to see Doone, only resigned. I made her some coffee and she sat and watched while Doone picked a piece of paper out of his breast pocket and handed it to Sam.

'A receipt, sir,' he said, 'for three lengths of floor-board retrieved from the dock in your boathouse.'

Sam unfolded the paper and looked at it dumbly.

'Why didn't they float?' Tremayne asked bluntly.

'Ah. So everyone knows about that?' Doone seemed disappointed.

'John just told us,' Tremayne nodded.

Doone gave me a sorrowful stare, but I hadn't given a thought to his wanting secrecy.

'They didn't float, sir, because they were weighted.'

'With what?' Sam asked.

'With pieces of paving stone. There are similar pieces of paving stone scattered on a portion of your boatyard property.'

'*Paving* stone?' Sam sounded bemused, then said doubtfully, 'Do you mean broken slabs of pink and grey marble?'

'Is that what it is, sir, marble?' Doone didn't know much about marble, it appeared.

'It might be.'

Doone pondered, made up his mind, went out to his

car and returned carrying a five-foot plank which he laid across the kitchen table. The old grey wood, though still dampish, looked as adequate for its purpose as its fellows still forming the boathouse floor and didn't seem to have been weakened in any way. Slightly towards one end, on the surface that was now upper-most on the table, rested a long, unevenly shaped dark-ish slab of what I might have thought was rough-faced granite.

'Yes,' Sam said, glancing at it. 'That's marble.' He stretched out his hand and tried to pick it up, and the plank came up an inch with it. Sam let it drop, frowning.

'It's stuck on,' Doone said, nodding. 'From the looks of the other pieces lying about, the surface that's stuck to the wood is smooth and polished.'

'Yes,' Sam said.

'Superglue, we think,' Doone said, 'would make a strong enough bond.'

'A lot of plastic adhesives would,' Sam said, nodding.

'And how do you happen to have chunks of marble lying about?' Doone asked, though not forbiddingly.

'It came with a job-lot of stuff I bought from a demolition firm,' Sam explained without stress. 'They had some panelling I wanted for a boat I did up, and some antique bathroom fittings. I had to take a lot of oddments as well, like the marble. It came from a mansion they were pulling down. They sell off things, you know. Fireplaces, doors, anything.'

Doone asked conversationally, 'Did you stick the marble on to the floorboards, sir?'

'No, I sodding well did *not*,' Sam said explosively.

'On to the underside of the floorboards,' I said. 'There were no slabs of marble in sight when Harry and I went into the upstairs room of the boathouse. I expect, if there are some other blocks still in place, that you can see them from underneath, in the dock.'

Doone with slight reluctance admitted that there seemed to be marble stuck to the underside of one more floorboard on each side of the hole.

The plank on the table was about eight inches across. Harry had taken three of them down with him; five altogether had been doctored. The trap with its missing section of beam had been three and a half feet across, and Harry, taking the envelope bait, had gone through its centre.

'Have you finished snooping round my place now?' Sam demanded, and Doone shook his head.

'I want to work on my boat,' Sam objected.

'Go ahead, sir. Never mind my men, if they're there.'

'Right.' Sam stood up with bouncing energy, quite unlike a patient suddenly stricken with flu. 'Bye, Tremayne. Bye, Mackie. See you, John.'

He went out to his car carrying his jazzy jacket and tooted as he drove away. The kitchen seemed a lot less alive without him.

'I'd like to talk to Mr Kendall alone,' Doone said placidly.

Tremayne's eyebrows rose but he made no objection. He suggested I took Doone into the dining-room while he told Mackie about Roydale's gallop, and Doone followed me docilely, bringing the plank.

The formality of the dining-room furnishings seemed at first to change his mood from ease to starch, but it appeared to me after a short while that he was troubled rather by indecision as to which side I was now on, them or us.

He seemed to settle finally for us, us being the police, or at least the fact-seekers and, clearing his throat, he told me that his men with grappling irons and magnets had missed finding the floorboards the first time, probably because the floorboards weren't magnetic. Did I, he wanted to know, think the trap-setter had taken magnetism into account.

I frowned. 'Stretching it a bit,' I said. 'I should think he looked around for something heavy that would take glue, and with all that junk lying around there was bound to be something. The marble happened to be perfect. But the whole thing was so thoroughly thought out, you really can't tell.'

'Do you know who did it?' he asked forthrightly.

'No,' I said truthfully.

'You must have opinions.' He shifted on his chair, looking around him. 'I'd like to hear them.'

'They're negative more than positive.'

'Often just as valuable.'

'I'd assume the trap-setter had been a guest at Sam

360

Yaeger's boatyard party,' I said, 'only you warned me never to assume.'

'Assume it,' he said, almost smiling and in some inner way contented.

'And,' I went on, 'I'd assume it was the person who killed Angela Brickell who wanted to fix the blame for ever on Harry by making him disappear, only . . .'

'Assume it,' he said.

'Anyone could have killed Angela Brickell, but only a hundred and fifty or so people went to Sam's party, and half of those were women.'

'Don't you think a woman could have set that trap?' he asked neutrally.

'Sure, a woman could have thought it out and done the carpentering. But what woman could have lured Angela Brickell and persuaded her to take all her clothes off in the middle of a wood?'

He sucked his teeth.

'All right,' he said, 'I agree, a man killed her.' He paused, 'Motive?'

'I'd guess . . . to keep a secret. I mean, suppose she was pregnant. Suppose she went out into the woods with . . . *him*, and they were going to make love . . . or they'd done it . . . and she said "I'm pregnant, you're the father, what are you going to do about it?" She was full of jumbled religious guilts but it was she who was the seducer . . .' I paused. 'I'd think perhaps she was killed because she wanted too much . . . and because she wouldn't have an abortion.'

361

He made a sound very like a purr in his throat.

'All right,' he said again. 'Method: strangulation. Guaranteed to work, as everyone around here knew, after the death of that other girl, Olympia.'

'Yes.'

'Opportunity?' he said.

'No one can remember what they were doing the day Angela Brickell disappeared.'

'Except the murderer,' he observed. 'What about opportunity on the day Mr Goodhaven fell through the floor?'

'Someone was there to drive his car away . . . no fingerprints, I suppose?'

'Gloves,' he said succinctly. 'Too few of Mr Goodhaven's prints are still there. No palm print on the gear lever, for instance. I don't know if we'd have worried about that if we'd thought he'd done a bunk. It was a cold day, after all. He might have worn gloves himself.'

'You might have guessed at collusion,' I suggested.

'Did you ever consider police work?'

'Not good at that sort of discipline.'

'You don't like taking orders, sir?'

'I prefer giving them to myself.'

He smiled without criticism. 'You'd be no good in uniform.'

'None at all.'

He was entitled, I supposed, to his small exploratory excursion around my character; and if he himself, I thought, had been wholly fulfilled by uniform, he would still be in it.

Perkin in his overalls appeared in the open doorway, hovering.

'Is Mackie over here?' he said. 'I can't find her.'

'In the kitchen with Tremayne,' I said.

'Thanks.' He swept a gaze over Doone and the plank and said with irony, 'Sorting it out, then?'

Doone said a shade heavily, 'Mr Kendall's always helpful,' and Perkin made a face and went off to join Mackie.

'About Harry's car,' I said to Doone. 'There must have been just a small problem of logistics. I mean, perhaps our man parked his own car in Reading station car park, then took a train to Maidenhead station and a bus from there to near the river, and went on foot from there to the boatyard... wouldn't that make sense?'

'It would, but so far we haven't found anyone who noticed anything useful.'

'Car park ticket?'

'There wasn't one in the car. We don't know when the car arrived in the car park. It could have been parked somewhere else on Wednesday and repositioned when our man discovered Mr Goodhaven was still alive.'

'Mm. It would mean that our man had a lot of time available for manoeuvring.'

'Racing people do have flexible hours,' he observed, 'and they mostly have free afternoons.'

'I don't suppose there's a hope that my jacket and boots were still in the car?' I asked.

'No sign of them. Sorry. They'll be in a dump somewhere, shouldn't wonder.' He was looking round the room again, and this time revealed his purpose. 'About those guide books of yours, I'd like to see them.'

They were in the family room. I went to fetch them and returned with only three I'd found, *Jungle*, *Safari* and *Ice*. The others, I explained, could be anywhere, as everyone had been reading them.

He opened *Jungle* and quickly flipped through the opening chapters, which were straightforward advice for well-equipped jungle holidays: 'Never put a bare foot on the earth. Shower in slip-ons. Sleep with your shoes inside your mosquito netting. Never drink untreated water . . . never brush your teeth with it . . . don't wash fruit or vegetables in it, avoid suspect ice-cubes.'

' "Never get exhausted"!' Doone said aloud. 'What sort of advice is that?'

'Exhausted people can't be bothered to stick to life-saving routines. If you don't drive yourself too hard you're more likely to survive. For instance, if you've a long way to go, it's better to get there slowly than not at all.'

'That's weak advice,' he said, shaking his head.

I didn't argue, but many died from exhaustion every

year through not understanding the strengths of weakness. It was better to stop every day's travel early so as to have good energy for raising a tent, digging an igloo, building a platform up a tree. Dropping down exhausted without shelter could bring new meaning to the expression 'dead tired'.

' "Food",' Doone read out. ' "Fishing, hunting, trapping." ' He flicked the pages. ' "In the jungle, hang fishhooks to catch birds. Don't forget bait. You always need bait." ' He looked up. 'That envelope was bait, wasn't it?'

I nodded. 'Good bait.'

'We haven't found it. That water's like liquid mud. You can't see an inch through it, my men say.'

'They're right.'

He stared for a second. 'Oh, yes. I'd forgotten you'd been in it.' He went back to the book. ' "It's possible to bring down game with a spear or a bow and arrow, but these take considerable practice and involve hours spent lying in wait. Let a trap do the waiting . . ." ' He read on. ' "The classic trap for large animals is a pit with sharpened staves pointing upwards. Cover the pit with natural-looking vegetation and earth, and suspend the bait over the top." ' He looked up. 'Very graphic illustrations and instructions.'

'Afraid so.'

Eyes down again to the book, he went on, ' "All sharpened staves for use in traps (and also spears and arrows) can be hardened to increase their powers of

penetration by being charred lightly in hot embers, a process which tightens and toughens the wood fibres." '
Doone stopped reading and remarked, 'You don't say anything about sharpening old bicycle frames and railings.'

'There aren't many bicycle frames in the jungle. Er . . . were they sharpened?'

He sighed. 'Not artificially.' He read on. ' "If digging or scraping out a pit is impracticable because of hard or waterlogged ground, try netting. Arrange a net to entangle game when it springs the trap. To make a strong net you can use tough plant fibres . . ." ' He silently read several pages, occasionally shaking his head, not, I gathered, in disagreement with the text, but in sorrow at its availability.

' "How to skin a snake" ,' he read. 'Dear God.'

'Roast rattlesnake tastes like chicken,' I said.

'You've eaten it?'

I nodded. 'Not at all bad.'

' "First aid. How to stop heavy bleeding. Pressure points . . . To close gaping wounds, use needle and thread. To help blood clot, apply cobwebs to the wound." *Cobwebs!* I don't believe it.'

'They're organic,' I said, 'and as sterile as most bandages.'

'Not for me, thanks.' He put down *Jungle* and flipped through *Safari* and *Ice*. Many of the same suggestions for traps appeared in all the books, modified only by terrain.

' "Don't eat polar bear liver," ' Doone read in amazement, ' "it stores enough vitamin A to kill humans." ' He smiled briefly. 'That would make a dandy new method for murder.'

First catch your polar bear . . .

'Well, sir,' Doone said, laying the books aside, 'we can trace the path of ideas about the trap, but who do you think put them into practice?'

I shook my head.

'If I throw names at you,' he said, 'give your reasons for or against.'

'All right,' I said, cautiously.

'Mr Vickers.'

'Tremayne?' I must have sounded astonished. 'All against.'

'Why, exactly?'

'Well, he's not like that.'

'As I told you before, I don't know these people the way you do. So give me reasons.'

I said, thinking, 'Tremayne Vickers is forceful, a bit old-fashioned, straightforward, often kind. Angela Brickell would not have been to his taste. If – and to my mind it's a colossal if – *if* she managed to seduce him and then told him he was the father-to-be, and if he believed it, it would have been more his style to pack her off home to her parents and provide for her. He doesn't shirk responsibility. Also, I can't imagine him taking any woman out into deep woods for sex.

Impossible. As for trying to kill Harry . . .' Words failed me.

'All right,' Doone said. He brought out a notebook and methodically wrote 'KENDALL'S ASSESSMENTS' at the top of the page. Underneath he wrote 'Tremayne Vickers', followed by a cross, and under Tremayne, 'Nolan Everard'.

'Nolan Everard,' he said.

Not so easy. 'Nolan is brave. He's dynamic and determined . . . and violent.'

'And he threatened to kill you,' Doone said flatly.

'Who told you that?'

'Half the racing world heard him.'

Sighing, I explained about my riding.

'And when he attacked you, you picked him up like a baby in front of all those people,' Doone said. 'A man might not forgive that.'

'We're talking about Angela Brickell and Harry,' I pointed out mildly.

'Talk about Nolan Everard then. *For*, first.'

'*For* . . . Well, he killed Olympia, not really meaning to, but definitely by putting her life at risk. He couldn't afford another scandal while waiting for trial. If Angela Brickell had seduced him – or the other way round – and she threatened a messy paternity suit . . . I don't know. That's again a big if, but not as impossible as Tremayne. Nolan and Sam Yaeger often bed the same girl, more or less to spite each other, it seems. Nolan regularly rides the horse, Chickweed, that Angela

Brickell had care of, and there would have been opportunities for sex at race meetings, like in a horse-box, if he wanted to take the risk. He could sue me for slander over this.'

'He won't hear of it,' Doone said positively. 'This conversation is just between you and me. I'll deny I ever discussed the case with you if anyone asks.'

'Fair enough.' I thought a bit. 'As for the trap for Harry, Nolan would be mentally and physically capable.'

'But? I hear your but.'

I nodded. '*Against*. He's Fiona's cousin, and they're close. He depends on Fiona's horses to clinch his amateur-champion status. He couldn't be sure she would have the heart to go on running racehorses if she were forced to believe Harry a murderer ... if she thought he had left her without warning, without a note, if she were worried sick by not knowing where he'd gone, and was also haunted by the thought of Harry with Angela Brickell.'

'Would Everard have stopped to consider all that?' he mused doubtfully.

'The trap was well thought out.'

Doone wrote a question mark after Nolan's name.

'Doesn't *anyone* have a solid alibi for Wednesday afternoon?' I asked. 'That's the one definite time our man has to explain away.'

'And don't think we don't know it,' Doone nodded. 'Not many of the men connected with this place can account for every hour of that afternoon, though the women can. We've been very busy this morning, making enquiries. Mrs Goodhaven went to a committee meeting, then home in time to be there when you telephoned. Mrs Perkin Vickers was at Ascot races, vouched for by saddling a horse in the three-mile chase. Mr Vickers' secretary Dee-Dee made several telephone calls from the office here and Mrs Ingrid Watson went shopping in Oxford with her mother and can produce receipts.'

'*Ingrid?*'

'She can't vouch for what her husband did.'

He wrote 'Bob Watson' under Nolan.

'*For* him being our man,' I said dubiously, 'is, I suppose, Ingrid herself. She wouldn't put up with shenanigans with Angela Brickell. But whether Bob would kill to stay married to Ingrid . . .' I shook my head. 'I don't know. He's a good head lad, Tremayne trusts him, but I wouldn't stake my life on his loyalty. Also he's an extremely competent carpenter, as you saw yourself. He was serving drinks at the party when Olympia died. He went to the boatyard party as a guest.'

'*Against?*'

I hesitated. 'Killing Angela Brickell might have been a moment's panic. Setting the trap for Harry took cunning and nerve. I don't know Bob Watson well enough for a real opinion. I don't know him like the others.'

Doone nodded and put a question mark after his name also.

370

'Gareth Vickers,' he wrote.

I smiled. 'It can't be him.'

'Why not?' Doone asked.

'Angela Brickell's sexuality frightened him. He would never have gone into the woods with her. Apart from that, he hasn't a driving licence, and he was at school on Wednesday afternoon.'

'Actually,' Doone said calmly, 'he is known to be able to drive his father's jeep on the Downs expertly, and my men have discovered he was out of school last Wednesday afternoon on a field trip to Windsor Safari Park. That's not miles from the boatyard. The teacher in charge is flustered over the number of boys who sloped off to buy food.'

I considered Gareth as a murderer. I said, 'You asked me for my knowledge of these people. Gareth couldn't possibly be our man.'

'Why are you so sure?'

'I just am.'

He wrote a cross against Gareth's name, and then as an afterthought, a question mark also.

I shook my head. Under Gareth's name he wrote 'Perkin Vickers'.

'What about *him*?' he asked.

'Perkin . . .' I sighed. 'He lives in another world half the time. He works hard. *For*, I suppose, is that he makes furniture, he's good with wood. I don't know that it's *for* or *against* that he dotes on his wife. He's very possessive of her. He's a bit childlike in some

371

ways. She loves him and looks after him. *Against* . . . he doesn't have much to do with the horses. Seldom goes racing. He didn't remember who Angela Brickell was, the first morning you were here.'

Doone pursed his lips judiciously, then nodded and wrote a cross against Perkin, and then again a question mark.

'Keeping your options open?' I asked dryly.

'You never know what we don't know,' he said.

'Deep.'

'It might be reasonable to assume that Mr Good-haven didn't set the trap himself, to persuade me of his innocence,' he said, writing 'Henry Goodhaven' on the list.

'A hundred per cent,' I agreed.

'However, he took you along as a witness.' He paused. 'Suppose he planned it and it all went wrong? Suppose he needed you there to assert he'd walked into a trap?'

'Impossible.'

He put a question mark against Harry, all the same.

'Who drove his car away?' I said, a shade aggressively.

'A casual thief.'

'I don't believe it.'

'You like him,' Doone said. 'You're unreliable.'

'That page is headed "KENDALL'S ASSESSMENTS".' I protested. 'My assessment of Harry merits a firm cross.'

He looked at what he'd written, shrugged and

changed the question mark to a negative. Then he made a question mark away to the right on the same line. 'My assessments,' he said.

I smiled a little ruefully and said reflectively, 'Have you worked out when the trap was set? Raising the floorboards, finding the marble and sticking it on, cutting out the bit of beam – and I bet that went floating down the river – remembering to lock the lower door . . . It would all have taken a fair time.'

'When would *you* say it was done, then?' he asked, giving nothing away.

'Any time Tuesday, or Wednesday morning, I suppose.'

'Why, exactly?'

'Anti-Harry fever was publicly at its height on Monday, Tuesday and Wednesday, but by the Sunday before, at least, you'd begun to spread your investigation outwards . . . which must horribly have alarmed our man. Sam Yaeger spent Monday at the boatyard because he'd been medically stood down from racing as a result of a fall, but by Tuesday he was racing again; on Wednesday he rode at Ascot, so the boathouse was vulnerable all day Tuesday and again Wednesday morning.'

Doone looked at me from under his eyelids.

'You're forgetting something,' he said, and added 'Sam Yaeger' to his list.

CHAPTER SEVENTEEN

'Put a cross,' I said.

Doone shook his head. 'You admire him. You could be blinded.'

I thought it over. 'I do in many ways admire him, I admit. I admire his riding, his professionalism. He's courageous. He's a realist.' I paused. 'I'll agree that on the *For* side you could put the things you listed the other day, that he has all the skills to set the trap and the perfect place to do it.'

'Go on,' Doone nodded.

'You'd begun actively investigating him,' I said.

'Yes, I had.'

'He'd rolled around a bit with Angela Brickell,' I said, 'and that's where we come to the biggest *Against*.'

'You're not saying he couldn't have had the irritation, the nerve, the strength to strangle her?'

'No, I'm not, though I don't think he did it. What I'm saying is that he wouldn't have taken her out into the woods. He told you himself he moves a mattress into the boathouse on such occasions. If he'd strangled her on impulse it would have been *there*, and he could have slid her weighted body into the river, no one the wiser.'

Doone listened with his head on one side. 'But what if he'd deliberately planned it? What if he'd suggested the woods as being far away from his own territory?'

'I wouldn't think he'd need to cover his sins with strangulation,' I said. 'Everyone knows he seduced anything that moves. He would pass off an Angela Brickell sort of scandal with a laugh.'

Doone disapproved, saying, 'Unsavoury,' and maybe thinking of his assailable daughters.

'We haven't got very far,' I said, looking at his list. All my own assessments were a cross except the question mark against Nolan. Not awfully helpful, I thought.

Doone clicked his pen a few times, then at the bottom wrote Lewis Everard.

'That's a long shot,' I said.

'Give me some *Fors* and *Againsts*.'

I pondered. '*Against* first. I don't think he's bold enough to have set that trap, but then . . .' I hesitated, 'there's no doubt he's both clever and cunning. I wouldn't have thought he would have gone into the woods with Angela Brickell. Can't exactly say why, but I'd think he'd be too fastidious, especially when he's sober.'

'*For?*' Doone prompted, when I stopped.

'He gets drunk . . . I don't know if he'd tumble Angela Brickell in that state or not.'

'But he knew her.'

'Even if not in the biblical sense,' I agreed.

'Sir!' he said with mock reproach.

'He would have seen her at the races,' I said, smiling. 'And *For* . . . he is a good liar. According to him, he's the best actor of the lot.'

'A question mark, then?' Doone's pen hovered.

I slowly shook my head. 'A cross.'

'The trouble with you,' Doone said with disillusion, looking at the column of negatives, 'is that you haven't met enough murderers.'

'None,' I agreed. 'You can't exactly count Nolan Everard.'

'And you wouldn't know a murderer if you tripped over one.'

'Your list is too short,' I said.

'It seems so.' He put away the notebook and stood up. 'Well, Mr Kendall, thank you for your time. I don't discount your impressions. You've helped me clarify my thoughts. Now we'll have to step up our enquiries. We'll get there in the end.'

The sing-song accent came to a stop and he shook my hand and let himself out, a grey man in grey clothes following his own informal, idiosyncratic path towards the truth.

I sat for a while thinking of what I'd said and of what he'd told me, and I still couldn't believe that any of the people I'd come to know so well was really a murderer.

No one was a villain, not even Nolan. There had to be someone else, someone we hadn't begun to consider.

I worked on and off on Tremayne's book for the rest of the morning but found it hard to concentrate.

Dee-Dee drifted in and out, offering coffee and company, and Tremayne put his head in to say he was going to Oxford to see his tailor, and to ask if I wanted an opportunity to shop.

I thanked him and declined. I would probably have liked to replace my boots and ski-jacket, but I still hadn't much personal money. It was easy at Shellerton House to get by without any. Tremayne would doubtless have lent me some of the quarter-advance due at the end of the month but my lack was my own choice, and as long as I could survive as I was, I wouldn't ask. It was all part of the game.

Mackie came through from her side to keep company with Dee-Dee, saying Perkin had gone to Newbury to collect some supplies, and presently the two women went out to lunch together, leaving me alone in the great sprawling house.

I tried again and harder to work and felt restless and uneasy. Stupid, I thought. Being alone never bothered me: in fact, I liked it. That day, I found the size of the silent house oppressive.

I went upstairs, showered and changed out of riding clothes into the more comfortable jeans and shirt I'd worn the day before and pulled on sneakers and the red sweater for warmth. After that I went down to the kitchen and made a cheese sandwich for lunch and wished I'd gone with Tremayne if only for the ride. It was the usual pattern of finding something to do – *anything* – rather than sit down and face the empty page, except that that day the uneasiness was extra.

I wandered in a desultory fashion into the family room which looked dead without the fire blazing and began to wonder what I could make for dinner. Gareth's 'BACK FOR GRUB' message was still pinned to the corkboard, and it was with a distinct sense of release that I remembered I'd said that I would go back for his camera.

The unease vanished. I found a piece of paper and left my own message: 'I'VE BORROWED THE LAND ROVER TO FETCH GARETH'S CAMERA. BACK FOR COOKING THE GRUB!' I pinned it to the corkboard with a red drawing pin and a light heart, and went upstairs again to change back into jodhpur boots to deal with the terrain and to pick up the map and the compass in case I couldn't find the trail. Then I skipped downstairs and went out to the wheels, locking the back door behind me.

It was a good day, sunny like the day before but with more wind. With a feeling of having been unexpectedly let out of school, I drove over the hills on the road to Reading and coasted along the unfenced part of the Quillersedge Estate until I thought I'd come more or less to where Gareth had dropped the paint: parked off the road there and searched more closely for the place on foot.

No one had driven the paint away on their tyres. The splash was dusty but still visible and, without much trouble, I found the beginning of the trail about twenty feet straight ahead in the wood and followed it as easily through the tangled trees and undergrowth as on the day before.

Gareth a murderer . . . I smiled to myself at the absurdity of it. As well suspect Coconut.

The pale paint splashes, the next one ahead visible all the time, weren't all that marked the trail: it showed signs in broken twigs and scuffed ground of our passage the day before. By the time I came back with the camera it would be almost a beaten track.

Wind rattled and swayed the trees and filled my ears with the old songs of the land, and the sun shone through the moving boughs in shimmering ever-changing patterns. I wound my slow way through the maze of unpruned growth and felt at one with things there and inexpressibly happy.

The trail strayed round and eventually reached the small clearing. Our improvised seats were frayed by the wind but still identified the place with certainty, and almost at once I spotted Gareth's camera, prominently hanging, as he'd said, from a branch.

I walked across to collect it and something hit me very hard indeed in the back.

Moments of disaster are disorientating. I didn't know

what had happened. The world had changed. I was falling. I was lying face down on the ground. There was something wrong with my breathing.

I had heard nothing but the wind, seen nothing but the moving trees but, I thought incredulously, *someone had shot me.*

From total instinct as much as from injury I lay as dead. There was a zipping noise beside my ear as something sped past it. I shut my eyes. There was another jolting thud in my back.

So this was death, I thought numbly; and I didn't even know who was killing me, and I didn't know why.

Breathing was terrible. My chest was on fire. A wave of clammy perspiration broke out on my skin.

I lay unmoving.

My face was on dead leaves and dried grass and pieces of twig. I could smell the musty earth. Earth-digested, come to dust.

Someone, I thought dimly, was waiting to see if I moved: and if I moved there would be a third thud and my heart would stop. If I didn't move someone would come and feel for a pulse and, finding one, finish me off. Either way, everything that had been beginning was now ending, ebbing away without hope.

I lay still. Not a twitch.

I couldn't hear anything but the wind in the trees. Could hear no one moving. Hadn't heard even the shots.

Breathing was dreadful. A shaft of pain. Minimum

air could go in, trickle out. Too little. In a while . . . I would go to sleep.

A long time seemed to pass, and I was still alive.

I had a vision of someone standing not far behind me with a gun, waiting for me to move. He was shadowy and had no face, and his patience was for ever.

Clammy nausea came again, enveloping and ominous. My skin sweated. I felt cold.

I didn't exactly try to imagine what was happening in my body.

Lying still was anyway easier than moving. I would slide unmoving into eternity. The man with the gun could wait for ever, but I would be gone. I would cheat him that way.

That's delirium, I thought.

Nothing happened in the clearing. I lay still. Time drifted.

After countless ages I seemed to come back to a real realization that I was continuing to breathe, even if with difficulty, and didn't seem in immediate danger of stopping. However ghastly I might feel, however feeble, I wasn't drowning in blood. Wasn't coughing it up. Coughing was a bleak thought, the way my chest hurt.

My certainty of the waiting gun had begun to fade. He wouldn't be there after all this time. He wouldn't stand for ever doing nothing. He hadn't felt my pulse. He must have thought it unnecessary.

He believed I was dead.

He had gone. I was alone.

It took me a while to believe those three things utterly and another while to risk acting on the belief.

If I didn't move I would die where I lay.

With dread, but in the end inevitability, I moved my left arm.

Christ, I thought, that *hurt*.

Hurt it might, but nothing else happened.

I moved my right arm. Just as bad. Even worse.

No more thuds in the back, though. No quick steps, no pounce, no final curtain.

Perhaps I really was alone. I let the thought lie there for comfort. Wouldn't contemplate a cat-and-mouse cruelty.

I put both palms flat on the decaying undergrowth and tried to heave myself up on to my knees.

Practically fainted. Not only could I not do it but the effort was so excruciating that I opened my mouth to scream and couldn't breathe enough for that either. My weight settled back on the earth and I felt nothing but staggering agony and couldn't think connectedly until it abated.

Something was odd, I thought finally. It wasn't only that I couldn't lift myself off the ground but that I was stuck to it in some way.

Cautiously, sweating, with fiery stabs in every inch, I wormed my right hand between my body and the earth and came to what seemed like a rod between the two.

I must have fallen on to a sharp stick, I thought.

Perhaps I hadn't been shot. But yes, I had. Hit in the back. Couldn't mistake it.

Slowly, trying to ration the pain into manageable portions, I slid my hand out again, and then after a while, hardly believing it, I bent my arm and felt round my back and came to the rod there also, and faced the grim certainty that someone had shot me not with a bullet but an *arrow*.

I lay for a while simply wrestling with the enormity of it.

I had an arrow right through my body from back to front somewhere in the region of my lower ribs. Through my right lung, which was why I was breathing oddly. Not, miraculously, through any major blood vessels, or I would by now have bled internally to death. About level with my heart, but to one side.

Bad enough. Awful. But I was still alive.

I'd been hit twice, I remembered. Maybe I had two arrows through me. One or two, I was still alive.

'*Survival begins in the mind.*'

I'd written that, and knew it to be true. But to survive an arrow a mile from a road with a killer around to make sure I didn't make it . . . where in one's mind did one search for the will to survive that? Where, when just getting to one's knees loomed as an unavoidable torture and to lie and wait to be rescued appeared to be merely common sense.

I thought about rescue. A long long way off. No one

would start looking for me for hours; not until after dark. The sun on my back was warm, but the February nights were still near zero and I was wearing only a sweater. Theoretically the luminous trail should lead rescuers to the clearing even at night ... but any sensible murderer would have obliterated the road end of it after he'd found his own way out.

I couldn't realistically be rescued before tomorrow. I thought I might die while I waited: might die in the night. People died of injuries sometimes because their bodies went into shock. General trauma, not just the wound, could kill.

One thought, one decision at a time.

Better die trying.

All right. Next decision.

Which way to go?

The trail seemed obvious enough, but my intended killer had come and gone that way – must have done – and if he should return for any reason I wouldn't want to meet him.

I had a compass in my pocket.

The distant road lay almost due north of the clearing and the straightest line to the road lay well to the left of the paint trail.

I waited for energy, but it didn't materialise.

Next decision: get up anyway.

The tip of the arrow couldn't be far into the earth, I thought. I'd fallen with it already through me. It could be only an inch or so in. No more than a centimetre, maybe.

I shut my mind to the consequences, positioned my hands, and pushed.

The arrow tip came free and I lay on my side in frightful suffering weakness, looking down at a sharp black point sticking out from scarlet wool.

Black. The length of a finger. Hard and sharp. I touched the needle tip of it and wished I hadn't.

Only one arrow. Only one all the way through, at least.

Not much blood, surprisingly. Or perhaps I couldn't tell, blood being the same colour as the jersey, but there was no great wet patch.

A mile to the road seemed an impossible distance. Moving an inch was taxing. Still, inches added up. Better get started.

First catch your compass . . .

With an inward smile and a mental sigh I retrieved the compass carefully from my pocket and took a bearing on north. North, it seemed, was where my feet were.

I rolled with effort to my knees and felt desperately, appallingly, overwhelmingly ill. The flicker of humour died fast. The waves of protest were so strong that I almost gave up there and then. Outraged tissues, invaded lungs, an overall warning.

I stayed on my knees, sitting back on my heels, head bowed, breathing as little as possible, staring at the protruding arrow, thinking the survival programme was too much.

There was a pale slim rod sticking into the ground beside me. I looked at it vaguely and then with more attention, remembering the thing that had sung past my ear.

An arrow that had missed me.

It was about as long as an arm. A peeled fine-grained stick, dead straight. A notch in its visible end, for slotting onto a bowstring. No feather to make a flight.

The guide books all gave instructions for making arrows.

'Char the tips in hot embers to shrink and toughen the fibres for better penetration . . .'

The charred black tip had penetrated all right.

'Cut two slots in the other end, one shallow one for the bowstring, one deep one to push a shaped feather into, to make a flight so that the arrow will travel straighter to the target.'

Illustrations thoughtfully provided.

If the three arrows had all had flights . . . if there'd been no wind . . .

I closed my eyes weakly. Even without flights, the aim had been deadly enough.

Gingerly, sweating, I curled my left hand behind my back and felt for the third arrow, and found it sticking out of my jersey though fairly loose in my hand. With trepidation I took a stronger hold of it and it came away altogether but with a sharp dagger of soreness, like digging out a splinter.

The black tip of that arrow was scarlet with blood, but I reckoned it hadn't gone in further than a rib or my spine. I only had the first one to worry about.

Only the one.

Quite enough.

It would have been madness to pull it out, even if I could have faced doing it. In duels of old, it hadn't always been the sword going *into* the lungs that had killed so much as the drawing of it out. The puncture let air rush in and out, spoiling nature's enclosed vacuum system. With holes to the outer air, the lungs collapsed and couldn't breathe. With the arrow still in place, the holes were virtually blocked. With the arrow in place, bleeding was held at bay. I might die with it in. I'd die quicker with it out.

The first rule of surviving a disaster, I had written, was to accept that it had happened and make the best of what was left. Self-pity, regrets, hopelessness and surrender would never get one home. Survival began, continued and was accomplished in the mind.

All right, I told myself, follow your own rules.

Accept the fact of the arrow. Accept your changed state. Accept that it hurts, that every moment will hurt for the foreseeable future. Take that for granted. Go on from there.

Still on my knees I edged round to face north.

The clearing was all mine: no man with a gun. No archer with a bow.

The day in some respects remained incredibly the same. The sun still threw its dappled mantle and the trees still creaked and resonantly vibrated in the oldest of symphonies. Many before me, I thought, had been shot by arrows in ancient woodland and faced their mortality in places that had looked like this before man started killing man.

But I, if I stirred myself, could reach surgeons and antibiotics and hooray for the National Health Service. I slowly shifted on my knees across the clearing, aiming to the left of the painted trail.

It wasn't so bad . . .

It was awful.

For God's sake, I told myself, ignore it. Get used to it. Think about north.

It wasn't possible to go all the way to the road on one's knees: the undergrowth was too thick, the saplings in places too close together. I would have to stand up.

So, OK, hauling on branches, I stood up.

Even my legs felt odd. I clung hard to a sapling with my eyes closed, waiting for things to get better, telling myself that if I fell down again it would be much much *much* worse.

North.

I opened my eyes eventually and took the compass out of my jeans pocket, where I'd stowed it to have hands free for standing up. Holding on still with one hand, I took a visual line ahead from the north needle to mark into memory the furthest small tree I could see, then put the compass away again and with infinite slowness clawed a way forward by inches and after a while reached the target and held on to it for dear life.

I had travelled perhaps ten yards. I felt exhausted.

'Never get exhausted', I had written. Dear God.

I rested out of necessity, out of weakness.

In a while I consulted the compass, memorised another young tree and made my way there. When I looked back I could no longer see the clearing.

I was committed, I thought. I wiped sweat off my forehead with my fingers and stood quietly, holding on, trying to let the oxygen level in my blood climb back to a functioning state.

A functioning mode, Gareth might have said.

Gareth . . .

Sherwood Forest, I thought, eight hundred years ago. Whose face should I pin on the Sheriff of Nottingham . . .

I went another ten yards, and another, careful always not to trip, holding onto branches as onto railings. My breath began wheezing from the exertion. Pain had finally become a constant. Ignore it. Weakness was more of a problem, and lack of breath.

Stopping again for things to calm down I began to do a few unwelcome sums. I had travelled perhaps fifty yards. It seemed a marathon to me but realistically it was roughly one thirty-fifth of a mile, which left thirty-four thirty-fifths still to go. I hadn't timed the fifty yards but it had been no sprint. According to my watch it was already after four o'clock, a rotten piece of information borne out by the angle of the sun. Darkness lay ahead.

I would have to go as fast as I could while I could still see the way, and then rest for longer, and then probably crawl. Sensible plan, but not enough strength to go fast.

Fifty more yards in five sections. One more thirty-fifth of the way. Marvellous. It had taken me fifteen minutes.

More sums. At a speed of fifty yards in fifteen minutes it would take me another eight hours to reach the road. It would then be half-past midnight, and that didn't take into account long rest or crawling.

Despair was easy. Survival wasn't.

To hell with despair, I thought. Get on and walk.

The shaft of the arrow protruding from my back occasionally knocked against something, bringing me to a gasping halt. I didn't know how long it was, couldn't feel as far as the end, and I couldn't always judge how much space I needed to keep it clear.

I'd come out on the simple camera-fetching errand without the complete zipped pouch of gadgets but I did have with me the belt holding my knife and the multi-purpose survival tool, and on the back of that tool there was a mirror. After the next fifty yards I drew it out and took a look at the bad news.

The shaft, straight, pale and rigid, stuck out about eighteen inches. There was a notch in the end for the bowstring, but no flight.

I didn't look at my face in the mirror. Didn't want to confirm how I felt. I returned the small tool to the pouch and went another fifty yards, taking care.

North. Ten yards visible at a time. Go ten yards. Five times ten yards. Short rest.

The sun sank lower on my left and the blue shadows of dusk began gathering on the pines and firs and creeping in among the sapling branches and the alders. In the wind, the shadows threw barred stripes and moved like prowling tigers.

Fifty yards, rest. Fifty yards, rest. Fifty yards, rest.

Think of nothing else.

There would be moonlight later, I thought. Full moon was three days back. If the sky remained clear, I could go on by moonlight.

Dusk deepened until I could no longer see ten yards ahead, and after I'd knocked the shaft of the arrow against an unseen hazard twice within a minute I stopped and sank slowly down to my knees, resting my forehead and the front of my left shoulder against a young birch trunk, drained as I'd never been before.

Perhaps I would write a book about this one day, I thought.

Perhaps I would call it . . . Longshot.

A long shot with an arrow.

Perhaps not so long, though. No doubt from only a

few yards out of the clearing, to get a straight view. A short shot, perhaps.

He'd been waiting there for me, I concluded. If he'd been following me he would have to have been close because I had gone straight to the camera, and I would have heard him, even in the wind. He'd been there first, waiting, and I'd walked up to the carefully prominent bait and presented him with a perfect target, a broad back in a scarlet sweater, an absolute cinch.

Traps.

I'd walked into one, as Harry had.

I leaned against the tree, sagging into it. I did feel comprehensively dreadful.

If I'd been the archer, I thought, I would have been waiting in position, crouched and camouflaged, endlessly patient, arrow notched on a bow. Along comes the target, happily unaware, going to the camera, putting himself in position. Stand up, aim . . . a whamming direct hit, first time lucky.

Shoot twice more at the fallen body. Pity to waste the arrows. Another nice hit.

Target obviously dead. Wait a bit to make sure. Maybe go near for a closer look. All well. Then retreat along the trail. Mission accomplished.

Who was the Sheriff of Nottingham . . .?

I tried to find a more comfortable position but there wasn't one, really. To save my knees a bit I slid down onto my left hip, leaning my head and my left side against the tree. It was better than walking, better than fighting the tangle of woodland, but whether it was better than lying in the clearing I couldn't decide. Yet he, the archer, might have gone back there to check again after all and if he had he would know I was alive, but he would never find me where I was now, deep in impenetrable shadow along a path he couldn't follow in the dark.

It was ironic, I thought, that for the expedition for Gareth and Coconut I'd deliberately chosen to aim for a spot on the map that looked as remote from any road as possible. I should have had more sense.

The darkness intensified down in the wood though I could see stars between the boughs. I listened to the wind. Grew cold. Felt extremely alone.

I let go of things a bit. Simply existed. Let thoughts drift. I felt formless, part of time and space, an essence, a piece of cosmos. The awareness of the world's antiquity which was often with me seemed to intensify, to be a solace. Everything was one. Every being was integral, but alone. One could dissolve and still exist . . . I hovered on the edge of consciousness, semi-asleep, making nonsense.

I relaxed too far. My weight shifted against the tree, slipping downwards, and the shaft of the arrow hit the ground. The explosive pain of it brought me hellishly back to full savage consciousness and to a revived desire not to become part of the eternal mystery just yet. I struggled back into equilibrium and tried to ride the pulverising waves of misery and found to my desperate dismay that the finger of arrow in front was almost an inch longer.

I'd pushed the arrow further through. I'd done hell knew what extra damage to my lung. I didn't know how to bear what my body felt.

I went on breathing. Went on living. That's all one could say.

The worst of it got better.

I sat for what seemed a long time in the cold darkness, breathing shallowly, not moving at all, just waiting, and eventually there was a lightening of the shadows and a luminosity in the wood, and the moon rose clear and bright in the east. To eyes long in the dark, it was as daylight.

Time to go. I pulled out the compass, held it horizontally close to my eyes, let the needle settle onto north, looked that way and mapped the first few feet in my mind.

Putting thought into action was an inevitable trial. Everything was sore, every muscle seemed wired directly to the arrow. Violent twinges shot up my nerves like steel lightning.

So what, I told myself. Stop bellyaching. Ignore what it feels like, concentrate on the journey.

Concentrate on the Sheriff . . .

I pulled myself to my feet again, rocked a bit, sweated, clung onto things, groaned a couple of times, gave myself lectures. Put one foot in front of the other, the only way home.

Knocking the arrow seemed after all not to have been the ultimate disaster. Moving seemed to require the same amount of breath as before, which was to say more than could be easily provided.

I couldn't always see so far ahead by moonlight and needed to consult the compass more often. It slowed things up to keep slipping it in and out of my jeans pocket so after a while I tucked it up the sleeve of my jersey. That improvement upset the old fifty-yard rhythm but it didn't much matter. I looked at my watch instead and stopped every fifteen minutes for a rest.

The moon rose high in the sky and shone unfalteringly into the woods, a silver goddess that I felt like worshipping. I became numb again to discomfort to a useful degree and plodded on methodically taking continual bearings, breathing carefully, aiming performance just below capability so as to last out to the end.

The archer had to have a face.

If I could think straight, if every scrap of attention didn't have to be focused on not falling, I could probably get nearer to knowing. Things had changed since the arrow. A whole lot of new factors had to be considered. I tripped over a root, half lost my balance, shoved the new factors into oblivion.

Slowly, slowly, I went north. Then one time when I put my hand in my sleeve to bring out the compass, it wasn't there.

I'd dropped it.

I couldn't go on without it. Had to go back. Doubted

if I could find it in the undergrowth. I felt swamped with liquefying despair, weak enough for tears.

Get a bloody grip on things, I told myself. Don't be stupid. Work it out.

I was facing north. If I turned precisely one hundred and eighty degrees I would be facing where I'd come from.

Elementary.

Think.

I stood and thought and made the panic recede until I could work out what to do, then I took my knife out of its sheath on my belt and carved an arrow in the bark of the tree I was facing. An arrow pointing skywards. I had arrows on the brain as well as through the lungs, I thought.

The tree pointed north.

The compass had to be somewhere in sight of that arrow. I would have to crawl to have any hope of finding it.

I went down on my knees carefully and as carefully turned to face the other way, south. The tangle of brown foot-long dried grass and dead leaves and the leafless shoots of new growth filled every space between saplings and established trees. Even in daylight with every faculty at full steam it wouldn't have been an easy search, and as things were it was abysmal.

I crawled a foot or two, casting about, trying to part the undergrowth, hoping desperate hopes. I looked back to the arrow on the tree, then crawled another foot. Nothing. Crawled another and another. Nothing. Crawled until I could see the arrow only because it was pale against the bark, and knew I was already further away than when I'd taken the last bearing.

I turned round and began to crawl back, still sweeping one hand at a time through the jumbled growth. Nothing. Nothing. Hope became a very thin commodity. Weakness was winning.

The compass had to be *somewhere*.

If I couldn't find it I would have to wait for morning and steer north by my watch and the sun. If the sun shone. If I lasted that long. The cold of the night was deepening and I was weaker than I'd been when I set out.

I crawled in a fruitless search all the way back to the tree and then turned and crawled away again in a slightly different line, looking, looking, hope draining away yard by yard in progressive debility, resolution ebbing with failure.

One time when I turned to check on the arrow on the tree, I couldn't see it. I no longer knew which way was north.

I stopped and slumped dazedly back on my heels, facing utter defeat.

Everything hurt unremittingly and I could no longer pretend I could ignore it. I was wounded to death and dying on my knees, scrabbling in dead grass, my time running out with the moonlight, shadows closing in.

I felt that I couldn't endure any more. I had no will

left. I had always believed that survival lay in the mind but now I knew there were things one couldn't survive. One couldn't survive unless one could believe one could, and belief had leaked out of me, gone with sweat and pain and weakness into the wind.

CHAPTER EIGHTEEN

Time . . . unmeasured time . . . slid away.

I moved in the end from discomfort, from stiffness: made a couple of circling shuffles on my knees, an unthought-out search for a nest to lie in, to die in, maybe.

I looked up and saw again the arrow cut into the tree. It hadn't been and wasn't far away, just out of sight behind a group of saplings.

Apathetically, I thought it of little use. The arrow pointed in the right direction, but ten feet past it, without a compass, which way was north?

The arrow on the tree pointed upwards.

I looked slowly in that direction, as if instructed. Looked upwards to the sky: and there, up there, glimpsed now and then between the moving boughs, was the constellation of the great bear . . . and the pole star.

No doubt from then on my route wasn't as straight or as accurate as earlier, but at least I was moving. It wasn't possible after all to curl up and surrender, not with an alternative. Clinging onto things, breathing little, inching a slow way forwards, I achieved again a sort of numbness to my basic state and in looking upwards to the stars at every pause felt lighter and more disembodied than before.

Light-headed, I dare say.

I looked at my watch and found it was after eleven o'clock, which meant nothing really. I couldn't reach the road by half past midnight. I didn't know how long I'd wasted looking for the compass or how long I'd knelt in capitulation. I didn't know at what rate I was now travelling and no longer bothered to work it out. All I was really clear about was that this time I would go on as long as my lungs and muscles would function. Survival or nothing. It was settled.

The face of the archer . . .

In splinters of thought, unconnectedly, I began to look back over the past three weeks.

I thought of how I must seem to them, the people I'd grown to know.

The writer, a stranger, set down in their midst. A person with odd knowledge, odd skills, physically fit. Someone Tremayne trusted and wanted around. Someone who'd been in the right place a couple of times. Someone who threatened.

I thought of Angela Brickell's death and of the attacks on Harry and me and it seemed that all three had had one purpose, which was to keep things as they were. They were designed not to achieve but to prevent.

One foot in front of the other . . .

Faint little star, half hidden, revealed now and then by the wind; flickering pin-point in a whirling galaxy, the prayer of navigators . . . see me home.

Angela Brickell had probably been killed to close her mouth. Harry was to have died to cement his guilt. I wasn't to be allowed to do what Fiona and Tremayne had both foretold, that I would find the truth for Doone.

They all expected too much of me.

Because of that expectation, I was half dead.

All guesses, I thought. All inferences. No actual objects that could prove guilt. No statements or admissions to go on, but only probability, only likelihood.

The archer had to be someone who knew I was going to go back for Gareth's camera. It had to be someone who knew how to find the trail. It had to be someone who could follow instructions to make an effective bow and sharp arrows, who had time to lie in wait, who wanted me gone, who had a universe to lose.

The way information zoomed round Shellerton, anyone theoretically could have heard of the lost camera and the way to find it. On the other hand the boys' expedition had occurred only yesterday . . . dear God, only *yesterday* . . . and if . . . *when* . . . I got back, I could find out for certain who had told who.

One step and another. There was fluid in my lungs,

rattling and wheezing at every breath. People lived a long time with fluid ... asthma ... emphysema ... years. Fluid took up air space ... you never saw anyone with emphysema run upstairs.

Angela Brickell had been small and light; a pushover.

Harry and I were tall and strong, not easy to attack at close quarters. Half the racing world had seen me pick up Nolan and knew I could defend myself. So, sharp spikes for Harry and arrows for John, and it was only luck in both cases that had saved us. I'd been there for Harry and the arrow had by-passed my heart.

Luck.

The clear sky was luck.

I didn't want to see the face of the archer.

The sudden admission was a revelation in itself. Even with his handiwork through me, I thought of the sadness inevitably awaiting the others; yet I would have to pursue him, for someone who had three times seen murder as a solution to problems couldn't be trusted never to try it again. Murder was habit-forming, so I'd been told.

Endless night. The moon moved in silver stateliness across the sky behind me. Left foot. Right foot. Hold on to branches. Breathe by fractions.

Midnight.

If ever this ended, I thought, I wouldn't go walking in woodland for a very long time. I would go back to my attic and not be too hard on my characters if they came to pieces on their knees.

I thought of Fringe and the Downs and wondered if I would ever ride in a race, and I thought of Ronnie Curzon and publishers and American rights and of Erica Upton's reviews and it all seemed as distant as Ursa Major but not one whit as essential to my continued existence.

Grapevine round Shellerton. A mass of common knowledge. Yet this time . . . this time . . .

I stopped.

The archer had a face.

Doone would have to juggle with alibis and charts, proving opportunity, searching for footprints. Doone would have to deal with a cunning mind in the best actor of them all.

Perhaps I was wrong. Doone could find out.

I tortoised onwards. A mile was sixty-three thousand three hundred and sixty inches. A mile was roughly one point six kilometres or one hundred and sixty thousand centimetres.

Who cared?

I might have travelled at almost eight thousand inches an hour if it hadn't been for the stops. Six hundred and sixty feet. Two hundred and twenty yards.

A furlong! Brilliant. One furlong an hour. A record for British racing.

Twinkle twinkle little star . . .

No one but a bloody fool would try to walk a mile with an arrow through his chest. Meet J. Kendall, bloody fool.

Light-headed.

One o'clock.

The moon, I thought briefly, had come down from the sky and was dancing about in the wood not far ahead. Rubbish, it couldn't be. It certainly was. I could see it shining.

Lights. I came to sensible awareness; to incredulous understanding. The lights were travelling along the road.

The road was real, was there, was not some lost myth in a witch-cursed forest. I had actually got there. I would have shouted with joy if I could have spared the oxygen.

I reached the last tree and leaned feebly against it, wondering what to do next. The road had for so long been the only goal that I'd given no thought to anything beyond it. It was dark now; no cars.

What to do? Crawl out onto the road and risk getting run over? Hitchhike? Give some poor passing motorist a nightmare?

I felt dreadfully spent. With the trunk's support I slid down to kneeling, leaning head and left shoulder against the bark. By my reckoning, if I'd steered anything like a true course, the Land Rover was way along the road to the right, but it was pointless and impossible to reach it.

Car lights came round a bend from that direction

and seemed not to be travelling too fast. I tried waving an arm to attract attention but only a weak flap of a hand was achieved.

Have to do better.

The car braked suddenly with screeching wheels, then backed rapidly until it was level with me. It was the Land Rover itself. How could it be?

Doors opened. People spilled out. People I knew.

Mackie.

Mackie running, calling, 'John, John,' and reaching me and stopping dead and saying, 'Oh my *God*.'

Perkin behind her, looking down, his mouth shocked open in speechlessness. Gareth saying, 'What's the matter,' urgently, and then seeing and coming down scared and wide-eyed on his knees beside me.

'We've been looking for you for *ages*,' he said. 'You've got an arrow . . .' His voice died.

I knew.

'Run and fetch Tremayne,' Mackie told him and he sprang instantly to his feet and sprinted away along the road to the right, his feet impelled as if by demons.

'Surely we must take that arrow out,' Perkin said, and put his hand on the shaft and gave it a tug. He hardly moved it in my chest but it felt like liquid fire.

I yelled . . . it came out as a croak only but it was a yell in my mind . . . 'Don't.'

I tried to move away from him but that made it worse. I shot out a hand and gripped Mackie's trouser leg and pulled with strength I didn't know I still had left. Strength of desperation.

Mackie's face came down to mine, frightened and caring.

'Don't ... move ... the arrow,' I said with terrible urgency. 'Don't let him.'

'Oh God.' She stood up. 'Don't touch it, Perkin. It's hurting him dreadfully.'

'It would hurt less out,' he said obstinately. The vibrations from his hand travelled through me, inducing terror as well.

'*No. No.*' Mackie pulled at his arm in a panic. 'You must leave it. You'll kill him. Darling, you *must* leave it alone.'

Without her, Perkin would have had his way but he finally took his dangerous hand off the shaft. I wondered if he believed that it would kill me. Wondered if he had any idea what force he would have needed to pull the arrow out, like a wooden skewer out of meat. Wondered if he could imagine the semi-asleep furies he'd already reawakened. The furies had claws and merciless teeth. I tried to breathe even less. I could feel the sweat running down my face.

Mackie leaned down again. 'Tremayne will get help.' Her voice was shaky with stress, with the barbarity of things.

I didn't answer: no breath.

A car pulled up behind the Land Rover and disgorged Gareth and then Tremayne who moved like a tank across the earthy verge and rocked to a halt a yard away.

'*Jesus Christ,*' he said blankly. 'I didn't believe Gareth.' He took charge of things then as a natural duty but also, it seemed, with an effort. 'Right, I'll call an ambulance on the car phone. Keep still,' he said to me, unnecessarily. 'We'll soon have you out of here.'

I didn't answer him either. He sped away back to the car and we could hear his urgent voice, though not the words. He returned shortly telling me to hang on, it wouldn't be for long; and the shock had made him breathless too, I noticed.

'We've looked for you for hours,' he said, anxious, I thought, to prove I hadn't been forgotten. 'We telephoned the police and the hospitals and they had no news of a car crash or anything, so then we came out here . . .'

'Because of your message,' Mackie said, 'on the corkboard.'

Oh, yes.

Gareth's camera was swinging from Perkin's hand. Mackie saw me watching it and said, 'We found the trail, you know.'

Gareth chimed in. 'The paint by the road had gone but we looked and looked in the woods. I remembered where we'd been.' He was earnest. 'I remembered pretty well where it started. And Perkin found it.'

'He went all the way along it with a torch,' Mackie

said, stroking her husband's arm, 'clever thing – and he came back after absolutely ages with Gareth's camera and said you weren't there. We didn't know what to do next.'

'I wouldn't let them go home,' Gareth said. A mixture of stubbornness and pride in his voice. Thank God for him, I thought.

'What happened exactly?' Tremayne asked me bluntly. 'How did you get like this?'

'Tell you ... later.' It came out not much above a whisper, lost in the sound of their movements around me.

'Don't bother him,' Mackie said. 'He can hardly speak.'

They waited beside me making worried encouragements until the ambulance arrived from the direction of Reading. Tremayne and Mackie went to meet the men in uniform, to tell them, I supposed, what to expect. Gareth took a step or two after them and I called him in an explosive croak, 'Gareth,' and he stopped and turned immediately and came back, bending down.

'Yes? What? What can I do?'

'Stay with me,' I said.

It surprised him but he said, 'Oh, OK,' and stayed a pace away looking troubled.

Perkin said irritably, 'Oh, go on, Gareth.'

I said, 'No,' hoarsely. 'Stay.'

After a pause Perkin put his back towards Gareth

and his face down near mine and asked with perfect calmncss, 'Do you know who shot you?' It sounded like a natural question in the circumstances, but it wasn't.

I didn't reply. I looked for the first time straight into his moonlit eyes, and I saw Perkin the son, the husband, the one who worked with wood. I looked deep, but I couldn't see his soul. Saw the man who thought he'd killed me . . . saw the archer.

'Do you really know?' he asked again.

He showed no feeling, yet my knowledge held the difference between his safety and destruction.

After a long moment, in which he read the answer for himself, I said, 'Yes.'

Something within him seemed to collapse but he didn't outwardly fall to pieces or rant and rave or even try to pull out the arrow again or finish me in any other way. He didn't explain or show remorse or produce justification. He straightened and looked across to where the men from the ambulance werc advancing with his father and his wife. Looked at his brother, a pace away, listening.

He said to me, 'I love Mackie very much.'

He'd said everything, really.

I spent the night thankfully unaware of the marathon needlework going on in my chest and drifted back late in the morning to a mass of tubes and machines and techniques I'd never heard of. It seemed I was going to live: the doctors were cheerful, not cautious.

'Constitution like a horse,' one said. 'We'll have you back on your feet in no time.'

A nurse told me a policeman wanted to see me, but visitors had been barred until tomorrow.

By tomorrow, which was Wednesday, I was breathing shallowly but without mechanical help, sitting propped up sideways and drinking soup; talking, attached to drainage tubes and feeling sore. Doing just fine, they said.

The first person who came to see me wasn't Doone at all but Tremayne. He came in the afternoon and he looked white, fatigued and many years older.

He didn't ask about my health. He went over to the window of the post-operation side-ward I was occupying alone and stood looking out for a while, then he turned and said, 'Something awful happened yesterday.'

He was trembling, I saw.

'What?' I asked apprehensively.

'Perkin . . .' His throat closed. His distress was overwhelming.

'Sit down,' I said.

He fumbled his way into the chair provided for visitors and put a hand over his lips so that I shouldn't see how close he was to tears.

'Perkin,' he said after a while. 'After all these years you'd think he'd be careful.'

'What happened?' I asked, when he stopped.

'He was carving part of a cabinet, by hand ... and he cut his leg open with the knife. He bled ... he tried to reach the door ... there was blood all over the floor ... pints of it. He's had cuts sometimes before but this was an artery ... Mackie found him.'

'Oh, no,' I said in protest.

'She's in a terrible state and she won't let them give her sedatives because of the baby.'

Despite his efforts, tears filled his eyes. He waited for his face to steady, then took out a handkerchief and fiercely blew his nose.

'Fiona's with her,' he said. 'She's been marvellous.' He swallowed. 'I didn't want to burden you with this but you'd soon have wondered why Mackie hadn't come.'

'That's the least of things.'

'I have to go back now, but I wanted to tell you myself.'

'Yes. Thank you.'

'There's so much to see to.' His voice wavered again. 'I wish you were there. The horses need to go out. I need your help.'

I wanted very much to give it but he could see I couldn't.

'In a few days,' I said, and he nodded.

'There has to be an inquest,' he said wretchedly.

He stayed for a while sitting exhaustedly as if loath to take up his burdens again, postponing the moment when he would have to go back to supporting everyone

411

else. Eventually he sighed deeply, pushed himself to his feet and with a wan smile departed.

Admirable man, Tremayne.

Doone arrived very soon after Tremayne had gone and came straight to the point.

'Who shot you?'

'Some kid playing Robin Hood,' I said.

'Be serious.'

'Seriously, I didn't see.'

He sat in the visitors' chair and looked at me broodingly.

'I saw Mr Tremayne Vickers in the car park,' he said. 'I suppose he told you their bad news?'

'Yes. Dreadful for them.'

'You wouldn't think, would you,' he added, 'that this could be another murder?'

He saw my surprise. 'I hadn't thought of it,' I said.

'It looks like an accident,' he said with a certain delicacy, 'but he was experienced with that knife, was young Mr Vickers, and after Angela Brickell, after Mr Goodhaven, after your little bit of trouble . . .' He left the thought hanging and I did nothing to bring it to earth. He sighed after a while and asked how I was feeling.

'Fine.'

'Hm.' He bent down and picked up a carrier that he'd lain on the floor. 'Thought you might like to see this.' He drew out a sturdy transparent plastic inner bag and held it up to the light to show me the contents.

An arrow, cut into two pieces.

One half was clean and pale, and the other stained and dark, with a long black section sharpened at the tip.

'We've had our lab take a look at this,' he said in his sing-song way, 'but they say there are no distinctive tool marks. It could have been sharpened by any straight blade in the kingdom.'

'Oh,' I said.

'But charring the point, now, that's in your books.'

'And in other books besides mine.'

He nodded. 'Yesterday morning, at Shellerton House, Mr Tremayne Vickers and young Mr and Mrs Perkin Vickers all told me they'd spent three or four hours looking for you on Monday night. Young Gareth didn't want them to give up, they said, but Mr Vickers senior told him you'd be all right even if you had got lost. You knew how to look after yourself, he said. They were just about to go home when they found you.'

'Lucky me.'

He nodded. 'An inch either way and you'd be history, so I hear. I told them all not to worry, I would go on working with you as soon as you were conscious and we would see our way together to a solution of the whole case.'

'Did you?' He took away what breath I still had.

'Mr Tremayne Vickers said he was delighted.' He paused. 'Did you follow that trail of paint towards the clearing they talk about?'

'Mm.'

'And was it along the trail that someone shot at you?'

'Mm.'

'We'll be taking a look at it ourselves, I shouldn't wonder.'

I made no comment and he looked disappointed.

'You should be wanting your assailant brought to justice.' Text book words again. 'You don't seem to care.'

'I'm tired,' I said.

'You wouldn't be interested then in the glue.'

'What glue?' I asked. 'Oh yes, glue.'

'For sticking marble to floorboards,' he said. 'We had it analysed. Regular impact adhesive. On sale everywhere. Untraceable.'

'And the alibis?'

'We're working on them, but everyone moved about so much except poor young Mr Vickers, who was in his workroom all the time.'

He seemed to be waiting for me to react, rather as if he'd floated a fly in front of a fish.

I smiled at him a little and displayed no interest. His moustache seemed to droop further from the lack of good results. He rose to go and told me to take care. Good advice, though a bit too late. He would proceed, he said, with his enquiries.

I wished him luck.

'You're too quiet,' he said.

When he'd gone I lay and thought for a long time about poor young Mr Vickers, and of what I should have told Doone, and hadn't.

Perkin, I thought, was one of the very few people who'd known about the camera and the trail. I'd listened to Gareth tell him in detail on Sunday evening.

Mackie had told Sam Yaeger on Monday morning.

Theoretically she could also have told Fiona on the telephone who could have told Nolan or Lewis, but it wasn't the sort of item one would naturally bother to pass on.

On Monday morning Doone had turned up at Shellerton House with the plank. Perkin knew it was I who had remembered that the floorboards should have floated, and on Monday he'd seen the plank on the dining-room table and heard Doone and me talking in close private consultation. Everything Fiona and Tremayne believed of me must have looked inevitable at that moment. John Kendall would lead Doone to the quarry, who was himself. Any quarry was entitled to take evasive action: to pre-empt discovery by striking first.

By lunchtime Perkin had driven off, going to Newbury for supplies, he'd said. Going to the Quillersedge woods, more like.

Tremayne had gone to Oxford to his tailor. Mackie was out to lunch with Dee-Dee. Gareth was at school.

I'd abandoned the empty house and walked joyfully into the woods and only by chance did I know what had hit me.

I imagined Perkin threading along that trail at night, following the paint quite easily as he'd been that way already in daylight, and being secretly pleased with himself because if he had inadvertently left any traces of his passage the first time they could be explained away naturally by the second. That satisfaction would smartly have evaporated when he reached the clearing and found me gone. A nasty shock, one might say. He might have been intending to go back to his family and appear utterly horrified while breaking the news of my death. Instead, he'd looked shocked and utterly horrified at seeing me still alive. Open-mouthed. Speechless. Too bad.

If I'd tried to walk out along the trail, I would have met Perkin face to face.

I shivered in the warm hospital room. Some things were better unimagined.

For Perkin, making arrows would have been like filing his nails, and he'd had a stove right in his workroom for the charring. He must have constructed a pretty good strong bow too (according to my detailed instructions) which would by now no doubt be broken into unidentifiable pieces in distant undergrowth, Perhaps he'd risked time to practise with a few shots before I got there. Couldn't tell unless I went back to look for spent arrows, which I wasn't going to do.

Random thoughts edged slowly into my mind for the rest of the day.

For instance, Perkin thought in wood, like a language. Any trap he made would be wooden.

Nolan had knocked Perkin down at Tremayne's dinner. I'd picked Nolan up and made a fool of him. Perkin wouldn't have risked any way to kill me that meant creeping up on me, not after what he'd seen.

Perkin had had to get over the shock of finding my familiar ski-jacket and boots in the boathouse and then the far worse shock of the cataclysmic reversal of his scheme when Harry and I both lived.

The best actor of them all, he had contained those shocks within himself with no screaming crises of nerves. Many a convicted murderer had displayed that sort of control. Maybe it was something to do with a divorce from reality. There were books on the subject. One day I might read them.

Perkin had resented Mackie's friendly feelings towards me. Not strongly enough to kill me for that, but certainly strongly enough to make killing me satisfying in that respect also.

Never assume . . .

Perkin had always been presumed to be busy in his workshop, and yet there were hours and days when he might not have been, when Mackie was out of the house seeing to the horses. On the Wednesday of Harry's trap, Mackie had been saddling Tremayne's runner in the three-mile chase at Ascot.

Perkin had made none of the classic mistakes. Hadn't scattered monogrammed handkerchiefs about or faked alibis or carelessly dropped dated train tickets or shown knowledge he shouldn't have had. Perkin had listened more than he'd talked, and he'd been cunning and careful.

I thought of Angela Brickell and of all the afternoons Perkin had spent alone in the house. She had tried to seduce even Gareth. Not hard to imagine she'd set her sights also on Perkin. Intelligent men in love with their wives weren't immune to blatantly offered temptations. Sudden arousal. Quick, casual gratification. End of episode.

Except not the end of the episode if there were a failure of a birth control measure and the result was conception. Not the end if the woman asked for money or threatened disclosure. Not the end if she could and would destroy the man's marriage.

Say Angela Brickell had definitely been pregnant. Say she was sure who the father was; and working in a racing stable with thoroughbreds she would know that proving paternity was increasingly an exact science. The father wouldn't be able to deny it. Say she enticed him into the woods and became demanding in every way and heavily emotional, piling on pressure.

Perkin had not long before seen Olympia lying dead at Nolan's feet. He'd heard over and over again how fast she'd died. Say that picture, that certainty, had flashed into his mind. The quick way out of all his troubles lay in his own two strong hands.

I imagined what Perkin might have been feeling. Might have been facing.

Mackie at that time had been unable to conceive and was troubled and unhappy because of it. Angela Brickell however was devastatingly carrying Perkin's child. Perkin loved Mackie and all too probably couldn't face her knowing what he'd done. Couldn't bear to hurt her so abominably. Was perhaps ashamed. Didn't want his father to find out.

Irresistible solution: a fast death for Angela too. Easy.

Perhaps he, not she, had chosen the woods. Perhaps he'd planned it, perhaps it hadn't been a lightning urge but the first of his traps.

Impossible to know now if either scenario were right. Possible, likely, probable; no more than one of those.

I wondered if he had gone home feeling anything but relief.

Long before Doone came knocking on the door, Perkin could have decided, in case the girl's body were ever found, to say he didn't remember her. No one had thought it odd that he didn't; he was seldom seen with the horses.

His one catastrophic mistake had been to try to settle the mystery for ever by making Harry disappear.

By his actions shall you know him . . .

By his arrows.

I thought that Doone would not think of looking in Perkin's workroom for a match to the arrow's wood. Perkin hadn't had much time to hunt elsewhere for anything suitable. He would have used a common wood, not exotic; but all the same there would be more of it to be found, perhaps even in the cabinet he was making of bleached oak.

He hadn't had any handy feathers, so no flights.

Perkin would have known that a wood match could be made. He knew more about wood than anyone else.

Doone, with his promise of instant detection once I woke up, must have been the end of hope.

He did love Mackie. His universe was lost. One way out remained.

I thought of Tremayne and his pride in Perkin's work. Thought of Gareth's vulnerable age. Thought of Mackie, her face alive with the wondrous joy of discovering she was pregnant. Thought of that child growing up, loved and safe.

Nothing could be gained by trying to prove what Perkin had done. Much would be smashed. They all would suffer. The families always suffered most.

No child would become a secure and balanced adult with a known murderer for a father. Without knowledge, Mackie's grief would heal normally in time. Tremayne and Gareth wouldn't be crippled by undeserved shame. All of them would live more happily if they and the world remained in ignorance, and try to achieve that I would give them the one gift I could.

Silence.

At the short uncomplicated inquest on Perkin a week later the coroner found unhesitatingly for 'Accident' and expressed sympathy with the family. Tremayne came to collect me from the hospital afterwards and told me on the way to Shellerton that Mackie had got through the court ordeal bravely.

'The baby?' I asked.

'The baby's fine. It's what's giving Mackie strength. She says Perkin is with her, will always be with her that way.'

'Mm.'

Tremayne glanced briefly across at me and back to the road.

'Has Doone found out yet who put that arrow through you?' he asked.

'I don't think so,' I said.

'You don't know, yourself?'

'No.'

He drove for a while in silence.

'I just wondered . . .' he said uncertainly.

After a while I said, 'Doone came to see me twice. I told him I didn't know who shot me. I told him I had no ideas of any sort any more.'

I certainly hadn't told him where to look for arrow wood.

Doone had been disgustedly disillusioned with me: I had closed ranks with *them*, he said. Goodhavens, Everards, Vickers and Kendall. 'Yes,' I'd agreed, 'I'm sorry.' Doone said there was no way of proving who had killed Angela Brickell. 'Let her lie,' I said, nodding. After a silence he'd risen greyly to his feet to leave and told me to look after myself. Wryly I'd said, 'I will.' He'd gone slowly, regretfully, seeing regret in my face also, an unexpected mutual liking, slipping away into memory.

'You don't think,' Tremayne said painfully, 'I mean, it had to be someone who knew you would fetch Gareth's camera, who shot you.'

'I told Doone it was a kid playing Robin Hood.'

'I'm . . . afraid . . .'

'Block it out,' I said. 'Some kid did it.'

'John . . .'

He knew, I thought. He was no fool. He could have worked things out the same way I had, and he'd have had a hellish time believing it all of his own son.

'About my book,' he said hesitating, 'I don't know that I want to go on with it.'

'I'm going to write it,' I said positively. 'It's going to be an affirmation of your life and your worth, just as was intended. It's all the more important now, for you especially, but for Gareth, for Mackie and your new grandchild as well. For you and for them, it's essential I do it.'

'You do know,' he said.

'It was a kid.'

He drove without speaking the rest of the way.

Fiona and Harry were with Mackie and Gareth in the family room. Perkin's absence was to me almost a shock, so accustomed had I become to his being there. Mackie looked pale but in charge of things, greeting me with a sisterly kiss.

'Hi,' Gareth said, very cool.

'Hi yourself.'

'I've got the day off from school.'

'Great.'

Harry said, 'How are you feeling?' and Fiona put her arms carefully round me and let her scent drift in my senses.

Harry said his Aunt Erica sent good wishes, his eyes ironic.

I asked Harry how his leg was. All on the surface and polite.

Mackie brought cups of tea for everyone; a very English balm in troubles. I remembered the way Harry had laced the coffee after the ditch, and would have preferred that, on the whole.

It was a month yesterday, I thought, that I came here.

A month in the country . . .

Harry said, 'Has anyone found out who shot at you?'

He was asking a simple unloaded question, not like Tremayne. I gave him a simple answer, the one that eventually became officially accepted.

'Doone is considering it was a child playing out a fantasy,' I said. 'Robin Hood, Cowboys and Indians. That sort of thing. No hope of ever really knowing.'

'Awful,' Mackie said, remembering.

I looked at her with affection and Tremayne patted my shoulder and told them I would be staying on as arranged to write his book.

They all seemed pleased, as if I belonged; but I knew I would leave them again before summer, would walk out of the brightly-lit play, and go back to the shadows and solitude of fiction. It was a compulsion I'd starved for, and even if I never went hungry again I would feel that compulsion for ever. I couldn't understand it or analyse it, but it was there.

After a while I left the family room and wandered through the great central hall and on into the far side of the house, into Perkin's workroom.

It smelled aromatically and only of wood. Tools lay neatly as always. The glue-pot was cold on the stove. Everything had been cleaned and tidied and there were no stains on the polished floor to show where his life had pumped out.

I felt no hatred for him. I thought instead of the extinction of his soaring talent. Thought of consequences and seduction. What's done is done, Tremayne would say, but one couldn't wipe out an enveloping feeling of pathetic waste.

A copy of *Return Safe from the Wilderness* lay on a workbench, and I picked it up idly and looked through it.

Traps. Bows and arrows. All the familiar ideas.

I flipped the pages resignedly and they fell open as if from use at the diagram in the first-aid section showing the pressure points for stopping arterial bleeding. I stared blankly at the carefully drawn and accurate illustration of exactly where the main arteries could be found nearest the surface in the arms and wrists . . . and in the legs.

Dear God, I thought numbly. I taught him that too.

STRAIGHT

My thanks especially to

JOSEPH and DANIELLE ZERGER
of ZARLENE IMPORTS
dealers in semi-precious stones

and also to

MARY BROMILEY – ankle specialist

BARRY PARK – veterinary surgeon

JEREMY THOMPSON – doctor, pharmacologist

ANDREW HEWSON – literary agent

and as always to

MERRICK and FELIX, our sons.

All the people in this story are imaginary.
All the gadgets exist.

CHAPTER ONE

I inherited my brother's life. Inherited his desk, his business, his gadgets, his enemies, his horses and his mistress. I inherited my brother's life, and it nearly killed me.

I was thirty-four at the time and walking about on elbow crutches owing to a serious disagreement with the last fence in a steeplechase at Cheltenham. If you've never felt your ankle explode, don't try it. As usual it hadn't been the high-speed tumble that had done the damage but the half-ton of one of the other runners coming over the fence after me, his forefoot landing squarely on my boot on the baked earth of an Indian summer. The hoof mark was imprinted on the leather. The doctor who cut the boot off handed it to me as a souvenir. Medical minds have a macabre sense of humour.

Two days after this occurrence, while I was reluctantly coming to terms with the fact that I was going to miss at least six weeks of the steeplechasing season and with them possibly my last chance of making it to champion again (the middle thirties being the beginning of the end for jump jockeys), I answered the telephone for about the tenth time that morning and found it was not another friend ringing to commiserate.

'Could I speak,' a female voice asked, 'to Derek Franklin?'

'I'm Derek Franklin,' I said.

'Right.' She was both brisk and hesitant, and one could understand why. 'We have you listed,' she said, 'as your brother Greville's next of kin.'

Those three words, I thought with an accelerating heart, must be among the most ominous in the language.

I said slowly, not wanting to know, 'What's happened?'

'I'm speaking from St Catherine's Hospital, Ipswich. Your brother is here, in the intensive care unit . . .'

At least he was alive, I thought numbly.

'. . . and the doctors think you should be told.'

'How is he?'

'I'm sorry I haven't seen him. This is the almoner's office. But I understand that his condition is very serious.'

'What's the matter with him?'

'He was involved in an accident,' she said. 'He has multiple injuries and is on life support.'

'I'll come,' I said.

'Yes. It might be best.'

I thanked her, not knowing exactly what for, and put

down the receiver, taking the shock physically in light-headedness and a constricted throat.

He would be all right, I told myself. Intensive care meant simply that he was being carefully looked after. He would recover, of course.

I shut out the anxiety to work prosaically instead on the practicalities of getting from Hungerford in Berkshire, where I lived, to Ipswich in Suffolk, about a hundred and fifty miles across country, with a crunched ankle. It was fortunately the left ankle, which meant I would soon be able to drive my automatic gears without trouble, but it was on that particular day at peak discomfort and even with painkillers and icepacks was hot, swollen and throbbing. I couldn't move it without holding my breath, and that was partly my own fault.

Owing to my hatred – not to say phobia – about the damaging immobility of plaster of Paris I had spent a good deal of the previous day persuading a long-suffering orthopaedic surgeon to give me the support of a plain crêpe bandage instead of imprisonment in a cast. He was himself a plate-and-screw man by preference and had grumbled as usual at my request. Such a bandage as I was demanding might be better in the end for one's muscles, but it gave no protection against knocks, as he had reminded me on other occasions, and it would be more painful, he said.

'I'll be racing much quicker with a bandage.'

'It's time you stopped breaking your bones,' he said, giving in with a shrug and a sigh and obligingly winding

433

the crêpe on tightly. 'One of these days you'll crack something serious.'

'I don't actually like breaking them.'

'At least I haven't had to pin anything this time,' he said. 'And you're mad.'

'Yes. Thanks very much.'

'Go home and rest it. Give those ligaments a chance.'

The ligaments took their chance along the back seat of my car while Brad, an unemployed welder, drove it to Ipswich. Brad, taciturn and obstinate, was unemployed by habit and choice but made a scratchy living doing odd jobs in the neighbourhood for anyone willing to endure his moods. As I much preferred his long silences to his infrequent conversation, we got along fine. He looked forty, hadn't reached thirty, and lived with his mother.

He found St Catherine's Hospital without much trouble and at the door helped me out and handed me the crutches, saying he would park and sit inside the reception area and I could take my time. He had waited for me similarly for hours the day before, expressing neither impatience nor sympathy but simply being restfully and neutrally morose.

The intensive care unit proved to be guarded by brisk nurses who looked at the crutches and said I'd come to the wrong department, but once I'd persuaded them of my identity they kitted me sympathetically with a mask and gown and let me in to see Greville.

I had vaguely expected Intensive Care to involve a

lot of bright lights and clanging bustle, but I found that it didn't, or at least not in that room in that hospital. The light was dim, the atmosphere peaceful, the noise level, once my ears adjusted to it, just above silence but lower than identification.

Greville lay alone in the room on a high bed with wires and tubes all over the place. He was naked except for a strip of sheeting lying loosely across his loins and they had shaved half the hair off his head. Other evidences of surgery marched like centipede tracks across his abdomen and down one thigh, and there were darkening bruises everywhere.

Behind his bed a bank of screens showed blank rectangular faces, as the information from the electrodes fed into other screens in a room directly outside. He didn't need, they said, an attendant constantly beside him, but they kept an eye on his reactions all the time.

He was unconscious, his face pale and calm, his head turned slightly towards the door as if expecting visitors. Decompression procedures had been performed on his skull, and that wound was covered by a large padded dressing which seemed more like a pillow to support him.

Greville Saxony Franklin, my brother. Nineteen years my senior; not expected to live. It had to be faced. To be accepted.

'Hi, guy,' I said.

It was an Americanism he himself used often, but it produced no response. I touched his hand, which was warm and relaxed, the nails, as always, clean and cared for. He had a pulse, he had circulation: his heart beat by electrical stimulus. Air went in and out of his lungs mechanically through a tube in his throat. Inside his head the synapses were shutting down. Where was his soul, I wondered: where was the intelligent, persistent, energetic spirit? Did he know that he was dying?

I didn't want just to leave him. No one should die alone. I went outside and said so.

A doctor in a green overall replied that when all the remaining brain activity had ceased, they would ask my consent before switching off the machines. I was welcome to be with my brother at this crisis point as well as before. 'But death,' he said austerely, 'will be for him an infinitesimal process, not a definitive moment.' He paused. 'There is a waiting room along the hall, with coffee and things.'

Bathos and drama, I thought: his everyday life. I crutched all the way down to the general reception area, found Brad, gave him an update and told him I might be a long time. All night, perhaps.

He waved a permissive hand. He would be around, he said, or he would leave a message at the desk. Either way, I could reach him. I nodded and went back upstairs, and found the waiting room already occupied by a very young couple engulfed in grief, whose baby was hanging on to life by threads not much stronger than Greville's.

The room itself was bright, comfortable and impersonal, and I listened to the mother's slow sobs and thought of the misery that soaked daily into those walls. Life has a way of kicking one along like a football, or so I've found. Fate had never dealt me personally a particularly easy time, but that was OK, that was normal. Most people, it seemed to me, took their turn to be football. Most survived. Some didn't.

Greville had simply been in the wrong place at the wrong time. From the scrappy information known to the hospital, I gleaned that he had been walking down Ipswich High Street when some scaffolding that was being dismantled had fallen on him from a considerable height. One of the construction workers had been killed, and a second had been taken to hospital with a broken hip.

I had been given my brother's clinical details. One metal bar had pierced his stomach, another had torn into his leg, something heavy had fallen on his head and caused brain damage with massive cerebral bleeding. It had happened late the previous afternoon, he had been deeply unconscious from the moment of the impact and he hadn't been identified until workmen dealing with the rubble in the morning had found his diary and given it to the police.

'Wallet?' I asked.

No, no wallet. Just the diary with, neatly filled in on the first page, next of kin, Derek Franklin, brother; telephone number supplied. Before that, they had no

437

clue except the initials G.S.F. embroidered above the pocket of his torn and blood-stained shirt.

'A *silk* shirt,' a nurse added disapprovingly, as if monogrammed silk shirts were somehow immoral.

'Nothing else in his pockets?' I asked.

'A bunch of keys and a handkerchief. That was all. You'll be given them, of course, along with the diary and his watch and signet ring.'

I nodded. No need to ask when.

The afternoon stretched out, strange and unreal, a time-warped limbo. I went again to spend some time with Greville, but he lay unmoving, oblivious in his dwindling twilight, already subtly not himself. If Wordsworth were right about immortality, it was the sleep and the forgetting that were slipping away and reawakening that lay ahead, and maybe I should be glad for him, not grieve.

I thought of him as he had been, and of our lives as brothers. We had never lived together in a family unit because, by the time I was born, he was away at university, building a life of his own. By the time I was six, he had married, by the time I was ten, he'd divorced. For years he was a semi-stranger whom I met briefly at family gatherings, celebrations which grew less and less frequent as our parents aged and died, and which stopped altogether when the two sisters who bridged the gap between Greville and me both emigrated, one to Australia and one to Japan.

It wasn't until I'd reached twenty-eight myself that

after a long Christmas-and-birthday-card politeness we'd met unexpectedly on a railway platform and during the journey ahead had become friends. Not close time-sharing friends even then, but positive enough for telephoning each other sporadically and exchanging restaurant dinners and feeling good about it.

We had been brought up in different environments, Greville in the Regency London house which went with our father's job as manager of one of the great landowning estates, I in the comfortable country cottage of his retirement. Greville had been taken by our mother to museums, art galleries and the theatre: I had been given ponies.

We didn't even look much alike. Greville, like our father, was six feet tall, I three inches shorter. Greville's hair, now greying, had been light brown and straight, mine darker brown and curly. We had both inherited amber eyes and good teeth from our mother and a tendency to leanness from our father, but our faces, though both tidy enough, were quite different.

Greville best remembered our parents' vigorous years; I'd been with them through their illnesses and deaths. Our father had himself been twenty years older than our mother, and she had died first, which had seemed monstrously unfair. The old man and I had lived briefly together after that in tolerant mutual non-comprehension, though I had no doubt that he'd loved me, in his way. He had been sixty-two when I was born and he died on my eighteenth birthday, leaving me a fund for my continued education and a letter of admonitions and instructions, some of which I'd carried out.

Greville's stillness was absolute. I shifted uncomfortably on the crutches and thought of asking for a chair. I wouldn't see him smile again, I thought: not the lightening of the eyes and the gleam of teeth, the quick appreciation of the black humour of life, the awareness of his own power.

He was a magistrate, a justice of the peace, and he imported and sold semi-precious stones. Beyond these bare facts I knew few details of his day-to-day existence, as whenever we met it seemed that he was always more interested in my doings than his own. He had himself owned horses from the day he telephoned to ask my opinion: someone who owed him money had offered his racehorse to settle the debt. What did I think? I told him I'd phone back, looked up the horse, thought it was a bargain and told Greville to go right ahead if he felt like it.

'Don't see why not,' he'd said. 'Will you fix the paperwork?'

I'd said yes, of course. It wasn't hard for anyone to say yes to my brother Greville: much harder to say no.

The horse had won handsomely and given him a taste for future ownership, though he seldom went to see his horses run, which wasn't particularly unusual in an owner but always to me mystifying. He refused absolutely to own jumpers on the grounds that he might buy something that would kill me. I was too big for Flat races; he'd felt safe with those. I couldn't persuade him that I would like to ride for him and in the end I stopped trying. When Greville made up his mind he was unshakable.

Every ten minutes or so a nurse would come quietly into the room to stand for a short while beside the bed, checking that all the electrodes and tubes were still in order. She gave me brief smiles and commented once that my brother was unaware of my presence and could not be comforted by my being there.

'It's as much for me as for him,' I said.

She nodded and went away, and I stayed for a couple more hours, leaning against a wall and reflecting that it was ironic that it was he who should meet death by chance when it was I who actively risked it half the days of the year.

Strange to reflect also, looking back now to that lengthening evening, that I gave no thought to the consequences of his death. The present was vividly alive still in the silent diminishing hours, and all I saw in the future was a pretty dreary programme of form-filling and funeral arrangements, which I didn't bother to think about in any detail. I would have to telephone the sisters, I vaguely supposed, and there might be a little long-distance grief, but I knew they would say, 'You can see to it, can't you? Whatever you decide will be all right with us,' and they wouldn't come back halfway round the world to stand in mournful drizzle at the graveside of a brother they'd seen perhaps twice in ten years.

Beyond that, I considered nothing. The tie of common blood was all that truly linked Greville and me, and once it was undone there would be nothing left of him but memory. With regret I watched the pulse that flickered in his throat. When it was gone I would go back to my own life and think of him warmly sometimes, and remember this night with overall sorrow, but no more.

I went along to the waiting room for a while to rest my legs. The desperate young parents were still there, hollow-eyed and entwined, but presently a sombre nurse came to fetch them, and in the distance, shortly after, I heard the rising wail of the mother's agonized loss. I felt my own tears prickle for her, a stranger. A dead baby, a dying brother, a universal uniting misery. I grieved for Greville most intensely then because of the death of the child, and realized I had been wrong about the sorrow level. I would miss him very much.

I put my ankle up on a chair and fitfully dozed, and sometime before daybreak the same nurse with the same expression came to fetch me in my turn.

I followed her along the passage and into Greville's room. There was much more light in there this time, and more people, and the bank of monitoring screens behind the bed had been switched on. Pale greenish lines moved across them, some in regular spasms, some uncompromisingly straight.

I didn't need to be told, but they explained all the same. The straight lines were the sum of the activity in Greville's brain. None at all.

There was no private goodbye. There was no point. I was there, and that was enough. They asked for, and received, my agreement to the disconnection of the machines, and presently the pulsing lines straightened out also, and whatever had been in the quiet body was there no longer.

It took a long time to get anything done in the morning because it turned out to be Sunday.

I thought back, having lost count of time. Thursday when I broke my ankle, Friday when the scaffolding fell on Greville, Saturday when Brad drove me to Ipswich. It all seemed a cosmos away: relativity in action.

There was the possibility, it seemed, of the scaffolding constructors being liable for damages. It was suggested that I should consult a solicitor.

Plodding through the paperwork, trying to make decisions, I realized that I didn't know what Greville would want. If he'd left a will somewhere, maybe he had given instructions that I ought to carry out. Maybe no one but I, I thought with a jolt, actually knew he was dead. There had to be people I should notify, and I didn't know who.

I asked if I could have the diary the police had found in the rubble, and presently I was given not only the diary but everything else my brother had had with him: keys, watch, handkerchief, signet ring, a small amount of change, shoes, socks, jacket. The rest of his clothes, torn and drenched with blood, had been incinerated, it appeared. I was required to sign for what I was taking, putting a tick against each item.

Everything had been tipped out of the large brown plastic bag in which they had been stored. The bag said 'St Catherine's Hospital' in white on the sides. I put the shoes, socks, handkerchief and jacket back into the bag and pulled the strings tight again, then I shovelled the large bunch of keys into my own trouser pocket, along with the watch, the ring and the money, and finally consulted the diary.

On the front page he had entered his name, his London home telephone number and his office number, but no addresses. It was near the bottom, where there was a space headed 'In case of accident please notify', that he had written 'Derek Franklin, brother, next of kin.'

The diary itself was one I had sent him at Christmas: the racing diary put out by the Jockeys' Association and the Injured Jockeys' Fund. That he should have chosen to use that particular diary when he must have been given several others I found unexpectedly moving. That he had put my name in it made me wonder what he had really thought of me; whether there was much we might have been to each other, and had missed.

With regret I put the diary into my other trouser pocket. The next morning, I supposed, I would have to telephone his office with the dire news. I couldn't forewarn anyone as I didn't know the names, let alone the phone numbers, of the people who worked for him. I knew only that he had no partners, as he had said several times that the only way he could run his business was by himself. Partners too often came to blows, he said, and he would have none of it.

When all the signing was completed, I looped the strings of the plastic bag a couple of times round my wrist and took it and myself on the crutches down to the reception area, which was more or less deserted on that early Sunday morning. Brad wasn't there, nor was there any message from him at the desk, so I simply sat down and waited. I had no doubt he would come back in his own good time, glowering as usual, and eventually he did, slouching in through the door with no sign of haste.

He saw me across the acreage, came to within ten feet, and said, 'Shall I fetch the car, then?' and when I nodded, wheeled away and departed. A man of very few words, Brad. I followed slowly in his wake, the plastic bag bumping against the crutch. If I'd thought faster I would have given it to Brad to carry, but I didn't seem to be thinking fast in any way.

Outside, the October sun was bright and warm. I breathed the sweet air, took a few steps away from the door and patiently waited some more, and was totally unprepared to be savagely mugged.

I scarcely saw who did it. One moment I was upright, leaning without concentration on the crutches, the next I'd received a battering-ram shove in the back and was sprawling face forward onto the hard black surface of the entrance drive. To try to save myself, I put my left foot down instinctively and it twisted beneath me, which was excruciating and useless. I fell flat down on my stomach in a haze and I hardly cared when someone kicked one of the fallen crutches away along the ground and tugged at the bag around my wrist.

He ... it had to be a he, I thought, from the speed and strength ... thumped a foot down on my back and put his weight on it. He yanked my arm up and back roughly, and cut through the plastic with a slash that took some of my skin with it. I scarcely felt it. The messages from my ankle obliterated all else.

A voice approached saying, 'Hey! Hey!' urgently, and my attacker lifted himself off me as fast as he'd arrived and sped away.

It was Brad who had come to my rescue. On any other day there might have been people constantly coming and going, but not on Sunday morning. No one else seemed to be around to notice a thing. No one but Brad had come running.

'Friggin' hell,' Brad said from above me. 'Are you all right?'

Far from it, I thought.

He went to fetch the scattered crutch and brought it

back. 'Your hand's bleeding,' he said with disbelief. 'Don't you want to stand up?'

I wasn't too sure that I did, but it seemed the only thing to do. When I'd made it to a moderately vertical position he looked impassively at my face and gave it as his opinion that we ought to go back into the hospital. As I didn't feel like arguing, that's what we did.

I sat on the end of one of the empty rows of seats and waited for the tide of woe to recede, and when I had more command of things I went across to the desk and explained what had happened.

The woman behind the reception window was horrified.

'Someone stole your plastic bag!' she said, round-eyed. 'I mean, everyone around here knows what those bags signify, they're always used for the belongings of people who've died or come here after accidents. I mean, everyone knows they can contain wallets and jewellery and so on, but I've never heard of one being snatched. How awful! How much did you lose? You'd better report it to the police.'

The futility of it shook me with weariness. Some punk had taken a chance that the dead man's effects would be worth the risk, and the police would take notes and chalk it up among the majority of unsolved muggings. I reckoned I'd fallen into the ultra-vulnerable bracket which included little old ladies, and however much I might wince at the thought, I on my crutches had looked and been a pushover, literally.

I shuffled painfully into the washroom and ran cold water over my slowly bleeding hand, and found that the cut was more extensive than deep and could sensibly be classified as a scratch. With a sigh, I dabbed a paper towel on the scarlety oozing spots and unwound the cut-off pieces of white and brown plastic which were still wrapped tightly round my wrist, throwing them in the bin. What a bloody stupid anti-climactic postscript, I thought tiredly, to the accident that had taken my brother.

When I went outside Brad said with a certain amount of anxiety, 'You going to the police, then?' and he relaxed visibly when I shook my head and said, 'Not unless you can give them a detailed description of who-ever attacked me.'

I couldn't tell from his expression whether he could or not. I thought I might ask him later, on the way home, but when I did, all that he said was, 'He had jeans on, and one of them woolly hats. And he had a knife. I didn't see his face, he sort of had his back turned my way, but the sun flashed on the knife, see? It all went down so fast. I did think you were a goner. Then he ran off with the bag. You were dead lucky, I'd say.'

I didn't feel lucky, but all things were relative.

Brad, having contributed what was for him a long speech, relapsed into his more normal silence, and I wondered what the mugger would think of the worth-less haul of shoes, socks, handkerchief and jacket whose loss hadn't been realistically worth reporting. Whatever of value Greville had set out with would have been in his wallet, which had fallen to an earlier predator.

I had been wearing, was still wearing, a shirt, tie and sweater, but no jacket. A sweater was better with the crutches than a jacket. It was pointless to wonder whether the thief would have dipped into my trouser pockets if Brad hadn't shouted. Pointless to wonder if he would have put his blade through my ribs. There was no way of knowing. I did know I couldn't have stopped him, but his prize in any case would have been meagre. Apart from Greville's things I was carrying only a credit card and a few notes in a small folder, from a habit of travelling light.

I stopped thinking about it and instead, to take my mind off the ankle, wondered what Greville had been doing in Ipswich.

Wondered if, ever since Friday, anyone had been waiting for him to arrive. Wondered how he had got there. Wondered if he had parked his car somewhere there and, if so, how I would find it, considering I didn't know its number and wasn't even sure if he still had a Porsche. Someone else would know, I thought easily. His office, his local garage, a friend. It wasn't really my worry.

By the time we reached Hungerford three hours later, Brad had said, in addition, only that the car was running out of juice (which we remedied) and, half an hour from home, that if I wanted him to go on driving me during the following week, he would be willing.

'Seven-thirty tomorrow morning?' I suggested, reflecting, and he said 'Yerss' on a growl which I took to mean assent.

He drove me to my door, helped me out as before, handed me the crutches, locked the car and put the keys into my hand all without speaking.

'Thanks,' I said.

He ducked his head, not meeting my eyes, and turned and shambled off on foot towards his mother's house. I watched him go; a shy difficult man with no social skills who had possibly that morning saved my life.

CHAPTER TWO

I had for three years rented the ground floor of an old house in a turning off the main road through the ancient country town. There was a bedroom and bathroom facing the street and the sunrise, and a large all-purpose room to the rear into which the sunset flooded. Beyond that, a small stream-bordered garden which I shared with the owners of the house, an elderly couple upstairs.

Brad's mother had cooked and cleaned for them for years; Brad mended, painted and chopped when he felt like it. Soon after I'd moved in, mother and son had casually extended their services to me, which suited me well. It was all in all an easy uncluttered existence, but if home was where the heart was, I really lived out on the windy Downs and in stable yards and on the raucous racetracks where I worked.

I let myself into the quiet rooms and sat with ice-packs along a sofa, watching the sun go down on the far side of the stream and thinking I might have done better to stay in the Ipswich hospital. From the knee down my left leg was hurting abominably, and it was still getting

451

clearer by the minute that falling had intensified Thursday's damage disastrously. My own surgeon had been going off to Wales for the weekend, but I doubted that he would have done very much except say 'I told you so', so in the end I simply took another Distalgesic and changed the icepacks and worked out the time zones in Tokyo and Sydney.

At midnight I telephoned to those cities where it was already morning and by good luck reached both of the sisters. 'Poor Greville,' they said sadly, and, 'Do whatever you think best.' 'Send some flowers for us.' 'Let us know how it goes.'

I would, I said. Poor Greville, they repeated, meaning it, and said they would love to see me in Tokyo, in Sydney, whenever. Their children, they said, were all fine. Their husbands were fine. Was I fine? Poor, poor Greville.

I put the receiver down ruefully. Families did scatter, and some scattered more than most. I knew the sisters by that time only through the photographs they sometimes sent at Christmas. They hadn't recognized my voice.

Taking things slowly in the morning, as nothing was much better, I dressed for the day in shirt, tie and sweater as before, with a shoe on the right foot, sock alone on the left, and was ready when Brad arrived five minutes early.

'We're going to London,' I said. 'Here's a map with the place marked. Do you think you can find it?'

'Got a tongue in my head,' he said, peering at the maze of roads. 'Reckon so.'

'Give it a go, then.'

He nodded, helped me inch onto the back seat, and drove seventy miles through the heavy morning traffic in silence. Then, by dint of shouting at street vendors via the driver's window, he zig-zagged across Holborn, took a couple of wrong turns, righted himself, and drew up with a jerk in a busy street round the corner from Hatton Garden.

'That's it,' he said, pointing. 'Number fifty-six. That office block.'

'Brilliant.'

He helped me out, gave me the crutches, and came with me to hold open the heavy glass entrance door. Inside, behind a desk, was a man in a peaked cap personifying security who asked me forbiddingly what floor I wanted.

'Saxony Franklin,' I said.

'Name?' he asked, consulting a list.

'Franklin.'

'Your name, I mean.'

I explained who I was. He raised his eyebrows, picked up a telephone, pressed a button and said, 'A Mr Franklin is on his way up.'

Brad asked where he could park the car and was told

453

there was a yard round the back. He would wait for me, he said. No hurry. No problem.

The office building, which was modern, had been built rubbing shoulders to the sixth floor with Victorian curlicued neighbours, soaring free to the tenth with a severe lot of glass.

Saxony Franklin was on the eighth floor, it appeared. I went up in a smooth lift and elbowed my way through some heavy double doors into a lobby furnished with a reception desk, several armchairs for waiting in and two policemen.

Behind the policemen was a middle-aged woman who looked definitely flustered.

I thought immediately that news of Greville's death had already arrived and that I probably hadn't needed to come, but it seemed the Force was there for a different reason entirely.

The flustered lady gave me a blank stare and said, 'That's not Mr Franklin. The guard said Mr Franklin was on his way up.'

I allayed the police suspicions a little by saying again that I was Greville Franklin's brother.

'Oh,' said the woman. 'Yes, he does have a brother.'

They all swept their gaze over my comparative immobility.

'Mr Franklin isn't here yet,' the woman told me.

'Er . . .' I said, 'what's going on?'

They all looked disinclined to explain. I said to her, 'I'm afraid I don't know your name.'

'Adams,' she said distractedly. 'Annette Adams. I'm your brother's personal assistant.'

'I'm sorry,' I said slowly, 'but my brother won't be coming at all today. He was involved in an accident.'

Annette Adams heard the bad news in my voice. She put a hand over her heart in the classic gesture as if to hold it still in her chest and with anxiety said, 'What sort of accident? A car crash? Is he hurt?'

She saw the answer clearly in my expression and with her free hand felt for one of the armchairs, buckling into it with shock.

'He died in hospital yesterday morning,' I said to her and to the policemen, 'after some scaffolding fell on him last Friday. I was with him in the hospital.'

One of the policemen pointed at my dangling foot. 'You were injured at the same time, sir?'

'No. This was different. I didn't see his accident. I meant, I was there when he died. The hospital sent for me.'

The two policemen consulted each other's eyes and decided after all to say why they were there.

'These offices were broken into during the weekend, sir. Mrs Adams here discovered it when she arrived early for work, and she called us in.'

'What does it matter? It doesn't matter now,' the lady said, growing paler.

'There's a good deal of mess,' the policeman went on, 'and Mrs Adams doesn't know what's been stolen. We were waiting for your brother to tell us.'

455

'Oh dear, oh dear,' said Annette, gulping.

'Is there anyone else here?' I asked her. 'Someone who could get you a cup of tea?' Before you faint, I thought, but didn't say it.

She nodded a fraction, glancing at a door behind the desk, and I swung over there and tried to open it. It wouldn't open: the knob wouldn't turn.

'It's electronic,' Annette said weakly. 'You have to put in the right numbers . . .' She flopped her head back against the chair and said she couldn't remember what today's number was; it was changed often. She and the policemen had come through it, it seemed, and let it swing shut behind them.

One of the policemen came over and pounded on the door with his fist, shouting 'Police' very positively which had the desired effect like a reflex. Without finesse he told the much younger woman who stood there framed in the doorway that her boss was dead and that Mrs Adams was about to pass out and was needing some strong hot sweet tea, love, like five minutes ago.

Wild-eyed, the young woman retreated to spread more consternation behind the scenes and the police-man nullified the firm's defences by wedging the electronic door open, using the chair from behind the reception desk.

I took in a few more details of the surroundings, beyond my first impression of grey. On the light greenish-grey of the carpet stood the armchairs in char-coal and the desk in matt black unpainted and unpolished wood. The walls, palest grey, were hung with a series of framed geological maps, the frames black and narrow and uniform in size. The propped-open door, and another similar door to one side, still closed, were painted the same colour as the walls. The total effect, lit by recessed spotlights in the ceiling, looked both straightforward and immensely sophisticated, a true representation of my brother.

Mrs Annette Adams, still flaccid from too many unpleasant surprises on a Monday morning, wore a cream shirt, a charcoal grey skirt and a string of knobbly pearls. She was dark haired, in her late forties, perhaps, and from the starkness in her eyes, just beginning to realize, I guessed, that the upheaval of the present would be permanent.

The younger woman returned effectively with a scarlet steaming mug and Annette Adams sipped from it obediently for a while, listening to the policemen telling me that the intruder had not come in this way up the front lift, which was for visitors, but up another lift at the rear of the building which was used by the staff of all floors of offices, and for freight. That lift went down into a rear lobby which, in its turn, led out to the yard where cars and vans were parked: where Brad was presumably waiting at that moment.

The intruder had apparently ridden to the tenth floor, climbed some service stairs to the roof, and by some means had come down outside the building to the eighth floor, where he had smashed a window to let himself in.

'What sort of means?' I asked.

'We don't know, sir. Whatever it was, he took it with him. Maybe a rope.' He shrugged. 'We've had only a quick preliminary look around up there. We wanted to know what's been stolen before we ... er ... See, we don't want to waste our time for nothing.'

I nodded. Like Greville's stolen shoes, I thought.

'This whole area round Hatton Garden is packed with the jewel trade. We get break-ins, or attempted break-ins, all the time.'

The other policeman said, 'This place here is loaded with stones, of course, but the vault's still shut and Mrs Adams says nothing seems to be missing from the other stock-rooms. Only Mr Franklin has a key to the vault which is where their more valuable faceted stones are kept.'

Mr Franklin had no keys at all. Mr Franklin's keys were in my own pocket. There was no harm, I supposed, in producing them.

The sight of what must have been a familiar bunch brought tears to Annette Adams's eyes. She put down the mug, searched around for a tissue and cried, 'He really is dead, then,' as if she hadn't thoroughly believed it before.

When she'd recovered a little I asked her to point out the vault key, which proved to be the longest and slenderest of the lot, and shortly afterwards we were all walking through the propped-open door and down a central corridor with spacious offices opening to either side. Faces showing shock looked out at our passing. We stopped at an ordinary looking door which might have been mistaken for a cupboard and certainly looked nothing like a vault.

'That's it,' Annette Adams insisted, nodding; so I slid the narrow key into the small ordinary keyhole, and found that it turned unexpectedly anti-clockwise. The thick and heavy door swung inwards to the right under pressure and a light came on automatically, shining in what did indeed seem exactly like a large walk-in cupboard, with rows of white cardboard boxes on several plain white-painted shelves stretching away along the left-hand wall.

Everyone looked in silence. Nothing seemed to have been disturbed.

'Who knows what should be in the boxes?' I asked, and got the expected answer: my brother.

I took a step into the vault and took the lid off one of the nearest boxes which bore a sticky label saying $MgA1_2O_4$, Burma. Inside the box there were about a dozen glossy white envelopes, each taking up the whole width. I lifted one out to open it.

'Be careful!' Annette Adams exclaimed, fearful of my clumsiness as I balanced on the crutches. 'The packets unfold.'

I handed to her the one I held, and she unfolded it carefully on the palm of her hand. Inside, cushioned by white tissue, lay two large red translucent stones, cut and polished, oblong in shape, almost pulsing with intense colour under the lights.

'Are they rubies?' I asked, impressed.

Annette Adams smiled indulgently. 'No, they're spinel. Very fine specimens. We rarely deal in rubies.'

'Are there any diamonds in here?' one of the policemen asked.

'No, we don't deal in diamonds. Almost never.'

I asked her to look into some of the other boxes, which she did, first carefully folding the two red stones into their packet and restoring them to their right place. We watched her stretch and bend, tipping up random lids on several shelves to take out a white packet here and there for inspection, but there were clearly no dismaying surprises, and at the end she shook her head and said that nothing at all was missing, as far as she could see.

'The real value of these stones is in quantity,' she said. 'Each individual stone isn't worth a fortune. We sell stones in tens and hundreds . . .' Her voice trailed off into a sort of forlornness. 'I don't know what to do,' she said, 'about the orders.'

The policemen weren't affected by the problem. If nothing was missing, they had other burglaries to look into, and they would put in a report, but goodbye for now, or words to that effect.

When they'd gone, Annette Adams and I stood in the passage and looked at each other.

'What do I do?' she said. 'Are we still in business?'

I didn't like to tell her that I hadn't the foggiest notion. I said, 'Did Greville have an office?'

'That's where most of the mess is,' she said, turning away and retracing her steps to a large corner room near the entrance lobby. 'In here.'

I followed her and saw what she meant about mess. The contents of every wide-open drawer seemed to be out on the floor, most of it paper. Pictures had been removed from the walls and dropped. One filing cabinet lay on its side like a fallen soldier. The desk top was a shambles.

'The police said the burglar was looking behind the pictures for a safe. But there isn't one . . . just the vault.' She sighed unhappily. 'It's all so pointless.'

I looked around. 'How many people work here altogether?' I said.

'Six of us. And Mr Franklin, of course.' She swallowed. 'Oh dear.'

'Mm,' I agreed. 'Is there anywhere I can meet everyone?'

She nodded mutely and led the way into another large office where three of the others were already gathered, wide-eyed and rudderless. Another two came when called; four women and two men, all worried and uncertain and looking to me for decisions.

Greville, I perceived, hadn't chosen potential leaders to work around him. Annette Adams herself was no aggressive waiting-in-the-wings manager but a true second-in-command, skilled at carrying out orders, incapable of initiating them. Not so good, all things considered.

I introduced myself and described what had happened to Greville.

They had liked him, I was glad to see. There were tears on his behalf. I said that I needed their help because there were people I ought to notify about his death, like his solicitor and his accountant, for instance, and his closest friends, and I didn't know who they were. I would like, I said, to make a list, and sat beside one of the desks, arming myself with paper and pen.

Annette said she would fetch Greville's address book from his office but after a while returned in frustration: in all the mess she couldn't find it.

'There must be other records,' I said. 'What about that computer?' I pointed across the room. 'Do you have addresses on that?'

The girl who had brought the tea brightened a good deal and informed me that this was the stock control room, and the computer in question was programmed to record 'stock in, stock out', statements, invoices and accounts. But, she said encouragingly, in her other domain across the corridor there was another computer which she used for letters. She was out of the door by the end of the sentence and Annette remarked that June was a whirlwind always.

June, blonde, long-legged, flat-chested, came back with a fast print-out of Greville's ten most frequent correspondents (ignoring customers) which included not only the lawyers and the accountants but also the bank, a stockbroker and an insurance company.

'Terrific,' I said. 'And could one of you get through to the big credit card companies, and see if Greville was a customer of theirs and say his cards have been stolen, and he's dead.' Annette agreed mournfully that she would do it at once.

I then asked if any of them knew the make and number of Greville's car. They all did. It seemed they saw it every day in the yard. He came to work in a ten-year-old Rover 3500 without radio or cassette player because the Porsche he'd owned before had been broken into twice and finally stolen altogether.

'The old car's still bursting with gadgets, though,' the younger of the two men said, 'but he keeps them all locked in the boot.'

Greville had always been a sucker for gadgets, full of enthusiasm for the latest fidgety way of performing an ordinary task. He'd told me more about those toys of his, when we'd met, than ever about his own human relationships.

'Why did you ask about his car?' the young man said. He had rows of badges attached to a black leather jacket and orange spiky hair set with gel. A need to prove he existed, I supposed.

'It may be outside his front door,' I said. 'Or it may be parked somewhere in Ipswich.'

'Yeah,' he said thoughtfully. 'See what you mean.'

463

The telephone rang on the desk beside me, and Annette after a moment's hesitation came and picked up the receiver. She listened with a worried expression and then, covering the mouthpiece, asked me, 'What shall I do? It's a customer who wants to give an order.'

'Have you got what he wants?' I asked.

'Yes, we're sure to have.'

'Then say it's OK.'

'But do I tell him about Mr Franklin?'

'No,' I said instinctively, 'just take the order.'

She seemed glad of the direction and wrote down the list, and when she'd disconnected I suggested to them all that for that day at least they should take and send out orders in the normal way, and just say if asked that Mr Franklin was out of the office and couldn't be reached. We wouldn't start telling people he was dead until after I'd talked to his lawyers, accountants, bank and the rest, and found out our legal position. They were relieved and agreed without demur, and the older man asked if I would soon get the broken window fixed, as it was in the packing and despatch room, where he worked.

With a feeling of being sucked feet first into quicksand I said I would try. I felt I didn't belong in that place or in those people's lives, and all I knew about the jewellery business was where to find two red stones in a box marked $MgA1_2O_4$, Burma.

At the fourth try among the Yellow Pages I got a promise of instant action on the window and after that, with office procedure beginning to tick over again all around me, I put a call through to the lawyers.

They were grave, they were sympathetic, they were at my service. I asked if by any chance Greville had made a will, as specifically I wanted to know if he had left any instructions about cremation or burial, and if he hadn't, did they know of anyone I should consult, or should I make whatever arrangements I thought best.

There was a certain amount of clearing of throats and a promise to look up files and call back, and they kept their word almost immediately, to my surprise.

My brother had indeed left a will: they had drawn it up for him themselves three years earlier. They couldn't swear it was his *last* will, but it was the only one they had. They had consulted it. Greville, they said, pedantically, had expressed no preference as to the disposal of his remains.

'Shall I just . . . go ahead, then?'

'Certainly,' they said. 'You are in fact named as your brother's sole executor. It is your duty to make the decisions.'

Hell, I thought, and I asked for a list of the beneficiaries so that I could notify them of the death and invite them to the funeral.

After a pause they said they didn't normally give out that information on the telephone. Could I not come to their office? It was just across the City, at Temple.

'I've broken an ankle,' I said, apologetically. 'It takes me all my time to cross the room.'

Dear, dear, they said. They consulted among themselves in guarded whispers and finally said they supposed there was no harm in my knowing. Greville's will was extremely simple; he had left everything he possessed to Derek Saxony Franklin, his brother. To my good self, in fact.

'What?' I said stupidly. 'He can't have.'

He had written his will in a hurry, they said, because he had been flying off to a dangerous country to buy stones. He had been persuaded by the lawyers not to go intestate, and he had given in to them, and as far as they knew, that was the only will he had ever made.

'He can't have meant it to be his last,' I said blankly.

Perhaps not, they agreed: few men in good health expected to die at fifty-three. They then discussed probate procedures discreetly and asked for my instructions, and I felt the quicksands rising above my knees.

'Is it legal,' I asked, 'for this business to go on running, for the time being?'

They saw no impediment in law. Subject to probate, and in the absence of any later will, the business would be mine. If I wanted to sell it in due course, it would be in my own interest to keep it running. As my brother's executor it would also be my duty to do my best for the estate. An interesting situation, they said with humour.

Not wholeheartedly appreciating the subtlety, I asked how long probate would take.

Always difficult to forecast, was the answer. Anything between six months or two years, depending on the complexity of Greville's affairs.

'Two years!'

More probably six months, they murmured soothingly. The speed would depend on the accountants and the Inland Revenue, who could seldom be hurried. It was in the lap of the gods.

I mentioned that there might be work to do over claiming damages for the accident. Happy to see to it, they said, and promised to contact the Ipswich police. Meanwhile, good luck.

I put the receiver down in sinking dismay. This business, like any other, might run on its own impetus for two weeks, maybe even for four, but after that . . . After that I would be back on horses, trying to get fit again to race.

I would have to get a manager, I thought vaguely, and had no idea where to start looking. Annette Adams with furrows of anxiety across her forehead asked if it would be all right to begin clearing up Mr Franklin's office, and I said yes, and thought that her lack of drive could sink the ship.

Please would someone, I asked the world in general, mind going down to the yard and telling the man in my car that I wouldn't be leaving for two or three hours; and June with her bright face whisked out of the door again and soon returned to relate that my man would lock the car, go on foot for lunch, and be back in good time to wait for me.

'Did he say all that?' I asked curiously.

June laughed. 'Actually he said, "Right. Bite to eat," and off he stomped.'

She asked if I would like her to bring me a sandwich when she went out for her own lunch and, surprised and grateful, I accepted.

'Your foot hurts, doesn't it?' she said judiciously.

'Mm.'

'You should put it up on a chair.'

She fetched one without ado and placed it in front of me, watching with a motherly air of approval as I lifted my leg into place. She must have been all of twenty, I thought.

A telephone rang beside the computer on the far side of the room and she went to answer it.

'Yes, sir, we have everything in stock. Yes, sir, what size and how many? A hundred twelve-by-ten milli-metre ovals . . . yes . . . yes . . . yes.'

She tapped the lengthy order rapidly straight on to the computer, not writing in longhand as Annette had done.

'Yes, sir, they will go off today. Usual terms, sir, of course.' She put the phone down, printed a copy of the order and laid it in a shallow wire tray. A fax machine simultaneously clicked on and whined away and switched off with little shrieks, and she tore off the emergent sheet and tapped its information also into the computer, making a print-out and putting it into the tray.

'Do you fill all the orders the day they come in?' I asked.

'Oh, sure, if we can. Within twenty-four hours without fail. Mr Franklin says speed is the essence of good business. I've known him stay here all evening by himself packing parcels when we're swamped.'

She remembered with a rush that he would never come back. It did take a bit of getting used to. Tears welled in her uncontrollably as they had earlier, and she stared at me through them, which made her blue eyes look huge.

'You couldn't help liking him,' she said. 'Working with him, I mean.'

I felt almost jealous that she'd known Greville better than I had; yet I could have known him better if I'd tried. Regret stabbed in again, a needle of grief.

Annette came to announce that Mr Franklin's room was at least partially clear so I transferred myself into there to make more phone calls in comparative privacy. I sat in Greville's black leather swivelling chunk of luxury and put my foot on the typist's chair June carried in after me, and I surveyed the opulent carpet, deep armchairs and framed maps as in the lobby, and smoothed a hand over the grainy black expanse of the oversized desk, and felt like a jockey, not a tycoon.

Annette had picked up from the floor and assembled at one end of the desk some of the army of gadgets, most of them matt black and small, as if miniaturization were part of the attraction. Easily identifiable at a glance were battery-operated things like pencil sharpener, hand-held copier, printing calculator, dictionary-thesaurus, but most needed investigation. I stretched out a hand to the nearest and found that it was a casing with a dial face, plus a head like a microphone on a lead.

'What's this?' I asked Annette who was picking up a stack of paper from the far reaches of the floor. 'Some sort of meter?'

She flashed a look at it. 'A Geiger counter,' she said matter-of-factly, as if everyone kept a Geiger counter routinely among their pens and pencils.

I flipped the switch from off to on, but apart from a couple of ticks, nothing happened.

Annette paused, sitting back on her heels as she knelt among the remaining clutter.

'A lot of stones change colour for the better under gamma radiation,' she said. 'They're not radioactive afterwards, but Mr Franklin was once accidentally sent a batch of topaz from Brazil that had been irradiated in a nuclear reactor and the stones were bordering on dangerous. A hundred of them. There was a terrible lot of trouble because, apart from being unsaleable, they had come in without a radioactivity import licence, or something like that, but it wasn't Mr Franklin's fault, of course. But he got the Geiger counter then.' She paused. 'He had an amazing flair for stones, you know. He just felt there was something wrong with that topaz.

470

Such a beautiful deep blue they'd made it, when it must have been almost colourless to begin with. So he sent a few of them to a lab for testing.' She paused again. 'He'd just been reading about some old diamonds that had been exposed to radium and turned green, and were as radioactive as anything . . .'

Her face crumpled and she blinked her eyes rapidly, turning away from me and looking down to the floor so that I shouldn't see her distress. She made a great fuss among the papers and finally, with a sniff or two, said indistinctly, 'Here's his desk diary,' and then, more slowly, 'That's odd.'

'What's odd?'

'October's missing.'

She stood up and brought me the desk diary, which proved to be a largish appointments calendar showing a week at a glance. The month on current display was November, with a few of the daily spaces filled in but most of them empty. I flipped back the page and came next to September.

'I expect October's still on the floor, torn off,' I said.

She shook her head doubtfully, and in fact couldn't find it.

'Has the address book turned up?' I asked.

'No.' She was puzzled. 'It hasn't.'

'Is anything else missing?'

'I'm not really sure.'

It seemed bizarre that anyone should risk breaking in via the roof simply to steal an address book and some pages from a desk diary. Something else had to be missing.

The Yellow-Pages glaziers arrived at that point, putting a stop to my speculation. I went along with them to the packing room and saw the efficient hole that had been smashed in the six-by-four-foot window. All the glass that must have been scattered over every surface had been collected and swept into a pile of dagger-sharp glittering triangles, and a chill breeze ruffled papers in clipboards.

'You don't break glass this quality by tapping it with a fingernail,' one of the workmen said knowledgeably, picking up a piece. 'They must have swung a weight against it, like a wrecking ball.'

CHAPTER THREE

While the workmen measured the window frame, I watched the oldest of Greville's employees take transparent bags of beads from one cardboard box, insert them into bubble-plastic sleeves and stack them in another brown cardboard box. When all was transferred he put a list of contents on top, crossed the flaps and stuck the whole box around with wide reinforced tape.

'Where do the beads come from?' I asked.

'Taiwan, I dare say,' he said briefly, fixing a large address label on the top.

'No . . . I meant, where do you keep them here?'

He looked at me in pitying astonishment, a white-haired grandfatherly figure in storemen's brown overalls. 'In the stock-rooms, of course.'

'Of course.'

'Down the hall,' he said.

I went back to Greville's office and in the interests of good public relations asked Annette if she would show me the stock-rooms. Her heavyish face lightened with pleasure and she led the way to the far end of the corridor.

'In here,' she said with obvious pride, passing through a central doorway into a small inner lobby, 'there are four rooms.' She pointed through open doorways. 'In there, mineral cabochons, oval and round; in there, beads; in there, oddities, and in there, organics.'

'What are organics?' I asked.

She beckoned me forward into the room in question, and I walked into a windowless space lined from floor to shoulder height with column after column of narrow grey metal drawers, each presenting a face to the world of about the size of a side of a shoebox. Each drawer, above a handle, bore a label identifying what it contained.

'Organics are things that grow,' Annette said patiently, and I reflected I should have worked that out for myself. 'Coral, for instance.' She pulled open a nearby drawer which proved to extend lengthily backwards, and showed me the contents: clear plastic bags, each packed with many strings of bright red twiglets. 'Italian,' she said. 'The best coral comes from the Mediterranean.' She closed that drawer, walked a few paces, pulled open another. 'Abalone, from abalone shells.' Another: 'Ivory. We still have a little, but we can't sell it now.' Another: 'Mother of pearl. We sell tons of it.' 'Pink mussel.' 'Freshwater pearls.' Finally, 'Imitation pearls. Cultured pearls are in the vault.'

Everything, it seemed, came in dozens of shapes and

sizes. Annette smiled at my bemused expression and invited me into the room next door.

Floor to shoulder height metal drawers, as before, not only lining the walls this time but filling the centre space with aisles, as in a supermarket.

'Cabochons, for setting into rings, and so on,' Annette said. 'They're in alphabetical order.'

Amethyst to turquoise via garnet, jade, lapis lazuli and onyx, with dozens of others I'd only half heard of. 'Semi-precious,' Annette said briefly. 'All genuine stones. Mr Franklin doesn't touch glass or plastic.' She stopped abruptly. Let five seconds lengthen. 'He didn't touch them,' she said lamely.

His presence was there strongly, I felt. It was almost as if he would walk through the door, all energy, saying 'Hello, Derek, what brings you here?' and if he seemed alive to me, who had seen him dead, how much more physical he must still be to Annette and June.

And to Lily too, I supposed. Lily was in the third stock-room pushing a brown cardboard box around on a thing like a tea-trolley, collecting bags of strings of beads and checking them against a list. With her centre-parted hair drawn back into a slide at her neck, with her small pale mouth and rounded cheeks, Lily looked like a Charlotte Brontë governess and dressed as if immolation were her personal choice. The sort to love the master in painful silence, I thought, and wondered what she'd felt for Greville.

Whatever it was, she wasn't letting it show. She raised

475

downcast eyes briefly to my face and at Annette's prompting told me she was putting together a consignment of rhodonite, jasper, aventurine and tiger eye, for one of the largest firms of jewellery manufacturers.

'We import the stones,' Annette said. 'We're wholesalers. We sell to about three thousand jewellers, maybe more. Some are big businesses. Many are small ones. We're at the top of the semi-precious trade. Highly regarded.' She swallowed. 'People trust us.'

Greville, I knew, had travelled the world to buy the stones. When we'd met he'd often been on the point of departing for Arizona or Hong Kong or had just returned from Israel, but he'd never told me more than the destinations. I at last understood what he'd been doing, and realized he couldn't easily be replaced.

Depressed, I went back to his office and telephoned to his accountant and his bank.

They were shocked and they were helpful, impressively so. The bank manager said I would need to call on him in the morning, but Saxony Franklin, as a limited company, could go straight on functioning. I could take over without trouble. All he would want was confirmation from my brother's lawyers that his will was as I said.

'Thank you very much,' I said, slightly surprised, and he told me warmly he was glad to be of service. Greville's affairs, I thought with a smile, must be amazingly healthy.

To the insurance company, also, my brother's death

seemed scarcely a hiccup. A limited company's insurance went marching steadily on, it seemed: it was the company that was insured, not my brother. I said I would like to claim for a smashed window. No problem. They would send a form.

After that I telephoned to the Ipswich undertakers who had been engaged to remove Greville's body from the hospital, and arranged that he should be cremated. They said they had 'a slot' at two o'clock on Friday: would that do? 'Yes,' I said, sighing. 'I'll be there.' They gave me the address of the crematorium in a hushed obsequious voice, and I wondered what it must be like to do business always with the bereaved. Happier by far to sell glittering baubles to the living or to ride jump-racing horses at thirty miles an hour, win, lose or break your bones.

I made yet another phone call, this time to the orthopaedic surgeon, and as usual came up against the barrier of his receptionist. He wasn't in his own private consulting rooms, she announced, but at the hospital.

I said, 'Could you ask him to leave me a prescription somewhere, because I've fallen on my ankle and twisted it, and I'm running out of Distalgesic.'

'Hold on,' she said, and I held until she returned. 'I've spoken to him,' she said. 'He'll be back here later. He says can you be here at five?'

I said gratefully that I could, and reckoned that I'd have to leave soon after two-thirty to be sure of making it. I told Annette, and asked what they did about locking up.

'Mr Franklin usually gets here first and leaves last.' She stopped, confused. 'I mean . . .'

'I know,' I said. 'It's all right. I think of him in the present tense too. So go on.'

'Well, the double front doors bolt on the inside. Then the door from the lobby to the offices has an electronic bolt, as you know. So does the door from the corridor to the stock-rooms. So does the rear door, where we all come in and out. Mr Franklin changes . . . changed . . . the numbers at least every week. And there's another electronic lock, of course, on the door from the lobby to the showroom, and from the corridor into the showroom . . .' She paused. 'It does seem a lot, I know, but the electronic locks are very simple, really. You only have to remember three digits. Last Friday they were five, three, two. They're easy to work. Mr Franklin installed them so that we shouldn't have too many keys lying around. He and I both have a key, though, that will unlock all the electronic locks manually, if we need to.'

'So you've remembered the numbers?' I asked.

'Oh, yes. It was just, this morning, with everything . . . they went out of my head.'

'And the vault,' I said. 'Does that have any electronics?'

'No, but it has an intricate locking system in that heavy door, though it looks so simple from the outside. Mr Franklin always locks . . . locked . . . the vault before

478

he left. When he went away on long trips, he made the key available to me.'

I wondered fleetingly about the awkward phrase, but didn't pursue it. I asked her instead about the showroom, which I hadn't seen and, again with pride, she went into the corridor, programmed a shining brass doorknob with the open sesame numbers, and ushered me into a windowed room that looked much like a shop, with glass-topped display counters and the firm's overall ambience of wealth.

Annette switched on powerful lights and the place came to life. She moved contentedly behind the counters, pointing out to me the contents now bright with illumination.

'In here are examples of everything we stock, except not all the sizes, of course, and not the faceted stones in the vault. We don't really use the showroom a great deal, only for new customers mostly, but I like being in here. I love the stones. They're fascinating. Mr Franklin says stones are the only things the human race takes from the earth and makes more beautiful.' She lifted a face heavy with loss. 'What will happen without him?'

'I don't know yet,' I said, 'but in the short term we fill the orders and despatch them, and order more stock from where you usually get it. We keep to all the old routines and practices. OK?'

She nodded, relieved at least for the present.

'Except,' I added, 'that it will be you who arrives first and leaves last, if you don't mind.'

'That's all right. I always do when Mr Franklin's away.'

We stared briefly at each other, not putting words to the obvious, then she switched off the showroom lights almost as if it were a symbolic act, and as we left pulled the self-locking door shut behind us.

Back in Greville's office I wrote down for her my own address and telephone number and said that if she felt insecure, or wanted to talk, I would be at home all evening.

'I'll come back here tomorrow morning, after I've seen the bank manager,' I said. 'Will you be all right until then?'

She nodded shakily. 'What do we call you? We can't call you Mr Franklin, it wouldn't seem right.'

'How about Derek?'

'Oh no.' She was instinctively against it. 'Would you mind, say . . . Mr Derek?'

'If you prefer it.' It sounded quaintly old-fashioned to me, but she was happy with it and said she would tell the others.

'About the others,' I said, 'sort everyone out for me, with their jobs. There's you, June, Lily . . .'

'June works the computers and the stock control,' she said. 'Lily fills the orders. Tina, she's a general assistant, she helps Lily and does some of the secretarial work. So does June. So do I, actually. We all do what's needed, really. There are few hard and fast divisions.

Except that Alfie doesn't do much except pack up the orders. It takes him all his time.'

'And that younger guy with the spiky orange halo?'

'Jason? Don't worry about the hair, he's harmless. He's our muscles. The stones are very heavy in bulk, you know. Jason shifts boxes, fills the stock-rooms, does odd jobs and hoovers the carpets. He helps Alfie sometimes, or Lily, if we're busy. Like I said, we all do anything, whatever's needed. Mr Franklin has never let anyone mark out a territory.'

'His words?'

'Yes, of course.'

Collective responsibility, I thought. I bowed to my brother's wisdom. If it worked, it worked. And from the look of everything in the place, it did indeed work, and I wouldn't disturb it.

I closed and locked the vault door with Greville's key and asked Annette which of his large bunch overrode the electronic locks. That one, she said, pointing, separating it.

'What are all the others, do you know?'

She looked blank. 'I've no idea.'

Car, house, whatever. I supposed I might eventually sort them out. I gave her what I hoped was a reassuring smile, sketched a goodbye to some of the others and rode down in the service lift to find Brad out in the yard.

'Swindon,' I said. 'The medical centre where we were on Friday. Would you mind?'

'Course not.' Positively radiant, I thought.

481

It was an eighty-mile journey, ten miles beyond home. Brad managed it without further communication and I spent the time thinking of all the things I hadn't yet done, like seeing to Greville's house and stopping delivery of his daily paper, wherever it might come from, and telling the post office to divert his letters . . . To hell with it, I thought wearily, why did the damned man have to die?

The orthopod X-rayed and unwrapped my ankle and tut-tutted. From toes to shin it looked hard, black and swollen, the skin almost shiny from the stretching.

'I advised you to rest it,' he said, a touch crossly.

'My brother died . . .' and I explained about the mugging, and also about having to see to Greville's affairs.

He listened carefully, a strong sensible man with prematurely white hair. I didn't know a jockey who didn't trust him. He understood our needs and our imperatives, because he treated a good many of us who lived in or near the training centre of Lambourn.

'As I told you the other day,' he said when I'd finished, 'you've fractured the lower end of the fibula, and where the tibia and fibula should be joined, they've sprung apart. Today, they are further apart. They're now providing no support at all for the talus, the heel bone. You've now completely ripped the lateral ligament which normally binds the ankle together. The whole joint is insecure and coming apart inside, like a mortise joint in a piece of furniture when the glue's given way.'

'So how long will it take?' I asked.

He smiled briefly. 'In a crêpe bandage it will hurt for about another ten days, and after that you can walk on it. You could be back on a horse in three weeks from now, if you don't mind the stirrup hurting you, which it will. About another three weeks after that, the ankle might be strong enough for racing.'

'Good,' I said, relieved. 'Not much worse than before, then.'

'It's worse, but it won't take much longer to mend.'

'Fine.'

He looked down at the depressing sight. 'If you're going to be doing all this travelling about, you'd be much more comfortable in a rigid cast. You could put your weight on it in a couple of days. You'd have almost no pain.'

'And wear it for six weeks? And get atrophied muscles?'

'Atrophy is a strong word.' He knew all the same that jump jockeys needed strong leg muscles above all else, and the way to keep them strong was to keep them moving. Inside plaster they couldn't move at all and weakened rapidly. If movement cost a few twinges, it was worth it.

'Delta-cast is lightweight,' he said persuasively. 'It's a polymer, not like the old plaster of Paris. It's porous, so air circulates, and you don't get skin problems. It's good.

And I could make you a cast with a zip in it so you could take it off for physiotherapy.'

'How long before I was racing?'

'Nine or ten weeks.'

I didn't say anything for a moment or two and he looked up fast, his eyes bright and quizzical.

'A cast, then?' he said.

'No.'

He smiled and picked up a roll of crêpe bandage. 'Don't fall on it again in the next month, or you'll be back to square one.'

'I'll try not to.'

He bandaged it all tight again from just below the knee down to my toes and back, and gave me another prescription for Distalgesic. 'No more than eight tablets in twenty-four hours and not with alcohol.' He said it every time.

'Right.'

He considered me thoughtfully for a moment and then rose and went over to a cabinet where he kept packets and bottles of drugs. He came back tucking a small plastic bag into an envelope which he held out to me.

'I'm giving you something known as DF 1–1–8s. Rather appropriate, as they're your own initials! I've given you three of them. They are serious painkillers, and I don't want you to use them unless something like yesterday happens again.'

'OK,' I said, putting the envelope in my pocket. 'Thanks.'

'If you take one, you won't feel a thing.' He smiled. 'If you take two at once, you'll be spaced out, high as a kite. If you take all three at once, you'll be unconscious. So be warned.' He paused. 'They are a last resort.'

'I won't forget,' I said, 'and I truly am grateful.'

Brad drove to a chemist's, took my prescription in, waited for it to be dispensed, and finished the ten miles home, parking outside my door.

'Same time tomorrow morning?' I asked. 'Back to London.'

'Yerss.'

'I'd be in trouble without you,' I said, climbing out with his help. He gave me a brief haunted glance and handed me the crutches. 'You drive great,' I said.

He was embarrassed, but also pleased. Nowhere near a smile, of course, but a definite twitch in the cheeks. He turned away, ducking my gaze, and set off doggedly towards his mother.

I let myself into the house and regretted the embargo on a large scotch. Instead, with June's lunchtime sandwich a distant memory, I refuelled with sardines on toast and ice-cream after, which more or less reflected my habitual laziness about cooking.

Then, aligned with icepacks along the sofa, I

telephoned the man in Newmarket who trained Greville's two racehorses.

He picked up the receiver as if he'd been waiting for it to ring.

'Yes?' he said. 'What are they offering?'

'I've no idea,' I said. 'Is that Nicholas Loder?'

'What? Who are you?' He was brusque and impatient, then took a second look at things and with more honey said, 'I beg your pardon, I was expecting someone else. I'm Loder, yes, who am I talking to?'

'Greville Franklin's brother.'

'Oh yes?'

It meant nothing to him immediately. I pictured him as I knew him, more by sight than face to face, a big light-haired man in his forties with enormous presence and self-esteem to match. Undoubtedly a good-to-great trainer, but in television interviews occasionally over-bearing and condescending to the interviewer, as I'd heard he could be also to his owners. Greville kept his horses with him because the original horse he'd taken as a bad debt had been in that stable. Nicholas Loder had bought Greville all his subsequent horses and done notably well with them, and Greville had assured me that he got on well with the man by telephone, and that he was perfectly friendly.

The last time I'd spoken to Greville myself on the telephone he'd been talking of buying another two-year-old, saying that Loder would get him one at the October sales, perhaps.

I explained to Loder that Greville had died and after the first sympathetic exclamations of dismay he reacted as I would have expected, not as if missing a close friend but on a practical business level.

'It won't affect the running of his horses,' he said. 'They're owned in any case by the Saxony Franklin company, not by Greville himself. I can run the horses still in the company name. I have the company's Authority to Act. There should be no problem.'

'I'm afraid there may be,' I began.

'No, no. Dozen Roses runs on Saturday at York. In with a great chance. I informed Greville of it only a few days ago. He always wanted to know when they were running, though he never went to see them.'

'The problem is,' I said, 'about my being his brother. He has left the Saxony Franklin company to me.'

The size of the problem suddenly revealed itself to him forcibly. 'You're not his brother *Derek* Franklin? That brother? The jockey?'

'Yes. So . . . could you find out from Weatherby's whether the horses can still run while the estate is subject to probate?'

'My God,' he said weakly.

Professional jockeys, as we both knew well, were not allowed to own runners in races. They could own other horses such as brood mares, foals, stallions, hacks, hunters, show-jumpers, anything in horseshoes; they could even own racehorses, but they couldn't run them.'

'Can you find out?' I asked again.

'I will.' He sounded exasperated. 'Dozen Roses should trot up on Saturday.'

Dozen Roses was currently the better of Greville's two horses whose fortunes I followed regularly in the newspapers and on television. A triple winner as a three-year-old, he had been disappointing at four, but in the current year, as a five-year-old, he had regained all his old form and had scored three times in the past few weeks. A 'trot-up' on Saturday was a reasonable expectation.

Loder said, 'If Weatherby's give the thumbs down to the horse running, will you sell it? I'll find a buyer by Saturday, among my owners.'

I listened to the urgency in his voice and wondered whether Dozen Roses was more than just another trot-up, of which season by season he had many. He sounded a lot more fussed than seemed normal.

'I don't know whether I can sell before probate,' I said. 'You'd better find that out, too.'

'But if you can, will you?'

'I don't know,' I said, puzzled. 'Let's wait and see, first.'

'You won't be able to hang on to him, you know,' he said, forcefully. 'He's got another season in him. He's still worth a good bit. But unless you do something like turn in your licence, you won't be able to run him, and he's not worth turning in your licence for. It's not as if he were favourite for the Derby.'

'I'll decide during the week.'

'But you're not thinking of turning in your licence, are you?' He sounded almost alarmed. 'Didn't I read in the paper that you're on the injured list but hope to be back racing well before Christmas?'

'You did read that, yes.'

'Well, then.' The relief was as indefinable as the alarm, but came clear down the wires. I didn't understand any of it. He shouldn't have been so worried.

'Perhaps Saxony Franklin could lease the horse to someone,' I said.

'Oh. Ah. To me?' He sounded as if it were the perfect solution.

'I don't know,' I said cautiously. 'We'll have to find out.'

I realized that I didn't totally trust him, and it wasn't a doubt I'd have felt before the phone call. He was one of the top five Flat race trainers in the country, automatically held to be reliable because of his rock-solid success.

'When Greville came to see his horses,' I asked, 'did he ever bring anyone with him? I'm trying to reach people he knew, to tell them of his death.'

'He never came here to see his horses. I hardly knew him personally myself, except on the telephone.'

'Well, his funeral is on Friday at Ipswich,' I said. 'What if I called in at Newmarket that day, as I'll be over your way, to see you and the horses and complete any paperwork that's necessary?'

'No,' he said instantly. Then, softening it, 'I always

discourage owners from visiting. They disrupt the stable routine. I can't make any exceptions. If I need you to sign anything I'll arrange it another way.'

'All right,' I agreed mildly, not crowding him into corners. 'I'll wait to hear from you about what Weatherby's decide.'

He said he would get in touch and abruptly disconnected, leaving me thinking that on the subject of his behaviour I didn't know the questions let alone the answers.

Perhaps I had been imagining things: but I knew I hadn't. One could often hear more nuances in someone's voice on the telephone than one could face to face. When people were relaxed, the lower vibrations of their voices came over the wires undisturbed; under stress, the lower vibrations disappeared because the vocal cords involuntarily tightened. After Loder had discovered I would be inheriting Dozen Roses, there had been no lower vibrations at all.

Shelving the enigma I pondered the persisting difficulty of informing Greville's friends. They had to exist, no one lived in a vacuum; but if it had been the other way round, I supposed that Greville would have had the same trouble. He hadn't known my friends either. Our worlds had scarcely touched except briefly when we met, and then we had talked a bit about horses, a bit about gadgets, a bit about the world in general and any interesting current events.

He'd lived alone, as I did. He'd told me nothing about any love life. He'd said merely, 'Bad luck' when three years earlier I'd remarked that my live-in girlfriend had gone to live-in somewhere else. It didn't matter, I said. It had been a mutual agreement, a natural ending. I'd asked him once about his long-ago divorced wife. 'She remarried. Haven't seen her since,' was all he'd said.

If it had been I that had died, I thought, he would have told the world I worked in: he'd have told, perhaps, the trainer I mostly rode for and maybe the racing papers. So I should tell his world: tell the semi-precious stone fraternity. Annette could do it, regardless of the absence of Greville's address book, because of June's computer. The computer made more and more nonsense of the break-in. I came back to the same conviction: something else had been stolen, and I didn't know what.

I remembered at about that point that I did have Greville's pocket diary, even if his desk diary had lost October, so I went and fetched it from the bedroom where I'd left it the night before. I thought I might find friends' names and phone numbers in the addresses section at the back, but he had been frugal in that department as everywhere in the slim brown book. I turned the pages, which were mostly unused, seeing only short entries like 'R arrives from Brazil' and 'B in Paris' and 'Buy citrine for P'.

In March I was brought up short. Because it was a racing diary, the race-meetings to be held on each day of the year were listed under the day's date. I came to Thursday 16 March which listed 'Cheltenham'. The word Cheltenham had been ringed with a ball-point pen, and Greville had written 'Gold Cup' in the day's space; and then, with a different pen, he had added the words 'Derek won it!!'

It brought me to sudden tears. I couldn't help it.

I longed for him to be alive so I could get to know him better. I wept for the lost opportunities, the time wasted. I longed to know the brother who had cared what I did, who had noted in his almost empty diary that I'd won one of the top races of the year.

CHAPTER FOUR

There were only three telephone numbers in the addresses section at the back, all identified merely by initials. One, NL, was Nicholas Loder's. I tried the other two, which were London numbers, and got no reply.

Scattered through the rest of the diary were three more numbers. Two of them proved to be restaurants in full evening flood, and I wrote down their names, recognizing one of them as the place I'd last dined with Greville, two or three months back. On 25 July, presumably, as that was the date on which he'd written the number. It had been an Indian restaurant, I remembered, and we had eaten ultra-hot curry.

Sighing, I turned the pages and tried a number occurring on 2 September, about five weeks earlier. It wasn't a London number, but I didn't recognize the code. I listened to the bell ringing continuously at the other end and had resigned myself to another blank when someone lifted the distant receiver and in a low breathy voice said, 'Hello?'

'Hello,' I replied. 'I'm ringing on behalf of Greville Franklin.'

'Who?'

'Greville Franklin.' I spoke the words slowly and clearly.

'Just a moment.'

There was a long uninformative silence and then someone else clattered on sharp heels up to the receiver and decisively spoke, her voice high and angry.

'How dare you!' she said. 'Don't ever do this again. I will not have your name spoken in this house.'

She put the receiver down with a crash before I could utter a word, and I sat bemusedly looking at my own telephone and feeling as if I'd swallowed a wasp.

Whoever she was, I thought wryly, she wouldn't want to send flowers to the funeral, though she might have been gladdened by the death. I wondered what on earth Greville could have done to raise such a storm, but that was the trouble, I didn't know him well enough to make a good guess.

Thankful on the whole that there weren't any more numbers to be tried I looked again at what few entries he had made, more out of curiosity than looking for helpful facts.

He had noted the days on which his horses had run, again only with initials. DR, Dozen Roses, appeared most, each time with a number following, like 300 at 8s, which I took to mean the amounts he'd wagered at what odds. Below the numbers he had put each time another number inside a circle which, when I compared them with the form book, were revealed as the placings of the horse at the finish. Its last three appearances, all with 5 in the circle, seemed to have netted Greville respectively 500 at 14s, 500 at 5s, 1000 at 6/4. The trot-up scheduled for Saturday, I thought, would be likely to be at odds-on.

Greville's second horse, Gemstones appearing simply as G, had run six times, winning only once but profitably: 500 at 100/6.

All in all, I thought, a moderate betting pattern for an owner. He had made, I calculated, a useful profit overall, more than most owners achieved. With his prize money in addition to offset both the training fees and the capital cost of buying the horses in the first place, I guessed that he had come out comfortably ahead, and it was in the business sense, I supposed, that owning horses had chiefly pleased him.

I flicked casually forward to the end of the book and in the last few pages headed 'NOTES' came across a lot of doodling and then a list of numbers.

The doodling was the sort one does while listening on the telephone, a lot of boxes and zig-zags, haphazard and criss-crossed with lines of shading. On the page facing, there was an equation: $CZ = C \times 1.7$. I supposed it had been of sparkling clarity to Greville, but of no use to me.

Overleaf I found the sort of numbers list I kept in my own diary: passport, bank account, national insurance.

After those, in small capital letters further down the page, was the single word DEREK. Another jolt, seeing it again in his writing.

I wondered briefly whether, from its placing, Greville had used my name as some sort of mnemonic, or whether it was just another doodle: there was no way of telling. With a sigh I riffled back through the pages and came to something I'd looked at before, a lightly-pencilled entry for the day before his death. Second time around, it meant just as little.

Koningin Beatrix? he had written. Just the two words and the question mark. I wondered idly if it were the name of a horse, if he'd been considering buying it; my mind tended to work that way. Then I thought that perhaps he'd written the last name first, such as Smith, Jane, and that maybe he'd been going to Ipswich to meet a Beatrix Koningin.

I returned to the horse theory and got through to the trainer I rode for, Milo Shandy, who enquired breezily about the ankle and said would I please waste no time in coming back.

'I could ride out in a couple of weeks,' I said.

'At least that's something, I suppose. Get some massage.'

The mere thought of it was painful. I said I would, not meaning it, and asked about Koningin Beatrix, spelling it out.

'Don't know of any horse called that, but I can find out for you in the morning. I'll ask Weatherby's if the name's available, and if they say yes, it means there isn't a horse called that registered for racing.'

'Thanks a lot.'

'Think nothing of it. I heard your brother died. Bad luck.'

'Yes . . . How did you know?'

'Nicholas Loder rang me just now, explaining your dilemma and wanting me to persuade you to lease him Dozen Roses.'

'But that's crazy. His ringing you, I mean.'

He chuckled. 'I told him so. I told him I could bend you like a block of teak. He didn't seem to take it in. Anyway, I don't think leasing would solve anything. Jockeys aren't allowed to own racing horses, period. If you lease a horse, you still own it.'

'I'm sure you're right.'

'Put your shirt on it.'

'Loder bets, doesn't he?' I asked. 'In large amounts?'

'So I've heard.'

'He said Dozen Roses would trot up at York on Saturday.'

'In that case, do you want me to put a bit on for you?'

Besides not being allowed to run horses in races, jockeys also were banned from betting, but there were always ways round that, like helpful friends.

'I don't think so, not this time,' I said, 'but thanks anyway.'

'You won't mind if I do?'

'Be my guest. If Weatherby's let it run, that is.'

'A nice little puzzle,' he said appreciatively. 'Come over soon for a drink. Come for evening stables.'

I would, I said.

'Take care.'

I put down the phone, smiling at his easy farewell colloquialism. Jump jockeys were paid not to take care, on the whole. Not too much care.

Milo would be horrified if I obeyed him.

In the morning, Brad drove me to Saxony Franklin's bank to see the manager who was young and bright and spoke with deliberate slowness, as if waiting for his clients' intelligence to catch up. Was there something about crutches, I wondered, that intensified the habit? It took him five minutes to suspect that I wasn't a moron. After that he told me Greville had borrowed a sizeable chunk of the bank's money, and he would be looking to me to repay it. 'One point five million United States dollars in cash, as a matter of fact.'

'One point five million dollars,' I repeated, trying not to show that he had punched most of the breath out of me. '*What for?*'

'For buying diamonds. Diamonds from the DTC of the CSO are, of course, normally paid for in cash, in dollars.'

Bank managers around Hatton Garden, it seemed, saw nothing extraordinary in such an exercise.

'He doesn't . . . didn't deal in diamonds,' I protested.

'He had decided to expand and, of course, we made the funds available. Your brother dealt with us for many years and as you'll know was a careful and conscientious businessman. A valued client. We have several times advanced him money for expansion and each time we have been repaid without difficulty. Punctiliously, in fact.' He cleared his throat. 'The present loan, taken out three months ago, is due for repayment progressively over a period of five years, and of course as the loan was made to the company, not to your brother personally, the terms of the loan will be unchanged by his death.'

'Yes,' I said.

'I understood from what you said yesterday that you propose to run the business yourself?' He seemed happy enough where I might have expected a shade of anxiety. So why no anxiety? What wasn't I grasping?

'Do you hold security for the loan?' I asked.

'An agreement. We lent the money against the stock of Saxony Franklin.'

'All the stones?'

'As many as would satisfy the debt. But our best security has always been your brother's integrity and his business ability.'

I said, 'I'm not a gemmologist. I'll probably sell the business after probate.'

He nodded comfortably. 'That might be the best course. We would expect the Saxony Franklin loan to be repaid on schedule, but we would welcome a dialogue with the purchasers.'

499

He produced papers for me to sign and asked for extra specimen signatures so that I could put my name to Saxony Franklin cheques. He didn't ask what experience I'd had in running a business. Instead, he wished me luck.

I rose to my crutches and shook his hand, thinking of the things I hadn't said.

I hadn't told him I was a jockey, which might have caused a panic in Hatton Garden. And I hadn't told him that, if Greville had bought one and a half million dollars' worth of diamonds, I didn't know where they were.

'Diamonds?' Annette said. 'No. I told you. We never deal in diamonds.'

'The bank manager believes that Greville bought some recently. From something called the DTC of the CSO.'

'The Central Selling Organization? That's De Beers. The DTC is their diamond trading company. No, no.' She looked anxiously at my face. 'He can't have done. He never said anything about it.'

'Well, has the stock-buying here increased over the past three months?'

'It usually does,' she said, nodding. 'The business always grows. Mr Franklin comes back from world trips with new stones all the time. Beautiful stones. He can't resist them. He sells most of the special ones to a jewellery designer who has several boutiques in places like Knightsbridge and Bond Street. Gorgeous costume jewellery, but with real stones. Many of his pieces are one-offs, designed for a single stone. He has a great name. People prize some of his pieces like Fabergé's.'

'Who is he?'

'Prospero Jenks,' she said, expecting my awe at least.

I hadn't heard of him, but I nodded all the same.

'Does he set the stones with diamonds?' I asked.

'Yes, sometimes. But he doesn't buy those from Saxony Franklin.'

We were in Greville's office, I sitting in his swivel chair behind the vast expanse of desk, Annette sorting yesterday's roughly heaped higgledy-piggledy papers back into the drawers and files that had earlier contained them.

'You don't think Greville would ever have kept diamonds in this actual office, do you?' I asked.

'Certainly not.' The idea shocked her. 'He was always very careful about security.'

'So no one who broke in here would expect to find anything valuable lying about?'

She paused with a sheaf of papers in one hand, her brow wrinkling.

'It's odd, isn't it? They wouldn't expect to find anything valuable lying about in an office if they knew anything about the jewellery trade. And if they didn't know anything about the jewellery trade, why pick this office?'

501

The same old unanswerable question.

June with her incongruous motherliness brought in the typist's chair again for me to put my foot on. I thanked her and asked if her stock control computer kept day-to-day tabs on the number and value of all the polished pebbles in the place.

'Goodness, yes,' she said with amusement. 'Dates and amounts in, dates and amounts out. Prices in, prices out, profit margin, VAT, tax, you name it, the computer will tell you what we've got, what it's worth, what sells slowly, what sells fast, what's been hanging around here wasting space for two years or more, which isn't much.'

'The stones in the vault as well?'

'Sure.'

'But no diamonds?'

'No, we don't deal in them.' She gave me a bright incurious smile and swiftly departed, saying over her shoulder that the Christmas rush was still going strong and they'd been bombarded by fax orders overnight.

'Who reorders what you sell?' I asked Annette.

'I do for ordinary stock. June tells me what we need. Mr Franklin himself ordered the faceted stones and anything unusual.'

She went on sorting the papers, basically unconcerned because her responsibility ended on her way home. She was wearing that day the charcoal skirt of the day before but topped with a black sweater, perhaps out of respect for Greville. Solid in body, but not large, she had good legs in black tights and a settled, well-groomed, middle-aged air. I couldn't imagine her being as buoyant as June even in her youth.

I asked her if she could lay her hands on the company's insurance policy and she said as it happened she had just refiled it. I read its terms with misgivings and then telephoned the insurance company. Had my brother, I asked, recently increased the insurance? Had he increased it to cover diamonds to the value of one point five million dollars? He had not. It had been discussed only. My brother had said the premium asked was too high, and he had decided against it. The voice explained that the premium had been high because the stones would be often in transit, which made them vulnerable. He didn't know if Mr Franklin had gone ahead with buying the diamonds. It had been an enquiry only, he thought, three or four months ago. I thanked him numbly and put down the receiver.

The telephone rang again immediately and as Annette seemed to be waiting for me to do so, I answered it.

'Hello?' I said.

A male voice said, 'Is that Mr Franklin? I want to speak to Mr Franklin, please.'

'Er . . . could I help? I'm his brother.'

'Perhaps you can,' he said. 'This is the clerk of the West London Magistrates Court. Your brother was due here twenty minutes ago and it is unlike him to be late. Could you tell me when to expect him?'

'Just a minute.' I put my hand over the mouthpiece

and told Annette what I'd just heard. Her eyes widened and she showed signs of horrified memory.

'It's his day for the Bench! Alternate Tuesdays. I'd clean forgotten.'

I returned to the phone and explained the situation.

'Oh. Oh. How dreadfully upsetting.' He did indeed sound upset, but also a shade impatient. 'It really would have been more helpful if you could have alerted me in advance. It's very short notice to have to find a replacement.'

'Yes,' I agreed, 'but this office was broken into during the weekend. My brother's appointments diary was stolen, and in fact we cannot alert anybody not to expect him.'

'How extremely inconvenient.' It didn't seem an inappropriate statement to him. I thought Greville might find it inconvenient to be dead. Maybe it wasn't the best time for black humour.

'If my brother had personal friends among the magistrates,' I said, 'I would be happy for them to get in touch with me here. If you wouldn't mind telling them.'

'I'll do that, certainly.' He hesitated. 'Mr Franklin sits on the licensing committee. Do you want me to inform the chairman?'

'Yes, please. Tell anyone you can.'

He said goodbye with all the cares of the world on his shoulders and I sighed to Annette that we had better begin telling everyone else as soon as possible, but the trade was to expect business as usual.

'What about the papers?' she asked. 'Shall we put it in *The Times* and so on?'

'Good idea. Can you do it?'

She said she could, but in fact showed me the paragraph she'd written before phoning the papers. 'Suddenly, as the result of an accident, Greville Saxony Franklin JP, son of . . .' She'd left a space after 'son of' which I filled in for her: 'the late Lt. Col. and Mrs Miles Franklin'. I changed 'brother of Derek' to 'brother of Susan, Miranda and Derek', and I added a few final words, 'Cremation, Ipswich, Friday'.

'Have you any idea,' I asked Annette, 'what he could have been doing in Ipswich?'

She shook her head. 'I've never heard him mention the place. But then he didn't ever tell me very much that wasn't business.' She paused. 'He wasn't exactly secretive, but he never chatted about his private life.' She hesitated. 'He never talked about you.'

I thought of all the times he'd been good company and told me virtually nothing, and I understood very well what she meant.

'He used to say that the best security was a still tongue,' she said. 'He asked us not to talk too much about our jobs to total strangers, and we all know it's safer not to, even though we don't have precious stones here. All the people in the trade are security mad and the diamantaires can be paranoid.'

'What,' I said, 'are diamantaires?'

'Not what, who,' she said. 'They're dealers in rough

diamonds. They get the stones cut and polished and sell them to manufacturing jewellers. Mr Franklin always said diamonds were a world of their own, quite separate from other gemstones. There was a ridiculous boom and a terrible crash in world diamond prices during the eighties and a lot of the diamantaires lost fortunes and went bankrupt and Mr Franklin was often saying that they must have been mad to over-extend the way they had.' She paused. 'You couldn't help but know what was happening all round us in this area, where every second business is in gemstones. No one in the pubs and restaurants talked of much else. So you see, I'm sure the bank manager must be wrong. Mr Franklin would never buy diamonds.'

If he hadn't bought diamonds, I thought, what the hell had he done with one point five million dollars in cash?

Bought diamonds. He had to have done. Either that or the money was still lying around somewhere, undoubtedly carefully hidden. Either the money or diamonds to the value were lying around uninsured, and if my semi-secretive ultra-security-conscious brother had left a treasure-island map with X marking the precious spot, I hadn't yet found it. Much more likely, I feared, that the knowledge had died under the scaffolding. If it had, the firm would be forfeited to the bank, the last thing Greville would have wanted.

If it had, a major part of the inheritance he'd left me had vanished like morning mist.

He should have stuck to his old beliefs, I thought gloomily, and let diamonds strictly alone.

The telephone on the desk rang again and this time Annette answered it, as she was beside it.

'Saxony Franklin, can I help you?' she said, and listened. 'No, I'm very sorry, you won't be able to talk to Mr Franklin personally ... Could I have your name, please?' She listened. 'Well, Mrs Williams, we must most unhappily inform you that Mr Franklin died as a result of an accident over the weekend. We are however continuing in business. Can I help you at all?'

She listened for a moment or two in increasing puzzlement, then said, 'Are you there? Mrs Williams, can you hear me?' But it seemed as though there was no reply, and in a while she put the receiver down, frowning. 'Whoever it was hung up.'

'Do I gather you don't know Mrs Williams?'

'No, I don't.' She hesitated. 'But I think she rang yesterday, too. I think I told her yesterday that Mr Franklin wasn't expected in the office all day, like I told everyone. I didn't ask for her name yesterday. But she has a voice you don't forget.'

'Why not?'

'Cut glass,' she said succinctly. 'Like Mr Franklin, but more so. Like you too, a bit.'

I was amused. She herself spoke what I thought of as unaccented English, though I supposed any way of speaking sounded like an accent to someone else. I wondered briefly about the cut-glass Mrs Williams who had received the news of the accident in silence and hadn't asked where, or how, or when.

Annette went off to her own office to get through to the newspapers and I picked Greville's diary out of my trouser pocket and tried the numbers that had been unreachable the night before. The two at the back of the book turned out to be first his bookmaker and second his barber, both of whom sounded sorry to be losing his custom, though the bookmaker less so because of Greville's habit of winning.

My ankle heavily ached; the result, I dared say, of general depression as much as aggrieved bones and muscle. Depression because whatever decisions I'd made to that point had been merely common sense, but there would come a stage ahead when I could make awful mistakes through ignorance. I'd never before handled finances bigger than my own bank balance and the only business I knew anything about was the training of racehorses, and that only from observation, not from hands-on experience. I knew what I was doing around horses: I could tell the spinel from the ruby. In Greville's world, I could be taken for a ride and never know it. I could lose badly before I'd learned even the elementary rules of the game.

Greville's great black desk stretched away to each side of me, the wide knee-hole flanked to right and left by twin stacks of drawers, four stacks in all. Most of them now contained what they had before the break-in, and I began desultorily to investigate the nearest on the left, looking vaguely for anything that would prompt me as to what I'd overlooked or hadn't known was necessary to be done.

I first found not tasks but the toys: the small black gadgets now tidied away into serried ranks. The Geiger counter was there, also the hand-held copier and a variety of calculators, and I picked out a small black contraption about the size of a paperback book and, turning it over curiously, couldn't think what it could be used for.

'That's an electric measurer,' June said, coming breezily into the office with her hands full of paper. 'Want to see how it works?'

I nodded and she put it flat on its back on the desk. 'It'll tell you how far it is from the desk to the ceiling,' she said, pressing knobs. 'There you are, seven feet five and a half inches. In metres,' she pressed another knob, 'two metres twenty-six centimetres.'

'I don't really need to know how far it is to the ceiling,' I said.

She laughed. 'If you hold it flat against a wall, it measures how far it is to the opposite wall. Does it in a flash, as you saw. You don't need to mess around with tape measures. Mr Franklin got it when he was redesigning the stock-rooms. And he worked out how much carpet we'd need, and how much paint for the walls. This gadget tells you all that.'

'You like computers, don't you?' I said.

'Love them. All shapes, all sizes.' She peered into the

509

open drawer. 'Mr Franklin was always buying the tiny ones.' She picked out a small grey leather slip-cover the size of a pack of cards and slid the contents onto her palm. 'This little dilly is a travel guide. It tells you things like phone numbers for taxis, airlines, tourist information, the weather, embassies, American Express.' She demonstrated, pushing buttons happily. 'It's an American gadget, it even tells you the TV channels and radio frequencies for about a hundred cities in the US, including Tucson, Arizona, where they hold the biggest gem fair every February. It helps you with fifty other cities round the world, places like Tel Aviv and Hong Kong and Taipei where Mr Greville was always going.'

She put the travel guide down and picked up something else. 'This little round number is a sort of telescope, but it also tells you how far you are away from things. It's for golfers. It tells you how far you are away from the flag on the green, Mr Franklin said, so that you know which club to use.'

'How often did he play golf?' I said, looking through the less than four-inch-long telescope and seeing inside a scale marked GREEN on the lowest line with diminishing numbers above, from 200 yards at the bottom to 40 yards at the top. 'He never talked about it much.'

'He sometimes played at weekends, I think,' June said doubtfully. 'You line up the word GREEN with the actual green, and then the flag stick is always eight feet high, I think, so wherever the top of the stick is on the scale, that's how far away you are. He said it was a

good gadget for amateurs like him. He said never to be
ashamed of landing in life's bunkers if you'd tried your
best shot.' She blinked a bit. 'He always used to show
these things to me when he bought them. He knew I
liked them too.' She fished for a tissue and without
apology wiped her eyes.

'Where did he get them all from?' I asked.

'Mail order catalogues, mostly.'

I was faintly surprised. Mail order and Greville didn't
seem to go together, somehow, but I was wrong about
that, as I promptly found out.

'Would you like to see our own new catalogue?' June
asked, and was out of the door and back again before I
could remember if I'd ever seen an old one and decide
I hadn't. 'Fresh from the printers,' she said. 'I was just
unpacking them.'

I turned the glossy pages of the 50-page booklet,
seeing in faithful colours all the polished goodies I'd
met in the stock-rooms and also a great many of lesser
breeding. Amulets, heart shapes, hoops and butterflies:
there seemed to be no end to the possibilities of adorn-
ment. When I murmured derogatorily that they were a
load of junk, June came fast and strongly to their
defence, a mother-hen whose chickens had been
snubbed.

'Not everyone can afford diamonds,' she said sharply,
'and, anyway, these things are pretty and we sell them in
thousands, and they wind up in hundreds of High Street
shops and department stores and I often see people

buying the odd shapes we've had through here. People do like them, even if they're not your taste.'

'Sorry,' I said.

Some of her fire subsided. 'I suppose I shouldn't speak to you like that,' she said uncertainly, 'but you're not Mr Franklin . . .' She stopped with a frown.

'It's OK,' I said. 'I am, but I'm not. I know what you mean.'

'Alfie says,' she said slowly, 'that there's a steeple-chase jockey called Derek Franklin.' She looked at my foot as if with new understanding. 'Champion jockey one year, he said. Always in the top ten. Is that . . . you?'

I said neutrally, 'Yes.'

'I *had* to ask you,' she said. 'The others didn't want to.'

'Why not?'

'Annette didn't think you could be a jockey. You're too tall. She said Mr Franklin never said anything about you being one. All she knew was that he had a brother he saw a few times a year. She said she was going to ignore what Alfie thought, because it was most unlikely.' She paused. 'Alfie mentioned it yesterday, after you'd gone. Then he said . . . they all said . . . they didn't see how a jockey could run a business of this sort. If you were one, that is. They didn't want it to be true, so they didn't want to ask.'

'You tell Alfie and the others that if the jockey doesn't run the business their jobs will be down the tubes and they'll be out in the cold before the week's over.'

Her blue eyes widened. 'You sound just like Mr Franklin!'

'And you don't need to mention my profession to the customers, in case I get the same vote of no confidence I've got from the staff.'

Her lips shaped the word 'Wow' but she didn't quite say it. She disappeared fast from the room and presently returned, followed by all the others who were only too clearly in a renewed state of anxiety.

Not one of them a leader. What a pity.

I said, 'You all look as if the ship's been wrecked and the lifeboat's leaking. Well, we've lost the captain, and I agree we're in trouble. My job is with horses and not in an office. But, like I said yesterday, this business is going to stay open and thrive. One way or another, I'll see that it does. So if you'll all go on working normally and keep the customers happy, you'll be doing yourselves a favour because if we get through safely you'll all be due for a bonus. I'm not my brother, but I'm not a fool either, and I'm a pretty fast learner. So just let's get on with the orders, and, er, cheer up.'

Lily, the Charlotte Brontë lookalike, said meekly, 'We don't really doubt your ability . . .'

'Of course we do,' interrupted Jason. He stared at me with half a snigger, with a suggestion of curling lip. 'Give us a tip for the three-thirty, then.'

I listened to the street-smart bravado which went with the spiky orange hair. He thought me easy game.

I said, 'When you are personally able to ride the winner of any three-thirty, you'll be entitled to your jeer. Until then, work or leave, it's up to you.'

There was a resounding silence. Alfie almost smiled. Jason looked merely sullen. Annette took a deep breath, and June's eyes were shining with laughter.

They all drifted away still wordless and I couldn't tell to what extent they'd been reassured, if at all. I listened to the echo of my own voice saying I wasn't a fool, and wondering ruefully if it were true: but until the diamonds were found or I'd lost all hope of finding them, I thought it more essential than ever that Saxony Franklin Ltd should stay shakily afloat. All hands, I thought, to the pumps.

June came back and said tentatively, 'The pep talk seems to be working.'

'Good.'

'Alfie gave Jason a proper ticking off, and Jason's staying.'

'Right.'

'What can I do to help?'

I looked at her thin alert face with its fair eyelashes and blonde-to-invisible eyebrows and realized that without her the save-the-firm enterprise would be a non-starter. She, more than her computer, was at the heart of things. She more than Annette, I thought.

'How long have you worked here?' I asked.

'Three years. Since I left school. Don't ask if I like the job, I love it. What can I do?'

'Look up in your computer's memory any reference to diamonds,' I said.

She was briefly impatient. 'I told you, we don't deal in diamonds.'

'All the same, would you?'

She shrugged and was gone. I got to my feet – foot – and followed her, and watched while she expertly tapped her keys.

'Nothing at all under diamonds,' she said finally. 'Nothing. I told you.'

'Yes.' I thought about the boxes in the vault with the mineral information on the labels. 'Do you happen to know the chemical formula for diamonds?'

'Yes, I do,' she said instantly. 'It's C. Diamonds are pure carbon.'

'Could you try again, then, under C?'

She tried. There was no file for C.

'Did my brother know how to use this computer?' I asked.

'He knew how to work all computers. Given five minutes or so to read the instructions.'

I pondered, staring at the blank unhelpful screen.

'Are there,' I asked eventually, 'any secret files in this?'

She stared. 'We never use secret files.'

'But you could do?'

'Of course. Yes. But we don't need to.'

515

'If,' I said, 'there were any secret files, would you know that they were there?'

She nodded briefly. 'I wouldn't know, but I could find out.'

'How?' I asked. 'I mean, please would you?'

'What am I looking for? I don't understand.'

'Diamonds.'

'But I told you, we don't . . .'

'I know,' I said, 'but my brother said he was going to buy diamonds and I need to know if he did. If there's any chance he made a private entry on this computer some day when he was first or last in this office, I need to find it.'

She shook her head but tapped away obligingly, bringing what she called menus to the screen. It seemed a fairly lengthy business but finally, frowning, she found something that gave her pause. Then her concentration increased abruptly until the screen was showing the word 'Password?' as before.

'I don't understand,' she said. 'We gave this computer a general password which is Saxony, though we almost never use it. But you can put in any password you like on any particular document to supersede Saxony. This entry was made only a month ago. The date is on the menu. But whoever made it didn't use Saxony as the password. So the password could be anything, literally any word in the world.'

I said, 'By document you mean file?'

'Yes, file. Every entry has a document name, like, say,

516

"oriental cultured pearls". If I load "oriental cultured pearls" onto the screen I can review our whole stock. I do it all the time. But this document with an unknown password is listed under pearl in the singular, not pearls in the plural, and I don't understand it. I didn't put it there.' She glanced at me. 'At any rate, it doesn't say diamonds.'

'Have another try to guess the password.'

She tried Franklin and Greville without result. 'It could be *anything*,' she said helplessly.

'Try Dozen Roses.'

'Why Dozen Roses?' She thought it extraordinary.

'Greville owned a horse – a racehorse – with that name.'

'Really? He never said. He was so nice, and awfully private.'

'He owned another horse called Gemstones.'

With visible doubt she tried 'Dozen Roses' and then 'Gemstones'. Nothing happened except another insistent demand for the password.

'Try "diamonds", then,' I said.

She tried 'diamonds'. Nothing changed.

'You knew him,' I said. 'Why would he enter something under "pearl"?'

'No idea.' She sat hunched over the keys, drumming her fingers on her mouth. 'Pearl. Pearl. Why pearl?'

'What is a pearl?' I said. 'Does it have a formula?'

'Oh.' She suddenly sat up straight. 'It's a birthstone.'

She typed in 'birthstone', and nothing happened.

Then she blushed slightly.

'It's one of the birthstones for the month of June,' she said. 'I could try it, anyway.'

She typed 'June', and the screen flashed and gave up its secrets.

CHAPTER FIVE

We hadn't found the diamonds.

The screen said:

> June, if you are reading this, come straight into my
> office for a rise. You are worth your weight in your
> birthstone, but I'm only offering to increase your
> salary by twenty per cent. Regards, Greville
> Franklin.

'Oh!' She sat transfixed. 'So that's what he meant.'

'Explain,' I said

'One morning . . .' She stopped, her mouth screwing
up in an effort not to cry. It took her a while to be able
to continue, then she said, 'One morning he told me
he'd invented a little puzzle for me and he would give
me six months to solve it. After six months it would self-
destruct. He was smiling so much.' She swallowed. 'I
asked him what sort of puzzle and he wouldn't tell me.
He just said he hoped I would find it.'

'Did you look?' I asked.

'Of course I did. I looked everywhere in the office, though I didn't know what I was looking for. I even looked for a new document in the computer, but I just never gave a thought to its being filed as a secret, and my eyes just slid over the word "pearl", as I see it so often. Silly of me. Stupid.'

I said, 'I don't think you're stupid, and I'll honour my brother's promise.'

She gave me a swift look of pleasure but shook her head a little and said, 'I didn't find it. I'd never have solved it except for you.' She hesitated. 'How about ten per cent?'

'Twenty,' I said firmly. 'I'm going to need your help and your knowledge, and if Annette is Personal Assistant, as it says on the door of her office, you can be Deputy Personal Assistant, with the new salary to go with the job.'

She turned a deeper shade of rose and busied herself with making a print-out of Greville's instruction, which she folded and put in her handbag.

'I'll leave the secret in the computer,' she said with misty fondness. 'No one else will ever find it.' She pressed a few buttons and the screen went blank, and I wondered how many times in private she would call up the magic words that Greville had left her.

I wondered if they would really self-destruct: if one could programme something on a computer to erase itself on a given date. I didn't see why not, but I thought

Greville might have given her strong clues before the six months were out.

I asked her if she would print out first a list of everything currently in the vault and then as many things as she thought would help me understand the business better, like the volume and value of a day's, a week's, a month's sales; like which items were most popular, and which least.

'I can tell you that what's very popular just now is black onyx. Fifty years ago they say it was all amber, now no one buys it. Jewellery goes in and out of fashion like everything else.' She began tapping keys. 'Give me a little while and I'll print you a crash course.'

'Thanks.' I smiled, and waited while the printer spat out a gargantuan mouthful of glittering facets. Then I took the list in search of Annette, who was alone in the stock-rooms, and asked her to give me a quick canter round the vault.

'There aren't any diamonds there,' she said positively.

'I'd better learn what is.'

'You don't seem like a jockey,' she said.

'How many do you know?'

She stared. 'None, except you.'

'On the whole,' I said mildly, 'jockeys are like anyone else. Would you feel I was better able to manage here if I were, say, a piano tuner? Or an actor? Or a clergyman?'

She said faintly, 'No.'

'OK, then. We're stuck with a jockey. Twist of fate. Do your best for the poor fellow.'

She involuntarily smiled a genuine smile which lightened her heavy face miraculously. 'All right.' She paused. 'You're really like Mr Franklin in some ways. The way you say things. Deal with honour, he said, and sleep at night.'

'You all remember what he said, don't you?'

'Of course.'

He would have been glad, I supposed, to have left so positive a legacy. So many precepts. So much wisdom. But so few signposts to his personal life. No visible signpost to the diamonds.

In the vault Annette showed me that, besides its chemical formula, each label bore a number: if I looked at that number on the list June had printed, I would see the formula again, but also the normal names of the stones, with colours, shapes and sizes and country of origin.

'Why did he label them like this?' I asked. 'It just makes it difficult to find things.'

'I believe that was his purpose,' she answered. 'I told you, he was very security conscious. We had a secretary working here once who managed to steal a lot of our most valuable turquoise out of the vault. The labels read "turquoise" then, which made it easy, but now they don't.'

'What do they say?'

She smiled and pointed to a row of boxes. I looked

at the labels and read $CuAl_6(PO_4)_4(OH)_8 \cdot 4-5(H_2O)$ on each of them.

'Enough to put anyone off for life,' I said.

'Exactly. That's the point. Mr Franklin could read formulas as easily as words, and I've got used to them myself now. No one but he and I handle these stones in here. We pack them into boxes ourselves and seal them before they go to Alfie for despatch.' She looked along the rows of labels and did her best to educate me. 'We sell these stones at so much per carat. A carat weighs two hundred milligrams, which means five carats to a gram, a hundred and forty-two carats to an ounce and five thousand carats to the kilo.'

'Stop right there,' I begged.

'You said you learned fast.'

'Give me a day or two.'

She nodded and said if I didn't need her any more she had better get on with the ledgers.

Ledgers, I thought, wilting internally. I hadn't even started on those. I thought of the joy with which I'd left Lancaster University with a degree in Independent Studies, swearing never again to pore dutifully over books and heading straight (against my father's written wishes) to the steeplechase stable where I'd been spending truant days as an amateur. It was true that at college I'd learned fast, because I'd had to, and learned all night often enough, keeping faith with at least the first half of my father's letter. He'd hoped I would grow out of the lure he knew I felt for race-riding, but it was all I'd ever wanted and I couldn't have settled to anything else. There was no long-term future in it, he'd written, besides a complete lack of financial security along with a constant risk of disablement. I ask you to be sensible, he'd said, to think it through and decide against.

Fat chance.

I sighed for the simplicity of the certainty I'd felt in those days, yet, given a second beginning, I wouldn't have lived any differently. I had been deeply fulfilled in racing and grown old in spirit only because of the way life worked in general. Disappointments, injustices, small betrayals, they were everyone's lot. I no longer expected everything to go right, but enough had gone right to leave me at least in a balance of content.

With no feeling that the world owed me anything, I applied myself to the present boring task of opening every packet in every box in the quest for little bits of pure carbon. It wasn't that I expected to find the diamonds there: it was just that it would be so stupid not to look, in case they were.

I worked methodically, putting the boxes one at a time on the wide shelf which ran along the right-hand wall, unfolding the stiff white papers with the soft inner linings and looking at hundreds of thousands of peridots, chrysoberyls, garnets and aquamarines until my head spun. I stopped in fact when I'd done only a third of the stock because apart from the airlessness of the vault it was physically tiring standing on one leg all the time, and the crutches got in the way as much as they helped. I refolded the last of the $XY_3Z_6[(O,OH,F)_4(BO_3)_3Si_6O_{18}]$ (tourmaline) and gave it best.

'What did you learn?' Annette asked when I reappeared in Greville's office. She was in there, replacing yet more papers in their proper files, a task apparently nearing completion.

'Enough to look at jewellery differently,' I said.

She smiled. 'When I read magazines I don't look at the clothes, I look at the jewellery.'

I could see that she would. I thought that I might also, despite myself, from then on. I might even develop an affinity with black onyx cufflinks.

It was by that time four o'clock in the afternoon of what seemed a very long day. I looked up the racing programme in Greville's diary, decided that Nicholas Loder might well have passed over going to Redcar, Warwick and Folkestone, and dialled his number. His secretary answered, and yes, Mr Loder was at home, and yes, he would speak to me.

He came on the line with almost none of the previous evening's agitation, bass resonances positively throbbing down the wire.

'I've been talking to Weatherby's and the Jockey Club,' he said easily, 'and there's fortunately no problem. They agree that before probate the horses belong to Saxony Franklin Limited and not to you, and they will not bar them from racing in that name.'

'Good,' I said, and was faintly surprised.

'They say of course that there has to be at least one registered agent appointed by the company to be responsible for the horses, such appointment to be sealed with the company's seal and registered at Weatherby's. Your brother appointed both himself and myself as registered agents, and although he has died I remain a registered agent as before and can act for the company on my own.'

'Ah,' I said.

'Which being so,' Loder said happily, 'Dozen Roses runs at York as planned.'

'And trots up?'

He chuckled. 'Let's hope so.'

That chuckle, I thought, was the ultimate in confidence.

'I'd be grateful if you could let Saxony Franklin know whenever the horses are due to run in the future,' I said.

'I used to speak to your brother personally at his home number. I can hardly do that with you, as you don't own the horses.'

'No,' I agreed. 'I meant, please will you tell the company? I'll give you the number. And would you ask for Mrs Annette Adams? She was Greville's second-in-command.'

He could hardly say he wouldn't, so I read out the number and he repeated it as he wrote it down.

'Don't forget though that there's only a month left of the Flat season,' he said. 'They'll probably run only once more each. Two at the very most. Then I'll sell them for you, that would be best. No problem. Leave it to me.'

He was right, logically, but I still illogically disliked his haste.

'As executor, I'd have to approve any sale,' I said, hoping I was right. 'In advance.'

'Yes, yes, of course.' Reassuring heartiness. 'Your injury,' he said, 'what exactly is it?'

'Busted ankle.'

'Ah. Bad luck. Getting on well, I hope?' The sympathy sounded more like relief to me than anything else, and again I couldn't think why.

'Getting on,' I said.

'Good, good. Goodbye then. The York race should be on the television on Saturday. I expect you'll watch it?'

'I expect so.'

'Fine.' He put down the receiver in great good humour and left me wondering what I'd missed.

Greville's telephone rang again immediately, and it was Brad to tell me that he had returned from his day's visit to an obscure aunt in Walthamstow and was downstairs in the front hall: all he actually said was, 'I'm back.'

'Great. I won't be long.'

I got a click in reply. End of conversation.

I did mean to leave almost at once but there were two more phone calls in fairly quick succession. The first was from a man introducing himself as Elliot Trelawney,

a colleague of Greville's from the West London Magistrates Court. He was extremely sorry, he said, to hear
about his death, and he truly sounded it. A positive
voice, used to attention: a touch of plummy accent.

'Also,' he said, 'I'd like to talk to you about some
projects Greville and I were working on. I'd like to have
his notes.'

I said rather blankly, 'What projects? What notes?'

'I could explain better face to face,' he said. 'Could I
ask you to meet me? Say tomorrow, early evening, over
a drink? You know that pub just round the corner from
Greville's house? The Rook and Castle? There. He and
I often met there. Five-thirty, six, either of those suit
you?'

'Five-thirty,' I said obligingly.

'How shall I know you?'

'By my crutches.'

It silenced him momentarily. I let him off embarrassment.

'They're temporary,' I said.

'Er, fine, then. Until tomorrow.'

He cut himself off, and I asked Annette if she knew
him, Elliot Trelawney? She shook her head. She
couldn't honestly say she knew anyone outside the
office who was known to Greville personally. Unless
you counted Prospero Jenks, she said doubtfully. And
even then, she herself had never really met him, only
talked to him frequently on the telephone.

'Prospero Jenks . . . alias Fabergé?'

'That's the one.'

I thought a bit. 'Would you mind phoning him now?' I said. 'Tell him about Greville and ask if I can go to see him to discuss the future. Just say I'm Greville's brother, nothing else.'

She grinned. 'No horses? Pas de gee-gees?'

Annette, I thought in amusement, was definitely loosening up.

'No horses,' I agreed.

She made the call but without results. Prospero Jenks wouldn't be reachable until morning. She would try then, she said.

I levered myself upright and said I'd see her tomorrow. She nodded, taking it for granted that I would be there. The quicksands were winning, I thought. I was less and less able to get out.

Going down the passage I stopped to look in on Alfie whose day's work stood in columns of loaded cardboard boxes waiting to be entrusted to the post.

'How many do you send out every day?' I asked, gesturing to them.

He looked up briefly from stretching sticky tape round yet another parcel. 'About twenty, twenty-five regular, but more from August to Christmas.' He cut off the tape expertly and stuck an address label deftly on the box top. 'Twenty-eight so far today.'

'Do you bet, Alfie?' I asked. 'Read the racing papers?'

He glanced at me with a mixture of defensiveness

and defiance, neither of which feeling was necessary. 'I *knew* you was him,' he said. 'The others said you couldn't be.'

'You know Dozen Roses too?'

A tinge of craftiness took over in his expression. 'Started winning again, didn't he? I missed him the first time, but yes, I've had a little tickle since.'

'He runs on Saturday at York, but he'll be odds-on,' I said.

'Will he win, though? Will they be trying with him? I wouldn't put my shirt on that.'

'Nicholas Loder says he'll trot up.'

He knew who Nicholas Loder was: didn't need to ask. With cynicism, he put his just-finished box on some sturdy scales and wrote the result on the cardboard with a thick black pen. He must have been well into his sixties, I thought, with deep lines from his nose to the corners of his mouth and pale sagging skin everywhere from which most of the elasticity had vanished. His hands, with the veins of age beginning to show dark blue, were nimble and strong however, and he bent to pick up another heavy box with a supple back. A tough old customer, I thought, and essentially more in touch with street awareness than the exaggerated Jason.

'Mr Franklin's horses run in and out,' he said pointedly. 'And as a jock you'd know about that.'

Before I could decide whether or not he was intentionally insulting me, Annette came hurrying down the passage calling my name.

'Derek . . . Oh there you are. Still here, good. There's another phone call for you.' She about-turned and went back towards Greville's office, and I followed her, noticing with interest that she'd dropped the Mister from my name. Yesterday's unthinkable was today's natural, now that I was established as a jockey, which was OK as far as it went, as long as it didn't go too far.

I picked up the receiver which was lying on the black desk and said, 'Hello? Derek Franklin speaking.'

A familiar voice said, 'Thank God for that. I've been trying your Hungerford number all day. Then I remembered about your brother . . .' He spoke loudly, driven by urgency.

Milo Shandy, the trainer I'd ridden most for during the past three seasons: a perpetual optimist in the face of world evidence of corruption, greed and lies.

'I've a crisis on my hands,' he bellowed, 'and can you come over? Will you pull out all stops to come over first thing in the morning?'

'Er, what for?'

'You know the Ostermeyers? They've flown over from Pittsburgh for some affair in London and they phoned me and I told them Datepalm is for sale. And you know that if they buy him I can keep him here, otherwise I'll lose him because he'll have to go to auction. And they want you here when they see him work on the Downs and they can only manage first lot tomorrow, and they think the sun twinkles out of your backside, so for God's sake *come*.'

531

Interpreting the agitation was easy. Datepalm was the horse on which I'd won the Gold Cup: a seven-year-old gelding still near the beginning of what with luck would be a notable jumping career. Its owner had recently dropped the bombshell of telling Milo she was leaving England to marry an Australian, and if he could sell Datepalm to one of his other owners for the astronomical figure she named, she wouldn't send it to public auction and out of his yard.

Milo had been in a panic most of the time since then because none of his other owners had so far thought the horse worth the price, his Gold Cup success having been judged lucky in the absence through coughing of a couple of more established stars. Both Milo and I thought Datepalm better than his press, and I had as strong a motive as Milo for wanting him to stay in the stable.

'Calm down,' I assured him. 'I'll be there.'

He let out a lot of breath in a rush. 'Tell the Ostermeyers he's a really good horse.'

'He is,' I said, 'and I will.'

'Thanks, Derek.' His voice dropped to normal decibels. 'Oh, and by the way, there's no horse called Koningin Beatrix, and not likely to be. Weatherby's say Koningin Beatrix means Queen Beatrix, as in Queen Beatrix of the Netherlands, and they frown on people naming racehorses after royal persons.'

'Oh,' I said. 'Well, thanks for finding out.'

'Any time. See you in the morning. For God's sake

don't be late. You know the Ostermeyers get up before larks.'

'What I need,' I said to Annette, putting down the receiver, 'is an appointments book, so as not to forget where I've said I'll be.'

She began looking in the drawerful of gadgets.

'Mr Franklin had an electric memory thing he used to put appointments in. You could use that for now.' She sorted through the black collection, but without result. 'Stay here a minute,' she said, closing the drawer, 'while I ask June if she knows where it is.'

She went away busily and I thought about how to convince the Ostermeyers, who could afford anything they set their hearts on, that Datepalm would bring them glory if not necessarily repay their bucks. They had had steeplechasers with Milo from time to time, but not for almost a year at the moment. I'd do a great deal, I thought, to persuade them it was time to come back.

An alarm like a digital watch alarm sounded faintly, muffled, and to begin with I paid it no attention, but as it persisted I opened the gadget drawer to investigate and, of course, as I did so it immediately stopped. Shrugging, I closed the drawer again, and Annette came back bearing a sheet of paper but no gadget.

'June doesn't know where the Wizard is, so I'll make out a rough calendar on plain paper.'

'What's the Wizard?' I asked.

'The calculator. Baby computer. June says it does everything but boil eggs.'

'Why do you call it the Wizard?' I asked.

'It has that name on it. It's about the size of a paper-back book and it was Mr Franklin's favourite object. He took it everywhere.' She frowned. 'Maybe it's in his car, wherever that is.'

The car. Another problem. 'I'll find the car,' I said, with more confidence than I felt. Somehow or other I would have to find the car. 'Maybe the Wizard was stolen out of this office in the break-in,' I said.

She stared at me with widely opening eyes. 'The thief would have to have known what it was. It folds up flat. You can't see any buttons.'

'All the gadgets were out on the floor, weren't they?'

'Yes.' It troubled her. 'Why the address book? Why the engagements for October? Why the Wizard?'

Because of diamonds, I thought instinctively, but couldn't rationalize it. Someone had perhaps been look-ing, as I was, for the treasure map marked X. Perhaps they'd known it existed. Perhaps they'd found it.

'I'll get here a couple of hours later tomorrow,' I said to Annette. 'And I must leave by five to meet Elliot Trelawney at five-thirty. So if you reach Prospero Jenks, ask him if I could go to see him in between. Or failing that, any time Thursday. Write off Friday because of the funeral.'

Greville died only the day before yesterday, I thought. It already seemed half a lifetime.

Annette said, 'Yes, Mr Franklin,' and bit her lip in dismay.

I half smiled at her. 'Call me Derek. Just plain Derek. And invest it with whatever you feel.'

'It's confusing,' she said weakly, 'from minute to minute.'

'Yes, I know.'

With a certain relief I rode down in the service lift and swung across to Brad in the car. He hopped out of the front seat and shovelled me into the back, tucking the crutches in beside me and waiting while I lifted my leg along the padded leather and wedged myself into the corner for the most comfortable angle of ride.

'Home?' he said.

'No. Like I told you on the way up, we'll stop in Kensington for a while, if you don't mind.'

He gave the tiniest of nods. I'd provided him in the morning with a detailed large-scale map of West London, asking him to work out how to get to the road where Greville had lived, and I hoped to hell he had done it, because I was feeling more drained than I cared to admit and not ready to ride in irritating traffic-clogged circles.

'Look out for a pub called The Rook and Castle, would you?' I asked, as we neared the area. 'Tomorrow at five-thirty I have to meet someone there.'

Brad nodded and with the unerring instinct of the beer drinker quickly found it, merely pointing vigor-ously to tell me.

'Great,' I said, and he acknowledged that with a wiggle of the shoulders.

He drew up so confidently outside Greville's address that I wondered if he had reconnoitred earlier in the day, except that his aunt lived theoretically in the opposite direction. In any case, he handed me the crutches, opened the gate of the small front garden and said loquaciously, 'I'll wait in the car.'

'I might be an hour or more. Would you mind having a quick recce up and down this street and those nearby to see if you can find an old Rover with this number?' I gave him a card with it on. 'My brother's car,' I said.

He gave me a brief nod and turned away, and I looked up at the tall townhouse that Greville had moved into about three months previously, and which I'd never visited. It was creamy-grey, gracefully proportioned, with balustraded steps leading up to the black front door, and businesslike but decorative metal grilles showing behind the glass in every window from semi-basement to roof.

I crossed the grassy front garden and went up the steps, and found there were three locks on the front door. Cursing slightly I yanked out Greville's half-ton of keys and by trial and error found the way into his fortress.

Late afternoon sun slanted yellowly into a long main drawing room which was on the left of the entrance hall, throwing the pattern of the grilles in shadows on the greyish-brown carpet. The walls, pale salmon, were adorned with vivid paintings of stained-glass cathedral windows, and the fabric covering sofa and armchairs was of a large broken herringbone pattern in dark

brown and white, confusing to the eye. I reflected ruefully that I didn't know whether it all represented
Greville's own taste or whether he'd taken it over from
the past owner. I knew only his taste in clothes, food,
gadgets and horses. Not very much. Not enough.

The drawing room was dustless and tidy; unlived in. I
returned to the front hall from where stairs led up and
down, but before tackling those I went through a door
at the rear which opened into a much smaller room
filled with a homely clutter of books, newspapers, magazines, black leather chairs, clocks, chrysanthemums in
pots, a tray of booze and framed medieval brass rub-
bings on deep green walls. This was all Greville, I
thought. This was home.

I left it for the moment and hopped down the stairs
to the semi-basement, where there was a bedroom,
unused, a small bathroom and decorator-style dining
room looking out through grilles to a rear garden, with
a narrow spotless kitchen alongside.

Fixed to the fridge by a magnetic strawberry was a
note.

Dear Mr Franklin,
    I didn't know you'd be away this weekend. I
brought in the papers, they're in the back room.
You didn't leave your laundry out, so I haven't
taken it. Thanks for the money. I'll be back next
Tuesday as usual.
    Mrs P

I looked around for a pencil, found a ball-point, pulled the note from its clip and wrote on the back, asking Mrs P to call the following number (Saxony Franklin's) and speak to Derek or Annette. I didn't sign it, but put it back under the strawberry where I supposed it would stay for another week, a sorry message in waiting.

I looked in the fridge which contained little but milk, butter, grapes, a pork pie and two bottles of champagne.

Diamonds in the ice cubes? I didn't think he would have put them anywhere so chancy: besides, he was security conscious, not paranoid.

I hauled myself upstairs to the hall again and then went on up to the next floor where there was a bedroom and bathroom suite in self-conscious black and white. Greville had slept there: the built-in cupboards and drawers held his clothes, the bathroom closet his privacy. He had been sparing in his possessions, leaving a single row of shoes, several white shirts on hangers, six assorted suits and a rack of silk ties. The drawers were tidy with sweaters, sports shirts, underclothes, socks. Our mother, I thought with a smile, would have been proud of him. She'd tried hard and unsuccessfully to instil tidiness into both of us as children, and it looked as if we'd both got better with age.

There was little else to see. The drawer in the bedside table revealed indigestion tablets, a torch and a paperback, John D. MacDonald. No gadgets and no treasure maps.

With a sigh I went into the only other room on that floor and found it unfurnished and papered with garish metallic silvery roses which had been half ripped off at one point. So much for the decorator.

There was another flight of stairs going upwards, but I didn't climb them. There would only be, by the looks of things, unused rooms to find there, and I thought I would go and look later when stairs weren't such a sweat. Anything deeply interesting in that house seemed likely to be found in the small back sitting room, so it was to there that I returned.

I sat for a while in the chair that was clearly Greville's favourite, from where he could see the television and the view over the garden. Places that people had left for ever should be seen through their eyes, I thought. His presence was strong in that room, and in me.

Beside his chair there was a small antique table with, on its polished top, a telephone and an answering machine. A red light for messages received was shining on the machine, so after a while I pressed a button marked 'rewind', followed by another marked 'play'.

A woman's voice spoke without preamble.

'Darling, where are you? Do ring me.'

There was a series of between-message clicks, then the same voice again, this time packed with anxiety.

'Darling, please please ring. I'm very worried. Where are you, darling? *Please* ring. I love you.'

Again the clicks, but no more messages.

Poor lady, I thought. Grief and tears waiting in the wings.

I got up and explored the room more fully, pausing by two drawers in a table beside the window. They contained two small black unidentified gadgets which baffled me and which I stowed in my pockets, and also a slotted tray containing a rather nice collection of small bears, polished and carved from shaded pink, brown and charcoal stone. I laid the tray on top of the table beside some chrysanthemums and came next to a box made of greenish stone, also polished and which, true to Greville's habit, was firmly locked. Thinking perhaps that one of the keys fitted it I brought out the bunch again and began to try the smallest.

I was facing the window with my back to the room, balancing on one foot and leaning a thigh against the table, my arms out of the crutches, intent on what I was doing and disastrously unheeding. The first I knew of anyone else in the house was a muffled exclamation behind me, and I turned to see a dark-haired woman coming through the doorway, her wild glance rigidly fixed on the green stone box. Without pause she came fast towards me, pulling out of a pocket a black object like a long fat cigar.

I opened my mouth to speak but she brought her hand round in a strong swinging arc, and in that travel the short black cylinder more than doubled its length into a thick silvery flexible stick which crashed with shattering force against my left upper arm, enough to stop a heavyweight in round one.

CHAPTER SIX

My fingers went numb and dropped the box. I swayed and spun on the force of the impact and overbalanced, toppling, thinking sharply that I mustn't this time put my foot on the ground. I dropped the bunch of keys and grabbed at the back of an upright black leather chair with my right hand to save myself, but it turned over under my weight and came down on top of me onto the carpet in a tangle of chair legs, table legs and crutches, the green box underneath and digging into my back.

In a spitting fury I tried to orientate myself and finally got enough breath for one single choice, charming and heartfelt word.

'*Bitch.*'

She gave me a baleful glare and picked up the telephone, pressing three fast buttons.

'Police,' she said, and in as short a time as it took the emergency service to connect her, 'Police, I want to report a burglary. I've caught a burglar.'

'I'm Greville's brother,' I said thickly, from the floor.

For a moment it didn't seem to reach her. I said again, more loudly, 'I'm Greville's brother.'

'What?' she said vaguely.

'For Christ's sake, are you deaf? I'm not a burglar, I'm Greville Franklin's brother.' I gingerly sat up into an L-shape and found no strength anywhere.

She put the phone down. 'Why didn't you say so?' she demanded.

'What chance did you give me? And who the hell are you, walking into my brother's house and belting people?'

She held at the ready the fearsome thing she'd hit me with, looking as if she thought I'd attack her in my turn, which I certainly felt like. In the last six days I'd been crunched by a horse, a mugger and a woman. All I needed was a toddler to amble up with a coup de grâce. I pressed the fingers of my right hand on my forehead and the palm against my mouth and considered the blackness of life in general.

'What's the matter with you?' she said after a pause.

I slid the hand away and drawled, 'Absolutely bloody nothing.'

'I only tapped you,' she said with criticism.

'Shall I give you a hefty clip with that thing so you can feel what it's like?'

'You're angry.' She sounded surprised.

'Dead right.'

I struggled up off the floor, straightened the fallen chair and sat on it. 'Who are you?' I repeated. But I knew who she was: the woman on the answering machine. The same voice. The cut-crystal accent. Darling, where are you? I love you.

'Did you ring his office?' I said. 'Are you Mrs Williams?'

She seemed to tremble and crumple inwardly and she walked past me to the window to stare out into the garden.

'Is he really dead?' she said.

'Yes.'

She was forty, I thought. Perhaps more. Nearly my height. In no way tiny or delicate. A woman of decision and power, sorely troubled.

She wore a leather-belted raincoat, though it hadn't rained for weeks, and plain black businesslike court shoes. Her hair, thick and dark, was combed smoothly back from her forehead to curl under on her collar, a cool groomed look achieved only by expert cutting. There was no visible jewellery, little remaining lipstick, no trace of scent.

'How?' she said eventually.

I had a strong impulse to deny her the information, to punish her for her precipitous attack, to hurt her and get even. But there was no point in it, and I knew I would end up with more shame than satisfaction, so after a struggle I explained briefly about the scaffolding.

'Friday afternoon,' I said. 'He was unconscious at once. He died early on Sunday.'

She turned her head slowly to look at me directly. 'Are you Derek?' she said.

'Yes.'

'I'm Clarissa Williams.'

Neither of us made any attempt to shake hands. It would have been incongruous, I thought.

'I came to fetch some things of mine,' she said. 'I didn't expect anyone to be here.'

It was an apology of sorts, I supposed: and if I had indeed been a burglar she would have saved the bric-à-brac.

'What things?' I asked.

She hesitated, but in the end said, 'A few letters, that's all.' Her gaze strayed to the answering machine and there was a definite tightening of muscles round her eyes.

'I played the messages,' I said.

'Oh God.'

'Why should it worry you?'

She had her reasons, it seemed, but she wasn't going to tell me what they were: or not then, at any rate.

'I want to wipe them off,' she said. 'It was one of the purposes of coming.'

She glanced at me, but I couldn't think of any urgent reason why she shouldn't, so I didn't say anything. Tentatively, as if asking my forbearance every step of the way, she walked jerkily to the machine, rewound the tape and pressed the record button, recording silence over what had gone before. After a while she rewound the tape again and played it, and there were no desperate appeals any more.

'Did anyone else hear . . .?'

'I don't think so. Not unless the cleaner was in the habit of listening. She came today, I think.'

'Oh God.'

'You left no name.' Why the hell was I reassuring her, I wondered. I still had no strength in my fingers. I could still feel that awful blow like a shudder.

'Do you want a drink?' she said abruptly. 'I've had a dreadful day.' She went over to the tray of bottles and poured vodka into a heavy tumbler. 'What do you want?'

'Water,' I said. 'Make it a double.'

She tightened her mouth and put down the vodka bottle with a clink. 'Soda or tonic?' she asked starchily.

'Soda.'

She poured soda into a glass for me and tonic into her own, diluting the spirit by not very much. Ice was downstairs in the kitchen. No one mentioned it.

I noticed she'd left her lethal weapon lying harmlessly beside the answering machine. Presumably I no longer represented any threat. As if avoiding personal contact, she set my soda water formally on the table beside me between the little stone bears and the chrysanthemums and drank deeply from her own glass. Better than tranquillizers, I thought. Alcohol loosened the stress, calmed the mental pain. The world's first anaesthetic. I could have done with some myself.

'Where are your letters?' I asked.

She switched on a table light. The on-creeping dusk in the garden deepened abruptly towards night and I wished she would hurry up because I wanted to go home.

She looked at a bookcase which covered a good deal of one wall.

'In there, I think. In a book.'

'Do start looking, then. It could take all night.'

'You don't need to wait.'

'I think I will,' I said.

'Don't you trust me?' she demanded.

'No.'

She stared at me hard. 'Why not?'

I didn't say that because of the diamonds I didn't trust anyone. I didn't know who I could safely ask to look out for them, or who would search to steal them, if they knew they might be found.

'I don't know you,' I said neutrally.

'But I . . .' She stopped and shrugged. 'I suppose I don't know you either.' She went over to the book-shelves. 'Some of these books are hollow,' she said.

Oh Greville, I thought. How would I ever find anything he had hidden? I liked straight paths. He'd had a mind like a labyrinth.

She began pulling out books from the lower shelves and opening the front covers. Not methodically book by book along any row but always, it seemed to me, those with predominantly blue spines. After a while, on her knees, she found a hollow one which she laid open on the floor with careful sarcasm, so that I could see she wasn't concealing anything.

The interior of the book was in effect a blue velvet box with a close-fitting lid that could be pulled out by a tab. When she pulled the lid out, the shallow blue velvet-lined space beneath was revealed as being entirely empty.

Shrugging, she replaced the lid and closed the book, which immediately looked like any other book, and returned it to the shelves: and a few seconds later found another hollow one, this time with red velvet interiors. Inside this one lay an envelope.

She looked at it without touching it, and then at me. 'It's not my letters,' she said. 'Not my writing paper.'

I said, 'Greville made a will leaving everything he possessed to me.'

She didn't seem to find it extraordinary, although I did: he had done it that way for simplicity when he was in a hurry, and he would certainly have changed it, given time.

'You'd better see what's in here, then,' she said calmly, and she picked the envelope out and stretched across to hand it to me.

The envelope, which hadn't been stuck down, contained a single ornate key, about four inches long, the top flattened and pierced like metal lace, the business end narrow with small but intricate teeth. I laid it on my palm and showed it to her, asking her if she knew what it unlocked.

She shook her head. 'I haven't seen it before.' She paused. 'He was a man of secrets,' she said.

I listened to the wistfulness in her voice. She might be strongly controlled at that moment, but she hadn't been before Annette told her Greville was dead. There had been raw panicky emotion on the tape. Annette had simply confirmed her frightful fears and put what I imagined was a false calmness in place of escalating despair. A man of secrets ... Greville had apparently not opened his mind to her much more than he had to me.

I put the key back in its envelope and handed it across.

'It had better stay in the book for now,' I said, 'until I find a keyhole it fits.'

She put the key in the book and returned it to the shelves, and shortly afterwards found her letters. They were fastened not with romantic ribbons but held together by a prosaic rubber band; not a great many of them by the look of things but carefully kept.

She stared at me from her knees. 'I don't want you to read them,' she said. 'Whatever Greville left you, they're mine, not yours.'

I wondered why she needed so urgently to remove all traces of herself from the house. Out of curiosity I'd have read the letters with interest if I'd found them myself, but I could hardly demand now to see her love letters . . . if they were love letters.

'Show me just a short page,' I said.

She looked bitter. 'You really don't trust me, do you? I'd like to know why.'

'Someone broke into Greville's office over the weekend,' I said, 'and I'm not quite sure what they were looking for.'

'Not my letters,' she said positively.

'Show me just a page,' I said, 'so I know they're what you say.'

I thought she would refuse altogether, but after a moment's thought she slid the rubber band off the letters and fingered through them, finally, with all expression repressed, handing me one small sheet.

It said:

. . . and until next Monday my life will be a desert. What am I to do? After your touch I shrink from him. It's dreadful. I am running out of headaches. I adore you.

C.

I handed the page back in silence, embarrassed at having intruded.

'Take them,' I said.

She blinked a few times, snapped the rubber band back round the small collection, and put them into a plain black leather handbag which lay beside her on the carpet.

I felt down onto the floor, collected the crutches and stood up, concentrating on at least holding the hand support of the left one, even if not putting much weight on it. Clarissa Williams watched me go over towards Greville's chair with a touch of awkwardness.

'Look,' she said, 'I didn't realize . . . I mean, when I came in here and saw you stealing things I thought you were stealing things . . . I didn't notice the crutches.'

I supposed that was the truth. Bona fide burglars didn't go around peg-legged, and I'd laid the supports aside at the time she'd come storming in. She'd been too fired up to ask questions: propelled no doubt by grief, anxiety and fear of the intruder. None of which lessened my contrary feeling that she damned well *ought* to have asked questions before waging war.

I wondered how she would have explained her presence to the police, if they had arrived, when she was urgent to remove all traces of herself from the house. Perhaps she would have realized her mistake and simply departed, leaving the incapacitated burglar on the floor.

I went over to the telephone table and picked up the brutal little man-tamer. The heavy handle, a black cigar-shaped cylinder, knurled for a good grip, was under an inch in diameter and about seven inches long. Protruding beyond that was a short length of solidly thick chromium-plated closely-coiled spring, with a similar but

551

narrower spring extending beyond that, the whole tipped with a black metal knob, fifteen or sixteen inches overall. A kick as hard as a horse.

'What is this?' I said, holding it, feeling its weight.

'Greville gave it to me. He said the streets aren't safe. He wanted me to carry it always ready. He said all women should carry them because of muggers and rapists . . . as a magistrate he heard so much about women being attacked . . . he said one blow would render the toughest man helpless and give me time to escape.'

I hadn't much difficulty in believing it. I bent the black knob to one side and watched the close heavy spring flex and straighten fast when I let it go. She got to her feet and said, 'I'm sorry. I've never used it before, not in anger. Greville showed me how . . . he just said to swing as hard as I could so that the springs would shoot out and do the maximum damage.'

My dear brother, I thought. Thank you very much.

'Does it go back into its shell?' I asked.

She nodded. 'Twist the bigger spring clockwise . . . it'll come loose and slide into the casing.' I did that, but the smaller spring with the black knob still stuck out. 'You have to give the knob a bang against something, then it will slide in.'

I banged the knob against the wall, and like a meek lamb the narrower spring slid smoothly into the wider, and the end of the knob became the harmless-looking end of yet another gadget.

'What makes it work?' I asked, but she didn't know.

I found that the end opposite the knob unscrewed if one tried, so I unscrewed it about twenty turns until the inch-long piece came off, and I discovered that the whole end section was a very strong magnet.

Simple, I thought. Ordinarily the magnet held the heavy springs inside the cylinder. Make a strong flicking arc, in effect throw the springs out, and the magnet couldn't hold them, but let them go, letting loose the full whipping strength of the thing.

I screwed back the cap, held the cylinder, swung it hard. The springs shot out, flexible, shining, horrific.

Wordlessly, I closed the thing up again and offered it to her.

'It's called a kiyoga,' she said.

I didn't care what it was called. I didn't care if I never saw it again. She put it familiarly into her raincoat pocket, every woman's ultimate reply to footpads, maniacs and assorted misogynists.

She looked unhappily and uncertainly at my face. 'I suppose I can't ask you to forget I came here?' she said.

'It would be impossible.'

'Could you just . . . not speak of it?'

If I'd met her in another way I suppose I might have liked her. She had generous eyes that would have looked better smiling, and an air of basic good humour which persisted despite her jumbling emotions.

With an effort she said, 'Please.'

'Don't beg,' I said sharply. It made me uncomfortable and it didn't suit her.

She swallowed. 'Greville told me about you. I guess . . . I'll have to trust to his judgement.'

She felt in the opposite pocket to the one with the kiyoga and brought out a plain keyring with three keys on it.

'You'd better have these,' she said. 'I won't be using them any more.' She put them down by the answering machine and in her eyes I saw the shininess of sudden tears.

'He died in Ipswich,' I said. 'He'll be cremated there on Friday afternoon. Two o'clock.'

She nodded speechlessly in acknowledgement, not looking at me, and went past me, through the doorway and down the hall and out of the front door, closing it with a quiet finality behind her.

With a sigh, I looked round the room. The book-box that had contained her letters still lay open on the floor and I bent down, picked it up, and restored it to the shelves. I wondered just how many books were hollow. Tomorrow evening, I thought, after Elliot Trelawney, I would come and look.

Meanwhile I picked up the fallen green stone box and put it on the table by the chrysanthemums, reflecting that the ornate key in the red-lined book-box was far too large to fit its tiny lock. Greville's bunch of keys was down on the carpet also. I returned to what I'd been doing before being so violently interrupted, but found that the smallest of the bunch was still too big for the green stone.

A whole load of no progress, I thought moodily.

I drank the soda water, which had lost its fizz.

I rubbed my arm, which didn't make it much better.

I wondered what judgement Greville had passed on me, that could be trusted.

There was a polished cupboard that I hadn't investigated underneath the television set and, not expecting much, I bent down and pulled one of the doors open by its brass ring handle. The other door opened of its own accord and the contents of the cupboard slid outwards as a unit; a video machine on top with, on two shelves below, rows of black boxes holding recording tapes. There were small uniform labels on the boxes bearing, not formulas this time, but dates.

I pulled one of the boxes out at random and was stunned to see the larger label stuck to its front: 'Race Video Club', it said in heavy print, and underneath, in typing, 'July 7th, Sandown Park, Dozen Roses.'

The Race Video Club, as I knew well, sold tapes of races to owners, trainers and anyone else interested. Greville, I thought in growing amazement as I looked further, must have given them a standing order: every race his horses had run in for the past two years, I judged, was there on his shelves to be watched.

He'd told me once, when I asked why he didn't go to see his runners, that he saw them enough on television;

and I'd thought he meant on the ordinary scheduled programmes, live from the racetracks in the afternoons.

The front doorbell rang, jarring and unexpected. I went along and looked through a small peephole and found Brad standing on the doorstep, blinking and blinded by two spotlights shining on his face. The lights came from above the door and lit up the whole path and the gate. I opened the door as he shielded his eyes with his arm.

'Hello,' I said. 'Are you all right?'

'Turn the lights off. Can't see.'

I looked for a switch beside the front door, found several, and by pressing them all upwards indiscriminately, put out the blaze.

'Came to see you were OK,' Brad explained. 'Those lights just went on.'

Of their own accord, I realized. Another manifestation of Greville's security, no doubt. Anyone who came up the path after dark would get illuminated for his pains.

'Sorry I've been so long,' I said. 'Now you're here, would you carry a few things?'

He nodded as if he'd let out enough words already to last the evening, and followed me silently, when I beckoned him, towards the small sitting room.

'I'm taking that green stone box and as many of those video tapes as you can carry, starting from that end,' I said, and he obligingly picked up about ten recent tapes, balancing the box on top.

I found a hall light, switched that on, and turned off the lamp in the sitting room. It promptly turned itself on again, unasked.

'Cor,' Brad said.

I thought that maybe it was time to leave before I tripped any other alarms wired direct after dark to the local constabulary. I closed the sitting-room door and we went along the hall to the outer world. Before leaving I pressed all the switches beside the front door downwards, and maybe I turned more on than I'd turned off: the spotlights didn't go on, but a dog started barking noisily behind us.

'Strewth,' Brad said, whirling round and clutching the video tapes to his chest as if they would defend him.

There was no dog. There was a loudspeaker like a bull horn on a low hall table emitting the deep-throated growls and barks of a determined Alsatian.

'Bleeding hell,' Brad said.

'Let's go,' I said in amusement, and he could hardly wait.

The barking stopped of its own accord as we stepped out into the air. I pulled the door shut, and we set off to go down the steps and along the path, and we'd gone barely three paces when the spotlights blazed on again.

'Keep going,' I said to Brad. 'I daresay they'll turn themselves off in time.'

It was fine by him. He'd parked the car round the corner, and I spent the swift journey to Hungerford wondering about Clarissa Williams; her life, love and adultery.

During the evening I failed both to open the green stone box and to understand the gadgets.

Shaking the box gave me no impression of contents and I supposed it could well be empty. A cigarette box, I thought, though I couldn't remember ever seeing Greville smoking. Perhaps a box to hold twin packs of cards. Perhaps a box for jewellery. Its tiny keyhole remained impervious to probes from nail scissors, suitcase keys and a piece of wire, and in the end I surrendered and laid it aside.

Neither of the gadgets opened or shut. One was a small black cylindrical object about the size of a thumb with one end narrowly ridged, like a coin. Turning the ridged end a quarter-turn clockwise, its full extent of travel, produced a thin faint high-pitched whine which proved to be the unexciting sum of the thing's activity. Shrugging, I switched the whine off again and stood the small tube upright on the green box.

The second gadget didn't even produce a whine. It was a flat black plastic container about the size of a pack of cards with a single square red button placed centrally on the front. I pressed the button: no results. A round chromiumed knob set into one of the sides of the cover revealed itself on further inspection as the end of a telescopic aerial. I pulled it out as far as it would go, about ten inches, and was rewarded with what I presumed was a small transmitter which transmitted I didn't know what to I didn't know where.

Sighing, I pushed the aerial back into its socket and added the transmitter to the top of the green box, and after that I fed Greville's tapes one by one into my video machine and watched the races.

Alfie's comment about in-and-out running had interested me more than I would have wanted him to know. Dozen Roses, from my own reading of the results, had had a long doldrum period followed by a burst of success, suggestive of the classic 'cheating' pattern of running a horse to lose and go on losing until he was low in the handicap and unbacked, then setting him off to win at long odds in a race below his latent abilities and wheeling away the winnings in a barrow.

All trainers did that in a mild way sometimes, whatever the rules might say about always running flat out. Young and inexperienced horses could be ruined by being pressed too hard too soon: one had to give them a chance to enjoy themselves, to let their racing instinct develop fully.

That said, there was a point beyond which no modern trainer dared go. In the bad old days before universal camera coverage, it had been harder to prove a horse hadn't been trying: many jockeys had been artists at waving their whips while hauling on the reins. Under the eagle lenses and fierce discipline of the current scene, even natural and unforeseen fluctuations in a horse's form could find the trainer yanked in before the Stewards for an explanation, and if the trainer couldn't explain why his short-priced favourite had turned leaden footed it could cost him a depressing fine.

No trainer, however industrious, was safe from suspicion, yet I'd never read or heard of Nicholas Loder getting himself into that sort of trouble. Maybe Alfie, I thought dryly, knew something the Stewards didn't. Maybe Alfie could tell me why Loder had all but panicked when he'd feared Dozen Roses might not run on Saturday next.

Brad had picked up the six most recent outings of Dozen Roses, interspersed by four of Gemstones's. I played all six of Dozen Roses's first, starting with the earliest, back in May, checking the details with what Greville had written in his diary.

On the screen there were shots of the runners walking round the parade ring and going down to the start, with Greville's pink and orange colours bright and easy to see. The May race was a ten-furlong handicap for three-year-olds and upwards, run at Newmarket on a Friday. Eighteen runners. Dozen Roses ridden by a second-string jockey because Loder's chief retained jockey was riding the stable's other runner which started favourite.

Down at the start there was some sort of fracas involving Dozen Roses. I rewound the tape and played it through in slow motion and couldn't help laughing.

Dozen Roses, his mind far from racing, had been showing unseemly interest in a mare.

I remembered Greville saying once that he thought it a shame and unfair to curb a colt's enthusiasm: no horse of his would ever be gelded. I remembered him vividly, leaning across a small table and saying it over a glass of brandy with a gleam in which I'd seen his own enjoyment of sex. So many glimpses of him in my mind, I thought. Too few, also. I couldn't really believe I would never eat with him again, whatever my senses said.

Trainers didn't normally run mares that had come into season, but sometimes one couldn't tell early on. Horses knew, though. Dozen Roses had been aroused. The mare was loaded into the stalls in a hurry and Dozen Roses had been walked around until the last minute to cool his ardour. After that, he had run without sparkle and finished mid-field, the mare to the rear of him trailing in last. Loder's other runner, the favourite, had won by a length.

Too bad, I thought, smiling, and watched Dozen Roses's next attempt three weeks later.

No distracting attractions this time. The horse had behaved quietly, sleepily almost, and had turned in the sort of moderate performance which set owners wondering if the game was worth it. The next race was much the same, and if I'd been Greville I would have decided it was time to sell.

Greville, it seemed, had had more faith. After seven weeks' rest Dozen Roses had gone bouncing down to the start, raced full of zest and zoomed over the finish-ing line in front, netting 14/1 for anyone ignorant enough to have backed him. Like Greville, of course.

Watching the sequence of tapes I did indeed wonder why the Stewards hadn't made a fuss, but Greville hadn't mentioned anything except his pleasure in the horse's return to his three-year-old form.

Dozen Roses had next produced two further copy-book performances of stamina and determination, which brought us up to date. I rewound and removed the last tape and could see why Loder thought it would be another trot-up on Saturday.

Gemstones's tapes weren't as interesting. Despite his name he wasn't of much value, and the one race he'd won looked more like a fluke than constructive engin-eering. I would sell them both, I decided, as Loder wanted.

CHAPTER SEVEN

Brad came early on Wednesday and drove me to Lambourn. The ankle was sore in spite of Distalgesics but less of a constant drag that morning and I could have driven the car myself if I'd put my mind to it. Having Brad around, I reflected on the way, was a luxury I was all too easily getting used to.

Clarissa Williams's attentions had worn off completely except for a little stiffness and a blackening bruise like a bar midway between shoulder and elbow. That didn't matter. For much of the year I had bruises somewhere or other, result of the law of averages operating in steeplechasing. Falls occurred about once every fourteen races, sometimes oftener, and while a few of the jockeys had bodies that hardly seemed to bruise at all, mine always did. On the other hand I healed everywhere fast, bones, skin and optimism.

Milo Shandy, striding about in his stable yard as if incapable of standing still, came over to my car as it rolled to a stop and yanked open the driver's door. The words he was about to say didn't come out as he stared first at Brad, then at me on the back seat, and what he eventually said was, 'A chauffeur, by God. Coddling yourself, aren't you?'

Brad got out of the car, gave Milo a neanderthal look and handed me the crutches as usual.

Milo, dark, short and squarely built, watched the proceedings with disgust.

'I want you to ride Datepalm,' he said.

'Well, I can't.'

'The Ostermeyers will want it. I told them you'd be here.'

'Gerry rides Datepalm perfectly well,' I said, Gerry being the lad who rode the horse at exercise as a matter of course most days of the week.

'Gerry isn't you.'

'He's better than me with a groggy ankle.'

Milo glared. 'Do you want to keep the horse here or don't you?'

I did.

Milo and I spent a fair amount of time arguing at the best of times. He was pugnacious by nature, mercurial by temperament, full of instant opinions that could be reversed the next day, didactic, dynamic and outspoken. He believed absolutely in his own judgement and was sure that everything would turn out all right in the end. He was moderately tactful to the owners, hard on his work-force and full of swearwords for his horses, which he produced as winners by the dozen.

I'd been outraged by the way he'd often spoken to

me when I first started to ride for him three years earlier, but one day I lost my temper and yelled back at him, and he burst out laughing and told me we would get along just fine, which in fact we did, though seldom on the surface.

I knew people thought ours an unlikely alliance, I neat and quiet, he restless and flamboyant, but in fact I liked the way he trained horses and they seemed to run well for him, and we had both prospered.

The Ostermeyers arrived at that point and they too had a chauffeur, which Milo took for granted. The bullishness at once disappeared from his manner to be replaced by the jocular charm that had owners regularly mesmerized, that morning being no exception. The Ostermeyers responded immediately, she with a roguish wiggle of the hips, he with a big handshake and a wide smile.

They were not so delighted about my crutches.

'Oh dear,' Martha Ostermeyer exclaimed in dismay. 'What have you done? Don't say you can't ride Datepalm. We only came, you know, because dear Milo said you'd be here to ride it.'

'He'll ride it,' Milo said before I had a chance of answering, and Martha Ostermeyer clapped her small gloved hands with relief.

'If we're going to buy him,' she said, smiling, 'we want to see him with his real jockey up, not some exercise rider.'

Harley Ostermeyer nodded in agreement, benignly.

Not really my week, I thought.

The Ostermeyers were all sweetness and light while people were pleasing them, and I'd never had any trouble liking them, but I'd also seen Harley Ostermeyer's underlying streak of ruthless viciousness once in a racecourse car-park where he'd verbally reduced to rubble an attendant who had allowed someone to park behind him, closing him in. He had had to wait half an hour. The attendant had looked genuinely scared. 'Goodnight, Derek,' he'd croaked as I went past, and Ostermeyer had whirled round and cooled his temper fifty per cent, inviting my sympathy in his trouble. Harley Ostermeyer liked to be thought a good guy, most of the time. He was the boss, as I understood it, of a giant supermarket chain. Martha Ostermeyer was also rich, a fourth-generation multi-millionaire in banking. I'd ridden for them often in the past years and been well rewarded, because generosity was one of their pleasures.

Milo drove them and me up to the Downs where Datepalm and the other horses were already circling, having walked up earlier. The day was bright and chilly, the Downs rolling away to the horizon, the sky clear, the horses' coats glossy in the sun. A perfect day for buying a champion chaser.

Milo sent three other horses down to the bottom of the gallop to work fast so that the Ostermeyers would know where to look and what to expect when Datepalm came up and passed them. They stood out on the grass, looking where Milo pointed, intent and happy.

Milo had brought a spare helmet with us in the big-wheeled vehicle that rolled over the mud and ruts on the Downs, and with an inward sigh I put it on. The enterprise was stupid really, as my leg wasn't strong enough and if anything wild happened to upset Date-palm, he might get loose and injure himself and we'd lose him surely one way or another.

On the other hand, I'd ridden races now and then with cracked bones, not just exercise gallops, and I knew one jockey who in the past had broken three bones in his foot and won races with it, sitting with it in an ice bucket in the changing room betweentimes and literally hopping out to the parade ring, supported by friends. The authorities had later brought in strict medical rules to stop that sort of thing as being unfair to the betting public, but one could still get away with it sometimes.

Milo saw me slide out of the vehicle with the helmet on and came over happily and said, 'I knew you would.'

'Mm,' I said. 'When you give me a leg up, put both hands round my knee and be careful, because if you twist my foot there'll be no sale.'

'You're such a wimp,' he said.

Nevertheless, he was circumspect and I landed in the saddle with little trouble. I was wearing jeans, and that morning for the first time I'd managed to get a shoe on, or rather one of the wide soft black leather moccasins I used as bedroom slippers. Milo threaded the stirrup

567

over the moccasin with unexpected gentleness and I wondered if he were having last-minute doubts about the wisdom of all this.

One look at the Ostermeyers' faces dispelled both his doubts and mine. They were beaming at Datepalm already with proprietary pride.

Certainly he looked good. He filled the eye, as they say. A bay with black points, excellent head, short sturdy legs with plenty of bone. The Ostermeyers always preferred handsome animals, perhaps because they were handsome themselves, and Datepalm was well-mannered besides, which made him a peach of a ride.

He and I and two others from the rest of the string set off at a walk towards the far end of the gallop but were presently trotting, which I achieved by standing in the stirrups with all my weight on my right foot while cursing Milo imaginatively for the sensations in my left. Datepalm, who knew how horses should be ridden, which was not lopsided like this, did a good deal of head and tail shaking but otherwise seemed willing to trust me. He and I knew each other well as I'd ridden him in all his races for the past three years. Horses had no direct way of expressing recognition, but occasionally he would turn his head to look at me when he heard my voice, and I also thought he might know me by scent as he would put his muzzle against my neck sometimes and make small whiffling movements of his nostrils. In any case we did have a definite rapport and that morning it stood us in good stead.

At the far end the two lads and I sorted out our three horses ready to set off at a working gallop back towards Milo and the Ostermeyers, a pace fast enough to be interesting but not flat out like racing.

There wasn't much finesse in riding a gallop to please customers, one simply saw to it that one was on their side of the accompanying horses, to give them a clear view of the merchandise, and that one finished in front to persuade them that that's what would happen in future.

Walking him around to get in position I chatted quietly as I often did to Datepalm, because in common with many racehorses he was always reassured by a calm human voice, sensing from one's tone that all was well. Maybe horses heard the lower resonances: one never knew.

'Just go up there like a pro,' I told him, 'because I don't want to lose you, you old bugger. I want us to win the National one day, so shine, boy. Dazzle. Do your bloody best.'

I shook up the reins as we got the horses going, and in fact Datepalm put up one of his smoothest performances, staying with his companions for most of the journey, lengthening his stride when I gave him the signal, coming away alone and then sweeping collectedly past the Ostermeyers with fluid power; and if the jockey found it an acutely stabbing discomfort all the way, it was a fair price for the result. Even before I'd pulled up, the Ostermeyers had bought the horse and shaken hands on the deal.

'Subject to a veterinarian's report, of course,' Harley was saying as I walked Datepalm back to join them. 'Otherwise, he's superb.'

Milo's smile looked as if it would split his face. He held the reins while Martha excitedly patted the new acquisition, and went on holding them while I took my feet out of the stirrups and lowered myself very carefully to the ground, hopping a couple of steps to where the crutches lay on the grass.

'What did you do to your foot?' Martha asked unworriedly.

'Wrenched it,' I said, slipping the arm cuffs on with relief. 'Very boring.'

She smiled, nodded and patted my arm. 'Milo said it was nothing much.'

Milo gave me a gruesome look, handed Datepalm back to his lad, Gerry, and helped the Ostermeyers into the big-wheeled vehicle for the drive home. We bumped down the tracks and I took off the helmet and ran my fingers through my hair, reflecting that although I wouldn't care to ride gallops like that every day of the week, I would do it again for as good an outcome.

We all went into Milo's house for breakfast, a ritual there as in many other racing stables, and over coffee, toast and scrambled eggs Milo and the Ostermeyers planned Datepalm's future programme, including all the top races with of course another crack at the Gold Cup.

'What about the Grand National?' Martha said, her eyes like stars.

'Well, now, we'll have to see,' Milo said, but his dreams too were as visible as searchlights. First thing on our return, he'd telephoned to Datepalm's former owner and got confirmation that she agreed to the sale and was pleased by it, and since then one had almost needed to pull him down from the ceiling with a string like a helium-filled balloon. My own feelings weren't actually much lower. Datepalm really was a horse to build dreams on.

After the food and a dozen repetitions of the horse's virtues, Milo told the Ostermeyers about my inheriting Dozen Roses and about the probate saga, which seemed to fascinate them. Martha sat up straighter and exclaimed, 'Did you say York?'

Milo nodded.

'Do you mean this Saturday? Why, Harley and I are going to York races on Saturday, aren't we, Harley?'

Harley agreed that they were. 'Our dear friends Lord and Lady Knightwood have asked us to lunch.'

Martha said, 'Why don't we give Derek a ride up there to see his horse run? What do you say, Harley?'

'Be glad to have you along,' Harley said to me genuinely. 'Don't give us no for an answer.'

I looked at their kind insistent faces and said lamely, 'I thought of going by train, if I went at all.'

'No, no,' Martha said. 'Come to London by train and we'll go up together. Do say you will.'

Milo was looking at me anxiously: pleasing the Ostermeyers was still an absolute priority. I said I'd be glad to accept their kindness and Martha, mixing gratification with sudden alarm, said she hoped the inheritance wouldn't persuade me to stop riding races.

'No,' I said.

'That's positive enough.' Harley was pleased. 'You're part of the package, fella. You and Datepalm together.'

Brad and I went on to London, and I was very glad to have him drive.

'Office?' he asked, and I said, 'Yes,' and we travelled there in silent harmony.

He'd told me the evening before that Greville's car wasn't parked anywhere near Greville's house: or rather he'd handed me back the piece of paper with the car's number on it and said, 'Couldn't find it.' I thought I'd better get on to the police and other towers-away in Ipswich, and I'd better start learning the company's finances and Greville's as well, and I had two-thirds of the vault still to check and I could feel the suction of the quicksands inexorably.

I took the two baffling little gadgets from Greville's sitting room upstairs to Greville's office and showed them to June.

'That one,' she said immediately, pointing to the

thumb-sized tube with the whine, 'is a device to discourage mosquitoes. Mr Franklin said it's the noise of a male mosquito, and it frightens the blood-sucking females away.' She laughed. 'He said every man should have one.'

She picked up the other gadget and frowned at it, pressing the red button with no results.

'It has an aerial,' I said.

'Oh yes.' She pulled it out to its full extent. 'I think . . .' She paused. 'He used to have a transmitter which started his car from a distance, so he could warm the engine up in cold weather before he left his house, but the receiver bit got stolen with his Porsche. Then he bought the old Rover, and he said a car-starter wouldn't work on it because it only worked with direct transmission or fuel injection, or something, which the Rover doesn't have.'

'So this is the car-starter?'

'Well . . . no. This one doesn't do so much. The car-starter had buttons that would also switch on the headlights so that you could see where your car was, if you'd left it in a dark car-park.' She pushed the aerial down again. 'I think this one only switches the lights on, or makes the car whistle, if I remember right. He was awfully pleased with it when he got it, but I haven't seen it for ages. He had so many gadgets, he couldn't take them all in his pockets and I think he'd got a bit tired of carrying them about. He used to leave them in his desk, mostly.'

'You just earned your twenty per cent all over again,'
I said.

'What?'

'Let's just check that the batteries work,' I said.

She opened the battery compartment and discovered
it was empty. As if it were routine, she then pulled
open a drawer in one of the other tiers of the desk
and revealed a large open box containing packet after
packet of new batteries in every possible size. She
pulled out a packet, opened it and fed the necessary
power packs into the slots, and although pressing the
red button still provided no visible results, I was pretty
confident we were in business.

June said suddenly, 'You're going to take this to
Ipswich, aren't you? To find his car? Isn't that what you
mean?'

I nodded. 'Let's hope it works.'

'Oh, it must.'

'It's quite a big town, and the car could be anywhere.'

'Yes,' she said, 'but it must be *somewhere*. I'm sure
you'll find it.'

'Mm.' I looked at her bright, intelligent face. 'June,' I
said slowly, 'don't tell anyone else about this gadget.'

'Why ever not?'

'Because,' I said, 'someone broke into this office
looking for something and we don't know if they found
it. If they didn't, and it is by any chance in the car, I
don't want anyone to realize that the car is still lost.'
I paused. 'I'd much rather you said nothing.'

574

'Not even to Annette?'

'Not to anyone.'

'But that means you think . . . you think . . .'

'I don't really think anything. It's just for security.'

Security was all right with her. She looked less troubled and agreed to keep quiet about the car-finder; and I hadn't needed to tell her about the mugger who had knocked me down to steal Greville's bag of clothes, which to me, in hindsight, was looking less and less a random hit and more and more a shot at a target.

Someone must have known Greville was dying, I thought. Someone who had organized or executed a mugging. I hadn't the faintest idea who could have done either, but it did seem to me possible that one of Greville's staff might have unwittingly chattered within earshot of receptive ears. Yet what could they have said? Greville hadn't told any of them he was buying diamonds. And why hadn't he? Secretive as he was, gems were his business.

The useless thoughts squirrelled around and got me nowhere. The gloomiest of them was that someone could have gone looking for Greville's car at any time since the scaffolding fell, and although I might find the engine and the wheels, the essential cupboard would be bare.

Annette came into the office carrying a fistful of papers which she said had come in the morning post and needed to be dealt with – by me, her manner inferred.

'Sit down, then,' I said, 'and tell me what they all mean.'

Thcrc were letters from insurance people, fund raisers, dissatisfied customers, gemmology forecasters, and a cable from a supplier in Hong Kong saying he didn't have enough African 12 mm amethyst AA quality round beads to fill our order and would we take Brazilian amethyst to make it up.

'What's the difference?' I asked. 'Does it matter?'

Annette developed worry lines over my ignorance. 'The best amethyst is found in Africa,' she said. 'Then it goes to Hong Kong or Taiwan for cutting and polishing into beads, then comes here. The amethyst from Brazil isn't such a good deep colour. Do you want me to order the Brazilian amethyst or wait until he has more of the African?'

'What do you think?' I said.

'Mr Franklin always decided.'

She looked at me anxiously. It's hopeless, I thought. The simplest decision was impossible without knowledge.

'Would the customers take the Brazilian instead?' I asked.

'Some would, some wouldn't. It's much cheaper. We sell a lot of the Brazilian anyway, in all sizes.'

'Well,' I said, 'if we run out of the African beads, offer the customers Brazilian. Or offer a different size of African. Cable the Chinese supplier to send just the

African AA 12 mm he's got now and the rest as soon as he can.'

She looked relieved. 'That's what I'd have said.'

Then why didn't you, I thought, but it was no use being angry. If she gave me bad advice I'd probably blame her for it: it was safer from her viewpoint, I supposed, not to stick her neck out.

'Incidentally,' she said, 'I did reach Prospero Jenks. He said he'd be in his Knightsbridge shop at two-thirty today, if you wanted to see him.'

'Great.'

She smiled. 'I didn't mention horses.'

I smiled back. 'Fine.'

She took the letters off to her own office to answer them, and I went from department to department on a round trip to the vault, watching everyone at work, all of them capable, willing and beginning to settle obligingly into the change of regime, keeping their inner reservations to themselves. I asked if one of them would go down and tell Brad I'd need him at two, not before: June went and returned like a boomerang.

I unlocked the vault and started on topaz: thousands of brilliant translucent slippery stones in a rainbow of colours, some bigger than acorns, some like peas.

No diamonds.

After that, every imaginable shape and size of garnet which could be yellow and green, I found, as well as red, and boxes of citrine.

Two and a half hours of unfolding and folding glossy white packets, and no diamonds.

June swirled in and out at one point with a long order for faceted stones which she handed to me without comment, and I remembered that only Greville and Annette packed orders from the vault. I went in search of Annette and asked if I might watch while she worked down the list, found what was needed from twenty or more boxes and assembled the total on the shelf. She was quick and sure, knowing exactly where to find everything. It was quite easy, she said, reassuring me. I would soon get the hang of it. God help me, I thought.

At two, after another of June's sandwich lunches, I went down to the car and gave Prospero Jenks's address to Brad. 'It's a shop somewhere near Harrods,' I said, climbing in.

He nodded, drove through the traffic, found the shop.

'Great,' I said. 'Now this time you'll have to answer the car phone whether you like it or not, because there's nowhere here to park.'

He shook his head. He'd resisted the suggestion several times before.

'Yes,' I said. 'It's very easy. I'll switch it on for you now. When it rings pick it up and press this button, SND, and you'll be able to hear me. OK? I'll ring when I'm ready to leave, then you just come back here and pick me up.'

He looked at the telephone as if it were contaminated.

It was a totally portable phone, not a fixture in the car, and it didn't receive calls unless one switched it on, which I quite often forgot to do and sometimes didn't do on purpose. I put the phone ready on the passenger seat beside him, to make it easy, and hoped for the best.

Prospero Jenks's shop window glittered with the sort of intense lighting that makes jewellery sparkle, but the lettering of his name over the window was neat and plain, as if ostentation there would have been superfluous.

I looked at the window with a curiosity I would never have felt a week earlier and found it filled not with conventional displays of rings and wristwatches but with joyous toys: model cars, aeroplanes, skiing figures, racing yachts, pheasants and horses, all gold and enamel and shining with gems. Almost every passer-by, I noticed, paused to look.

Pushing awkwardly through the heavy glass front door I stepped into a deep-carpeted area with chairs at the ready before every counter. Apart from the plushness, it was basically an ordinary shop, not very big, quiet in decor, all the excitement in the baubles.

There was no one but me in there and I swung over to one of the counters to see what was on display. Rings, I found, but not simple little circles. These were huge, often asymmetric, all colourful eyecatchers supreme.

'Can I help you?' a voice said.

A neutral man, middle-aged, in a black suit, coming from a doorway at the rear.

'My name's Franklin,' I said. 'Came to see Prospero Jenks.'

'A minute.'

He retreated, returned with a half-smile and invited me through the doorway to the privacies beyond. Shielded from customers' view by a screening partition lay a much longer space which doubled as office and workroom and contained a fearsome-looking safe and several tiers of little drawers like the ones in Saxony Franklin. On one wall a large framed sign read: 'NEVER TURN YOUR BACK TO CUSTOMERS. ALWAYS WATCH THEIR HANDS.' A fine statement of no trust, I thought in amusement.

Sitting on a stool by a workbench, a jeweller's lens screwed into one eye, was a hunched man in pale pink and white striped shirtsleeves, fiddling intently with a small gold object fixed into a vice. Patience and expert workmanship were much on view, all of it calm and painstaking.

He removed the lens with a sigh and rose to his feet, turning to inspect me from crown to crutches to toecaps with growing surprise. Whatever he'd been expecting, I was not it.

The feeling, I supposed, was mutual. He was maybe fifty but looked younger in a Peter Pan sort of way; a boyish face with intense bright blue eyes and a lot of lines developing across the forehead. Fairish hair, no beard, no moustache, no personal display. I had expected someone fancier, more extravagant, temperamental.

'Grev's brother?' he said. 'What a turn-up. There I was, thinking you'd be his age, his height.' He narrowed his eyes. 'He never said he had a brother. How do I know you're legit?'

'His assistant, Annette Adams, made the appointment.'

'Yes, so she did. Fair enough. Told me Grev was dead, long live the King. Said his brother was running the shop, life would go on. But I'll tell you, unless you know as much as Grev, I'm in trouble.'

'I came to talk to you about that.'

'It don't look like tidings of great joy,' he said, watching me judiciously. 'Want a seat?' He pointed at an office chair for me and took his place on the stool. His voice was a long way from cut-glass. More like East End London tidied up for West; the sort that came from nowhere with no privileges and made it to the top from sheer undeniable talent. He had the confident manner of long success, a creative spirit who was also a tradesman, an original artist without airs.

'I'm just learning the business,' I said cautiously. 'I'll do what I can.'

'Grev was a genius,' he said explosively. 'No one like him with stones. He'd bring me oddities, one-offs from all over the world, and I've made pieces . . .' He stopped and spread his arms out. 'They're in palaces,' he said, 'and museums and mansions in Palm Beach. Well, I'm in business. I sell them to wherever the money's coming from. I've got my pride, but it's in the pieces. They're good, I'm expensive, it works a treat.'

'Do you make everything you sell?' I asked.

He laughed. 'No, not myself personally, I couldn't. I design everything, don't get me wrong, but I have a workshop making them. I just make the special pieces myself, the unique ones. In between, I invent for the general market. Grev said he had some decent spinel, have you still got it?'

'Er,' I said, 'red?'

'Red,' he affirmed. 'Three, four or five carats. I'll take all you've got.'

'We'll send it tomorrow.'

'By messenger,' he said. 'Not post.'

'All right.'

'And a slab of rock crystal like the Eiger. Grev showed me a photo. I've got a commission for a fantasy . . . Send the crystal too.'

'All right,' I said again, and hid my doubts. I hadn't seen any slab of rock crystal. Annette would know, I thought.

He said casually, 'What about the diamonds?'

I let the breath out and into my lungs with conscious control.

'What about them?' I said.

'Grev was getting me some. He'd got them, in fact.

582

He told me. He'd sent a batch off to be cut. Are they back yet?'

'Not yet,' I said, hoping I wasn't croaking. 'Are those the diamonds he bought a couple of months ago from the Central Selling Organization that you're talking about?'

'Sure. He bought a share in a sight from a sight-holder. I asked him to. I'm still running the big chunky rings and necklaces I made my name in, but I'm setting some of them now with bigger diamonds, making more profit per item since the market will stand it, and I wanted Grev to get them because I trust him. Trust is like gold dust in this business, even though diamonds weren't his thing really. You wouldn't want to buy two-to three-carat stones from just anyone, even if they're not D or E flawless, right?'

'Er, right.'

'So he bought the share of the sight and he's having them cut in Antwerp as I require them, as I expect you know.'

I nodded. I did know, but only since he'd just told me.

'I'm going to make stars of some of them to shine from the rock crystal . . .' He broke off, gave a self-deprecating shrug of the shoulders, and said, 'And I'm making a mobile, with diamonds on gold trembler wires that move in the lightest air. It's to hang by a window and flash fire in the sunlight.' Again the self-deprecation, this time in a smile. 'Diamonds are ravishing in sunlight, they're at their best in it, and all the social

583

snobs in this city scream that it's so frightfully vulgar, darling, to wear diamond earrings or bracelets in the daytime. It makes me sick, to be honest. Such a waste.'

I had never thought about diamonds in sunlight before, though I suppose I would in future. Vistas opened could never be closed, as maybe Greville would have said.

'I haven't caught up with everything yet,' I said, which was the understatement of the century. 'Have any of the diamonds been delivered to you so far?'

He shook his head. 'I haven't been in a hurry for them before.'

'And . . . er . . . how many are involved?'

'About a hundred. Like I said, not the very best colour in the accepted way of things but they can look warmer with gold sometimes if they're not ultra blue-white. I work with gold mostly. I like the feel.'

'How much,' I said slowly, doing sums, 'will your rock crystal fantasy sell for?'

'Trade secret. But then, I guess you're trade. It's commissioned, I've got a contract for a quarter of a million if they like it. If they don't like it, I get it back, sell it somewhere else, dismantle it, whatever. In the worst event I'd lose nothing but my time in making it, but don't you worry, they'll like it.'

His certainty was absolute, built on experience.

I said, 'Do you happen to know the name of the Antwerp cutter Greville sent the diamonds to? I mean, it's bound to be on file in the office, but if I know who to look for . . .' I paused. 'I could try to hurry him up for you, if you like.'

'I'd like you to, but I don't know who Grev knew there, exactly.'

I shrugged. 'I'll look it up, then.'

Exactly where was I going to look it up, I wondered? Not in the missing address book, for sure.

'Do you know the name of the sightholder?' I asked.

'Nope.'

'There's a ton of paper in the office,' I said in explanation. 'I'm going through it as fast as I can.'

'Grev never said a word he didn't have to,' Jenks said unexpectedly. 'I'd talk, he listened. We got on fine. He understood what I do better than anybody.'

The sadness of his voice was my brother's universal accolade, I thought. He'd been liked. He'd been trusted. He would be missed.

I stood up and said, 'Thank you, Mr Jenks.'

'Call me Pross,' he said easily. 'Everyone does.'

'My name's Derek.'

'Right,' he said, smiling. 'Now I'll keep on dealing with you, I won't say I won't, but I'm going to have to find me another traveller like Grev, with an eye like his . . . He's been supplying me ever since I started on my own, he gave me credit when the banks wouldn't, he had faith in what I could do . . . Near the beginning he brought me two rare sticks of watermelon tourmaline that were each over two inches long and were half pink, half green mixed all the way up and transparent

585

with the light shining through them and changing while you watched. It would have been a sin to cut them for jewellery. I mounted them in gold and platinum to hang and twist in sunlight.' He smiled his deprecating smile. 'I like gemstones to have life. I didn't have to pay Grev for that tourmaline ever. It made my name for me, the piece was reviewed in the papers and won prizes, and he said the trade we'd do together would be his reward.' He clicked his mouth. 'I do go on a bit.'

'I like to hear it,' I said. I looked down the room to his workbench and said, 'Where did you learn all this? How does one start?'

'I started in metalwork classes at the local comprehensive,' he said frankly. 'Then I stuck bits of glass in gold-plated wire to give to my mum. Then her friends wanted some. So when I left school I took some of those things to show to a jewellery manufacturer and asked for a job. Costume jewellery, they made. I was soon designing for them, and I never looked back.'

CHAPTER EIGHT

I borrowed Prospero's telephone to get Brad, but although I could hear the ringing tone in the car, he didn't answer. Cursing slightly, I asked Pross for a second call and got through to Annette.

'Please keep on trying this number,' I said, giving it to her. 'When Brad answers, tell him I'm ready to go.'

'Are you coming back here?' she asked.

I looked at my watch. It wasn't worth going back as I had to return to Kensington by five-thirty. I said no, I wasn't.

'Well, there are one or two things . . .'

'I can't really tie this phone up,' I said. 'I'll go to my brother's house and ring you from there. Just keep trying Brad.'

I thanked Pross again for the calls. Any time, he said vaguely. He was sitting again in front of his vice, thinking and tinkering, producing his marvels.

There were customers in the shop being attended to by the black-suited salesman. He glanced up very briefly in acknowledgement as I went through and

587

immediately returned to watching the customers' hands. A business without trust; much worse than racing. But then, it was probably impossible to slip a racehorse into a pocket when the trainer wasn't looking.

I stood on the pavement and wondered pessimistically how long it would take Brad to answer the telephone but in the event he surprised me by arriving within a very few minutes. When I opened the car door, the phone was ringing.

'Why don't you answer it?' I asked, wriggling my way into the seat.

'Forgot which button.'

'But you came,' I said.

'Yerss.'

I picked up the phone myself and talked to Annette. 'Brad apparently reckoned that if the phone rang it meant I was ready, so he saw no need to answer it.'

Brad gave a silent nod.

'So now we're setting off to Kensington.' I paused. 'Annette, what's a sightholder, and what's a sight?'

'You're back to diamonds again!'

'Yes. Do you know?'

'Of course I do. A sightholder is someone who is permitted to buy rough diamonds from the CSO. There aren't so many sightholders, only about a hundred and fifty world-wide, I think. They sell the diamonds then to other people. A sight is what they call the sales CSO hold every five weeks, and a sight-box is a packet of stones they sell, though that's often called a sight too.'

'Is a sightholder the same as a diamantaire?' I asked.

'All sightholders are diamantaires, but all diamantaires are not sightholders. Diamantaires buy from the
sightholders, or share in a sight, or buy somewhere else,
not from De Beers.'

Ask a simple question, I thought.

Annette said, 'A consignment of cultured pearls has
come from Japan. Where shall I put them?'

'Um . . . Do you mean where because the vault is
locked?'

'Yes.'

'Where did you put things when my brother was
travelling?'

She said doubtfully, 'He always said to put them in
the stock-room under "miscellaneous beads".'

'Put them in there, then.'

'But the drawer is full with some things that came
last week. I wouldn't want the responsibility of putting
the pearls anywhere Mr Franklin hadn't approved.' I
couldn't believe she needed direction over the simplest
thing, but apparently she did. 'The pearls are valuable,'
she said. 'Mr Franklin would never leave them out in
plain view.'

'Aren't there any empty drawers?'

'Well, I . . .'

'Find an empty drawer or a nearby empty drawer
and put them there. We'll see to them properly in the
morning.'

'Yes, all right.'

She seemed happy with it and said everything else could wait until I came back. I switched off the telephone feeling absolutely swamped by the prospect she'd opened up: if Greville hid precious things under 'miscellaneous beads', where else might he not have hidden them? Would I find a hundred diamonds stuffed in at the back of rhodocrosite or jasper, if I looked?

The vault alone was taking too long. The four big stock-rooms promised a nightmare.

Brad miraculously found a parking space right outside Greville's house, which seemed obscurely to disappoint him.

'Twenty past five,' he said, 'for the pub?'

'If you wouldn't mind. And . . . er . . . would you just stand there now while I take a look-see?' I had grown cautious, I found.

He ducked his head in assent and watched me manoeuvre the few steps up to the front door. No floodlights came on and no dog barked, presumably because it was daylight. I opened the three locks and pushed the door.

The house was still. No movements of air. I propped the door open with a bronze horse clearly lying around for the purpose and went down the passage to the small sitting room.

No intruders. No mess. No amazons waving riot sticks, no wrecking balls trying to get past the grilles on the windows. If anyone had attempted to penetrate Greville's fortress, they hadn't succeeded.

I returned to the front door. Brad was still standing beside the car, looking towards the house. I gave him a thumbs-up sign, and he climbed into the driver's seat while I closed the heavy door, and in the little sitting room, started taking all of the books off the shelves methodically, riffling the pages and putting each back where I found it.

There were ten hollow books altogether, mostly with titles like *Tales of the Outback* and *With a Mule in Patagonia*. Four were empty, including the one which had held Clarissa Williams's letters. One held the big ornate key. One held an expensive-looking gold watch, the hands pointing to the correct time.

The watch Greville had been wearing in Ipswich was one of those affairs with more knobs than instructions. It lay now beside my bed in Hungerford emitting bleeps at odd intervals and telling me which way was north. The slim gold elegance in the hollow box was for a different mood, a different man, and when I turned it over on my palm I found the inscription on the back: G my love C.

She couldn't have known it was there, I thought. She hadn't looked for it. She'd looked only for the letters, and by chance had come to them first. I put the watch back into the box and back on the shelf. There was no way I could return it to her, and perhaps she wouldn't want it, not with that inscription.

Two of the remaining boxes contained large keys, again unspecified, and one contained a folded

instruction leaflet detailing how to set a safe in a concrete nest. The last revealed two very small plastic cases
containing baby recording tapes, each adorned with the
printed legend 'microcassette'. The cassette cases were
all of two inches long by one and a half wide, the
featherweight tapes inside a fraction smaller.

I tossed one in my hand indecisively. Nowhere
among Greville's tidy belongings had I so far found a
microcassette player, which didn't mean I wouldn't in
time. Sufficient to the day, I thought in the end, and left
the tiny tapes in the book.

With the scintillating titles and their secrets all back
on the shelves I stared at them gloomily. Not a diamond
in the lot.

Instructions for concrete nests were all very well, but
where was the safe? Tapes were OK, but where was the
player? Keys were fine, but where were the keyholes?
The most frustrating thing about it was that Greville
hadn't meant to leave such puzzles. For him, the
answers were part of his fabric.

I'd noticed on my way in and out of the house that
mail was accumulating in the wire container fixed inside
the letter-box on the front door, so to fill in the time
before I was due at the pub I took the letters along to
the sitting room and began opening the envelopes.

It seemed all wrong. I kept telling myself it was
necessary but I still felt as if I were trespassing on
ground Greville had surrounded with keep-out fences.
There were bills, requests from charities, a bank state-

ment for his private account, a gemmology magazine and two invitations. No letters from sightholders, diamantaires or cutters in Antwerp. I put the letters into the gemmology magazine's large envelope and added to them some similar unfinished business that I'd found in the drawer under the telephone, and reflected ruefully, putting it all ready to take to Hungerford, that I loathed paperwork at the best of times. My own had a habit of mounting up into increasingly urgent heaps. Perhaps having to do Greville's would teach me some sense.

Brad whisked us round to The Rook and Castle at five-thirty and pointed to the phone to let me know how I could call him when I'd finished, and I saw from his twitch of a smile that he found it a satisfactory amusement.

The Rook and Castle was old fashioned inside as well as out, an oasis of drinking peace without a juke-box. There was a lot of dark wood and tiffany lampshades and small tables with beer mats. A clientele of mostly business-suited men was beginning to trickle in and I paused inside the door both to get accustomed to the comparative darkness and to give anyone who was interested a plain view of the crutches.

The interest level being nil, I judged Elliot Trelawney to be absent. I went over to the bar, ordered some Perrier and swallowed a Distalgesic, as it was time. The morning's gallop had done no good to the ankle department but it wasn't to be regretted.

A bulky man of about fifty came into the place as if

familiar with his surroundings and looked purposefully around, sharpening his gaze on the crutches and coming without hesitation to the bar.

'Mr Franklin?'

I shook his offered hand.

'What are you drinking?' he said briskly, eyeing my glass.

'Perrier. That's temporary also.'

He smiled swiftly, showing white teeth. 'You won't mind if I have a double Glenlivet? Greville and I drank many of them together here. I'm going to miss him abominably. Tell me what happened.'

I told him. He listened intently, but at the end he said merely, 'You look very uncomfortable propped against that stool. Why don't we move to a table?' And without more ado he picked up my glass along with the one the bartender had fixed for him, and carried them over to two wooden armchairs under a multicoloured lampshade by the wall.

'That's better,' he said, taking a sip and eyeing me over the glass. 'So you're the brother he talked about. You're Derek.'

'I'm Derek. His only brother, actually. I didn't know he talked about me.'

'Oh, yes. Now and then.'

Elliot Trelawney was big, almost bald, with half-moon glasses and a face that was fleshy but healthy looking. He had thin lips but laugh lines around his eyes, and I'd have said on a snap judgement that he was a realist with a sense of humour.

'He was proud of you,' he said.

'Proud?' I was surprised.

He glimmered. 'We often played golf together on Saturday mornings and sometimes he would be wanting to finish before the two o'clock race at Sandown or somewhere, and it would be because you were riding and it was on the box. He liked to watch you. He liked you to win.'

'He never told me,' I said regretfully.

'He wouldn't, would he? I watched with him a couple of times and all he said after you'd won was, "That's all right then." '

'And when I lost?'

'When you lost?' He smiled. 'Nothing at all. Once you had a crashing fall and he said he'd be glad on the whole when you retired, as race-riding was so dangerous. Ironic, isn't it?'

'Yes.'

'By God, I'll miss him.' His voice was deep. 'We were friends for twenty years.'

I envied him. I wanted intolerably what it was too late to have, and the more I listened to people remembering Greville the worse it got.

'Are you a magistrate?' I asked.

He nodded. 'We often sat together. Greville introduced me to it, but I've never had quite his gift. He seemed to know the truth of things by instinct. He said goodness was visible, therefore in its absence one sought for answers.'

'What sort of cases did . . . do you try?'

'All sorts.' He smiled again briefly. 'Shoplifters. Vagrants. Possession of drugs. TV licence fee evaders. Sex offenders . . . that's prostitution, rape, sex with minors, kerb crawlers. Greville always seemed to know infallibly when those were lying.'

'Go on,' I said, when he stopped. 'Anything else?'

'Well, there are a lot of diplomats in West London, in all the embassies. You'd be astonished what they get away with by claiming diplomatic immunity. Greville hated diplomatic immunity, but we have to grant it. Then we have a lot of small businessmen who "forget" to pay the road tax on the company vehicles, and there are TDAs by the hundred – that's Taking and Driving Away cars. Other motoring offences, speeding and so on, are dealt with separately, like domestic offences and juveniles. And then occasionally we get the preliminary hearings in a murder case, but of course we have to refer those to the Crown Court.'

'Does it all ever depress you?' I said.

He took a sip and considered me. 'It makes you sad,' he said eventually. 'We see as much inadequacy and stupidity as downright villainy. Some of it makes you laugh. I wouldn't say it's depressing, but one learns to see the world from underneath, so to speak. To see the dirt and the delusions, to see through the offenders' eyes and understand their weird logic. But one's disillusion is sporadic because we don't have a bench every day. Twice a month, in Greville's and my cases, plus a little committee work. And that's what I really want from you: the notes Greville was making on the licensing of a new-style gambling club. He said he'd learned disturbing allegations against one of the organizers and he was going to advise turning down the application at the next committee meeting even though it was a project we'd formerly looked on favourably.'

'I'm afraid,' I said, 'that I haven't so far found any notes like that.'

'Damn . . . Where would he have put them?'

'I don't know. I'll look for them, though.' No harm in keeping an eye open for notes while I searched for C.

Elliot Trelawney reached into an inner jacket pocket and brought out two flat black objects, one a notebook, the other a folded black case a bit like a cigarette case.

'These were Greville's,' he said. 'I brought them for you.' He put them on the small table and moved them towards me with plump and deliberate fingers 'He lent me that one,' he pointed, 'and the notebook he left on the table after a committee meeting last week.'

'Thank you,' I said. I picked up the folded case and opened it and found inside a miniature electronic chess set, the sort that challenged a player to beat it. I looked up. Trelawney's expression, unguarded, was intensely sorrowful. 'Would you like it?' I said. 'I know it's not much, but would you like to keep it?'

'If you mean it.'

597

I nodded and he put the chess set back in his pocket. 'Greville and I used to play . . . *dammit* . . .' he finished explosivcly. 'Why should such a futile thing happen?'

No answer was possible. I regretfully picked up the black notebook and opened it at random.

'The bad scorn the good,' I read aloud, 'and the crooked despise the straight.'

'The thoughts of Chairman Mao,' Trelawney said dryly, recovering himself. 'I used to tease him . . . he said it was a habit he'd had from university when he'd learned to clarify his thoughts by writing them down. When I knew he was dead I read that notebook from cover to cover. I've copied down some of the things in it, I hope you won't mind.' He smiled. 'You'll find parts of it especially interesting.'

'About his horses?'

'Those too.'

I stowed the notebook in a trouser pocket which was already pretty full and brought out from there the racing diary, struck by a thought. I explained what the diary was, showing it to Trelawney.

'I phoned that number,' I said, turning pages and pointing, 'and mentioned Greville's name, and a woman told me in no uncertain terms never to telephone again as she wouldn't have the name Greville Franklin spoken in her house.'

Elliot Trelawney blinked. 'Greville? Doesn't sound like Greville.'

'I didn't think so, either. So would it have had something to do with one of your cases? Someone he found guilty of something?'

'Hah. Perhaps.' He considered. 'I could probably find out whose number it is, if you like. Strange he would have had it in his diary, though. Do you want to follow it up?'

'It just seemed so odd,' I said.

'Quite right.' He unclipped a gold pencil from another inner pocket and in a slim notebook of black leather with gold corners wrote down the number.

'Do you make enemies much, because of the court?' I asked.

He looked up and shrugged. 'We get cursed now and then. Screamed at, one might say. But usually not. Mostly they plead guilty because it's so obvious they are. The only real enemy Greville might have had is the gambling club organizer who's not going to get his licence. A drugs baron is what Greville called him. A man suspected of murder but not tried through lack of evidence. He might have had very hard feelings.' He hesitated. 'When I heard Greville was dead, I even wondered about Vaccaro. But it seems clear the scaffolding was a sheer accident . . . wasn't it?'

'Yes, it was. The scaffolding broke high up. One man working on it fell three storeys to his death. Pieces just rained down on Greville. A minute earlier, a minute later . . .' I sighed. 'Is Vaccaro the gambling-licence man?'

'He is. He appeared before the committee and

seemed perfectly straightforward. Subject to screening, we said. And then someone contacted Greville and uncovered the muck. But we don't ourselves have any details, so we need his notes.'

'I'll look for them,' I promised again. I turned more pages in the diary. 'Does Koningin Beatrix mean anything to you?' I showed him the entry. 'Or CZ = C × 1.7?'

C, I thought, looking at it again, stood for diamond.

'Nothing,' Elliot Trelawney said. 'But as you know, Greville could be as obscure as he was clear-headed. And these were private notes to himself, after all. Same as his notebook. It was never for public consumption.'

I nodded and put away the diary and paid for Elliot Trelawney's repeat Glenlivet but felt waterlogged myself. He stayed for a while, seeming to be glad to talk about Greville, as I was content to listen. We parted eventually on friendly terms, he giving me his card with his phone number for when I found Greville's notes.

If, I silently thought. If I find them.

When he'd gone I used the pub's telephone to ring the car, and after five unanswered brr-brrs disconnected and went outside, and Brad with almost a grin reappeared to pick me up.

'Home,' I said, and he said, 'Yerss,' and that was that.

On the way I read bits of Greville's notebook, pausing often to digest the passing thoughts which had clearly been chiefly prompted by the flotsam drifting through the West London Magistrates Court.

'Goodness is sickening to the evil,' he wrote, 'as evil is sickening to the good. Both the evil and the good may be complacent.'

'In all income groups you find your average regulation slob who sniggers at anarchy but calls the police indignantly to his burglarized home, who is actively anti-authority until he needs to be saved from someone with a gun.'

'The palm outstretched for a hand-out can turn in a flash into a cursing fist. A nation's palm, a nation's fist.'

'Crime to many is not crime but simply a way of life. If laws are inconvenient, ignore them, they don't apply to you.'

'Infinite sadness is not to trust an old friend.'

'Historically, more people have died of religion than cancer.'

'I hate rapists. I imagine being anally assaulted myself, and the anger overwhelms me. It's essential to make my judgement cold.'

Further on I came unexpectedly to what Elliot Trelawney must have meant.

Greville had written, 'Derek came to dinner very stiff with broken ribs. I asked him how he managed to live with all those injuries. "Forget the pain and get on with the party," he said. So we drank fizz.'

I stopped reading and stared out at the autumn countryside which was darkening now, lights going on. I remembered that evening very well, up to a point. Greville had been good fun. I'd got pretty high on

the cocktail of champagne and painkillers and I hadn't
felt a thing until I'd woken in the morning. I'd driven
myself seventy miles home and forgotten it, which
frightening fact was roughly why I was currently and
obediently sticking to water.

It was almost too dark to read more, but I flicked
over one more page and came to what amounted to a
prayer, so private and impassioned that I felt my mouth
go dry. Alone on the page were three brief lines:

> May I deal with honour.
> May I act with courage.
> May I achieve humility.

I felt as if I shouldn't have read it; knew he hadn't meant
it to be read. May I achieve humility . . . that prayer was
for saints.

When we reached my house I told Brad I would go to
London the next day by train, and he looked
devastated.

'I'll drive you for nowt,' he said, hoarsely.

'It isn't the money.' I was surprised by the strength of
his feelings. 'I just thought you'd be tired of all the
waiting about.'

He shook his head vigorously, his eyes positively
pleading.

'All right, then,' I said. 'London tomorrow, Ipswich on Friday. OK?'

'Yerss,' he said with obvious relief.

'And I'll pay you, of course.'

He looked at me dumbly for a moment, then ducked his head into the car to fetch the big brown envelope from Greville's house, and he waited while I unlocked my door and made sure that there were no unwelcome visitors lurking.

Everything was quiet, everything orderly. Brad nodded at my all-clear, gave me the envelope and loped off into the night more tongue-tied than ever. I'd never wondered very much about his thoughts during all the silent hours; had never tried, I supposed, to understand him. I wasn't sure that I wanted to. It was restful the way things were.

I ate a microwaved chicken pie from the freezer and made an unenthusiastic start on Greville's letters, paying his bills for him, closing his accounts, declining his invitations, saying sorry, sorry, very sorry.

After that, in spite of good resolutions, I did not attack my own backlog but read right through Greville's notebook looking for diamonds. Maybe there were some solid gold nuggets, maybe some pearls of wisdom, but no helpful instructions like turn right at the fourth apple tree, walk five paces and dig.

I did however find the answer to one small mystery, which I read with wry amusement.

The green soapstone box pleases me as an exercise in misdirection and deviousness. The keyhole
has no key because it has no lock. It's impossible
to unlock men's minds with keys, but guile and
pressure will do it, as with the box.

Even with the plain instruction to be guileful and devious it took me ages to find the secret. I tried pressing
each of the two hinges, pressing the lock, twisting, pressing everything again with the box upside down. The
green stone stayed stubbornly shut.

Misdirection, I thought. If the keyhole wasn't a lock,
maybe the hinges weren't hinges. Maybe the lid wasn't a
lid. Maybe the whole thing was solid.

I tried the box upside down again, put my thumbs on
its bottom surface with firm pressure and tried to push it
out endways, like a slide. Nothing happened. I reversed
it and pushed the other way and as if with a sigh for the
length of my stupidity the bottom of the box slid out
reluctantly to halfway, and stopped.

It was beautifully made, I thought. When it was shut
one couldn't see the bottom edges weren't solid stone,
so closely did they fit. I looked with great curiosity to
see what Greville had hidden in his ingenious hiding
place, not really expecting diamonds, and brought out
two well-worn chamois leather pouches with draw-
strings, the sort jewellers use, with the name of the
jeweller indistinctly stamped on the front.

Both of the pouches were empty, to my great disappointment. I stuffed them back into the hole and shut the box, and it sat on the table beside the telephone all evening, an enigma solved but useless.

It wasn't until I'd decided to go to bed that some switch or other clicked in my brain and a word half-seen became suddenly a conscious thought. Van Ekeren, stamped in gold. Perhaps the jeweller's name stamped on the chamois pouches was worth another look.

I opened the box and pulled the pouches out again and in the rubbed and faded lettering read the full name and address.

> Jacob van Ekeren
> Pelikanstraat 70
> Antwerp

There had to be, I thought, about ten thousand jewellers in Antwerp. The pouches were far from new, certainly not only a few weeks old. All the same ... better find out.

I took one and left one, closing the box again, and in the morning bore the crumpled trophy to London and through international telephone enquiries found Jacob van Ekeren's number.

The voice that answered from Antwerp spoke either Dutch or Flemish, so I tried in French, '*Je veux parler avec Monsieur Jacob van Ekeren, s'il vous plaît.*'

'*Ne quittez pas.*'

I held on as instructed until another voice spoke, this time in French, of which I knew far too little.

'*Monsieur van Ekeren n'est pas ici maintenant, monsieur.*'

'*Parlez vous anglais*?' I asked. 'I'm speaking from England.'

'*Attendez.*'

I waited again and was rewarded with an extremely English voice asking if he could help.

I explained that I was speaking from Saxony Franklin Ltd, gemstone importers in London.

'How can I help you?' He was courteous and non-committal.

'Do you,' I said baldly, 'cut and polish rough diamonds?'

'Yes, of course,' he answered. 'But before we do business with any new client we need introductions and references.'

'Um,' I said. 'Wouldn't Saxony Franklin Ltd be a client of yours already? Or Greville Saxony Franklin, maybe? Or just Greville Franklin? It's really important.'

'May I have your name?'

'Derek Franklin. Greville's brother.'

'One moment.' He returned after a while and said he would call me back shortly with an answer.

'Thank you very much,' I said.

'*Pas du tout.*' Bilingual besides.

I put down the phone and asked both Annette and June, who were busily moving around, if they could find

Jacob van Ekeren anywhere in Greville's files. 'See if you can find any mention of Antwerp in the computer,' I added to June.

'Diamonds again!'

'Yup. The van Ekeren address is 70 Pelikanstraat.'

Annette wrinkled her brow. 'That's the Belgian equivalent of Hatton Garden,' she said.

It disrupted their normal work and they weren't keen, but Annette was very soon able to say she had no record of any Jacob van Ekeren, but the files were kept in the office for only six years, and any contact before that would be in storage in the basement. June whisked in to confirm that she couldn't find van Ekeren or Pelikanstraat or Antwerp in the computer.

It wasn't exactly surprising. If Greville had wanted his diamond transaction to be common knowledge in the office he would have conducted it out in the open. Very odd, I thought, that he hadn't. If it had been anyone but Greville one would have suspected him of something underhand, but as far as I knew he always had dealt with honour, as he'd prayed.

The telephone rang and Annette answered it. 'Saxony Franklin, can I help you?' She listened. 'Derek Franklin? Yes, just a moment.' She handed me the receiver and I found it was the return of the smooth French–English voice from Belgium. I knew as well as he did that he had spent the time between the two calls getting our number from international enquiries so that he could check back and be sure I was who I'd said. Merely prudent. I'd have done the same.

'Mr Jacob van Ekeren has retired,' he said. 'I am his nephew Hans. I can tell you now after our researches that we have done no business with your firm within the past six or seven years, but I can't speak for the time before that, when my uncle was in charge.'

'I see,' I said. 'Could you, er, ask your uncle?'

'I will if you like,' he said civilly. 'I did telephone his house, but I understand that he and my aunt will be away from home until Monday, and their maid doesn't seem to know where they went.' He paused. 'Could I ask what all this is about?'

I explained that my brother had died suddenly, leaving a good deal of unfinished business which I was trying to sort out. 'I came across the name and address of your firm. I'm following up everything I can.'

'Ah,' he said sympathetically. 'I will certainly ask my uncle on Monday, and let you know.'

'I'm most grateful.'

'Not at all.'

The uncle, I thought morosely, was a dead-end.

I went along and opened the vault, telling Annette that Prospero Jenks wanted all the spinel. 'And he says we have a piece of rock crystal like the Eiger.'

'The what?'

'Sharp mountain. Like Mont Blanc.'

'Oh.' She moved down the rows of boxes and chose a heavy one from near the bottom at the far end. 'This is it,' she said, humping it on to the shelf and opening the lid. 'Beautiful.'

The Eiger, filling the box, was lying on its side and had a knobbly base so that it wouldn't stand up, but I supposed one could see in the lucent faces and angled planes that, studded with diamond stars and given the Jenks's sunlight treatment, it could make the basis of a fantasy worthy of the name.

'Do we have a price for it?' I asked.

'Double what it cost,' she said cheerfully. 'Plus VAT, plus packing and transport.'

'He wants everything sent by messenger.'

She nodded. 'He always does. Jason takes them in a taxi. Leave it to me, I'll see to it.'

'And we'd better put the pearls away that came yesterday.'

'Oh, yes.'

She went off to fetch them and I moved down to where I'd given up the day before, feeling certain that the search was futile but committed to it all the same. Annette returned with the pearls, which were at least in plastic bags on strings, not in the awkward open envelopes, so while she counted and stored the new intake, I checked my way through the old.

Boxes of pearls, all sizes. No diamonds.

'Does CZ mean anything to you?' I asked Annette idly.

'CZ is cubic zirconia,' she said promptly. 'We sell a fair amount of it.'

'Isn't that, um, imitation diamond?'

'It's a manufactured crystal very like diamond,' she said, 'but about ten thousand times cheaper. If it's in a ring, you can't tell the difference.'

'Can't anyone?' I asked. 'They must do.'

'Mr Franklin said that most high-street jewellers can't at a glance. The best way to tell the difference, he said, is to take the stones out of their setting and weigh them.'

'*Weigh* them?'

'Yes. Cubic zirconia's much heavier than diamond, so one carat of cubic zirconia is smaller than a one-carat diamond.'

'CZ equals C times one point seven,' I said slowly.

'That's right,' she said, surprised. 'How did you know?'

CHAPTER NINE

From noon on, when I closed the last box-lid unproductively on the softly changing colours of rainbow opal from Oregon, I sat in Greville's office reading June's print-out of a crash course in business studies, beginning to see the pattern of a cash flow that ended on the side of the angels. Annette, who as a matter of routine had been banking the receipts daily, produced a sheaf of cheques for me to sign, which I did, feeling that it was the wrong name on the line, and she brought the day's post for decisions, which I strugglingly made.

Several people in the jewellery business telephoned in response to the notices of Greville's death which had appeared in the papers that morning. Annette, reassuring them that the show would go on, sounded more confident than she looked. 'They all say Ipswich is too far, but they'll be there in spirit,' she reported.

At four there was a phone call from Elliot Trelawney, who said he'd cracked the number of the lady who didn't want Greville's name spoken in her house.

'It's sad, really,' he said with a chuckle. 'I suppose I

611

shouldn't laugh. That lady can't and won't forgive Greville because he sent her upper-crust daughter to jail for three months for selling cocaine to a friend. The mother was in court, I remember her, and she talked to the press afterwards. She couldn't believe that selling cocaine to a friend was an offence. Drug peddlers were despicable, of course, but that wasn't the same as selling to a friend.'

'If a law is inconvenient, ignore it, it doesn't apply to you.'

'What?'

'Something Greville wrote in his notebook.'

'Oh yes. It seems Greville got the mother's phone number to suggest ways of rehabilitation for the daughter, but mother wouldn't listen. Look,' he hesitated. 'Keep in touch now and then, would you? Have a drink in The Rook and Castle occasionally?'

'All right.'

'And let me know as soon as you find those notes.'

'Sure,' I said.

'We want to stop Vaccaro, you know.'

'I'll look everywhere,' I promised.

When I put the phone down I asked Annette.

'Notes about his cases?' she said. 'Oh no, he never brought those to the office.'

Like he never bought diamonds, I thought dryly. And there wasn't a trace of them in the spreadsheets or the ledgers.

The small insistent alarm went off again, muffled

inside the desk. Twenty past four, my watch said. I reached over and pulled open the drawer and the alarm stopped, as it had before.

'Looking for something?' June said, breezing in.

'Something with an alarm like a digital watch.'

'It's bound to be the world clock,' she said. 'Mr Franklin used to set it to remind himself to phone suppliers in Tokyo, and so on.'

I reflected that as I wouldn't know what to say to suppliers in Tokyo I hardly needed the alarm.

'Do you want me to send a fax to Tokyo to say the pearls arrived OK?' she said.

'Do you usually?'

She nodded. 'They worry.'

'Then please do.'

When she'd gone Jason with his orange hair appeared through the doorway and without any trace of insolence told me he'd taken the stuff to Prospero Jenks and brought back a cheque, which he'd given to Annette.

'Thank you,' I said neutrally.

He gave me an unreadable glance, said, 'Annette said to tell you,' and took himself off. An amazing improvement, I thought.

I stayed behind that evening after they'd all left and went slowly round Greville's domain looking for hiding places that were guileful and devious and full of misdirection.

It was impossible to search the hundreds of shallow

drawers in the stock-rooms and I concluded he wouldn't have used them because Lily or any of the others might easily have found what they weren't meant to. That was the trouble with the whole place, I decided in the end. Greville's own policy of not encouraging private territories had extended also to himself, as all of his staff seemed to pop in and out of his office familiarly whenever the need arose.

Hovering always was the uncomfortable thought that if any pointer to the diamonds' whereabouts had been left by Greville in his office, it could have vanished with the break-in artist, leaving nothing for me to find; and indeed I found nothing of any use. After a fruitless hour I locked everything that locked and went down to the yard to find Brad and go home.

The day of Greville's funeral dawned cold and clear and we were heading east when the sun came up. The run to Ipswich taking three hours altogether, we came into the town with generous time to search for Greville's car.

Enquiries from the police had been negative. They hadn't towed, clamped or ticketed any ancient Rover. They hadn't spotted its number in any public road or car-park, but that wasn't conclusive, they'd assured me. Finding the car had no priority with them as it hadn't been stolen but they would let me know if, if.

I explained the car-finder to Brad en route, producing a street map to go with it.

'Apparently when you press this red button the car's lights switch on and a whistle blows,' I said. 'So you drive and I'll press, OK?'

He nodded, seeming amused, and we began to search in this slightly bizarre fashion, starting in the town centre near to where Greville had died and very slowly rolling up and down the streets, first to the north, then to the south, checking them off on the map. In many of the residential streets there were cars parked nose to tail outside houses, but nowhere did we get a whistle. There were public car-parks and shop car-parks and the station car-park, but nowhere did we turn lights on. Rover 3500s in any case were sparse: when we saw one we stopped to look at the plates, even if the paint wasn't grey, but none of them was Greville's.

Disappointment settled heavily. I'd seriously intended to find that car. As lunchtime dragged towards two o'clock I began to believe that I shouldn't have left it so long, that I should have started looking as soon as Greville died. But last Sunday, I thought, I hadn't been in any shape to, and anyway it wasn't until Tuesday that I knew there was anything valuable to look for. Even now I was sure that he wouldn't have left the diamonds themselves vulnerable, but some reason for being in Ipswich at all . . . given luck, why not?

The crematorium was set in a garden with neatly planted rose trees: Brad dropped me at the door and drove away to find some food. I was met by two blacksuited men, both with suitable expressions, who introduced themselves as the undertaker I'd engaged and one of the crematorium's officials. A lot of flowers had arrived, they said, and which did I want on the coffin.

In some bemusement I let them show me where the flowers were, which was in a long covered cloister beside the building, where one or two weeping groups were looking at wreaths of their own.

'These are Mr Franklin's,' the official said, indicating two long rows of bright bouquets blazing with colourful life in that place of death.

'All of these?' I said, astonished.

'They've been arriving all morning. Which do you want inside, on the coffin?'

There were cards on the bunches, I saw.

'I sent some from myself and our sisters,' I said doubtfully. 'The card has Susan, Miranda and Derek on it. I'll have that.'

The official and the undertaker took pity on the crutches and helped me find the right flowers; and I came first not to the card I was looking for but to another that shortened my breath.

'I will think of you every day at four-twenty. Love, C.'

The flowers that went with it were velvety red roses arranged with ferns in a dark green bowl. Twelve sweet-smelling blooms. Dozen Roses, I thought. Heavens above.

'I've found them,' the undertaker called, picking up a large display of pink and bronze chrysanthemums. 'Here you are.'

'Great. Well, we'll have these roses as well, and this wreath next to them, which is from the staff in his office. Is that all right?'

It appeared to be. Annette and June had decided on all-white flowers after agonizing and phoning from the office, and they'd made me promise to notice and tell them that they were pretty. We had decided that all the staff should stay behind and keep the office open as trade was so heavy, though I'd thought from her down-cast expression that June would have liked to have made the journey.

I asked the official where all the other flowers had come from: from businesses, he said, and he would col-lect all the cards afterwards and give them to me.

I supposed for the first time that perhaps I should have taken Greville back to London to be seen off by colleagues and friends, but during the very quiet half-hour that followed had no single regret. The clergyman engaged by the undertakers asked if I wanted the whole service read as I appeared to be the only mourner, and I said yes, go ahead, it was fitting.

His voice droned a bit. I half listened and half watched the way the sunshine fell onto the flowers on the coffin from the high windows along one wall and thought mostly not of Greville as he'd been alive but what he had become to me during the past week.

His life had settled on my shoulders like a mantle. Through Monday, Tuesday, Wednesday and Thursday I'd learned enough of his business never to forget it.

People who'd relied on him had transferred their reliance onto me, including in a way his friend Elliot Trelawney who wanted me as a Greville substitute to drink with. Clarissa Williams had sent her flowers knowing I would see them, wanting me to be aware of her, as if I weren't already. Nicholas Loder aimed to manipulate me for his own stable's ends. Prospero Jenks would soon be pressing hard for the diamonds for his fantasy, and the bank loan hung like a thundercloud in my mind.

Greville, lying cold in the coffin, hadn't meant any of it to happen.

A man of honour, I thought. I mentally repeated his own prayer for him, as it seemed a good time for it. May I deal with honour. May I act with courage. May I achieve humility. I didn't know if he'd managed that last one; I knew that I couldn't.

The clergyman droned to a halt. The official removed the three lots of flowers from the coffin to put them on the floor and, with a whirring and creaking of machinery that sounded loud in the silence, the coffin slid away forward, out of sight, heading for fire.

Goodbye, pal, I said silently. Goodbye, except that you are with me now more than ever before.

I went outside into the cold fresh air and thanked everyone and paid them and arranged for all of the flowers to go to St Catherine's Hospital, which seemed to be no problem. The official gave me the severed cards and asked what I wanted to do with my brother's ashes, and I had a ridiculous urge to laugh, which I saw from his hushed face would be wildly inappropriate. The business of ashes had always seemed to me an embarrassment.

He waited patiently for a decision. 'If you have any tall red rose trees,' I said finally, 'I daresay that would do, if you plant one along there with the others. Put the ashes there.'

I paid for the rose tree and thanked him again, and waited for a while for Brad to return, which he did looking smug and sporting a definite grin.

'I found it,' he said.

'What?' I was still thinking of Greville.

'Your brother's wheels.'

'You didn't!'

He nodded, highly pleased with himself.

'Where?'

He wouldn't say. He waited for me to sit and drove off in triumph into the centre of town, drawing up barely three hundred yards from where the scaffolding had fallen. Then, with his normal economy, he pointed to the forecourt of a used car sales business where under strips of fluttering pennants rows of offerings stood with large white prices painted on their windscreens.

'One of those?' I asked in disbelief.

Brad gurgled; no other word for the delight in his throat. 'Round the back,' he said.

He drove into the forecourt, then along behind the cars, and turned a corner, and we found ourselves outside the wide-open doors of a garage advertising repairs, oil changes, MOT tests and Ladies and Gents. Brad held the car-finder out of his open window and pressed the red button, and somewhere in the shadowy depths of the garage a pair of headlights began flashing on and off and a piercing whistle shrieked.

A cross-looking mechanic in oily overalls came hurrying out. He told me he was the foreman in charge and he'd be glad to see the back of the Rover 3500, and I owed him a week's parking besides the cleaning of the sparking plugs of the V.8 engine, plus a surcharge for inconvenience.

'What inconvenience?'

'Taking up space for a week when it was meant to be for an hour, and having that whistle blast my eardrums three times today.'

'Three times?' I said, surprised.

'Once this morning, twice this afternoon. This man came here earlier, you know. He said he'd bring the Rover's new owner.'

Brad gave me a bright glance. The car-finder had done its best for us early on in the morning, it seemed: it was our own eyes and ears that had missed it, out of sight as the car had been.

I asked the foreman to make out a bill and, getting out of my own car, swung over to Greville's. The Rover's doors would open, I found, but the boot was locked.

'Here,' said the foreman, coming over with the

account and the ignition keys. 'The boot won't open. Some sort of fancy lock. Custom made. It's been a bloody nuisance.'

I mollifyingly gave him a credit card in settlement and he took it off to his cubby-hole of an office.

I looked at the Rover. 'Can you drive that?' I asked Brad.

'Yerss,' he said gloomily.

I smiled and pulled Greville's keys out of my pocket to see if any of them would unlock the boot; and one did, to my relief, though not a key one would normally have associated with cars. More like the keys to a safe, I thought; and the lock revealed was intricate and steel. Its installation was typically Greville, ultra security-conscious after his experiences with the Porsche.

The treasure so well guarded included an expensive-looking set of golf clubs, with a trolley and a new box of golf balls, a large brown envelope, an overnight bag with pyjamas, clean shirt, toothbrush and a scarlet can of shaving cream, a portable telephone like my own, a personal computer, a portable fax machine, an opened carton of spare fax paper, a polished wooden box containing a beautiful set of brass scales with featherlight weights, an anti-thief device for locking onto the steering wheel, a huge torch, and a heavy complicated-looking orange metal contraption that I recognized from Greville's enthusiastic description as a device for sliding under flat tyres so that one could drive to a garage on it instead of changing a wheel by the roadside.

'Cor,' Brad said, looking at the haul, and the foreman too, returning with the paperwork, was brought to an understanding of the need for the defences.

I shut the boot and locked it again, which seemed a very Greville-like thing to do, and took a quick look round inside the body of the car, seeing the sort of minor clutter which defies the tidiest habit: matchbooks, time-clock parking slips, blue sunglasses, and a cellophane packet of tissues. In the door pocket on the driver's side, jammed in untidily, a map.

I picked it out. It was a road map of East Anglia, the route from London to Ipswich drawn heavily in black with, written down one side, the numbers of the roads to be followed. The marked route, I saw with interest, didn't stop at Ipswich but went on beyond, to Harwich.

Harwich, on the North Sea, was a ferry port. Harwich to the Hook of Holland; the route of one of the historic crossings, like Dover to Calais, Folkestone to Ostend. I didn't know if the Harwich ferries still ran, and I thought that if Greville had been going to Holland he would certainly have gone by air. All the same he had, presumably, been going to Harwich.

I said abruptly to the foreman, who was showing impatience for our departure, 'Is there a travel agent near here?'

'Three doors along,' he said, pointing, 'and you can't park here while you go there.'

I gave him a tip big enough to change his mind, and left Brad keeping watch over the cars while I peg-legged along the street. Right on schedule the travel agents came up, and I went in to enquire about ferries for the Hook of Holland.

'Sure,' said an obliging girl. 'They run every day and every night. Sealink operate them. When do you want to go?'

'I don't know, exactly.'

She thought me feeble. 'Well, the *St Nicholas* goes over to Holland every morning, and the *Koningin Beatrix* every night.'

I must have looked as stunned as I felt. I closed my open mouth.

'What's the matter?' she said.

'Nothing at all. Thank you very much.'

She shrugged as if the lunacies of the travelling public were past comprehension, and I shunted back to the garage with my chunk of new knowledge which had solved one little conundrum but posed another, such as what was Greville doing with Queen Beatrix, not a horse but a boat.

Brad drove the Rover to London and I drove my own car, the pace throughout enough to make a snail weep. Whatever the Ipswich garage had done to Greville's plugs hadn't cured any trouble, the V.8 running more like a V.4 or even a V.1½ as far as I could see. Brad stopped fairly soon after we'd left the town and, cursing, cleaned the plugs again himself, but to no avail.

'Needs new ones,' he said.

I used the time to search thoroughly through the golf bag, the box of golf balls, the overnight bag and all the gadgets.

No diamonds.

We set off again, the Rover going precariously slowly in very low gear up hills, with me staying on its tail in case it petered out altogether. I didn't much mind the slow progress except that resting my left foot on the floor sent frequent jabs up my leg and eventually reawoke the overall ache in the ankle, but in comparison with the ride home from Ipswich five days earlier it was chickenfeed. I still mended fast, I thought gratefully. By Tuesday at the latest I'd be walking. Well, limping, maybe, like Greville's car.

There was no joy in reflecting, as I did, that if the sparking plugs had been efficient he wouldn't have stopped to have them fixed and he wouldn't have been walking along a street in Ipswich at the wrong moment. If one could foresee the future, accidents wouldn't happen. 'If only' were wretched words.

We reached Greville's road eventually and found two spaces to park, though not outside the house. I'd told Brad in the morning that I would sleep in London that night to be handy for going to York with the Ostermeyers the next day. I'd planned originally that if we found the Rover he would take it on the orbital route direct to Hungerford and I would drive into London and go on home from there after I got back from York. The plugs having changed that plan near Ipswich, it was now Brad who would go to Hungerford in my car, and I would finish the journey by train. Greville's car, ruin that it was, could decorate the street.

We transferred all the gear from Greville's boot into the back of my car, or rather Brad did the transferring while I mostly watched. Then, Brad carrying the big brown envelope from the Rover and my own overnight grip, we went up the path to the house in the dark and set off the lights and the barking. No one in the houses around paid any attention. I undid the three locks and went in cautiously but, as before, once I'd switched the dog off the house was quiet and deserted. Brad, declining food and drink, went home to his mum, and I, sitting in Greville's chair, opened the big brown envelope and read all about Vaccaro who had been a very bad boy indeed.

Most of the envelope's contents were a copy of Vaccaro's detailed application, but on an attached sheet in abbreviated prose Greville had hand-written:

Ramón Vaccaro, wanted for drug-running, Florida, USA.

Suspected of several murders, victims mostly pilots, wanting out from flying drug crates. Vaccaro leaves no mouths alive to chatter. My info from scared-to-death pilot's widow. She won't come to the committee meeting but gave enough insider details for me to believe her.

Vaccaro seduced private pilots with a big pay-off, then when they'd done one run to Colombia and got away with it, they'd be hooked and do it again and again until they finally got rich enough to have cold feet. Then the poor sods would die from being shot on their own doorsteps from passing cars, no sounds because of silencers, no witnesses and no clues. But all were pilots owning their own small planes, too many for coincidence. Widow says her husband scared stiff but left it too late. She's remarried, lives in London, always wanted revenge, couldn't believe it was the same man when she saw local newspaper snippet, Vaccaro's Family Gaming, with his photo. Family! She went to Town Hall anonymously, they put her on to me.

We don't have to find Vaccaro guilty. We just don't give him a gaming licence. Widow says not to let him know who turned his application down, he's dangerous and vengeful, but how can he silence a whole committee? The Florida police might like to know his whereabouts. Extradition?

I telephoned Elliot Trelawney at his weekend home, told him I'd found the red-hot notes and read them to him, which brought forth a whistle and a groan.

'But Vaccaro didn't kill Greville,' I said.

'No.' He sighed. 'How did the funeral go?'

'Fine. Thank you for your flowers.'

'Just sorry I couldn't get there – but on a working day, and so far . . .'

'It was fine,' I said again, and it had been. I'd been relieved, on the whole, to be alone.

'Would you mind,' he said, diffidently, 'If I arranged a memorial service for him? Sometime soon. Within a month?'

'Go right ahead,' I said warmly. 'A great idea.'

He hoped I would send the Vaccaro notes by messenger on Monday to the Magistrates Court, and he asked if I played golf.

In the morning, after a dream-filled night in Greville's black and white bed, I took a taxi to the Ostermeyers' hotel, meeting them in the foyer as arranged on the telephone the evening before.

They were in very good form, Martha resplendent in a red wool tailored dress with a mink jacket, Harley with a new English-looking hat over his easy grin, binoculars and racing paper ready. Both of them seemed determined to enjoy whatever the day brought forth and Harley's occasional ill-humour was far out of sight.

The driver, a different one from Wednesday, brought a huge super-comfortable Daimler to the front door exactly on time, and with all auspices pointing to felicity, the Ostermeyers arranged themselves on the rear seat, I sitting in front of them beside the chauffeur.

The chauffeur, who announced his name as Simms,

kindly stowed my crutches in the boot and said it was no trouble at all, sir, when I thanked him. The crutches themselves seemed to be the only tiny cloud on Martha's horizon, bringing a brief frown to the proceedings.

'Is that foot still bothering you? Milo said it was nothing to worry about.'

'No, it isn't, and it's much better,' I said truthfully.

'Oh, good. Just as long as it doesn't stop you riding Datepalm.'

'Of course not,' I assured her.

'We're so pleased to have him. He's just darling.'

I made some nice noises about Datepalm, which wasn't very difficult, as we nosed through the traffic to go north on the M1.

Harley said, 'Milo says Datepalm might go for the Charisma 'Chase at Kempton next Saturday. What do you think?'

'A good race for him,' I said calmly. I would kill Milo, I thought. A dicey gallop was one thing, but no medic on earth was going to sign my card in one week to say I was fit; and I wouldn't be, because half a ton of horse over jumps at thirty-plus miles an hour was no puffball matter.

'Milo might prefer to save him for the Mackeson at Cheltenham next month,' I said judiciously, sowing the idea. 'Or of course for the Hennessy Cognac Gold Cup two weeks later.' I'd definitely be fit for the Hennessy, six weeks ahead. The Mackeson, at four weeks, was a toss-up.

'Then there's that big race the day after Christmas,' Martha sighed happily. 'It's all so exciting. Harley promises we can come back to see him run.'

They talked about horses for another half hour and then asked if I knew anything about a Dick Turpin.

'Oh, sure.'

'Some guy said he was riding to York. I didn't understand any part of it.'

I laughed. 'It happened a couple of centuries ago. Dick Turpin was a highwayman, a real villain, who rode his mare Black Bess north to escape the law. They caught him in York and flung him in gaol and for a fortnight he held a sort of riotous court in his cell, making jokes and drinking with all the notables of the city who came to see the famous thief in his chains. Then they took him out and hanged him on a piece of land called the Knavesmire, which is now the racecourse.'

'Oh, my,' Martha said, ghoulishly diverted. 'How perfectly grisly.'

In time we left the M1 and travelled north-east to the difficult old A1, and I thought that no one in their senses would drive from London to York when they could go by train. The Ostermeyers, of course, weren't doing the driving.

Harley said as we neared the city, 'You're expected at lunch with us, Derek.'

Expected, in Ostermeyer speech, meant invited. I protested mildly that it wasn't so.

'It sure is. I talked with Lord Knightwood yesterday

629

evening, told him we'd have you with us. He said right away to have you join us for lunch. They're giving their name to one of the races, it'll be a big party.'

'Which race?' I asked with curiosity. Knightwood wasn't a name I knew.

'Here it is.' Harley rustled the racing newspaper. 'The University of York Trophy. Lord Knightwood is the University's top man, president or governor, some kind of figurehead. A Yorkshire VIP. Anyway, you're expected.'

I thanked him. There wasn't much else to do, though a sponsor's lunch on top of no exercise could give me weight problems if I wasn't careful. However, I could almost hear Milo's agitated voice in my ear: 'Whatever the Ostermeyers want, for Christ's sake give it to them.'

'There's also the York Minster Cup,' Harley said, reading his paper, 'and the Civic Pride Challenge. Your horse Dozen Roses is in the York Castle Champions.'

'My brother's horse,' I said.

Harley chuckled. 'We won't forget.'

Simms dropped us neatly at the Club entrance. One could get addicted to chauffeurs, I thought, accepting the crutches gravely offered. No parking problems. Someone to drive one home on crunch days. But no spontaneity, no real privacy ... No thanks, not even long-term Brad.

Back the first horse you see, they say. Or the first jockey. Or the first trainer.

The first trainer we saw was Nicholas Loder. He

looked truly furious and, I thought in surprise, alarmed when I came face to face with him after he'd watched our emergence from the Daimler.

'What are you doing here?' he demanded brusquely. 'You've no business here.'

'Do you know Mr and Mrs Ostermeyer?' I asked politely, introducing them. 'They've just bought Date-palm. I'm their guest today.'

He glared; there wasn't any other word for it. He had been waiting for a man, perhaps one of his owners, to collect a Club badge from the allotted window and, the transaction achieved, the two of them marched off into the racecourse without another word.

'Well!' Martha said, outraged. 'If Milo ever behaved like that we'd whisk our horses out of his yard before he could say goodbye.'

'It isn't my horse,' I pointed out. 'Not yet.'

'When it is, what will you do?'

'The same as you, I think, though I didn't mean to.'

'Good,' Martha said emphatically.

I didn't really understand Loder's attitude or reaction. If he wanted a favour from me, which was that I'd let him sell Dozen Roses and Gemstones to others of his owners either for the commission or to keep them in his yard, he should at least have shown an echo of Milo's feelings for the Ostermeyers.

If Dozen Roses had been cleared by the authorities to run, why was Loder scared that I was there to watch it?

Crazy, I thought. The only thing I'd wholly learned was that Loder's ability to dissimulate was underdeveloped for a leading trainer.

Harley Ostermeyer said the York University's lunch was to be held at one end of the Club members' dining room in the grandstand, so I showed the way there, reflecting that it was lucky I'd decided on a decent suit for that day, not just a sweater. I might have been a last-minute addition to the party but I was happy not to look it.

There was already a small crowd of people, glasses in hand, chatting away inside a temporary white-lattice-fenced area, a long buffet set out behind them with tables and chairs to sit at for eating.

'There are the Knightwoods,' said the Ostermeyers, clucking contentedly, and I found myself being introduced presently to a tall white-haired kindly-looking man who had benevolence shining from every perhaps seventy-year-old wrinkle. He shook my hand amicably as a friend of the Ostermeyers with whom, it seemed, he had dined on a reciprocal visit to Harley's alma mater, the University of Pennsylvania. Harley was endowing a Chair there. Harley was a VIP in Pittsburgh, Pennsylvania.

I made the right faces and listened to the way the world went round, and said I thought it was great of the city of York to support its industry on the turf.

'Have you met my wife?' Lord Knightwood said vaguely. 'My dear,' he touched the arm of a woman

632

with her back to us, 'you remember Harley and Martha Ostermeyer? And this is their friend Derek Franklin that I told you about.'

She turned to the Ostermeyers smiling and greeting them readily, and she held out a hand for me to shake, saying, 'How do you do. So glad you could come.'

'How do you do, Lady Knightwood,' I said politely. She gave me a very small smile, in command of herself.

Clarissa Williams was Lord Knightwood's wife.

CHAPTER TEN

She had known I would be there, it was clear, and if she hadn't wanted me to find out who she was she could have developed a strategic illness in plenty of time.

She was saying graciously, 'Didn't I see you on television winning the Gold Cup?' and I thought of her speed with that frightful kiyoga and the tumult of her feelings on Tuesday, four days ago. She seemed to have no fear that I would give her away, and indeed, what could I say? Lord Knightwood, my brother was your wife's lover? Just the right sort of thing to get the happy party off to a good start.

The said Lord was introducing the Ostermeyers to a professor of physics who with twinkles said that as he was the only true aficionado of horse-racing among the teaching academics he had been pressed into service to carry the flag, although there were about fifty undergraduates out on the course ready to bet their socks off in the cause.

'Derek has a degree,' Martha said brightly, making conversation.

The professorial eyeballs swivelled my way speculatively. 'What university?'

'Lancaster,' I said dryly, which raised a laugh. Lancaster and York had fought battles of the red and white roses for many a long year.

'And subject?'

'Independent Studies.'

His desultory attention sharpened abruptly.

'What are Independent Studies?' Harley asked, seeing his interest.

'The student designs his own course and invents his own final subject,' the professor said. 'Lancaster is the only university offering such a course and they let only about eight students a year do it. It's not for the weak-willed or the feeble-minded.'

The Knightwoods and the Ostermeyers listened in silence and I felt embarrassed. I had been young then, I thought.

'What did you choose as your subject?' asked the professor, intent now on an answer. 'Horses, in some way?'

I shook my head. 'No. . . er. . . "Roots and Results of War".'

'My dear chap,' Lord Knightwood said heartily, 'sit next to the professor at lunch.' He moved away benignly, taking his wife and the Ostermeyers with him, and the professor, left behind, asked what I fancied for the races.

Clarissa, by accident or design, remained out of

talking distance throughout the meal and I didn't try to approach her. The party broke up during and after the first race, although everyone was invited to return for tea, and I spent most of the afternoon, as I'd spent so many others, watching horses stretch and surge and run as their individual natures dictated. The will to win was born and bred in them all, but some cared more than others: it was those with the implacable impulse to lead a wild herd who fought hardest and oftenest won. Sports writers tended to call it courage but it went deeper than that, right down into the gene pool, into instinct, into the primordial soup on the same evolutionary level as the belligerence so easily aroused in Homo sapiens, that was the taproot of water.

I was no stranger to the thought that I sought battle on the turf because, though the instinct to fight and conquer ran strong, I was averse to guns. Sublimation, the pundits would no doubt call it. Datepalm and I both, on the same primitive plane, wanted to win.

'What are you thinking?' someone asked at my shoulder.

I would have known her voice anywhere, I thought. I turned to see her half-calm half-anxious expression, the Lady Knightwood social poise explicit in the smooth hair, the patrician bones and the tailoring of her clothes, the passionate woman merely a hint in the eyes.

'Thinking about horses,' I said.

'I suppose you're wondering why I came today, after I learned last night that you'd not only be at the races, which I expected you might be anyway because of Dozen Roses, but actually be coming to our lunch . . .' She stopped, sounding uncertain.

'I'm not Greville,' I said. 'Don't think of me as Greville.'

Her eyelids flickered. 'You're too damned perceptive.' She did a bit of introspection. 'Yes, all right, I wanted to be near you. It's a sort of comfort.'

We were standing by the rails of the parade ring watching the runners for the next race walk round, led by their lads. It was the race before the University Trophy, two races before that of Dozen Roses, a period without urgency for either of us. There were crowd noises all around and the clip-clop of horses walking by, and we could speak quietly as in an oasis of private space without being overheard.

'Are you still angry with me for hitting you?' she said a shade bitterly, as I'd made no comment after her last remark.

I half smiled. 'No.'

'I did think you were a burglar.'

'And what would you have explained to the police, if they'd come?'

She said ruefully, 'I hope I would have come to my senses and done a bunk before they got there.' She sighed. 'Greville said if I ever had to use the kiyoga in earnest to escape at once and not worry what I'd done to my attacker, but he never thought of a burglar in his own house.'

'I'm surprised he gave you a weapon like that,' I said mildly. 'Aren't they illegal? And him a magistrate.'

'I'm a magistrate too,' she said unexpectedly. 'That's how we originally met, at a magistrates' conference. I've not enquired into the legality of kiyogas. If I were prosecuted for carrying and using an offensive weapon, well, that would be much preferable to being a victim of the appalling assaults that come before us every week.'

'Where did he get it?' I asked curiously.

'America.'

'Do you have it with you here?'

She nodded and touched her handbag. 'It's second nature, now.'

She must have been thirty years younger than her husband, I thought inconsequentially, and I knew what she felt about him. I didn't know whether or not I liked her, but I did recognize there was a weird sort of intimacy between us and that I didn't resent it.

The jockeys came out and stood around the owners in little groups. Nicholas Loder was there with the man he'd come in with, a thickset powerful-looking man in a dark suit, the pink cardboard Club badge fluttering from his lapel.

'Dozen Roses,' I said, watching Loder talking to the owner and his jockey, 'was he named for you?'

'Oh, God,' she said, disconcerted. 'How ever . . .?'

I said, 'I put your roses on the coffin for the service.'

'Oh . . .' she murmured with difficulty, her throat closing, her mouth twisting, 'I . . . can't . . .'

'Tell me how York University came to be putting its name to a race.' I made it sound conversational, to give her composure time.

She swallowed, fighting for control, steadying her breathing. 'I'm sorry. It's just that I can't even mourn for him except inside; can't let it show to anyone except you, and it sweeps over me, I can't help it.' She paused and answered my unimportant question. 'The Clerk of the Course wanted to involve the city. Some of the bigwigs of the University were against joining in, but Henry persuaded them. He and I have always come here to meetings now and then. We both like it, for a day out with friends.'

'Your husband doesn't actually lecture at the University, does he?'

'Oh, no, he's just a figurehead. He's chairman of a fair number of things in York. A public figure here.'

Vulnerable to scandal, I thought: as she was herself, and Greville also. She and he must have been unwaveringly discreet.

'How long since you first met Greville?' I asked noncommittally.

'Four years.' She paused. 'Four marvellous years. Not enough.'

The jockeys swung up onto the horses and moved away to go out onto the course. Nicholas Loder and his owner, busily talking, went off to the stands.

'May I watch the race with you?' Clarissa said. 'Do you mind?'

'I was going to watch from the grass.' I glanced down apologetically at the crutches. 'It's easier.'

'I don't mind the grass.'

So we stood side by side on the grass in front of the grandstand and she said, 'Whenever we could be together, he bought twelve red roses. It just . . . well . . .' She stopped, swallowing again hard.

'Mm,' I said. I thought of the ashes and the red rose tree and decided to tell her about that another time. It had been for him, anyway, not for her.

Nicholas Loder's two-year-old won the sprint at a convincing clip and I caught a glimpse of the owner afterwards looking heavily satisfied but unsmiling. Hardly a jolly character, I thought.

Clarissa went off to join her husband for the University race and after that, during their speeches and presentations, I went in search of Dozen Roses who was being led round in the pre-parade ring before being taken into a box or a stall to have his saddle put on.

Dozen Roses looked docile to dozy, I thought. An unremarkable bay, he had none of the looks or presence of Datepalm, nor the chaser's alert interest in his surroundings. He was a good performer, of that there was no question, but he didn't at that moment give an impression of going to be a 'trot-up' within half an hour, and he was vaguely not what I'd expected. Was this the colt that on the video tapes had won his last three races full of verve? Was this the young buck who had tried to mount a filly at the starting gate at Newmarket?

No, I saw with a sense of shock, he was not. I peered under his belly more closely, as it was sometimes difficult to tell, but there seemed to be no doubt that he had lost the essential tackle; that he had in fact been gelded.

I was stunned, and I didn't know whether to laugh or be furious. It explained so much: the loss of form when he had his mind on procreation rather than racing, and the return to speed once the temptation was removed. It explained why the Stewards hadn't called Loder in to justify the difference in running: horses very often did better after the operation.

I unfolded my racecard at Dozen Roses's race, and there, sure enough, against his name stood not c for colt or h for horse, but g for gelding.

Nicholas Loder's voice, vibrating with fury, spoke from not far behind me, 'That horse is not your horse. Keep away from him.'

I turned. Loder was advancing fast with Dozen Roses's saddle over his arm and full-blown rage in his face. The heavily unjoyful owner, still for some reason in tow, was watching the proceedings with puzzlement.

'Mine or not, I'm entitled to look at him,' I said. 'And look at him I darned well have, and either he is not Dozen Roses or you have gelded him against my brother's express wishes.'

His mouth opened and snapped shut.

'What's the matter, Nick?' the owner said. 'Who is this?'

Loder failed to introduce us. Instead he said to me

vehemently, 'You can't do anything about it. I have an Authority to Act. I am the registered agent for this horse and what I decide is none of your business.'

'My brother refused to have any of his horses gelded. You knew it well. You disobeyed him because you were sure he wouldn't find out, as he never went to the races.'

He glared at me. He was aware that if I lodged a formal complaint he would be in a good deal of trouble, and I thought he was certainly afraid that as my brother's executor I could and quite likely would do just that. Even if I only talked about it to others, it could do him damage: it was the sort of titbit the hungry racing press would pounce on for a giggle, and the owners of all the princely colts in his prestigious stable would get cold feet that the same might happen to their own property without their knowledge or consent.

He had understood all that, I thought, in the moment I'd told him on the telephone that it was I who would be inheriting Dozen Roses. He'd known that if I ever saw the horse I would realize at once what had been done. No wonder he'd lost his lower resonances.

'Greville was a fool,' he said angrily. 'The horse has done much better since he was cut.'

'That's true,' I agreed, 'but it's not the point.'

'How much do you want, then?' he demanded roughly.

My own turn, I thought, to gape like a fish. I said feebly, 'It's not a matter of money.'

'Everything is,' he declared. 'Name your price and get out of my way.'

I glanced at the attendant owner who looked more phlegmatic than riveted, but might remember and repeat this conversation, and I said merely, 'We'll discuss it later, OK?' and hitched myself away from them without aggression.

Behind me the owner was saying, 'What was that all about, Nick?' and I heard Loder reply, 'Nothing, Rollo. Don't worry about it,' and when I looked back a few seconds later I saw both of them stalking off towards the saddling boxes followed by Dozen Roses in the grasp of his lad.

Despite Nicholas Loder's anxious rage, or maybe because of it, I came down on the side of amusement. I would myself have had the horse gelded several months before the trainer had done it out of no doubt unbearable frustration: Greville had been pigheaded on the subject from both misplaced sympathy and not knowing enough about horses. I thought I would make peace with Loder that evening on the telephone, whatever the outcome of the race, as I certainly didn't want a fight on my hands for so rocky a cause. Talk about the roots of war, I thought wryly: there had been sillier reasons for bloody strife in history than the castration of a thoroughbred.

At York some of the saddling boxes were open to public view, some were furnished with doors. Nicholas

Loder seemed to favour the privacy and took Dozen Roses inside away from my eyes.

Harley and Martha Ostermeyer, coming to see the horses saddle, were full of beaming anticipation. They had backed the winner of the University Trophy and had wagered all the proceeds on my, that was to say, my *brother*'s horse.

'You won't get much return,' I warned them. 'It's favourite.'

'We know that, dear,' Martha said happily, looking around. 'Where is he? Which one?'

'He's inside that box,' I pointed, 'being saddled.'

'Harley and I have had a marvellous idea,' she said sweetly, her eyes sparkling.

'Now, Martha,' Harley said. He sounded faintly alarmed as if Martha's marvellous ideas weren't always the best possible news.

'We went you to dine with us when we get back to London,' she finished.

Harley relaxed, relieved. 'Yes. Hope you can.' He clearly meant that this particular marvellous idea was passable, even welcome. 'London at weekends is a graveyard.'

With a twitching of an inward grin I accepted my role as graveyard alleviator and, in the general good cause of cementing Ostermeyer–Shandy–Franklin relations, said I would be very pleased to stay to dinner. Martha and Harley expressed such gratification as to make me wonder whether when they were alone they bored each other to silence.

Dozen Roses emerged from his box with his saddle on and was led along towards the parade ring. He walked well, I thought, his good straight hocks encouraging lengthy strides, and he also seemed to have woken up a good deal, now that the excitement was at hand.

In the horse's wake hurried Nicholas Loder and his friend Rollo, and it was because they were crowding him, I thought, that Dozen Roses swung round on his leading rein and pulled backwards from his lad, and in straightening up again hit the Rollo man a hefty buffet with his rump and knocked him to his knees.

Martha with instinctive kindness rushed forward to help him, but he floundered to his feet with a curse that made her blink. All the same she bent and picked up a thing like a blue rubber ball which had fallen out of his jacket and held it towards him, saying, 'You dropped this, I think.'

He ungraciously snatched it from her, gave her an unnecessarily fierce stare as if she'd frightened the horse into knocking him over, which she certainly hadn't, and hurried into the parade ring after Nicholas Loder. He, looking back and seeing me still there, reacted with another show of fury.

'What perfectly horrid people,' Martha said, making a face. 'Did you hear what that man said? Disgusting! Fancy saying it aloud!'

Dear Martha, I thought, that word was everyday

coinage on racecourses. The nicest people used it: it made no one a villain. She was brushing dust off her gloves fastidiously as if getting rid of contamination and I half expected her to go up to Rollo and in the tradition of the indomitable American female to tell him to wash his mouth out with soap.

Harley had meanwhile picked something else up off the grass and was looking at it helplessly. 'He dropped this too,' he said. 'I think.'

Martha peered at his hands and took the object out of them.

'Oh, yes,' she said with recognition, 'that's the other half of the baster. You'd better have it, Derek, then you can give it back to that obnoxious friend of your trainer, if you want to.'

I frowned at what she'd given me, which was a rigid plastic tube, semi-transparent, about an inch in diameter, nine inches long, open at one end and narrowing to half the width at the other.

'A baster,' Martha said again. 'For basting meat when it's roasting. You know them, don't you? You press the bulb thing and release it to suck up the juices which you then squirt over the meat.'

I nodded. I knew what a baster was.

'What an extraordinary thing to take to the races,' Martha said wonderingly.

'Mm,' I agreed. 'He seems an odd sort of man altogether.' I tucked the plastic tube into an inside jacket pocket, from which its nozzle end protruded a couple of inches, and we went first to see Dozen Roses joined with his jockey in the parade ring and then up onto the stands to watch him race.

The jockey was Loder's chief stable jockey, as able as any, as honest as most. The stable money was definitely on the horse, I thought, watching the forecast odds on the information board change from 2/1 on to 5/2 on. When a gambling stable didn't put its money up front, the whisper went round and the price eased dramatically. The whisper where it mattered that day had to be saying that Loder was in earnest about the 'trot-up', and Alfie's base imputation would have to wait for another occasion.

Perhaps as a result of his year-by-year successes, Loder's stable always, it was well-known in the racing world, attracted as owners serious gamblers whose satisfaction was more in winning money than in winning races: and that wasn't the truism it seemed, because in steeplechasing the owners tended to want to win the races more than the money. Steeplechasing owners only occasionally made a profit overall and realistically expected to have to pay for their pleasure.

Wondering if the Rollo man was one of the big Loder gamblers, I flicked back the pages of the racecard and looked up his name beside the horse of his that had won the sprint. Owner, Mr T. Rollway, the card read. Rollo for short to his friends. Never heard of him, I thought, and wondered if Greville had.

Dozen Roses cantered down to the start with at least

as much energy and enthusiasm as any of the seven other runners and was fed into the stalls without fuss. He'd been striding out well, I thought, and taking a good hold of the bit. An old hand at the game by now, of course, as I was also, I thought dryly.

I'd ridden in several Flat races in my teens as an amateur, learning that the hardest and most surprising thing about the unrelenting Flat race crouch over the withers was the way it cramped one's lungs and affected one's breathing. The first few times I'd almost fallen off at the finish from lack of oxygen. A long time ago, I thought, watching the gates fly open in the distance and the colours spill out, long ago when I was young and it all lay ahead.

If I could find Greville's diamonds, I thought, I would in due course be able to buy a good big yard in Lambourn and start training free of a mortgage and on a decent scale, providing of course I could get owners to send me horses, and I had no longer any doubt that one of these years, when my body packed up mending fast, as everyone's did in the end, I would be content with the new life, even though the consuming passion I still felt for race-riding couldn't be replaced by anything tamer.

Dozen Roses was running with the pack, all seven bunched after the first three furlongs, flying along the far side of the track at more than cruising speed but with acceleration still in reserve.

If I didn't find Greville's diamonds, I thought, I

would just scrape together whatever I could and borrow the rest, and still buy a place and set my hand to the future. But not yet, not yet.

Dozen Roses and the others swung left-handed into the long bend round the far end of the track, the bunch coming apart as the curve element hit them. Turning into the straight five furlongs from the winning post Dozen Roses was in fourth place and making not much progress. I wanted him quite suddenly to win and was surprised by the strength of the feeling; I wanted him to win for Greville, who wouldn't care anyway, and perhaps also for Clarissa, who would. Sentimental fool, I told myself. Anyway, when the crowd started yelling home their fancy I yelled for mine also, and I'd never done that before as far as I could remember.

There was not going to be a trot-up, whatever Nicholas Loder might have thought. Dozen Roses was visibly struggling as he took second place at a searing speed a furlong from home and he wouldn't have got the race at all if the horse half a length in front, equally extended and equally exhausted, hadn't veered from a straight line at the last moment and bumped into him.

'Oh dear,' Martha exclaimed sadly, as the two horses passed the winning post. 'Second. Oh well, never mind.'

'He'll get the race on an objection,' I said. 'Which I suppose is better than nothing. Your winnings are safe.'

'Are you sure?'

'Certain,' I said, and almost immediately the loudspeakers were announcing 'Stewards' enquiry'.

More slowly than I would have liked to be able to manage, the three of us descended to the area outside the weighing room where the horse that was not my horse stood in the place for the unsaddling of the second, a net rug over his back and steam flowing from his sweating skin. He was moving about restlessly, as horses often do after an all-out effort, and his lad was holding tight to the reins, trying to calm him.

'He ran a great race,' I said to Martha, and she said, 'Did he, dear?'

'He didn't give up. That's really what matters.'

Of Nicholas Loder there was no sign: probably inside the Stewards' room putting forward his complaint. The Stewards would show themselves the views from the side camera and the head-on camera, and at any moment now . . .

'Result of Stewards' enquiry,' said the loudspeakers. 'Placing of first and second reversed.' Hardly justice, but inevitable: the faster horse had lost. Nicholas Loder came out of the weighing room and saw me standing with the Ostermeyers, but before I could utter even the first conciliatory words like, 'Well done,' he'd given me a sick look and hurried off in the opposite direction. No Rollo in his shadow, I noticed.

Martha, Harley and I returned to the luncheon room for the University's tea where the Knightwoods were being gracious hosts and Clarissa, at the sight of me, developed renewed trouble with the tear glands. I left the Ostermeyers taking cups and saucers from a wait-ress and drifted across to her side.

'So silly,' she said crossly, blinking hard as she offered me a sandwich. 'But wasn't he great?'

'He was.'

'I wish . . .' She stopped. I wished it too. No need at all to put it into words. But Greville never went to the races.

'I go to London fairly often,' she said. 'May I phone you when I'm there?'

'Yes, if you like.' I wrote my home number on my racecard and handed it to her. 'I live in Berkshire,' I said, 'not in Greville's house.'

She met my eyes, hers full of confusion.

'I'm not Greville,' I said.

'My dear chap,' said her husband boomingly, coming to a halt beside us, 'delighted your horse finally won. Though, of course, not technically your horse, what?'

'No, sir.'

He was shrewd enough, I thought, looking at the intelligent eyes amid the bonhomie. Not easy to fool. I wondered fleetingly if he'd ever suspected his wife had a lover, even if he hadn't known who. I thought that if he had known who, he wouldn't have asked me to lunch.

He chuckled. 'The professor says you tipped him three winners.'

'A miracle.'

'He's very impressed.' He looked at me benignly. 'Join us at any time, my dear chap.' It was the sort of vague invitation, not meant to be accepted, that was a mild seal of approval, in its way.

'Thank you,' I said, and he nodded, knowing he'd been understood.

Martha Ostermeyer gushed up to say how marvellous the whole day had been, and gradually from then on, as such things always do, the University party evaporated.

I shook Clarissa's outstretched hand in farewell, and also her husband's who stood beside her. They looked good together, and settled, a fine couple on the surface.

'We'll see you again,' she said to me, and I wondered if it were only I who could hear her smothered desperation.

'Yes,' I said positively. 'Of course.'

'My dear chap,' her husband said. 'Any time.'

Harley, Martha and I left the racecourse and climbed into the Daimler, Simms following Brad's routine of stowing the crutches.

Martha said reproachfully, 'Your ankle's broken, not twisted. One of the guests told us. I said you'd ridden a gallop for us on Wednesday and they couldn't believe it.'

'It's practically mended,' I said weakly.

'But you won't be able to ride Datepalm in that race next Saturday, will you?'

'Not really. No.'

She sighed. 'You're very naughty. We'll simply have to wait until you're ready.'

I gave her a fast smile of intense gratitude. There weren't many owners who would have dreamed of waiting. No trainer would; they couldn't afford to. Milo was currently putting up one of my arch-rivals on the horses I usually rode, and I just hoped I would get all of them back once I was fit. That was the main trouble with injuries, not the injury itself but losing one's mounts to other jockeys. Permanently, sometimes, if they won.

'And now,' Martha said as we set off south towards London, 'I have had another simply marvellous idea, and Harley agrees with me.'

I glanced back to Harley who was sitting behind Simms. He was nodding indulgently. No anxiety this time.

'We think,' she said happily, 'that we'll buy Dozen Roses and send him to Milo to train for jumping. That is,' she laughed, 'if your brother's executor will sell him to us.'

'Martha!' I was dumbstruck and used her first name without thinking, though I'd called her Mrs Ostermeyer before, when I'd called her anything.

'There,' she said, gratified at my reaction, 'I told you it was a marvellous idea. What do you say?'

'My brother's executor is speechless.'

'But you will sell him?'

'I certainly will.'

'Then let's use the car phone to call Milo and tell him.' She was full of high good spirits and in no mood for waiting, but when she reached Milo he apparently didn't immediately catch fire. She handed the phone to me with a frown, saying, 'He wants to talk to you.'

'Milo,' I said, 'what's the trouble?'

'That horse is an entire. They don't jump well.'

'He's a gelding,' I assured him.

'You told me your brother wouldn't ever have it done.'

'Nicholas Loder did it without permission.'

'You're kidding!'

'No,' I said. 'Anyway the horse got the race today on a Stewards' enquiry but he ran gamely, and he's fit.'

'Has he ever jumped?'

'I shouldn't think so. But I'll teach him.'

'All right then. Put me back to Martha.'

'Don't go away when she's finished. I want another word.'

I handed the phone to Martha who listened and spoke with a return to enthusiasm, and eventually I talked to Milo again.

'Why,' I asked, 'would one of Nicholas Loder's owners carry a baster about at the races?'

'A what?'

'Baster. Thing that's really for cooking. You've got one. You use it as a nebuliser.'

'Simple and effective.'

He used it, I reflected, on the rare occasions when it was the best way to give some sort of medication to a horse. One dissolved or diluted the medicine in water and filled the rubber bulb of the baster with it. Then one fitted the tube onto that, slid the tube up the horse's nostril, and squeezed the bulb sharply. The liquid came out in a vigorous spray straight onto the mucous membranes and from there passed immediately into the bloodstream. One could puff out dry powder with the same result. It was the fastest way of getting some drugs to act.

'At the races?' Milo was saying. 'An owner?'

'That's right. His horse won the five-furlong sprint.'

'He'd have to be mad. They dope-test two horses in every race, as you know. Nearly always the winner, and another at random. No owner is going to pump drugs into his horse at the races.'

'I don't know that he did. He had a baster with him, that's all.'

'Did you tell the Stewards?'

'No, I didn't. Nicholas Loder was with his owner and he would have exploded as he was angry with me already for spotting Dozen Roses's alteration.'

Milo laughed. 'So that was what all the heat was about this past week?'

'You've got it.'

'Will you kick up a storm?'

'Probably not.'

'You're too soft,' he said, 'and oh yes, I almost forgot. There was a phone message for you. Wait a tick. I wrote it down.' He went away for a bit and returned. 'Here you are. Something about your brother's diamonds.' He sounded doubtful. 'Is that right?'

'Yes. What about them?'

He must have heard the urgency in my voice because he said, 'It's nothing much. Just that someone had been trying to ring you last night and all day today, but I said you'd slept in London and gone to York.'

'Who was it?'

'He didn't say. Just said that he had some info for you. Then he hummed and hahed and said if I talked to you would I tell you he would telephone your brother's house, in case you went there, at about ten tonight, or later. Or it might have been a she. Difficult to tell. One of those middle-range voices. I said I didn't know if you would be speaking to me, but I'd tell you if I could.'

'Well, thanks.'

'I'm not a message service,' he said testily. 'Why don't you switch on your answer phone like everyone else?'

'I do sometimes.'

'Not enough.'

I switched off the phone with a smile and wondered who'd been trying to reach me. It had to be someone who knew Greville had bought diamonds. It might even be Annette, I thought: her voice had a mid-range quality.

I would have liked to have gone to Greville's house as soon as we got back to London, but I couldn't exactly renege on the dinner after Martha's truly marvellous idea, so the three of us ate together as planned and I tried to please them as much as they'd pleased me.

Martha announced yet another marvellous idea during dinner. She and Harley would get Simms or another of the car firm's chauffeurs to drive us all down to Lambourn the next day to take Milo out to lunch, so that they could see Datepalm again before they went back to the States on Tuesday. They could drop me at my house afterwards, and then go on to visit a castle in Dorset they'd missed last time around. Harley looked resigned. It was Martha, I saw, who always made the decisions, which was maybe why the repressed side of him needed to lash out sometimes at car-park attendants who boxed him in.

Milo, again on the telephone, told me he'd do practically anything to please the Ostermeyers, definitely including Sunday lunch. He also said that my informant had rung again and he had told him/her that I'd got the message.

'Thanks,' I said.

'See you tomorrow.'

I thanked the Ostermeyers inadequately for everything and went to Greville's house by taxi. I did think of asking the taxi driver to stay, like Brad, until I'd reconnoitred, but the house was quiet and dark behind the impregnable grilles, and I thought the taxi driver would think me a fool or a coward or both, so I paid him off and, fishing out the keys, opened the gate in the hedge and went up the path until the lights blazed on and the dog started barking.

Everyone can make mistakes.

CHAPTER ELEVEN

I didn't get as far as the steps up to the front door. A dark figure, dimly glimpsed in the floodlight's glare, came launching itself at me from behind in a cannonball rugger tackle and when I reached the ground something very hard hit my head.

I had no sensation of blacking out or of time passing. One moment I was awake, and the next moment I was awake also, or so it seemed, but I knew in a dim way that there had been an interval.

I didn't know where I was except that I was lying face down on grass. I'd woken up concussed on grass several times in my life, but never before in the dark. They couldn't have all gone home from the races, I thought, and left me alone out on the course all night.

The memory of where I was drifted back quietly. In Greville's front garden. Alive. Hooray for small mercies.

I knew from experience that the best way to deal with being knocked out was not to hurry. On the other hand, this time I hadn't come off a horse, not on

Greville's pocket handkerchief turf. There might be urgent reasons for getting up quickly, if I could think of them.

I remembered a lot of things in a rush and groaned slightly, rolling up onto my knees, wincing and groping about for the crutches. I felt stupid and went on behaving stupidly, acting on fifty per cent brainpower. Looking back afterwards, I thought that what I ought to have done was slither silently away through the gate to go to any neighbouring house and call the police. What I actually did was to start towards Greville's front door, and of course the lights flashed on again and the dog started barking and I stood rooted to the spot expecting another attack, swaying unsteadily on the crutches, absolutely dim and pathetic.

The door was ajar, I saw, with lights on in the hall, and while I stood dithering it was pulled wide open from inside and the cannonball figure shot out.

The cannonball was a motor-cycle helmet, shiny and black, its transparent visor pulled down over the face. Behind the visor the face also seemed to be black, but a black balaclava, I thought, not black skin. There was an impression of jeans, denim jacket, gloves, black running shoes, all moving fast. He turned his head a fraction and must have seen me standing there insecurely, but he didn't stop to give me another unbalancing shove. He vaulted the gate and set off at a run down the street and I simply stood where I was in the garden waiting for my head to clear a bit more and start working.

659

When that happened to some extent, I went up the short flight of steps and in through the front door. The keys, I found, were still in the lowest of the locks; the small bunch of three keys that Clarissa had had, which I'd been using instead of Greville's larger bunch as they were easier. I'd made things simple for the intruder, I thought, by having them ready in my hand.

With a spurt of alarm I felt my trouser pocket to find if Greville's main bunch had been stolen, but to my relief they were still there, clinking.

I switched off the floodlights and the dog and in the sudden silence closed the front door. Greville's small sitting room, when I reached it, looked like the path of a hurricane. I surveyed the mess in fury rather than horror and picked the tumbled phone off the floor to call the police. A burglary, I said. The burglar had gone.

Then I sat in Greville's chair with my head in my hands and said '*Shit*' aloud with heartfelt rage and gingerly felt the sore bump swelling on my scalp. A bloody pushover, I thought. Like last Sunday. Too like last Sunday to be a coincidence. The cannonball had known both times that I wouldn't be able to stand upright against a sudden unexpected rush. I supposed I should be grateful he hadn't smashed my head in altogether this time while he had the chance. No knife, this time, either.

After a bit I looked wearily round the room. The pictures were off the walls, most of the glass smashed. The drawers had been yanked out of the tables and the tables themselves overturned. The little pink and brown stone bears lay scattered on the floor, the chrysanthemum plant and its dirt were trampled into the carpet, the chrysanthemum pot itself was embedded in the smashed screen of the television, the video recorder had been torn from from its unit and dropped, the video cassettes of the races lay pulled out in yards of ruined tape. The violence of it all angered me as much as my own sense of failure in letting it happen.

Many of the books were out of the bookshelves, but I saw with grim satisfaction that none of them lay open. Even if none of the hollow books had contained diamonds, at least the burglar hadn't known the books were hollow. A poor consolation, I thought.

The police arrived eventually, one in uniform, one not. I went along the hall when they rang the doorbell, checked through the peep-hole and let them in, explaining who I was and why I was there. They were both of about my own age and they'd seen a great many break-ins.

Looking without emotion at Greville's wrecked room, they produced notebooks and took down an account of the assault in the garden. (Did I want a doctor for the bump? No, I didn't.) They knew of this house, they said. The new owner, my brother, had installed all the window grilles and had them wired on a direct alarm to the police station so that if anyone tried to enter that way they would be nicked. Police specialists had given their advice over the defences and had considered the house as secure as was possible, up to now: but shouldn't there have been active floodlights and a dog alarm? They'd worked well, I said, but before they came I'd turned them off.

'Well, sir,' they said, not caring much, 'what's been stolen?'

I didn't know. Nothing large, I said, because the burglar had had both hands free, when he vaulted the gate.

Small enough to go in a pocket, they wrote.

What about the rest of the house? Was it in the same state?

I said I hadn't looked yet. Crutches. Bang on head. That sort of thing. They asked about the crutches. Broken ankle, I said. Paining me, perhaps? Just a bit.

I went with them on a tour of the house and found the tornado had blown through all of it. The long drawing room on the ground floor was missing all the pictures from the walls and all the drawers from chests and tables.

'Looking for a safe,' one of the policemen said, turning over a ruined picture. 'Did your brother have one here, do you know?'

'I haven't seen one,' I said.

They nodded and we went upstairs. The black and white bedroom had been ransacked in the same fashion and the bathroom also. Clothes were scattered everywhere. In the bathroom, aspirins and other pills were scattered on the floor. A toothpaste tube had been squeezed flat by a shoe. A can of shaving cream lay in the wash basin, with some of the contents squirted out in loops on the mirror. They commented that as there was no graffiti and no excrement smeared over everything, I had got off lightly.

'Looking for something small,' the non-uniformed man said. 'Your brother was a gem merchant, wasn't he?'

'Yes.'

'Have you found any jewels here yourself?'

'No, I haven't.'

They looked into the empty bedroom on that floor, still empty, and went up the stairs to look round above, but coming down reported nothing to see but space. It's one big attic room, they explained, when I said I hadn't been up there. Might have been a studio once, perhaps.

We all descended to the semi-basement where the mess in the kitchen was indescribable. Every packet of cereal had been poured out, sugar and flour had been emptied and apparently sieved in a strainer. The fridge's door hung open with the contents gutted. All liquids had been poured down the sinks, the cartons and bottles either standing empty or smashed by the draining boards. The ice cubes I'd wondered about were missing, presumably melted. Half of the floor of carpet tiles had been pulled up from the concrete beneath.

The policemen went phlegmatically round looking at things but touching little, leaving a few footprints in the floury dust.

I said uncertainly, 'How long was I unconscious? If he did all this . . .'

'Twenty minutes, I'd say,' one said, and the other nodded. 'He was working fast, you can see. He was probably longest down here. I'd say he was pulling up these tiles looking for a floor safe when you set the alarms off again. I'd reckon he panicked then, he'd been here long enough. And also, if it's any use to you, I'd guess that if he was looking for anything particular, he didn't find it.'

'Good news, is that?' asked the other, shrewdly, watching me.

'Yes, of course.' I explained about the Saxony Franklin office being broken into the previous weekend. 'We weren't sure what had been stolen, apart from an address book. In view of this,' I gestured to the shambles, 'probably nothing was.'

'Reasonable assumption,' one said.

'When you come back here another time in the dark,' the other advised, 'shine a good big torch all around the garden before you come through the gate. Sounds as if he was waiting there for you, hiding in the shadow of the hedge, out of range of the body-heat detecting mechanism of the lights.'

'Thank you,' I said.

'And switch all the alarms on again, when we leave.'

'Yes.'

'And draw all the curtains. Burglars sometimes wait about outside, if they haven't found what they're after, hoping that the householders, when they come home, will go straight to the valuables to check if they're there. Then they come rampaging back to steal them.'

'I'll draw the curtains,' I said.

They looked around in the garden on the way out and found half a brick lying on the grass near where I'd woken up. They showed it to me. Robbery with violence, that made it.

'If you catch the robber,' I said.

They shrugged. They were unlikely to, as things stood. I thanked them for coming and they said they'd be putting in a report, which I could refer to for insurance purposes when I made a claim. Then they retreated to the police car doubled-parked outside the gate and presently drove away, and I shut the front door, switched on the alarms, and felt depressed and stupid and without energy, none of which states was normal.

The policemen had left lights on behind them everywhere. I went slowly down the stairs to the kitchen meaning merely to turn them off, but when I got there I stood for a while contemplating the mess and the reason for it.

Whoever had come had come because the diamonds were still somewhere to be found. I supposed I should be grateful at least for that information; and I was also inclined to believe the policeman who said the burglar hadn't found what he was looking for. But could I find it, if I looked harder?

I hadn't particularly noticed on my first trip downstairs that the kitchen's red carpet was in fact carpet
tiles, washable squares that were silent and warmer
underfoot than conventional tiles. I'd been brought up
on such flooring in our parents' house.

The big tiles, lying flat and fitting snugly, weren't
stuck to the hard surface beneath, and the intruder had
had no trouble in pulling them up. The intruder hadn't
been certain there was a safe, I thought, or he wouldn't
have sieved the sugar. And if he'd been successful and
found a safe, what then? He hadn't given himself time
to do anything about it. He hadn't killed me. Hadn't
tied me. Must have known I would wake up.

All it added up to, I thought, was a frantic and rather
unintelligent search, which didn't make the bump on
my head or my again knocked-about ankle any less
sore. Mincing machines had no brains either. Nor, I
thought dispiritedly, had the mince.

I drew the curtains as advised and bent down and
pulled up another of the red tiles, thinking about Greville's security complex. It would be just like him to build a
safe into the solid base of the house and cover it with
something deceptive. Setting a safe in concrete, as the
pamphlet had said. People tended to think of safes as
being built into walls: floors were less obvious and more
secure, but far less convenient. I pulled up a few
more tiles, doubting my conclusions, doubting my
sanity.

The same sort of feeling as in the vaults kept me

going. I didn't expect to find anything but it would be stupid not to make sure, just in case. This time it took half an hour, not three days, and in the end the whole area was up except for a piece under a serving table on wheels. Under that carpet square, when I'd moved the table, I found a flat circular piece of silvery metal flush with the hard base floor, with a recessed ring in it for lifting.

Amazed and suddenly unbearably hopeful I knelt and pulled the ring up and tugged, and the flat piece of metal came away and off like the lid of a biscuit-tin, revealing another layer of metal beneath: an extremely solid-looking circular metal plate the size of a dinner plate in which there was a single keyhole and another handle for lifting.

I pulled the second handle. As well try to pull up the house by its roots. I tried all of Greville's bunch of keys in the keyhole but none of them came near to fitting.

Even Greville, I thought, must have kept the key reasonably handy, but the prospect of searching anew for anything at all filled me with weariness. Greville's affairs were a maze with more blind alleys than Hampton Court.

There were keys in the hollow books, I remembered. Might as well start with those. I shifted upstairs and dug out *With a Mule in Patagonia* and the others, rediscovering the two businesslike keys and also the decorative one which looked too flamboyant for sensible use. True to Greville's mind, however, it was that one whose wards slid easily into the keyhole of the safe and under pressure turned the mechanism inside.

Even then the circular lid wouldn't pull out. Seesawing between hope and frustration I found that, if one turned instead of pulling, the whole top of the safe went round like a wheel until it came against stops; and at that point it finally gave up the struggle and came up loose in my grasp.

The space below was big enough to hold a case of champagne but to my acute disappointment it contained no nest-egg, only a clutch of business-like brown envelopes. Sighing deeply I took out the top two and found the first contained the freehold deeds of the house and the second the paperwork involved in raising a mortgage to buy it. I read the latter with resignation. Greville's house belonged in essence to a finance company, not to me.

Another of the envelopes contained a copy of his will, which was as simple as the lawyers had said, and in another there was his birth certificate and our parents' birth and marriage certificates. Another yielded an endowment insurance policy taken out long ago to provide him with an income at sixty-five: but inflation had eaten away its worth and he had apparently not bothered to increase it. Instead, I realized, remembering what I'd learned of his company's finances, he had ploughed back his profits into expanding his business which would itself ride on the tide of inflation and provide him with a munificent income when he retired and sold.

A good plan, I thought, until he'd knocked the props out by throwing one point five million dollars to the winds. Only he hadn't, of course. He'd had a sensible plan for a sober profit. Deal with honour . . . He'd made a good income, lived a comfortable life and run his racehorses, but he had stacked away no great personal fortune. His wealth, whichever way one looked at it, was in the stones.

Hell and damnation, I thought. If I couldn't find the damned diamonds I'd be failing him as much as myself. He would long for me to find them, but where the bloody *hell* had he put them?

I stuffed most of the envelopes back into their private basement, keeping out only the insurance policy, and replaced the heavy circular lid. Turned it, turned the key, replaced the upper piece of metal and laid a carpet tile on top. Fireproof the hiding place undoubtedly was, and thiefproof it had proved, and I couldn't imagine why Greville hadn't used it for jewels.

Feeling defeated, I climbed at length to the bedroom where I found my own overnight bag had, along with everything else, been tipped up and emptied. It hardly seemed to matter. I picked up my sleeping shorts and changed into them and went into the bathroom. The mirror was still half covered with shaving cream and by the time I'd wiped that off with a face cloth and swallowed a Distalgesic and brushed my teeth and swept a lot of the crunching underfoot junk to one side with a towel, I had used up that day's ration of stamina pretty thoroughly.

Even then, though it was long past midnight. I couldn't sleep. Bangs on the head were odd, I thought. There had been one time when I'd dozed for a week afterwards, going to sleep in mid-sentence as often as not. Another time I'd apparently walked and talked rationally to a doctor but hadn't any recollection of it half an hour later. This time, in Greville's bed, I felt shivery and unsettled, and thought that that had probably as much to do with being attacked as concussed.

I lay still and let the hours pass, thinking of bad and good and of why things happened, and by morning felt calm and much better. Sitting on the lid of the loo in the bathroom I unwrapped the crêpe bandage and by hopping and holding on to things took a long, luxurious and much needed shower, washing my hair, letting the dust and debris and the mental tensions of the week run away in the soft bombardment of water. After that, loin-clothed in a bath towel, I sat on the black and white bed and more closely surveyed the ankle scenery.

It was better than six days earlier, one could confidently say that. On the other hand, it was still black, still fairly swollen and still sore to the touch. Still vulnerable to knocks. I flexed my calf and foot muscles several times: the bones and ligaments still violently protested, but none of it could be helped. To stay strong, the muscles had to move, and that was that. I kneaded the calf muscle a bit to give it some encouragement and thought about borrowing an apparatus called Elcctro-vet which Milo had tucked away somewhere, which he used on his horses' legs to give their muscles electrical stimuli to bring down swelling and get them fit again. What worked on horses should work on me, I reckoned.

Eventually I wound the bandage on again, not as neatly as the surgeon, but I hoped as effectively. Then I dressed, borrowing one of Greville's clean white shirts and, down in the forlorn little sitting room, telephoned to Nicholas Loder.

He didn't sound pleased to hear my voice.

'Well done with Dozen Roses,' I said.

He grunted.

'To solve the question of who owns him,' I continued, 'I've found a buyer for him.'

'Now look here!' he began angrily. 'I—'

'Yes, I know,' I interrupted, 'you'd ideally like to sell him to one of your own owners and keep him in your yard, and I do sympathize with that, but Mr and Mrs Ostermeyer, the people I was with yesterday at York, they've told me they would like the horse themselves.'

'I strongly protest,' he said.

'They want to send him to Milo Shandy to be trained for jumping.'

'You owe it to me to leave him here,' he said obstinately. 'Four wins in a row . . . it's downright dishonourable to take him away.'

'He's suitable for jumping, now that he's been

gelded.' I said it without threat, but he knew he was in an awkward position. He'd had no right to geld the horse. In addition, there was in fact nothing to stop Greville's executor selling the horse to whomever he pleased, as Milo had discovered for me, and which Nicholas Loder had no doubt discovered for himself, and in the racing world in general the sale to the Ostermeyers would make exquisite sense as I would get to ride the horse even if I couldn't own him.

Into Loder's continued silence I said, 'If you find a buyer for Gemstones, though, I'll give my approval.'

'He's not as good.'

'No, but not useless. No doubt you'd take a commission, I wouldn't object to that.'

He grunted again, which I took to mean assent, but he also said grittily, 'Don't expect any favours from me, ever.'

'I've done one for you,' I pointed out, 'in not lodging a complaint. Anyway, I'm lunching with the Ostermeyers at Milo's today and we'll do the paperwork of the sale. So Milo should be sending a box to collect Dozen Roses sometime this week. No doubt he'll fix a day with you.'

'Rot you,' he said.

'I don't want to quarrel.'

'You're having a damn good try.' He slammed down his receiver and left me feeling perplexed as much as anything else by his constant rudeness. All trainers lost horses regularly when owners sold them and, as he'd said himself, it wasn't as if Dozen Roses were a Derby hope. Nicholas Loder's stable held far better prospects than a five-year-old gelding, prolific winner though he might be.

Shrugging, I picked up my overnight bag and felt vaguely guilty at turning my back on so much chaos in the house. I'd done minimum tidying upstairs, hanging up Greville's suits and shirts and so on, and I'd left my own suit and some other things with them because it seemed I might spend more nights there, but the rest was physically difficult and would have to wait for the anonymous Mrs P, poor woman, who was going to get an atrocious shock.

I went by taxi to the Ostermeyers' hotel and again found them in champagne spirits, and it was again Simms, fortyish, with a moustache, who turned up as chauffeur. When I commented on his working Sunday as well as Saturday he smiled faintly and said he was glad of the opportunity to earn extra; Monday to Friday he developed films in the dark.

'Films?' Martha asked. 'Do you mean movies?'

'Family snapshots, madam, in a one-hour photo shop.'

'Oh.' Martha sounded as if she couldn't envisage such a life. 'How interesting.'

'Not very, madam,' Simms said resignedly, and set off smoothly into the sparse Sunday traffic. He asked me for directions as we neared Lambourn and we arrived without delay at Milo's door, where Milo himself greeted me with the news that Nicholas Loder wanted me to phone him at once.

'It sounded to me,' Milo said, 'like a great deal of agitation pretending to be casual.'

'I don't understand him.'

'He doesn't want me to have Dozen Roses, for some reason.'

'Oh, but,' Martha said to him anxiously, overhearing, 'you are going to, aren't you?'

'Of course, yes, don't worry. Derek, get it over with while we go and look at Datepalm.' He bore the Ostermeyers away, dazzling them with twinkling charm, and I went into his kitchen and phoned Nicholas Loder, wondering why I was bothering.

'Look,' he said, sounding persuasive. 'I've an owner who's very interested in Dozen Roses. He says he'll top whatever your Ostermeyers are offering. What do you say?'

I didn't answer immediately, and he said forcefully, 'You'll make a good clear profit that way. There's no guarantee the horse will be able to jump. You can't ask a high price for him, because of that. My owner will top their offer and add a cash bonus for you personally. Name your figure.'

'Um,' I said slowly, 'this owner wouldn't be yourself, would it?'

He said sharply, 'No, certainly not.'

'The horse that ran at York yesterday,' I said even more slowly, 'does he fit Dozen Roses's passport?'

674

'That's slanderous!'

'It's a question.'

'The answer is yes. The horse is Dozen Roses. Is that good enough for you?'

'Yes.'

'Well, then,' he sounded relieved, 'name your figure.'

I hadn't yet discussed any figure at all with Martha and Harley and I'd been going to ask a bloodstock agent friend for a snap valuation. I said as much to Nicholas Loder who, sounding exasperated, repeated that his owner would offer more, plus a tax-free sweetener for myself.

I had every firm intention of selling Dozen Roses to the Ostermeyers and no so-called sweetener that I could think of would have persuaded me otherwise.

'Please tell your owner I'm sorry,' I said, 'but the Ostermeyers have bought Datepalm, as I told you, and I am obligated to them, and loyalty to them comes first. I'm sure you'll find your owner another horse as good as Dozen Roses.'

'What if he offered double what you'd take from the Ostermeyers?'

'It's not a matter of money.'

'Everyone can be bought,' he said.

'Well, no. I'm sorry, but no.'

'Think it over,' he said, and slammed the receiver down again. I wondered in amusement how often he broke them. But he hadn't in fact been amusing, and the situation as a whole held no joy. I was going to have to meet him on racecourses for ever once I was a trainer myself, and I had no appetite for chronic feuds.

I went out into the yard where, seeing me, Milo broke away from the Ostermeyers who were feasting their eyes as Datepalm was being led round on the gravel to delight them.

'What did Loder want?' Milo demanded, coming towards me.

'He offered double whatever I was asking the Ostermeyers to pay for Dozen Roses.'

Milo stared. 'Double! Without knowing what it was?'

'That's right.'

'What are you going to do?'

'What do you think?' I asked.

'If you've accepted, I'll flatten you.'

I laughed. Too many people that past week had flattened me and no doubt Milo could do it with the best.

'Well?' he said belligerently.

'I told him to stuff it.'

'Good.'

'Mm, perhaps. But you'd better arrange to fetch the horse here at once. Like tomorrow morning, as we don't want him having a nasty accident and ending up at the knackers, do you think?'

'Christ!' He was appalled. 'He wouldn't! Not Nicholas Loder.'

'One wouldn't think so. But no harm in removing the temptation.'

'No.' He looked at me attentively. 'Are you all right?' he asked suddenly. 'You don't look too well.'

I told him briefly about being knocked out in Greville's garden. 'Those phone calls you took,' I said, 'were designed to make sure I turned up in the right place at the right time. So I walked straight into an ambush and, if you want to know, I feel a fool.'

'Derek!' He was dumbfounded, but also of course practical. 'It's not going to delay your getting back on a horse?'

'No, don't worry.'

'Did you tell the Ostermeyers?'

'No, don't bother them. They don't like me being unfit.'

He nodded in complete understanding. To Martha, and to Harley to a lesser but still considerable extent, it seemed that proprietorship in the jockey was as important as in the horse. I'd met that feeling a few times before and never undervalued it: they were the best owners to ride for, even if often the most demanding. The quasi-love relationship could however turn to dust and damaging rejection if one ever put them second, which was why I would never jeopardize my place on Datepalm for a profit on Dozen Roses. It was hard to explain to more rational people, but I rode races, as every jump jockey did, from a different impetus than making money, though the money was nice enough and thoroughly earned besides.

When Martha and Harley at length ran out of questions and admiration of Datepalm we all returned to the house, where over drinks in Milo's comfortable sitting room we telephoned to the bloodstock agent for an opinion and then agreed on a price which was less than he'd suggested. Milo beamed. Martha clapped her hands together with pleasure. Harley drew out his chequebook and wrote in it carefully, 'Saxony Franklin Ltd.'

'Subject to a vet's certificate,' I said.

'Oh yes, dear,' Martha agreed, smiling. 'As if you would ever sell us a lemon.'

Milo produced the 'Change of Ownership' forms which Martha and Harley and I all signed, and Milo said he would register the new arrangements with Weatherby's in the morning.

'Is Dozen Roses ours, now?' Martha asked, shiny-eyed.

'Indeed he is,' Milo said, 'subject to his being alive and in good condition when he arrives here. If he isn't the sale is void and he still belongs to Saxony Franklin.'

I wondered briefly if he were insured. Didn't want to find out the hard way.

With business concluded, Milo drove us all out to lunch at a nearby restaurant which as usual was crammed with Lambourn people: Martha and Harley held splendid court as the new owners of Gold Cup winner Datepalm and were pink with gratification over the compliments to their purchase. I watched their stimulated faces, hers rounded and still pretty under the blonde-rinsed grey hair, his heavily handsome, the square jaw showing the beginning of jowls. Both now looking sixty, they still displayed enthusiasms and enjoyments that were almost childlike in their simplicity, which did no harm in the weary old world.

Milo drove us back to rejoin the Daimler and Simms, who'd eaten his lunch in a village pub, and Martha in farewell gave Milo a kiss with flirtation but also real affection. Milo had bound the Ostermeyers to his stable with hoops of charm and all we needed now was for the two horses to carry on winning.

Milo said 'Thanks' to me briefly as we got into the car, but in truth I wanted what he wanted, and securing the Ostermeyers had been a joint venture. We drove out of the yard with Martha waving and then settling back into her seat with murmurs and soft remarks of pleasure.

I told Simms the way to Hungerford so that he could drop me off there, and the big car purred along with Sunday afternoon somnolence.

Martha said something I didn't quite catch and I turned my face back between the headrests, looking towards her and asking her to say it again. I saw a flash of raw horror begin on Harley's face, and then with a

679

crash and a bang the car rocketed out of control across
the road towards a wall and there was blood and shred-
ded glass everywhere and we careered off the wall back
onto the road and into the path of a fifty-seater touring
coach which had been behind us and was now bearing
down on us like a runaway cliff.

CHAPTER TWELVE

In a split second before the front of the bus hit the side of the car where I was sitting, in the freeze-frame awareness of the tons of bright metal thundering inexorably towards us, I totally believed I would be mangled to pulp within a breath.

There was no time for regrets or anger or any other emotion. The bus plunged into the Daimler and turned it again forwards and both vehicles screeched along the road together, monstrously joined wheel to wheel, the white front wing of the coach buried deep in the black Daimler's engine, the noise and buffeting too much for thinking, the speed of everything truly terrifying and the nearness of death an inevitability merely postponed.

Inertia dragged the two vehicles towards a halt, but they were blocking the whole width of the road. Towards us, round the bend, came a family car travelling too fast to stop in the space available. The driver in a frenzy braked so hard that his rear end swung round and hit the front of the Daimler broadside with a sickening jolt and a crunching bang and behind us, somewhere, another car ran into the back of the bus.

About that time I stopped being clear about the sequence of events. Against all catastrophe probability, I was still alive and that seemed enough. After the first stunned moments of silence when the tearing of metal had stopped, there were voices shouting everywhere, and people screaming and a sharp petrifying smell of raw petrol.

The whole thing was going to burn, I thought. Explode. Fireballs coming. Greville had burned two days ago. Greville had at least been dead at the time. Talk about delirious. I had half a car in my lap and in my head the warmed-up leftovers of yesterday's concussion.

The heat of the dead engine filled the cracked-open body of the car, forewarning of worse. There would be oil dripping out of it. There were electrical circuits . . . sparks . . . there was dread and despair and a vision of hell.

I couldn't escape. The glass had gone from the window beside me and from the windscreen, and what might have been part of the frame of the door had bent somehow across my chest, pinning me deep against the seat. What had been the fascia and the glove compartment seemed to be digging into my waist. What had been ample room for a dicky ankle was now as constricting as any cast. The car seemed to have wrapped itself around me in an iron-maiden embrace and the only parts free to move at all were my head and the arm nearest Simms. There was intense pressure rather than active agony, but what I felt most was fear.

Almost automatically, as if logic had gone on working on its own, I stretched as far as I could, got my fingers on the keys, twisted and pulled them out of the ignition. At least, no more sparks. At most, I was breathing.

Martha, too, was alive, her thoughts probably as abysmal as my own. I could hear her whimpering behind me, a small moaning without words. Simms and Harley were silent; and it was Simms's blood that had spurted over everything, scarlet and sticky. I could smell it under the smell of petrol; it was on my arm and face and clothes and in my hair.

The side of the car where I sat was jammed tight against the bus. People came in time to the opposite side and tried to open the doors, but they were immovably buckled. Dazed people emerged from the family car in front, the children weeping. People from the coach spread along the roadside, all of them elderly, most of them, it seemed to me, with their mouths open. I wanted to tell them all to keep away, to go further to safety, far from what was going to be a conflagration at any second, but I didn't seem to be able to shout, and the croak I achieved got no further than six inches.

Behind me Martha stopped moaning. I thought wretchedly that she was dying, but it seemed to be the opposite. In a quavery small voice she said, 'Derek?'

683

'Yes.' Another croak.

'I'm frightened.'

So was I, by God. I said futilely, hoarsely, 'Don't worry.'

She scarcely listened. She was saying 'Harley? Harley, honey?' in alarm and awakening anguish. 'Oh, get us out, please, someone get us out.'

I turned my head as far as I could and looked back sideways at Harley. He was cold to the world but his eyes were closed, which was a hopeful sign on the whole.

Simms's eyes were half open and would never blink again. Simms, poor man, had developed his last one-hour photo. Simms wouldn't feel any flames.

'Oh God, honey. Honey, wake up.' Her voice cracked, high with rising panic. 'Derek, get us out of here, can't you smell the gas?'

'People will come,' I said, knowing it was of little comfort. Comfort seemed impossible, out of reach.

People and comfort came, however, in the shape of a works foreman-type of man, used to getting things done. He peered through the window beside Harley and was presently yelling to Martha that he was going to break the rear window to get her out and she should cover her face in case of flying glass.

Martha hid her face against Harley's chest, calling to him and weeping, and the rear window gave way to determination and a metal bar.

'Come on, Missis,' encouraged the best of British

workmen. 'Climb up on the seat, we'll have you out of there in no time.'

'My husband . . .' she wailed.

'Him too. No trouble. Come on, now.'

It appeared that strong arms hauled Martha out bodily. Almost at once her rescuer was himself inside the car, lifting the still unconscious Harley far enough to be raised by other hands outside. Then he put his head forward near to mine, and took a look at me and Simms.

'Christ,' he said.

He was smallish, with a moustache and bright brown eyes.

'Can you slide out of there?' he asked.

'No.'

He tried to pull me, but we could both see it was hopeless.

'They'll have to cut you out,' he said, and I nodded. He wrinkled his nose. 'The smell of petrol's very strong in here. Much worse than outside.'

'It's vapour,' I said. 'It ignites.'

He knew that, but it hadn't seemed to worry him until then.

'Clear all those people further away,' I said. I raised perhaps a twitch of a smile. 'Ask them not to smoke.'

He gave me a sick look and retreated through the rear window, and soon I saw him outside delivering a warning which must have been the quickest crowd control measure on record.

Perhaps because with more of the glass missing there

was a through current of air, the smell of petrol did begin to abate, but there was still, I imagined, a severed fuel line somewhere beneath me, with freshly-released vapour continually seeping through the cracks. How much liquid bonfire, I wondered numbly, did a Daimler's tank hold?

There were a great many more cars now ahead in the road, all stopped, their occupants out and crash-gazing. No doubt to the rear it would be the same thing. Sunday afternoon entertainment at its worst.

Simms and I sat on in our silent immobility and I thought of the old joke about worrying, that there was no point in it. If one worried that things would get bad and they didn't, there was no point in worrying. If they got bad and one worried they would get worse, and they didn't, there was no point in worrying. If they got worse and one worried that one might die, and one didn't, there was no point in worrying, and if one died one could no longer worry, so why worry?

For worry read fear, I thought; but the theory didn't work. I went straight on being scared silly.

It was odd, I thought, that for all the risks I took, I very seldom felt any fear of death. I thought about physical pain, as indeed one often had to in a trade like mine, and remembered things I'd endured, and I didn't know why the imagined pain of burning should fill me with a terror hard to control. I swallowed and felt lonely, and hoped that if it came it would be over quickly.

There were sirens at length in the distance and the best sight in the world, as far as I was concerned, was the red fire-engine which slowly forced its way forward, scattering spectator cars to either side of the road. There was room, just, for three cars abreast, a wall on one side of the road, a row of trees on the other. Behind the fire-engine I could see the flashing blue light of a police car and beyond that another flashing light which might betoken an ambulance.

Figures in authority uniforms appeared from the vehicles, the best being in flameproof suits lugging a hose. They stopped in front of the Daimler, seeing the bus wedged into one side of it and the family car on the other and one of them shouted to me through the space where the windscreen should have been.

'There's petrol running from these vehicles,' he said. 'Can't you get out?'

What a damn silly question, I thought. I said, 'No.'

'We're going to spray the road underneath you. Shut your eyes and hold something over your mouth and nose.'

I nodded and did as I was bid, managing to shield my face inside the neck of my jersey. I listened to the long whooshing of the spray and thought no sound could be sweeter. Incineration faded progressively from near certainty to diminishing probability to unlikely outcome, and the release from fear was almost as hard to manage as the fear itself. I wiped blood and sweat off my face and felt shaky.

After a while some of the firemen brought up metal-cutting gear and more or less tore out of its frame the buckled door next to where Harley had been sitting. Into this new entrance edged a policeman who took a preliminary look at Simms and me and then perched on the rear seat where he could see my head. I turned it as far as I could towards him, seeing a serious face under the peaked cap: about my own age, I judged, and full of strain.

'A doctor's coming,' he said, offering crumbs. 'He'll deal with your wounds.'

'I don't think I'm bleeding,' I said. 'It's Simms's blood that's on me.'

'Ah.' He drew out a notebook and consulted it. 'Did you see what caused this . . . all this?'

'No,' I said, thinking it faintly surprising that he should be asking at this point. 'I was looking back at Mr and Mrs Ostermeyer, who were sitting where you are now. The car just seemed to go out of control.' I thought back, remembering. 'I think Harley . . . Mr Ostermeyer . . . may have seen something. For a second he looked horrified . . . then we hit the wall and rebounded into the path of the bus.'

He nodded, making a note.

'Mr Ostermeyer is now conscious,' he said, sounding carefully noncommittal. 'He says you were shot.'

'We were *what*?'

'Shot. Not all of you. You, personally.'

'No.' I must have sounded as bewildered as I felt. 'Of course not.'

'Mr and Mrs Ostermeyer are very distressed but he is quite clear he saw a gun. He says the chauffeur had just pulled out to pass a car that had been in front of you for some way, and the driver of that car had the window down and was pointing a gun out of it. He says the gun was pointing at you, and you were shot. Twice at least, he says. He saw the spurts of flame.'

I looked from the policeman to Simms, and at the chauffeur's blood over everything and at the solidly scarlet congealed mess below his jaw.

'No,' I protested, not wanting to believe it. 'It can't be right.'

'Mrs Ostermeyer is intensely worried that you are sitting here bleeding to death.'

'I feel squeezed, not punctured.'

'Can you feel your feet?'

I moved my toes, one foot after another. There wasn't the slightest doubt, particularly about the left.

'Good,' he said. 'Well, sir, we are treating this from now on as a possible murder enquiry, and apart from that I'm afraid the firemen say it may be some time before they can get you loose. They need more gear. Can you be patient?' He didn't wait for a reply, and went on, 'As I said, a doctor is here and will come to you, but if you aren't in urgent need of him there are two other people back there in a very bad way, and I hope you can be patient about that also.'

I nodded slightly. I could be patient for hours if I wasn't going to burn.

'Why,' I asked, 'would anyone shoot at us?'

'Have you no idea?'

'None at all.'

'Unfortunately,' he said, 'there isn't always an understandable reason.'

I met his eyes. 'I live in Hungerford,' I said.

'Yes, sir, so I've been told.' He nodded and slithered out of the car, and left me thinking about the time in Hungerford when a berserk man had gunned down many innocent people, including some in cars, and turned the quiet country town into a place of horror. No one who lived in Hungerford would ever discount the possibility of being randomly slaughtered.

The bullet that had torn into Simms would have gone through my own neck or head, I thought, if I hadn't turned round to talk to Martha. I'd put my head between the headrests, the better to see her. I tried to sort out what had happened next, but I hadn't seen Simms hit. I'd heard only the bang and crash of the window breaking and felt the hot spray of the blood that had fountained out of his smashed main artery in the time it had taken him to die. He had been dead, I thought, before anyone had started screaming: the jet of blood had stopped by then.

The steering wheel was now rammed hard against his chest with the instrument panel slanting down across his knees, higher my end than his. The edge of it pressed uncomfortably into my stomach, and I could see that if it had travelled back another six inches, it would have cut me in half.

A good many people arrived looking official with measuring tapes and cameras, taking photographs of Simms particularly and consulting in low tones. A police surgeon solemnly put a stethoscope to Simms's chest and declared him dead, and without bothering with the stethoscope declared me alive.

How bad was the compression, he wanted to know. Uncomfortable, I said.

'I know you, don't I?' he said, considering me. 'Aren't you one of the local jockeys? The jumping boys?'

'Mm.'

'Then you know enough about being injured to give me an assessment of your state.'

I said that my toes, fingers and lungs were OK and that I had cramp in my legs, the trapped arm was aching and the instrument panel was inhibiting the digestion of a good Sunday lunch.

'Do you want an injection?' he asked, listening.

'Not unless it gets worse.'

He nodded, allowed himself a small smile and wriggled his way out onto the road. It struck me that there was much less leg-room for the back seat than there had been when we set out. A miracle Martha's and Harley's legs hadn't been broken. Three of us, I thought, had been incredibly lucky.

691

Simms and I went on sitting quietly side by side for what seemed several more ages but finally the extra gear to free us appeared in the form of winches, cranes and an acetylene torch, which I hoped they would use around me with discretion.

Large mechanics scratched their heads over the problems. They couldn't get to me from my side of the car because it was tight against the bus. They decided that if they tried to cut through the support under the front seats and pull them backwards they might upset the tricky equilibrium of the engine and instead of freeing my trapped legs bring the whole weight of the front of the car down to crush them. I was against the idea, and said so.

In the end, working from inside the car in fireproof suits and with thick foam pumped all around, using a well-sheltered but still scorching hot acetylene flame, which roared and threw terrifying sparks around like matches, they cut away most of the driver's side, and after that, because he couldn't feel or protest, they forcefully pulled Simms's stiffening body out and laid it on a stretcher. I wondered greyly if he had a wife, who wouldn't know yet.

With Simms gone, the mechanics began fixing chains and operating jacks and I sat and waited without bothering them with questions. From time to time they said, 'You all right, mate?' and I answered 'Yes,' and was grateful to them.

After a while they fastened chains and a winch to the

family car still impacted broadside on the Daimler's wing and with inching care began to pull it away. There was almost instantly a fearful shudder through the Daimler's crushed body and also through mine, and the pulling stopped immediately. A little more head-scratching went on, and one of them explained to me that their crane couldn't get a good enough stabilizing purchase on the Daimler because the family car was in the way, and they would have to try something else. Was I all right? Yes, I said.

One of them began calling me Derek. 'Seen you in Hungerford, haven't I,' he said, 'and on the telly?' He told the others, who made jolly remarks like, 'Don't worry, we'll have you out in time for the three-thirty tomorrow. Sure to.' One of them seriously told me that it sometimes did take hours to free people because of the dangers of getting it wrong. Lucky, he said, that it was a Daimler I was in, with its tank-like strength. In anything less I would have been history.

They decided to rethink the rear approach. They wouldn't disturb the seat anchorages from their pushed-back position: the seats were off their runners, they said, and had dug into the floor. Also the recliner-mechanism had jammed and broken. However they were going to cut off the back of Simms's seat to give themselves more room to work. They were then going to extract the padding and springs from under my bottom and see if they could get rid of the back of my seat also, and draw me out backwards so that they wouldn't have to manoeuvre me out sideways past the steering column, which they didn't want to remove as it was the anchor for one of the chief stabilizing chains. Did I understand? Yes, I did.

They more or less followed this plan, although they had to dismantle the back of my seat before the cushion, the lowering effect of having the first spring removed from under me having jammed me even tighter against the fascia and made breathing difficult. They yanked padding out from behind me to relieve that, and then with a hacksaw took the back of the seat off near the roots; and, finally, with one of them supporting my shoulders, another pulled out handfuls of springs and other seat innards, the bear-hug pressure on my abdomen and arm and legs lessened and went away, and I had only blessed pins and needles instead.

Even then the big car was loath to let me go. With my top half free the two men began to pull me backwards, and I grunted and stiffened, and they stopped at once.

'What's the matter?' one asked anxiously.

'Well, nothing. Pull again.'

In truth, the pulling hurt the left ankle but I'd sat there long enough. It was at least an old, recognizable pain, nothing threateningly new. Reassured, my rescuers hooked their arms under my armpits and used a bit of strength, and at last extracted me from the car's crushing embrace like a breeched calf from a cow.

Relief was an inadequate word. They gave me a minute's rest on the back seat, and sat each side of me, all three of us breathing deeply.

'Thanks,' I said briefly.

'Think nothing of it.'

I guessed they knew the depths of my gratitude, as I knew the thought and care they'd expended. Thanks, think nothing of it: it was enough.

One by one we edged out onto the road, and I was astonished to find that after all that time there was still a small crowd standing around waiting: policemen, fire-men, mechanics, ambulance men and assorted civilians, many with cameras. There was a small cheer and applause as I stood up free, and I smiled and moved my head in a gesture of both embarrassment and thanks-giving.

I was offered a stretcher but said I'd much rather have the crutches that might still be in the boot, and that caused a bit of general consternation, but someone brought them out unharmed, about the only thing still unbent in the whole mess. I stood for a bit with their support simply looking at all the intertwined wreckage; at the bus and the family car and above all at the Daimler's buckled-up roof, at its sheared-off bonnet, its dislodged engine awry at a tilted angle, its gleaming black paintwork now unrecognizable scrap, its former shape mangled and compressed like a stamped-on toy. I thought it incredible that I'd sat where I'd sat and lived. I reckoned that I'd used up a lifetime's luck.

The Ostermeyers had been taken to Swindon Hospital and treated for shock, bruises and concussion. From there, recovering a little, they had telephoned Milo and told him what had happened and he, reacting I guessed with spontaneous generosity but also with strong business sense, had told them they must stay with him for the night and he would collect them. All three were on the point of leaving when I in my turn arrived.

There was a predictable amount of fussing from Martha over my rescue, but she herself looked as exhausted as I felt and she was pliably content to be supported on Harley's arm on their way to the door.

Milo, coming back a step, said, 'Come as well, if you like. There's always a bed.'

'Thanks, I'll let you know.'

He stared at me. 'Is it true Simms was shot?'

'Mm.'

'It could have been you.'

'Nearly was.'

'The police took statements here from Martha and Harley, it seems.' He paused, looking towards them as they reached the door. 'I'll have to go. How's the ankle?'

'Be back racing as scheduled.'

'Good.'

He bustled off and I went through the paperwork

routines, but there was nothing wrong with me that a small application of time wouldn't fix and I got myself discharged pretty fast as a patient and was invited instead to give a more detailed statement to the police I couldn't add much more than I'd told them in the first place, but some of their questions were in the end disturbing.

Could we have been shot at for any purpose?

I knew of no purpose.

How long had the car driven by the man with the gun been in front of us?

I couldn't remember: hadn't noticed.

Could anyone have known we would be on that road at that time? I stared at the policeman. Anyone, perhaps, who had been in the restaurant for lunch. Anyone there could have followed us from there to Milo's house, perhaps, and waited for us to leave, and passed us, allowing us then to pass again. But why ever should they?

Who else might know?

Perhaps the car company who employed Simms.

Who else?

Milo Shandy, and he'd have been as likely to shoot himself as the Ostermeyers.

Mr Ostermeyer said the gun was pointing at you, sir.

With all due respect to Mr Ostermeyer, he was looking through the car and both cars were moving, and at

697

different speeds presumably, and I didn't think one could be certain.

Could I think of any reason why anyone should want to kill me?

Me, personally? No ... I couldn't.

They pounced on the hesitation I could hear in my own voice, and I told them I'd been attacked and knocked out the previous evening. I explained about Greville's death. I told them he had been dealing in precious stones as he was a gem merchant and I thought my attacker had been trying to find and steal part of the stock. But I had no idea why the would-be thief should want to shoot me today when he could easily have bashed my head in yesterday.

They wrote it down without comment. Had I any idea who had attacked me the previous evening?

No, I hadn't.

They didn't say they didn't believe me, but something in their manner gave me the impression they thought anyone attacked twice in two days had to know who was after him.

I would have liked very much to be able to tell them. It had just occurred to me, if not to them, that there might be more to come.

I'd better find out soon, I thought.

I'd better not find out too late.

CHAPTER THIRTEEN

I didn't go to Milo's house nor to my own bed, but stayed in an anonymous hotel in Swindon where unknown enemies wouldn't find me.

The urge simply to go home was strong, as if one could retreat to safety into one's den, but I thought I would probably be alarmed and wakeful all night there, when what I most wanted was sleep. All in all it had been a rough ten days, and however easily my body usually shook off bumps and bangs, the accumulation was making an insistent demand for rest.

RICE, I thought wryly, RICE being the acronym of the best way to treat sports injuries: rest, ice, compression, elevation. I rarely seemed to be managing all of them at the same time, though all, in one way or another, separately. With elevation in place, I phoned Milo from the hotel to say I wouldn't be coming and asked how Martha and Harley were doing.

'They're quavery. It must have been some crash. Martha keeps crying. It seems a car ran into the back of the bus and two people in the car were terribly injured.

She saw them, and it's upsetting her almost as much as knowing Simms was shot. Can't you come and comfort her?'

'You and Harley can do it better.'

'She thought you were dying too. She's badly shocked. You'd better come.'

'They gave her a sedative at the hospital, didn't they?'

'Yes,' he agreed grudgingly. 'Harley too.'

'Look . . . persuade them to sleep. I'll come in the morning and pick them up and take them back to their hotel in London. Will that do?'

He said unwillingly that he supposed so.

'Say goodnight to them from me,' I said. 'Tell them I think they're terrific.'

'Do you?' He sounded surprised.

'It does no harm to say it.'

'Cynic.'

'Seriously,' I said, 'they'll feel better if you tell them.'

'All right then. See you at breakfast.'

I put down the receiver and on reflection a few minutes later got through to Brad.

'Cor,' he said, 'you were in that crash.'

'How did you hear about it?' I asked, surprised.

'Down the pub. Talk of Hungerford. Another madman. It's shook everyone up. My mum won't go out.'

It had shaken his tongue loose, I thought in amusement. 'Have you still got my car?' I said.

700

'Yerss.' He sounded anxious. 'You said keep it here.'

'Yes. I meant keep it there.'

'I walked down your house earlier. There weren't no one there then.'

'I'm not there now,' I said. 'Do you still want to go on driving?'

'Yerss.' Very positive. 'Now?'

'In the morning.' I said I would meet him at eight outside the hotel near the railway station at Swindon, and we would be going to London. 'OK?'

'Yerss,' he said, signing off, and it sounded like a cat purring over the resumption of milk.

Smiling and yawning, a jaw-cracking combination, I ran a bath, took off my clothes and the bandage and lay gratefully in hot water, letting it soak away the fatigue along with Simms's blood. Then, my overnight bag having survived unharmed along with the crutches, I scrubbed my teeth, put on sleeping shorts, rewrapped the ankle, hung a 'Do not disturb' card outside my door and was in bed by nine and slept and dreamed of crashes and fire and hovering unidentified threats.

Brad came on the dot in the morning and we went first to my place in a necessary quest for clean clothes. His mum, Brad agreed, would wash the things I'd worn in the crash.

My rooms were still quiet and unransacked and no

701

dangers lurked outside in daylight. I changed uneventfully and repacked the travelling bag and we drove in good order to Lambourn, I sitting beside Brad and thinking I could have done the driving myself, except that I found his presence reassuring and I'd come to grief on both of the days he hadn't been with me.

'If a car passes us and sits in front of us,' I said, 'don't pass it. Fall right back and turn up a side road.'

'Why?'

I told him that the police thought we'd been caught in a deliberate moving ambush. Neither the Ostermeyers nor I, I pointed out, would be happy to repeat the experience, and Brad wouldn't be wanting to double for Simms. He grinned, an unnerving sight, and gave me to understand with a nod that he would follow the instruction.

The usual road to Lambourn turned out to be still blocked off, and I wondered briefly, as we detoured, whether it was because of the murder enquiry or simply technical difficulties in disentangling the omelette.

Martha and Harley were still shaking over breakfast, the coffee cups trembling against their lips. Milo with relief shifted the burden of their reliance smartly from himself to me, telling them that now Derek was here, they'd be safe. I wasn't so sure about that, particularly if both Harley and the police were right about me personally being yesterday's target. Neither Martha nor Harley seemed to suffer such qualms and gave me the instant status of surrogate son/nephew, the one to be naturally leaned on, psychologically if not physically, for succour and support.

I looked at them with affection. Martha had retained enough spirit to put on lipstick. Harley was making light of a sticking plaster on his temple. They couldn't help their nervous systems' reaction to mental trauma, and I hoped it wouldn't be long before their habitual preference for enjoyment resurfaced.

'The only good thing about yesterday,' Martha said with a sigh, 'was buying Dozen Roses. Milo says he's already sent a van for him.'

I'd forgotten about Dozen Roses. Nicholas Loder and his tizzies seemed a long way off and unimportant. I said I was glad they were glad, and that in about a week or so, when he'd settled down in his new quarters, I would start teaching him to jump.

'I'm sure he'll be brilliant,' Martha said bravely, trying hard to make normal conversation. 'Won't he?'

'Some horses take to it better than others,' I said neutrally. 'Like humans.'

'I'll believe he'll be brilliant.'

Averagely good, I thought, would be good enough for me: but most racehorses could jump if started patiently over low obstacles like logs.

Milo offered fresh coffee and more toast, but they were ready to leave and in a short while we were on the road to London. No one passed us and slowed, no one ambushed or shot us, and Brad drew up with a flourish outside their hotel, at least the equal of Simms.

Martha with a shine of tears kissed my cheek in goodbye, and I hers: Harley gruffly shook my hand. They would come back soon, they said, but they were sure glad to be going home tomorrow. I watched them go shakily into the hotel and thought uncomplicated thoughts, like hoping Datepalm would cover himself with glory for them, and Dozen Roses also, once he could jump.

'Office?' I suggested to Brad, and he nodded, and made the now familiar turns towards the environs of Hatton Garden.

Little in Saxony Franklin appeared to have changed. It seemed extraordinary that it was only a week since I'd walked in there for the first time, so familiar did it feel on going back. The staff said, 'Good morning, Derek,' as if they'd been used to me for years, and Annette said there were letters left over from Friday which needed decisions.

'How was the funeral?' she asked sadly, laying out papers on the desk.

A thousand light years ago, I thought. 'Quiet,' I said. 'Good. Your flowers were good. They were on top of his coffin.'

She looked pleased and said she would tell the others, and received the news that there would be a memorial service with obvious satisfaction. 'It didn't seem right, not being at his funeral, not on Friday. We had a minute's silence here at two o'clock. I suppose you'll think us silly.'

'Far from it.' I was moved and let her see it. She smiled sweetly in her heavy way and went off to relay to the others and leave me floundering in the old treacle of deciding things on a basis of no knowledge.

June whisked in looking happy with a pink glow on both cheeks and told me we were low in blue lace agate chips and snowflake obsidian and amazonite beads.

'Order some more, same as before.'

'Yes, right.'

She turned and was on her way out again when I called her back and asked her if there was an alarm clock among all the gadgets. I pulled open the deep drawer and pointed downwards.

'An alarm clock?' She was doubtful and peered at the assorted black objects. 'Telescopes, dictionaries, Geiger counter, calculators, spy juice . . .'

'What's spy juice?' I asked, intrigued.

'Oh, this.' She reached in and extracted an aerosol can. 'That's just my name for it. You squirt this stuff on anyone's envelopes and it makes the paper transparent so you can read the private letters inside.' She looked at my face and laughed. 'Banks have got round it by printing patterns all over the insides of their envelopes. If you spray their envelopes, all you see is the pattern.'

'Whatever did Greville use it for?'

'Someone gave it to him, I think. He didn't use it much, just to check if it was worth opening things that looked like advertisements.'

She put a plain sheet of paper over one of the letters

705

lying on the desk and squirted a little liquid over it. The plain paper immediately became transparent so that one could read the letter through it, and then slowly went opaque again as it dried.

'Sneaky,' she said, 'isn't it?'

'Very.'

She was about to replace the can in the drawer but I said to put it on top of the desk, and I brought out all the other gadgets and stood them around in plain sight. None of them, as far as I could see, had an alarm function.

'You mentioned something about a world clock,' I said, 'but there isn't one here.'

'I've a clock with an alarm in my room,' she said helpfully. 'Would you like me to bring that?'

'Um, yes, perhaps. Could you set it to four-fifteen?'

'Sure, anything you like.'

She vanished and returned fiddling with a tiny thing like a black credit card which turned out to be a highly versatile timepiece.

'There you are,' she said. 'Four-fifteen – pm, I suppose you mean.' She put the clock on the desk.

'This afternoon, yes. There's an alarm somewhere here that goes off every day at four-twenty. I thought I might find it.'

Her eyes widened. 'Oh, but that's Mr Franklin's watch.'

'Which one?' I asked.

'He only ever wore one. It's a computer itself, a calendar and a compass.'

That watch, I reflected, was beside my bed in Hungerford.

'I think,' I said, 'that he may have had more than one alarm set to four-twenty.'

The fair eyebrows lifted. 'I did sometimes wonder why,' she said. 'I mean, why four-twenty? If he was in the stock-room and his watch alarm went off he would stop doing whatever it was for a few moments. I sort of asked him once, but he didn't really answer, he said it was a convenient time for communication, or something like that. I didn't understand what he meant, but that was all right, he didn't mean me to.'

She spoke without resentment and with regret. I thought that Greville must have enjoyed having June around him as much as I did. All that bright intelligence and unspoiled good humour and common sense. He'd liked her enough to make puzzles for her and let her share his toys.

'What's this one?' I asked, picking up a small grey contraption with black ear sponges on a headband with a cord like a walkabout cassette player, but with no provision for cassettes in what might have been a holder.

'That's a sound-enhancer. It's for deaf people, really, but Mr Franklin took it away from someone who was using it to listen to a private conversation he was having with another gem merchant. In Tucson, it was. He said he was so furious at the time that he just snatched the amplifier and headphones off the man who was listening and walked away with them uttering threats about commercial espionage, and he said the man hadn't even tried to get them back.' She paused. 'Put the earphones on. You can hear everything everyone's saying anywhere in the office. It's pretty powerful. Uncanny, really.'

I put on the ultra-light earphones and pressed the ON switch on the cigarette-packet-sized amplifier and sure enough I could straightaway hear Annette across the hallway talking to Lily about remembering to ask Derek for time off for the dentist.

I removed the earphones and looked at June.

'What did you hear?' she asked. 'Secrets?'

'Not that time, no.'

'Scary, though?'

'As you say.'

The sound quality was in fact excellent, astonishingly sensitive for so small a microphone and amplifier. Some of Greville's toys, I thought, were decidedly unfriendly.

'Mr Franklin was telling me that there's a voice transformer that you can fix on the telephone that can change the pitch of your voice and make a woman sound like a man. He said he thought it was excellent for women living alone so that they wouldn't be bothered by obscene phone calls and no one would think they were alone and vulnerable.'

I smiled. 'It might disconcert a bona fide boyfriend innocently ringing up.'

'Well, you'd have to warn them,' she agreed. 'Mr Franklin was very keen on women taking precautions.'

'Mm,' I said wryly.

'He said the jungle came into his court.'

'Did you get a voice changer?' I asked.

'No. We were only talking about it just before ...' She stopped. 'Well ... anyway, do you want a sandwich for lunch?'

'Yes, please.'

She nodded and was gone. I sighed and tried to apply myself to the tricky letters and was relieved at the interruption when the telephone rang.

It was Elliot Trelawney on the line, asking if I would messenger round the Vaccaro notes at once if I wouldn't mind as they had a committee meeting that afternoon.

'Vaccaro notes,' I repeated. I'd clean forgotten about them. I couldn't remember, for a moment, where they were.

'You said you would send them this morning,' Trelawney said with a tinge of civilized reproach. 'Do you remember?'

'Yes.' I did, vaguely.

Where the hell were they? Oh yes, in Greville's sitting room. Somewhere in all that mess. Somewhere there, unless the thief had taken them.

I apologized. I didn't actually say I'd come near to being killed twice since I'd last spoken to him and it was

709

playing tricks with my concentration. I said things had cropped up. I was truly sorry. I would try to get them to the court by . . . when?

'The committee meets at two and Vaccaro is first on the agenda,' he said.

'The notes are still in Greville's house,' I replied, 'but I'll get them to you.'

'Awfully good of you.' He was affable again. 'It's frightfully important we turn this application down.'

'Yes, I know.'

Vaccaro, I thought uncomfortably, replacing the receiver, was alleged to have had his wanting-out cocaine-smuggling pilots murdered by shots from moving cars.

I stared into space. There was no reason on earth for Vaccaro to shoot me, even supposing he knew I existed. I wasn't Greville, and I had no power to stand in the way of his plans. All I had, or probably had, were the notes on his transgressions, and how could he know that? And how could he know I would be in a car between Lambourn and Hungerford on Sunday afternoon? And couldn't the notes be gathered again by someone else besides Greville, even if they were now lost?

I shook myself out of the horrors and went down to the yard to see if Brad was sitting in the car, which he was, reading a magazine about fishing.

Fishing? 'I didn't know you fished,' I said.

'I don't.'

End of conversation.

Laughing inwardly I invited him to go on the journey. I gave him the simple keyring of three keys and explained about the upheaval he would find. I described the Vaccaro notes in and out of their envelope and wrote down Elliot Trelawney's name and the address of the court.

'Can you do it?' I asked, a shade doubtfully.

'Yerss.' He seemed to be slighted by my tone and took the paper with the address with brusqueness.

'Sorry,' I said.

He nodded without looking at me and started the car, and by the time I'd reached the rear entrance to the offices he was driving out of the yard.

Upstairs, Annette said there had just been a phone call from Antwerp and she had written down the number for me to ring back.

Antwerp.

With an effort I thought back to Thursday's distant conversations. What was it I should remember about Antwerp?

Van Ekeren. Jacob. His nephew, Hans.

I got through to the Belgian town and was rewarded with the smooth bilingual voice telling me that he had been able now to speak to his uncle on my behalf.

'You're very kind,' I said.

'I'm not sure that we will be of much help. My uncle says he knew your brother for a long time, but not very well. However, about six months ago your brother telephoned my uncle for advice about a sightholder.' He paused. 'It seems your brother was considering buying diamonds and trusted my uncle's judgement.'

'Ah,' I said hopefully. 'Did your uncle recommend anyone?'

'Your brother suggested three or four possible names. My uncle said they were all trustworthy. He told your brother to go ahead with any of them.'

I sighed. 'Does he possibly remember who they were?'

Hans said, 'He knows one of them was Guy Servi here in Antwerp, because we ourselves do business with him often. He can't remember the others. He doesn't know which one your brother decided on, or if he did business at all.'

'Well, thank you, anyway.'

'My uncle wishes to express his condolences.'

'Very kind.'

He disconnected with politeness, having dictated to me carefully the name, address and telephone number of Guy Servi, the one sightholder Greville had asked about that his uncle remembered.

I dialled the number immediately and again went through the rigmarole of being handed from voice to voice until I reached someone who had both the language and the information.

Mr Greville Saxony Franklin, now deceased, had been my brother? They would consult their files and call me back.

I waited without much patience while they went through whatever security checks they considered necessary but finally, after a long hour, they came back on the line.

What was my problem, they wanted to know.

'My problem is that our offices were ransacked and a lot of paperwork is missing. I've taken over since Greville's death, and I'm trying to sort out his affairs. Could you please tell me if it was your firm who bought diamonds for him?'

'Yes,' the voice said matter-of-factly. 'We did.'

Wow, I thought. I quietened my breath and I tried not to sound eager.

'Could you, er, give me the details?' I asked.

'Certainly. Your brother wanted colour H diamonds of approximately three carats each. We bought a normal sight-box of mixed diamonds at the July sight at the CSO in London and from it and from our stocks chose one hundred colour H stones, total weight three hundred and twenty carats, which we delivered to your brother.'

'He . . . er . . . paid for them in advance didn't he?'

'Certainly. One point five million United States dollars in cash. You don't need to worry about that.'

'Thank you,' I said, suppressing irony. 'Um, when you delivered them, did you send any sort of, er, packing note?'

It seemed he found the plebeian words 'packing note' faintly shocking.

'We sent the diamonds by personal messenger,' he said austerely. 'Our man took them to your brother at his private residence in London. As is our custom, your brother inspected the merchandise in our messenger's presence and weighed it, and when he was satisfied he signed a release certificate. He would have the carbon copy of that release. There was no other – uh – packing note.'

'Unfortunately I can't find the carbon copy.'

'I assure you, sir . . .'

'I don't doubt it,' I said hastily. 'It's just that the tax people have a habit of wanting documentation.'

'Ah.' His hurt feelings subsided. 'Yes, of course.'

I thought a bit and asked, 'When you delivered the stones to him, were they rough or faceted?'

'Rough, of course. He was going to get them cut and polished over a few months, as he needed them, I believe, but it was more convenient for us and for him to buy them all at once.'

'You don't happen to know who he was getting to polish them?'

'I understood they were to be cut for one special client who had his own requirements, but no, he didn't say who would be cutting them.'

I sighed. 'Well, thank you anyway.'

'We'll be happy to send you copies of the paperwork of the transaction, if it would be of any use?'

'Yes, please,' I said. 'It would be most helpful.'

'We'll put them in the post this afternoon.'

I put the receiver down slowly. I might now know where the diamonds had come *from* but was no nearer knowing where they'd gone *to*. I began to hope that they were safely sitting somewhere with a cutter who would kindly write to tell me they were ready for delivery. Not an impossible dream, really. But if Greville had sent them to a cutter, why was there no record?

Perhaps there had been a record, now stolen. But if the record had been stolen the thief would know the diamonds were with a cutter, and there would be no point in searching Greville's house. Unprofitable thoughts, chasing their own tails.

I straightened my neck and back and eased a few of the muscles which had developed small aches since the crash.

June came in and said, 'You look fair knackered,' and then put her hand to her mouth in horror and said, 'I'd never have said that to Mr Franklin.'

'I'm not him.'

'No, but . . . you're the boss.'

'Then think of someone who could supply a list of cutters and polishers of diamonds, particularly those specializing in unusual requirements, starting with Antwerp. What we want is a sort of Yellow Pages directory. After Antwerp, New York, Tel Aviv and Bombay, isn't that right? Aren't those the four main centres?' I'd been reading his books.

'But we don't deal—'

'Don't say it,' I said. 'We do. Greville bought some

for Prospero Jenks who wants them cut to suit his sculptures or fantasy pieces, or whatever one calls them.'

'Oh.' She looked first blank and then interested. 'Yes, all right, I'm sure I can do that. Do you want me to do it now?'

'Yes, please.'

She went as far as the door and looked back with a smile. 'You still look fair . . .'

'Mm. Go and get on with it.'

I watched her back view disappear. Grey skirt, white shirt. Blonde hair held back with combs behind the ears. Long legs. Flat shoes. Exit June.

The day wore on. I assembled three orders in the vault by myself and got Annette to check they were all right, which it seemed they were. I made a slow tour of the whole place, calling in to see Alfie pack his parcels, watching Lily with her squashed governess air move endlessly from drawer to little drawer collecting orders, seeing Jason manhandle heavy boxes of newly arrived stock, stopping for a moment beside strong-looking Tina, whom I knew least, as she checked the new intake against the packing list and sorted it into trays.

None of them paid me great attention. I was already wallpaper. Alfie made no more innuendoes about Dozen Roses and Jason, though giving me a dark sideways look, again kept his cracks to himself. Lily said, 'Yes, Derek,' meekly, Annette looked anxious, June was busy. I returned to Greville's office and made another effort with the letters.

By four o'clock, in between her normal work with the stock movements on the computer, June had received answers to her 'feelers', as she described them, in the shape of a long list of Antwerp cutters and a shorter one so far for New York. Tel Aviv was 'coming' but had language difficulties and she had nothing for Bombay, though she didn't think Mr Franklin would have sent anything to Bombay because with Antwerp so close there was no point. She put the lists down and departed.

At the rate all the cautious diamond-dealers worked, I thought, picking up the roll call, it would take a week just to get yes or no answers from the Antwerp list. Maybe it would be worth trying. I was down to straws. One of the letters was from the bank, reminding me that interest on the loan was now due.

June's tiny alarm clock suddenly began bleeping. All the other mute gadgets on top of the desk remained unmoved. June returned through my doorway at high speed and paid them vivid attention.

'Five minutes to go,' I said calmingly. 'Is every single gadget in sight?'

She checked all the drawers swiftly and peered into filing cabinets, leaving everything wide open, as I asked.

'Can't find any more,' she said. 'Why does it matter?'

'I don't know,' I said. 'I try everything.'

She stared. I smiled lopsidedly.

'Greville left me a puzzle too,' I said. 'I try to solve it, though I don't know where to look.'

717

'Oh.' It made a sort of sense to her, even without more explanation. 'Like my rise?'

I nodded. 'Something like that.' But not so positive, I thought. Not so certain. He had at least assured her that the solution was there to find.

The minutes ticked away and at four-twenty by June's clock the little alarm duly sounded. Very distant, not at all loud. Insistent. June looked rather wildly at the assembled gadgets and put her ear down to them.

'I will think of you every day at four-twenty.'

Clarissa had written it on her card at the funeral. Greville had apparently done it every day in the office. It had been their own private language, a long way from diamonds. I acknowledged with regret that I would learn nothing from whatever he'd used to jog his aware-ness of loving and being loved.

The muffled alarm stopped. June raised her head, frowning.

'It wasn't any of these,' she said.

'No. It was still inside the desk.'

'But it can't have been.' She was mystified. 'I've taken everything out.'

'There must be another drawer.'

She shook her head, but it was the only reasonable explanation.

'Ask Annette,' I suggested.

Annette, consulted, said with a worried frown that she knew nothing at all about another drawer. The three of us looked at the uninformative three-inch-deep slab of black grainy wood that formed the enormous top surface. There was no way it could be a drawer, but there wasn't any other possibility.

I thought back to the green stone box. To the keyhole that wasn't a keyhole, to the sliding base.

To the astonishment of Annette and June I lowered myself to the floor and looked upwards at the desk from under the knee-hole part. The wood from there looked just as solid, but in the centre, three inches in from the front, there was what looked like a sliding switch. With satisfaction I regained the black leather chair and felt under the desk top for the switch. It moved away from one under pressure, I found. I pressed it, and absolutely nothing happened.

Something had to have happened, I reasoned. The switch wasn't there for nothing. Nothing about Greville was for nothing. I pressed it back hard again and tried to raise, slide or otherwise move anything else I could reach. Nothing happened. I banged my fist with frustration down on the desk top, and a section of the front edge of the solid-looking slab fell off in my lap.

Annette and June gasped. The piece that had come off was like a strip of veneer furnished with metal clips for fastening it in place. Behind it was more wood, but this time with a keyhole in it. Watched breathlessly by Annette and June, I brought out Greville's bunch of keys and tried those that looked the right size: and one of them turned obligingly with hardly a click. I pulled

719

the key, still in the hole, towards me, and like silk a wide shallow drawer slid out.

We all looked at the contents. Passport. Little flat black gadgets, four or five of them.

No diamonds.

June was delighted. 'That's the Wizard,' she said.

CHAPTER FOURTEEN

'Which is the Wizard?' I asked.

'That one.'

She pointed at a black rectangle a good deal smaller than a paperback, and when I picked it up and turned it over, sure enough, it had WIZARD written on it in gold. I handed it to June who opened it like a book, laying it flat on the desk. The right-hand panel was covered with buttons and looked like an ultra-versatile calculator. The left-hand side had a small screen at the top and a touch panel at the bottom with headings like 'expense record', 'time accounting', 'reports' and 'reference'.

'It does everything,' June said. 'It's a diary, a phone directory, a memo pad, an appointments calendar, an accounts keeper . . . a world clock.'

'And does it have an alarm system set to four-twenty?'

She switched the thing on, pressed three keys and showed me the screen. Daily alarm, it announced. 4.20 pm, set.

'Fair enough.'

For Annette the excitement seemed to be over. There were things she needed to see to, she said, and went away. June suggested she should tidy away all the gadgets and close all the doors, and while she did that I investigated further the contents of the one drawer we left open.

I frowned a bit over the passport. I'd assumed that in going to Harwich, Greville had meant to catch the ferry. The *Koningin Beatrix* sailed every night . . .

If one looked at it the other way round, the *Koningin Beatrix* must sail from Holland to Harwich every day. If he hadn't taken the passport with him, perhaps he'd been going to *meet* the *Koningin Beatrix*, not leave on her.

Meet *who*?

I looked at his photograph which, like all passport photographs, wasn't very good but good enough to bring him vividly into the office; his office, where I sat in his chair.

June looked over my shoulder and said, 'Oh,' in a small voice. 'I do miss him, you know.'

'Yes.'

I put the passport with regret back into the drawer and took out a flat square object hardly larger than the Wizard, that had a narrow curl of paper coming out of it.

'That's the printer,' June said.

'A printer? So small?'

'It'll print everything stored in the Wizard.'

She plugged the printer's short cord into a slot in the side of the Wizard and dexterously pressed a few keys. With a whirr the tiny machine went into action and began printing out a strip of half the telephone directory, or so it seemed.

'Lovely, isn't it?' June said, pressing another button to stop it. 'When he was away on trips, Mr Franklin would enter all his expenses on here and we would print them out when he got home, or sometimes transfer them from the Wizard to our main computer through an interface . . . oh, dear.' She smothered the uprush of emotion and with an attempt at controlling her voice said, 'He would note down in there a lot of things he wanted to remember when he got home. Things like who had offered him unusual stones. Then he'd tell Prospero Jenks, and quite often I'd be writing to the addresses to have the stones sent.'

I looked at the small black electronic marvel. So much information quiescent in its circuits.

'Is there an instruction manual?' I asked.

'Of course. All the instruction manuals for everything are in this drawer.' She opened one on the outer right-hand stack. 'So are the warranty cards, and everything.' She sorted through a rank of booklets. 'Here you are. One for the Wizard, one for the printer, one for the expenses organizer.'

'I'll borrow them,' I said.

'They're yours now,' she replied blankly. 'Aren't they?'

'I can't get used to it any more than you can.'

I laid the manuals on top of the desk next to the Wizard and the printer and took a third black object out of the secret drawer.

This one needed no explanation. This was the microcassette recorder that went with the tiny tapes I'd found in the hollowed-out books.

'That's voice activated,' June said, looking at it. 'It will sit quietly around doing nothing for hours, then when anyone speaks it will record what's said. Mr Franklin used it sometimes for dictating letters or notes because it let him say a bit, think a bit, and say a bit more, without using up masses of tape. I used to listen to the tapes and type straight onto the word processor.'

Worth her weight in pearls, Greville had judged. I wouldn't quarrel with that.

I put the microcassette player beside the other things and brought out the last two gadgets. One was a tiny Minolta camera which June said Greville used quite often for pictures of unusual stones for Prospero Jenks, and the last was a grey thing one could hold in one's hand that had an on/off switch but no obvious purpose.

'That's to frighten dogs away,' June said with a smile. 'Mr Franklin didn't like dogs, but I think he was ashamed of not liking them, because at first he didn't want to tell me what that was, when I asked him.'

I hadn't known Greville didn't like dogs. I fiercely wanted him back, if only to tease him about it. The real trouble with death was what it left unsaid: and knowing that that thought was a more or less universal regret made it no less sharp.

I put the dog frightener back beside the passport and also the baby camera, which had no film in it. Then I closed and locked the shallow drawer and fitted the piece of veneer back in place, pushing it home with a click. The vast top again looked wholly solid, and I wondered if Greville had bought that desk simply because of the drawer's existence, or whether he'd had the whole piece especially made.

'You'd never know that drawer was there,' June said. 'I wonder how many fortunes have been lost by people getting rid of hiding places they didn't suspect?'

'I read a story about that once. Something about money stuffed in an old armchair that was left to some-one.' I couldn't remember the details: but Greville had left me more than an old armchair, and more than one place to look, and I too could get rid of the treasure from not suspecting the right hiding place, if there were one at all to find.

Meanwhile there was the problem of staying healthy while I searched. There was the worse problem of sort-ing out ways of taking the war to the enemy, if I could identify the enemy in the first place.

I asked June if she could find something I could carry the Wizard and the other things in and she was back in a flash with a soft plastic bag with handles. It reminded me fleetingly of the bag I'd had snatched at Ipswich but this time, I thought, when I carried the booty to the car,

I would take with me an invincible bodyguard, a long-legged flat-chested twenty-one-year-old blonde half in love with my brother.

The telephone rang. I picked up the receiver and said, 'Saxony Franklin' out of newly acquired habit.

'Derek? Is that you?'

'Yes, Milo, it is.'

'I'm not satisfied with this horse.' He sounded aggressive, which wasn't unusual, and also apologetic, which was.

'Which horse?' I asked.

'Dozen Roses, of course. What else?'

'Oh.'

'What do you mean, oh? You knew damn well I was fetching it today. The damn thing's half asleep. I'm getting the vet round at once and I'll want urine and blood tests. The damn thing looks doped.'

'Maybe they gave him a tranquillizer for the journey.'

'They've no right to, you know that. If they have, I'll have Nicholas Loder's head on a platter, like you should, if you had any sense. The man does what he damn well likes. Anyway, if the horse doesn't pass my vet he's going straight back, Ostermeyers or no Ostermeyers. It's not fair on them if I accept shoddy goods.'

'Um,' I said calmingly, 'perhaps Nicholas Loder wants you to do just that.'

'What? What do you mean?'

'Wants you to send him straight back.'

'Oh.'

'And,' I said, 'Dozen Roses was the property of Saxony Franklin Ltd, not Nicholas Loder, and if you think it's fair to the Ostermeyers to void the sale, so be it, but my brother's executor will direct you to send the horse anywhere else but back to Loder.'

There was a silence. Then he said with a smothered laugh, 'You always were a bright tricky bastard.'

'Thanks.'

'But get down here, will you? Take a look at him. Talk to the vet. How soon can you get here?'

'Couple of hours. Maybe more.'

'No, come on, Derek.'

'It's a long way to Tipperary,' I said. 'It never gets any nearer.'

'You're delirious.'

'I shouldn't wonder.'

'Soon as you can, then,' he said. 'See you.'

I put down the receiver with an inward groan. I did not want to go belting down to Lambourn to a crisis, however easily resolved. I wanted to let my aches unwind.

I telephoned the car and heard the ringing tone, but Brad, wherever he was, didn't answer. Then, as the first step towards leaving, I went along and locked the vault. Alfie in the packing room was stretching his back, his day's load finished. Lily, standing idle, gave me a repressed look from under her lashes. Jason goosed Tina in the doorway to the stock-rooms, which she didn't seem to mind. There was a feeling of afternoon

727

ending, of abeyance in the offing, of corporate activity drifting to suspense. Like the last race on an October card.

Saying goodnights and collecting the plastic bag I went down to the yard and found Brad there waiting.

'Did you find those papers OK?' I asked him, climbing in beside him after storing the crutches on the back seat.

'Yerss,' he said.

'And delivered them?'

'Yerss.'

'Thanks. Great. How long have you been back?'

He shrugged. I left it. It wasn't important.

'Lambourn,' I said, as we turned out of the yard. 'But on the way, back to my brother's house to collect something else. OK?'

He nodded and drove to Greville's house skilfully, but slowed just before we reached it and pointed to Greville's car, still standing by the kerb.

'See?' he said. 'It's been broken into.'

He found a parking place and we went back to look. The heavily locked boot had been jemmied open and now wouldn't close again.

'Good job we took the things out,' I said. 'I suppose they are still in my car.'

He shook his head. 'In our house, under the stairs. Our Mum said to do it, with your car outside our door all night. Dodgy neighbourhood, round our part.'

'Very thoughtful,' I said.

He nodded. 'Smart, our Mum.'

He came with me into Greville's garden, holding the gate open.

'They done this place over proper,' he said, producing the three keys from his pocket. 'Want me to?'

He didn't wait for particular assent but went up the steps and undid the locks. Daylight: no floods, no dog.

He waited in the hall while I went along to the little sitting room to collect the tapes. It all looked forlorn in there, a terrible mess made no better by time. I put the featherweight cassettes in my pocket and left again, thinking that tidying up was a long way down my urgency list. When the ankle had altogether stopped hurting; maybe then. When the insurance people had seen it, if they wanted to.

I had brought with me a note which I left prominently on the lowest step of the staircase, where anyone coming into the house would see it.

'Dear Mrs P. I'm afraid there is bad news for you. Don't clean the house. Telephone Saxony Franklin Ltd instead.'

I'd added the number in case she didn't know it by heart, and I'd warned Annette to go gently with anyone ringing. Nothing else I could do to cushion the shock.

Brad locked the front door and we set off again to Lambourn. He had done enough talking for the whole journey and we travelled in customary silence, easy if not comrades.

Milo was striding about in the yard, expending

energy to no purpose. He yanked the passenger side door of my car open and scowled in at Brad, more as a reflection of his general state of mind, I gathered, than from any particular animosity.

I retrieved the crutches and stood up, and he told me it was high time I threw them away.

'Calm down,' I said.

'Don't patronize me.'

'Is Phil here?'

Phil was Phil Urquhart, veterinary surgeon, pill pusher to the stable.

'No, he isn't,' Milo said crossly, 'but he's coming back. The damned horse won't give a sample. And for a start, you can tell me whether it is or isn't Dozen Roses. His passport matches, but I'd like to be sure.'

He strode away towards a box in one corner of the yard and I followed and looked where he looked, over the bottom half of the door.

Inside the box were an obstinate-looking horse and a furious red-faced lad. The lad held a pole which had on one end of it an open plastic bag on a ring, like a shrimping net. The plastic bag was clean and empty.

I chuckled.

'It's all right for you,' Milo said sharply. 'You haven't been waiting for more than two hours for the damned animal to stale.'

'On Singapore racecourse, one time,' I said, 'they got a sample with nicotine in it. The horse didn't smoke, but the lad did. He got tired of waiting for the horse and just supplied the sample himself.'

'Very funny,' Milo said repressively.

'This often takes hours, though, so why the rage?'

It sounded always so simple, of course, to take a regulation urine sample from two horses after every race, one nearly always from the winner. In practice, it meant waiting around for the horses to oblige. After two hours of non-performance, blood samples were taken instead, but blood wasn't as easy to come by. Many tempers were regularly lost while the horses made up their minds.

'Come away,' I said, 'he'll do it in the end. And he's definitely the horse that ran at York. Dozen Roses without doubt.'

He followed me away reluctantly and we went into the kitchen where Milo switched lights on and asked me if I'd like a drink.

'Wouldn't mind some tea,' I said.

'Tea? At this hour? Well, help yourself.' He watched me fill the kettle and set it to boil. 'Are you off booze for ever?'

'No.'

'Thank God.'

Phil Urquhart's car scrunched into the yard and pulled up outside the window, and he came breezing into the kitchen asking if there were any results. He read Milo's scowl aright and laughed.

'Do you think the horse is doped?' I asked him.

'Me? No, not really. Hard to tell. Milo thinks so.'

He was small and sandy-haired, and about thirty, the grandson of a three-generation family practice, and to my mind the best of them. I caught myself thinking that when I in the future trained here in Lambourn, I would want him for my horses. An odd thought. The future planning itself behind my back.

'I hear we're lucky you're still with us,' he said. 'An impressive crunch, so they say.' He looked at me assessingly with friendly professional eyes. 'You've a few rough edges, one can see.'

'Nothing that will stop him racing,' Milo said crisply.

Phil smiled. 'I detect more alarm than sympathy.'

'Alarm?'

'You've trained more winners since he came here.'

'Rubbish,' Milo said.

He poured drinks for himself and Phil, and I made my tea; and Phil assured me that if the urine passed all tests he would give the thumbs up to Dozen Roses.

'He may just be showing the effects of the hard race he had at York,' he said. 'It might be that he's always like this. Some horses are, and we don't know how much weight he lost.'

'What will you get the urine tested for?' I asked.

He raised his eyebrows. 'Barbiturates, in this case.'

'At York,' I said thoughtfully, 'one of Nicholas Loder's owners was walking around with a nebulizer in his pocket. A kitchen baster, to be precise.'

'An owner?' Phil asked, surprised.

'Yes. He owned the winner of the five-furlong sprint. He was also in the saddling box with Dozen Roses.'

Phil frowned. 'What are you implying?'

'Nothing. Merely observing. I can't believe he interfered with the horse. Nicholas Loder wouldn't have let him. The stable money was definitely on. They wanted to win, and they knew if it won it would be tested. So the only question is, what could you give a horse that wouldn't disqualify it? Give it via a nebulizer just before a race?'

'Nothing that would make it go faster. They test for all stimulants.'

'What if you gave it, say, sugar? Glucose? Or adrenalin?'

'You've a criminal mind!'

'I just wondered.'

'Glucose would give energy, as to human athletes. It wouldn't increase speed, though. Adrenalin is more tricky. If it's given by injection you can see it, because the hairs stand up all round the puncture. But straight into the mucous membranes ... well, I suppose it's possible.'

'And no trace.'

He agreed. 'Adrenalin pours into a horse's bloodstream naturally anyway, if he's excited. If he wants to win. If he feels the whip. Who's to say how much? If you suspected a booster, you'd have to take a blood sample in the winner's enclosure, practically, and even then you'd have a hard job proving any reading was excessive.

733

Adrenalin levels vary too much. You'd even have a hard job proving extra adrenalin made any difference at all.' He paused and considered me soberly. 'You do realize that you're saying that if anything was done, Nicholas Loder condoned it?'

'Doesn't seem likely, does it?'

'No, it doesn't,' he said. 'If he were some tin-pot little crook, well then, maybe, but not Nicholas Loder with his Classic winners and everything to lose.'

'Mm.' I thought a bit. 'If I asked, I could get some of the urine sample that was taken from Dozen Roses at York. They always make it available to owners for private checks. To my brother's company, that is to say, in this instance.' I thought a bit more. 'When Nicholas Loder's friend dropped his baster, Martha Ostermeyer handed the bulb part back to him, but then Harley Ostermeyer picked up the tube part and gave it to me. But it was clean. No trace of liquid. No adrenalin. So I suppose it's possible he might have used it on his own horse and still had it in his pocket, but did nothing to Dozen Roses.'

They considered it.

'You could get into a lot of trouble making unfounded accusations,' Phil said.

'So Nicholas Loder told me.'

'Did he? I'd think twice, then, before I did. It wouldn't do you much good generally in the racing world, I shouldn't think.'

'Wisdom from babes,' I said, but he echoed my thoughts.

'Yes, old man.'

'I kept the baster tube,' I said, shrugging, 'but I guess I'll do just what I did at the races, which was nothing.'

'As long as Dozen Roses tests clean both at York and here, that's likely best,' Phil said, and Milo, for all his earlier pugnaciousness, agreed.

A commotion in the darkening yard heralded the success of the urine mission and Phil went outside to unclip the special bag and close its patented seal. He wrote and attached the label giving the horse's name, the location, date and time and signed his name.

'Right,' he said, 'I'll be off. Take care.' He loaded himself, the sample and his gear into his car and with economy of movement scrunched away. I followed soon after with Brad still driving, but decided again not to go home.

'You saw the mess in London,' I said. 'I got knocked out by whoever did that. I don't want to be in if they come to Hungerford. So let's go to Newbury instead, and try The Chequers.'

Brad slowed, his mouth open.

'A week ago yesterday,' I said, 'you saved me from a man with a knife. Yesterday someone shot at the car I was in and killed the chauffeur. It may not have been your regulation madman. So last night I slept in Swindon, tonight in Newbury.'

'Yerss,' he said, understanding.

735

'If you'd rather not drive me any more, I wouldn't blame you.'

After a pause, with a good deal of stalwart resolution, he made a statement. 'You need me.'

'Yes,' I said. 'Until I can walk properly, I do.'

'I'll drive you, then.'

'Thanks,' I said, and meant it wholeheartedly, and he could hear that, because he nodded twice to himself emphatically and seemed even pleased.

The Chequers Hotel having a room free, I booked in for the night. Brad took himself home in my car, and I spent most of the evening sitting in an armchair upstairs learning my way round the Wizard.

Computers weren't my natural habitat like they were Greville's and I hadn't the same appetite for them. The Wizard's instructions seemed to take it for granted that everyone reading them would be computer-literate, so it probably took me longer than it might have done to get results.

What was quite clear was that Greville had used the gadget extensively. There were three separate telephone and address lists, the world-time clock, a system for entering daily appointments, a prompt for anniversaries, a calendar flashing with the day's date, and provision for storing oddments of information. By plugging in the printer, and after a few false starts, I ended with long printed lists of everything held listed under all the headings, and read them with growing frustration.

None of the addresses or telephone numbers seemed to have anything to do with Antwerp or with diamonds, though the 'Business Overseas' list contained many gem merchants' names from all round the world. None of the appointments scheduled, which stretched back six weeks or more, seemed to be relevant, and there were no entries at all for the Friday he'd gone to Ipswich. There was no reference to *Koningin Beatrix*.

I thought of my question to June the day she'd found her way to 'pearl': what if it were all in there, but stored in secret?

The Wizard's instruction manual, two hundred pages long, certainly did give lessons in how to lock things away. Entries marked 'secret' could only be retrieved by knowing the password which could be any combination of numbers and letters up to seven in all. Forgetting the password meant bidding farewell to the entries: they could never be seen again. They could be deleted unseen, but not printed or brought to the screen.

One could tell if secret files were present, the book said, by the small symbol s, which could be found on the lower right-hand side of the screen. I consulted Greville's screen and found the s there, sure enough.

It would be, I thought. It would have been totally unlike him to have had the wherewithal for secrecy and not used it.

Any combination of numbers or letters up to seven . . .

The book suggested 1234, but once I'd sorted out the

opening moves for unlocking and entered 1234 in the space headed 'Secret Off', all I got was a quick dusty answer, 'Incorrect Password'.

Damn him, I thought, wearily defeated. Why couldn't he make any of it easy?

I tried every combination of letters and numbers I thought he might have used but got absolutely nowhere. Clarissa was too long, 12Roses should have been right but wasn't. To be right, the password had to be entered exactly as it had been set, whether in capital letters or lower case. It all took time. In the end I was ready to throw the confounded Wizard across the room, and stared at its perpetual 'Incorrect Password' with hatred.

I finally laid it aside and played the tiny tape recorder instead. There was a lot of office chat on the tapes and I couldn't think why Greville should have bothered to take them home and hide them. Long before I reached the end of the fourth side, I was asleep.

I woke stiffly after a while, unsure for a second where I was. I rubbed my face, looked at my watch, thought about all the constructive thinking I was supposed to be doing and wasn't, and rewound the second of the baby tapes to listen to what I'd missed. Greville's voice, talking business to Annette.

The most interesting thing, the only interesting thing about those tapes, I thought, was Greville's voice. The only way I would ever hear him again.

'. . . going out to lunch,' he was saying. 'I'll be back by two-thirty.'

Annette's voice said, 'Yes, Mr Franklin.'

A click sounded on the tape.

Almost immediately, because of the concertina-ing of time by the voice-activated mechanism, a different voice said, 'I'm in his office now and I can't find them. He hides everything, he's security mad, you know that.' Click. 'I can't ask. He'd never tell me, and I don't think he trusts me.' Click. 'Po-faced Annette doesn't sneeze unless he tells her to. She'd never tell me anything.' Click. 'I'll try. I'll have to go, he doesn't like me using this phone, he'll be back from lunch any second.' Click.

End of tape.

Bloody hell, I thought. I rewound the end of the tape and listened to it again. I knew the voice, as Greville must have done. He'd left the recorder on, I guessed by mistake, and he'd come back and listened, with I supposed sadness, to treachery. It opened up a whole new world of questions and I went slowly to bed groping towards answers.

I lay a long time awake. When I slept, I dreamed the usual surrealist muddle and found it no help, but around dawn, awake again and thinking of Greville, it occurred to me that there was one password I hadn't tried because I hadn't thought of his using it.

The Wizard was across the room by the armchair. Impelled by curiosity I turned on the light, rolled out of bed and hopped over to fetch it. Taking it back with me, I switched it on, pressed the buttons, found 'Secret Off' and into the offered space typed the word Greville had written on the last page of his racing diary, below the numbers of his passport and national insurance.

DEREK, all in capital letters.

I typed DEREK and pressed Enter, and the Wizard with resignation let me into its data.

CHAPTER FIFTEEN

I began printing out everything in the secret files as it seemed from the manual that, particularly as regarded the expense organizer, it was the best way to get at the full information stored there.

Each category had to be printed separately, the baby printer clicking away line by line and not very fast. I watched its steady output with fascination, hoping the small roll of paper would last to the end, as I hadn't any more.

From the Memo section, which I printed first, came a terse note, 'Check, don't trust.'

Next came a long list of days and dates which seemed to bear no relation to anything. Monday, 30 January, Wednesday, 8 March ... Mystified I watched the sequence lengthen, noticing only that most of them were Mondays, Tuesdays or Wednesdays, five or six weeks apart, sometimes less, sometimes longer. The list ended five weeks before his death, and it began ... It began, I thought blankly, four years earlier. Four years ago; when he first met Clarissa.

I felt unbearable sadness for him. He'd fallen in love with a woman who wouldn't leave home for him, whom he hadn't wanted to compromise: he'd kept a record, I was certain, of every snatched day they'd spent together, and hidden it away as he had hidden so much else. A whole lot of roses, I thought.

The Schedule section, consulted next, contained appointments not hinted at earlier, including the delivery of the diamonds to his London house. For the day of his death there were two entries: the first, 'Ipswich. Orwell Hotel, P. 3.30 pm', and the second, 'Meet *Koningin Beatrix* 6.30 pm, Harwich.' For the following Monday he had noted, 'Meet C King's Cross 12.10 Lunch Luigi's.'

Meet C at King's Cross . . . He hadn't turned up, and she'd telephoned his house, and left a message on his answering machine, and sometime in the afternoon she'd telephoned his office to ask for him. Poor Clarissa. By Monday night she'd left the ultra-anxious second message, and on Tuesday she had learned he was dead.

The printer whirred and produced another entry, for the Saturday after. 'C and Dozen Roses both at York! Could I go? Not wise. Check TV.'

The printer stopped, as Greville's life had done. No more appointments on record.

Next I printed the Telephone sections, Private, Business and Business Overseas. Private contained only Knightwood. Business was altogether empty, but from Business Overseas I watched with widening eyes the emergence of five numbers and addresses in Antwerp. One was van Ekeren, one was Guy Servi: three were so far unknown to me. I breathed almost painfully with exultation, unable to believe Greville had entered them there for no purpose.

I printed the Expense Manager's secret section last as it was the most complicated and looked the least promising, but the first item that emerged was galvanic.

> Antwerp say 5 of the first
> batch of rough are CZ.
> Don't want to believe it.
> Infinite sadness.
> Priority 1.
> Arrange meetings. Ipswich?
> Undecided. Damnation!

I wished he had been more explicit, more specific, but he'd seen no need to be. It was surprising he'd written so much. His feelings must have been strong to have been entered at all. No other entries afterwards held any comment but were short records of money spent on courier services with a firm called Euro-Securo, telephone number supplied. In the middle of those the paper ran out. I brought the rest of the stored information up on to the screen and scrolled through it, but there was nothing else disturbing.

I switched off both baby machines and reread the long curling strip of printing from the beginning, afterwards flattening it out and folding it to fit a shirt pocket. Then I dressed, packed, breakfasted, waited for Brad and travelled to London hopefully.

The telephone calls to Antwerp had to be done from the Saxony Franklin premises because of the precautionary checking back. I would have preferred more privacy than Greville's office but couldn't achieve it, and one of the first things I asked Annette that morning was whether my brother had had one of those gadgets that warned you if someone was listening to your conversation on an extension. The office phones were all interlinked.

'No, he didn't,' she said, troubled.

'He could have done with one,' I said.

'Are you implying that we listened when he didn't mean us to?'

'Not you,' I assured her, seeing her resentment of the suggestion. 'But yes, I'd think it happened. Anyway, at some point this morning, I want to make sure of not being overheard, so when that call comes through perhaps you'll all go into the stock-room and sing Rule Britannia.'

Annette never made jokes. I had to explain I didn't mean sing literally. She rather huffily agreed that when I wanted it, she would go round the extensions checking against eavesdroppers.

I asked her why Greville hadn't had a private line in any case, and she said he had had one earlier but they now used that for the fax machine.

'If he wanted to be private,' she said, 'he went down to the yard and telephoned from his car.'

There, I supposed, he would have been safe also from people with sensitive listening devices, if he'd suspected their use. He had been conscious of betrayal, that was for sure.

I sat at Greville's desk with the door closed and matched the three unknown Antwerp names from the Wizard with the full list June had provided, and found that all three were there.

The first and second produced no results, but from the third, once I explained who I was, I got the customary response about checking the files and calling back. They did call back, but the amorphous voice on the far end was cautious to the point of repression.

'We at Maarten-Pagnier cannot discuss anything at all with you, monsieur,' he said. 'Monsieur Franklin gave express orders that we were not to communicate with anyone in his office except himself.'

'My brother is dead,' I said.

'So you say, monsieur. But he warned us to beware of any attempt to gain information about his affairs and we cannot discuss them.'

'Then please will you telephone to his lawyers and get their assurance that he's dead and that I am now managing his business?'

After a pause the voice said austerely, 'Very well, monsieur. Give us the name of his lawyers.'

I did that and waited for ages during which time

three customers telephoned with long orders which I wrote down, trying not to get them wrong from lack of concentration.

Then there was a frantic call from a nearly incoherent woman who wanted to speak to Mr Franklin urgently.

'Mrs P?' I asked tentatively.

Mrs P it was. Mrs Patterson, she said. I gave her the abysmal news and listened to her telling me what a fine nice gentleman my brother had been, and oh dear, she felt faint, had I seen the mess in the sitting room?

I warned her that the whole house was the same. 'Just leave it,' I said. 'I'll clean it up later. Then if you could come after that to hoover and dust, I'd be very grateful.'

Calming a little, she gave me her phone number. 'Let me know, then,' she said. 'Oh dear, oh dear.'

Finally the Antwerp voice returned and, begging him to hold on, I hopped over to the door, called Annette, handed her the customers' orders and said this was the moment for securing the defences. She gave me a disapproving look as I again closed the door.

Back in Greville's chair I said to the voice, 'Please, monsieur, tell me if my brother had any dealings with you. I am trying to sort out his office but he has left too few records.'

'He asked us particularly not to send any records of the work we were doing for him to his office.'

'He, er, what?' I said.

746

'He said he could not trust everyone in his office as he would like. Instead, he wished us to send anything necessary to the fax machine in his car, but only when he telephoned from there to arrange it.'

'Um,' I said, blinking, 'I found the fax machine in his car but there were no statements or invoices or anything from you.'

'I believe if you ask his accountants, you may find them there.'

'Good grief.'

'I beg your pardon, monsieur?'

'I didn't think of asking his accountants,' I said blankly.

'He said for tax purposes . . .'

'Yes, I see.' I hesitated. 'What exactly were you doing for him?'

'Monsieur?'

'Did he,' I asked a shade breathlessly, 'send you a hundred diamonds, colour II, average uncut weight three point two carats, to be cut and polished?'

'No, monsieur.'

'Oh.' My disappointment must have been audible.

'He sent twenty-five stones, monsieur, but five of them were not diamonds.'

'Cubic zirconia,' I said, enlightened.

'Yes, monsieur. We told Monsieur Franklin as soon as we discovered it. He said we were wrong, but we were not, monsieur.'

'No,' I agreed. 'He did leave a note saying five of the first batch were CZ.'

'Yes, monsieur. He was extremely upset. We made several enquiries for him, but he had bought the stones from a sightholder of impeccable honour and he had himself measured and weighed the stones when they were delivered to his London house. He sent them to us in a sealed Euro-Securo courier package. We assured him that the mistake could not have been made here by us, and it was then, soon after that, that he asked us not to send or give any information to anyone in his ... your ... office.' He paused. 'He made arrangements to receive the finished stones from us, but he didn't meet our messenger.'

'Your messenger?'

'One of our partners, to be accurate. We wished to deliver the stones to him ourselves because of the five disputed items, and Monsieur Franklin thought it an excellent idea. Our partner dislikes flying, so it was agreed he should cross by boat and return the same way. When Monsieur Franklin failed to meet him he came back here. He is elderly and had made no provision to stay away. He was ... displeased ... at having made a tiring journey for nothing. He said we should wait to hear from Monsieur Franklin. Wait for fresh instructions. We have been waiting, but we've been puzzled. We didn't try to reach Monsieur Franklin at his office as he had forbidden us to do that, but we were considering asking someone else to try on our behalf. We are very sorry to hear of his death. It explains everything, of course.'

I said, 'Did your partner travel to Harwich on the *Koningin Beatrix*?'

'That's right, monsieur.'

'He brought the diamonds with him?'

'That's right, monsieur. And he brought them back. We will now wait your instructions instead.'

I took a deep breath. Twenty of the diamonds at least were safe. Five were missing. Seventy-five were . . . *where*?

The Antwerp voice said, 'It's to be regretted that Monsieur Franklin didn't see the polished stones. They cut very well. Twelve tear drops of great brilliance, remarkable for that colour. Eight were not suitable for tear drops, as we told Monsieur Franklin, but they look handsome as stars. What shall we do with them, monsieur?'

'When I've talked to the jeweller they were cut for, I'll let you know.'

'Very good, monsieur. And our account? Where shall we send that?' He mentioned considerately how much it would be.

'To this office,' I said, sighing at the prospect. 'Send it to me marked "Personal".'

'Very good, monsieur.'

'And thank you,' I said. 'You've been very helpful.'

'At your service, monsieur.'

I put the receiver down slowly, richer by twelve

glittering tear drops destined to hang and flash in sun-light, and by eight handsome stars that might twinkle in a fantasy of rock crystal. Better than nothing, but not enough to save the firm.

Using the crutches, I went in search of Annette and asked her if she would please find Prospero Jenks, wherever he was, and make another appointment for me, that afternoon if possible. Then I went down to the yard, taking a tip from Greville, and on the telephone in my car put a call through to his accountants.

Brad, reading a golfing magazine, paid no attention.

Did he play golf, I asked?

No, he didn't.

The accountants helpfully confirmed that they had received envelopes both from my brother and from Antwerp, and were holding them unopened, as requested, pending further instructions.

'You'll need them for the general accounts,' I said. 'So would you please just keep them?'

Absolutely no problem.

'On second thoughts,' I said, 'please open all the envelopes and tell me who all the letters from Antwerp have come from.'

Again no problem: but the letters were all either from Guy Servi, the sightholder, or from Maarten-Pagnier, the cutters. No other firms. No other safe havens for seventy-five rocks.

I thanked them, watched Brad embark on a learned

comparison of Ballesteros and Faldo, and thought about disloyalty and the decay of friendship.

It was restful in the car, I decided. Brad went on reading. I thought of robbery with violence and violence without robbery, of being laid out with a brick and watching Simms die of a bullet meant for me, and I wondered whether, if I were dead, anyone could find what I was looking for, or whether they reckoned they now couldn't find it if I were alive.

I stirred and fished in a pocket and gave Brad a cheque I'd written out for him upstairs.

'What's this?' he said, peering at it.

I usually paid him in cash, but I explained I hadn't enough for what I owed him, and cash dispensers wouldn't disgorge enough all at once and we hadn't recently been in Hungerford when the banks were open, as he might have noticed.

'Give me cash later,' he said, holding the cheque out to me. 'And you paid me double.'

'For last week and this week,' I nodded. 'When we get to the bank I'll swap it for cash. Otherwise, you could bring it back here. It's a company cheque. They'd see you got cash for it.'

He gave me a long look.

'Is this because of guns and such? In case you never get to the bank?'

I shrugged. 'You might say so.'

He looked at the cheque, folded it deliberately and stowed it away. Then he picked up the magazine and stared blindly at a page he'd just read. I was grateful for the absence of comment or protest, and in a while said matter-of-factly that I was going upstairs for a bit, and why didn't he get some lunch.

He nodded.

'Have you got enough money for lunch?'

'Yerss.'

'You might make a list of what you've spent. I've enough cash for that.'

He nodded again.

'OK, then,' I said. 'See you.'

Upstairs, Annette said she had opened the day's post and put it ready for my attention, and she'd found Prospero Jenks and he would be expecting me in the Knightsbridge shop any time between three and six.

'Great.'

She frowned. 'Mr Jenks wanted to know if you were taking him the goods Mr Franklin bought for him. Grev – he always calls Mr Franklin, Grev. I do wish he wouldn't – I asked what he meant about goods and he said you would know.'

'He's talking about diamonds,' I said.

'But we haven't ...' She stopped and then went on with a sort of desperate vehemence. 'I *wish* Mr Franklin was here. Nothing's the same without him.'

She gave me a look full of her insecurity and doubt of my ability and plodded off into her own domain and I thought that with what lay ahead I'd have preferred a vote of confidence: and I too, with all my heart, wished Greville back.

The police from Hungerford telephoned, given my number by Milo's secretary. They wanted to know if I had remembered anything more about the car driven by the gunman. They had asked the family in the family car if they had noticed the make and colour of the last car they'd seen coming towards them before they rounded the bend and crashed into the Daimler, and one of the children, a boy, had given them a description. They had also, while the firemen and others were trying to free me, walked down the row of spectator cars asking them about the last car they'd seen coming towards them. Only the first two drivers had seen a car at all, that they could remember, and they had no helpful information. Had I any recollection, however vague, as they were trying to piece together all the impressions they'd been given?

'I wish I could help,' I said, 'but I was talking to Mr and Mrs Ostermeyer, not concentrating on the road. It winds a bit, as you know, and I think Simms had been waiting for a place where he could pass the car in front, but all I can tell you, as on Sunday, is that it was a greyish colour and fairly large. Maybe a Mercedes. It's only an impression.'

'The child in the family car says it was a grey Volvo travelling fast. The bus driver says the car in question was travelling slowly before the Daimler tried to pass it, and he was aiming to pass also at that point, and was accelerating to do so, which was why he rammed the Daimler so hard. He says the car was silver grey and accelerated away at high speed, which matched what the child says.'

'Did the bus driver,' I asked, 'see the gun or the shots?'

'No, sir. He was looking at the road ahead and at the Daimler, not at the car he intended to pass. Then the Daimler veered sharply, and bounded off the wall straight into his path. He couldn't avoid hitting it, he said. Do you confirm that, sir?'

'Yes. It happened so fast. He hadn't a chance.'

'We are asking in the neighbourhood for anyone to come forward who saw a grey four-door saloon, possibly a Volvo, on that road on Sunday afternoon, but so far we have heard nothing new. If you remember anything else, however minor, let us know.'

I would, I said.

I put the phone down wondering if Vaccaro's shot-down pilots had seen the make of car from which their deaths had come spitting. Anyone seeing those murders would, I supposed, have been gazing with uncomprehending horror at the falling victims, not dashing into the road to peer at a fast disappearing number plate.

No one had heard any shots on Sunday. No one had heard the shots, the widow had told Greville, when her husband was killed. A silencer on a gun in a moving car . . . a swift pfftt . . . curtains.

It couldn't have been Vaccaro who shot Simms. Vaccaro didn't make sense. Someone with the same anti-social habits, as in Northern Ireland and elsewhere. A copycat. Plenty of precedent.

Milo's secretary had been busy and given my London number also to Phil Urquhart who came on the line to tell me that Dozen Roses had tested clean for barbiturates and he would give a certificate of soundness for the sale.

'Fine,' I said.

'I've been to examine the horse again this morning. He's still very docile. It seems to be his natural state.'

'Mm.'

'Do I hear doubt?'

'He's excited enough every time cantering down to the start.'

'Natural adrenalin,' Phil said.

'If it was anyone but Nicholas Loder . . .'

'He would never risk it,' Phil said, agreeing with me. 'But look . . . there are things that potentiate adrenalin, like caffeine. Some of them are never tested for in racing, as they are not judged to be stimulants. It's your money that's being spent on the tests I've done for you. We have some more of that sample of urine. Do you want me to get different tests done, for things not usually looked for? I mean, do you really think Nicholas Loder gave the horse something, and if you do, do you want to know about it?'

'It was his owner, a man called Rollway, who had the baster, not Loder himself.'

755

'Same decision. Do you want to spend more, or not bother? It may be money down the drain, anyway. And if you get any results, what then? You don't want to get the horse disqualified, that wouldn't make sense.'

'No . . . it wouldn't.'

'What's your problem?' he asked. 'I can hear it in your voice.'

'Fear,' I said. 'Nicholas Loder was afraid.'

'Oh.' He was briefly silent. 'I could get the tests done anonymously, of course.'

'Yes. Get them done, then. I particularly don't want to sell the Ostermeyers a lemon, as she would say. If Dozen Roses can't win on his own merits, I'll talk them out of the idea of owning him.'

'So you'll pay for negative results?'

'I will indeed.'

'While I was at Milo's this morning,' he said, 'he was talking to the Ostermeyers in London, asking how they were and wishing them a good journey. They were still a bit wobbly from the crash, it seems.'

'Surprising if they weren't.'

'They're coming back to England though to see Datepalm run in the Hennessy. How's your ankle?'

'Good as new by then.'

'Bye then.' I could hear his smile. 'Take care.'

He disconnected and left me thinking that there still were good things in the world, like the Ostermeyers' faith and riding Datepalm in the Hennessy, and I stood up and put my left foot flat on the floor for a progress report.

It wasn't so bad if I didn't lean any weight on it, but there were still jabbingly painful protests against attempts to walk. Oh well, I thought, sitting down again, give it another day or two. It hadn't exactly had a therapeutic week and was no doubt doing its best against odds. On Thursday, I thought, I would get rid of the crutches. By Friday, definitely. Any day after that I'd be running. Ever optimistic. It was the belief that cured.

The ever-busy telephone rang again, and I answered it with 'Saxony Franklin?' as routine.

'Derek?'

'Yes,' I said.

Clarissa's unmistakable voice said, 'I'm in London. Could we meet?'

I hadn't expected her so soon, I thought. I said, 'Yes, of course. Where?'

'I thought ... perhaps ... Luigi's. Do you know Luigi's bar and restaurant?'

'I don't,' I said slowly, 'but I can find it.'

'It's in Swallow Street near Piccadilly Circus. Would you mind coming at seven, for a drink?'

'And dinner?'

'Well ...'

'And dinner,' I said.

I heard her sigh, 'Yes. All right,' as she disconnected, and I was left with a vivid understanding both of her compulsion to put me where she had been going to

757

meet Greville and of her awareness that perhaps she ought not to.

I could have said no, I thought. I could have, but hadn't. A little introspection revealed ambiguities in my response to her also, like did I want to give comfort, or to take it.

By three-thirty I'd finished the paperwork and filled an order for pearls and another for turquoise and relocked the vault and got Annette to smile again, even if faintly. At four, Brad pulled up outside Prospero Jenks's shop in Knightsbridge and I put the telephone ready to let him know when to collect me.

Prospero Jenks was where I'd found him before, sitting in shirtsleeves at his workbench. The discreet dark-suited man, serving customers in the shop, nodded me through.

'He's expecting you, Mr Franklin.'

Pross stood up with a smile on his young-old Peter Pan face and held out his hand, but let it fall again as I waggled a crutch handle at him instead.

'Glad to see you,' he said, offering a chair, waiting while I sat. 'Have you brought my diamonds?' He sat down again on his own stool.

'No. Afraid not.'

He was disappointed. 'I thought that was what you were coming for.'

'No, not really.'

I looked at his long efficient workroom with its little drawers full of unset stones and thought of the marvels he produced. The big notice on the wall still read 'NEVER TURN YOUR BACK TO CUSTOMERS. ALWAYS WATCH THEIR HANDS.'

I said, 'Greville sent twenty-five rough stones to Antwerp to be cut for you.'

'That's right.'

'Five of them were cubic zirconia.'

'No, no.'

'Did you,' I asked neutrally, 'swap them over?'

The half-smile died out of his face, which grew stiff and expressionless. The bright blue eyes stared at me and the lines deepened across his forehead.

'That's rubbish,' he said. 'I'd never do anything stupid like that.'

I didn't say anything immediately and it seemed to give him force.

'You can't come in here making wild accusations. Go on, get out, you'd better leave.' He half-rose to his feet.

I said, not moving, 'When the cutters told Greville five of the stones were cubic zirconia, he was devastated. Very upset.'

I reached into my shirt pocket and drew out the print-out from the Wizard.

'Do you want to see?' I asked. 'Read there.'

After a hesitation he took the paper, sat back on the stool and read the entry:

> Antwerp say 5 of the first
> batch of rough are CZ.

Don't want to believe it.
Infinite sadness.
Priority 1.
Arrange meetings. Ipswich?
Undecided. Damnation!

'Greville used to write his thoughts in a notebook,' I said. 'In there it says, "Infinite sadness is not to trust an old friend." '

'So what?'

'Since Greville died,' I said, 'someone has been trying to find his diamonds, to steal them from me. That someone had to be someone who knew they were there to be found. Greville kept the fact that he'd bought them very quiet for security reasons. He didn't tell even his staff. But of course you yourself knew, as it was for you he bought them.'

He said again, 'So what?'

'If you remember,' I said, still conversationally, 'someone broke into Greville's office after he died and stole things like an address book and an appointments diary. I began to think the thief had also stolen any other papers which might point to where the diamonds were, like letters or invoices. But I know now there weren't any such papers to be found there, because Greville was full of distrust. His distrust dated from the day the Antwerp cutters told him five of his stones were cubic zirconia, which was about three weeks before he died.'

Pross, Greville's friend, said nothing.

'Greville bought the diamonds,' I went on, 'from a sightholder based in Antwerp who sent them by messenger to his London house. There he measured them and weighed them and signed for them. Then it would be reasonable to suppose that he showed them to you, his customer. Or showed you twenty-five of them, perhaps. Then he sent that twenty-five back to Antwerp by the Euro-Securo couriers. Five diamonds had mysteriously become cubic zirconia, and yes, it was an entirely stupid thing to do, because the substitution was bound to be discovered almost at once, and you knew it would be. Had to be. I'd think you reckoned Greville would never believe it of you, but would swear the five stones had to have been swapped by someone in the couriers or the cutters in Antwerp, and he would collect the insurance in due course, and that would be that. You would be five diamonds to the good, and he would have lost nothing.'

'You can't prove it,' he said flatly.

'No, I can't prove it. But Greville was full of sorrow and distrust, and why should he be if he thought his stones had been taken by strangers?'

I looked with some of Greville's own sadness at Prospero Jenks. A likeable, entertaining genius whose feelings for my brother had been strong and long-lasting, whose regret at his death had been real.

'I'd think,' I said, 'that after your long friendship, after all the treasures he'd brought you, after the pink and green tourmaline, after your tremendous success, that he could hardly bear your treachery.'

'Stop it,' he said sharply. 'It's bad enough . . .'

He shut his mouth tight and shook his head, and seemed to sag internally.

'He forgave me,' he said.

He must have thought I didn't believe him.

He said wretchedly, 'I wished I hadn't done it almost from the beginning, if you want to know. It was just an impulse. He left the diamonds here while he went off to do a bit of shopping, and I happened to have some rough CZ the right size in those drawers, as I often do, waiting for when I want special cutting, and I just . . . exchanged them. Like you said. I didn't think he'd lose by it.'

'He knew, though,' I said. 'He knew you, and he knew a lot about thieves, being a magistrate. Another of the things he wrote was, "If laws are inconvenient, ignore them, they don't apply to you." '

'Stop it. Stop it. He forgave me.'

'When?'

'In Ipswich. I went to meet him there.'

I lifted my head. 'Ipswich. Orwell Hotel, P. 3.30 pm,' I said.

'What? Yes.' He seemed unsurprised that I should know. He seemed to be looking inwards to an unendurable landscape.

'I saw him die,' he said.

CHAPTER SIXTEEN

'I saw the scaffolding fall on him,' he said.

He'd stunned me to silence.

'We talked in the hotel. In the lounge there. It was almost empty . . . then we walked down the street to where I'd left my car. We said goodbye. He crossed the road and walked on, and I watched him. I wanted him to look back and wave . . . but he didn't.'

Forgiveness was one thing, I thought, but friendship had gone. What did he expect? Absolution and comfort? Perhaps Greville in time would have given those too, but I couldn't.

Prospero Jenks with painful memory said, 'Grev never knew what happened . . . There wasn't any warning. Just a clanging noise and metal falling and men with it. Crashing down fast. It buried him. I couldn't see him . . . I ran across the road to pull him and there were bodies . . . and he . . . he . . . I thought he was dead already. His head was bleeding . . . there was a metal bar in his stomach and another had ripped into his leg . . . it was . . . I can't . . . I try to forget but I see it all the time.'

I waited and in a while he went on.

'I didn't move him. Couldn't. There was so much blood . . . and a man lying over his legs . . . and another man groaning. People came running . . . then the police . . . it was just chaos . . .'

He stopped again, and I said, 'When the police came, why didn't you stay with Greville and help him? Why didn't you identify him to them, even?'

His genuine sorrow was flooded with a shaft of alarm. The dismay was momentary, and he shrugged it off.

'You know how it is.' He gave me a little-boy shame-faced look, much the same as when he'd admitted to changing the stones. 'Don't get involved. I didn't want to be dragged in . . . I thought he was dead.'

Somewhere along the line, I thought, he was lying to me. Not about seeing the accident: his description of Greville's injuries had been piercingly accurate.

'Did you simply . . . drive off?' I asked bleakly.

'No, I couldn't. Not for ages. The police cordoned off the street and took endless statements. Something about criminal responsibility and insurance claims. But I couldn't help them. I didn't see why the scaffolding fell. I felt sick because of the blood . . . I sat in my car till they let us drive out. They'd taken Grev off in an ambulance before that . . . and the bar was still sticking out of his stomach . . .'

The memory was powerfully reviving his nausea.

'You knew by then that he was still alive,' I said.

He was shocked. 'How? How could I have known?'

'They hadn't covered his face.'

'He was dying. Anyone could see. His head was dented . . . and bleeding . . .'

Dead men don't bleed, I thought, but didn't say it. Prospero Jenks already looked about to throw up, and I wondered how many times he actually had, in the past eleven days.

Instead, I said, 'What did you talk about in the Orwell Hotel?'

He blinked. 'You know what.'

'He accused you of changing the stones.'

'Yes.' He swallowed. 'Well, I apologized. Said I was sorry. Which I was. He could see that. He said why did I do it when I was bound to be found out, but when I did it, it was an impulse, and I didn't think I'd be found out, like I told you.'

'What did he say?'

'He shook his head as if I were a baby. He was sad more than angry. I said I would give the diamonds back, of course, and I begged him to forgive me.'

'Which he did?'

'Yes, I told you. I asked if we could go on trading together. I mean, no one was as good as Grev at finding marvellous stones, and he always loved the things I made. It was good for both of us. I wanted to go back to that.'

Going back was one of life's impossibilities, I thought. Nothing was ever the same.

'Did Greville agree?' I asked.

'Yes. He said he had the diamonds with him but he had arrangements to make. He didn't say what. He said he would come here to the shop at the beginning of the week and I would give him his five stones and pay for the tear drops and stars. He wanted cash for them, and he was giving me a day or two to find the money.'

'He didn't usually want cash for things, did he? You sent a cheque for the spinel and rock crystal.'

'Yes, well . . .' Again the quick look of shame, 'He said cash in future, as he couldn't trust me. But you didn't know that.'

Greville certainly hadn't trusted him, and it sounded as if he'd said he had the diamonds with him when he knew they were at that moment on a boat crossing the North Sea. Had he said that, I wondered? Perhaps Prospero Jenks had misheard or misunderstood, but he'd definitely believed Greville had had the diamonds with him.

'If I give you those diamonds now, then that will be the end of it?' he said. 'I mean, as Grev had forgiven me, you won't go back on that and make a fuss, will you? Not the police . . . Grev wouldn't have wanted that, you know he wouldn't.'

I didn't answer. Greville would have to have balanced his betrayed old friendship against his respect for the law, and I supposed he wouldn't have had Prospero prosecuted, not for a first offence, admitted and regretted.

Prospero Jenks gave my silence a hopeful look, rose from his stool and crossed to the ranks of little drawers. He pulled one open, took out several apparently unimportant packets and felt deep inside with a searching hand. He brought out a twist of white gauze fastened with a band of sticky tape and held it out for me.

'Five diamonds,' he said. 'Yours.'

I took the unimpressive little parcel which most resembled the muslin bag of herbs cooks put in stews, and weighed it in my hand. I certainly couldn't myself tell CZ from C and he could see the doubt in my face.

'Have them appraised,' he said with unjustified bitterness, and I said we would weigh them right there and then and he would write out the weight and sign it.

'Grev didn't . . .'

'More fool he. He should have done. But he trusted you. I don't.'

'Come on, Derek.' He was cajoling; but I was not Greville.

'No. Weigh them,' I said.

With a sigh and an exaggerated shrug he cut open the little bag when I handed it back to him, and on small fine scales weighed the contents.

It was the first time I'd actually seen what I'd been searching for, and they were unimposing, to say the least. Five dull-looking greyish pieces of crystal the size of large misshapen peas without a hint of the fire waiting within. I watched the weighing carefully and took them myself off the scales, wrapping them in a fresh

767

square of gauze which Prospero handed me and fastening them safely with sticky tape.

'Satisficd?' he said with a touch of sarcasm, watching me stow the bouquet garni in my trouser pocket.

'No. Not really.'

'They're the genuine article,' he protested. He signed the paper on which he'd written their combined weight, and gave it to me. 'I wouldn't make that mistake again.' He studied me. 'You're much harder than Grev.'

'I've reason to be.'

'What reason?'

'Several attempts at theft. Sundry assaults.'

His mouth opened.

'Who else?' I said.

'But I've never ... I didn't ...' He wanted me to believe him. He leaned forward with earnestness. 'I don't know what you're talking about.'

I sighed slightly. 'Greville hid the letters and invoices dealing with the diamonds because he distrusted someone in his office. Someone that he guessed was running to you with little snippets of information. Someone who would spy for you.'

'Nonsense.' His mouth seemed dry, however.

I pulled out of a pocket the microcassette recorder and laid it on his workbench.

'This is voice activated,' I said. 'Greville left it switched on one day when he went to lunch, and this is what he found on the tape when he returned.' I pressed the switch and the voice that was familiar to both of us spoke revealing forth:

'I'm in his office now and I can't find them. He hides everything, he's security mad, you know that. I can't ask. He'd never tell me, and I don't think he trusts me. Po-faced Annette doesn't sneeze unless he tells her to . . .'

Jason's voice, full of the cocky street-smart aggression that went with the orange spiky hair, clicked off eventually into silence. Prospero Jenks worked some saliva into his mouth and carefully made sure the recorder was not still alive and listening.

'Jason wasn't talking to me,' he said unconvincingly. 'He was talking to someone else.'

'Jason was the regular messenger between you and Greville,' I said. 'I sent him round here myself last week. Jason wouldn't take much seducing to bring you information along with the merchandise. But Greville found out. It compounded his sense of betrayal. So when you and he were talking in the Orwell at Ipswich, what was his opinion of Jason?'

He made a gesture of half-suppressed fury.

'I don't know how you know all this,' he said.

It had taken nine days and a lot of searching and a good deal of guessing at possibilities and probabilities, but the pattern was now a reliable path through at least part of the maze, and no other interpretation that I could think of explained the facts.

I said again, 'What did he say about Jason?'

Prospero Jenks capitulated. 'He said he'd have to leave Saxony Franklin. He said it was a condition of us ever doing business again. He said I was to tell Jason not to turn up for work on the Monday.'

'But you didn't do that,' I said.

'Well, no.'

'Because when Greville died, you decided to try to steal not only five stones but the lot.'

The blue eyes almost smiled. 'Seemed logical, didn't it?' he said. 'Grev wouldn't know. The insurance would pay. No one would lose.'

Except the underwriters, I thought. But I said, 'The diamonds weren't insured. Are not now insured. You were stealing them directly from Greville.'

He was almost astounded, but not quite.

'Greville told you that, didn't he?' I guessed.

Again the little-boy shame. 'Well, yes, he did.'

'In the Orwell?'

'Yes.'

'Pross,' I said, 'did you ever grow up?'

'You don't know what growing up is. Growing up is being ahead of the game.'

'Stealing without being found out?'

'Of course. Everyone does it. You have to make what you can.'

'But you have this marvellous talent,' I said.

'Sure. But I make things for money. I make what people like. I take their bread, whatever they'll pay. Sure, I get a buzz when what I've made is brilliant, but I wouldn't starve in a garret for art's sake. Stones sing to me. I give them life. Gold is my paintbrush. All that, sure. But I'll laugh behind people's backs. They're gullible. The day I understood all customers are suckers is the day I grew up.'

I said, 'I'll bet you never said all that to Greville.'

'Do me a favour. Grev was a saint, near enough. The only truly good person through and through I've ever known. I wish I hadn't cheated him. I regret it something rotten.'

I listened to the sincerity in his voice and believed him, but his remorse had been barely skin deep, and nowhere had it altered his soul.

'Jason,' I said, 'knocked me down outside St Catherine's Hospital and stole the bag containing Greville's clothes.'

'No.' The Jenks' denial was automatic, but his eyes were full of shock.

I said, 'I thought at the time it was an ordinary mugging. The attacker was quick and strong. A friend who was with me said the mugger wore jeans and a woolly hat, but neither of us saw his face. I didn't bother to report it to the police because there was nothing of value in the bag.'

'So how can you say it was Jason?'

I answered his question obliquely.

'When I went to Greville's firm to tell them he was dead,' I said, 'I found his office had been ransacked. As you know. The next day I discovered that Greville had bought diamonds. I began looking for them, but there was no paperwork, no address book, no desk diary, no reference to or appointments with diamond dealers. I couldn't physically find the diamonds either. I spent three days searching in the vault, with Annette and June, her assistant, telling me that there never were any diamonds in the office, Greville was far too security-conscious. You yourself told me the diamonds were intended for you, which I didn't know until I came here. Everyone in the office knew I was looking for diamonds, and at that point Jason must have told you I was looking for them, which informed you that I didn't know where they were.'

He watched my face with his mouth slightly open, no longer denying, showing only the stunned disbelief of the profoundly found out.

'The office staff grew to know I was a jockey,' I said, 'and Jason behaved to me with an insolence I thought inappropriate, but I now think his arrogance was the result of his having had me face down on the ground under his foot. He couldn't crow about that, but his belief in his superiority was stamped all over him. I asked the office staff not to unsettle the customers by telling them that they were now trading with a jockey not a gemmologist, but I think it's certain that Jason told *you.*'

'What makes you think that?' He didn't say it hadn't happened.

'You couldn't get into Greville's house to search it,' I

said, 'because it's a fortress. You couldn't swing any sort of wrecking ball against the windows because the grilles inside made it pointless, and anyway they're wired on a direct alarm to the police station. The only way to get into that house is by key, and I had the keys. So you worked out how to get me there, and you set it up through the trainer I ride for, which is how I know you were aware I was a jockey. Apart from the staff, no one else who knew I was a jockey knew I was looking for diamonds, because I carefully didn't tell them. Come to the telephone in Greville's house for information about the diamonds, you said, and I obediently turned up, which was foolish.'

'But I never went to Greville's house . . .' he said.

'No, not you, Jason. Strong and fast in the motor-cycle helmet which covered his orange hair, butting me over again just like old times. I saw him vault the gate on the way out. That couldn't have been you. He turned the house upside down but the police didn't think he'd found what he was looking for, and I'm sure he didn't.'

'Why not?' he asked, and then said, 'That's to say . . .'

'Did you mean Jason to kill me?' I asked flatly.

'No! Of course not!' The idea seemed genuinely to shock him.

'He could have done,' I said.

'I'm not a murderer!' His indignation, as far as I could tell, was true and without reservation, quite different from his reaction to my calling him a thief.

'What were you doing two days ago, on Sunday afternoon?' I said.

'What?' He was bewildered by the question but not alarmed.

'Sunday afternoon,' I said.

'What about Sunday afternoon? What are you talking about?'

I frowned. 'Never mind. Go back to Saturday night. To Jason giving me concussion with half a brick.'

The knowledge of that was plain to read. We were again on familiar territory.

'You can kill people,' I said, 'hitting them with bricks.'

'But he said . . .' He stopped dead.

'You might as well go on,' I said reasonably, 'we both know that what I've said is what happened.'

'Yes, but . . . what are you going to do about it?'

'I don't know yet.'

'I'll deny everything.'

'What did Jason say about the brick?'

He gave a hopeless little sigh. 'He said he knew how to knock people out for half an hour. He'd seen it done in street riots, he said, and he'd done it himself. He said it depended on where you hit.'

'You can't time it,' I objected.

'Well, that's what he said.'

He hadn't been so wrong, I supposed. I'd beaten his estimate by maybe ten minutes, not more.

'He said you'd be all right afterwards,' Pross said.

'He couldn't be sure of that.'

'But you are, aren't you?' There seemed to be a tinge of regret that I hadn't emerged punch drunk and unable to hold the present conversation. Callous and irresponsible, I thought, and unforgivable, really. Greville had forgiven treachery; and which was worse?

'Jason knew which office window to break,' I said, 'and he came down from the roof. The police found marks up there.' I paused. 'Did he do that alone, or were you with him?'

'Do you expect me to tell you?' he said incredulously.

'Yes, I do. Why not? You know what plea bargaining is, you just tried it with five diamonds.'

He gave me a shattered look and searched his common sense; not that he had much of it, when one considered.

Eventually, without shame, he said, 'We both went.'

'When?'

'That Sunday. Late afternoon. After he brought Grev's things back from Ipswich and they were a waste of time.'

'You found out which hospital Greville was in,' I said, 'and you sent Jason to steal his things because you believed they would include the diamonds which Greville had told you he had with him, is that right?'

He rather miserably nodded. 'Jason phoned me from the hospital on the Saturday and said Grev wasn't dead yet but that this brother had turned up, some frail old creature on crutches, and it was good because he'd be an easy mark . . . which you were.'

'Yes.'

He looked at me and repeated, 'Frail old creature,' and faintly smiled, and I remembered his surprise at my physical appearance when I'd first come into this room. Jason, I supposed, had seen only my back view and mostly at a distance. I certainly hadn't noticed anyone lurking, but I probably wouldn't at the time have noticed half a ship's company standing at attention. Being with the dying, seeing the death, had made ordinary life seem unreal and unimportant, and it had taken me until hours after Jason's attack to lose that feeling altogether.

'All right,' I said, 'so Jason came back empty-handed. What then?'

He shrugged. 'I thought I'd probably got it wrong. Grev couldn't have meant that he had the diamonds with him.' He frowned. 'I thought that was what he said, though.'

I enlightened him. 'Greville was on his way to Harwich to meet a diamond cutter coming from Antwerp by ferry, who was bringing your diamonds with him. Twelve tear drops and eight stars.'

'Oh.' His face cleared momentarily with pleasure but gloom soon returned. 'Well, I thought it was worth looking in his office, though Jason said he never kept anything valuable there. But for diamonds . . . so many diamonds . . . it was worth a chance. Jason didn't take much persuading. He's a violent young bugger . . .'

I wondered fleetingly if that description mightn't be positively and scatologically accurate.

'So you went up to the roof in the service lift,' I said, 'and swung some sort of pendulum at the packing room window.'

He shook his head. 'Jason brought grappling irons and a rope ladder and climbed down that to the window, and broke the glass with a baseball bat. Then when he was inside I threw the hooks and the ladder down into the yard, and went down in the lift to the eighth floor, and Jason let me in through the staff door. But we couldn't get into the stock-rooms because of Grev's infernal electronic locks or into the showroom, same reason. And that vault . . . I wanted to try to beat it open with the bat but Jason said the door is six inches thick.' He shrugged. 'So we had to make do with papers . . . and we couldn't find anything about diamonds. Jason got angry . . . we made quite a mess.'

'Mm.'

'And it was all a waste of time. Jason said what we really needed was something called a Wizard, but we couldn't find that either. In the end, we simply left. I gave up. Grev had been too careful. I got resigned to not having the diamonds unless I paid for them. Then Jason said you were hunting high and low for them, and I got interested again. Very. You can't blame me.'

I could and did, but I didn't want to switch off the fountain.

'And then,' he said, 'like you guessed, I inveigled you into Grev's garden, and Jason had been waiting ages there getting furious you took so long. He let his anger out on the house, he said.'

'He made a mess there too, yes.'

'Then you woke up and set the alarms off and Jason said he was getting right nervous by then and he wasn't going to wait around for the handcuffs. So Grev had beaten us again . . . and he's beaten you too, hasn't he?' He looked at me shrewdly. 'You haven't found the diamonds either.'

I didn't answer him. I said, 'When did Jason break into Greville's car?'

'Well . . . when he finally found it in Greville's road. I'd looked for it at the hotel and round about in Ipswich, but Grev must have hired a car to drive there because his own car won't start.'

'When did you discover that?'

'Saturday. If the diamonds had been in it, we wouldn't have needed to search the house.'

'He wouldn't have left a fortune in the street,' I said.

Pross shook his head resignedly. 'You'd already looked there, I suppose.'

'I had.' I considered him. 'Why Ipswich?' I said.

'What?'

'Why the Orwell Hotel at Ipswich, particularly? Why did he want you to go there?'

'No idea,' he said blankly. 'He didn't say. He'd often ask me to meet him in odd places. It was usually because he'd found some heirloom or other and wanted to know if the stones would be of use to me. An ugly old tiara once, with a boring yellow diamond centrepiece filthy from neglect. I had the stone recut and set it as the crest of a rock crystal bird and hung it in a golden cage . . . it's in Florida, in the sun.'

I was shaken with the pity of it. So much soaring priceless imagination and such grubby, perfidious greed.

I said, 'Had he found you a stone in Ipswich?'

'No. He told me he'd asked me to come there because he didn't want us to be interrupted. Somewhere quiet, he said. I suppose it was because he was going to Harwich.'

I nodded. I supposed so also, though it wasn't on the most direct route which was further south, through Colchester. But Ipswich was where Greville had chosen, by freak mischance.

I thought of all Pross had told me, and was struck by one unexplored and dreadful possibility.

'When the scaffolding fell,' I said slowly, 'when you ran across the road and found Greville lethally injured . . . when he was lying there bleeding with the metal bar in him . . . did you steal his wallet?'

Pross's little-boy face crumpled and he put up his hands to cover it as if he would weep. I didn't believe in the tears and the remorse. I couldn't bear him any longer. I stood up to go.

779

'You thought he might have diamonds in his wallet,' I said bitterly. 'And then, even then, when he was dying, you were ready to rob him.'

He said nothing. He in no way denied it.

I felt such anger on Greville's behalf that I wanted suddenly to hurt and punish the man before me with a ferocity I wouldn't have expected in myself, and I stood there trembling with the self-knowledge and the essential restraint, and felt my throat close over any more words.

Without thinking, I put my left foot down to walk out and felt the pain as an irrelevance, but then after three steps used the crutches to make my way to his doorway and round the screen into the shop and through there out onto the pavement, and I wanted to yell and scream at the bloody injustice of Greville's death and the wickedness of the world and call down the rage of angels.

CHAPTER SEVENTEEN

I stood blindly on the pavement oblivious to the passers-by finding me an obstacle in their way. The swamping tidal wave of fury and desolation swelled and broke and gradually ebbed, leaving me still shaking from its force, a tornado in the spirit.

I loosened a jaw I hadn't realized was clamped tight shut and went on feeling wretched.

A grandmotherly woman touched my arm and said, 'Do you need help?' and I shook my head at her kindness because the help I needed wasn't anyone's to give. One had to heal from the inside: to knit like bones.

'Are you all right?' she asked again, her eyes concerned.

'Yes.' I made an effort. 'Thank you.'

She looked at me uncertainly, but finally moved on, and I took a few sketchy breaths and remembered with bathos that I needed a telephone if I were ever to move from that spot.

A hairdressing salon having (for a consideration) let me use their instrument, Brad came within five minutes to pick me up. I shoved the crutches into the back and climbed wearily in beside him, and he said, 'Where to?' giving me a repeat of the grandmotherly solicitude in his face if not his words.

'Uh,' I said. 'I don't know.'

'Home?'

'No . . .' I gave it a bit of thought. I had intended to go to Greville's house to change into my suit that was hanging in his wardrobe before meeting Clarissa at seven, and it still seemed perhaps the best thing to do, even if my energy for the project had evaporated.

Accordingly we made our way there, which wasn't far, and when Brad stopped outside the door, I said, 'I think I'll sleep here tonight. This house is as safe as anywhere. So you can go on to Hungerford now, if you like.'

He didn't look as if he liked, but all he said was, 'I come back tomorrow?'

'Yes, please,' I agreed.

'Pick you up. Take you to the office?'

'Yes, please.'

He nodded, seemingly reassured that I still needed him. He got out of the car with me and opened the gate, brought my overnight bag and came in with me to see, upstairs and down, that the house was safely empty of murderers and thieves. When he'd departed I checked that all the alarms were switched on and went up to Greville's room to change.

I borrowed another of his shirts and a navy silk tie,

and shaved with his electric razor which was among the things I'd picked up from the floor and had put on his white chest of drawers, and brushed my hair with his brushes for the same reason, and thought with an odd frisson that all of these things were mine now, that I was in his house, in his room, in his clothes . . . in his life.

I put on my own suit, because his anyway were too long, and came across the tube of the baster, still there in an inner breast pocket. Removing it, I left it among the jumble on the dressing chest and checked in the looking glass on the wall that Franklin, Mark II, wouldn't entirely disgrace Franklin, Mark I. He had looked in that mirror every day for three months, I supposed. Now his reflection was my reflection and the man that was both of us had dark marks of tiredness under the eyes and a taut thinness in the cheeks, and looked as if he could do with a week's lying in the sun. I gave him a rueful smile and phoned for a taxi, which took me to Luigi's with ten minutes to spare.

She was there before me all the same, sitting at a small table in the bar area to one side of the restaurant, with an emptyish glass looking like vodka on a prim mat in front of her. She stood up when I went in and offered me a cool cheek for a polite social greeting, inviting me with a gesture to sit down.

'What will you drink?' she asked formally, but battling, I thought, with an undercurrent of diffidence.

I said I would pay for our drinks and she said no, no, this was her suggestion. She called the waiter and said,

'Double water?' to me with a small smile and when I nodded ordered Perrier with ice and fresh lime-juice for both of us.

I was down by then to only two or three Distalgesics a day and would soon have stopped taking them, though the one I'd just swallowed in Greville's house was still an inhibitor for the evening. I wondered too late which would have made me feel better, a damper for the ankle or a large scotch everywhere else.

Clarissa was wearing a blue silk dress with a double-strand pearl necklace, pearl, sapphire and diamond ear-rings and a sapphire and diamond ring. I doubted if I would have noticed those, in the simple old jockey days. Her hair, smooth as always, curved in the expensive cut and her shoes and handbag were quiet black calf. She looked as she was, a polished, well-bred woman of forty or so, nearly beautiful, slender, with generous eyes.

'What have you been doing since Saturday?' she asked, making conversation.

'Peering into the jaws of death. What have you?'

'We went to . . .' She broke off. '*What* did you say?'

'Martha and Harley Ostermeyer and I were in a car crash on Sunday. They're OK, they went back to America today, I believe. And I, as you see, am here in one piece. Well . . . almost one piece.'

She was predictably horrified and wanted to hear all the details, and the telling at least helped to evaporate any awkwardness either of us had been feeling at the meeting.

'Simms was *shot*?'

'Yes.'

'But . . . do the police know who did it?'

I shook my head. 'Someone in a large grey Volvo, they think, and there are thousands of those.'

'Good heavens.' She paused. 'I didn't like to comment, but you look . . .' She hesitated, searching for the word.

'Frazzled?' I suggested.

'Smooth.' She smiled. 'Frazzled underneath.'

'It'll pass.'

The waiter came to ask if we would be having dinner and I said yes, and no argument, the dinner was mine. She accepted without fuss, and we read the menus.

The fare was chiefly Italian, the decor cosmopolitan, the ambience faintly European tamed by London. A lot of dark red, lamps with glass shades, no wallpaper music. A comfortable place, nothing dynamic. Few diners yet, as the hour was early.

It was not, I was interested to note, a habitual rendez-vous place for Clarissa and Greville: none of the waiters treated her as a regular. I asked her about it and, startled, she said they had been there only two or three times, always for lunch.

'We never went to the same place often,' she said. 'It wouldn't have been wise.'

'No.'

She gave me a slightly embarrassed look. 'Do you disapprove of me and Greville?'

'No,' I said again. 'You gave him joy.'

'Oh.' She was comforted and pleased. She said with a certain shyness, 'It was the first time I'd fallen in love. I suppose you'll think that silly. But it was the first time for him, too, he said. It was ... truly *wonderful*. We were like ... as if twenty years younger ... I don't know if I can explain. Laughing. Lit up.'

'As far as I can see,' I said, 'the thunderbolt strikes at any age. You don't have to be teenagers.'

'Has it ... struck you?'

'Not since I was seventeen and fell like a ton of bricks for a trainer's daughter.'

'What happened?'

'Nothing much. We laughed a lot. Slept together, a bit clumsily at first. She married an old man of twenty-eight. I went to college.'

'I met Henry when I was eighteen. He fell in love with me ... pursued me ... I was flattered ... and he was so very good looking ... and kind.'

'He still is,' I said.

'He'd already inherited his title. My mother was ecstatic ... she said the age difference didn't matter ... so I married him.' She paused. 'We had a son and a daughter, both grown up now. It hasn't been a bad life, but before Greville, incomplete.'

'A better life than most,' I said, aiming to comfort.

'You're very like Greville,' she said unexpectedly. 'You look at things straight, in the same way. You've his sense of proportion.'

'We had realistic parents.'

'He didn't speak about them much, only that he became interested in gemstones because of the museums his mother took him to. But he lived in the present and he looked outward, not inward, and I loved him to distraction and in a way I didn't know him . . .' She stopped and swallowed and seemed determined not to let emotion intrude further.

'He was like that with me too,' I said. 'With everyone, I think. It didn't occur to him to give running commentaries on his actions and feelings. He found everything else more interesting.'

'I do miss him,' she said.

'What will you eat?' I asked.

She gave me a flick of a look and read the menu without seeing it for quite a long time. In the end she said with a sigh, 'You decide.'

'Did Greville?'

'Yes.'

'If I order fried zucchini as a starter, then fillet steak in pepper sauce with linguine tossed in olive oil with garlic, will that do?'

'I don't like garlic. I like everything else. Unusual. Nice.'

'OK. No garlic.'

We transferred to the dining room before seven-thirty and ate the proposed programme, and I asked if she were returning to York that night: if she had a train to catch, if that was why we were eating early.

787

'No, I'm down here for two nights. Tomorrow I'm going to an old friend's wedding, then back to York on Thursday morning.' She concentrated on twirling linguine onto her fork. 'When Henry and I come to London together we always stay at the Selfridge Hotel, and when I come alone I stay there also. They know us well there. When I'm there alone they don't present me with an account, they send it to Henry.' She ate the forkful of linguine. 'I tell him I go to the cinema and eat in snack bars . . . and he knows I'm always back in the hotel before midnight.'

There was a good long stretch of time between this dinner and midnight.

I said, 'Every five weeks or so, when you came down to London alone, Greville met you at King's Cross, isn't that right, and took you to lunch?'

She said in surprise, 'Did he tell you?'

'Not face to face. Did you ever see that gadget of his, the Wizard?'

'Yes, but . . .' She was horrified. 'He surely didn't put me in it?'

'Not by name, and only under a secret password. You're quite safe.'

She twiddled some more with the pasta, her eyes down, her thoughts somewhere else.

'After lunch,' she said, with pauses, 'if I had appointments, I'd keep them, or do some shopping . . . something to take home. I'd register at the hotel and change, and go to Greville's house. He used to have the flat, of course, but the house was much better. When he came, we'd have drinks . . . talk . . . maybe make love. We'd go to dinner early, then back to his house.' Her voice stopped. She still didn't look up.

I said, 'Do you want to go to his house now, before midnight?'

After a while, she said, 'I don't know.'

'Well . . . would you like coffee?'

She nodded, still not meeting my eyes, and pushed the linguine away. We sat in silence while waiters took away the plates and poured into cups, and if she couldn't make up her mind, nor could I.

In the end I said, 'If you like, come to Greville's house now. I'm sleeping there tonight, but that's not a factor. Come if you like, just to be near him, to be with him as much as you can for maybe the last time. Lie on his bed. Weep for him. I'll wait for you downstairs . . . and take you safely to your hotel before the fairy coach changes back to a pumpkin.'

'Oh!' She turned what had been going to be a sob into almost a laugh. 'Can I really?'

'Whenever you like.'

'Thank you, then. Yes.'

'I'd better warn you,' I said, 'it's not exactly tidy.' I told her what she would find, but she was inconsolable at the sight of the reality.

'He would have hated this,' she said. 'I'm so glad he didn't see it.'

We were in the small sitting room, and she went

round picking up the pink and brown stone bears, restoring them to their tray.

'I gave him these,' she said. 'He loved them. They're rhodonite, he said.'

'Take them to remember him by. And there's a gold watch you gave him, if you'd like that too.'

She paused with the last bear in her hand and said, 'You're very kind to me.'

'It's not difficult. And he'd have been furious with me if I weren't.'

'I'd love the bears. You'd better keep the watch, because of the engraving.'

'OK,' I said.

'I think,' she said with diffidence, 'I'll go upstairs now.'

I nodded.

'Come with me,' she said.

I looked at her. Her eyes were wide and troubled, but not committed, not hungry. Undecided. Like myself.

'All right,' I said.

'Is there chaos up there too?'

'I picked some of it up.'

She went up the stairs ahead of me at about four times my speed, and I heard her small moan of distress at the desecration of the bedroom. When I joined her, she was standing forlornly looking around, and with naturalness she turned to me and put her arms loosely round my waist, laying her head on my shoulder. I shed the confounded crutches and hugged her tight in grief

790

for her and for Greville and we stood there for a long minute in mutual and much needed comfort.

She let her arms fall away and went over to sit on the bed, smoothing a hand over the black and white chequer-board counterpane.

'He was going to change this room,' she said. 'All this drama . . .' She waved a hand at the white furniture, the black carpet, one black wall . . . 'It came with the house. He wanted me to choose something softer, that I would like. But this is how I'll always remember it.'

She lay down flat, her head on the pillows, her legs toward the foot of the bed, ankles crossed. I half-hopped, half-limped across the room and sat on the edge beside her.

She watched me with big eyes. I put my hand flat on her stomach and felt the sharp internal contraction of muscles.

'Should we do this?' she said.

'I'm not Greville.'

'No . . . Would he mind?'

'I shouldn't think so.' I moved my hand, rubbing a little. 'Do you want to go on?'

'Do you?'

'Yes,' I said.

She sat up fast and put her arms round my neck in a sort of released compulsion.

'I do want this,' she said. 'I've wanted it all day. I've been pretending to myself, telling myself I shouldn't, but yes, I do want this passionately, and I know you're not Greville, I know it will be different, but this is the only way I can love him . . . and can you bear it, can you understand it, if it's him I love?'

I understood it well, and I minded not at all.

I said, smiling, 'Just don't *call* me Greville. It would be the turn-off of the century.'

She took her face away from the proximity of my ear and looked me in the eyes, and her lips too, after a moment, were smiling.

'Derek,' she said deliberately, 'make love to me. Please.'

'Don't beg,' I said.

I put my mouth on hers and took my brother's place.

As a memorial service it was quite a success. I lay in the dark laughing in my mind at that disgraceful pun, wondering whether or not to share it with Clarissa.

The catharsis was over, and her tears. She lay with her head on my chest, lightly asleep, contented, as far as I could tell, with the substitute loving. Women said men were not all the same in the dark, and I knew both where I'd surprised her and failed her, known what I'd done like Greville and not done like Greville from the instinctive releases and tensions of her reactions.

Greville, I now knew, had been a lucky man, though whether he had himself taught her how to give exquisite pleasure was something I couldn't quite ask. She knew, though, and she'd done it, and the feeling of her featherlight tattooing fingers on the base of my spine at the moment of climax had been a revelation. Knowledge marched on, I thought. Next time, with anyone else, I'd know what to suggest.

Clarissa stirred and I turned my wrist over, seeing the fluorescent hands of my watch.

'Wake up,' I said affectionately. 'It's Cinderella time.'

'Ohh . . .'

I stretched out a hand and turned on a bedside light. She smiled at me sleepily, no doubts remaining.

'That was all right,' she said.

'Mm. Very.'

'How's the ankle?'

'What ankle?'

She propped herself on one elbow, unashamed of nakedness, and laughed at me. She looked younger and sweeter, and I was seeing, I knew, what Greville had seen, what Greville had loved.

'Tomorrow,' she said, 'my friend's wedding will be over by six or so. Can I come here again?' She put her fingers lightly on my mouth to stop me answering at once. 'This time was for him,' she said. 'Tomorrow for us. Then I'll go home.'

'For ever?'

'Yes, I think so. What I had with Greville was unforgettable and unrepeatable. I decided on the train coming down here that whatever happened with you, or didn't happen, I would live with Henry, and do my best there.'

'I could easily love you,' I said.

'Yes, but don't.'

I knew she was right. I kissed her lightly.

'Tomorrow for us,' I agreed. 'Then goodbye.'

When I went into the office in the morning, Annette told me crossly that Jason hadn't turned up for work, nor had he telephoned to say he was ill.

Jason had been prudent, I thought. I'd have tossed him down the lift shaft, insolence, orange hair and all, given half an ounce of provocation.

'He won't be coming back,' I said, 'so we'll need a replacement.'

She was astonished. 'You can't sack him for not turning up. You can't sack him for anything without paying compensation.'

'Stop worrying,' I said, but she couldn't take that advice.

June came zooming into Greville's office waving a tabloid newspaper and looking at me with wide incredulous eyes.

'Did you know you're in the paper? Lucky to be alive, it says here. You didn't say anything about it!'

'Let's see,' I said, and she laid the *Daily Sensation* open on the black desk.

There was a picture of the smash in which one could more or less see my head inside the Daimler, but not recognizably. The headline read: 'Driver shot, jockey lives', and the piece underneath listed the lucky-to-be-alive passengers as Mr and Mrs Ostermeyer of Pittsburgh, America, and ex-champion steeplechase jockey Derek Franklin. The police were reported to be interested in a grey Volvo seen accelerating from the scene, and also to have recovered two bullets from the bodywork of the Daimler. After that titbit came a rehash of the Hungerford massacre and a query, 'Is this a copycat killing?' and finally a picture of Simms looking happy: 'Survived by wife and two daughters who were last night being comforted by relatives'.

Poor Simms. Poor family. Poor every shot victim in Hungerford.

'It happened on Sunday,' June exclaimed, 'and you came here on Monday and yesterday as if nothing was wrong. No wonder you looked knackered.'

'June!' Annette disapproved of the word.

'Well, he did. Still does.' She gave me a critical, kindly, motherly-sister inspection. 'He could have been killed, and then what would we all have done here?'

The dismay in Annette's face was a measure, I supposed, of the degree to which I had taken over. The place no longer felt like a quicksand to me either and I was beginning by necessity to get a feel of its pulse.

But there was racing at Cheltenham that day. I turned the pages of the newspaper and came to the runners and riders. That was where my name belonged, not on Saxony Franklin cheques. June looked over my shoulder and understood at least something of my sense of exile.

'When you go back to your own world,' she said, rephrasing her thought and asking it seriously, 'what will we do here?'

'We have a month,' I said. 'It'll take me that time to get fit.' I paused. 'I've been thinking about that problem, and, er, you might as well know, both of you, what I've decided.'

They both looked apprehensive, but I smiled to reassure them.

'What we'll do,' I said, 'is this. Annette will have a new title, which will be Office Manager. She'll run things generally and keep the keys.'

She didn't look displeased. She repeated 'Office Manager' as if trying it on for size.

I nodded. 'Then I'll start looking from now on for a business expert, someone to oversee the cash flow and do the accounts and try to keep us afloat. Because it's going to be a struggle, we can't avoid that.'

They both looked shocked and disbelieving. Cash flow seemed never to have been a problem before.

'Greville did buy diamonds,' I said regretfully, 'and so far we are only in possession of a quarter of them. I can't find out what happened to the rest. They cost the firm altogether one and a half million dollars, and we'll still owe the bank getting on for three-quarters of that sum when we've sold the quarter we have.'

Their mouths opened in unhappy unison.

'Unless and until the other diamonds turn up,' I said, 'we have to pay interest on the loan and persuade the bank that somehow or other we'll climb out of the hole. So we'll want someone we'll call the Finance Manager, and we'll pay him out of part of what used to be Greville's own salary.'

They began to understand the mechanics, and nodded.

'Then,' I said, 'we need a gemmologist who has a feeling for stones and understands what the customers like and need. There's no good hoping for another Greville, but we will create the post of Merchandise Manager, and that,' I looked at her, 'will be June.'

She blushed a fiery red. 'But I can't . . . I don't know enough.'

'You'll go on courses,' I said. 'You'll go to trade fairs. You'll travel. You'll do the buying.'

I watched her expand her horizons abruptly and saw the sparkle appear in her eyes.

'She's too young,' Annette objected.

'We'll see,' I said, and to June I added, 'You know what sells. You and the Finance Manager will work together to make us the best possible profit. You'll still work the computer, and teach Lily or Tina how to use it for when you're away.'

'Tina,' she said, 'she's quicker.'

'Tina, then.'

'What about you?' she asked.

'I'll be General Manager. I'll come when I can, at

least twice a week for a couple of hours. Everyone will tell me what's going on and we will all decide what is best to be done, though if there's a disagreement I'll have the casting vote. Right or wrong will be my responsibility, not yours.'

Annette, nevertheless troubled, said, 'Surely you yourself will need Mr Franklin's salary.'

I shook my head. 'I earn enough riding horses. Until we're solvent here, we need to save every penny.'

'It's an adventure!' June said, enraptured.

I thought it might be a very long haul and even in the end impossible, but I couldn't square it with the consciousness of Greville all around me not to try.

'Well,' I said, putting a hand in a pocket and bringing out a twist of gauze, 'we have here five uncut diamonds which cost about seventy-five thousand dollars altogether.'

They more or less gasped.

'How do we sell them?' I said.

After a pause, Annette said, 'Interest a diamantaire.'

'Do you know how to do that?'

After another moment's hesitation, she nodded.

'We can give provenance,' I said. 'Copies of the records of the original sale are on their way here from Guy Servi in Antwerp. They might be here tomorrow. Sight-box number and so on. We'll put these stones in the vault until the papers arrive, then you can get cracking.'

She nodded, but fearfully.

'Cheer up,' I said. 'It's clear from the ledgers that Saxony Franklin is normally a highly successful and profitable business. We'll have to cut costs where we can, that's all.'

'We could cut out Jason's salary,' Annette said unexpectedly. 'Half the time Tina's been carrying the heavy boxes, anyway, and I can do the hoovering myself.'

'Great,' I said with gratitude. 'If you feel like that, we'll succeed.'

The telephone rang and Annette answered it briefly.

'A messenger has left a packet for you down at the front desk,' she said.

'I'll go for it,' June said, and was out of the door on the words, returning in her usual short time with a brown padded jiffy bag, not very large, addressed simply to Derek Franklin in neat handwriting, which she laid before me with a flourish.

'Mind it's not a bomb,' she said facetiously as I picked it up, and I thought with an amount of horror that it was a possibility I hadn't thought of.

'I didn't mean it,' she said teasingly, seeing me hesitate. 'Do you want me to open it?'

'And get your hands blown off instead?'

'Of course it's not a bomb,' Annette said uneasily.

'Tell you what,' June said, 'I'll fetch the shears from the packing room.' She was gone for a few seconds. 'Alfie says,' she remarked, returning, 'we ought to put it in a bucket of water.'

She gave me the shears, which were oversized scissors that Alfie used for cutting cardboard, and for all her disbelief she and Annette backed away across the room while I sliced the end off the bag.

There was no explosion. Complete anti-climax. I shook out the contents which proved to be two objects and one envelope.

One of the objects was the microcassette recorder that I'd left on Prospero Jenks's workbench in my haste to be gone.

The other was a long black leather wallet almost the size of the Wizard, with gold initials G.S.F. in one corner and an ordinary brown rubber band holding it shut.

'That's Mr Franklin's,' Annette said blankly, and June, coming to inspect it, nodded.

I peeled off the rubber band and laid the wallet open on the desk. There was a business card lying loose inside it with Prospero Jenks's name and shops on the front, and on the reverse the single word, 'Sorry.'

'Where did he get Mr Franklin's wallet from?' Annette asked, puzzled, looking at the card.

'He found it,' I said.

'He took his time sending it back,' June said tartly.

'Mm.'

The wallet contained a Saxony Franklin chequebook, four credit cards, several business cards and a small pack of banknotes, which I guessed were fewer in number than when Greville set out.

The small excitement over, Annette and June went off to tell the others the present and future state of the nation, and I was alone when I opened the envelope.

CHAPTER EIGHTEEN

Pross had sent me a letter and a certified bank draft: instantly cashable money.

I blinked at the numbers on the cheque and reread them very carefully. Then I read the letter.

It said:

Derek,

This is a plea for a bargain, as you more or less said. The cheque is for the sum I agreed with Grev for the twelve tear drops and eight stars. I know you need the money, and I need those stones.

Jason won't be troubling you again. I'm giving him a job in one of my workrooms.

Grev wouldn't have forgiven the brick, though he might the wallet. For you it's the other way round. You're very like him. I wish he hadn't died.

Pross.

What a mess, I thought. I did need the money, yet if I accepted it I was implicitly agreeing not to take any action against him. The trouble about taking action against him was that however much I might want to I didn't know that I could. Apart from difficulties of evidence, I had more or less made a bargain that for information he would get inaction, but that had been before the wallet. It was perceptive of him, I thought, to see that it was betrayal and attacks on our *brother* that would anger both Greville and me most.

Would Greville want me to extend, if not forgiveness, then at least suspended revenge? Would Greville want me to confirm his forgiveness or to rise up in wrath and tear up the cheque . . .

In the midst of these sombre squirrelling thoughts the telephone rang and I answered it.

'Elliot Trelawney here,' the voice said.

'Oh, hello.'

He asked me how things were going and I said life was full of dilemmas. Ever so, he said with a chuckle.

'Give me some advice,' I said on impulse, 'as a magistrate.'

'If I can, certainly.'

'Well. Listen to a story, then say what you think.'

'Fire away.'

'Someone knocked me out with a brick . . .' Elliot made protesting noises on my behalf, but I went on, 'I know now who it was, but I didn't then, and I didn't see his face because he was masked. He wanted to steal a particular thing from me, but although he made a mess in the house searching, he didn't find it, and so didn't rob me of anything except consciousness. I guessed later who it was, and I challenged another man with having sent him to attack me. That man didn't deny it to me, but he said he would deny it to anyone else. So . . . what do I do?'

'Whew.' He pondered. 'What do you want to do?'

'I don't know. That's why I need the advice.'

'Did you report the attack to the police at the time?'

'Yes.'

'Have you suffered serious after-effects?'

'No.'

'Did you see a doctor?'

'No.'

He pondered some more. 'On a practical level you'd find it difficult to get a conviction, even if the prosecution service would bring charges of actual bodily harm. You couldn't swear to the identity of your assailant if you didn't see him at the time, and as for the other man, conspiracy to commit a crime is one of the most difficult charges to make stick. As you didn't consult a doctor, you're on tricky ground. So, hard as it may seem, my advice would be that the case wouldn't get to court.'

I sighed. 'Thank you,' I said.

'Sorry not to have been more positive.'

'It's all right. You confirmed what I rather feared.'

'Fine then,' he said. 'I rang to thank you for sending the Vaccaro notes. We held the committee meeting and turned down Vaccaro's application, and now we find we needn't have bothered because on Saturday night he was arrested and charged with attempting to import illegal substances. He's still in custody, and America is asking for him to be extradited to Florida where he faces murder charges and perhaps execution. And we nearly gave him a gambling licence! Funny old world.'

'Hilarious.'

'How about our drink in The Rook and Castle?' he suggested. 'Perhaps one evening next week?'

'OK.'

'Fine,' he said. 'I'll ring you.'

I put the phone down thinking that if Vaccaro had been arrested on Saturday evening and held in custody, it was unlikely he'd shot Simms from a moving car in Berkshire on Sunday afternoon. But then, I'd never really thought he had.

Copycat. Copycat, that's what it had been.

Pross hadn't shot Simms either. Had never tried to kill me. The Peter-Pan face upon which so many emotions could be read had shown a total blank when I'd asked him what he was doing on Sunday afternoon.

The shooting of Simms, I concluded, had been random violence like the other murders in Hungerford. Pointless and vicious; malignant, lunatic and impossible to explain.

I picked up the huge cheque and looked at it. It would solve all immediate problems: pay the interest already due, the cost of cutting the diamonds and more than a fifth of the capital debt. If I didn't take it, we would no doubt sell the diamonds later to someone else, but they had been cut especially for Prospero Jenks's fantasies and might not easily fit necklaces and rings.

A plea. A bargain. A chance that the remorse was at least half real. Or was he taking me again for a sucker?

I did some sums with a calculator and when Annette came in with the day's letters I showed her my figures and the cheque and asked her what she thought.

'That's the cost price,' I pointed. 'That's the cost of cutting and polishing. That's for delivery charges. That's for loan interest and VAT. If you add those together and subtract them from the figure on this cheque, is that the sort of profit margin Greville would have asked?'

Setting prices was something she well understood, and she repeated my steps on the calculator.

'Yes,' she said finally; 'it looks about right. Not over-generous, but Mr Franklin would have seen this as a service for commission, I think. Not like the rock crystal, which he bought on spec, which had to help pay for his journeys.' She looked at me anxiously. 'You understand the difference?'

'Yes,' I said. 'Prospero Jenks says this is what he and Greville agreed on.'

'Well then,' she said, relieved, 'he wouldn't cheat you.'

I smiled with irony at her faith. 'We'd better bank this cheque, I suppose,' I said, 'before it evaporates.'

'I'll do it at once,' she declared. 'With a loan as big as you said, every minute costs us money.'

She put on her coat and took an umbrella to go out

with, as the day had started off raining and showed no signs of relenting.

It had been raining the previous night when Clarissa had been ready to leave, and I'd had to ring three times for a taxi, a problem Cinderella didn't seem to have encountered. Midnight had come and gone when the wheels had finally arrived, and I'd suggested meanwhile that I lend her Brad and my car for going to her wedding.

I didn't need to, she said. When she and Henry were in London, they were driven about by a hired car firm. The car was already ordered to take her to the wedding which was in Surrey. The driver would wait for her and return her to the hotel, and she'd better stick to the plan, she said, because the bill for it would be sent to her husband.

'I always do what Henry expects,' she said, 'then there are no questions.'

'Suppose Brad picks you up from the Selfridge after you get back?' I said, packing the little stone bears and giving them to her in a carrier. 'The forecast is lousy and if it's raining you'll have a terrible job getting a taxi at that time of day.'

She liked the idea except for Brad's knowing her name. I assured her he never spoke unless he couldn't avoid it, but I told her I would ask Brad to park somewhere near the hotel. Then she could call the car phone's number when she was ready to leave, and Brad would beetle up at the right moment and not need to know her name or ask for her at the desk.

As that pleased her, I wrote down the phone number and the car's number plate so that she would recognize the right pumpkin, and described Brad to her; going bald, a bit morose, an open-necked shirt, a very good driver.

I couldn't tell Brad's own opinion of the arrangement. When I'd suggested it in the morning on the rainy way to the office, he had merely grunted which I'd taken as preliminary assent.

When he'd brought Clarissa, I thought as I looked through the letters Annette had given me, he could go on home, to Hungerford, and Clarissa and I might walk along to the restaurant at the end of Greville's street where he could have been known but I was not, and after an early dinner we would return to Greville's bed, this time for us, and we'd order the taxi in better time . . . perhaps.

I was awoken from this pleasant daydream by the ever-demanding telephone, this time with Nicholas Loder on the other end spluttering with rage.

'Milo says you had the confounded cheek,' he said, 'to have Dozen Roses dope-tested.'

'For barbiturates, yes. He seemed very sleepy. Our vet said he'd be happier to know the horse hadn't been tranquillized for the journey before he gave him an all-clear certificate.'

'I'd never give a horse tranquillizers,' he declared.

'No, none of us really thought so,' I said pacifyingly, 'but we decided to make sure.'

'It's shabby of you. Offensive. I expect an apology.'

'I apologize,' I said sincerely enough, and thought guiltily of the further checks going on at that moment.

'That's not good enough,' Nicholas Loder said huffily.

'I was selling the horse to good owners of Milo, people I ride for,' I said reasonably. 'We all know you disapproved. In the same circumstances, confronted by a sleepy horse, you'd have done the same, wouldn't you? You'd want to be sure what you were selling.'

Weigh the merchandise, I thought. Cubic zirconia, size for size, was one point seven times heavier than diamond. Greville had carried jewellers' scales in his car on his way to Harwich, presumably to check what the *Koningin Beatrix* was bringing.

'You've behaved disgustingly,' Nicholas Loder said. 'When did you see the horse last? And when next?'

'Monday evening, last. Don't know when next. As I told you, I'm tied up a bit with Greville's affairs.'

'Milo's secretary said I'd find you in Greville's office,' he grumbled. 'You're never at home. I've got a buyer for Gemstones, I think, though you don't deserve it. Where will you be this evening, if he makes a definite offer?'

'In Greville's house, perhaps.'

'Right, I have the number. And I want a written apology from you about those dope tests. I'm so angry I can hardly be civil to you.'

He hardly was, I thought, but I was pleased enough about Gemstones. The money would go into the firm's coffers and hold off bankruptcy a little while longer. I still held the Ostermeyers' cheque for Dozen Roses, waiting for Phil Urquhart's final clearance before cashing it. The horses would make up for a few of the missing diamonds. Looking at it optimistically, saying it quickly, the millstone had been reduced to near one million dollars.

June out of habit brought me a sandwich for lunch. She was walking with an extra bounce, with unashamed excitement. Way down the line, I thought, if we made it through the crisis, what then? Would I simply sell the whole of Saxony Franklin as I'd meant or keep it and borrow against it to finance a stable, as Greville had financed the diamonds? I wouldn't hide the stable! Perhaps I would know enough by then to manage both businesses on a sound basis: I'd learned a good deal in ten days. I had also, though I found it surprising, grown fond of Greville's firm. If we saved it, I wouldn't want to let it go.

If I went on riding until solvency dawned I might be the oldest jump jockey in history . . .

Again the telephone interrupted the daydreams, and I'd barely made a start on the letters.

It was a man with a long order for cabochons and beads. I hopped to the door and yelled for June to pick up the phone and to put the order on the computer, and Alfie came along to complain we were running out of heavy duty binding tape and to ask why we'd ever needed Jason. Tina did his work in half the time without the swear words.

Annette almost with gaiety hoovered everywhere, though I thought I would soon ask Tina to do it instead. Lily came with downcast eyes to ask meekly if she could have a title also. Stock-room Manager? she suggested.

'Done!' I said with sincere pleasure; and before the day was out we had a Shipment Manager (Alfie) and an Enabling Manager (Tina), and it seemed to me that such a spirit had been released there that the enterprise was now flying. Whether the euphoria would last or not was next week's problem.

I telephoned Maarten-Pagnier in Antwerp and discussed the transit of twelve tear drops, eight stars and five fakes.

'Our customer has paid us for the diamonds,' I said. 'I'd like to be able to tell him when we could get them to him.'

'Do you want them sent direct to him, monsieur?'

'No. Here to us. We'll pass them on.' I asked if he would insure them for the journey and send them by Euro-Securo; no need to trouble his partner again personally as we did not dispute that five of the stones sent to him had been cubic zirconia. The real stones had been returned to us, I said.

'I rejoice for you, monsieur. And shall we expect a further consignment for cutting? Monsieur Franklin intended it.'

'Not at the moment, I regret.'

'Very well, monsieur. At any time, we are at your service.'

After that I asked Annette if she could find Prospero Jenks to tell him his diamonds would be coming. She ran him to earth in one of his workrooms and appeared in my doorway saying he wanted to speak to me personally.

With inner reluctance I picked up the receiver. 'Hello, Pross,' I said.

'Truce, then?' he asked.

'We've banked the cheque. You'll get the diamonds.'

'When?'

'When they get here from Antwerp. Friday, maybe.'

'Thanks.' He sounded fervently pleased. Then he said with hesitation, 'You've got some light blue topaz, each fifteen carats or more, emerald cut, glittering like water . . . can I have it? Five or six big stones, Grev said. I'll take them all.'

'Give it time,' I said, and God, I thought, what unholy nerve.

'Yes, well, but you and I need each other,' he protested.

'Symbiosis?' I said.

'What? Yes.'

It had done Greville no harm in the trade, I'd gathered, to be known as the chief supplier of Prospero Jenks. His firm still needed the cachet as much as the cash. I'd taken the money once. Could I afford pride?

'If you try to steal from me one more time,' I said, 'I not only stop trading with you, I make sure everyone knows why. Everyone from Hatton Garden to Pelikanstraat.'

'Derek!' He sounded hurt, but the threat was a dire one.

'You can have the topaz,' I said. 'We have a new gemmologist who's not Greville, I grant you, but who knows what you buy. We'll still tell you what special stones we've imported. You can tell us what you need. We'll take it step by step.'

'I thought you wouldn't!' He sounded extremely relieved. 'I thought you'd never forgive me the wallet. Your face . . .'

'I don't forgive it. Or forget. But after wars, enemies trade.'

It always happened, I thought, though cynics might mock. Mutual benefit was the most powerful of bridgebuilders, even if the heart remained bitter. 'We'll see how we go,' I said again.

'If you find the other diamonds,' he said hopefully, 'I still want them.' Like a little boy in trouble, I thought, trying to charm his way out.

Disconnecting, I ruefully smiled. I'd made the same inner compromise that Greville had, to do business with the treacherous child, but not to trust him. To supply the genius in him, and look to my back.

June came winging in and I asked her to go along to the vault to look at the light blue large-stone topaz which I well remembered. 'Get to know it while it's still here. I've sold it to Prospero Jenks.'

'But I don't go into the vault,' she said.

'You do now. You'll go in there every day from now on at spare moments to learn the look and feel of the faceted stones, like I have. Topaz is slippery, for instance. Learn the chemical formulas, learn the cuts and the weights, get to know them so that if you're offered unusual faceted stones anywhere in the world, you can check them against your knowledge for probability.'

Her mouth opened.

'You're going to buy the raw materials for Prospero Jenks's museum pieces,' I said. 'You've got to learn fast.'

Her eyes stretched wide as well, and she vanished.

With Annette I finished the letters.

At four o'clock I answered the telephone yet again, and found myself talking to Phil Urquhart, whose voice sounded strained.

'I've just phoned the lab for the results of Dozen Roses's tests.' He paused. 'I don't think I believe this.'

'What's the matter?' I asked.

'Do you know what a metabolite is?'

'Only vaguely.'

'What then?' he said.

'The result of metabolism, isn't it?'

'It is,' he said. 'It's what's left after some substance or other has broken down in the body.'

'So what?'

'So,' he said reasonably, 'if you find a particular metabolite in the urine, it means a particular substance was earlier present in the body. Is that clear?'

'Like viruses produce special antibodies, so the presence of the antibodies proves the existence of the viruses?'

'Exactly,' he said, apparently relieved I understood. 'Well, the lab found a metabolite in Dozen Roses's urine. A metabolite known as benzyl ecognine.'

'Go on,' I urged, as he paused. 'What is it the metabolite *of*?'

'Cocaine,' he said.

I sat in stunned disbelieving silence.

'Derek?' he said.

'Yes.'

'Racehorses aren't routinely tested for cocaine because it isn't a stimulant. Normally a racehorse could be full of cocaine and no one would know.'

'If it isn't a stimulant,' I said, loosening my tongue, 'why give it to them?'

'If you *believed* it was a stimulant, you might. Knowing it wouldn't be tested for.'

'How could you believe it?'

'It's one of the drugs that potentiates adrenalin. I particularly asked the lab to test for all drugs like that because of what you said about adrenalin yourself. What happens with a normal adrenalin surge is that after a while an enzyme comes along to disperse some of it while much gets stored for future use. Cocaine blocks the storage uptake, so the adrenalin goes roaring round the body for much longer. When the cocaine decays, its chief metabolic product is benzyl ecognine which is what the lab found in its gas chromatograph analyser this afternoon.'

'There were some cases in America...' I said vaguely.

'It's still not part of a regulation dope test even there.'

'But my God,' I said blankly, 'Nicholas Loder must have known.'

'Almost certainly, I should think. You'd have to administer the cocaine very soon before the race, because its effect is short lived. One hour, an hour and a half at most. It's difficult to tell, with a horse. There's no data. And although the metabolite would appear in the blood and the urine soon after that, the metabolite itself would be detectable for probably not much longer than forty-eight hours, but with a horse, that's still a guess. We took the sample from Dozen Roses on Monday evening about fifty-two hours after he'd raced. The lab said the metabolite was definitely present, but they could make no estimate of how much cocaine had been assimilated. They told me all this very carefully. They have much more experience with humans. They say in humans the rush from cocaine is fast, lasts about forty minutes and brings little post-exhilaration depression.'

'Nice,' I said.

'In horses,' he went on, 'they think it would probably induce skittishness at once.'

I thought back to Dozen Roses's behaviour both at York and on the TV tapes. He'd certainly woken up dramatically between saddling box and starting gate.

'But,' Phil added, 'they say that at the most it might give more stamina, but not more speed. It wouldn't make the horse go faster, but just make the adrenalin push last longer.'

That might be enough sometimes, I thought. Sometimes you could feel horses 'die' under you near the finish, not from lack of ability, but from lack of perseverance, of fight. Some horses were content to be second. In them, uninhibited adrenalin might perhaps tip the balance.

Caffeine, which had the same potentiating effect, was a prohibited substance in racing.

'Why don't they test for cocaine?' I asked.

'Heaven knows,' Phil said. 'Perhaps because enough to wind up a horse would cost the doper too much to be practicable. I mean . . . more than one could be sure of winning back on a bet. But cocaine's getting cheaper, I'm told. There's more and more of it around.'

'I don't know much about drugs,' I said.

'Where have you been?'

'Not my scene.'

'Do you know what they'd call you in America?'

'What?'

'Straight,' he said.

'I thought that meant heterosexual.'

He laughed. 'That too. You're straight through and through.'

'Phil,' I said, 'what do I do?'

He sobered abruptly. 'God knows. My job ends with passing on the facts. The moral decisions are yours. All I can tell you is that some time before Monday evening Dozen Roses took cocaine into his bloodstream.'

'Via a baster?' I said.

After a short silence he said, 'We can't be sure of that.'

'We can't be sure he didn't.'

'Did I understand right, that Harley Ostermeyer picked up the tube of the baster and gave it to you?'

'That's right,' I said. 'I still have it, but like I told you, it's clean.'

'It might look clean,' he said slowly, 'but if cocaine was blown up it in powder form, there may be particles clinging.'

I thought back to before the race at York.

'When Martha Ostermeyer picked up the blue bulb end and gave it back to Rollway,' I said, 'she was brushing her fingers together afterwards . . . she seemed to be getting rid of dust from her gloves.'

'Oh glory,' Phil said.

I sighed and said, 'If I give the tube to you, can you get it tested without anyone knowing where it came from?'

'Sure. Like the urine, it'll be anonymous. I'll get the lab to do another rush job, if you want. It costs a bit more, though.'

'Get it done, Phil,' I said. 'I can't really decide anything unless I know for sure.'

'Right. Are you coming back here soon?'

'Greville's business takes so much time. I'll be back at the weekend, but I think I'll send the tube to you by carrier, to be quicker. You should get it tomorrow morning.'

'Right,' he said. 'We might get a result late tomorrow. Friday at the latest.'

'Good, and er . . . don't mention it to Milo.'

'No, but why not?'

'He told Nicholas Loder we tested Dozen Roses for tranquillizers and Nicholas Loder was on my phone hitting the roof.'

'Oh God.'

'I don't want him knowing about tests for cocaine. I mean, neither Milo nor Nicholas Loder.'

'You may be sure,' Phil said seriously, 'they won't learn it from me.'

It was the worst dilemma of all, I thought, replacing the receiver.

Was cocaine a stimulant or was it not? The racing authorities didn't think so: didn't test for it. If I believed it didn't effect speed then it was all right to sell Dozen Roses to the Ostermeyers. If I thought he wouldn't have got the race at York without help, then it wasn't all right.

Saxony Franklin needed the Ostermeyers' money.

The worst result would be that, if I banked the money and Dozen Roses never won again and Martha and Harley ever found out I knew the horse had been given cocaine, I could say goodbye to any future Gold Cups or Grand Nationals on Datepalm. They wouldn't forgive the unforgivable.

Dozen Roses had seemed to me to run gamely at York and to battle to the end. I was no longer sure. I wondered now if he'd won all his four races spaced out, as the orthopod would have described it; as high as a kite.

At the best, if I simply kept quiet, banked the money and rode Dozen Roses to a couple of respectable victories, no one would ever know. Or I could inform the Ostermeyers privately, which would upset them.

There would be precious little point in proving to the world that Dozen Roses had been given cocaine (and of course I could do it by calling for a further analysis of the urine sample taken by the officials at York) because if cocaine weren't a specifically banned substance, neither was it a normal nutrient. Nothing that was not a normal nutrient was supposed to be given to thoroughbreds racing in Britain.

If I disclosed the cocaine, would Dozen Roses be disqualified for his win at York? If he were, would Nicholas Loder lose his licence to train?

If I caused so much trouble, I would be finished in racing. Whistleblowers were regularly fired from their jobs.

My advice to myself seemed to be, take the money, keep quiet, hope for the best.

Coward, I thought. Maybe stupid as well.

My thoughts made me sweat.

CHAPTER NINETEEN

June, her hands full of pretty pink beads from the stock-room, said, 'What do we do about more rhodocrosite? We're running out and the suppliers in Hong Kong aren't reliable any more. I was reading in a trade magazine that a man in Germany has some of good quality. What do you think?'

'What would Greville have done?' I asked.

Annette said regretfully, 'He'd have gone to Germany to see. He'd never start buying from a new source without knowing who he was trading with.'

I said to June, 'Make an appointment, say who we are, and book an air ticket.'

They both simultaneously said, 'But . . .' and stopped.

I said mildly, 'You never know whether a horse is going to be a winner until you race it. June's going down to the starting gate.'

June blushed and went away. Annette shook her head doubtfully.

'I wouldn't know rhodocrosite from granite,' I said.

'June does. She knows its price, knows what sells. I'll trust that knowledge until she proves me wrong.'

'She's too young to make decisions,' Annette objected.

'Decisions are easier when you're young.'

Isn't that the truth, I thought wryly, rehearsing my own words. At June's age I'd been full of certainties. At June's age, what would I have done about cocaine-positive urine tests? I didn't know. Impossible to go back.

I said I would be off for the day and would see them all in the morning. Dilemmas could be shelved, I thought. The evening was Clarissa's.

Brad, I saw, down in the yard, had been reading the *Racing Post* which had the same photograph as the *Daily Sensation*. He pointed to the picture when I eased in beside him, and I nodded.

'That's your head,' he said.

'Mm.'

'Bloody hell,' he said.

I smiled. 'It seems a long time ago.'

He drove to Greville's house and came in with me while I went upstairs and put the baster tube into an envelope and then into a jiffy bag brought from the office for the purpose and addressed it to Phil Urquhart.

To Brad, downstairs again, I said, 'The Euro-Securo couriers' main office is in Oxford Street not very far from the Selfridge Hotel. This is the actual address . . .' I gave it to him. 'Do you think you can find it?'

'Yerss.' He was again affronted.

'I phoned them from the office. They're expecting this. You don't need to pay, they're sending the bill. Just get a receipt. OK?'

'Yerss.'

'Then pick up my friend from the Selfridge Hotel and bring her here. She'll phone for you, so leave it switched on.'

'Yerss.'

'Then go home, if you like.'

He gave me a glowering look but all he said was, 'Same time tomorrow?'

'If you're not bored.'

He gave me a totally unexpected grin. Unnerving, almost, to see that gloom-ridden face break up.

'Best time o' my life,' he said, and departed, leaving me literally gasping.

In bemusement, I went along to the little sitting room and tidied up a bit more of the mess. If Brad enjoyed waiting for hours reading improbable magazines it was all right by me, but I no longer felt in imminent danger of assault or death, and I could drive my car myself if I cared to, and Brad's days as bodyguard/chauffeur were numbered. He must realize it, I thought: he'd clung on to the job several times.

By that Wednesday evening there was a rapid improvement also in the ankle. Bones, as I understood it, always grew new soft tissue at the site of a fracture, as if to stick the pieces together with glue. After eight or nine days, the soft tissue began to harden, the bone getting progressively stronger from then on, and it was in that phase that I'd by then arrived. I laid one of the crutches aside in the sitting room and used the other like a walking stick, and put my left toe down to the carpet for balance if not to bear my full weight.

Distalgesic, I decided, was a thing of the past. I'd drink wine for dinner with Clarissa.

The front door bell rang, which surprised me. It was too early to be Clarissa: Brad couldn't have done the errand and got to the Selfridge and back in the time he'd been gone.

I hopped along to the door and looked through the peep-hole and was astounded to see Nicholas Loder on the doorstep. Behind him, on the path, stood his friend Rollo Rollway, looking boredly around at the small garden.

In some dismay I opened the door and Nicholas Loder immediately said, 'Oh, good. You're in. We happened to be dining in London so as we'd time to spare I thought we'd come round on the off-chance to discuss Gemstones, rather than negotiate on the telephone.'

'But I haven't named a price,' I said.

'Never mind. We can discuss that. Can we come in?'

I shifted backwards reluctantly.

'Well, yes,' I said, looking at my watch. 'But not for long. I have another appointment pretty soon.'

'So have we,' he assured me. He turned round and

waved a beckoning arm to his friend. 'Come on, Rollo, he has time to see us.'

Rollway, looking as if the enterprise were not to his liking, came up the steps and into the house. I turned to lead the way along the passage, ostentatiously not closing the front door behind them as a big hint to them not to stay long.

'The room's in a mess,' I warned them over my shoulder, 'we had a burglar.'

'We?' Nicholas Loder said.

'Greville and I.'

'Oh.'

He said, 'Oh' again when he saw the chrysanthemum pot wedged in the television, but Rollway blinked around in an uninterested fashion as if he saw houses in chaos every day of the week.

Rollway at close quarters wasn't any more attractive than Rollway at a distance: a dull dark lump of a man, thickset, middle-aged and humourless. One could only explain his friendship with the charismatic Loder, I thought, in terms of trainer-owner relationship.

'This is Thomas Rollway,' Nicholas Loder said to me, making belated introductions. 'One of my owners. He's very interested in buying Gemstones.'

Rollway didn't look very interested in anything.

'I'd offer you a drink,' I said, 'but the burglar broke all the bottles.'

Nicholas Loder looked vaguely at the chunks of glass

on the carpet. There had been no diamonds in the bottles. Waste of booze.

'Perhaps we could sit down,' he said.

'Sure.'

He sat in Greville's armchair and Rollway perched on the arm of the second armchair which effectively left me the one upright hard one. I sat on the edge of it, wanting them to hurry, laying the second crutch aside.

I looked at Loder, big, light-haired with brownish eyes, full of ability and not angry with me as he had been in the recent past. It was almost with guilt that I thought of the cocaine analyses going on behind his back when his manner towards me was more normal than at any time since Greville's death. If he'd been like that from the beginning, I'd have seen no reason to have had the tests done.

'Gemstones,' he said, 'what do you want for him?'

I'd seen in the Saxony Franklin ledgers what Gemstones had cost as a yearling, but that had little bearing on his worth two years later. He'd won one race. He was no bright star. I doubled his cost and asked for that.

Nicholas Loder laughed with irony. 'Come on, Derek. Half.'

'Half is what he cost Greville originally,' I said.

His eyes narrowed momentarily and then opened innocently. 'So we've been doing our homework!' He actually smiled. 'I've promised Rollo a reasonable horse at a reasonable price. We all know Gemstones is no world-beater, but there are more races in him. His cost price is perfectly fair. More than fair.'

I thought it quite likely was indeed fair, but Saxony Franklin needed every possible penny.

'Meet me halfway,' I said, 'and he's yours.'

Nicholas raised his eyebrows at his friend for a decision. 'Rollo?'

Rollo's attention seemed to be focused more on the crutch I'd earlier propped unused against a wall rather than on the matter in hand.

'Gemstones is worth that,' Nicholas Loder said to him judiciously, and I thought in amusement that he would get me as much as he could in order to earn himself a larger commission. Trade with the enemy, I thought: build mutual-benefit bridges.

'I don't want Gemstones at any price,' Rollo said, and they were the first words he'd uttered since arriving. His voice was harsh and curiously flat, without inflection. Without emotion, I thought.

Nicholas Loder protested, 'But that's why you wanted to come here! It was your idea to come here.'

Thomas Rollway, as if absentmindedly, stood and picked up the abandoned crutch, turning it upside down and holding it by the end normally near the floor. Then, as if the thought had at that second occurred to him, he bent his knees and swung the crutch round forcefully in a scything movement a bare four inches above the carpet.

It was so totally unexpected that I wasn't quick

enough to avoid it. The elbow-rest and cuff crashed into my left ankle and Rollway came after it like a bull, kicking, punching, overbalancing me, knocking me down.

I was flabbergasted more than frightened, and then furious. It seemed senseless, without reason, unprovoked, out of any sane proportion. Over Rollway's shoulder I glimpsed Nicholas Loder looking dumbfounded, his mouth and eyes stretched open, uncomprehending.

As I struggled to get up, Thomas Rollway reached inside his jacket and produced a handgun; twelve inches of it at least, with the thickened shape of a silencer on the business end.

'Keep still,' he said to me, pointing the barrel at my chest.

A gun ... Simms ... I began dimly to understand and to despair pretty deeply.

Nicholas Loder was shoving himself out of his armchair. 'What are you doing?' His voice was high with alarm, with rising panic.

'Sit down, Nick,' his friend said. 'Don't get up.' And such was the grindingly heavy tone of his unemotional voice that Nicholas Loder subsided, looking overthrown, not believing what was happening.

'But you came to buy his horse,' he said weakly.

'I came to kill him.'

Rollway said it dispassionately, as if it were nothing. But then, he'd tried to before.

Loder's consternation became as deep as my own.

Rollway moved his gun and pointed it at my ankle. I immediately shifted it, trying desperately to get up, and he brought the spitting end back fast into alignment with my heart.

'Keep still,' he said again. His eyes coldly considered me as I half-sat, half-lay on the floor, propped on my elbow and without any weapon within reach, not even the one crutch I'd been using. Then, with as little warning as for his first attack, he stamped hard on my ankle and for good measure ground away with his heel as if putting out a cigarette butt. After that he left his shoe where it was, pressing down on it with his considerable weight.

I swore at him and couldn't move, and thought idiotically, feeling things give way inside there, that it would take me a lot longer now to get fit, and that took my mind momentarily off a bullet that I would feel a lot less, anyway.

'But *why*?' Nicholas Loder asked, wailing. 'Why are you doing this?'

Good question.

Rollway answered it.

'The only successful murders,' he said, 'are those for which there appears to be no motive.'

It sounded like something he'd learned on a course. Something surrealistic. Monstrous.

Nicholas Loder, sitting rigidly to my right in Greville's chair, said with an uneasy attempt at a laugh,

'You're kidding, Rollo, aren't you? This is some sort of joke?'

Rollo was not kidding. Rollo, standing determinedly on my ankle between me and the door, said to me, 'You picked up a piece of my property at York races. When I found it was missing I went back to look for it. An official told me you'd put it in your pocket. I want it back.'

I said nothing.

Damn the official, I thought. So helpful. So deadly. I hadn't even noticed one watching.

Nicholas Loder, bewildered, said, 'What piece of property?'

'The tube part of the nebulizer,' Rollway told him.

'But that woman, Mrs Ostermeyer, gave it back to you.'

'Only the bulb. I didn't notice the tube had dropped as well. Not until after the race. After the Stewards' enquiry.'

'But what does it matter?'

Rollway pointed his gun unwaveringly at where it would do me fatal damage and answered the question without taking his gaze from my face.

'You yourself, Nick,' he informed him, 'told me you were worried about Franklin, he was observant and too bright.'

'But that was because I gelded Dozen Roses.'

'So when I found he had the nebulizer, I asked one or two other people their opinion of Derek Franklin as a person, not a jockey, and they all said the same. Brainy. Intelligent. Bright.' He paused. 'I don't like that.'

I was thinking that through the door, down the passage and in the street there was sanity and Wednesday and rain and rush hour all going on as usual. Saturn was just as accessible.

'I don't believe in waiting for trouble,' Rollway said. 'And dead men can't make accusations.' He stared at me. 'Where's the tube?'

I didn't answer for various reasons. If he took murder so easily in his stride and I told him I'd sent the tube to Phil Urquhart I could be sentencing Phil to death too, and besides, if I opened my mouth for any reason, what might come out wasn't words at all but something between a yell and a groan, a noise I could hear loudly in my head but which wasn't important either, or not as important as getting out of the sickening prospect of the next few minutes.

'But he would never have suspected . . .' Loder feebly said.

'Of course he did. Anyone would. Why do you think he's had that bodyguard glued to him? Why do you think he's been dodging about so I can't find him and not going home? And he had the horse's urine taken in Lambourn for testing, and there's the official sample too at York. I tell you, I'm not waiting for him to make trouble. I'm not going to gaol, I'll tell you.'

'But you wouldn't.'

'Be your age, Nick,' Rollway said caustically, 'I import the stuff. I take the risks. And I get rid of trouble as soon as I see it. If you wait too long, trouble can destroy you.'

Nicholas Loder said in wailing protest, 'I told you it wasn't necessary to give it to horses. It doesn't make them go faster.'

'Rubbish. You can't tell, because it isn't much done. No one can afford it except people like me. I'm swamped with the stuff at the moment, it's coming in bulk from the Medellin cartel in Madrid ... *Where's the tube?*' he finished, bouncing his weight up and down.

If not telling him would keep me alive a bit longer, I wasn't going to try telling him I'd thrown it away.

'You can't just shoot him,' Nicholas Loder said despairingly. 'Not with me watching.'

'You're no danger to me, Nick,' Rollway said flatly. 'Where would you go for your little habit? One squeak from you would mean your own ruin. I'd see you went down for possession. For conniving with me to drug horses. They'd take your licence away for that. Nicholas Loder, trainer of Classic winners, down in the gutter.' He paused. 'You'll keep quiet, we both know it.'

The threats were none the lighter for being uttered in a measured unexcited monotone. He made my hair bristle. Heaven knew what effect he had on Loder.

He wouldn't wait much longer, I thought, for me to tell him where the tube was: and maybe the tube would in the end indeed be his downfall because Phil knew whose it was, and that the Ostermeyers had been witnesses, and if I were found shot perhaps he would light a long fuse ... but it wasn't of much comfort at that moment.

With the strength of desperation I rolled my body and with my right foot kicked hard at Rollway's leg. He grunted and took his weight off my ankle and I pulled away from him, shuffling backwards, trying to reach the chair I'd been sitting on to use it as a weapon against him, or at least not to lie there supinely waiting to be slaughtered, and I saw him recover his rocked balance and begin to straighten his arm, aiming and looking along the barrel so as not to miss.

That unmistakable stance was going to be the last thing I would see: and the last emotion I would feel would be the blazing fury of dying for so pointless a cause.

Nicholas Loder, also seeing that it was the moment of irretrievable crisis, sprang with horror from the armchair and shouted urgently, 'No, no, Rollo. No, don't do it!'

It might have been the droning of a gnat for all the notice Rollo paid him.

Nicholas Loder took a few paces forward and grabbed at Rollway and at his aiming arm.

I took the last opportunity to get my hands on something ... anything ... got my fingers on a crutch.

'I won't let you,' Nicholas Loder frantically persisted. 'You mustn't!'

Rollo shook him off and swung his gun back to me.

'No.' Loder was terribly disturbed. Shocked. Almost frenzied. 'It's wrong. I won't let you.' He put his body against Rollway's, trying to push him away.

Rollway shrugged him off, all bull-muscle and undeterrable. Then, very fast, he pointed the gun straight at Nicholas Loder's chest and without pausing pulled the trigger. Pulled it twice.

I heard the rapid phut, phut. Saw Nicholas Loder fall, saw the blankness on his face, the absolute astonishment.

There was no time to waste on terror, though I felt it. I gripped the crutch I'd reached and swung the heavier end of it at Rollway's right hand, and landed a blow fierce enough to make him drop the gun.

It fell out of my reach.

I stretched for it and rolled and scrambled but he was upright and much faster, and he bent down and took it into his hand again with a tight look of fury as hot as my own.

He began to lift his arm again in my direction and again I whipped at him with the crutch and again hit him. He didn't drop the gun that time but transferred it to his left hand and shook out the fingers of his right hand as if they hurt, which I hoped to God they did.

I slashed at his legs. Another hit. He retreated a couple of paces and with his left hand began to take aim. I slashed at him. The gun barrel wavered. When he pulled the trigger, the flame spat out and the bullet missed me.

He was still between me and the door.

Ankle or not, I thought, once I was on my feet I'd smash him down and out of the way and run, run . . . run into the street . . .

I had to get up. Got as far as my knees. Stood up on my right foot. Put down the left. It wasn't a matter of pain. I didn't feel it. It just buckled. It needed the crutch's help . . . and I needed the crutch to fight against his gun, to hop and shuffle forward and hack at him, to put off the inevitable moment, to fight until I was dead.

A figure appeared abruptly in the doorway, seen peripherally in my vision.

Clarissa.

I'd forgotten she was coming.

'Run,' I shouted agonizedly. 'Run. Get away.'

It startled Rollway. I'd made so little noise. He seemed to think the instructions were for himself. He sneered. I kept my eyes on his gun and lunged at it, making his aim swing wide again at a crucial second. He pulled the trigger. Flame. Phut. The bullet zipped over my shoulder and hit the wall.

'Run,' I yelled again with fearful urgency. 'Quick. Oh, be quick.'

Why didn't she run? He'd see her if he turned.

He would kill her.

Clarissa didn't run. She brought her hand out of her raincoat pocket holding a thing like a black cigar and she swung her arm in a powerful arc like an avenging fury. Out of the black tube sprang the fearsome telescopic silvery springs with a knob on the end, and the kiyoga smashed against the side of Rollway's skull.

He fell without a sound. Fell forward, cannoning into me, knocking me backwards. I ended on the floor, sitting, his inert form stomach-down over my shins.

Clarissa came down on her knees beside me, trembling violently, very close to passing out. I was breathless, shattered, trembling like her. It seemed ages before either of us was able to speak. When she could, it was a whisper, low and distressed.

'Derek . . .'

'Thanks,' I said jerkily, 'for saving my life.'

'Is he dead?' She was looking with fear at Rollway's head, strain in her eyes, in her neck, in her voice.

'I don't care if he is,' I said truthfully.

'But I . . . I hit him.'

'I'll say I did it. Don't worry. I'll say I hit him with the crutch.'

She said waveringly, 'You can't.'

'Of course I can. I meant to, if I could.'

I glanced over at Nicholas Loder, and Clarissa seemed to see him for the first time. He was on his back, unmoving.

'Dear God,' she said faintly, her face even paler. 'Who's that?'

I introduced her posthumously to Nicholas Loder, racehorse trainer, and then to Thomas Rollway, drug baron. They'd squirted cocaine into Dozen Roses, I said, struggling for lightness. I'd found them out. Rollway wanted me dead rather than giving evidence against him. He'd said so.

Neither of the men contested the charges, though Rollway at least was alive, I thought. I could feel his breathing on my legs. A pity, on the whole. I told Clarissa which made her feel a shade happier.

Clarissa still held the kiyoga. I touched her hand, brushing my fingers over hers, grateful beyond expression for her courage. Greville had given her the kiyoga. He couldn't have known it would keep me alive. I took it gently out of her grasp and let it lie on the carpet.

'Phone my car,' I said. 'If Brad hasn't gone too far, he'll come back.'

'But . . .'

'He'll take you safely back to the Selfridge. Phone quickly.'

'I can't just . . . leave you.'

'How would you explain being here, to the police?'

She looked at me in dismay and obstinacy. 'I can't . . .'

'You must,' I said. 'What do you think Greville would want?'

'Oh . . .' It was a long sigh of grief, both for my brother and, I thought, for the evening together that she and I were not now going to have.

'Do you remember the number?' I said.

'Derek . . .'

'Go and do it, my dear love.'

She got blindly to her feet and went over to the telephone. I told her the number, which she'd forgotten. When the impersonal voice of the radio-phone operator said as usual after six or seven rings that there was no reply, I asked her to dial the number again, and yet again. With luck, Brad would reckon three calls spelled emergency.

'When we got here,' Clarissa said, sounding stronger, 'Brad told me there was a grey Volvo parked not far from your gate. He was worried, I think. He asked me to tell you. Is it important?'

God in heaven . . .

'Will that phone stretch over here?' I said. 'See if it will. Push the table over. Pull the phone over here. If I ring the police from here, and they find me here, they'll take the scene for granted.'

She tipped the table on its side, letting the answering machine fall to the floor, and pulled the phone to the end of its cord. I still couldn't quite reach it, and edged round a little in order to do so, and it hurt, which she saw.

'Derek!'

'Never mind.' I smiled at her, twistedly, making a joke of it. 'It's better than death.'

'I can't leave you.' Her eyes were still strained and she was still visibly trembling, but her composure was on the way back.

'You damned well can,' I said. 'You have to. Go out to the gate. If Brad comes, get him to toot the horn, then I'll know you're away and I'll phone the police. If he doesn't come ... give him five minutes, then walk ... walk and get a taxi ... Promise?'

I picked up the kiyoga and fumbled with it, trying to concertina it shut. She took it out of my hands, twisted it, banged the knob on the carpet and expertly returned it closed to her pocket.

'I'll think of you, and thank you,' I said, 'every day that I live.'

'At four-twenty,' she said as if automatically, and then paused and looked at me searchingly. 'It was the time I met Greville.'

'Four-twenty,' I said, and nodded. 'Every day.'

She knelt down again beside me and kissed me, but it wasn't passion. More like farewell.

'Go on,' I said. 'Time to go.'

She rose reluctantly and went to the doorway, pausing there and looking back. Lady Knightwood, I thought, a valiant deliverer with not a hair out of place.

'Phone me,' I said, 'one day soon?'

'Yes.'

She went quietly down the passage but wasn't gone long. Brad himself came bursting into the room with Clarissa behind him like a shadow.

Brad almost skidded to a halt, the prospect before him enough to shock even the garrulous to silence.

'Strewth,' he said economically.

'As you say,' I replied.

Rollway had dropped his gun when he fell but it still lay not far from his left hand. I asked Brad to move it further away in case the drug man woke up.

'Don't touch it,' I said sharply as he automatically reached out a hand, bending down. 'Your prints would be an embarrassment.'

He made a small grunt of acknowledgement and Clarissa wordlessly held out a tissue with which Brad gingerly took hold of the silencer and slid the gun across the room to the window.

'What if he does wake up?' he said, pointing to Rollway.

'I give him another clout with the crutch.'

He nodded as if that were normal behaviour.

'Thanks for coming back,' I said.

'Didn't go far. You've got a Volvo . . .'

I nodded.

'Is it the one?'

'Sure to be,' I said.

'Strewth.'

'Take my friend back to the Selfridge,' I said. 'Forget she was here. Forget you were here. Go home.'

'Can't leave you,' he said. 'I'll come back.'

'The police will be here.'

As ever, the thought of policemen made him uneasy. 'Go on home,' I said. 'The dangers are over.'

He considered it. Then he said hopefully, 'Same time tomorrow?'

841

I moved my head in amused assent and said wryly, 'Why not?'

He seemed satisfied in a profound way, and he and Clarissa went over to the doorway, pausing there and looking back, as she had before. I gave them a brief wave, and they waved back before going. They were both, incredibly, smiling.

'Brad!' I yelled after him.

He came back fast, full of instant alarm.

'Everything's fine,' I said. 'Just fine. But don't shut the front door behind you. I don't want to have to get up to let the police in. I don't want them smashing the locks. I want them to walk in here nice and easy.'

CHAPTER TWENTY

It was a long dreary evening, but not without humour.

I sat quietly apart most of the time in Greville's chair, largely ignored while relays of people came and efficiently measured, photographed, took fingerprints and dug bullets out of the walls.

There had been a barrage of preliminary questions in my direction which had ended with Rollway groaning his way back to consciousness. Although the police didn't like advice from a civilian, they did, at my mild suggestion, handcuff him before he was fully awake, which was just as well, as the bullish violence was the first part of his personality to surface. He was on his feet, threshing about, mumbling, before he knew where he was.

While a policeman on each side of him held his arms, he stared at me, his eyes slowly focusing. I was still at that time on the floor, thankful to have his weight off me. He looked as if he couldn't believe what was happening, and in the same flat uninflected voice as before, called me a bastard, among other things not as innocuous.

'I knew you were trouble,' he said. He was still too groggy to keep a rein on his tongue. 'You won't live to give evidence, I'll see to that.'

The police phlegmatically arrested him formally, told him his rights and said he would get medical attention at the police station. I watched him stumble away, thinking of the irony of the decision I'd made earlier not to accuse him of anything at all, much less, as now, of shooting people. I hadn't known he'd shot Simms. I hadn't feared him at all. It didn't seem to have occurred to him that I might not act against him on the matter of cocaine. He'd been ready to kill to prevent it. Yet I hadn't suspected him even of being a large-scale dealer until he'd boasted of it.

While the investigating activity went on around me, I wondered if it were because drug runners cared so little for the lives of others that they came so easily to murder.

Like Vaccaro, I thought, gunning down his renegade pilots from a moving car. Perhaps that was an habitual mode of clean-up among drug kings. Copycat murder, everyone had thought about Simms, and everyone had been right.

People like Rollway and Vaccaro held other people's lives cheap because they aimed anyway at destroying them. They made addiction and corruption their business, wilfully intended to profit from the collapse and unhappiness of countless lives, deliberately enticed young people onto a one-way misery trail. I'd read that people could snort cocaine for two or three years before the physical damage hit. The drug growers, shippers, wholesalers knew that. It gave them time for steady selling. Their greed had filthy feet.

The underlying immorality, the aggressive callousness had themselves to be corrupting; addictive. Rollway had self destructed, like his victims.

I wondered how people grew to be like him. I might condemn them, but I didn't understand them. They weren't happy-go-lucky dishonest, like Pross. They were uncaring and cold. As Eliot Trelawney had said, the logic of criminals tended to be weird. If I ever added to Greville's notebook, I thought, it would be something like 'The ways of the crooked are mysterious to the straight', or even 'What makes the crooked crooked and the straight straight?' One couldn't trust the sociologists' easy answers.

I remembered an old story I'd heard sometime. A scorpion asked a horse for a ride across a raging torrent. Why not? said the horse, and obligingly started to swim with the scorpion on his back. Halfway across, the scorpion stung the horse. The horse, fatally poisoned, said, 'We will both drown now. Why did you do that?' And the scorpion said, 'Because it's my nature.'

Nicholas Loder wasn't going to worry or wonder about anything any more; and his morality, under stress, had risen up unblemished and caused his death. Injustice and irony everywhere, I thought, and felt regret for the man who couldn't acquiesce in my murder.

He had taken cocaine himself, that much was clear. He'd become perhaps dependent on Rollway, had perhaps been more or less blackmailed by him into allowing his horses to be tampered with. He'd been frightened I would find him out: but in the end he hadn't been evil, and Rollway had seen it, had seen he couldn't trust him to keep his mouth shut after all.

Through Loder, Rollway had known where to find me on Sunday afternoon, and through him he'd known where to find me this Wednesday evening. Yet Nicholas Loder hadn't knowingly set me up. He'd been used by his supposed friend; and I hadn't seen any danger in reporting on Sunday morning that I'd be lunching with Milo and the Ostermeyers or saying I would be in Greville's house ready for Gemstones bids.

I hadn't specifically been keeping myself safe from Rollway, whatever he might believe, but from an unidentified enemy, someone *there* and dangerous, but unrecognized.

Irony everywhere . . .

I thought about Martha and Harley and the cocaine in Dozen Roses. I would ask them to keep the horse and race him, and I'd promise that if he never did any good I would give them their money back and send him to auction. What the Jockey Club and the racing press would have to say about the whole mess boggled the mind. We might still lose the York race: would have to, I guessed.

I thought of Clarissa in the Selfridge Hotel struggling to behave normally with a mind filled with visions of violence. I hoped she would ring up her Henry, reach back to solid ground, mourn Greville peacefully, be glad she'd saved his brother. I would leave the Wizard's alarm set to four-twenty pm, and remember them both when I heard it: and one could say it was sentimental, that their whole affair had been packed with sentimental behaviour, but who cared, they'd enjoyed it, and I would endorse it.

At some point in the evening's proceedings, a highly senior plain-clothes policeman arrived whom everyone else deferred to and called sir.

He introduced himself as Superintendent Ingold and invited a detailed statement from me, which a minion wrote down. The superintendent was short, piercing, businesslike, and considered what I said with pauses before his next question, as if internally computing my answers. He was also, usefully, a man who liked racing: who sorrowed over Nicholas Loder and knew of my existence.

I told him pretty plainly most of what had happened, omitting only a few things: the precise way Rollway had asked for his tube, and Clarissa's presence, and the dire desperation of the minutes before she'd arrived. I made that hopeless fight a lot shorter, a lot easier, a rapid knock-out.

'The crutches?' he enquired. 'What are they for?'

'A spot of trouble with an ankle at Cheltenham.'

'When was that?'

'Nearly two weeks ago.'

He merely nodded. The crutch handles were quite heavy enough for clobbering villains, and he sought no other explanation.

It all took a fair while, with the pauses and the writing. I told him about the car crash near Hungerford. I said I thought it possible that it had been Rollway who shot Simms. I said that of course they would compare the bullets the Hungerford police had taken from the Daimler with those just now dug out of Greville's walls, and those no doubt to be retrieved from Nicholas Loder's silent form. I wondered innocently what sort of car Rollway drove. The Hungerford police, I told the superintendent, were looking for a grey Volvo.

After a pause a policeman was despatched to search the street. He came back wide-eyed with his news and was told to put a cordon round the car and keep the public off.

It was by then well past dark. Every time the police or officials came into the house, the mechanical dog started barking and the lights repeatedly blazed on. I thought it amusing which says something for my light-headed state of mind but it wore the police nerves to irritation.

'The switches are beside the front door,' I said to one of them eventually. 'Why don't you flip them all up?'

They did, and got peace.

'Who threw the flower-pot into the television?' the superintendent wanted to know.

'Burglars. Last Saturday. Two of your men came round.'

'Are you ill?' he said abruptly.

'No. Shaken.'

He nodded. Anyone would be, I thought.

One of the policemen mentioned Rollway's threat that I wouldn't live to give evidence. To be taken seriously, perhaps.

Ingold looked at me speculatively. 'Does it worry you?'

'I'll try to be careful.'

He smiled faintly. 'Like on a horse?' The smile disappeared. 'You could do worse than hire someone to mind your back for a while.'

I nodded my thanks. Brad, I thought dryly, would be ecstatic.

They took poor Nicholas Loder away. I would emphasize his bravery, I thought, and save what could be saved of his reputation. He had given me, after all, a chance of life.

Eventually the police wanted to seal the sitting room, although the superintendent said it was a precaution only: the events of the evening seemed crystal clear.

He handed me the crutches and asked where I would be going.

'Upstairs to bed,' I said.

'Here?' He was surprised. 'In this house?'

'This house,' I said, 'is a fortress. Until one lowers the drawbridge, that is.'

They sealed the sitting room, let themselves out, and left me alone in the newly quiet hallway.

I sat on the stairs and felt awful. Cold. Shivery. Old and grey. What I needed was a hot drink to get warm from inside, and there was no way I was going down to the kitchen. Hot water from the bathroom tap upstairs would do fine, I thought.

As happened in many sorts of battle, it wasn't the moment of injury that was worst, but the time a couple of hours later when the body's immediate natural anaesthetic properties subsided and let pain take over: nature's marvellous system for allowing a wild animal to flee to safety before hiding to lick its wounds with healing saliva. The human animal was no different. One needed the time to escape, and one needed the pain afterwards to say something was wrong.

At the moment of maximum adrenalin, fight-or-flight, I'd believed I could run on that ankle. It had been mechanics that had defeated me, not instinct, not willingness. Two hours later, the idea of even standing on it was impossible. Movement alone became breathtaking. I'd sat in Greville's chair for another two long hours after that, concentrating on policemen, blanking out feeling.

With them gone, there was no more pretending. However much I might protest in my mind, however much rage I might feel, I knew the damage to bones and ligaments was about as bad as before. Rollway had cracked them apart again. Back to square one . . . and the Hennessy only four and a half weeks away . . . and I was bloody well going to ride Datepalm in it, and I wasn't going to tell anyone about tonight's little stamping-ground, no one knew except Rollway and he wouldn't boast about that.

If I stayed away from Lambourn for two weeks, Milo wouldn't find out; not that he would himself care all that much. If he didn't know, though, he couldn't mention it to anyone else. No one expected me to be racing again for another four weeks. If I simply stayed in London for two of those and ran Greville's business, no one would comment. Then once I could walk I'd go down to Lambourn and ride every day . . . get physiotherapy, borrow the Electrovet . . . it could be done . . . piece of cake.

Meanwhile there were the stairs.

Up in Greville's bathroom, in a zipped bag with my washing things, I would find the envelope the orthopaedic surgeon had given me, which I'd tucked into a waterproof pocket and travelled around with ever since. In the envelope, three small white tablets not as big as aspirins, more or less with my initials on: DF 1–1–8s. Only as a last resort, the orthopod had said.

Wednesday evening, I reckoned, qualified.

I went up the stairs slowly, backwards, sitting down,

hooking the crutches up with me. If I dropped them, I thought, they would slither down to the bottom again. I wouldn't drop them.

It was pretty fair hell. I reminded myself astringently that people had been known to crawl down mountains with much worse broken bones: they wouldn't have made a fuss over one little flight upwards. Anyway, there had to be an end to everything, and eventually I sat on the top step, with the crutches beside me, and thought that the DF 1–1–8s weren't going to fly along magically to my tongue. I had still got to get them.

I shut my eyes and put both hands round my ankle on top of the bandage. I could feel the heat and it was swelling again already, and there was a pulse hammering somewhere.

Damn it, I thought. God bloody damn it. I was used to this sort of pain, but it never made it any better. I hoped Rollway's head was banging like crazy.

I made it to the bathroom, ran the hot water, opened the door of the capacious medicine cabinet, pulled out and unzipped my bag.

One tablet, no pain, I thought. Two tablets, spaced out. Three tablets, unconscious.

Three tablets had definite attractions but I feared I might wake in the morning needing them again and wishing I'd been wiser. I swallowed one with a glassful of hot water and waited for miracles.

The miracle that actually happened was extraordinary but had nothing to do with the pills.

I stared at my grey face in the looking glass over the basin. Improvement, I thought after a while, was a long time coming. Perhaps the damned things didn't work.

Be patient.

Take another . . .

No. Be patient.

I looked vaguely at the objects in the medicine cupboard. Talc. Deodorant. Shaving cream. Shaving cream. Most of one can of shaving cream had been squirted all over the mirror by Jason. A pale blue and grey can: 'Unscented,' it said.

Greville had an electric razor as well, I thought inconsequentially. It was on the dressing chest. I'd borrowed it that morning. Quicker than a wet shave, though not so long lasting.

The damn pill wasn't working.

I looked at the second one longingly.

Wait a bit.

Think about something else.

I picked up the second can of shaving cream which was scarlet and orange and said: 'Regular Fragrance'. I shook the can and took off the cover and tried to squirt foam onto the mirror.

Nothing happened. I shook it. Tried again. Nothing at all.

Guile and misdirection, I thought. Hollow books and green stone boxes with keyholes but no keys. Safes in concrete, secret drawers in desks . . . Take nothing at face value. Greville's mind was a maze ... *and he wouldn't have used scented shaving cream.*

I twisted the shaving cream can this way and that and the bottom ring moved and began to turn in my hand. I caught my breath. Didn't really believe it. I went on turning ... unscrewing.

It would be another empty hiding place, I told myself. Get a grip on hope. I unscrewed the whole bottom off the can, and from a nest of cottonwool a chamois leather pouch fell out into my hand.

Well, all right, I thought, but it wouldn't be diamonds.

With the help of the crutches I took the pouch into the bedroom and sat on Greville's bed, and poured onto the counterpane a little stream of dullish-looking pea-sized lumps of carbon.

I almost stopped breathing. Time stood still. I couldn't believe it. Not after everything ...

With shaking fingers I counted them, setting them in small clumps of five.

Ten ... fifteen ... twenty ... twenty-five.

Twenty-five meant I'd got fifty per cent. Half of what Greville had bought. With half, Saxony Franklin would be safe. I offered heartbursting thanks to the fates. I came dangerously near to crying.

Then, with a sense of revelation, I knew where the rest were. Where they had to be. Greville really had taken them with him to Ipswich, as he'd told Pross. I guessed he'd taken them thinking he might give them to the Maarten-Pagnier partner to take back to Antwerp for cutting.

I'd searched through the things in his car and had found nothing, and I'd held his diamonds in my hand and not known it.

They were . . . they had to be . . . in that other scarlet and orange can, in the apparent can of shaving cream in his overnight bag, safe as Fort Knox under the stairs of Brad's mum's house in Hungerford. She'd taken all Greville's things in off the street out of my car to keep them safe in a dodgy neighbourhood. In memory, I could hear Brad's pride in her.

'Smart, our Mum . . .'

The DF 1–1–8 was at last taking the edge off the worst.

I rolled the twenty-five precious pebbles around under my fingers with indescribable joy and thought how relieved Greville would have been. Sleep easy, pal, I told him, uncontrollably smiling. I've finally found them.

He'd left me his business, his desk, his gadgets, his enemies, his horses, his mistress. Left me Saxony Franklin, the Wizard, the shaving cream cans, Prospero Jenks and Nicholas Loder, Dozen Roses, Clarissa.

I'd inherited his life and laid him to rest; and at that moment, though I might hurt and I might throb, I didn't think I had ever been happier.

HIGH STAKES

INTRODUCTION

It's impossible sometimes for an author to remember exactly what sight or sound kicked his imagination's starter-motor into life. I think that for *High Stakes* the basic idea arose simply from an abstract contemplation of the consequences of a betrayal of trust – in this case the blind trust of an enthusiastic but ignorant owner of racehorses in the friendship, good faith and honesty of his trainer.

I grafted on to this concept the all-too-common phenomenon of the sinner being seen as the victim in the public mind, while the real victim is cast as the sinner. I was much taken at that time by a bitter joke about a man who fell among thieves who robbed him, beat him and left him for dead in the gutter. Along came two social workers who looked at his wounds and said, 'The man who did this needs our help.'

My betrayed racehorse owner, victim cast as sinner, became Steven Scott, chief character of *High Stakes*. I gave him a mind that worked more comfortably in circles than in straight lines, and I made him an inventor of rotary gadgets and toys.

To defeat his enemies Scott gathered round him a circle of friends, and devised a circular conjuring trick with horses.

By this time thinking in circles myself, I borrowed the essentials of a belt-driven power system installed in my father-in-law's printing factory and translated them into a simplified version for Steven Scott's workshop.

On the ground floor of the factory, the thunder of the monster rollers on the huge printing presses made talking impossible. On the next floor came medium machines with, on the top floor, quietly clack-clacking contraptions that sorted, cut, glued and counted. All the machines on the two upper floors were driven by a weighty ground-floor engine that set heavy belts revolving on central spindles running the lengths of the upper-floor ceilings. Though nowadays no doubt every machine is individually powered by electricity, the centrally powered belt system ran economically for generations.

A man was killed in my father-in-law's factory. I used that, too, in *High Stakes*.

CHAPTER ONE

I looked at my friend and saw a man who had robbed me. Deeply disturbing. The ultimate in rejection.

Jody Leeds looked back at me, half smiling, still disbelieving.

'You're *what*?'

'Taking my horses away,' I said.

'But . . . I'm your *trainer*.' He sounded bewildered. Owners, his voice and expression protested, never deserted their trainers. It simply wasn't done. Only the eccentric or the ruthless shifted their horses from stable to stable, and I had shown no signs of being either.

We stood outside the weighing room of Sandown Park racecourse on a cold windy day with people scurrying past us carrying out saddles and number cloths for the next steeplechase. Jody hunched his shoulders inside his sheepskin coat and shook his bare head. The wind blew straight brown hair in streaks across his eyes and he pulled them impatiently away.

'Come on, Steven,' he said. 'You're kidding me.'

'No.'

Jody was short, stocky, twenty-eight, hardworking, clever, competent and popular. He had been my constant adviser since I had bought my first racehorses three years earlier, and right from the beginning he had robbed me round the clock and smiled while doing it.

'You're crazy,' he said. 'I've just won you a race.'

We stood, indeed, on the patch of turf where winners were unsaddled: where Energise, my newest and glossiest hurdler, had recently decanted his smiling jockey, had stamped and steamed and tossed his head with pride and accepted the crowd's applause as simply his due.

The race he had won had not been important, but the way he had won it had been in the star-making class. The sight of him sprinting up the hill to the winning post, a dark brown streak of rhythm, had given me a rare bursting feeling of admiration, of joy... probably even of love. Energise was beautiful and courageous and chockfull of will to win and it was because he had won, and won in that fashion, that my hovering intention to break with Jody had hardened into action.

I should, I suppose, have chosen a better time and place.

'I picked out Energise for you at the Sales,' he said.

'I know.'

'And all your other winners.'

'Yes.'

'And I moved into bigger stables because of you.'

I nodded briefly.

'Well . . . You can't let me down now.'

Disbelief had given way to anger. His bright blue eyes sharpened to belligerence and the muscles tightened round his mouth.

'I'm taking the horses away,' I repeated. 'And we'll start with Energise. You can leave him here when you go home.'

'You're mad.'

'No.'

'Where's he going then?'

I actually had no idea. I said, 'I'll make all the arrangements. Just leave him in the stable here and go home without him.'

'You've no right to do this.' Full-scale anger blazed in his eyes. 'You're a bloody rotten *shit*.'

But I had every right. He knew it and I knew it. Every owner had the right at any time to withdraw his custom if he were dissatisfied with his trainer. The fact that the right was seldom exercised was beside the point.

Jody was rigid with fury. 'I am taking that horse home with me and nothing is going to stop me.'

His very intensity stoked up in me an answering determination that he should not. I shook my head decisively. I said, 'No, Jody. The horse stays here.'

'Over my dead body.'

His body, alive, quivered with pugnaciousness.

'As of this moment,' I said, 'I'm cancelling your authority to act on my behalf, and I'm going straight into the weighing room to make that clear to all the authorities who need to know.'

He glared. 'You owe me money,' he said. 'You can't take your horses away until you've paid.'

I paid my bills with him on the nail every month and owed him only for the current few weeks. I pulled my cheque book out of my pocket and unclipped my pen.

'I'll give you a cheque right now.'

'No you bloody well won't.'

He snatched the whole cheque book out of my hand and ripped it in two. Then in the same movement he threw the pieces over his shoulder, and all the loose halves of the cheques scattered in the wind. Faces turned our way in astonishment and the eyes of the Press came sharply to life. I couldn't have chosen anywhere more public for what was developing into a first class row.

Jody looked around him. Looked at the men with notebooks. Saw his allies.

His anger grew mean.

'You'll be sorry,' he said. 'I'll chew you into little bits.'

The face that five minutes earlier had smiled with cheerful decisive friendliness had gone for good. Even if I now retracted and apologised, the old relationship could not be re-established. Confidence, like Humpty Dumpty, couldn't be put together again.

His fierce opposition had driven me further than I

had originally meant. All the same I still had the same objective, even if I had to fight harder to achieve it.

'Whatever you do,' I said, 'you won't keep my horses.'

'You're ruining me,' Jody shouted.

The Press advanced a step or two.

Jody cast a quick eye at them. Maliciousness flooded through him and twisted his features with spite. 'You big rich bastards don't give a damn who you hurt.'

I turned abruptly away from him and went into the weighing room, and there carried out my promise to disown him officially as my trainer. I signed forms cancelling his authority to act for me, and for good measure also included a separate handwritten note to say that I had expressly forbidden him to remove Energise from Sandown Park. No one denied I had the right: there was just an element of coolness towards one who was so vehemently and precipitately ridding himself of the services of the man who had ten minutes ago given him a winner.

I didn't tell them that it had taken a very long time for the mug to face the fact that he was being conned. I didn't tell them how I had thrust the first suspicions away as disloyalty and had made every possible allowance before being reluctantly convinced.

I didn't tell them either that the reason for my determination now lay squarely in Jody's first reaction to my saying I was removing my horses.

Because he hadn't, not then or afterwards, asked the one natural question.

He hadn't asked *why*.

When I left the weighing room, both Jody and the Press had gone from the unsaddling enclosure. Racegoers were hurrying towards the stands to watch the imminent steeplechase, the richest event of the afternoon, and even the officials with whom I'd just been dealing were dashing off with the same intent.

I had no appetite for the race. Decided, instead, to go down to the racecourse stables and ask the gatekeeper there to make sure Energise didn't vanish in a puff of smoke. But as the gatekeeper was there to prevent villainous strangers walking *in*, not any bona fide racehorses walking *out*, I wasn't sure how much use he would be, even if he agreed to help.

He was sitting in his sentry box, a middle-aged sturdy figure in a navy blue serge uniform with brass buttons. Various lists on clip-boards hung on hooks on the walls, alongside an electric heater fighting a losing battle against the December chill.

'Excuse me,' I said. 'I want to ask you about my horse . . .'

'Can't come in here,' he interrupted bossily. 'No owners allowed in without trainers.'

'I know that,' I said. 'I just want to make sure my horse stays here.'

'What horse is that?'

He was adept at interrupting, like many people in small positions of power. He blew on his fingers and looked at me over them without politeness.

'Energise,' I said.

He screwed up his mouth and considered whether to answer. I supposed that he could find no reason against it except natural unhelpfulness, because in the end he said grudgingly, 'Would it be a black horse trained by Leeds?'

'It would.'

'Gone then,' he said.

'Gone?'

'S'right. Lad took him off, couple of minutes ago.' He jerked his head in the general direction of the path down to the area where the motor horseboxes were parked. 'Leeds was with him. Ask me, they'll have driven off by now.' The idea seemed to cheer him. He smiled.

I left him to his sour satisfaction and took the path at a run. It led down between bushes and opened abruptly straight on to the gravelled acre where dozens of horseboxes stood in haphazard rows.

Jody's box was fawn with scarlet panels along the sides: and Jody's box was already manoeuvring out of its slot and turning to go between two of the rows on its way to the gate.

I slid my binoculars to the ground and left them, and fairly sprinted. Ran in front of the first row of boxes and raced round the end to find Jody's box completing its turn from between the rows about thirty yards away, and accelerating straight towards me.

I stood in its path and waved my arms for the driver to stop.

The driver knew me well enough. His name was Andy-Fred. He drove my horses regularly. I saw his face, looking horrified and strained, as he put his hand on the horn button and punched it urgently.

I ignored it, sure that he would stop. He was advancing between a high wooden fence on one side and the flanks of parked horseboxes on the other, and it wasn't until it became obvious that he didn't know what his brakes were for that it occurred to me that maybe Energise was about to leave over *my* dead body, not Jody's.

Anger, not fear, kept me rooted to the spot.

Andy-Fred's nerve broke first, thank God, but only just. He wrenched the wheel round savagely when the massive radiator grill was a bare six feet from my annihilation and the diesel throb was a roar in my ears.

He had left it too late for braking. The sudden swerve took him flatly into the side of the foremost of the parked boxes and with screeching and tearing sounds of metal the front corner of Jody's box ploughed forwards and inwards until the colliding doors of the cabs of both vehicles were locked in one crumpled mess. Glass smashed and tinkled and flew about with razor edges. The engine stalled and died.

The sharp bits on the front of Jody's box had missed me but the smooth wing caught me solidly as I leapt belatedly to get out of the way. I lay where I'd bounced, half against the wooden fence, and wholly winded.

Andy-Fred jumped down unhurt from the unsmashed side of his cab and advanced with a mixture of fear, fury and relief.

'What the bloody hell d'you think you're playing at?' he yelled.

'Why . . .' I said weakly, 'didn't . . . you . . . stop?'

I doubt if he heard me. In any case, he didn't answer. He turned instead to the exploding figure of Jody, who arrived at a run along the front of the boxes, the same way that I had come.

He practically danced when he saw the crushed cabs and rage poured from his mouth like fire.

'You stupid *bugger*,' he shouted at Andy-Fred. 'You stupid sodding effing . . .'

The burly box driver shouted straight back.

'He stood right in my way.'

'I told you not to stop.'

'I'd have killed him.'

'No you wouldn't.'

'I'm telling you. He stood there. Just stood there . . .'

'He'd have jumped if you'd kept on going. You stupid bugger. Just look what you've done. You stupid . . .'

Their voices rose, loud and acrimonious, into the wind. Further away the commentator's voice boomed over the tannoy system, broadcasting the progress of the steeplechase. On the other side of the high wooden fence the traffic pounded up and down the London to Guildford road. I gingerly picked myself off the cold gravel and leaned against the weathered planks.

Nothing broken. Breath coming back. Total damage, all the buttons missing from my overcoat. There was a row of small right-angled tears down the front where the buttons had been. I looked at them vaguely and knew I'd been lucky.

Andy-Fred was telling Jody at the top of a raucous voice that he wasn't killing anyone for Jody's sake, he was bloody well not.

'You're fired,' Jody yelled.

'Right.'

He took a step back, looked intensely at the mangled horseboxes, looked at me, and looked at Jody. He thrust his face close to Jody's and yelled at him again.

'*Right.*'

Then he stalked away in the direction of the stables and didn't bother to look back.

Jody's attention and fury veered sharply towards me. He took three or four purposeful steps and yelled, 'I'll sue you for this.'

I said, 'Why don't you find out if the horse is all right?'

He couldn't hear me for all the day's other noises.

'What?'

'Energise,' I said loudly. 'Is he all right?'

He gave me a sick hot look of loathing and scudded away round the side of the box. More slowly, I followed. Jody yanked open the groom's single door and hauled himself up inside and I went after him.

Energise was standing in his stall quivering from head to foot and staring wildly about with a lot of white round his eyes. Jody had packed him off still sweating from his race and in no state anyway to travel and the crash had clearly terrified him: but he was none the less on his feet and Jody's anxious search could find no obvious injury.

'No thanks to you,' Jody said bitterly.

'Nor to you.'

We faced each other in the confined space, a quiet oasis out of the wind.

'You've been stealing from me,' I said. 'I didn't want to believe it. But from now on . . . I'm not giving you the chance.'

'You won't be able to prove a thing.'

'Maybe not. Maybe I won't even try. Maybe I'll write off what I've lost as the cost of my rotten judgement in liking and trusting you.'

He said indignantly, 'I've done bloody well for you.'

'And out of me.'

'What do you expect? Trainers aren't in it for love, you know.'

'Trainers don't all do what you've done.'

871

A sudden speculative look came distinctly into his eyes. 'What have I done, then?' he demanded.

'You tell me,' I said. 'You haven't even pretended to deny you've been cheating me.'

'Look, Steven, you're so bloody unworldly. All right, so maybe I have added a bit on here and there. If you're talking about the time I charged you travelling expenses for Hermes to Haydock the day they abandoned for fog before the first . . . well, I know I didn't actually *send* the horse . . . he went lame that morning and couldn't go. But trainer's perks. Fair's fair. And you could afford it. You'd never miss thirty measly quid.'

'What else?' I said.

He seemed reassured. Confidence and a faint note of defensive wheedling seeped into his manner and voice.

'Well . . .' he said. 'If you ever disagreed with the totals of your bills, why didn't you query it with me? I'd have straightened things out at once. There was no need to bottle it all up and blow your top without warning.'

Ouch, I thought. I hadn't even checked that all the separate items on the monthly bills did add up to the totals I'd paid. Even when I was sure he was robbing me, I hadn't suspected it would be in any way so ridiculously simple.

'What else?' I said.

He looked away for a second, then decided that I couldn't after all know a great deal.

'Oh all right,' he said, as if making a magnanimous concession. 'It's Raymond, isn't it?'

'Among other things.'

Jody nodded ruefully. 'I guess I did pile it on a bit, charging you for him twice a week when some weeks he only came once.'

'And some weeks not at all.'

'Oh well . . .' said Jody deprecatingly. 'I suppose so, once or twice.'

Raymond Child rode all my jumpers in races and drove fifty miles some mornings to school them over fences on Jody's gallops. Jody gave him a fee and expenses for the service and added them to my account. The twice a week schooling session fees had turned up regularly for the whole of July, when in fact, as I had very recently and casually discovered, no horses had been schooled at all and Raymond himself had been holidaying in Spain.

'A tenner here or there,' Jody said persuasively. 'It's nothing to you.'

'A tenner plus expenses twice a week for July came to over a hundred quid.'

'Oh.' He tried a twisted smile. 'So you really have been checking up.'

'What did you expect?'

'You're so easy going. You've always paid up without question.'

'Not any more.'

'No . . . Look, Steven, I'm sorry about all this. If I give you my word there'll be no more fiddling on your account . . . If I promise every item will be strictly accurate . . . why don't we go on as before? I've won a lot of races for you, after all.'

He looked earnest, sincere and repentant. Also totally confident that I would give him a second chance. A quick canter from confession to penitence, and a promise to reform, and all could proceed as before.

'It's too late,' I said.

He was not discouraged; just piled on a bit more of the ingratiating manner which announced 'I know I've been a bad bad boy but now I've been found out I'll be angelic.'

'I suppose having so much extra expense made me behave stupidly,' he said. 'The mortgage repayments on the new stables are absolutely bloody, and as you know I only moved there because I needed more room for all your horses.'

My fault, now, that he had had to steal.

I said, 'I offered to build more boxes at the old place.'

'Wouldn't have done,' he interrupted hastily: but the truth of it was that the old place had been on a plain and modest scale where the new one was frankly opulent. At the time of the move I had vaguely wondered how he could afford it. Now, all too well, I knew.

'So let's call this just a warning, eh?' Jody said cajolingly. 'I don't want to lose your horses, Steven. I'll say so frankly. I don't want to lose them. We've been good friends all this time, haven't we? If you'd just *said* I mean, if you'd just said, "Jody, you bugger, you've been careless about a bill or two . . ." Well, I mean, we could have straightened it out in no time. But . . . well . . . When you blew off without warning, just said you were taking the horses away, straight after Energise won like that . . . well, I lost my temper real and proper. I'll admit I did. Said things I didn't mean. Like one does. Like everyone does when they lose their temper.'

He was smiling in a counterfeit of the old way, as if nothing at all had happened. As if Energise were not standing beside us sweating in a crashed horsebox. As if my overcoat were not torn and muddy from a too close brush with death.

'Steven, you know me,' he said. 'Got a temper like a bloody rocket.'

When I didn't answer at once he took my silence as acceptance of his explanations and apologies, and briskly turned to practical matters.

'Well now, we'll have to get this lad out of here.' He slapped Energise on the rump. 'And we can't get the ramp down until we get this box moved away from that other one.' He made a sucking sound through his teeth. 'Look, I'll try to back straight out again. Don't see why it shouldn't work.'

He jumped out of the back door and went round to

the front of the cab. Looking forward through the stalls I could see him climb into the driver's seat, check the gear lever, and press the starter: an intent, active, capable figure dealing with an awkward situation.

The diesel starter whirred and the engine roared to life. Jody settled himself, found reverse gear, and carefully let out the clutch. The horsebox shuddered and stood still. Jody put his foot down on the accelerator.

Through the windscreen I could see two or three men approaching, faces a mixture of surprise and anger. One of them began running and waving his arms about in the classic reaction of the chap who comes back to his parked car to find it dented.

Jody ignored him. The horsebox rocked, the crushed side of the cab screeched against its mangled neighbour, and Energise began to panic.

'Jody, stop,' I yelled.

He took no notice. He raced the engine harder, then took his foot off the accelerator, then jammed it on again. Off, on, repeatedly.

Inside the box it sounded as if the whole vehicle were being ripped in two. Energise began whinnying and straining backwards on his tethering rope and stamping about with sharp hooves. I didn't know how to begin to soothe him and could hardly get close enough for a pat, even if that would have made the slightest difference. My relationship with horses was along the lines of admiring them from a distance and giving them carrots while they were safely tied up. No one had briefed me about dealing with a hysterical animal at close quarters in a bucketing biscuit tin.

With a final horrendous crunch the two entwined cabs tore apart and Jody's box, released from friction, shot backwards. Energise slithered and went down for a moment on his hind-quarters and I too wound up on the floor. Jody slammed on the brakes, jumped out of the cab and was promptly clutched by the three newcomers, one now in a full state of apoplectic rage.

I stood up and picked bits of hay off my clothes and regarded my steaming, foam-flaked, terrified, four-footed property.

'All over, old fellow,' I said.

It sounded ridiculous. I smiled, cleared my throat, tried again.

'You can cool off, old lad. The worst is over.'

Energise showed no immediate signs of getting the message. I told him he was a great horse, he'd won a great race, he'd be king of the castle in no time and that I admired him very much. I told him he would soon be rugged up nice and quiet in a stable somewhere though I hadn't actually yet worked out exactly which one, and that doubtless someone would give him some excessively expensive hay and a bucket of nice cheap water and I dared say some oats and stuff like that. I told him I was sorry I hadn't a carrot in my pocket at that moment but I'd bring him one next time I saw him.

After a time this drivel seemed to calm him. I put

out a hand and gave his neck a small pat. His skin was wet and fiery hot. He shook his head fiercely and blew out vigorously through black moist nostrils, but the staring white no longer showed round his eye and he had stopped trembling. I began to grow interested in him in a way which had not before occurred to me: as a person who happened also to be a horse.

I realised I had never before been alone with a horse. Extraordinary, really, when Energise was the twelfth I'd owned. But racehorse owners mostly patted their horses in stables with lads and trainers in attendance, and in parade rings with all the world looking on, and in unsaddling enclosures with friends pressing round to congratulate. Owners who like me were not riders themselves and had nowhere of their own to turn horses out to grass seldom ever spent more than five consecutive minutes in a horse's company.

I spent longer with Energise in that box than in all the past five months since I'd bought him.

Outside, Jody was having troubles. One of the men had fetched a policeman who was writing purposefully in a notebook. I wondered with amusement just how Jody would lay the blame on my carelessness in walking in front of the box and giving the driver no choice but to swerve. If he thought he was keeping my horses, he would play it down. If he thought he was losing them, he'd be vitriolic. Smiling to myself I talked it over with Energise.

'You know,' I said, 'I don't know why I haven't told

him yet that I know about his other fraud, but as it
turns out I'm damn glad I haven't. Do you know?' I
said. 'All those little fiddles he confessed to, they're just
froth.'

Energise was calm enough to start drooping with
tiredness. I watched him sympathetically.

'It isn't just a few hundred quid he's pinched,' I said.
'It's upwards of thirty-five thousand.'

CHAPTER TWO

The owner of the crunched box accepted my apologies, remembered he was well insured and decided not to press charges. The policeman sighed, drew a line through his notes and departed. Jody let down the ramp of his box, brought out Energise and walked briskly away with him in the direction of the stables. And I returned to my binoculars, took off my battered coat and went thoughtfully back towards the weighing room.

The peace lasted for all of ten minutes – until Jody returned from the stables and found I had not cancelled my cancellation of his authority to act.

He sought me out among the small crowd standing around talking on the weighing room verandah.

'Look, Steven,' he said. 'You've forgotten to tell them I'm still training for you.'

He showed no anxiety, just slight exasperation at my oversight. I weakened for one second at the thought of the storm which would undoubtedly break out again and began to make all the old fatal allowances: he *was* a good trainer, and my horses *did* win, now and again.

And I could keep a sharp eye on the bills and let him know I was doing it. And as for the other thing ... I could easily avoid being robbed in future.

I took a deep breath. It had to be now or never.

'I haven't forgotten,' I said slowly. 'I meant what I said. I'm taking the horses away.'

'*What?*'

'I am taking them away.'

The naked enmity that filled his face was shocking.

'You *bastard*,' he said.

Heads turned again in our direction.

Jody produced several further abusive epithets, all enunciated very clearly in a loud voice. The Press notebooks sprouted like mushrooms in little white blobs on the edge of my vision and I took the only way I knew to shut him up.

'I backed Energise today on the Tote,' I said.

Jody said 'So what?' very quickly in the second before the impact of what I meant hit him like a punch.

'I'm closing my account with Ganser Mays,' I said.

Jody looked absolutely murderous, but he didn't ask *why*. Instead he clamped his jaws together, cast a less welcoming glance at the attentive Press and said very quietly and with menace, 'If you say anything I'll sue you for libel.'

'Slander,' I said automatically.

'What?'

'Libel is written, slander is spoken.'

'I'll have you,' he said, 'if you say anything.'

881

'Some friendship,' I commented.

His eyes narrowed. 'It was a pleasure,' he said, 'to take you for every penny I could.'

A small silence developed. I felt that racing had gone thoroughly sour and that I would never get much fun from it again. Three years of uncomplicated enjoyment had crumbled to disillusionment.

In the end I simply said, 'Leave Energise here. I'll fix his transport,' and Jody turned on his heel with a stony face and plunged in through the weighing room door.

The transport proved no problem. I arranged with a young owner-driver of a one-box transport firm that he should take Energise back to his own small transit yard overnight and ferry him on in a day or two to whichever trainer I decided to send him.

'A dark brown horse. Almost black,' I said. 'The gatekeeper will tell you which box he's in. But I don't suppose he'll have a lad with him.'

The owner-driver, it transpired, could provide a lad to look after Energise. 'He'll be right as rain,' he said. 'No need for you to worry.' He had brought two other horses to the course, one of which was in the last race, and he would be away within an hour afterwards, he said. We exchanged telephone numbers and addresses and shook hands on the deal.

After that, more out of politeness than through any

great appetite for racing, I went back to the private box of the man who had earlier given me lunch and with whom I'd watched my own horse win.

'Steven, where have you been? We've been waiting to help you celebrate.'

Charlie Canterfield, my host, held his arms wide in welcome, with a glass of champagne in one hand and a cigar in the other. He and his eight or ten other guests sat on dining chairs round a large central table, its white cloth covered now not with the paraphernalia of lunch, but with a jumble of half full glasses, race cards, binoculars, gloves, handbags and betting tickets. A faint haze of Havana smoke and the warm smell of alcohol filled the air, and beyond, on the other side of snugly closed glass, lay the balcony overlooking the fresh and windy racecourse.

Four races down and two to go. Mid afternoon. Everyone happy in the interval between coffee-and-brandy and cake-and-tea. A cosy little roomful of chat and friendliness and mild social smugness. Well-intentioned people doing no one any harm.

I sighed inwardly and raised a semblance of enjoyment for Charlie's sake, and sipped champagne and listened to everyone telling me it was *great* that Energise had won. They'd all backed it, they said. Lots of lovely lolly, Steven dear. Such a clever horse... and such a clever little trainer, Jody Leeds.

'Mm,' I said, with a dryness no one heard.

Charlie waved me to the empty chair between himself and a lady in a green hat.

'What do you fancy for the next race?' he asked.

I looked at him with a mind totally blank.

'Can't remember what's running,' I said.

Charlie's leisured manner skipped a beat. I'd seen it in him before, this split-second assessment of a new factor, and I knew that therein lay the key to his colossal business acumen. His body might laze, his bonhomie might expand like softly whipped cream, but his brain never took a moment off.

I gave him a twisted smile.

Charlie said, 'Come to dinner.'

'Tonight, do you mean?'

He nodded.

I bit my thumb and thought about it. 'All right.'

'Good. Let's say Parkes, Beauchamp Place, eight o'clock.'

'All right.'

The relationship between Charlie and me had stood for years in that vague area between acquaintanceship and active friendship where chance meetings are enjoyed and deliberate ones seldom arranged. That day was the first time he had invited me to his private box. Asking me for dinner as well meant a basic shift to new ground.

I guessed he had misread my vagueness, but all the same I liked him, and no one in his right mind would pass up a dinner at Parkes. I hoped he wouldn't think it a wasted evening.

Charlie's guests began disappearing to put on bets for the next race. I picked up a spare race card which was lying on the table and knew at once why Charlie had paid me such acute attention: two of the very top hurdlers were engaged in battle and the papers had been talking about it for days.

I looked up and met Charlie's gaze. His eyes were amused.

'Which one, then?' he asked.

'Crepitas.'

'Are you betting?'

I nodded. 'I did it earlier. On the Tote.'

He grunted. 'I prefer the bookmakers. I like to know what odds I'm getting before I lay out my cash.' And considering his business was investment banking that was consistent thinking. 'I can't be bothered to walk down, though.'

'You can have half of mine, if you like,' I said.

'Half of how much?' he said cautiously.

'Ten pounds.'

He laughed. 'Rumour says you can't think in anything less than three noughts.'

'That was an engineering joke,' I said, 'which escaped.'

'How do you mean?'

'I sometimes use a precision lathe. You can just about set it to an accuracy of three noughts ... point nought nought nought one. One ten-thousandth of an inch. That's my limit. Can't think in less than three noughts.'

He chuckled. 'And you never have a thousand on a horse?'

'Oh, I did that too, once or twice.'

He definitely did, that time, hear the arid undertone. I stood up casually and moved towards the glass door to the balcony.

'They're going down to the post,' I said.

He came without comment, and we stood outside watching the two stars, Crepitas and Waterboy, bouncing past the stands with their jockeys fighting for control.

Charlie was a shade shorter than I, a good deal stouter, and approximately twenty years older. He wore top quality clothes as a matter of course and no one hearing his mellow voice would have guessed his father had been a lorry driver. Charlie had never hidden his origins. Indeed he was justly proud of them. It was simply that under the old educational system he'd been sent to Eton as a local boy on Council money, and had acquired the speech and social habits along with the book learning. His brains had taken him along all his life like a surf rider on the crest of a roller, and it was probably only a modest piece of extra luck that he'd happened to be born within sight of the big school.

His other guests drifted out on to the balcony and claimed his attention. I knew none of them well, most of them by sight, one or two by reputation. Enough for the occasion, not enough for involvement.

The lady in the green hat put a green glove on my arm. 'Waterboy looks wonderful, don't you think?'

'Wonderful,' I agreed.

She gave me a bright myopic smile from behind think lensed glasses. 'Could you just tell me what price they're offering now in the ring?'

'Of course.'

I raised my binoculars and scanned the boards of the bookmakers ranged in front of a sector of stands lying some way to our right. 'It looks like evens Waterboy and five to four Crepitas, as far as I can see.'

'So kind,' said the green lady warmly.

I swung the binoculars round a little to search out Ganser Mays: and there he stood, half way down the row of bookmakers lining the rails separating the Club Enclosure from Tattersall's, a thin man of middle height with a large sharp nose, steel-rimmed spectacles and the manner of a high church clergyman. I had never liked him enough to do more than talk about the weather, but I had trusted him completely, and that had been foolish.

He was leaning over the rails, head bent, talking earnestly to someone in the Club Enclosure, someone hidden from me by a bunch of other people. Then the bunch shifted and moved away and the person behind them was Jody.

The anger in Jody's body came over sharp and clear

and his lower jaw moved vigorously in speech. Ganser Mays' responses appeared more soothing than fierce and when Jody finally strode furiously away, Ganser Mays raised his head and looked after him with an expression more thoughtful than actively worried.

Ganser Mays had reached that point in a book-maker's career where outstanding personal success began to merge into the status of a large and respect-able firm. In gamblers' minds he was moving from an individual to an institution. A multiplying host of betting shops bore his name from Glasgow southwards, and recently he had announced that next Flat season he would sponsor a three-year-old sprint.

He still stood on the rails himself at big meetings to talk to his more affluent customers and keep them faithful. To open his big shark jaws and suck in all the new unwary little fish.

With a wince I swung my glasses away. I would never know exactly how much Jody and Ganser Mays had stolen from me in terms of cash, but in terms of dented self-respect they had stripped me of all but crumbs.

The race started, the super-hurdlers battled their hearts out, and Crepitas beat Waterboy by a length. The Tote would pay me a little because of him, and a great deal because of Energise, but two winning bets in one afternoon weren't enough to dispel my depression. I dodged the tea-and-cakes, thanked Charlie for the lunch and said I'd see him later, and went down towards the weighing room again to see if inspiration would strike in the matter of a choice of trainers.

I heard hurrying footsteps behind me and a hand grabbed my arm.

'Thank goodness I've found you.'

He was out of breath and looking worried. The young owner-driver I'd hired for Energise.

'What is it? Box broken down?'

'No . . . look, you did say your horse was black, didn't you? I mean, I did get that right, didn't I?'

Anxiety sharpened my voice. 'Is there anything wrong with him?'

'No . . . at least . . . not with him, no. But the horse which Mr Leeds has left for me to take is . . . well . . . a chestnut mare.'

I went with him to the stables. The gatekeeper still smiled with pleasure at things going wrong.

'S'right,' he said with satisfaction. 'Leeds went off a quarter of an hour ago in one of them hire boxes, one horse. Said his own box had had an accident and he was leaving Energise here, instructions of the owner.'

'The horse he's left is not Energise,' I said.

'Can't help that, can I?' he said virtuously.

I turned to the young man. 'Chestnut mare with a big white blaze?'

He nodded.

'That's Asphodel. She ran in the first race today. Jody Leeds trains her. She isn't mine.'

'What will I do about her then?'

'Leave her here,' I said. 'Sorry about this. Send me a bill for cancellation fees.'

He smiled and said he wouldn't, which almost restored my faith in human nature. I thanked him for bothering to find me instead of keeping quiet, taking the wrong horse and then sending me a bill for work done. He looked shocked that anyone could be so cynical, and I reflected that until I learnt from Jody, I wouldn't have been.

Jody had taken Energise after all.

I burnt with slow anger, partly because of my own lack of foresight. If he had been prepared to urge Andy-Fred to risk running me down I should have known that he wouldn't give up at the first setback. He had been determined to get the better of me and whisk Energise back to his own stable and I'd underestimated both his bloody-mindedness and his nerve.

I could hardly wait to be free of Jody. I went back to my car and drove away from the racecourse with no thoughts but of which trainer I would ask to take my horses and how soon I could get them transferred from one to the other.

Charlie smiled across the golden polished wood of the table in Parkes and pushed away his empty coffee cup. His cigar was half smoked, his port half drunk, and his stomach, if mine were anything to go by, contentedly full of some of the best food in London.

I wondered what he had looked like as a young man, before the comfortable paunch and the beginning of jowls. Big businessmen were all the better for a little weight, I thought. Lean-and-hungry was for the starters, the hotheads in a hurry. Charlie exuded maturity and wisdom with every excess pound.

He had smooth greying hair, thin on top and brushed back at the sides. Eyes deep set, nose large, mouth firmly straight. Not conventionally a good-looking face, but easy to remember. People who had once met Charlie tended to know him next time.

He had come alone, and the restaurant he had chosen consisted of several smallish rooms with three or four tables in each; a quiet place where privacy was easy. He had talked about racing, food, the Prime Minister and the state of the Stock Market, and still had not come to the point.

'I get the impression,' he said genially, 'that you are waiting for something.'

'You've never asked me to dine before.'

'I like your company.'

'And that's all?'

He tapped ash off the cigar. 'Of course not,' he said.

'I thought not,' I smiled. 'But I've probably eaten your dinner under false pretences.'

'Knowingly?'

'Maybe. I don't know exactly what's in your mind.'

'Your vagueness,' he said. 'When someone like you goes into a sort of trance . . .'

'I thought so,' I sighed. 'Well, that was no useful productive otherwhereness of mind, that was the aftermath of a practically mortal row I'd just had with Jody Leeds.'

He sat back in his chair. 'What a pity.'

'Pity about the row, or a pity about the absence of inspiration?'

'Both, I dare say. What was the row about?'

'I gave him the sack.'

He stared. 'What on earth for?'

'He said if I told anyone that, he'd sue me for slander.'

'Oh, did he indeed!' Charlie looked interested all over again, like a horse taking fresh hold of its bit. 'And could he?'

'I expect so.'

Charlie sucked a mouthful of smoke and trickled it out from one corner of his mouth.

'Care to risk it?' he said.

'Your discretion's better than most . . .'

'Absolute,' he said. 'I promise.'

I believed him. I said, 'He found a way of stealing huge sums from me so that I didn't know I was being robbed.'

'But you must have known that *someone* . . .'

I shook my head. 'I dare say I'm not the first the trick's been played on. It's so deadly simple.'

'Proceed,' Charlie said. 'You fascinate me.'

'Right. Now suppose you are basically a good racehorse trainer but you've got a large and crooked thirst for unearned income.'

'I'm supposing,' Charlie said.

'First of all, then,' I said, 'you need a silly mug with a lot of money and enthusiasm and not much knowledge of racing.'

'You?' Charlie said.

'Me.' I nodded ruefully. 'Someone recommends you to me as a good trainer and I'm impressed by your general air of competence and dedication, so I toddle up and ask you if you could find me a good horse, as I'd like to become an owner.'

'And do I buy a good horse cheaply and charge you a fortune for it?'

'No. You buy the very best horse you can. I am delighted, and you set about the training and very soon the horse is ready to run. At this point you tell me you know a very reliable bookmaker and you introduce me to him.'

'Oh hum.'

'As you say. The bookmaker however is eminently respectable and respected and as I am not used to betting in large amounts I am glad to be in the hands of so worthy a fellow. You, my trainer, tell me the horse shows great promise and I might think of a small each way bet on his first race. A hundred pounds each way, perhaps.'

'A small bet!' Charlie exclaimed.

'You point out that is scarcely more than three weeks' training fees,' I said.

'I do?'

'You do. So I gulp a little as I've always bet in tenners before and I stake a hundred each way. But sure enough the horse does run well and finishes third, and the bookmaker pays out a little instead of me paying him.'

I drank the rest of my glass of port. Charlie finished his and ordered more coffee.

'Next time the horse runs,' I went on, 'you say it is really well and sure to win and if I ever want to have a big bet, now's the time, before everyone else jumps on the bandwagon. The bookmaker offers me a good price and I feel euphoric and take the plunge.'

'A thousand?'

I nodded. 'A thousand.'

'And?'

'The word goes round and the horse starts favourite. It is not his day, though. He runs worse than the first time and finishes fifth. You are very upset. You can't understand it. I find myself comforting you and telling you he is bound to run better next time.'

'But he doesn't run better next time?'

'But he does. Next time he wins beautifully.'

'But you haven't backed it?'

'Yes, I have. The price this time isn't five to two as it was before, but six to one. I stake five hundred pounds and win three thousand. I am absolutely delighted. I have regained all the money I had lost and more besides, and I have also gained the prize money for the race. I pay the training bills out of the winnings and I have recouped part of the purchase price of the horse, and I am very happy with the whole business of being an owner. I ask you to buy me another horse. Buy two or three, if you can find them.'

'And this time you get expensive duds?'

'By no means. My second horse is a marvellous two-year-old. He wins his very first race. I have only a hundred on him, mind you, but as it is at ten to one, I am still very pleased. So next time out, as my horse is a hot favourite and tipped in all the papers, you encourage me to have a really big bet. Opportunities like this seldom arise, you tell me, as the opposition is hopeless. I am convinced, so I lay out three thousand pounds.'

'My God,' Charlie said.

'Quite so. My horse sprints out of the stalls and takes the lead like the champion he is and everything is going splendidly. But then half way along the five furlongs a buckle breaks on the saddle and the girths come loose and the jockey has to pull up as best he can because by now he is falling off.'

'Three thousand!' Charlie said.

'All gone,' I nodded. 'You are inconsolable. The strap was new, the buckle faulty. Never mind, I say kindly, gulping hard. Always another day.'

'And there is?'

'You're learning. Next time out the horse is favourite again and I have five hundred on. He wins all right, and although I have not this time won back all I lost, well, it's the second time the horse has brought home a decent prize, and taking all in all I am not out of pocket and I have had a great deal of pleasure and excitement. And I am well content.'

'And so it goes on?'

'And so, indeed, it goes on. I find I get more and more delight from watching horses. I get particular delight if the horses are my own, and although in time of course my hobby costs me a good deal of money, because owners on the whole don't make a profit, I am totally happy and consider it well spent.'

'And then what happens?'

'Nothing really,' I said. 'I just begin to get these niggling suspicions and I thrust them out of my head and think how horribly disloyal I am being to you, after all the winners you have trained for me. But the suspicions won't lie down. I've noticed, you see, that when I have my biggest bets, my horses don't win.'

'A lot of owners could say the same,' Charlie said.

'Oh sure. But I tot up all the big bets which didn't come up, and they come to nearly forty thousand pounds.'

'Good God.'

'I am really ashamed of myself, but I begin to *wonder*. I say to myself, suppose ... just suppose ... that every time I stake anything over a thousand, my trainer and my bookmaker conspire together and simply keep the money and make sure my horse doesn't win. Just suppose ... that if I stake three thousand, they split it fifty fifty, and the horse runs badly, or is left, or the buckle on the girth breaks. Just suppose that next time out my horse is trained to the utmost and the race is carefully chosen and he duly wins, and I am delighted ... just suppose that this time my bookmaker and my trainer are betting on the horse themselves ... with the money they stole from me last time.'

Charlie looked riveted.

'If my horse wins, they win. If my horse loses, they haven't lost their own money, but only mine.'

'Neat.'

'Yes. So the weeks pass and now the Flat season is finished, and we are back with the jumpers. And you, my trainer, have found and bought for me a beautiful young hurdler, a really top class horse. I back him a little in his first race and he wins it easily. I am thrilled. I am also worried, because you tell me there is a race absolutely made for him at Sandown Park which he is certain to win, and you encourage me to have a very big bet on him. I am by now filled with horrid doubts and fears, and as I particularly admire this horse I do not want his heart broken by trying to win when he isn't allowed to ... which I am sure happened to one or two of the others ... so I say I will not back him.'

'Unpopular?'

'Very. You press me harder than ever before to lay out a large stake. I refuse. You are obviously annoyed and warn me that the horse will win and I will be sorry. I say I'll wait till next time. You say I am making a big mistake.'

'When do I say all this?'

'Yesterday.'

'And today?' Charlie asked.

'Today I am suffering from suspicion worse than ever. Today I think that maybe you will let the horse win if he can, just to prove I was wrong not to back him, so that next time you will have no difficulty at all in persuading me to have a bigger bet than ever.'

'Tut tut.'

'Yes. So today I don't tell you that a little while ago ... because of my awful doubts ... I opened a credit account with the Tote, and today I also don't tell you that I have backed my horse for a thousand pounds on my credit account.'

'Deceitful of you.'

'Certainly.'

'And your horse wins,' Charlie said, nodding.

'He looked superb ...' I smiled wryly. 'You tell me after the race that it is my own fault I didn't back him. You say you did try to get me to. You say I'd do better to take your advice next time.'

'And then?'

'Then,' I sighed, 'all the weeks of suspicion just jelled into certainty. I knew he'd been cheating me in other ways too. Little ways. Little betrayals of friendship. Nothing enormous. I told him there wasn't going to be a next time. I said I would be taking the horses away.'

'What did he say to that?'

'He didn't ask why.'

'Oh dear,' Charlie said.

CHAPTER THREE

I told Charlie everything that had happened that day. All amusement died from his expression and by the end he was looking grim.

'He'll get away with it,' he said finally.

'Oh yes.'

'You remember, I suppose, that his father's a member of the Jockey Club?'

'Yes.'

'Above suspicion, is Jody Leeds.'

Jody's father, Quintus Leeds, had achieved pillar-of-the-Turf status by virtue of being born the fifth son of a sporting peer, owning a few racehorses and knowing the right friends. He had a physically commanding presence, tall, large and handsome, and his voice and handshake radiated firm confidence. He was apt to give people straight piercing looks from fine grey eyes and to purse his mouth thoughtfully and shake his head as if pledged to secrecy when asked for an opinion. I privately thought his appearance and mannerisms were a lot of glossy window-dressing concealing a marked absence of goods, but there was no doubting that he was basically well-meaning and honest.

He was noticeably proud of Jody, puffing up his chest and beaming visibly in unsaddling enclosures from Epsom to York.

In his father's eyes, Jody, energetic, capable and clever, could do no wrong. Quintus would believe him implicitly, and for all his suspect shortness of intelligence he carried enough weight to sway official opinion.

As Jody had said, I couldn't prove a thing. If I so much as hinted at theft he'd slap a lawsuit on me, and the bulk of the Jockey Club would be ranged on his side.

'What will you do?' Charlie said.

'Don't know.' I half smiled. 'Nothing, I suppose.'

'It's bloody unfair.'

'All crime is bloody unfair on the victim.'

Charlie made a face at the general wickedness of the world and called for the bill.

Outside we turned left and walked down Beauchamp Place together, having both, as it happened, parked our cars round the corner in Walton Street. The night was cold, cloudy, dry and still windy. Charlie pulled his coat collar up round his ears and put on thick black leather gloves.

'I hate the winter,' he said.

'I don't mind it.'

'You're young,' he said. 'You don't feel the cold.'

'Not that young. Thirty-five.'

'Practically a baby.'

We turned the corner and the wind bit sharply with Arctic teeth. 'I hate it,' Charlie said.

His car, a big blue Rover 3500, was parked nearer than my Lamborghini. We stopped beside his and he unlocked the door. Down the street a girl in a long dress walked in our direction, the wind blowing her skirt sideways and her hair like flags.

'Very informative evening,' he said, holding out his hand.

'Not what you expected, though,' I said, shaking it.

'Better perhaps.'

He opened his door and began to lower himself into the driver's seat. The girl in the long dress walked past us, her heels brisk on the pavement. Charlie fastened his seat belt and I shut his door.

The girl in the long dress stopped, hesitated and turned back.

'Excuse me,' she said. 'But I wonder...' She stopped, appearing to think better of it.

'Can we help you?' I said.

She was American, early twenties, and visibly cold. Round her shoulders she wore only a thin silk shawl, and under that a thin silk shirt. No gloves. Gold sandals. A small gold mesh purse. In the street lights her skin looked blue and she was shivering violently.

'Get in my car,' Charlie suggested, winding down his window, 'out of the wind.'

She shook her head. 'I guess . . .' She began to turn away.

'Don't be silly,' I said. 'You need help. Accept it.'

'But . . .'

'Tell us what you need.'

She hesitated again and then said with a rush, 'I need some money.'

'Is that all?' I said and fished out my wallet. 'How much?'

'Enough for a taxi . . . to Hampstead.'

I held out a fiver. 'That do?'

'Yes. I . . . where shall I send it back to?'

'Don't bother.'

'But I must.'

Charlie said, 'He's got wads of the stuff. He won't miss it.'

'That's not the point,' the girl said. 'If you won't tell me how to repay it, I can't take it.'

'It is ridiculous to argue about morals when you're freezing,' I said. 'My name is Steven Scott. Address, Regent's Park Malthouse. That'll find me.'

'Thanks.'

'I'll drive you, if you like. I have my car.' I pointed along the street.

'No thanks,' she said. 'How d'you think I got *into* this mess?'

'How then?'

She pulled the thin shawl close. 'I accepted a simple invitation to dinner and found there were strings attached. So I left him at the soup stage and blasted out, and it was only when I was walking away that I realised that I'd no money with me. He'd collected me, you see.' She smiled suddenly, showing straight white teeth. 'Some girls are dumber than others.'

'Let Steven go and find you a taxi, then,' Charlie said.

'Okay.'

It took me several minutes, but she was still huddled against the outside of Charlie's car, sheltering as best she could from the worst of the wind, when I got back. I climbed out of the taxi and she climbed in and without more ado drove away.

'A fool and his money,' Charlie said.

'That was no con trick.'

'It would be a good one,' he said. 'How do you know she's not hopping out of the cab two blocks away and shaking a fiver out of the next Sir Galahad?'

He laughed, wound up the window, waved and pointed his Rover towards home.

Monday morning brought the good news and the bad.

The good was a letter with a five pound note enclosed. Sucks to Charlie, I thought.

Dear Mr Scott,
I was so grateful for your help on Saturday night. I
guess I'll never go out on a date again without the
cab fare home.
Yours sincerely,
Alexandra Ward.

The bad news was in public print: comments in both
newspapers delivered to my door (one sporting, one
ordinary) about the disloyalty of owners who shed their
hardworking trainers. One said:

> Particularly hard on Jody Leeds that after all he
> had done for Mr Scott the owner should see fit to
> announce he would be sending his horses elsewhere.
> As we headlined in this column a year ago, Jody
> Leeds took on the extensive Berksdown Court
> Stables especially to house the expanding Scott
> string. Now without as much as half an hour's
> warning, the twenty-eight-year-old trainer is left flat,
> with all his new liabilities still outstanding. Treachery
> may sound a harsh word. Ingratitude is not.

And the other in more tabloid vein:

> Leeds (28) smarting from the sack delivered by
> ungrateful owner Steven Scott (35) said at Sandown
> on Saturday, 'I am right in the cart now. Scott
> dumped me while still collecting back-slaps for the

win on his hurdler Energise, which I trained. I am sick at heart. You sweat your guts out for an owner, and he kicks you in the teeth.'

High time trainers were protected from this sort of thing. Rumour has it Leeds may suc.

All those Press note books, all those extended Press ears had not been there for nothing. Very probably they did all genuinely believe that Jody had had a raw deal, but not one single one had bothered to ask what the view looked like from where I stood. Not one single one seemed to think that there might have been an overpowering reason for my action.

I disgustedly put down both papers, finished my breakfast and settled down to the day's work, which as usual consisted mostly of sitting still in an armchair and staring vacantly into space.

Around mid-afternoon, stiff and chilly, I wrote to Miss Ward.

Dear Miss Ward,
Thank you very much for the fiver. Will you have dinner with me? No strings attached. I enclose five pounds for the cab fare home.
Yours sincerely,
Steven Scott.

In the evening I telephoned three different race-horse trainers and offered them three horses each. They all accepted, but with the reservations blowing cool in their voices. None actually asked why I had split with Jody though all had obviously read the papers.

One, a blunt north countryman, said, 'I'll want a guarantee you'll leave them with me for at least six months, so long as they don't go lame or something.'

'All right.'

'In writing.'

'If you like.'

'Ay, I do like. You send 'em up with a guarantee and I'll take 'em.'

For Energise I picked a large yard in Sussex where hurdlers did especially well, and under the guarded tones of the trainer Rupert Ramsey I could hear that he thought almost as much of the horse as I did.

For the last three I chose Newmarket, a middle-sized stable of average achievement. No single basket would ever again contain all the Scott eggs.

Finally with a grimace I picked up the receiver and dialled Jody's familiar number. It was not he who answered, however, but Felicity, his wife.

Her voice was sharp and bitter. 'What do you want?'

I pictured her in their luxuriously furnished drawing-room, a thin positive blonde girl, every bit as competent and hardworking as Jody. She would be wearing tight blue jeans and an expensive shirt, there would be six gold bracelets jingling on her wrist and she would smell of a musk-based scent. She held intolerant views on most things and stated them forthrightly, but she had never, before that evening, unleashed on me personally the scratchy side of her mind.

'To talk about transport,' I said.

'So you really are kicking our props away.'

'You'll survive.'

'That's bloody complacent claptrap,' she said angrily. 'I could kill you. After all Jody's done for you.'

I paused. 'Did he tell you why I'm breaking with him?'

'Some stupid little quarrel about ten quid on a bill.'

'It's a great deal more than that,' I said.

'Rubbish.'

'Ask him,' I said. 'In any case, three horseboxes will collect my horses on Thursday morning. The drivers will know the ones each of them has to take and where to take them. You tell Jody that if he mixes them up he can pay the bills for sorting them out.'

The names she called me would have shaken Jody's father to the roots.

'Thursday,' I said. 'Three horseboxes, different destinations. And goodbye.'

No pleasure in it. None at all.

I sat gloomily watching a play on television and hearing hardly a word. At nine forty-five the telephone interrupted and I switched off.

' . . . Just want to know, sir, where I stand.'

Raymond Child. Jump jockey. Middle-ranker, thirty years old, short on personality. He rode competently enough, but the longer I went racing and the more I learnt, the more I could see his short-comings. I was certain also that Jody could not have manipulated my horses quite so thoroughly without help at the wheel.

'I'll send you an extra present for Energise,' I said. Jockeys were paid an official percentage of the winning prize money through a central system, but especially grateful owners occasionally came across with more.

'Thank you, sir.' He sounded surprised.

'I had a good bet on him.'

'Did you, sir?' The surprise was extreme. 'But Jody said . . .' He stopped dead.

'I backed him on the Tote.'

'Oh.'

The silence lengthened. He cleared his throat. I waited.

'Well, sir. Er . . . about the future . . .'

'I'm sorry,' I said, half meaning it. 'I'm grateful for the winners you've ridden. I'll send you the present for Energise. But in the future he'll be ridden by the jockey attached to his new stable.'

This time there was no tirade of bad language. This time, just a slow defeated sigh and the next best thing to an admission.

'Can't really blame you, I suppose.'

He disconnected before I could reply.

Tuesday I should have had a runner at Chepstow, but since I'd cancelled Jody's authority he couldn't send it.

I kicked around my rooms unproductively all morning and in the afternoon walked from Kensington Gardens to the Tower of London. Cold grey damp air with seagulls making a racket over the low-tide mud. Coffee-coloured river racing down on the last of the ebb. I stood looking towards the City from the top of little Tower Hill and thought of all the lives that had ended there under the axe. December mood, through and through. I bought a bag of roast chestnuts and went home by bus.

Wednesday brought a letter.

> Dear Mr Scott,
> When and where?
> Alexandra Ward.

She had kept the five pound note.

On Thursday evening the three new trainers confirmed that they had received the expected horses; on Friday I did a little work and on Saturday I drove down to Cheltenham races. I had not, it was true, exactly expected a rousing cheer, but the depth and extent of the animosity shown to me was acutely disturbing.

Several backs were turned, not ostentatiously but decisively. Several acquaintances lowered their eyes in embarrassment when talking to me and hurried away as soon as possible. The Press looked speculative, the trainers wary and the Jockey Club coldly hostile.

Charlie Canterfield alone came up with a broad smile and shook me vigorously by the hand.

'Have I come out in spots?' I said.

He laughed. 'You've kicked the underdog. The British never forgive it.'

'Even when the underdog bites first?'

'Underdogs are never in the wrong.'

He led me away to the bar. 'I've been taking a small poll for you. Ten per cent think it would be fair to hear your side. Ten per cent think you ought to be shot. What will you drink?'

'Scotch. No ice or water. What about the other eighty per cent?'

'Enough righteous indignation to keep the Mothers' Union going for months.' He paid for the drinks. 'Cheers.'

'And to you too.'

'It'll blow over,' Charlie said.

'I guess so.'

'What do you fancy in the third?'

We discussed the afternoon's prospects and didn't refer again to Jody, but later, alone, I found it hard to ignore the general climate. I backed a couple of horses on the Tote for a tenner each, and lost. That sort of day.

All afternoon I was fiercely tempted to protest that it was I who was the injured party, not Jody. Then I thought of the further thousands he would undoubtedly screw out of me in damages if I opened my mouth, and I kept it shut.

The gem of the day was Quintus himself, who planted his great frame solidly in my path and told me loudly that I was a bloody disgrace to the good name of racing. Quintus, I reflected, so often spoke in clichés.

'I'll tell you something,' he said. 'You would have been elected to the Jockey Club if you hadn't served Jody such a dirty trick. Your name was up for consideration. You won't be invited now, I'll see to that.'

He gave me a short curt nod and stepped aside. I didn't move.

'Your son is the one for dirty tricks.'

'How dare you!'

'You'd best believe it.'

'Absolute nonsense. The discrepancy on your bill was a simple secretarial mistake. If you try to say it was anything else . . .'

'I know,' I said. 'He'll sue.'

'Quite right. He has a right to every penny he can get.'

I walked away. Quintus might be biased, but I knew I'd get a straight answer from the Press.

I asked the senior columnist of a leading daily, a fiftyish man who wrote staccato prose and sucked peppermints to stop himself smoking.

'What reason is Jody Leeds giving for losing my horses?'

The columnist sucked and breathed out a gust of sweetness.

'Says he charged you by mistake for some schooling Raymond Child didn't do.'

'That all?'

'Says you accused him of stealing and were changing your trainer.'

'And what's your reaction to that?'

'I haven't got one.' He shrugged and sucked contemplatively. 'Others ... The consensus seems to be it was a genuine mistake and you've been unreasonable ... to put it mildly.'

'I see,' I said. 'Thanks.'

'Is that all? No story?'

'No,' I said. 'Sorry.'

He put another peppermint in his mouth, nodded non-committally, and turned away to more fertile prospects. As far as he was concerned, I was last week's news. Others, this Saturday, were up for the chop.

I walked thoughtfully down on the Club lawn to watch the next race. It really was not much fun being cast as everyone's villain, and the clincher was delivered by a girl I'd once taken to Ascot.

'Steven dear,' she said with coquettish reproof, 'you're a big rich bully. That poor boy's struggling to make ends meet. Even if he did pinch a few quid off you, why get into such a tizz? So uncool, don't you think?'

'You believe the rich should lie down for Robin Hood?'

'What?'

'Never mind.'

I gave it up and went home.

The evening was a great deal better. At eight o'clock I collected Miss Alexandra Ward from an address in Hampstead and took her to dinner in the red and gold grill room of the Café Royal.

Seen again in kinder light, properly warm and not blown to rags by the wind, she was everything last week's glimpse had suggested. She wore the same long black skirt, the same cream shirt, the same cream silk shawl. Also the gold sandals, gold mesh purse and no gloves. But her brown hair was smooth and shining, her skin glowing, her eyes bright, and over all lay the indefinable extra, a typically American brand of grooming.

She opened the door herself when I rang the bell and for an appreciable pause we simply looked at each other. What she saw was, I supposed, about six feet of solidly built chap, dark hair, dark eyes, no warts to speak of. Tidy, clean, house-trained and dressed in a conventional dinner jacket.

'Good evening,' I said.

She smiled, nodded as if endorsing a decision,

914

stepped out through the door, and pulled it shut behind her.

'My sister lives here,' she said, indicating the house. 'I'm on a visit. She's married to an Englishman.'

I opened the car door for her. She sat smoothly inside, and I started the engine and drove off.

'A visit from the States?' I asked.

'Yes. From Westchester . . . outside New York.'

'Executive ladder-climbing country?' I said, smiling.

She gave me a quick sideways glance. 'You know Westchester?'

'No. Been to New York a few times, that's all.'

We stopped at some traffic lights. She remarked that it was a fine night. I agreed.

'Are you married?' she said abruptly.

'Did you bring the fiver?'

'Yes, I did.'

'Well . . . No, I'm not.'

The light changed to green. We drove on.

'Are you truthful?' she said.

'In that respect, yes. Not married now. Never have been.'

'I like to know,' she said with mild apology.

'I don't blame you.'

'For the sakes of the wives.'

'Yes.'

I pulled up in due course in front of the Café Royal at Piccadilly Circus, and helped her out of the car. As we went in she looked back and saw a small thin man taking my place in the driving seat.

'He works for me,' I said. 'He'll park the car.'

She looked amused. 'He waits around to do that?'

'On overtime, Saturday nights.'

'So he likes it?'

'Begs me to take out young ladies. Other times I do my own parking.'

In the full light inside the hall she stopped for another straight look at what she'd agreed to dine with.

'What do you expect of me?' she said.

'Before I collected you, I expected honesty, directness and prickles. Now that I've known you for half an hour I expect prickles, directness and honesty.'

She smiled widely, the white teeth shining and little pouches of fun swelling her lower eyelids.

'That isn't what I meant.'

'No . . . So what do you expect of me?'

'Thoroughly gentlemanly conduct and a decent dinner.'

'How dull.'

'Take it or leave it.'

'The bar,' I said, pointing, 'is over there. I take it.'

She gave me another flashing smile, younger sister to the first, and moved where I'd said. She drank vodka martini, I drank scotch, and we both ate a few black olives and spat out the stones genteelly into fists.

'Do you usually pick up girls in the street?' she said.

'Only when they fall.'

'Fallen girls?'

I laughed. 'Not those, no.'

'What do you do for a living?'

I took a mouthful of scotch. 'I'm a sort of engineer.' It sounded boring.

'Bridges and things?'

'Nothing so permanent or important.'

'What then?'

I smiled wryly. 'I make toys.'

'You make . . . *what*?'

'Toys. Things to play with.'

'I know what toys are, damn it.'

'What do you do?' I asked, 'In Westchester.'

She gave me an amused glance over her glass. 'You take it for granted that I work?'

'You have the air.'

'I cook, then.'

'Hamburgers and French fries?'

Her eyes gleamed. 'Weddings and stuff. Parties.'

'A lady caterer.'

She nodded. 'With a girl friend. Millie.'

'When do you go back?'

'Thursday.'

Thursday suddenly seemed rather close. After a noticeable pause she added almost defensively, 'It's Christmas, you see. We've a lot of work then and around New Year. Millie couldn't do it all alone.'

'Of course not.'

We went into dinner and ate smoked trout and steak

wrapped in pastry. She read the menu from start to finish with professional interest and checked with the head waiter the ingredients of two or three dishes.

'So many things are different over here,' she explained.

She knew little about wine. 'I guess I drink it when I'm given it, but I've a better palate for spirits.' The wine waiter looked sceptical, but she wiped that look off his face later by correctly identifying the brandy he brought with the coffee as Armagnac.

'Where is your toy factory?' she asked.

'I don't have a factory.'

'But you said you made toys.'

'Yes, I do.'

She looked disbelieving. 'You don't mean you actually *make* them. I mean, with your own hands?'

I smiled. 'Yes.'

'But . . .' She looked round the velvety room with the thought showing as clear as spring water: if I worked with my hands how often could I afford such a place.

'I don't often make them,' I said. 'Most of the time I go to the races.'

'Okay,' she said. 'I give in. You've got me hooked. Explain the mystery.'

'Have some more coffee.'

'Mr Scott . . .' She stopped. 'That sounds silly, doesn't it?'

'Yes, Miss Ward, it does.'

'Steven . . .'

'Much better.'

'My mother calls me Alexandra, Millie calls me Al. Take your pick.'

'Allie?'

'For God's sakes.'

'I invent toys,' I said. 'I patent them. Other people manufacture them. I collect royalties.'

'Oh.'

'Does "oh" mean enlightenment, fascination, or boredom to death?'

'It means oh how extraordinary, oh how interesting, and oh I never knew people did things like that.'

'Quite a lot do.'

'Did you invent Monopoly?'

I laughed. 'Unfortunately not.'

'But that sort of thing?'

'Mechanical toys, mostly.'

'How odd . . .' She stopped, thinking better of saying what was in her mind. I knew the reaction well, so I finished the sentence for her.

'How odd for a grown man to spend his life in toyland?'

'You said it.'

'Children's minds have to be fed.'

She considered it. 'And the next bunch of leaders are children today?'

'You rate it too high. The next lot of parents, teachers, louts and layabouts are children today.'

'And you are fired with missionary zeal?'

'All the way to the bank.'

'Cynical.'

'Better than pompous.'

'More honest,' she agreed. Her eyes smiled in the soft light, half mocking, half friendly, greeny-grey and shining, the whites ultra white. There was nothing wrong with the design of her eyebrows. Her nose was short and straight, her mouth curved up at the corners, and her cheeks had faint hollows in the right places. Assembled, the components added up not to a standard type of beauty, but to a face of character and vitality. Part of the story written, I thought. Lines of good fortune, none of discontent. No anxiety, no inner confusion. A good deal of self assurance, knowing she looked attractive and had succeeded in the job she'd chosen. Definitely not a virgin: a girl's eyes were always different, after.

'Are all your days busy,' I asked, 'between now and Thursday?'

'There are some minutes here and there.'

'Tomorrow?'

She smiled and shook her head. 'Not a chink tomorrow. Monday if you like.'

'I'll collect you,' I said. 'Monday morning, at ten.'

CHAPTER FOUR

Rupert Ramsey's voice on the telephone sounded resigned rather than welcoming.

'Yes, of course, do come down to see your horses, if you'd like to. Do you know the way?'

He gave me directions which proved easy to follow, and at eleven thirty, Sunday morning, I drove through his white painted stone gateposts and drew up in the large gravelled area before his house.

He lived in a genuine Georgian house, simple in design, with large airy rooms and elegant plaster-worked ceilings. Nothing self-consciously antique about the furnishings: all periods mingled together in a working atmosphere that was wholly modern.

Rupert himself was about forty-five, intensely ener-getic under a misleadingly languid exterior. His voice drawled slightly. I knew him only by sight and it was to all intents the first time we had met.

'How do you do?' He shook hands. 'Care to come into my office?'

I followed him through the white painted front door,

across the large square hall and into the room he called his office, but which was furnished entirely as a sitting-room except for a dining table which served as a desk, and a grey filing cabinet in one corner.

'Do sit down.' He indicated an armchair. 'Cigarette?'

'Don't smoke.'

'Wise man.' He smiled as if he didn't really think so and lit one for himself.

'Energise,' he said, 'is showing signs of having had a hard race.'

'But he won easily,' I said.

'It looked that way, certainly.' He inhaled, breathing out through his nose. 'All the same, I'm not too happy about him.'

'In what way?'

'He needs building up. We'll do it, don't you fear. But he looks a bit thin at present.'

'How about the other two?'

'Dial's jumping out of his skin. Ferryboat needs a lot of work yet.'

'I don't think Ferryboat likes racing any more.'

The cigarette paused on its way to his mouth.

'Why do you say that?' he asked.

'He's had three races this autumn. I expect you'll have looked up his form. He's run badly every time. Last year he was full of enthusiasm and won three times out of seven starts, but the last of them took a lot of winning... and Raymond Child cut him raw with his whip... and during the summer out at grass

Ferryboat seems to have decided that if he gets too near the front he's in for a beating, so it's only good sense *not* to get near the front . . . and he consequently isn't trying.'

He drew deeply on the cigarette, giving himself time. 'Do you expect me to get better results than Jody?'

'With Ferryboat, or in general?'

'Let's say . . . both.'

I smiled. 'I don't expect much from Ferryboat. Dial's a novice, an unknown quantity. Energise might win the Champion Hurdle.'

'You didn't answer my question,' he said pleasantly.

'No . . . I expect you to get different results from Jody. Will that do?'

'I'd very much like to know why you left him.'

'Disagreements over money,' I said. 'Not over the way he trained the horses.'

He tapped ash off with the precision that meant his mind was elsewhere. When he spoke, it was slowly.

'Were you always satisfied with the way your horses ran?'

The question hovered delicately in the air, full of inviting little traps. He looked up suddenly and met my eyes and his own widened with comprehension. 'I see you understand what I'm asking.'

'Yes. But I can't answer. Jody says he will sue me for slander if I tell people why I left him, and I've no reason to doubt him.'

'That remark in itself is a slander.'

'Indubitably.'

He got cheerfully to his feet and stubbed out the cigarette. A good deal more friendliness seeped into his manner.

'Right then. Let's go out and look at your horses.'

We went out into his yard, which showed prosperity at every turn. The thin cold December sun shone on fresh paint, wall-to-wall tarmac, tidy flower tubs and well-kept stable lads. There was none of the clutter I was accustomed to at Jody's; no brooms leaning against walls, no rugs, rollers, brushes and bandages lying in ready heaps, no straggles of hay across the swept ground. Jody liked to give owners the impression that work was being done, that care for the horses was non-stop. Rupert, it seemed, preferred to tuck the sweat and toil out of sight. At Jody's, the muck heap was always with you. At Rupert's it was invisible.

'Dial is here.'

We stopped at a box along a row outside the main quadrangle, and with an unobtrusive flick of his fingers Rupert summoned a lad hovering twenty feet away.

'This is Donny,' he said. 'Looks after Dial.'

I shook hands with Donny, a young tough-looking boy of about twenty with unsmiling eyes and a you-can't-con-me expression. From the look he directed first at Rupert and then later at the horse I gathered that this was his overall attitude to life, not an announcement of no confidence in me personally. When we'd looked at and admired the robust little

924

chestnut I tried Donny with a fiver. It raised a nod of thanks, but no smile.

Further along the same row stood Ferryboat, looking out on the world with a lack lustre eye and scarcely shifting from one leg to the other when we went into his box. His lad, in contrast to Donny, gave him an indulgent smile, and accepted his gift from me with a beam.

'Energise is in the main yard,' Rupert said, leading the way. 'Across in the corner.'

When we were half way there two other cars rolled up the drive and disgorged a collection of men in sheep-skin coats and ladies in furs and jangly bracelets. They saw Rupert and waved and began to stream into the yard.

Rupert said, 'I'll show you Energise in just a moment.'

'It's all right,' I said. 'You tell me which box he's in. I'll look at him myself. You see to your other owners.'

'Number fourteen, then. I'll be with you again shortly.'

I nodded and walked on to number fourteen. Unbolted the door. Went in. The near-black horse was tied up inside. Ready, I supposed, for my visit.

Horse and I looked at each other. My old friend, I thought. The only one of them all with whom I'd ever had any real contact. I talked to him, as in the horsebox, looking guiltily over my shoulder at the open door, for fear someone should hear me and think me nuts.

I could see at once why Rupert had been unhappy about him. He looked thinner. All that crashing about in the horsebox could have done him no good.

Across the yard I could see Rupert talking to the newcomers and shepherding them to their horses. Owners came en masse on Sunday mornings.

I was content to stay where I was. I spent probably twenty minutes with my black horse, and he instilled in me some very strange ideas.

Rupert came back hurrying and apologising. 'You're still here . . . I'm so sorry.'

'Don't be,' I assured him.

'Come into the house for a drink.'

'I'd like to.'

We joined the other owners and returned to his office for lavish issues of gin and scotch. Drinks for visiting owners weren't allowable as a business expense for tax purposes unless the visiting owners were foreign. Jody had constantly complained of it to all and sundry while accepting cases of the stuff from me with casual nods. Rupert poured generously and dropped no hints, and I found it a refreshing change.

The other owners were excitedly making plans for the Christmas meeting at Kempton Park. Rupert made introductions, explaining that Energise, too, was due to run there in the Christmas Hurdle.

'After the way he won at Sandown,' remarked one of the sheepskin coats, 'he must be a cast-iron certainty.'

I glanced at Rupert for an opinion but he was busy with bottles and glasses.

'I hope so,' I said.

The sheepskin coat nodded sagely.

His wife, a cosy looking lady who had shed her ocelot and now stood five-feet-nothing in bright green wool, looked from him to me in puzzlement.

'But George honey, Energise is trained by that nice young man with the pretty little wife. You know, the one who introduced us to Ganser Mays.'

She smiled happily and appeared not to notice the pole-axed state of her audience. I must have stood immobile for almost a minute while the implications fizzed around my brain, and during that time the conversation between George-honey and the bright green wool had flowed on into the chances of their own chaser in a later race. I dragged them back.

'Excuse me,' I said, 'but I didn't catch your names.'

'George Vine,' said the sheepskin coat, holding out a chunky hand, 'and my wife, Poppet.'

'Steven Scott,' I said.

'Glad to know you.' He gave his empty glass to Rupert, who amiably refilled it with gin and tonic. 'Poppet doesn't read the racing news much, so she wouldn't know you've left Jody Leeds.'

'Did you say,' I asked carefully, 'that Jody Leeds introduced you to Ganser Mays?'

'Oh no,' Poppet said, smiling. 'His wife did.'

'That's right,' George nodded. 'Bit of luck.'

'You see,' Poppet explained conversationally, 'the prices on the Tote are sometimes so awfully small and it's all such a lottery isn't it? I mean, you never know really what you're going to get for your money, like you do with the bookies.'

'Is that what she said?' I asked.

'Who? Oh . . . Jody Leeds' wife. Yes, that's right, she did. I'd just been picking up my winnings on one of our horses from the Tote, you see, and she was doing the same at the next window, the Late-Pay window that was, and she said what a shame it was that the Tote was only paying three to one when the bookies' starting price was five to one, and I absolutely agreed with her, and we just sort of stood there chatting. I told her that only last week we had bought the steeplechaser which had just won and it was our first ever racehorse, and she was so interested and explained that she was a trainer's wife and that sometimes when she got tired of the Tote paying out so little she bet with a bookie. I said I didn't like pushing along the rows with all those men shoving and shouting and she laughed and said she meant one on the rails, so you could just walk up to them and not go through to the bookies' enclosure at all. But of course you have to know them, I mean, they have to know *you*, if you see what I mean. And neither George nor I knew any of them, as I explained to Mrs Leeds.'

She stopped to take a sip of gin. I listened in fascination.

'Well,' she went on, 'Mrs Leeds sort of hesitated and then I got this great idea of asking her if she could possibly introduce us to *her* bookie on the rails.'

'And she did?'

'She thought it was a great idea.'

She would.

'So we collected George and she introduced us to dear Ganser Mays. And,' she finished triumphantly, 'he gives us much better odds than the Tote.'

George Vine nodded several times in agreement.

'Trouble is,' he said, 'you know what wives are, she bets more than ever.'

'George honey.' A token protest only.

'You know you do, love.'

'It isn't worth doing in sixpences,' she said smiling. 'You never win enough that way.'

He patted her fondly on the shoulder and said man-to-man to me, 'When Ganser Mays' account comes, if she's won, she takes the winnings, and if she's lost, I pay.'

Poppet smiled happily. 'George honey, you're sweet.'

'Which do you do most?' I asked her. 'Win or lose?'

She made a face. 'Now that's a naughty question, Mr Scott.'

Next morning, ten o'clock to the second, I collected Allie from Hampstead.

Seen in daylight for the first time she was sparkling

929

as the day was rotten. I arrived at her door with a big
black umbrella holding off slanting sleet, and she
opened it in a neat white mackintosh and knee-high
black boots. Her hair bounced with new washing, and
the bloom on her skin had nothing to do with Max
Factor.

I tried a gentlemanly kiss on the cheek. She smelled
of fresh flowers and bath soap.

'Good morning,' I said.

She chuckled. 'You English are so formal.'

'Not always.'

She sheltered under the umbrella down the path to
the car and sat inside with every glossy hair dry and in
place.

'Where are we going?'

'Fasten your lap straps,' I said. 'To Newmarket.'

'Newmarket?'

'To look at horses.' I let in the clutch and pointed
the Lamborghini roughly north-east.

'I might have guessed.'

I grinned. 'Is there anything you'd really rather do?'

'I've visited three museums, four picture galleries,
six churches, one Tower of London, two Houses of
Parliament and seven theatres.'

'In how long?'

'Sixteen days.'

'High time you saw some real life.'

The white teeth flashed. 'If you'd lived with my two

small nephews for sixteen days you couldn't wait to get away from it.'

'Your sister's children?'

She nodded. 'Ralph and William. Little devils.'

'What do they play with?'

She was amused. 'The toy maker's market research?'

'The customer is always right.'

We crossed the North Circular road and took the AI towards Baldock.

'Ralph dresses up a doll in soldier's uniforms and William makes forts on the stairs and shoots dried beans at anyone going up.'

'Healthy aggressive stuff.'

'When I was little I hated being given all those educational things that were supposed to be good for you.'

I smiled. 'It's well known there are two sorts of toys. The ones that children like and the ones their mothers buy. Guess which there are more of?'

'You're cynical.'

'So I'm often told,' I said. 'It isn't true.'

The wipers worked overtime against the sleet on the windscreen and I turned up the heater. She sighed with what appeared to be contentment. The car purred easily across Cambridgeshire and into Suffolk, and the ninety minute journey seemed short.

It wasn't the best of weather but even in July the stable I'd chosen for my three young flat racers would have looked depressing. There were two smallish quadrangles side by side, built tall and solid in Edwardian brick. All the doors were painted a dead dull dark brown. No decorations, no flowers, no grass, no gaiety of spirit in the whole place.

Like many Newmarket yards it led straight off the street and was surrounded by houses. Allie looked around without enthusiasm and put into words exactly what I was thinking.

'It looks more like a prison.'

Bars on the windows of the boxes. Solid ten foot tall gates at the road entrance. Jagged glass set in concrete along the top of the boundary wall. Padlocks swinging on every bolt on every door in sight. All that was missing was a uniformed figure with a gun, and maybe they had those too, on occasion.

The master of all this security proved pretty dour himself. Trevor Kennet shook hands with a smile that looked an unaccustomed effort for the muscles involved and invited us into the stable office out of the rain.

A bare room; linoleum, scratched metal furniture, strip lighting and piles of paper work. The contrast between this and the grace of Rupert Ramsey was remarkable. A pity I had taken Allie to the wrong one.

'They've settled well, your horses.' His voice dared me to disagree.

'Splendid,' I said mildly.

'You'll want to see them, I expect.'

As I'd come from London to do so, I felt his remark silly.

'They're doing no work yet, of course.'

'No,' I agreed. The last Flat season had finished six weeks ago. The next lay some three months ahead. No owner in his senses would have expected his Flat horses to be in full work in December. Trevor Kennet had a genius for the obvious.

'It's raining,' he said. 'Bad day to come.'

Allie and I were both wearing macs, and I carried the umbrella. He looked lengthily at these preparations and finally shrugged.

'Better come on, then.'

He himself wore a raincoat and a droopy hat that had suffered downpours for years. He led the way out of the office and across the first quadrangle with Allie and me close under my umbrella behind him.

He flicked the bolts on one of the dead chocolate doors and pulled both halves open.

'Wrecker,' he said.

We went into the box. Wrecker moved hastily away across the peat which covered the floor, a leggy bay yearling colt with a nervous disposition. Trevor Kennet made no effort to reassure him but stood four square looking at him with an assessing eye. Jody for all his faults had been good with young stock, fondling them and talking to them with affection. I thought I might have chosen badly, sending Wrecker here.

'He needs a gentle lad,' I said.

933

Kennet's expression was open to scorn. 'Doesn't do to molly coddle them. Soft horses win nothing.'

End of conversation.

We went out into the rain and he slammed the bolts home. Four boxes further along he stopped again.

'Hermes.'

Again the silent appraisal. Hermes, from the experience of two full racing seasons, could look at humans without anxiety and merely stared back. Ordinary to look at, he had won several races in masterly fashion ... and lost every time I'd seriously backed him. Towards the end of the Flat season he had twice trailed in badly towards the rear of the field. Too much racing, Jody had said. Needed a holiday.

'What do you think of him?' I asked.

'He's eating well,' Kennet said.

I waited for more, but nothing came. After a short pause we trooped out again into the rain and more or less repeated the whole depressing procedure in the box of my third colt, Bubbleglass.

I had great hopes of Bubbleglass. A late-developing two-year-old, he had run only once so far, and without much distinction. At three, though, he might be fun. He had grown and filled out since I'd seen him last. When I said so, Kennet remarked that it was only to be expected.

We all went back to the office, Kennet offered us coffee and looked relieved when I said we'd better be going.

'What an utterly dreary place,' Allie said, as we drove away.

'Designed to discourage owners from calling too often, I dare say.'

She was surprised. 'Do you mean it?'

'Some trainers think owners should pay their bills and shut up.'

'That's crazy.'

I glanced sideways at her.

She said positively, 'If I was spending all that dough, I'd sure expect to be welcomed.'

'Biting the hand that feeds is a national sport.'

'You're all nuts.'

'How about some lunch?'

We stopped at a pub which did a fair job for a Monday, and in the afternoon drove comfortably back to London. Allie made no objections when I pulled up outside my own front door and followed me in through it with none of the prickly reservations I'd feared.

I lived in the two lower floors of a tall narrow house in Prince Albert Road overlooking Regent's Park. At street level, garage, cloakroom, workshop. Upstairs, bed, bath, kitchen and sitting-room, the last with a balcony half as big as itself. I switched on lights and led the way.

'A bachelor's pad if ever I saw one,' Allie said, looking around her. 'Not a frill in sight.' She walked across and looked out through the sliding glass wall to the balcony. 'Don't you just hate all that traffic?'

Cars drove incessantly along the road below, yellow sidelights shining through the glistening rain.

'I quite like it,' I said. 'In the summer I practically live out there on the balcony ... breathing in great lungfuls of exhaust fumes and waiting for the clouds to roll away.'

She laughed, unbuttoned her mac and took it off. The red dress underneath looked as unruffled as it had at lunch. She was the one splash of bright colour in that room of creams and browns, and she was feminine enough to know it.

'Drink?' I suggested.

'It's a bit early ...' She looked around her as if she had expected to see more than sofas and chairs. 'Don't you keep any of your toys here?'

'In the workshop,' I said. 'Downstairs.'

'I'd love to see them.'

'All right.'

We went down to the hall again and turned towards the back of the house. I opened the civilised wood-panelled door which led straight from carpet to concrete, from white collar to blue, from champagne to tea breaks. The familiar smell of oil and machinery waited there in the dark. I switched on the stark bright lights and stood aside for her to go through.

'But it *is* ... a factory.' She sounded astonished.

'What did you expect?'

'Oh, I don't know. Something much smaller, I guess.'

The workshop was fifty feet long and was the reason

I had bought the house on my twenty-third birthday with money I had earned myself. Selling off the three top floors had given me enough back to construct my own first floor flat, but the heart of the matter lay here, legacy of an old-fashioned light engineering firm that had gone bust.

The pulley system that drove nearly the whole works from one engine was the original, even if now powered by electricity instead of steam, and although I had replaced one or two and added another, the old machines still worked well.

'Explain it to me,' Allie said.

'Well ... this electric engine here ...' I showed her its compact floor-mounted shape. ' ... drives that endless belt, which goes up there round that big wheel.'

'Yes.' She looked up where I pointed.

'The wheel is fixed to that long shaft which stretches right down the workshop, near the ceiling. When it rotates, it drives all those other endless belts going down to the machines. Look, I'll show you.'

I switched on the electric motor and immediately the big belt from it turned the wheel, which rotated the shaft, which set the other belts circling from the shaft down to the machines. The only noises were the hum of the engines, the gentle whine of the spinning shaft and the soft slapping of the belts.

'It looks alive,' Allie said. 'How do you make the machines work?'

'Engage a sort of gear inside the belt, then the belt revolves the spindle of the machine.'

'Like a sewing machine,' Allie said.

'More or less.'

We walked down the row. She wanted to know what job each did, and I told her.

'That's a milling machine, for flat surfaces. That's a speed lathe; I use that for wood as well as metal. That tiny lathe came from a watchmaker for ultra-fine work. That's a press. That's a polisher. That's a hacksaw. And that's a drilling machine; it bores holes downwards.'

I turned round and pointed to the other side of the workshop.

'That big one on its own is an engine lathe, for heavier jobs. It has its own electric power.'

'It's incredible. All this.'

'Just for toys?'

'Well . . .'

'These machines are all basically simple. They just save a lot of time.'

'Do toys have to be so . . . well . . . *accurate*?'

'I mostly make the prototypes in metal and wood. Quite often they reach the shops in plastic, but unless the engineering's right in the first place the toys don't work very well, and break easily.'

'Where do you keep them?' She looked around at the bare well-swept area with no work in sight.

'Over there. In the right-hand cupboard.'

I went over with her and opened the big double doors. She pulled them wider with outstretched arms.

'Oh!' She looked utterly astounded.

She stood in front of the shelves with her mouth open and her eyes staring, just like a child.

'Oh,' she said again, as if she could get no breath to say anything else. 'Oh . . . They're the Rola toys!'

'Yes, that's right.'

'Why didn't you say so?'

'Habit, really. I never do.'

She gave me a smile without turning her eyes away from the bright coloured rows in the cupboard. 'Do so many people ask for free samples?'

'It's just that I get tired of talking about them.'

'But I played with them myself.' She switched her gaze abruptly in my direction, looking puzzled. 'I had a lot of them in the States ten or twelve years ago.' Her voice plainly implied that I was too young to have made those.

'I was only fifteen when I did the first one,' I explained. 'I had an uncle who had a workshop in his garage . . . he was a welder, himself. He'd shown me how to use tools from the time I was six. He was pretty shrewd. He made me take out patents before I showed my idea to anyone, and he raised and lent me the money to pay for them.'

'Pay?'

'Patents are expensive and you have to take out one

939

for each different country, if you don't want your idea pinched. Japan, I may say, costs the most.'

'Good heavens.' She turned back to the cupboard, put out her hand and lifted out the foundation of all my fortunes, the merry-go-round.

'I had the carousel,' she said. 'Just like this, but different colours.' She twirled the centre spindle between finger and thumb so that the platform revolved and the little horses rose and fell on their poles. 'I simply can't believe it.'

She put the merry-go-round back in its slot and one by one lifted out several of the others, exclaiming over old friends and investigating the strangers. 'Do you have a Rola-base down here?'

'Sure,' I said, lifting it from the bottom of the cupboard.

'Oh do let me . . . please?' She was as excited as if she'd still been little. I carried the base over to the workbench and laid it there, and she came over with four of the toys.

The Rola-base consisted of a large flat box, in this case two feet square by six inches deep, though several other sizes had been made. From one side protruded a handle for winding, and one had to have that side of the Rola-base aligned with the edge of the table, so that winding was possible. Inside the box were the rollers which gave the toy its phonetic Rola name; wide rollers carrying a long flat continuous belt inset with many rows of sideways facing cogwheel teeth. In the top of the box were corresponding rows of holes: dozen of holes altogether. Each of the separate mechanical toys, like the merry-go-round and a hundred others, had a central spindle which protruded down from beneath the toy and was grooved like a cog-wheel. When one slipped any spindle through any hole it engaged on the belt of cog teeth below, and when one turned the single handle in the Rola-base, the wide belt of cog teeth moved endlessly round and all the spindles rotated and all the toys performed their separate tasks. A simple locking device on the base of each toy engaged with stops by each hole to prevent the toy rotating as a whole.

Allie had brought the carousel and the roller-coaster from the fairground set, and a cow from the farm set, and the firing tank from the army set. She slotted the spindles through random holes and turned the handle. The merry-go-round went round and round, the trucks went up and down the roller-coaster, the cow nodded its head and swished its tail, and the tank rotated with sparks coming out of its gun barrel.

She laughed with pleasure.

'I don't believe it. I simply don't believe it. I never dreamt you could have made the Rola toys.'

'I've made others, though.'

'What sort?'

'Um . . . the latest in the shops is a coding machine. It's doing quite well this Christmas.'

'You don't mean the Secret Coder?'

'Yes.' I was surprised she knew of it.

'Do show me. My sister's giving one each to the boys, but they were already gift-wrapped.'

So I showed her the coder, which looked like providing me with racehorses for some time to come, as a lot of people besides children had found it compulsive. The new adult version was much more complicated but also much more expensive, which somewhat increased the royalties.

From the outside the children's version looked like a box, smaller than a shoe box, with a sloping top surface. Set in this were letter keys exactly like a conventional typewriter, except that there were no numbers, no punctuation and no space bar.

'How does it work?' Allie asked.

'You type your message and it comes out in code.'

'Just like that?'

'Try it.'

She gave me an amused look, turned so that I couldn't see her fingers, and with one hand expertly typed about twenty-five letters. From the end of the box a narrow paper strip emerged, with letters typed on it in groups of five.

'What now?'

'Tear the strip off,' I said.

She did that. 'It's like ticker-tape,' she said.

'It is. Same size, anyway.'

She held it out to me. I looked at it and came as close to blushing as I'm ever likely to.

'Can you read it just like that?' she exclaimed. 'Some coder, if you can read it at a glance.'

'I invented the damn thing,' I said. 'I know it by heart.'

'How does it work?'

'There's a cylinder inside with twelve complete alphabets on it, each arranged in a totally random manner and all different. You set this dial here . . . see,' I showed her, 'to any number from one to twelve. Then you type your message. Inside, the keys don't print the letter you press on the outside, but the letter that's aligned with it inside. There's an automatic spring which jumps after every five presses, so the message comes out in groups of five.'

'It's fantastic. My sister says the boys have been asking for them for weeks. Lots of children they know have them, all sending weird messages all over the place and driving their mothers wild.'

'You can make more involved codes by feeding the coded message through again, or backwards,' I said. 'Or by switching the code number every few letters. All the child receiving the message needs to know is the numbers he has to set on his own dial.'

'How do I decode this?'

'Put that tiny lever . . . there . . . down instead of up, and just type the coded message. It will come out as it went in, except still in groups of five letters, of course. Try it.'

She herself looked confused. She screwed up the tape and laughed, 'I guess I don't need to.'

'Would you like one?' I asked diffidently.

'I sure would.'

'Blue or red?'

'Red.'

In another cupboard I had a pile of manufactured coders packed like those in the shops. I opened one of the cartons, checked that the contents had a bright red plastic casing and handed it over.

'If you write me a Christmas message,' she said, 'I'll expect it in code number four.'

I took her out to dinner again as I was on a bacon-and-egg level myself as a cook, and she was after all on holiday to get away from the kitchen.

There was nothing new in taking a girl to dinner. Nothing exceptional, I supposed, in Allie herself. I liked her directness, her naturalness. She was supremely easy to be with, not interpreting occasional silences as personal insults, not coy or demanding, nor sexually a tease. Not a girl of hungry intellect, but certainly of good sense.

That wasn't all, of course. The spark which attracts one person to another was there too, and on her side also, I thought.

I drove her back to Hampstead and stopped outside her sister's house.

'Tomorrow?' I said.

She didn't answer directly. 'I go home on Thursday.'

'I know. What time is your flight?'

'Not till the evening. Six-thirty.'

'Can I drive you to the airport?'

'I could get my sister . . .'

'I'd like to.'

'Okay.'

We sat in a short silence.

'Tomorrow,' she said finally. 'I guess . . . If you like.'

'Yes.'

She nodded briefly, opened the car door, and spoke over her shoulder. 'Thank you for a fascinating day.'

She was out on the pavement before I could get round to help her. She smiled. Purring and contented, as far as I could judge.

'Good night.' She held out her hand.

I took it, and at the same time leant down and kissed her cheek. We looked at each other, her hand still in mine. One simply cannot waste such opportunities. I repeated the kiss, but on her lips.

She kissed as I'd expected, with friendliness and reservations. I kissed her twice more on the same terms.

'Good night,' she said again, smiling.

I watched her wave before she shut her sister's front door, and drove home wishing she were still with me. When I got back I went into the workshop and retrieved the screwed up piece of code she'd thrown in the litter bin. Smoothing it, I read the jumbled up letters again.

No mistake. Sorted out, the words were still a pat on the ego.

The toy man is as great as his toys.

I put the scrap of paper in my wallet and went upstairs to bed feeling the world's biggest fool.

CHAPTER FIVE

On Wednesday morning Charlie Canterfield telephoned at seven-thirty. I stretched a hand sleepily out of bed and groped for the receiver.

'Hullo?'

'Where the hell have you been?' Charlie said. 'I've been trying your number since Sunday morning.'

'Out.'

'I know that.' He sounded more amused than irritated. 'Look ... can you spare me some time today?'

'All of it, if you like.'

My generosity was solely due to the unfortunate fact that Allie had felt bound to spend her last full day with her sister, who had bought tickets and made plans. I had gathered that she'd only given me Monday and Tuesday at the expense of her other commitments, so I couldn't grumble. Tuesday had been even better than Monday, except for ending in exactly the same way.

'This morning will do,' Charlie said. 'Nine-thirty?'

'Okay. Amble along.'

'I want to bring a friend.'

'Fine. Do you know how to get here?'

'A taxi will find it,' Charlie said and disconnected.

Charlie's friend turned out to be a large man of Charlie's age with shoulders like a docker and language to match.

'Bert Huggerneck,' Charlie said, making introductions.

Bert Huggerneck crunched my bones in his muscular hand. 'Any friend of Charlie's is a friend of mine,' he said, but with no warmth or conviction.

'Come upstairs,' I said. 'Coffee? Or breakfast?'

'Coffee,' Charlie said. Bert Huggerneck said he didn't mind, which proved in the end to be bacon and tomato ketchup on toast twice, with curried baked beans on the side. He chose the meal himself from my meagre store cupboard and ate with speed and relish.

'Not a bad bit of bleeding nosh,' he observed, 'considering.'

'Considering what?' I asked.

He gave me a sharp look over a well-filled fork and made a gesture embracing both the flat and its neighbourhood. 'Considering you must be a rich bleeding capitalist, living here.' He pronounced it 'ca*pit*alist', and clearly considered it one of the worst of insults.

'Come off it,' Charlie said amiably. 'His breeding's as impeccable as yours and mine.'

'Huh.' Total disbelief didn't stop Bert Huggerneck accepting more toast. 'Got any jam?' he said.

'Sorry.'

He made do with half a jar of marmalade.

'What's that about breeding?' he said suspiciously to Charlie. 'Capitalists are all snobs.'

'His grandfather was a mechanic,' Charlie said. 'Same as mine was a milkman and yours a navvie.'

I was amused that Charlie had glossed over my father and mother, who had been school teacher and nurse. Far more respectable to be able to refer to the grandfather-mechanic, the welder-uncle and the host of card-carrying cousins. If politicians of all sorts searched diligently amongst their antecedents for proletarianism and denied aristocratic contacts three times before cockcrow every week-day morning, who was I to spoil the fun? In truth the two seemingly divergent lines of manual work and schoolmastering had given me the best of both worlds, the ability to use my hands and the education to design things for them to make. Money and experience had done the rest.

'I gather Mr Huggerneck is here against his will,' I observed.

'Don't you believe it,' Charlie said. 'He wants your help.'

'How does he act if he wants to kick you in the kidneys?'

'He wouldn't eat your food.'

Fair enough, I thought. Accept a man's salt, and you didn't boot him. Times hadn't collapsed altogether where that still held good.

We were sitting round the kitchen table with Charlie smoking a cigarette and using his saucer as an ashtray and me wondering what he considered so urgent. Bert wiped his plate with a spare piece of toast and washed that down with coffee.

'What's for lunch?' he said.

I took it as it was meant, as thanks for breakfast.

'Bert,' said Charlie, coming to the point, 'is a bookie's clerk.'

'Hold on,' Bert said. 'Not is. Was.'

'Was,' Charlie conceded, 'and will be again. But at the moment the firm he worked for is bankrupt.'

'The boss went spare,' Bert said, nodding. 'The bums come and took away all the bleeding office desks and that.'

'And all the bleeding typists?'

'Here,' said Bert, his brows suddenly lifting as a smile forced itself at last into his eyes. 'You're not all bad, then.'

'Rotten to the core,' I said. 'Go on.'

'Well, see, the boss got all his bleeding sums wrong, or like he said, his mathematical computations were based on a misconception.'

'Like the wrong horse won?'

Bert's smile got nearer. 'Cotton on quick, don't you? A whole bleeding row of wrong horses. Here, see, I've been writing for him for bleeding years. All the big courses, he was ... well, he had ... a pitch in Tatt's and down in the Silver Ring too, and I've been writing for him myself most of the time, for him personally, see?'

'Yes.' Bookmakers always took a clerk to record all bets as they were made. A bookmaking firm of any size sent out a team of two men or more to every allowed enclosure at most race meetings in their area: the bigger the firm, the more meetings they covered.

'Well, see, I warned him once or twice there was a leary look to his book. See, after bleeding years you get a nose for trouble, don't you? This last year or so he's made a right bleeding balls-up more than once and I told him he'd have the bums in if he went on like that, and I was right, wasn't I?'

'What did he say?'

'Told me to mind my own bleeding business,' Bert said. 'But it was my bleeding business, wasn't it? I mean, it was my job at stake. My livelihood, same as his. Who's going to pay my H.P. and rent and a few pints with the lads, I asked him, and he turned round and said not to worry, he had it all in hand, he knew what he was doing.' His voice held total disgust.

'And he didn't,' I remarked.

'Of course he bleeding didn't. He didn't take a blind bit of notice of what I said. Bleeding stupid, he was. Then ten days ago he really blew it. Lost a bleeding packet. The whole works. All of us got the push. No redundancy either. He's got a bleeding big overdraft in the bank and he's up to the eyeballs in debt.'

951

I glanced at Charlie who seemed exclusively interested in the ash on his cigarette.

'Why,' I asked Bert, 'did your boss ignore your warnings and rush headlong over the cliff?'

'He didn't jump over no cliff, he's getting drunk every night down the boozer.'

'I meant . . .'

'Hang on, I get you. Why did he lose the whole bleeding works? Because someone fed him the duff gen, that's my opinion. Cocky as all get out, he was, on the way to the races. Then coming home he tells me the firm is all washed up and down the bleeding drain. White as chalk, he was. Trembling, sort of. So I told him I'd warned him over and over. And that day I'd warned him too that he was laying too much on that Energise and not covering himself, and he'd told me all jolly like to mind my own effing business. So I reckon someone had told him Energise was fixed not to win, but it bleeding did win, and that's what's done for the firm.'

Bert shut his mouth and the silence was as loud as bells. Charlie tapped the ash off and smiled.

I swallowed.

'Er . . .' I said eventually.

'That's only half of it,' Charlie said, interrupting smoothly. 'Go on, Bert, tell him the rest.'

Bert seemed happy to oblige. 'Well, see, there I was in the boozer Saturday evening. Last Saturday, not the day Energise won. Four days ago, see? After the bums had been, and all that. Well, in walks Charlie like he sometimes does and we had a couple of jars together, him and me being old mates really on account of we lived next door to each other when we were kids and he was going to that la-di-da bleeding Eton and someone had to take him down a peg or two in the holidays. So, anyway, there we were in the boozer and I pour out all my troubles and Charlie says he has another friend who'd like to hear them, so ... well ... here we are.'

'What are the other troubles, then?' I asked.

'Oh ... Yeah. Well, see, the boss had a couple of betting shops. Nothing fancy, just a couple of betting shops in Windsor and Staines, see. The office, now, where the bailiffs came and took everything, that was behind the shop in Staines. So there's the boss holding his head and wailing like a siren because all his bleeding furniture's on its way out, when the phone rings. Course by this time the phone's down on the floor because the desk it was on is out on the pavement. So the boss squats down beside it and there's some geezer on the other end offering to buy the lease.'

He paused more for dramatic effect than breath.

'Go on,' I said encouragingly.

'Manna from Heaven for the boss, that was,' said Bert, accepting the invitation. 'See, he'd have had to go on paying the rent for both places even if they were shut. He practically fell on the neck of this geezer in a manner of speaking, and the geezer came round and paid him in cash on the nail, three hundred smackers, that very morning and the boss has been getting drunk on it ever since.'

A pause. 'What line of business,' I asked, 'is this geezer in?'

'Eh?' said Bert, surprised. 'Bookmaking, of course.' Charlie smiled.

'I expect you've heard of him,' Bert said. 'Name of Ganser Mays.'

It was inevitable, I supposed.

'In what way,' I asked, 'do you want me to help?'

'Huh?'

'Charlie said you wanted my help.'

'Oh that. I dunno, really. Charlie just said it might help to tell you what I'd told him, so I done it.'

'Did Charlie tell you,' I asked, 'who owns Energise?'

'No, Charlie didn't,' Charlie said.

'What the bleeding hell does it matter who owns it?' Bert demanded.

'I do,' I said.

Bert looked from one of us to the other several times. Various thoughts took their turn behind his eyes, and Charlie and I waited.

'Here,' he said at last. 'Did you bleeding fix that race?'

'The horse ran fair and square, and I backed it on the Tote,' I said.

'Well, how come my boss thought ...'

'I've no idea,' I said untruthfully.

Charlie lit another cigarette from the stub of the last. They were his lungs, after all.

'The point is,' I said, 'who gave your boss the wrong information?'

'Dunno.' He thought it over, but shook his head. 'Dunno.'

'Could it have been Ganser Mays?'

'Blimey!'

'Talk about slander,' Charlie said. 'He'd have you for that.'

'I merely ask,' I said. 'I also ask whether Bert knows of any other small firms which have gone out of business in the same way.'

'Blimey,' Bert said again, with even more force.

Charlie sighed with resignation, as if he hadn't engineered the whole morning's chat.

'Ganser Mays,' I said conversationally, 'has opened a vast string of betting shops during the past year or so. What has happened to the opposition?'

'Down the boozer getting drunk,' Charlie said.

Charlie stayed for a while after Bert had gone, sitting more comfortably in one of my leather armchairs and reverting thankfully to his more natural self.

'Bert's a great fellow,' he said. 'But I find him tiring.' His Eton accent, I noticed, had come back in force and I realised with mild surprise how much he tailored voice and manner to suit his company. The Charlie

Canterfield I knew, the powerful banker smoking a cigar who thought of a million as everyday currency, was not the face he had shown to Bert Huggerneck. It occurred to me that of all the people I had met who had moved from one world to another, Charlie had done it with most success. He swam through big business like a fish in water but he could still feel completely at home with Bert in a way that I, who had made a less radical journey, could not.

'Which is the villain,' Charlie asked, 'Ganser Mays or Jody Leeds?'

'Both.'

'Equal partners?'

We considered it. 'No way of knowing at the moment,' I said.

'At the moment?' His eyebrows went up.

I smiled slightly. 'I thought I might have a small crack at . . . would you call it justice?'

'The law's a bad thing to take into your own hands.'

'I don't exactly aim to lynch anyone.'

'What, then?'

I hesitated. 'There's something I ought to check. I think I'll do it today. After that, if I'm right, I'll make a loud fuss.'

'Slander actions notwithstanding?'

'I don't know.' I shook my head. 'It's infuriating.'

'What are you going to check?' he asked.

'Telephone tomorrow morning and I'll tell you.'

Charlie, like Allie, asked before he left if I would

show him where I made the toys. We went down to the workshop and found Owen Idris, my general helper, busy sweeping the tidy floor.

'Morning, Owen.'

'Morning, sir.'

'This is Mr Canterfield, Owen.'

'Morning, sir.'

Owen appeared to have swept without pause but I knew the swift glance he had given Charlie was as good as a photograph. My neat dry little Welsh factotum had a phenomenal memory for faces.

'Will you want the car today, sir?' he said.

'This evening.'

'I'll just change the oil, then.'

'Fine.'

'Will you be wanting me for the parking?'

I shook my head. 'Not tonight.'

'Very good, sir.' He looked resigned. 'Any time,' he said.

I showed Charlie the machines but he knew less about engineering than I did about banking.

'Where do you start, in the hands or in the head?'

'Head,' I said. 'Then hands, then head.'

'So clear.'

'I think of something, I make it, I draw it.'

'Draw it?'

'Machine drawings, not an artistic impression.'

'Blue prints,' said Charlie, nodding wisely.

'Blue prints are copies . . . The originals are black on white.'

'Disillusioning.'

I slid open one of the long drawers which held them and showed him some of the designs. The fine spidery lines with a key giving details of materials and sizes of screw threads looked very different from the bright shiny toys which reached the shops, and Charlie looked from design to finished article with a slowly shaking head.

'Don't know how you do it.'

'Training,' I said. 'Same way that you switch money round ten currencies in half an hour and end up thousands richer.'

'Can't do that so much these days,' he said gloomily. He watched me put designs and toys away. 'Don't forget though that my firm can always find finances for good ideas.'

'I won't forget.'

'There must be a dozen merchant banks,' Charlie said, 'all hoping to be nearest when you look around for cash.'

'The manufacturers fix the cash. I just collect the royalties.'

He shook his head. 'You'll never make a million that way.'

'I won't get ulcers either.'

'No ambition?'

'To win the Derby and get even with Jody Leeds.'

*

I arrived at Jody's expensive stable uninvited, quietly, at half past midnight, and on foot. The car lay parked half a mile behind me, along with prudence.

Pale fitful moonlight lit glimpses of the large manor house with its pedimented front door and rows of uniform windows. No lights shone upstairs in the room Jody shared with Felicity, and none downstairs in the large drawing-room beneath. The lawn, rough now and scattered with a few last dead leaves, stretched peacefully from the house to where I stood hidden in the bushes by the gate.

I watched for a while. There was no sign of anyone awake or moving, and I hadn't expected it. Jody like most six-thirty risers was usually asleep by eleven at the latest, and telephone calls after ten were answered brusquely if at all. On the other hand he had no reservations about telephoning others in the morning before seven. He had no patience with life-patterns unlike his own.

To the right and slightly to the rear of the house lay the dimly gleaming roofs of the stables. White railed paddocks lay around and beyond them, with big planned trees growing at landscaped corners. When Berksdown Court had been built, cost had come second to excellence.

Carrying a large black rubber-clad torch, unlit, I walked softly up the drive and round towards the horses. No dogs barked. No all-night guards sprang out to ask my business. Silence and peace bathed the whole place undisturbed.

My breath, all the same, came faster. My heart thumped. It would be bad if anyone caught me. I had tried reassuring myself that Jody would do me no actual physical harm, but I hadn't found myself convinced. Anger, as when I'd stood in the path of the horsebox, was again thrusting me into risk.

Close to the boxes one could hear little more than from a distance. Jody's horses stood on sawdust now that straw prices had trebled, and made no rustle when they moved. A sudden equine sneeze made me jump.

Jody's yard was not a regular quadrangle but a series of three-sided courts of unequal size and powerful charm. There were forty boxes altogether, few enough in any case to support such a lavish establishment, but since my horses had left I guessed there were only about twenty inmates remaining. Jody was in urgent need of another mug.

He had always economised on labour, reckoning that he and Felicity between them could do the work of four. His inexhaustible energy in fact ensured that no lads stayed in the yard very long as they couldn't stand the pace. Since the last so-called head lad had left in dudgeon because Jody constantly usurped his authority, there had been no one but Jody himself in charge. It was unlikely, I thought, that in present circumstances he would have taken on another man, which meant that the cottage at the end of the yard would be empty.

There were at any rate no lights in it, and no anxious figure came scurrying out to see about the stranger in the night. I went with care to the first box in the first court and quietly slid back the bolts.

Inside stood a large chestnut mare languidly eating hay. She turned her face unexcitedly in the torchlight. A big white blaze down her forehead and nose. Asphodel.

I shut her door, inching home the bolts. Any sharp noise would carry clearly through the cold calm air and Jody's subconscious ears would never sleep. The second box contained a heavy bay gelding with black points, the third a dark chestnut with one white sock. I went slowly round the first section of stables, shining the torch at each horse.

Instead of settling, my nerves got progressively worse. I had not yet found what I'd come for, and every passing minute made discovery more possible. I was careful with the torch. Careful with the bolts. My breath was shallow. I decided I'd make a rotten burglar.

Box number nine, in the next section, contained a dark brown gelding with no markings. The next box housed an undistinguished bay, the next another and the next another. After that came an almost black horse, with a slightly Arab looking nose, another very dark horse, and two more bays. The next three boxes all contained chestnuts, all unremarkable to my eyes. The last inhabited box held the only grey.

I gently shut the door of the grey and returned to the box of the chestnut next door. Went inside. Shone my torch over him carefully inch by inch.

I came to no special conclusion except that I didn't know enough about horses.

I'd done all I could. Time to go home. Time for my heart to stop thudding at twice the speed of sound. I turned for the door.

Lights came on in a blaze. Startled I took one step towards the door. Only one.

Three men crowded into the opening.

Jody Leeds.

Ganser Mays.

Another man whom I didn't know, whose appearance scarcely inspired joy and confidence. He was large, hard and muscular, and he wore thick leather gloves, a cloth cap pulled forward and, at two in the morning, sunglasses.

Whomever they had expected, it wasn't me. Jody's face held a mixture of consternation and anger, with the former winning by a mile.

'What the bloody hell are you doing here?' he said.

There was no possible answer.

'He isn't leaving,' Ganser Mays said. The eyes behind the metal rims were narrowed with ill intent and the long nose protruded sharply like a dagger. The urbane manner which lulled the clients while he relieved them of their cash had turned into the naked viciousness of the threatened criminal. Too late to worry that I'd cast myself in the role of threat.

'What?' Jody turned his face to him, not understanding.

'He isn't leaving.'

Jody said, 'How are you going to stop him?'

Nobody told him. Nobody told me, either. I took two steps towards the exit and found out.

The large man said nothing at all, but it was he who moved. A large gloved fist crashed into my ribs at the business end of a highly efficient short jab. Breath left my lungs faster than nature intended and I had difficulty getting it back.

Beyond schoolboy scuffles I had never seriously had to defend myself. No time to learn. I slammed an elbow at Jody's face, kicked Ganser Mays in the stomach and tried for the door.

Muscles in cap and sunglasses knew all that I didn't. An inch or two taller, a stone or two heavier, and warmed to his task. I landed one respectable punch on the junction of his nose and mouth in return for a couple of bangs over the heart, and made no progress towards freedom.

Jody and Ganser Mays recovered from my first onslaught and clung to me like limpets, one on each arm. I staggered under their combined weight. Muscles measured his distance and flung his bunched hand at my jaw. I managed to move my head just in time and felt the leather glove burn my cheek. Then the other

963

fist came round, faster and crossing, and hit me square. I fell reeling across the box, released suddenly by Ganser Mays and Jody, and my head smashed solidly into the iron bars of the manger.

Total instant unconsciousness was the result.

Death must be like that, I suppose.

CHAPTER SIX

Life came back in an incomprehensible blur.

I couldn't see properly. Couldn't focus. Heard strange noises. Couldn't control my body, couldn't move my legs, couldn't lift my head. Tongue paralysed. Brain whirling. Everything disconnected and hazy.

'Drunk,' someone said distinctly.

The word made no sense. It wasn't I who was drunk.

'Paralytic.'

The ground was wet. Shining. Dazzled my eyes. I was sitting on it. Slumped on it, leaning against something hard. I shut my eyes against the drizzle and that made the whirling worse. I could feel myself falling. Banged my head. Cheek in the wet. Nose in the wet. Lying on the hard wet ground. There was a noise like rain.

'Bloody amazing,' said a voice.

'Come on, then, let's be having you.'

Strong hands slid under my armpits and grasped my ankles. I couldn't struggle. Couldn't understand where I was or what was happening.

It seemed vaguely that I was in the back of a car. I could smell the upholstery. My nose was on it. Someone was breathing very loudly. Almost snoring. Someone spoke. A jumbled mixture of sounds that made no words. It couldn't have bccn me. Couldn't have been.

The car jerked to a sudden stop. The driver swore. I rolled off the seat and passed out.

Next thing, bright lights and people carrying me as before.

I tried to say something. It came out in a jumble. This time I knew the jumble came from my own mouth.

'Waking up again,' someone said.

'Get him out of here before he's sick.'

March, march. More carrying. Loud boots on echoing floors.

'He's bloody heavy.'

'Bloody nuisance.'

The whirling went on. The whole building was spinning like a merry-go-round.

Merry-go-round.

The first feeling of identity came back. I wasn't just a lump of weird disorientated sensations. Somewhere, deep inside, I was . . . somebody.

Merry-go-rounds swam in and out of consciousness. I found I was lying on a bed. Bright lights blinded me every time I tried to open my eyes. The voices went away.

Time passed.

I began to feel exceedingly ill. Heard someone moaning. Didn't think it was me. After a while, I knew it was, which made it possible to stop.

Feet coming back. March march. Two pairs at least.

'What's your name?'

What was my name? Couldn't remember.

'He's soaking wet.'

'What do you expect? He was sitting on the pavement in the rain.'

'Take his jacket off.'

They took my jacket off, sitting me up to do it. I lay down again. My trousers were pulled off and someone put a blanket over me.

'He's dead drunk.'

'Yes. Have to make sure though. They're always an infernal nuisance like this. You simply can't risk that they haven't bumped their skulls and got a hairline fracture. You don't want them dying on you in the night.'

I tried to tell him I wasn't drunk. Hairline fracture . . . Christ . . . I didn't want to wake up dead in the morning.

'What did you say?'

I tried again. 'Not drunk,' I said.

Someone laughed without mirth.

'Just smell his breath.'

How did I know I wasn't drunk? The answer eluded me. I just knew I wasn't drunk . . . because I knew I hadn't drunk enough ... or any ... alcohol. How did I know? I just knew. How did I know?

While these hopeless thoughts spiralled around in the chaos inside my head a lot of strange fingers were feeling around in my hair.

'He *has* banged his head, damn it. There's quite a large swelling.'

'He's no worse than when they brought him in, doc. Better if anything.'

'Scott,' I said suddenly.

'What's that?'

'Scott.'

'Is that your name?'

I tried to sit up. The lights whirled giddily.

'Where ... am I?'

'That's what they all say.'

'In a cell, my lad, that's where.'

In a cell.

'What?' I said.

'In a cell at Savile Row police station. Drunk and incapable.'

I couldn't be.

'Look, constable, I'll just take a blood test. Then I'll do those other jobs, then come back and look at him, to make sure. I don't think we've a fracture here, but we can't take the chance.'

'Right, doc.'

The prick of a needle reached me dimly. Waste of time, I thought. Wasn't drunk. What was I ... besides ill, giddy, lost and stuck in limbo? Didn't know. Couldn't be bothered to think. Slid without struggling into a whirling black sleep.

The next awakening was in all ways worse. For a start, I wasn't ready to be dragged back from the dark. My head ached abominably, bits of my body hurt a good deal and overall I felt like an advanced case of seasickness.

'Wakey, wakey, rise and shine. Cup of tea for you and you don't deserve it.'

I opened my eyes. The bright light was still there but now identifiable not as some gross moon but as a simple electric bulb near the ceiling.

I shifted my gaze to where the voice had come from. A middle-aged policeman stood there with a paper cup in one hand. Behind him, an open door to a corridor. All round me, the close walls of a cell. I lay on a reasonably comfortable bed with two blankets keeping me warm.

'Sobering up, are you?'

'I wasn't . . . drunk.' My voice came out hoarse and my mouth felt as furry as a mink coat.

The policeman held out the cup. I struggled on to one elbow and took it from him.

'Thanks.' The tea was strong, hot and sweet. I wasn't sure it didn't make me feel even sicker.

'The doc's been back twice to check on you. You were drunk all right. Banged your head, too.'

'But I wasn't . . .'

'You sure were. The doc did a blood test to make certain.'

'Where are my clothes?'

'Oh yeah. We took 'em off. They were wet. I'll get them.'

He went out without shutting the door and I spent the few minutes he was away trying to sort out what was happening. I could remember bits of the night, but hazily. I knew who I was. No problem there. I looked at my watch: seven-thirty. I felt absolutely lousy.

The policeman returned with my suit which was wrinkled beyond belief and looked nothing like the one I'd set out in.

Set out ... Where to?

'Is this ... Savile Row? West end of London?'

'You remember being brought in then?'

'Some of it. Not much.'

'The patrol car picked you up somewhere in Soho at around four o'clock this morning.'

'What was I doing there?'

'I don't know, do I? Nothing, as far as I know. Just sitting dead drunk on the pavement in the pouring rain.'

'Why did they bring me here if I wasn't doing anything?'

'To save you from yourself,' he said without rancour. 'Drunks make more trouble if we leave them than if we bring them in, so we bring them in. Can't have drunks wandering out into the middle of the road and causing accidents or breaking their silly skulls falling over or waking up violent and smashing shop windows as some of them do.'

'I feel ill.'

'What d'you expect? If you're going to be sick there's a bucket at the end of the bed.'

He gave me a nod in which sympathy wasn't entirely lacking, and took himself away.

About an hour later I was driven with three other gentlemen in the same plight to attend the Marlborough Street Magistrates' Court. Drunks, it seemed, were first on the agenda. Every day's agenda.

In the interim I had become reluctantly convinced of three things.

First was that even though I could not remember drinking, I had at four a.m. that morning been hopelessly intoxicated. The blood test, analysed at speed because of the bang on my head, had revealed a level of two hundred and ninety milligrammes of alcohol per centilitre of blood which, I had been assured, meant that I had drunk the equivalent of more than half a bottle of spirits during the preceding few hours.

The second was that it would make no difference at all if I could convince anyone that at one-thirty I had been stone cold sober seventy miles away in Berkshire. They would merely say I had plenty of time to get drunk on the journey.

971

And the third and perhaps least welcome of all was that I seemed to have collected far more sore spots than I could account for.

I had remembered, bit by bit, my visit to Jody. I remembered trying to fight all three men at once, which was an idiotic sort of thing to attempt in the first place, even without the casual expertise of the man in sun glasses. I remembered the squashy feel when my fist connected with his nose and I knew all about the punches he'd given me in return. Even so . . .

I shrugged. Perhaps I didn't remember it all, like I didn't remember getting drunk. Or perhaps . . . Well, Ganser Mays and Jody both had reason to dislike me, and Jody had been wearing jodhpur boots.

The court proceedings took ten minutes. The charge was 'drunk in charge'. In charge of what, I asked. In charge of the police, they said.

'Guilty or not guilty?'

'Guilty,' I said resignedly.

'Fined five pounds. Do you need time to pay?'

'No, sir.'

'Good. Next, please.'

Outside, in the little office where I was due to pay the fine, I telephoned Owen Idris. Paying after all had been a problem, as there had proved to be no wallet in my rough-dried suit. No cheque book either, nor, when I came to think of it, any keys. Were they all by any chance at Savile Row, I asked. Someone telephoned. No, they weren't. I had nothing at all in my pockets when picked up. No means of identification, no money, no keys, no pen, no handkerchief.

'Owen? Bring ten pounds and a taxi to Marlborough Street Court.'

'Very good, sir.'

'Right away.'

'Of course.'

I felt hopelessly groggy. I sat in an upright chair to wait and wondered how long it took for half a bottle of spirits to dry out.

Owen came in thirty minutes and handed me the money without comment. Even his face showed no surprise at finding me in such a predicament and unshaven into the bargain. I wasn't sure that I appreciated his lack of surprise. I also couldn't think of any believable explanation. Nothing to do but shrug it off, pay the five pounds and get home as best I could. Owen sat beside me in the taxi and gave me small sidelong glances every hundred yards.

I made it upstairs to the sitting-room and lay down flat on the sofa. Owen had stayed downstairs to pay the taxi and I could hear him talking to someone down in the hall. I could do without visitors, I thought. I could do without everything except twenty-four hours of oblivion.

The visitor was Charlie.

'Your man says you're in trouble.'

'Mm.'

'Good God.' He was standing beside me, looking down. 'What on earth have you been doing?'

'Long story.'

'Hm. Will your man get us some coffee?'

'Ask him . . . he'll be in the workshop. Intercom over there.' I nodded towards the far door and wished I hadn't. My whole brain felt like a bruise.

Charlie talked to Owen on the intercom and Owen came up with his ultra-polite face and messed around with filters in the kitchen.

'What's the matter with you?' Charlie asked.

'Knocked out, drunk and . . .' I stopped.

'And what?'

'Nothing.'

'You need a doctor.'

'I saw a police surgeon. Or rather . . . he saw me.'

'You can't see the state of your eyes,' Charlie said seriously. 'And whether you like it or not, I'm getting you a doctor.' He went away to the kitchen to consult Owen and I heard the extension bell there tinkling as he kept his promise. He came back.

'What's wrong with my eyes?'

'Pinpoint pupils and glassy daze.'

'Charming.'

Owen brought the coffee, which smelled fine, but I found I could scarcely drink it. Both men looked at me with what I could only call concern.

'How did you get like this?' Charlie asked.

'Shall I go, sir?' Owen said politely.

'No. Sit down, Owen. You may as well know too . . .'
He sat comfortably in a small armchair, neither per-
ching on the front nor lolling at ease in the depths. The
compromise of Owen's attitude to me was what made
him above price, his calm understanding that although
I paid for work done, we each retained equal dignity
in the transaction. I had employed him for less than a
year: I hoped he would stay till he dropped.

'I went down to Jody Leeds' stable, last night, after
dark,' I said. 'I had no right at all to be there. Jody and
two other men found me in one of the boxes looking
at a horse. There was a bit of a struggle and I banged
my head . . . on the manger, I think . . . and got knocked
out.'

I stopped for breath. My audience said nothing at
all.

'When I woke up, I was sitting on a pavement in
Soho, dead drunk.'

'Impossible,' Charlie said.

'No. It happened. The police scooped me up, as they
apparently do to all drunks littering the footpaths. I
spent the remains of the night in a cell and got fined
five pounds, and here I am.'

There was a long pause.

Charlie cleared his throat. 'Er . . . various questions
arise.'

'They do indeed.'

Owen said calmly, 'The car, sir. Where did you leave

the car?' The car was his especial love, polished and cared for like silver.

I told him exactly where I'd parked it. Also that I no longer had its keys. Nor the keys to the flat or the workshop, for that matter.

Both Charlie and Owen showed alarm and agreed between themselves that the first thing Owen would do, even before fetching the car, would be to change all my locks.

'I made those locks,' I protested.

'Do you want Jody walking in here while you're asleep?'

'No.'

'Then Owen changes the locks.'

I didn't demur any more. I'd been thinking of a new form of lock for some time, but hadn't actually made it. I would soon, though. I would patent it and make it as a toy for kids to lock up their secrets, and maybe in twenty years' time half the doors in the country would be keeping out burglars that way. My lock didn't need keys or electronics, and couldn't be picked. It stood there, clear and sharp in my mind, with all its working parts meshing neatly.

'Are you all right?' Charlie said abruptly.

'What?'

'For a moment you looked . . .' He stopped and didn't finish the sentence.

'I'm not dying, if that's what you think. It's just that I've an idea for a new sort of lock.'

Charlie's attention sharpened as quickly as it had at Sandown.

'Revolutionary?' he asked hopefully.

I smiled inside. The word was apt in more ways than one, as some of the lock's works would revolve.

'You might say so,' I agreed.

'Don't forget . . . my bank.'

'I won't.'

'No one but you would be inventing things when he's half dead.'

'I may look half dead,' I said, 'but I'm not.' I might feel half dead, too, I thought, but it would all pass.

The door bell rang sharply.

'If it's anyone but the doctor,' Charlie told Owen, 'tell them our friend is out.'

Owen nodded briefly and went downstairs, but when he came back he brought not the doctor but a visitor less expected and more welcome.

'Miss Ward, sir.'

She was through the door before he had the words out, blowing in like a gust of fresh air, her face as smooth and clean and her clothes as well-groomed as mine were dirty and squalid. She looked like life itself on two legs, her vitality lighting the room.

'Steven!'

She stopped dead a few feet from the sofa, staring down. She glanced at Charlie and at Owen. 'What's the matter with him?'

'Rough night on the tiles,' I said. 'D'you mind if I don't get up?'

'How do you do?' Charlie said politely. 'I am Charlie Canterfield. Friend of Steven's.' He shook hands with her.

'Alexandra Ward,' she replied, looking bemused.

'You've met,' I said.

'What?'

'In Walton Street.'

They looked at each other and realised what I meant. Charlie began to tell Allie how I had arrived in this sorry state and Owen went out shopping for locks. I lay on the sofa and drifted. The whole morning seemed disjointed and jerky to me, as if my thought processes were tripping over cracks.

Allie pulled up a squashy leather stool and sat beside me, which brought recovery nearer. She put her hand on mine. Better still.

'You're crazy,' she said.

I sighed. Couldn't have everything.

'Have you forgotten I'm going home this evening?'

'I have not,' I said. 'Though it looks now as though I'll have to withdraw my offer of driving you to the airport. I don't think I'm fit. No car, for another thing.'

'That's actually what I came for.' She hesitated. 'I have to keep peace with my sister . . .' She stopped, leaving a world of family tensions hovering unspoken. 'I came to say goodbye.'

'What sort of goodbye?'

'What do you mean?'

'Goodbye for now,' I said, 'or goodbye for ever?'

'Which would you like?'

Charlie chuckled. 'Now there's a double-edged question if I ever heard one.'

'You're not supposed to be listening,' she said with mock severity.

'Goodbye for now,' I said.

'All right.' She smiled the flashing smile. 'Suits me.'

Charlie wandered round the room looking at things but showed no signs of going. Allie disregarded him. She stroked my hair back from my forehead and kissed me gently. I can't say I minded.

After a while the doctor came. Charlie went down to let him in and apparently briefed him on the way up. He and Allie retired to the kitchen where I heard them making more coffee.

The doctor helped me remove all clothes except underpants. I'd have been much happier left alone. He tapped my joints for reflexes, peered through lights into my eyes and ears and prodded my many sore spots. Then he sat on the stool Allie had brought, and pinched his nose.

'Concussion,' he said. 'Go to bed for a week.'

'Don't be silly,' I protested.

'Best,' he said succinctly.

'But the jump jockeys get concussion one minute and ride winners the next.'

'The jump jockeys are bloody fools.' He surveyed

me morosely. 'If you'd been a jump jockey I'd say you'd been trampled by a field of horses.'

'But as I'm not?'

'Has someone been beating you?'

It wasn't the sort of question somehow that one expected one's doctor to ask. Certainly not as matter-of-factly as this.

'I don't know,' I said.

'You must do.'

'I agree it feels a bit like it, but if they did, I was unconscious.'

'With something big and blunt,' he added. 'They're large bruises.' He pointed to several extensive reddening patches on my thighs, arms and trunk.

'A boot?' I said.

He looked at me soberly. 'You've considered the possibility?'

'Forced on me.'

He smiled. 'Your friend, the one who let me in, told me you say you got drunk also while unconscious.'

'Yes. Tube down the throat?' I suggested.

'Tell me the time factors.'

I did as nearly as I could. He shook his head dubiously. 'I wouldn't have thought pouring neat alcohol straight into the stomach would produce that amount of intoxication so quickly. It takes quite a while for a large quantity of alcohol to be absorbed into the bloodstream through the stomach wall.' He pondered, thinking aloud. 'Two hundred and ninety milligrammes ... and you were maybe unconscious from the bang on the head for two hours or a little more. Hm.'

He leaned forward, picked up my left forearm and peered at it closely, front and back. Then he did the same thing with the right, and found what he was looking for.

'There,' he exclaimed. 'See that? The mark of a needle. Straight into the vein. They've tried to disguise it by a blow on top to bruise all the surrounding tissue. In a few more hours the needle mark will be invisible.'

'Anaesthetic?' I said dubiously.

'My dear fellow. No. Probably gin.'

'*Gin!*'

'Why not? Straight into the bloodstream. Much more efficient than a tube to the stomach. Much quicker results. Deadly, really. And less effort, on the whole.'

'But ... how? You can't harness a gin bottle to a hypodermic.'

He grinned. 'No, no. You'd set up a drip. Sterile glucose saline drip. Standard stuff. You can buy it in plastic bags from any chemist. Pour three quarters of a pint of gin into one bag of solution, and drip it straight into the vein.'

'But, how long would that take?'

'Oh, about an hour. Frightful shock to the system.'

I thought about it. If it had been done that way I had been transported to London with gin dripping into my blood for most of the journey. There hadn't been time to do it first and set off after.

'Suppose I'd started to come round?' I asked.

'Lucky you didn't, I dare say. Nothing to stop someone bashing you back to sleep, as far as I can see.'

'You take it very calmly,' I said.

'So do you. And it's interesting, don't you think?'

'Oh very,' I said dryly.

CHAPTER SEVEN

Charlie and Allie stayed for lunch, which meant that they cooked omelettes for themselves and found some reasonable cheese to follow. Out in the kitchen Charlie seemed to have been filling in gaps because when they carried their trays into the sitting-room it was clear that Allie knew all that Charlie did.

'Do you feel like eating?' Charlie asked.

'I do not.'

'Drink?'

'Shut up.'

'Sorry.'

The body rids itself of alcohol very slowly, the doctor had said. Only at a rate of ten milligrammes per hour. There was no way of hastening the process and nothing much to be done about hangovers except endure them. People who normally drank little suffered worst, he said, because their bodies had no tolerance. Too bad, he'd said, smiling about it.

Two hundred and ninety milligrammes came into the paralytic bracket. Twenty-nine hours to be rid of it. I'd lived through about ten so far. No wonder I felt so awful.

Round a mouthful of omelette Charlie said, 'What are you going to do about all this?' He waved his fork from my heels to my head, still prostrate on the sofa.

'Would you suggest going to the police?' I asked neutrally.

'Er . . .'

'Exactly. The very same police who gave me hospitality last night and know for a certainty that I was so drunk that anything I might complain of could be explained away as an alcoholic delusion.'

'Do you think that's why Jody and Ganser Mays did it?'

'Why else? And I suppose I should be grateful that all they did was discredit me, not bump me right off altogether.'

Allie looked horrified, which was nice. Charlie was more prosaic.

'Bodies are notoriously difficult to get rid of,' he said. 'I would say that Jody and Ganser Mays made a rapid assessment and reckoned that dumping you drunk in London was a lot less dangerous than murder.'

'There was another man as well,' I said, and described my friend with sunglasses and muscles.

'Ever seen him before?' Charlie asked.

'No, never.'

'The brawn of the organisation?'

'Maybe he has brain, too. Can't tell.'

'One thing is sure,' Charlie said. 'If the plan was to discredit you, your little escapade will be known all round the racecourse by tomorrow afternoon.'

How gloomy, I thought. I was sure he was right. It would make going to the races more uninviting than ever.

Allie said, 'I guess you won't like it, but if I were trying to drag your name through the mud I'd have made sure there was a gossip columnist in court this morning.'

'Oh hell.' Worse and worse.

'Are you just going to lie there,' Charlie said, 'and let them crow?'

'He's got a problem,' Allie said with a smile. 'How come he was wandering around Jody's stable at that time anyway?'

'Ah,' I said. 'Now that's the nub of the matter, I agree. And if I tell you, you must both promise me on your souls that you will not repeat it.'

'Are you serious?' Allie said in surprise.

'You don't sound it,' Charlie commented.

'I am, though. Deadly serious. Will you promise?'

'You play with too many toys. It's childish.'

'Many civil servants swear an oath of secrecy.'

'Oh all right,' Charlie said in exasperation. 'On my soul.'

'And on mine,' Allie said lightheartedly. 'Now do get on with it.'

'I own a horse called Energise,' I said. They both

nodded. They knew. 'I spent half an hour alone with him in a crashed horsebox at Sandown.' They both nodded again. 'Then I sent him to Rupert Ramsey and last Sunday morning I spent half an hour alone with him again.'

'So what?' Charlie said.

'So the horse at Rupert Ramsey's is not Energise.'

Charlie sat bolt upright so quickly that his omelette plate fell on the carpet. He bent down, feeling around for bits of egg with his astounded face turned up to mine.

'Are you sure?'

'Definitely. He's very like him, and if I hadn't spent all that time in the crashed horsebox I would never have known the difference. Owners often don't know which their horse is. It's a standing joke. But I *learnt* Energise that day at Sandown. So when I visited Rupert Ramsey's I knew he had a different horse.'

'So,' said Charlie slowly, 'you went to Jody's stable last night to see if Energise was still there.'

'Yes.'

'And is he?'

'Yes.'

'Absolutely certain?'

'Positive. He has a slightly Arab nose, a nick near the tip of his left ear, a bald spot about the size of a twopenny piece on his shoulder. He was in box number thirteen.'

'Is that where they found you?'

'No. You remember, Allie, that we went to New-market?'

'How could I forget?'

'Do you remember Hermes?'

She wrinkled her nose. 'Was that the chestnut?'

'That's right. Well, I went to Trevor Kennet's stable that day with you because I wanted to see if I could tell whether the Hermes he had was the Hermes Jody had had . . . if you see what I mean.'

'And was he?' she said, fascinated.

'I couldn't tell. I found I didn't know Hermes well enough and anyway if Jody did switch Hermes he probably did it before his last two races last summer, because the horse did no good at all in those and trailed in at the back of the field.'

'Good God,' Charlie said. 'And did you find Hermes at Jody's place too?'

'I don't know. There were three chestnuts there. No markings, same as Hermes. All much alike. I couldn't tell if any of them was Hermes. But it was in one of the chestnuts' boxes that Jody and the others found me, and they were certainly alarmed as well as angry.'

'But what would he get out of it?' Allie asked.

'He owns some horses himself,' I said. 'Trainers often do. They run them in their own names, then if they're any good, they sell them at a profit, probably to owners who already have horses in the stable.'

'You mean . . .' she said, 'that he sent a horse he owned himself to Rupert Ramsey and kept Energise,

Then when Energise wins another big race he'll sell him to one of the people he trains for, for a nice fat sum, and keep on training him himself?'

'That's about it.'

'Wow.'

'I'm not so absolutely sure,' I said with a sardonic smile, 'that he hasn't in the past sold me my own horse back after swopping it with one of his own.'

'Je-*sus*,' Charlie said.

'I had two bay fillies I couldn't tell apart. The first one won for a while, then turned sour. I sold her on Jody's advice and bought the second, which was one of his own. She started winning straight away.'

'How are you going to prove it?' Allie said.

'I don't see how you can,' said Charlie. 'Especially not after this drinking charge.'

We all three contemplated the situation in silence.

'Gee, dammit,' said Allie finally and explosively. 'I just don't see why that guy should be allowed to rob you and make people despise you and get away with it.'

'Give me time,' I said mildly, 'and he won't.'

'Time?'

'For thinking,' I explained. 'If a frontal assault would land me straight into a lawsuit for slander, which it would, I'll have to come up with a sneaky scheme which will creep up on him from the rear.'

Allie and Charlie looked at each other.

Charlie said to her, 'A lot of the things he's invented as children's toys get scaled up very usefully.'

'As if Cockerell had made the first Hovercraft for the bath tub?'

'Absolutely.' Charlie nodded at her with approval. 'And I dare say it was a gentle-seeming man who thought up gunpowder.'

She flashed a smiling look from him to me and then looked suddenly at her watch and got to her feet in a hurry.

'Oh golly! I'm late. I should have gone an hour ago. My sister will be so mad. Steven . . .'

Charlie looked at her resignedly and took the plates out to the kitchen. I shifted my lazy self off the sofa and stood up.

'I wish you weren't going,' I said.

'I really have to.'

'Do you mind kissing an unshaven drunk?'

It seemed she didn't. It was the best we'd achieved.

'The Atlantic has shrunk,' I said, 'since Columbus.'

'Will you cross it?'

'Swim, if necessary.'

She briefly kissed my bristly cheek, laughed and went quickly. The room seemed darker and emptier. I wanted her back with a most unaccustomed fierceness. Girls had come and gone in my life and each time afterwards I had relapsed thankfully into singleness. Maybe at thirty-five, I thought fleetingly, what I wanted was a wife.

Charlie returned from the kitchen carrying a cup and saucer.

'Sit down before you fall down,' he said. 'You're swaying about like the Empire State.'

I sat on the sofa.

'And drink this.'

He had made a cup of tea, not strong, not weak, and with scarcely any milk. I took a couple of sips and thanked him.

'Will you be all right if I go?' he said. 'I've an appointment.'

'Of course, Charlie.'

'Take care of your damned silly self.'

He buttoned his overcoat, gave me a sympathetic wave and departed. Owen had long since finished changing the locks and had set off with a spare set of keys to fetch the car. I was alone in the flat. It seemed much quieter than usual.

I drank the rest of the tea, leaned back against the cushions, and shut my eyes, sick and uncomfortable from head to foot. Damn Jody Leeds, I thought. Damn and blast him to hell.

No wonder, I thought, that he had been so frantically determined to take Energise back with him from Sandown. He must already have had the substitute in his yard, waiting for a good moment to exchange them. When I'd said I wanted Energise to go elsewhere immediately he had been ready to go to any lengths to prevent it. I was pretty sure now that had Jody been driving the horsebox instead of Andy-Fred I would have ended up in hospital if not the morgue.

I thought about the passports which were the identity cards of British thoroughbreds. A blank passport form bore three stylised outlines of a horse, one from each side and one from head on. At the time when a foal was named, usually as a yearling or two-year-old, the veterinary surgeon attending the stable where he was being trained filled in his markings on the form and completed a written description alongside. The passport was then sent to the central racing authorities who stamped it, filed it and sent a photocopy back to the trainer.

I had noticed from time to time that my horses had hardly a blaze, star or white sock between them. It had never struck me as significant. Thousands of horses had no markings. I had even preferred them without.

The passports, once issued, were rarely used. As far as I knew, apart from travelling abroad, they were checked only once, which was on the day of the horse's very first race; and that not out of suspicion, but simply to make sure the horse actually did match the vet's description.

I didn't doubt that the horse now standing instead of Energise at Rupert Ramsey's stable matched Energise's passport in every way. Details like the shape of the nose, the slant of the stomach, the angle of the hock, wouldn't be on it.

I sighed and shifted a bit to relieve various aches. Didn't succeed. Jody had been generous with his boots.

I remembered with satisfaction the kick I'd landed in Ganser Mays' stomach. But perhaps he too had taken revenge.

It struck me suddenly that Jody wouldn't have had to rely on Raymond Child to ride crooked races. Not every time, anyway. If he had a substitute horse of poor ability, all he had to do was send him instead of the good one whenever the race had to be lost.

Racing history was packed with rumours of ringers, the good horses running in the names of the bad. Jody, I was sure, had simply reversed things and run bad horses in the names of good.

Every horse I'd owned, when I looked back, had followed much the same pattern. There would be at first a patch of sporadic success, but with regular disasters every time I staked a bundle, and then a long tail-off with no success at all. It was highly likely that the no success was due to my now having the substitute, which was running way out of its class.

It would explain why Ferryboat had run badly all autumn. Not because he resented Raymond Child's whip, but because he wasn't Ferryboat. Wrecker, too. And at least one of the three older horses I'd sent up north.

Five at least, that made. Also the filly. Also the first two, now sold as flops. Eight. I reckoned I might still have the real Dial and I might still have the real Bubbleglass, because they were novices who had yet to prove their worth. But they too would have been matched, when they had.

A systematic fraud. All it needed was a mug.

I had been ignorantly happy. No owner expected to win all the time and there must have been many days when Jody's disappointment too had been genuine. Even the best-laid bets went astray if the horses met faster opposition.

The money I'd staked with Ganser Mays had been small change compared with the value of the horses.

Impossible ever to work out just how many thousands had vanished from there. It was not only that the re-sale value of the substitutes after a string of bad races was low, but there was also the prize money the true horses might have won for me and even, in the case of Hermes, the possibility of stud fees. The real Hermes might have been good enough. The substitute would fail continually as a four-year-old and no one would want to breed from him. In every way, Jody had bled every penny he could.

Energise . . .

Anger deepened in me abruptly. For Energise I felt more admiration and affection than for any of the others. He wasn't a matter of cash value. He was a person I'd got to know in a horsebox. One way or another I was going to get him back.

I moved restlessly, standing up. Not wise. The head-ache I'd had all day began imitating a pile-driver. Whether it was still alcohol, or all concussion, it made little difference to the wretched end result. I went impatiently into the bedroom, put on a dressing-gown over shirt and trousers and lay down on the bed. The short December afternoon began to close in with creeping grey shadows and I reckoned it was twelve hours since Jody had dumped me in the street.

I wondered whether the doctor was right about the gin dripping into my vein. The mark he had said was a needle prick had, as predicted, vanished into a larger area of bruising. I doubted whether it had ever been there. When one thought it over it seemed an unlikely method because of one simple snag: the improbability of Jody just happening to have a bag of saline lying around handy. Maybe it was true one could buy it from any chemist, but not in the middle of the night.

The only all-night chemists were in London. Would there have been time to belt up the M4, buy the saline, and drip it in while parked in central London? Almost certainly not. And why bother? Any piece of rubber tubing down the throat would have done instead.

I massaged my neck thoughtfully. No soreness around the tonsils. Didn't prove anything either way.

It was still less likely that Ganser Mays, on a visit to Jody, would be around with hypodermic and drip. My absolutely stinking luck, I reflected gloomily, that I had chosen to snoop around on one of the rare evenings Jody had not been to bed by ten thirty. I supposed that for all my care the flash of my torch had been visible from outside. I supposed that Jody had come out of his house to see off his guests and they'd spotted the wavering light.

Ganser Mays. I detested him in quite a different way from Jody because I had never at any time liked him personally. I felt deeply betrayed by Jody, but the trust I'd given Ganser Mays had been a surface thing, a matter of simple expectation that he would behave with professional honour.

From Bert Huggerneck's description of the killing-off of one small bookmaking business it was probable Ganser Mays had as much professional honour as an octopus. His tentacles stretched out and clutched and sucked the victim dry. I had a vision of a whole crowd of desperate little men sitting on their office floors because the bailiffs had taken the furniture, sobbing with relief down their telephones while Ganser Mays offered to buy the albatross of their lease for peanuts: and another vision of the same crowd of little men getting drunk in dingy pubs, trying to obliterate the pain of seeing the bright new shop fronts glowing over the ashes of their closed books.

Very likely the little men had been stupid. Very likely they should have had more sense than to believe even the most reliable-seeming information, even though the reliable-seeming information had in the past proved to be correct. Every good card-sharper knew that the victim who had been allowed to win to begin with would part with the most in the end.

If on a minor level Ganser Mays had continually

worked that trick on me, and others like me, then how much more had he stood to gain by entangling every vulnerable little firm he could find. He'd sucked the juices, discarded the husks, and grown fat.

Proof, I thought, was impossible. The murmurs of wrong information could never be traced and the crowd of bankrupt little men probably thought of Ganser Mays as their saviour, not the architect of the skids.

I imagined the sequence of events as seen by Jody and Ganser Mays when Energise ran at Sandown. To begin with, they must have decided that I should have a big bet and the horse would lose. Or even ... that the substitute would run instead. Right up until the day before the race, that would have been the plan. Then I refused to bet. Persuasion failed. Quick council of war. I should be taught a lesson, to bet when my trainer said so. The horse ... Energise himself ... was to run to win.

Fine. But Bert Huggerneck's boss went off to Sandown expecting, positively *knowing*, that Energise would lose. The only people who could have told him so were Ganser Mays and Jody. Or perhaps Raymond Child. I thought it might be informative to find out just when Bert Huggerneck's boss had been given the news. I might get Bert to ask him.

My memory wandered to Rupert Ramsey's office and the bright green wool of Poppet Vine. She and her husband had started to bet with Ganser Mays and Felicity Leeds had engineered it. Did Felicity, I wondered sourly, know all about Jody's plundering ways? I supposed that she must, because she knew all their horses. Lads might come and go, discouraged by having to work too hard, but Felicity rode out twice every morning and groomed and fed in the evenings. Felicity assuredly would know if a horse had been switched.

She might be steering people to Ganser Mays out of loyalty, or for commission, or for some reason unguessed at; but everything I heard or learned seemed to make it certain that although Jody Leeds and Ganser Mays might benefit in separate ways, everything they did was a joint enterprise.

There was also, I supposed, the third man, old muscle and sunglasses. The beef of the organisation. I didn't think I would ever forget him: raincoat over heavy shoulders, cloth cap over forehead, sunglasses over eyes... almost a disguise. Yet I hadn't known him. I was positive I'd never seen him anywhere before. So why had he needed a disguise at one-thirty in the morning when he hadn't expected to be seen by me in the first place?

All I knew of him was that at some point he had learned to box. That he was of sufficient standing in the trio to make his own decisions, because neither of the others had told him to hit me: he'd done it of his own accord. That Ganser Mays and Jody felt they needed his extra muscle, because neither of them was large, though Jody in his way was strong, in case any of the swindled victims cut up rough.

The afternoon faded and became night. All I was doing, I thought, was sorting through the implications and explanations of what had happened. Nothing at all towards getting myself out of trouble and Jody in. When I tried to plan that, all I achieved was a blank.

In the silence I clearly heard the sound of the street door opening. My heart jumped. Pulse raced again, as in the stable. Brain came sternly afterwards like a schoolmaster, telling me not to be so bloody silly.

No one but Owen had the new keys. No one but Owen would be coming in. All the same I was relieved when the lights were switched on in the hall and I could hear his familiar tread on the stairs.

He came into the dark sitting-room.

'Sir?'

'In the bedroom,' I called.

He came into the doorway, silhouetted against the light in the passage.

'Shall I turn the light on?'

'No, don't bother.'

'Sir . . .' His voice suddenly struck me as being odd. Uncertain. Or distressed.

'What's the matter?'

'I couldn't find the car.' The words came out in a rush. The distress was evident.

'Go and get yourself a stiff drink and come back and tell me about it.'

He hesitated a fraction but went away to the sitting-room and clinked glasses. I fumbled around with an outstretched hand and switched on the bedside light. Squinted at my watch. Six-thirty. Allie would be at Heathrow, boarding her aeroplane, waving to her sister, flying away.

Owen returned with two glasses, both containing scotch and water. He put one glass on my bedside table and interrupted politely when I opened my mouth to protest.

'The hair of the dog. You know it works, sir.'

'It just makes you drunker.'

'But less queasy.'

I waved towards my bedroom armchair and he sat in it easily as before, watching me with a worried expression. He held his glass carefully, but didn't drink. With a sigh I propped myself on one elbow and led the way. The first sip tasted vile, the second passable, the third familiar.

'Okay,' I said. 'What about the car?'

Owen took a quick gulp from his glass. The worried expression intensified.

'I went down to Newbury on the train and hired a taxi, like you said. We drove to where you showed me on the map, but the car didn't seem to be there. So I got the taxi driver to go along every possible road leading away from Mr Leeds' stable and I still couldn't find it. The taxi driver got pretty ratty in the end. He said there wasn't anywhere else to look. I got him to drive around in a larger area, but you said you'd walked from the car to the stables so it couldn't have been more than a mile away, I thought.'

'Half a mile, no further,' I said.

'Well, sir, the car just wasn't there.' He took another swig. 'I didn't really know what to do. I got the taxi to take me to the police in Newbury, but they knew nothing about it. They rang around two or three local nicks because I made a bit of a fuss, sir, but no one down there had seen hair or hide of it.'

I thought a bit. 'They had the keys, of course.'

'Yes, I thought of that.'

'So the car could be more or less anywhere by now.'

He nodded unhappily.

'Never mind,' I said. 'I'll report it stolen. It's bound to turn up somewhere. They aren't ordinary car thieves. When you come to think of it we should have expected it to be gone, because if they were going to deny I had ever been in the stables last night they wouldn't want my car found half a mile away.'

'Do you mean they went out looking for it?'

'They would know I hadn't dropped in by parachute.'

He smiled faintly and lowered the level in his glass to a spoonful.

'Shall I get you something to eat, sir?'

'I don't feel . . .'

'Better to eat. Really it is. I'll pop out to the take-away.' He put his glass down and departed before I could argue and came back in ten minutes with a wing of freshly roasted chicken.

'Didn't think you'd fancy the chips,' he said. He put the plate beside me, fetched knife, fork and napkin, and drained his own glass.

'Be going now, sir,' he said, 'if you're all right.'

CHAPTER EIGHT

Whether it was Owen's care or the natural course of events, I felt a great deal better in the morning. The face peering back at me from the bathroom mirror, though adorned now with two days' stubble, had lost the grey look and the dizzy eyes. Even the bags underneath were retreating to normal.

I shaved first and bathed after, and observed that at least twenty per cent of my skin was now showing bruise marks. I supposed I should have been glad I hadn't been awake when I collected them. The bothersome aches they had set up the day before had more or less abated, and coffee and breakfast helped things along fine.

The police were damping on the matter of stolen Lamborghinis. They took particulars with pessimism and said I might hear something in a week or so; then within half an hour they were back on the line bristling with irritation. My car had been towed away by colleagues the night before last because I'd parked it on a space reserved for taxis in Leicester Square. I could find it in the pound at Marble Arch and there would be a charge for towing.

Owen arrived at nine with a long face and was hugely cheered when I told him about the car.

'Have you seen the papers, sir?'

'Not yet.'

He held out one of his own. 'You'd better know,' he said. I unfolded it. Allie had been right about the gossip columnist. The paragraph was short and sharp and left no one in any doubt.

Red-face day for Steven Scott (35), wealthy race-horse owner, who was scooped by police from a Soho gutter early yesterday. At Marlborough Street Court, Scott, looking rough and crumpled, pleaded guilty to a charge of drunk and incapable. Save your sympathy. Race-followers will remember Scott recently dumped Jody Leeds (28), trainer of all his winners, without a second's notice.

I looked through my own two dailies and the *Sporting Life*. They all carried the story and in much the same vein, even if without the tabloid heat. Smug satisfaction that the kicker-of-underdogs had himself bitten the dust.

It was fair to assume that the story had been sent to every newspaper and that most of them had used it. Even though I'd expected it, I didn't like it. Not a bit.

'It's bloody unfair,' Owen said, reading the piece in the *Life*.

I looked at him with surprise. His usually non-committal face was screwed into frustrated anger and I wondered if his expression was a mirror-image of my own.

'Kind of you to care.'

'Can't help it, sir.' The features returned more or less to normal, but with an effort. 'Anything I can do, sir?'

'Fetch the car?'

He brightened a little. 'Right away.'

His brightness was short-lived because after half an hour he came back white-faced and angrier than I would have thought possible.

'Sir!'

'What is it?'

'The car, sir. The car.'

His manner said it all. He stammered with fury over the details. The nearside front wing was crumpled beyond repair. Headlights smashed. Hub cap missing. Bonnet dented. All the paintwork on the nearside scratched and scored down to the metal. Nearside door a complete write-off. Windows smashed, handle torn away.

'It looks as if it was driven against a brick wall, sir. Something like that.'

I thought coldly of the nearside of Jody's horsebox,

identically damaged. My car had been smashed for vengeance.

'Were the keys in it?' I asked.

He shook his head. 'It wasn't locked. Couldn't be, with one lock broken. I looked for your wallet, like you said, but it wasn't there. None of your things, sir.'

'Is the car drivable?'

He calmed down a little. 'Yes, the engine's all right. It must have been going all right when it was driven into Leicester Square. It looks a proper wreck, but it must be going all right, otherwise how could they have got it there?'

'That's something, anyway.'

'I left it in the pound, sir. It'll have to go back to the coach builders, and they might as well fetch it from there.'

'Sure,' I agreed. I imagined he couldn't have borne to have driven a crumbed car through London; he was justly proud of his driving.

Owen took his tangled emotions down to the workshop and I dealt with mine upstairs. The fresh blight Jody had laid on my life was all due to my own action in creeping into his stable by night. Had it been worth it, I wondered. I'd paid a fairly appalling price for a half-minute's view of Energise: but at least I now *knew* Jody had swapped him. It was a fact, not a guess.

I spent the whole morning on the telephone straightening out the chaos. Organising car repairs and arranging a hired substitute. Telling my bank manager and about ten assorted others that I had lost my cheque book and credit cards. Assuring various enquiring relatives, who had all of course read the papers, that I was neither in jail nor dipsomaniac. Listening to a shrill lady, whose call inched in somehow, telling me it was disgusting for the rich to get drunk in gutters. I asked her if it was okay for the poor, and if it was, why should they have more rights than I. Fair's fair, I said. Long live equality. She called me a rude word and rang off. It was the only bright spot of the day.

Last of all I called Rupert Ramsey.

'What do you mean, you don't want Energise to run?' His voice sounded almost as surprised as Jody's at Sandown.

'I thought,' I said diffidently, 'that he might need more time. You said yourself he needed building up. Well, it's only a week or so to that Christmas race and I don't want him to run below his best.'

Relief distinctly took the place of surprise at the other end of the wire.

'If you feel like that, fine,' he said. 'To be honest, the horse has been a little disappointing on the gallops. I gave him a bit of fast work yesterday upsides a hurdler he should have made mincemeat of, and he couldn't even lie up with him. I'm a bit worried about him. I'm sorry not to be able to give you better news.'

'It's all right,' I said. 'If you'll just keep him and do your best, that'll be fine with me. But don't run him anywhere. I don't mind waiting. I just don't want him raced.'

'You made your point.' The smile came down the wire with the words. 'What about the other two?'

'I'll leave them to your judgement. Nothing Ferry-boat does will disappoint me, but I'd like to bet on Dial whenever you say he's ready.'

'He's ready now. He's entered at Newbury in a fort-night. He should run very well there, I think.'

'Great,' I said.

'Will you be coming?' There was a load of meaning in the question. He too had read the papers.

'Depends on the state of my courage,' I said flip-pantly. 'Tell you nearer the day.'

In the event, I went.

Most people's memories were short and I received no larger slice than I expected of the cold shoulder. Christmas had come and gone, leaving perhaps a trace of goodwill to all men even if they had been beastly to poor Jody Leeds and got themselves fined for drunken-ness. I collected more amused sniggers than active disapproval, except of course from Quintus Leeds, who went out of his way to vent himself of his dislike. He told me again that I would certainly never be elected to the Jockey Club. Over his dead body, he said. He and Jody were both addicted to the phrase.

I was in truth sorry about the Jockey Club. Whatever

one thought of it, it was still a sort of recognition to be asked to become a member. Racing's freedom of the city: along those lines. If I had meekly allowed Jody to carry on robbing, I would have been in. As I hadn't, I was out. Sour joke.

Dial made up for a lot by winning the four-year-old hurdle by a length, and not even Quintus telling everyone it was solely due to Jody's groundwork could dim my pleasure in seeing him sprint to the post.

Rupert Ramsey, patting Dial's steaming sides, sounded all the same apologetic.

'Energise isn't his old self yet, I'm afraid.'

Truer than you know, I thought. I said only, 'Never mind. Don't run him.'

He said doubtfully, 'He's entered for the Champion Hurdle. I don't know if it's worth leaving him in at the next forfeit stage.'

'Don't take him out,' I said with haste. 'I mean . . . I don't mind paying the extra entrance fee. There's always hope that he'll come right.'

'Ye-es.' He was unconvinced, as well he might be. 'As you like, of course.'

I nodded. 'Drink?' I suggested.

'A quick one, then. I've some other runners.'

He gulped his scotch in friendly fashion, refused a refill, and cantered away to the saddling boxes. I wandered alone to a higher point in the stands and looked idly over the cold windy racecourse.

During the past fortnight I'd been unable to work

out just which horse was doubling for Energise. Nothing on Jody's list of horses-in-training seemed to match. Near-black horses were rarer than most, and none on his list were both the right colour and the right age. The changeling at Rupert's couldn't be faulted on colour, age, height, or general conformation. Jody, I imagined, hadn't just happened to have him lying around: he would have had to have searched for him diligently. How, I wondered vaguely, would one set about buying a ringer? One could hardly drift about asking if anyone knew of a spitting image at bargain prices.

My wandering gaze jolted to a full stop. Down among the crowds among the rows of bookmakers' stands I was sure I had seen a familiar pair of sunglasses.

The afternoon was grey. The sky threatened snow and the wind searched every crevice between body and soul. Not a day, one would have thought, for needing to fend off dazzle to the eyes.

There they were again. Sitting securely on the nose of a man with heavy shoulders. No cloth cap, though. A trilby. No raincoat; sheepskin.

I lifted my race glasses for a closer look. He had his back towards me with his head slightly turned to the left. I could see a quarter profile of one cheek and the tinted glasses which showed plainly as he looked down to a race card.

Mousey brown hair, medium length. Hands in

pigskin gloves. Brownish tweed trousers. Binoculars slung over one shoulder. A typical racegoer among a thousand others. Except for those sun specs.

I willed him to turn round. Instead he moved away, his back still towards me, until he was lost in the throng. Impossible to know without getting closer.

I spent the whole of the rest of the afternoon looking for a man, any man, wearing sunglasses, but the only thing I saw in shades was an actress dodging her public.

Inevitably, at one stage, I came face to face with Jody.

Newbury was his local meeting and he was running three horses, so I had been certain he would be there. A week earlier I had shrunk so much from seeing him that I had wanted to duck going, but in the end I had seen that it was essential. Somehow or other I had to convince him that I had forgotten most of my nocturnal visit, that the crack on the head and concussion had between them wiped the memory slate clean.

I couldn't afford for him to be certain I had seen and recognised Energise and knew about the swap. I couldn't afford it for exactly the same reason that I had failed to go to the police. For the same reason that I had quite seriously sworn Charlie and Allie to secrecy.

Given a choice of prosecution for fraud and getting rid of the evidence, Jody would have jettisoned the evidence faster than sight. Energise would have been dead and dogmeat long before an arrest.

The thought that Jody had already killed him was

one I tried continually to put out of my head. I reasoned that he couldn't be sure I'd seen the horse, or recognised him even if I had. They had found me down one end of the line of boxes: they couldn't be sure that I hadn't started at that far end and was working back. They couldn't really be sure I had been actually searching for a ringer, or even that I suspected one. They didn't know for certain why I'd been in the yard.

Energise was valuable, too valuable to destroy in needless panic. I guessed, and I hoped, that they wouldn't kill him unless they had to. Why else would they have gone to such trouble to make sure my word would be doubted. Transporting me to London and making me drunk had given them ample time to whisk Energise to a safer place, and I was sure that if I'd gone belting back there at once with the police I would have been met by incredulous wide-eyed innocence.

'Come in, come in, search where you like,' Jody would have said.

No Energise anywhere to be seen.

'Of course, if you were drunk, you dreamt it all, no doubt.'

End of investigation, and end of Energise, because after that it would have been too risky to keep him.

Whereas if I could convince Jody I knew nothing, he might keep Energise alive and somehow or other I might get him back.

I accidentally bumped into him outside the weighing

room. We both half-turned to each other to apologise, and recognition froze the words in our mouths.

Jody's eyes turned stormy and I suppose mine also.

'Get out of my bloody way,' he said.

'Look, Jody,' I said, 'I want your help.'

'I'm as likely to help you as kiss your arse.'

I ignored that and put on a bit of puzzle. 'Did I, or didn't I, come to your stables a fortnight ago?'

He was suddenly a great deal less violent, a great deal more attentive.

'What d'you mean?'

'I know it's stupid . . . but somehow or other I got drunk and collected concussion from an almighty bang on the head, and I thought . . . it seemed to me, that the evening before, I'd set out to visit you, though with things as they are between us I can't for the life of me think why. So what I want to know is, did I arrive at your place, or didn't I?'

He gave me a straight narrow-eyed stare.

'If you came, I never saw you,' he said.

I looked down at the ground as if disconsolate and shook my head. 'I can't understand it. In the ordinary way I never drink much. I've been trying to puzzle it out ever since, but I can't remember anything between about six one evening and waking up in a police station next morning with a frightful headache and a lot of bruises. I wondered if you could tell me what I'd done in between, because as far as I'm concerned it's a blank.'

I could almost feel the procession of emotions flowing out of him. Surprise, elation, relief and a feeling that this was a totally unexpected piece of luck.

He felt confident enough to return to abuse.

'Why the bloody hell should you have wanted to visit me? You couldn't get shot of me fast enough.'

'I don't know,' I said glumly. 'I suppose you didn't ring me up and ask me . . .'

'You're so right I didn't. And don't you come hanging round. I've had a bellyful of you and I wouldn't have you back if you crawled.'

He scowled, turned away and strode off, and only because I knew what he must be thinking could I discern the twist of satisfied smile that he couldn't entirely hide. He left me in much the same state. If he was warning me so emphatically to stay away from his stables there was the best of chances that Energise was back there, alive and well.

I watched his sturdy backview threading through the crowd, with people smiling at him as he passed. Everyone's idea of a bright young trainer going places. My idea of a ruthless little crook.

At Christmas I had written to Allie in code four.

'Which is the first night you could have dinner with me and where? I enclose twenty dollars for cab fare home.'

On the morning after Newbury races I received her reply, also in groups of five letters, but not in code four. She had jumbled her answer ingeniously enough for it to take me two minutes to unravel it. Very short messages were always the worst, and this was brief indeed.

'January fifth in Miami.'

I laughed aloud. And she had kept the twenty bucks.

The *Racing Calendar* came in the same post. I took it and a cup of coffee over to the big window on the balcony and sat in an armchair there to read. The sky over the Zoo in Regent's Park looked as heavy and grey as the day before, thick with the threat of snow. Down by the canal the bare branches of trees traced tangled black lines across the brown water and grassy banks, and the ribbon traffic as usual shattered the illusion of rural peace. I enjoyed this view of life which, like my work, was a compromise between old primitive roots and new glossy technology. Contentment, I thought, lay in being succoured by the first and cosseted by the second. If I'd had a pagan god, it would have been electricity, which sprang from the skies and galvanised machines. Mysterious lethal force of nature, harnessed and insulated and delivered on tap. My welder-uncle had made electricity seem a living person

1014

to me as a child. 'Electricity will catch you if you don't look out.' He said it as a warning; and I thought of Electricity as a fiery monster hiding in the wires and waiting to pounce.

The stiff yellowish pages of the *Racing Calendar* crackled familiarly as I opened their double spread and folded them back. The *Calendar*, racing's official weekly publication, contained lists of horses entered for forthcoming races, pages and pages of them, four columns to a page. The name of each horse was accompanied by the name of its owner and trainer, and also by its age and the weight it would have to carry if it ran.

With pencil in hand to act as insurance against skipping a line with the eye, I began painstakingly, as I had the previous week and the week before that, to check the name, owner and trainer of every horse entered in hurdle races.

Grapevine (Mrs R. Wantage) B. Fritwell 6 11 11
Pirate Boy (Lord Dresden) A. G. Barnes 10 11 4
Hopfield (Mr Paul Hatheleigh) K. Poundsgate 5 11 2

There were reams of them. I finished the Worcester entries with a sigh. Three hundred and sixty-eight down for one novice hurdle and three hundred and forty-nine for another, and not one of them what I was looking for.

My coffee was nearly cold. I drank it anyway and got on with the races scheduled for Taunton.

Hundreds more names, but nothing.

Ascot, nothing. Newcastle, nothing. Warwick, Teesside, Plumpton, Doncaster, nothing.

I put the *Calendar* down for a bit and went out onto the balcony for some air. Fiercely cold air, slicing down to the lungs. Primeval arctic air carrying city gunge: the mixture as before. Over in the Park the zoo creatures were quiet, sheltering in warmed houses. They always made more noise in the summer.

Return to the task.

Huntingdon, Market Rasen, Stratford on Avon . . . I sighed before starting Stratford and checked how many more still lay ahead. Nottingham, Carlisle and Wetherby. I was in for another wasted morning, no doubt.

Turned back to Stratford, and there it was.

I blinked and looked again carefully, as if the name would vanish if I took my eyes off it.

Half way down among sixty-four entries for the Shakespeare Novice Hurdle.

Padellic (Mr J. Leeds) J. Leeds 5 10   7

Padellic.

It was the first time the name had appeared in association with Jody. I knew the names of all his usual horses well, and what I had been searching for was a new one, an unknown. Owned, if my theories were right, by Jody himself. And here it was.

Nothing in the *Calendar* to show Padellic's colour or markings. I fairly sprinted over to the shelf where I kept a few form books and looked him up in every index.

Little doubt, I thought. He was listed as a black or brown gelding, five years old, a half-bred by a thoroughbred sire out of a hunter mare. He had been trained by a man I'd never heard of and he had run three times in four-year-old hurdles without being placed.

I telephoned to the trainer at once, introducing myself as a Mr Robinson trying to buy a cheap novice.

'Padellic?' he said in a forthright Birmingham accent. 'I got shot of that bugger round October time. No bloody good. Couldn't run fast enough to keep warm. Is he up for sale again? Can't say as I'm surprised. He's a right case of the slows, that one.'

'Er . . . where did you sell him?' I asked tentatively.

'Sent him to Doncaster mixed sales. Right bloody lot they had there. He fetched four hundred quid and I reckon he was dear at that. Only the one bid, you see. I reckon the bloke could've got him for three hundred if he'd tried. I was right pleased to get four for him, I'll tell you.'

'Would you know who bought him?'

'Eh?' He sounded surprised at the question. 'Can't say. He paid cash to the auctioneers and didn't give his name. I saw him make his bid, that's all. Big fellow. I'd never clapped eyes on him before. Wearing sunglasses. I didn't see him after. He paid up and took the horse away and I was right glad to be shot of him.'

'What is the horse like?' I asked.

'I told you, bloody slow.'

'No, I mean to look at.'

'Eh? I thought you were thinking of buying him.'

'Only on paper, so to speak. I thought,' I lied, 'that he still belonged to you.'

'Oh, I see. He's black, then. More or less black, with a bit of brown round the muzzle.'

'Any white about him?'

'Not a hair. Black all over. Black 'uns are often no good. I bred him, see? Meant to be bay, he was, but he turned out black. Not a bad looker, mind. He fills the eye. But nothing where it matters. No speed.'

'Can he jump?'

'Oh ay. In his own good time. Not bad.'

'Well, thanks very much.'

'You'd be buying a monkey,' he said warningly. 'Don't say as I didn't tell you.'

'I won't buy him,' I assured him. 'Thanks again for your advice.'

I put down the receiver reflectively. There might of course be dozens of large untraceable men in sunglasses going round the sales paying cash for slow black horses with no markings; and then again there might not.

The telephone bell rang under my hand. I picked up the receiver at the first ring.

'Steven?'

No mistaking that cigar-and-port voice. 'Charlie.'

'Have you lunched yet?' he said. 'I've just got off a train round the corner at Euston and I thought . . .'

'Here or where?' I said.

'I'll come round to you.'

'Great.'

He came, beaming and expansive, having invested three million somewhere near Rugby. Charlie, unlike some merchant bankers, liked to see things for himself. Reports on paper were all very well, he said, but they didn't give you the smell of a thing. If a project smelt wrong, he didn't disgorge the cash. Charlie followed his nose and Charlie's nose was his fortune.

The feature in question buried itself gratefully in a large scotch and water.

'How about some of that nosh you gave Bert?' he suggested, coming to the surface. 'To tell you the truth I get tired of eating in restaurants.'

We repaired amicably to the kitchen and ate bread and bacon and curried beans and sausages, all of which did no good at all to anyone's waistline, least of all Charlie's. He patted the bulge affectionately. 'Have to get some weight off, one of these days. But not today,' he said.

We took coffee back to the sitting-room and settled comfortably in armchairs.

'I wish I lived the way you do,' he said. 'So easy and relaxed.'

I smiled. Three weeks of my quiet existence would have driven him screaming to the madhouse. He thrived on bustle, big business, fast decisions, financial juggling and the use of power. And three weeks of all *that*, I thought in fairness, would have driven me mad even quicker.

'Have you made that lock yet?' he asked. He was lighting a cigar round the words and they sounded casual, but I wondered all of a sudden if that was why he had come.

'Half,' I said.

He shook his match to blow it out. 'Let me know,' he said.

'I promise.'

He drew in a lungful of Havana and nodded, his eyes showing unmistakably now that his mind was on duty for his bank.

'Which would you do most for,' I asked. 'Friendship or the lock?'

He was a shade startled. 'Depends what you want done.'

'Practical help in a counter-offensive.'

'Against Jody?'

I nodded.

'Friendship,' he said. 'That comes under the heading of friendship. You can count me in.'

His positiveness surprised me. He saw it and smiled.

'What he did to you was diabolical. Don't forget, I was here. I saw the state you were in. Saw the humiliation of that drink charge, and the pain from God knows what else. You looked a little below par and that's a fact.'

'Sorry.'

'Don't be. If it was just your pocket he'd bashed, I would probably be ready with cool advice but not active help.'

I hadn't expected anything like this. I would have thought it would have been the other way round, that the loss of property would have angered him more than the loss of face.

'If you're sure . . .' I said uncertainly.

'Of course.' He was decisive. 'What do you want done?'

I picked up the *Racing Calendar*, which was lying on the floor beside my chair, and explained how I'd looked for and found Padellic.

'He was bought at Doncaster sales for cash by a large man in sunglasses and he's turned up in Jody's name.'

'Suggestive.'

'I'd lay this house to a sneeze,' I said, 'that Rupert Ramsey is worrying his guts out trying to train him for the Champion Hurdle.'

Charlie smoked without haste. 'Rupert Ramsey has Padellic, but thinks he has Energise. Is that right?'

I nodded.

1021

'And Jody is planning to run Energise at Stratford on Avon in the name of Padellic?'

'I would think so,' I said.

'So would I.'

'Only it's not entirely so simple.'

'Why not?'

'Because,' I said, 'I've found two other races for which Padellic is entered, at Nottingham and Lingfield. All the races are ten to fourteen days ahead and there's no telling which Jody will choose.'

He frowned. 'What difference does it make, which he chooses?'

I told him.

He listened with his eyes wide open and the eyebrows disappearing upwards into his hair. At the end, he was smiling.

'So how do you propose to find out which race he's going for?' he asked.

'I thought,' I said, 'that we might mobilise your friend Bert. He'd do a lot for you.'

'What, exactly?'

'Do you think you could persuade him to apply for a job in one of Ganser Mays' betting shops?'

Charlie began to laugh. 'How much can I tell him?'

'Only what to look for. Not why.'

'You slay me, Steven.'

'And another thing,' I said, 'how much do you know about the limitations of working hours for truck drivers?'

CHAPTER NINE

Snow was falling when I flew out of Heathrow, thin scurrying flakes in a driving wind. Behind me I left a half-finished lock, a half-mended car and a half-formed plan.

Charlie had telephoned to say Bert Huggerneck had been taken on at one of the shops formerly owned by his ex-boss and I had made cautious enquiries from the auctioneers at Doncaster. I'd had no success. They had no record of the name of the person who'd bought Padellic. Cash transactions were common. They couldn't possibly remember who had bought one par ticular cheap horse three months earlier. End of enquiry.

Owen had proclaimed himself as willing as Charlie to help in any way he could. Personal considerations apart, he said, whoever had bent the Lamborghini deserved hanging. When I came back, he would help me build the scaffold.

The journey from snow to sunshine took eight hours. Seventy-five degrees at Miami airport and only a shade cooler outside the hotel on Miami Beach; and it felt great. Inside the hotel the air-conditioning brought things nearly back to an English winter, but my sixth-floor room faced straight towards the afternoon sun. I drew back the closed curtains and opened the window, and let heat and light flood in.

Below, round a glittering pool, tall palm trees swayed in the sea wind. Beyond, the concrete edge to the hotel grounds led immediately down to a narrow strip of sand and the frothy white waves edging the Atlantic, with mile upon mile of deep blue water stretching away to the lighter blue horizon.

I had expected Miami Beach to be garish and was unprepared for its beauty. Even the ranks of huge white slabs of hotels with rectangular windows piercing their façades in a uniform geometrical pattern held a certain grandeur, punctuated and softened as they were by scattered palms.

Round the pool people lay in rows on day beds beside white fringed sun umbrellas, soaking up ultra-violet like a religion. I changed out of my travel-sticky clothes and went for a swim in the sea, paddling lazily in the warm January water and sloughing off cares like dead skin. Jody Leeds was five thousand miles away, in another world. Easy, and healing, to forget him.

Upstairs again, showered and dressed in slacks and cotton shirt I checked my watch for the time to tele-phone Allie. After the letters, we had exchanged cables, though not in code because the cable company didn't like it.

I sent, 'What address Miami?'

She replied: 'Telephone four two six eight two after six any evening.'

When I called her it was five past six on January fifth, local time. The voice which answered was not hers and for a soggy moment I wondered if the Western Union had jumbled the message as they often did, and that I should never find her.

'Miss Ward? Do you mean Miss Alexandra?'

'Yes,' I said with relief.

'Hold the line, please.'

After a pause came the familiar voice, remembered but suddenly fresh. 'Hallo?'

'Allie ... It's Steven.'

'Hi.' Her voice was laughing. 'I've won close on fifty dollars if you're in Miami.'

'Collect it,' I said.

'I don't believe it.'

'We have a date,' I said reasonably.

'Oh sure.'

'Where do I find you?'

'Twelve twenty-four Garden Island,' she said. 'Any cab will bring you. Come right out, it's time for cocktails.'

Garden Island proved to be a shady offshoot of land with wide enough channels surrounding it to justify its name. The cab rolled slowly across twenty yards of decorative iron bridge and came to a stop outside twelve twenty-four. I paid off the driver and rang the bell.

From the outside the house showed little. The white-washed walls were deeply obscured by tropical plants and the windows by insect netting. The door itself looked solid enough for a bank.

Allie opened it. Smiled widely. Gave me a non-committal kiss.

'This is my cousin's house,' she said. 'Come in.'

Behind its secretive front the house was light and large and glowing with clear, uncomplicated colours. Blue, sea-green, bright pink, white and orange; clear and sparkling.

'My cousin Minty,' Allie said, 'and her husband, Warren Barbo.'

I shook hands with the cousins. Minty was neat, dark and utterly self-possessed in lemon-coloured beach pyjamas. Warren was large, sandy and full of noisy good humour. They gave me a tall, iced, unspecified drink and led me into a spacious glass-walled room for a view of the setting sun.

Outside in the garden the yellowing rays fell on a lush lawn, a calm pool and white painted lounging chairs. All peaceful and prosperous and a million miles from blood, sweat and tears.

'Alexandra tells us you're interested in horses,' Warren said, making host-like conversation. 'I don't know how long you reckon on staying, but there's a racemeet at Hialeah right now, every day this week. And the bloodstock sales, of course, in the evenings. I'll be going myself some nights and I'd be glad to have you along.'

The idea pleased me, but I turned to Allie.

'What are your plans?'

'Millie and I split up,' she said without visible regret. 'She said when we were through with Christmas and New Year she would be off to Japan for a spell, so I grabbed a week down here with Minty and Warren.'

'Would you come to the races, and the sales?'

'Sure.'

'I have four days,' I said.

She smiled brilliantly but without promise. Several other guests arrived for drinks at that point and Allie said she would fetch the canapés. I followed her to the kitchen.

'You can carry the stone crabs,' she said, putting a large dish into my hands. 'And okay, after a while we can sneak out and eat some place else.'

For an hour I helped hand round those understudies for a banquet, American-style canapés. Allie's delicious work. I ate two or three and like a true male chauvinist meditated on the joys of marrying a good cook.

I found Minty at my side, her hand on my arm, her gaze following mine.

'She's a great girl,' she said. 'She swore you would come.'

'Good,' I said with satisfaction.

Her eyes switched sharply to mine with a grin breaking out. 'She told us to be careful what we said to you, because you always understood the implications, not just the words. And I guess she was right.'

'You've only told me that she wanted me to come and thought I liked her enough to do it.'

'Yeah, but . . .' She laughed. 'She didn't actually say all that.'

'I see what you mean.'

She took out of my hands a dish of thin pastry boats filled with pink chunks of lobster in pale green mayonnaise. 'You've done more than your duty here,' she smiled. 'Get on out.'

She lent us her car. Allie drove it northwards along the main boulevard of Collins Avenue and pulled up at a restaurant called Stirrup and Saddle.

'I thought you might feel at home here,' she said teasingly.

The place was crammed. Every table in sight was taken, and as in many American restaurants, the tables were so close together that only emaciated waiters could inch around them. Blow-ups of racing scenes decorated the walls and saddles and horseshoes abounded.

Dark decor, loud chatter and, to my mind, too much light.

A slightly harassed head waiter intercepted us inside the door.

'Do you have reservations, sir?'

I began to say I was sorry, as there were dozens of people already waiting round the bar, when Allie interrupted.

'Table for two, name of Barbo.'

He consulted his lists, smiled, nodded. 'This way, sir.'

There was miraculously after all one empty table, tucked in a corner but with a good view of the busy room. We sat comfortably in dark wooden-armed chairs and watched the head waiter turn away the next customers decisively.

'When did you book this table?' I asked.

'Yesterday. As soon as I got down here.' The white teeth gleamed. 'I got Warren to do it; he likes this place. That's when I made the bets. He and Minty said it was crazy, you wouldn't come all the way from England just to take me out to eat.'

'And you said I sure was crazy enough for anything.'

'I sure did.'

We ate bluepoint oysters and barbecued baby ribs with salad alongside. Noise and clatter from other tables washed around us and waiters towered above with huge loaded trays. Business was brisk.

'Do you like it here?' Allie asked, tackling the ribs.

'Very much.'

She seemed relieved. I didn't add that some quiet candlelight would have done even better. 'Warren says all horse people like it, the same way he does.'

'How horsey is Warren?'

'He owns a couple of two-year-olds. Has them in

training with a guy in Aiken, North Carolina. He was hoping they'd be running here at Hialeah but they've both got chipped knees and he doesn't know if they'll be any good any more.'

'What are chipped knees?' I asked.

'Don't you have chipped knees in England?'

'Heaven knows.'

'So will Warren.' She dug into the salad, smiling down at the food. 'Warren's business is real estate but his heart beats out there where the hooves thunder along the homestretch.'

'Is that how he puts it?'

Her smile widened. 'It sure is.'

'He said he'd take us to Hialeah tomorrow, if you'd like.'

'I might as well get used to horses, I suppose.' She spoke with utter spontaneity and then in a way stood back and looked at what she'd said. 'I mean . . .' she stuttered.

'I know what you mean,' I said smiling.

'You always do, dammit.'

We finished the ribs and progressed to coffee. She asked how fast I'd recovered from the way she had seen me last and what had happened since. I told her about the gossip columns and the car, and she was fiercely indignant; mostly, I gathered, because of the car.

'But it was so beautiful!'

'It will be again.'

'I'd like to murder that Jody Leeds.'

She scarcely noticed, that time, that she was telling me what she felt for me. The sense of a smoothly deepening relationship filled me with contentment: and it was also great fun.

After three cups of dawdled coffee I paid the bill and we went out to the car.

'I can drop you off at your hotel,' Allie said. 'It's quite near here.'

'Certainly not. I'll see you safely home.'

She grinned. 'There isn't much danger. All the alligators in Florida are a hundred miles away in the Everglades.'

'Some alligators have two feet.'

'Okay, then.' She drove slowly southwards, the beginnings of a smile curling her mouth all the way. Outside her cousin's house she put on the handbrake but left the engine running.

'You'd better borrow this car to go back. Minty won't mind.'

'No, I'll walk.'

'You can't. It's all of four miles.'

'I like seeing things close. Seeing how they're made.'

'You sure are nuts.'

I switched off the engine, put my arm round her shoulders and kissed her the same way as at home, several times. She sighed deeply but not, it seemed, with boredom.

*

I hired an Impala in the morning and drove down to Garden Island. A cleaner answered the door and showed me through to where Warren and Minty were in swimsuits, standing by the pool in January sunshine as warm as July back home.

'Hi,' said Minty in welcome. 'Alexandra said to tell you she'll be right back. She's having her hair fixed.'

The fixed hair, when it appeared, looked as smooth and shining as the girl underneath. A black-and-tan sleeveless cotton dress did marvellous things for her waist and stopped in plenty of time for the legs. I imagine appreciation was written large on my face because the wide smile broke out as soon as she saw me.

We sat by the pool drinking cold fresh orange juice while Warren and Minty changed into street clothes. The day seemed an interlude, a holiday, to me, but not to the Barbos. Warren's life, I came to realise, was along the lines of perpetual summer vacation interrupted by short spells in the office. Droves of sharp young men did the leg-work of selling dream retirement homes to elderly sun-seekers and Warren, the organiser, went to the races.

Hialeah Turf Club was a sugar-icing racecourse, as pretty as lace. Miami might show areas of cracks and rust and sun-peeled poverty on its streets, but in the big green park in its suburb the lush life survived and seemingly flourished.

Bright birds in cages beguiled visitors the length

of the paddock, and a decorative pint-sized railway trundled around. Tons of ice cream added to weight problems and torn up Tote tickets fluttered to the ground like snow.

The racing itself that day was moderate, which didn't prevent me losing my bets. Allie said it served me right, gambling was a nasty habit on a par with jumping off cliffs.

'And look where it's got you,' she pointed out.

'Where?'

'In Ganser Mays' clutches.'

'Not any more.'

'Which came first,' she said, 'the gamble or the race?'

'All life's a gamble. The fastest sperm fertilizes the egg.'

She laughed. 'Tell that to the chickens.'

It was the sort of day when nonsense made sense. Minty and Warren met relays of drinking pals and left us much alone, which suited me fine, and at the end of the racing programme we sat high up on the stands looking over the course while the sunlight died to yellow and pink and scarlet. Drifts of flamingoes on the small lakes in the centre of the track deepened from pale pink to intense rose and the sky on the water reflected silver and gold.

'I bet it's snowing in London,' I said.

After dark and after dinner Warren drove us round to the sales paddock on the far side of the racecourse, where spotlights lit a scene that was decidedly more rustic than the stands. Sugar icing stopped with the tourists: horse-trading had its feet on the grass.

There were three main areas linked by short undefined paths and well-patronised open-fronted bars; there was the sale ring, the parade ring and long barns lined with stalls, where the merchandise ate hay and suffered prods and insults and people looking at its teeth.

Warren opted for the barns first and we wandered down the length of the nearest while he busily consulted his catalogue. Minty told him they were definitely not buying any more horses until the chipped knees were all cleared up. 'No dear,' Warren said soothingly, but with a gleam in his eye which spelt death to the bank balance.

I looked at the offerings with interest. A mixed bunch of horses which had been raced, from three years upwards. Warren said the best sales were those for two-year-olds at the end of the month and Minty said why didn't he wait awhile and see what they were like.

The lights down the far end of the barn were dim and the horse in the last stall of all was so dark that at first I thought the space was empty. Then an eye shimmered and a movement showed a faint gleam on a rounded rump.

A black horse. Black like Energise.

I looked at him first because he was black, and then more closely, with surprise. He was indeed very like Energise. Extremely like him.

The likeness abruptly crystallised an idea I'd already been turning over in my mind. A laugh fluttered in my throat. The horse was a gift from the gods and who was I to look it in the mouth.

'What have you found?' Warren asked, advancing with good humour.

'I've a hurdler like this at home.'

Warren looked at the round label stuck onto one hindquarter which bore the number sixty-two.

'Hip number sixty-two,' he said, flicking the pages of the catalogue. 'Here it is. Black Fire, five-year-old gelding. Humph.' He read quickly down the page through the achievements and breeding. 'Not much good and never was much good, I guess.'

'Pity.'

'Yeah.' He turned away. 'Now there's a damned nice looking chestnut colt along there . . .'

'No, Warren,' said Minty despairingly.

We all walked back to look at the chestnut colt. Warren knew no more about buying horses than I did, and besides, the first thing I'd read on the first page of the catalogue was the clear warning that the auctioneers didn't guarantee the goods were of merchantable quality. In other words, if you bought a lame duck it was your own silly fault.

'Don't pay no attention to that,' said Warren expansively. 'As long as you don't take the horse out of the sales paddock, you can get a veterinarian to check a horse you've bought, and if he finds anything wrong you can call the deal off. But you have to do it within twenty-four hours.'

'Sounds fair.'

'Sure. You can have x-rays even. Chipped knees would show on an x-ray. Horses can walk and look okay with chipped knees but they sure can't race.'

Allie said with mock resignation, 'So what exactly are chipped knees?'

Warren said, 'Cracks and compressions at the ends of the bones at the knee joint.'

'From falling down?' Allie asked.

Warren laughed kindly. 'No. From too much hard galloping on dirt. The thumping does it.'

I borrowed the sales catalogue from Warren again for a deeper look at the regulations and found the twenty-four hour inspection period applied only to brood mares, which wasn't much help. I mentioned it diffidently to Warren. 'It says here,' I said neutrally, 'that it's wise to have a vet look at a horse for soundness before you bid. After is too late.'

'Is that so?' Warren retrieved his book and peered at the small print. 'Well, I guess you're right.' He received the news good-naturedly. 'Just shows how easy it is to go wrong at horse sales.'

'And I hope you remember it,' Minty said with meaning.

Warren did in fact seem a little discouraged from his chestnut colt but I wandered back for a second look at Black Fire and found a youth in jeans and grubby sweat shirt bringing him a bucket of water.

'Is this horse yours?' I asked.

'Nope. I'm just the help.'

'Which does he do most, bite or kick?'

The boy grinned. 'Reckon he's too lazy for either.'

'Would you take him out of that dark stall so I could have a look at him in the light?'

'Sure.' He untied the halter from the tethering ring and brought Black Fire out into the central alley, where the string of electric lights burned without much enthusiasm down the length of the barn.

'There you go, then,' he said, persuading the horse to arrange its legs as if for a photograph. 'Fine looking fella, isn't he?'

'What you can see of him,' I agreed.

I looked at him critically, searching for differences. But there was no doubt he was the same. Same height, same elegant shape, even the same slightly dished Arab-looking nose. And black as coal, all over. When I walked up and patted him he bore it with fortitude. Maybe his sweet nature, I thought. Or maybe tranquillisers.

On the neck or head of many horses the hair grew in one or more whorls, making a pattern which was entered as an identifying mark on the passports. Energise had no whorls at all. Nor had Padellic. I looked carefully at the forehead, cheeks, neck and shoulders of Black Fire and ran my fingers over his coat. As far as I could feel or see in that dim light, there were no whorls on him either.

'Thanks a lot,' I said to the boy, stepping back.

He looked at me with surprise. 'You don't aim to look at his teeth or feel his legs?'

'Is there something wrong with them?'

'I guess not.'

'Then I won't bother,' I said and left unsaid the truth understood by us both, that even if I'd inspected those extremities I wouldn't have been any the wiser.

'Does he have a tattoo number inside his lip?' I asked.

'Yeah, of course.' The surprise raised his eyebrows to peaks like a clown. 'Done when he first raced.'

'What is it?'

'Well, gee, I don't know.' His tone said he couldn't be expected to and no one in his senses would have bothered to ask.

'Take a look.'

'Well, okay.' He shrugged and with the skill of practice opened the horse's mouth and turned down the lower lip. He peered closely for a while during which time the horse stood suspiciously still, and then let him go.

'Far as I can see there's an F and a six and some others, but it's not too light in here and anyway the numbers get to go fuzzy after a while, and this fella's five now so the tattoo would be all of three years old.'

'Thanks anyway.'

'You're welcome.' He pocketed my offered five bucks and took the very unfiery Black Fire back to his stall.

I turned to find Allie, Warren and Minty standing in a row, watching. Allie and Minty both wore indulgent feminine smiles and Warren was shaking his head.

'That horse has won a total of nine thousand three hundred dollars in three years' racing,' he said. 'He won't have paid the feed bills.' He held out the catalogue opened at Black Fire's page, and I took it and read the vaguely pathetic race record for myself.

'At two, unplaced. At three, three wins, four times third. At four, twice third. Total: three wins, six times third, earned $9,326.'

A modest success as a three-year-old, but all in fairly low-class races. I handed the catalogue back to Warren with a smile of thanks, and we moved unhurriedly out of that barn and along to the next. When even Warren had had a surfeit of peering into stalls we went outside and watched the first entries being led into the small wooden-railed collecting ring.

A circle of lights round the rails lit the scene, aided by spotlights set among the surrounding trees. Inside, as on a stage, small bunches of people anxiously added the finishing touches of gloss which might wring a better price from the unperceptive. Some of the horses' manes were decorated with a row of bright wool pompoms, arching along the top of the neck from ears to withers as if ready for the circus. Hip No. 1, resplendent in scarlet pompoms, raised his long bay head and whinnied theatrically.

I told Allie and the Barbos I would be back in a minute and left them leaning on the rails. A couple of enquiries and one misdirection found me standing in the cramped office of the auctioneers in the sale ring building.

'A report from the veterinarian? Sure thing. Pay in advance, please. If you don't want to wait, return for the report in half an hour.'

I paid and went back to the others. Warren was deciding it was time for a drink and we stood for a while in the fine warm night near one of the bars drinking Bacardi and Coke out of throwaway cartons.

Brilliant light poured out of the circular sales building in a dozen places through open doors and slatted windows. Inside, the banks of canvas chairs were beginning to fill up, and down on the rostrum in the centre the auctioneers were shaping up to starting the evening's business. We finished the drinks, duly threw away the cartons and followed the crowd into the show.

Hip No. 1 waltzed in along a ramp and circled the rostrum with all his pompoms nodding. The auctioneer began his sing-song selling, amplified and insistent, and to me, until my ears adjusted, totally unintelligible. Hip No. 1 made five thousand dollars and Warren said the prices would all be low because of the economic situation.

Horses came and went. When Hip No. 15 in orange pompoms had fetched a figure which had the crowd murmuring in excitement I slipped away to the office and found that the veterinary surgeon himself was there, dishing out his findings to other enquiries.

'Hip number sixty-two?' he echoed. 'Sure, let me find my notes.' He turned over a page or two in a notebook. 'Here we are. Dark bay or brown gelding, right?'

'Black,' I said.

'Uh, uh. Never say black.' He smiled briefly, a busy middle-aged man with an air of a clerk. 'Five years. Clean bill of health.' He shut the notebook and turned to the customer.

'Is that all?' I said blankly.

'Sure,' he said briskly. 'No heart murmur, legs cool, teeth consistent with given age, eyes normal, range of movement normal, trots sound. No bowed tendons, no damaged knees.'

'Thanks,' I said.

'You're welcome.'

'Is he tranquillised?'

He looked at me sharply, then smiled. 'I guess so. Acepromazine probably.'

'Is that usual, or would he be a rogue?'

'I wouldn't think he'd had much. He should be okay.'

'Thanks again.'

I went back to the sale ring in time to see Warren fidgeting badly over the sale of the chestnut colt. When the price rose to fifteen thousand Minty literally clung on to his hands and told him not to be a darned fool.

'He must be sound,' Warren protested, 'to make that money.'

The colt made twenty-five thousand in thirty seconds' brisk bidding and Warren's regrets rumbled on all evening. Minty relaxed as if the ship of state had safely negotiated a killing reef and said she would like a breath of air. We went outside and leaned again on the collecting ring rails.

There were several people from England at the sales. Faces I knew, faces which knew me. No close friends, scarcely acquaintances, but people who would certainly notice and remark if I did anything unexpected.

I turned casually to Warren.

'I've money in New York,' I said. 'I can get it tomorrow. Would you lend me some tonight?'

'Sure,' he said good-naturedly, fishing for his wallet. 'How much do you need?'

'Enough to buy that black gelding.'

'What?' His hand froze and his eyes widened.

'Would you buy it for me?'

'You're kidding.'

'No.'

He looked at Allie for help. 'Does he mean it?'

'He's sure crazy enough for anything,' she said.

'That's just what it is,' Warren said. 'Crazy. Crazy to

buy some goddamned useless creature, just because he looks like a hurdler you've got back home.'

To Allie this statement suddenly made sense. She smiled vividly and said, 'What are you going to do with him?'

I kissed her forehead. 'I tend to think in circles,' I said.

CHAPTER TEN

Warren, enjoying himself hugely, bought Black Fire for four thousand six hundred dollars. Bid for it, signed for it, and paid for it.

With undiminished good nature he also contracted for its immediate removal from Hialeah and subsequent shipment by air to England.

'Having himself a ball,' Minty said.

His good spirits lasted all the way back to Garden Island and through several celebratory nightcaps.

'You sure bought a stinker,' he said cheerfully, 'but boy, I haven't had so much fun in years. Did you see that guy's face, the one I bid against? He thought he was getting it for a thousand.' He chuckled. 'At four thousand five he sure looked mad and he could see I was going on for ever.'

Minty began telling him to make the most of it, it was the last horse he'd be buying for a long time, and Allie came to the door to see me off. We stood outside for a while in the dark, close together.

'One day down. Three to go,' she said.

'No more horses,' I promised.

'Okay.'

'And fewer people.'

A pause. Then again, 'Okay.'

I smiled and kissed her good night and pushed her indoors before my best intentions should erupt into good old-fashioned lust. The quickest way to lose her would be to snatch.

She said how about Florida Keys and how about a swim and how about a picnic. We went in the Impala with a cold box of goodies in the boot and the Tropic of Cancer flaming away over the horizon ahead.

The highway to Key West stretched for mile after mile across a linked chain of causeways and small islands. Palm trees, sand dunes, sparkling water and scrubby grass. Few buildings. Sun-bleached wooden huts, wooden landing stages, fishing boats. Huge skies, hot sun, vast seas. Also Greyhound buses on excursions and noisy families in station wagons with Mom in pink plastic curlers.

Allie had brought directions from Warren about one of the tiny islands where he fished, and when we reached it we turned off the highway on to a dusty side road that was little more than a track. It ended abruptly under two leaning palms, narrowing to an Indian file path through sand dunes and tufty grass towards the sea. We took the picnic box and walked, and found ourselves surprisingly in a small sandy hollow from which neither the car nor the road could be seen.

'That,' said Allie, pointing at the sea, 'is Hawk Channel.'

'Can't see any hawks.'

'You'd want cooks in Cook Strait.'

She took off the loose white dress she'd worn on the way down and dropped it on the sand. Underneath she wore a pale blue and white bikini, and underneath that, warm honey coloured skin.

She took the skin without more ado into the sea and I stripped off shirt and trousers and followed her. We swam in the free warm-cool water and it felt the utmost in luxury.

'Why are these islands so uninhabited?' I asked.

'Too small, most of them. No fresh water. Hurricanes, as well. It isn't always so gentle here. Sizzling hot in the summer and terrible storms.'

The wind in the palm tree tops looked as if butter wouldn't melt in its mouth. We splashed in the shallows and walked up the short beach to regain the warm little hollow, Allie delivering on the way a fairly non-stop lecture about turtles, bonefish, marlin and tarpon. It struck me in the end that she was talking fast to hide that she was feeling self-conscious.

I fished in my jacket pocket and brought out a twenty dollar bill.

'Bus fare home,' I said, holding it out to her.

She laughed a little jerkily. 'I still have the one you sent from England.'

'Did you bring it?'

She smiled, shook her head, took the note from me, folded it carefully and pushed it into the wet top half of her bikini.

'It'll be safe there,' she said matter-of-factly. 'How about a vodka martini?'

She had brought drinks, ice and delicious food. The sun in due course shifted thirty degrees round the sky, and I lay lazily basking in it while she put the empties back in the picnic box and fiddled with spoons.

'Allie?'

'Mm?'

'How about now?'

She stopped the busy rattling. Sat back on her ankles. Pushed the hair out of her eyes and finally looked at my face.

'Try sitting here,' I said, patting the sand beside me with an unemphatic palm.

She tried it. Nothing cataclysmic seemed to happen to her in the way of fright.

'You've done it before,' I said persuasively, stating a fact.

'Yeah ... but ...'

'But what?'

'I didn't really like it.'

'Why not?'

'I don't know. I didn't like the boy enough, I expect.'

1047

'Then why the hell sleep with him?'

'You make it sound so simple. But at college, well, one sort of had to. Three years ago, most of one summer. I haven't done it since. I've been not exactly afraid to, but afraid I would ... be unfair ...' She stopped.

'You can catch a bus whenever you like,' I said.

She smiled and bit by bit lay down beside me. I knew she wouldn't have brought me to this hidden place if she hadn't been willing at least to try. But acquiescence, in view of what she'd said, was no longer enough. If she didn't enjoy it, I couldn't.

I went slowly, giving her time. A touch. A kiss. An undemanding smoothing of hand over skin. She breathed evenly through her nose, trusting but unaroused.

'Clothes off?' I suggested. 'No one can see us.'

'... Okay.'

She unhitched the bikini top, folded it over the twenty dollars, and put it on the sand beside her. The pants in a moment followed. Then she sat with her arms wrapped round her knees, staring out to sea.

'Come on,' I said, smiling, my shorts joining hers. 'The fate worse than death isn't all that bad.'

She laughed with naturalness and lay down beside me, and it seemed as if she'd made up her mind to do her best, even if she found it unsatisfactory. But in a while she gave the first uncontrollable shiver of authentic pleasure, and after that it became not just all right but very good indeed.

'Oh God,' she said in the end, half laughing, half gasping for air. 'I didn't know . . .'

'Didn't know what?' I said, sliding lazily down beside her.

'At college . . . he was clumsy. And too quick.'

She stretched out her hand, fumbled in the bikini and picked up the twenty dollar note.

She waved it in the air, holding it between finger and thumb. Then she laughed and opened her hand and the wind blew her fare home away along the beach.

CHAPTER ELEVEN

London was cold enough to encourage emigration. I arrived back early Tuesday morning with sand in my shoes and sympathy for Eskimos, and Owen collected me with a face pinched and blue.

'We've had snow and sleet and the railways are on strike,' he said, putting my suitcase in the hired Cortina. 'Also the mild steel you ordered hasn't come and there's a cobra loose somewhere in Regent's Park.'

'Thanks very much.'

'Not at all, sir.'

'Anything else?'

'A Mr Kennet rang from Newmarket to say Hermes has broken down. And . . . sir . . .'

'What?' I prompted, trying to dredge up resignation.

'Did you order a load of manure, sir?'

'Of course not.'

The total garden in front of my house consisted of three tubs of fuchsia, an old walnut tree and several square yards of paving slabs. At the rear, nothing but workshop.

'Some has been delivered, sir.'

'How much?'

'I can't see the dustmen moving it.'

He drove steadily from Heathrow to home, and I dozed from the jet-lag feeling that it was midnight. When we stopped it was not in the driveway but out on the road, because the driveway was completely blocked by a dung-hill five feet high.

It was even impossible to walk round it without it sticking to one's shoes. I crabbed sideways with my suitcase to the door, and Owen drove off to find somewhere else to park.

Inside, on the mat, I found the delivery note. A postcard handwritten in ball point capitals, short and unsweet.

'*Shit to the shit.*'

Charming little gesture. Hardly original, but disturbing all the same, because it spoke so eloquently of the hatred prompting it.

Felicity, I wondered?

There was something remarkably familiar about the consistency of the load. A closer look revealed half rotted horse droppings mixed with a little straw and a lot of sawdust. Straight from a stable muck heap, not from a garden supplier: and if looked exactly like Jody's own familiar muck heap, that wasn't in itself conclusive. I dared say one vintage was much like another.

Owen came trudging back and stared at the smelly obstruction in disgust.

'If I hadn't been using the car to go home, like you said, I wouldn't have been able to get out of the garage this morning to fetch you.'

'When was it dumped?'

'I was here ycsterday morning, sir. Keeping an eye on things. Then this morning I called round to switch on the central heating, and there it was.'

I showed him the card. He looked, read, wrinkled his nose in distaste, but didn't touch.

'There'll be fingerprints on that, I shouldn't wonder.'

'Do you think it's worth telling the police?' I asked dubiously.

'Might as well, sir. You never know, this nutter might do something else. I mean, whoever went to all this trouble is pretty sick.'

'You're very sensible, Owen.'

'Thank you, sir.'

We went indoors and I summoned the constabulary, who came in the afternoon, saw the funny side of it, and took away the card in polythene.

'What are we going to do with the bloody stuff?' said Owen morosely. 'No one will want it on their flower beds, it's bung full of undigested hay seeds and that means weeds.'

'We'll shift it tomorrow.'

'There must be a ton of it.' He frowned gloomily.

'I didn't mean spadeful by spadeful,' I said. 'Not you and I. We'll hire a grab.'

Hiring things took the rest of the day. Extraordinary

what one could hire if one tried. The grab proved to be one of the easiest on a long list.

At about the time merchant bankers could reasonably be expected to be reaching for their hats, I telephoned to Charlie.

'Are you going straight home?' I asked.

'Not necessarily.'

'Care for a drink?'

'On my way,' he said.

When he arrived, Owen took his Rover to park it and Charlie stood staring at the muck heap, which looked no more beautiful under the street lights and was moreover beginning to ooze round the edges.

'Someone doesn't love me,' I said with a grin. 'Come on in and wipe your feet rather thoroughly on the mat.'

'What a stink.'

'Lavatory humour,' I agreed.

He left his shoes alongside mine on the tray of newspaper Owen had prudently positioned near the front door and followed me upstairs in his socks.

'Who?' he said, shaping up to a large scotch.

'A shit is what Jody's wife Felicity called me after Sandown.'

'Do you think she did it?'

'Heaven knows. She's a capable girl.'

'Didn't anyone see the ... er ... delivery?'

'Owen asked the neighbours. No one saw a thing. No one ever does, in London. All he discovered was that the muck wasn't there at seven yesterday evening when the man from two doors along let his labrador make use of my fuchsia tubs.'

He drank his whisky and asked what I'd done in Miami. I couldn't stop the smile coming. 'Besides that,' he said.

'I bought a horse.'

'You're a glutton for punishment.'

'An understudy,' I said, 'for Energise.'

'Tell all to your Uncle Charlie.'

I told, if not all, most.

'The trouble is though, that although we must be ready for Saturday at Stratford, he might choose Nottingham on Monday or Lingfield on Wednesday,' I said.

'Or none of them.'

'And it might freeze.'

'How soon would we know?' Charlie asked.

'He'll have to declare the horse to run four days before the race, but he then has three days to change his mind and take him out again. We wouldn't know for sure until the runners are published in the evening papers the day before. And even then we need the nod from Bert Huggerneck.'

He chuckled. 'Bert doesn't like the indoor life. He's itching to get back on the racecourse.'

'I hope he'll stick to the shop.'

'My dear fellow!' Charlie lit a cigar and waved the match. 'Bert's a great scrapper by nature and if you could cut him in on the real action he'd be a lot happier. He's taken a strong dislike to Ganser Mays, and he says that for a capitalist you didn't seem half bad. He knows there's something afoot and he said if there's a chance of anyone punching Ganser Mays on the long bleeding nose he would like it to be him.'

I smiled at the verbatim reporting. 'All right. If he really feels like that, I do indeed have a job for him.'

'Doing what?'

'Directing the traffic.'

He puffed at the cigar. 'Do you know what your plan reminds me of?' he said. 'Your own Rola toys. There you are, turning the single handle, and all the little pieces will rotate on their spindles and go through their allotted acts.'

'You're no toy,' I said.

'Of course I am. But at least I know it. The real trick will be programming the ones who don't.'

'Do you think it will all work?'

He regarded me seriously. 'Given ordinary luck, I don't see why not.'

'And you don't have moral misgivings?'

His sudden huge smile warmed like a fire. 'Didn't you know that merchant bankers are pirates under the skin?'

Charlie took Wednesday off and we spent the whole day prospecting the terrain. We drove from London to Newbury, from Newbury to Stratford on Avon, from Stratford to Nottingham, and from Nottingham back to Newbury. By that time the bars were open, and we repaired to the Chequers for revivers.

'There's only the one perfect place,' Charlie said, 'and it will do for both Stratford and Nottingham.'

I nodded. 'By the fruit stall.'

'Settle on that, then?'

'Yes.'

'And if he isn't down to run at either of those courses we spend Sunday surveying the road to Lingfield?'

'Right.'

He smiled vividly. 'I haven't felt so alive since my stint in the army. However this turns out, I wouldn't have missed it for the world.'

His enthusiasm was infectious and we drove back to London in good spirits.

Things had noticeably improved in the garden. The muck heap had gone and Owen had sloshed to some effect with buckets of water, though without obliterating the smell. He had also stayed late, waiting for my return. All three of us left our shoes in the hall and went upstairs.

'Too Japanese for words,' Charlie said.

'I stayed, sir,' Owen said, 'because a call came from America.'

'Miss Ward?' I said hopefully.

'No, sir. About a horse. It was a shipping firm. They said a horse consigned to you would be on a flight to Gatwick Airport tonight as arranged. Probable time of arrival, ten a.m. tomorrow morning. I wrote it down.'

He pointed to the pad beside the telephone. 'But I thought I would stay in case you didn't see it. They said you would need to engage transport to have the horse met.'

'You,' I said, 'will be meeting it.'

'Very good, sir,' he said calmly.

'Owen,' Charlie said, 'if he ever kicks you out, come to me.'

We all sat for a while discussing the various arrangements and Owen's part in them. He was as eager as Charlie to make the plan work, and he too seemed to be plugged into some inner source of excitement.

'I'll enjoy it, sir,' he said, and Charlie nodded in agreement. I had never thought of either of them as being basically adventurous and I had been wrong.

I was wrong also about Bert Huggerneck, and even in a way about Allie, for they too proved to have more fire than reservations.

Charlie brought Bert with him after work on Thursday and we sat round the kitchen table poring over a large scale map.

'That's the A34,' I said, pointing with a pencil to a red line running south to north. 'It goes all the way from Newbury to Stratford. For Nottingham, you branch off just north of Oxford. The place we've chosen is some way south of that. Just here . . .' I marked it with the pencil. 'About a mile before you reach the Abingdon by-pass.'

'I know that bleeding road,' Bert said. 'Goes past the Harwell atomic.'

'That's right.'

'Yeah. I'll find that. Easy as dolly-birds.'

'There's a roadside fruit stall there,' I said. 'Shut, at this time of year. A sort of wooden hut.'

'Seen dozens of 'em,' Bert nodded.

'It has a good big space beside it for cars.'

'Which side of the road?'

'On the near side, going north.'

'Yeah. I get you.'

'It's on a straight stretch after a fairly steep hill. Nothing will be going very fast there. Do you think you could manage?'

'Here,' he complained to Charlie. 'That's a bleeding insult.'

'Sorry,' I said.

'Is that all I do, then? Stop the bleeding traffic?' He sounded disappointed; and I'd thought he might have needed to be persuaded.

'No,' I said. 'After that you do a lot of hard work extremely quickly.'

'What, for instance?'

When I told him, he sat back on his chair and positively beamed.

'That's more bleeding like it,' he said. 'Now that's a daisy, that is. Now you might think I'm slow on my feet, like, with being big, but you'd be bleeding wrong.'

'I couldn't do it at all without you.'

'Hear that?' he said to Charlie.

'It might even be true,' Charlie said.

Bert at that point described himself as peckish and moved in a straight line to the store cupboard. 'What've you got here, then? Don't you ever bleeding eat? Do you want this tin of ham?'

'Help yourself,' I said.

Bert made a sandwich inch-deep in mustard and ate it without blinking. A couple of cans of beer filled the cracks.

'Can I chuck the betting shop, then?' he asked between gulps.

'What have you learned about Ganser Mays?'

'He's got a bleeding nickname, that's one thing I've learned. A couple of smart young managers run his shops now, you'd never know they was the same place. All keen and sharp and not a shred of soft heart like my old boss.'

'A soft-hearted bookmaker?' Charlie said. 'There's no such thing.'

'Trouble was,' Bert said, ignoring him, 'he had a bleeding soft head and all.'

'What is Ganser Mays' nickname?' I asked.

'Eh? Oh yeah. Well, these two smart alecs, who're sharp enough to cut themselves, they call him Squeezer. Squeezer Mays. When they're talking to each other, of course, that is.'

'Squeezer because he squeezes people like your boss out of business?'

'You don't hang about, do you? Yeah, that's right. There's two sorts of squeezer. The one they did on my boss, telling him horses were fixed to lose when they wasn't. And the other way round, when the smart alecs know a horse that's done no good before is fixed to win. Then they go round all the little men putting thousands on, a bit here and a bit there, and all the little men think it's easy pickings because they think the bad horse can't win in a month of bleeding Sundays. And then of course it does, and they're all down the bleeding drain.'

'They owe Ganser Mays something like the National Debt.'

'That's right. And they can't raise enough bread. So then Mr pious bleeding Mays comes along and says he'll be kind and take the shop to make up the difference. Which he does.'

'I thought small bookies were more clued up nowadays,' I said.

'You'd bleeding well think so, wouldn't you? They'll tell you they are, but they bleeding well aren't. Oh sure, if they find afterwards there's been a right fiddle, like, they squeal blue murder and refuse to pay up, but take the money in the first place, of course they do. Like bleeding innocent little lambs.'

'I don't think there would be any question of anyone thinking it a fiddle, this time,' I said.

'There you are, then. Quite a few would all of a

bleeding sudden be finding they were swallowed up by that smarmy bastard. Just like my poor old boss.'

I reflected for a minute or two. 'I think it would be better if you stayed in the betting shop until we're certain which day the horse is going to run. I don't imagine they would risk letting him loose without backing him, so we must suppose that his first race is IT. But if possible I'd like to be sure. And you might hear something, if you're still in the shop.'

'Keep my ears flapping, you mean?'

'Absolutely. And eyes open.'

'Philby won't have nothing on me,' Bert said.

Charlie stretched out to the makings of the sandwich and assembled a smaller edition for himself.

'Now, transport,' I said. 'I've hired all the vehicles we need from a firm in Chiswick. I was there this morning, looking them over. Owen took a Land-Rover and trailer from there to Gatwick to meet Black Fire and ferry him to his stable, and he's coming back by train. Then there's the caravan for you, Charlie, and the car to pull it. Tomorrow Owen is driving those to Reading and leaving them in the station car park, again coming back by train. I got two sets of keys for the car and caravan, so I'll give you yours now.' I went through to the sitting-room and came back with the small jingling bunch. 'Whichever day we're off, you can go down to Reading by train and drive from there.'

'Fine,' Charlie said, smiling broadly.

'The caravan is one they hire out for horse shows

and exhibitions and things like that. It's fitted out as a sort of office. No beds or cookers, just a counter, a couple of desks, and three or four folding chairs. Owen and I will load it with all the things you'll need before he takes it to Reading.'

'Great.'

'Finally there's the big van for Owen. I'll bring that here tomorrow and put the shopping in it. Then we should be ready.'

'Here,' said Bert. 'How's the cash, like?'

'Do you want some, Bert?'

'It's only, well, seeing as how you're hiring things left right and centre, well, I wondered if it wouldn't be better to hire a car for me too, like. Because my old banger isn't all that bleeding reliable, see? I wouldn't like to miss the fun because of a boiling bleeding radiator or some such.'

'Sure,' I said. 'Much safer.' I went back to the sitting-room, fetched some cash, and gave it to Bert.

'Here,' he said. 'I don't need that much. What do you think I'm going to hire, a bleeding golden coach?'

'Keep it anyway.'

He looked at me dubiously. 'I'm not doing this for bread, mate.'

I felt humbled. 'Bert ... Give me back what you don't use. Or send it to the Injured Jockeys' Fund.'

His face lightened. 'I'll take my old boss down the boozer a few times. Best bleeding charity there is!'

Charlie finished his sandwich and wiped his fingers

on his handkerchief. 'You won't forget the sign-writing, will you?' he said.

'I did it today,' I assured him. 'Want to see?'

We trooped down to the workshop, where various painted pieces of the enterprise were standing around drying.

'Blimey,' Bert said. 'They look bleeding real.'

'They'd have to be,' Charlie nodded.

'Here,' Bert said, 'seeing these makes it seem, well, as if it's all going to happen.'

Charlie went home to a bridge-playing wife in an opulent detached in Surrey and Bert to the two-up two-down terraced he shared with his fat old mum in Staines. Some time after their departure I got the car out and drove slowly down the M4 to Heathrow.

I was early. About an hour early. I had often noticed that I tended to arrive prematurely for things I was looking forward to, as if by being there early one could make them happen sooner. It worked in reverse that time. Allie's aeroplane was half an hour late.

'Hi,' she said, looking as uncrushed as if she'd travelled four miles, not four thousand. 'How's cold little old England?'

'Warmer since you're here.'

The wide smile had lost none of its brilliance, but now there was also a glow in the eyes, where the Miami sun shone from within.

'Thanks for coming,' I said.

'I wouldn't miss this caper for the world.' She gave me a kiss of excitement and warmth. 'And I haven't told my sister I'm coming.'

'Great,' I said with satisfaction; and took her home to the flat.

The change of climate was external. We spent the night, our first together, warmly entwined under a goosefeather quilt: more comfortable, more relaxed and altogether more cosy than the beach or the fishing boat or my hotel bedroom on an air-conditioned afternoon in Miami.

We set off early next morning while it was still dark, shivering in the chill January air and impatient for the car heater to make an effort. Allie drove, concentrating fiercely on the left-hand business, telling me to watch out that she didn't instinctively turn the wrong way at crossings. We reached the fruit stall on the A34 safely in two hours and drew up there in the wide sweep of car-parking space. Huge lorries ground past on the main route from the docks at Southampton to the heavy industry area at Birmingham; a road still in places too narrow for its traffic.

Each time a heavy truck breasted the adjoining hill and drew level with us, it changed its gears, mostly with a good deal of noise. Allie raised her voice. 'Not the quietest of country spots.'

I smiled. 'Every decibel counts.'

We drank hot coffee from a thermos flask and

watched the slow grey morning struggle from gloomy to plain dull.

'Nine o'clock,' said Allie, looking at her watch. 'The day sure starts late in these parts.'

'We'll need you here by nine,' I said.

'You just tell me when to start.'

'Okay.'

She finished her coffee. 'Are you certain sure he'll come this way?'

'It's the best road and the most direct, and he always does.'

'One thing about having an ex-friend for an enemy,' she said. 'You know his habits.'

I packed away the coffee and we started again, turning south.

'This is the way you'll be coming,' I said. 'Straight up the A34.'

'Right.'

She was driving now with noticeably more confidence, keeping left without the former steady frown of anxiety. We reached a big crossroads and stopped at the traffic lights. She looked around and nodded. 'When I get here, there'll only be a couple of miles to go.'

We pressed on for a few miles, the road climbing and descending over wide stretches of bare downlands, bleak and windy and uninviting.

'Slow down a minute,' I said. 'See that turning there, to the left? That's where Jody's stables are. About a mile along there.'

'I really hate that man,' she said.

'You've never met him.'

'You don't have to know snakes to hate them.'

We went round the Newbury by-pass, Allie screwing her head round alarmingly to learn the route from the reverse angle.

'Okay,' she said. 'Now what?'

'Still the A34. Signposts to Winchester. But we don't go that far.'

'Right.'

Through Whitchurch, and six miles beyond we took a narrow side road on the right, and in a little while turned into the drive of a dilapidated looking country house with a faded paint job on a board at the gate.

HANTSFORD MANOR RIDING SCHOOL.
FIRST CLASS INSTRUCTION. RESIDENTIAL ACCOMMODATION.
PONIES AND HORSES FOR HIRE OR AT LIVERY.

I had chosen it from an advertisement in the *Horse and Hound* because of its location, to make the drive from there to the fruit stall as simple as possible for Allie, but now that I saw it, I had sinking doubts.

There was an overall air of life having ended, of dust settling, weeds growing, wood rotting and hope dead. Exaggerated, of course. Though the house indoors smelt faintly of fungus and decay, the proprietors were still alive. They were two much-alike sisters, both about seventy, with thin wiry bodies dressed in jodhpurs,

1066

hacking jackets and boots. They both had kind faded blue eyes, long strong lower jaws, and copious iron grey hair in businesslike hairnets.

They introduced themselves as Miss Johnston and Mrs Fairchild-Smith. They were glad to welcome Miss Ward. They said they hoped her stay would be comfortable. They never had many guests at this time of year. Miss Ward's horse had arrived safely the day before and they were looking after him.

'Yourselves?' I asked doubtfully.

'Certainly, ourselves.' Miss Johnston's tone dared me to imply they were incapable. 'We always cut back on staff at this time of year.'

They took us out to the stables, which like everything else were suffering from advancing years and moreover appeared to be empty. Among a ramshackle collection of wooden structures whose doors any self-respecting toddler could have kicked down, stood three or four brick-built boxes in a sturdy row; in one of these we found Black Fire.

He stood on fresh straw. There was clean water in his bucket and good-looking hay in his net, and he had his head down to the manger, munching busily at oats and bran. All too clear to see where any profits of the business disappeared: into the loving care of the customers.

'He looks fine,' I said, and to myself, with relief, confirmed that he really was indeed the double of

Energise, and that in the warm distant Miami night I hadn't been mistaken.

Allie cleared her throat. 'Er . . . Miss Johnston, Mrs Fairchild-Smith . . . Tomorrow morning I may be taking Black Fire over to some friends, to ride with them. Would that be okay?'

'Of course,' they said together.

'Leaving at eight o'clock?'

'We'll see he's ready for you, my dear,' said Miss Johnston.

'I'll let you know for sure when I've called my friends. If I don't go tomorrow, it may be Monday, or Wednesday.'

'Whenever you say, my dear.' Miss Johnston paused delicately. 'Could you give us any idea how long you'll be staying?'

Allie said without hesitation, 'I guess a week's board would be fair, both for Black Fire and me, don't you think? We may not be here for all of seven days, but obviously at this time of year you won't want to be bothered with shorter reservations.'

The sisters looked discreetly pleased and when Allie produced cash for the bulk of the bill in advance, a faint flush appeared on their thin cheeks and narrow noses.

'Aren't they the weirdest?' Allie said as we drove out of the gates. 'And how do you shift these damned gears?'

She sat this time at the wheel of the Land-Rover I'd

hired from Chiswick, learning her way round its unusual levers.

'That one with the red knob engages four-wheeled drive, and the yellow one is for four ultra-low gears, which you shouldn't need as we're not aiming to cross ploughed fields or drag tree stumps out of the ground.'

'I wouldn't rule them out when you're around.'

She drove with growing ease, and before long we returned to hitch on the two-horse trailer. She had never driven with a trailer before and reversing, as always, brought the worst problems. After a fair amount of swearing on all sides and the best part of an hour's trundling around Hampshire she said she guessed she would reach the fruit stall if it killed her. When we returned to Hantsford Manor after refuelling she parked with the Land-Rover's nose already facing the road, so that at least she wouldn't louse up the linkage, as she put it, before she'd even started.

'You'll find the trailer a good deal heavier with a horse in it,' I said.

'You don't say.'

Without encountering the sisters we returned to Black Fire and I produced from an inner pocket a hair-cutting gadget in the form of a razor blade incorporated into a comb.

'What are you going to do with that?' Allie said.

'If the two old girls materialise, keep them chatting,' I said. 'I'm just helping the understudy to look like the star.'

I went into the box and as calmly as possible approached Black Fire. He wore a head collar, but was not tied up, and the first thing I did was attach him to the tethering chain. I ran my hand down his neck and patted him a few times and said a few soothing non-senses. He didn't seem to object to my presence, so rather gingerly I laid the edge of the hair-cutting comb against his black coat.

I had been told often that nervous people made horses nervous also. I wondered if Black Fire could feel my fumbling inexperience. I thought that after all this I would really have to spend more time with horses, that owning them should entail the obligation of intimacy.

His muscles twitched. He threw his head up and down. He whinnied. He also stood fairly still, so that when I'd finished my delicate scraping he had a small bald patch on his right shoulder, the same size and in the same place as the one on Energise.

Allie leant her elbows on the closed bottom half of the stable door and watched through the open top half.

'Genius,' she said smiling, 'is nine tenths an infinite capacity for taking pains.'

I straightened, grinned, patted Black Fire almost familiarly, and shook my head. 'Genius is infinite pain,' I said. 'I'm happy. Too bad.'

'How do you know, then? About genius being pain?'

'Like seeing glimpses of a mountain from the valley.'

'And you'd prefer to suffer on the peaks?'

I let myself out of the loose box and carefully fastened all the bolts.

'You're either issued with climbing boots, or you aren't,' I said. 'You can't choose. Just as well.'

The sisters reappeared and invited us to take sherry: a double thimbleful in unmatched cut glasses. I looked at my watch and briefly nodded, and Allie asked if she might use the telephone to call the friends.

In the library, they said warmly. This way. Mind the hole in the carpet. Over there, on the desk. They smiled, nodded and retreated.

Beside the telephone stood a small metal box with a stuck-on notice. *Please pay for calls.* I dialled the London number of the Press Association and asked for the racing section.

'Horses knocked out of the novice hurdle at Stratford?' said a voice. 'Well, I suppose so, but we prefer people to wait for the evening papers. These enquiries waste our time.'

'Arrangements to make as soon as possible . . .' I murmured.

'Oh, all right. Wait a sec. Here we are . . .' He read out about seven names rather fast. 'Got that?'

'Yes, thank you very much,' I said.

I put down the telephone slowly, my mouth suddenly dry. Jody had declared Padellic as a Saturday Stratford runner three days ago. If he intended not to go there, he would have had to remove his name by a Friday morning deadline of eleven o'clock . . .

Eleven o'clock had come and gone. None of the horses taken out of the novice hurdle had been Padellic. 'Tomorrow,' I said. 'He runs tomorrow.'

'Oh.' Allie's eyes were wide. 'Oh golly!'

CHAPTER TWELVE

Eight o'clock, Saturday morning.

I sat in my hired Cortina in a lay-by on the road over the top of the Downs, watching the drizzly dawn take the eye-strain out of the passing headlights.

I was there much too early because I hadn't been able to sleep. The flurry of preparations all Friday afternoon and evening had sent me to bed still in top gear and from then on my brain had whirred relentlessly, thinking of all the things which could go wrong.

Snatches of conversation drifted back.

Rupert Ramsey expressing doubts and amazement on the other end of the telephone.

'You want to do *what*?'

'Take Energise for a ride in a horsebox. He had a very upsetting experience in a horsebox at Sandown, in a crash . . . I thought it might give him confidence to go for an uneventful drive.'

'I don't think it would do much good,' he said.

'All the same I'm keen to try. I've asked a young chap called Pete Duveen, who drives his own box, just to pick him up and take him for a ride. I thought tomorrow would be a good day. Pete Duveen says he can collect him at seven thirty in the morning. Would you have the horse ready?'

'You're wasting your money,' he said regretfully. 'I'm afraid there's more wrong with him than nerves.'

'Never mind. And . . . will you be at home tomorrow evening?'

'After I get back from Chepstow races, yes.'

The biggest race meeting of the day was scheduled for Chepstow, over on the west side of the Bristol Channel. The biggest prizes were on offer there and most of the top trainers, like Rupert, would be going.

'I hope you won't object,' I said, 'but after Energise returns from his ride, I'd like to hire a security firm to keep an eye on him.'

Silence from the other end. Then his voice, carefully polite. 'What on earth for?'

'To keep him safe,' I said reasonably. 'Just a guard to patrol the stable and make regular checks. The guard wouldn't be a nuisance to anybody.'

I could almost feel the shrug coming down the wire along with the resigned sigh. Eccentric owners should be humoured. 'If you want to, I suppose . . . But why?'

'If I called at your house tomorrow evening,' I suggested diffidently, 'I could explain.'

'Well . . .' He thought for a bit. 'Look, I'm having a few friends to dinner. Would you care to join us?'

'Yes, I would,' I said positively. 'I'd like that very much.'

I yawned in the car and stretched. Despite anorak, gloves and thick socks the cold encroached on fingers and toes, and through the drizzle-wet windows the bare rolling Downs looked thoroughly inhospitable. Straight ahead through the windscreen wipers I could see a good two miles of the A34. It came over the brow of a distant hill opposite, swept down into a large valley and rose again higher still to cross the Downs at the point where I sat.

A couple of miles to my rear lay the crossroads with the traffic lights, and a couple of miles beyond that, the fruit stall.

Bert Huggerneck, wildly excited, had telephoned at six in the evening.

'Here, know what? There's a squeezer on tomorrow!'

'On Padellic?' I said hopefully.

'What else? On bleeding little old Padellic.'

'How do you know?'

'Listened at the bleeding door,' he said cheerfully. 'The two smart alecs was talking. Stupid bleeding gits. All over the whole bleeding country Ganser Mays is going to flood the little bookies' shops with last minute bets on Padellic. The smart alecs are all getting their girl friends, what the little guys don't know by sight, to go round putting on the dough. Hundreds of them, by the sound of it.'

'You're a wonder, Bert.'

'Yeah,' he said modestly. 'Missed my bleeding vocation.'

Owen and I had spent most of the afternoon loading the big hired van from Chiswick and checking that we'd left nothing out. He worked like a demon, all energy and escaping smiles.

'Life will seem flat after this,' he said.

I had telephoned Charlie from Hantsford Manor and caught him before he went to lunch.

'We're off,' I said. 'Stratford, tomorrow.'

'Tally bloody ho!'

He rang me from his office again at five. 'Have you seen the evening papers?'

'Not yet,' I said.

'Jody has two definite runners at Chepstow as well.'

'Which ones?'

'Cricklewood in the big race and Asphodel in the handicap chase.'

Cricklewood and Asphodel both belonged to the same man, who since I'd left had become Jody's number one owner. Cricklewood was now also ostensibly the best horse in the yard.

'That means,' I said, 'that Jody himself will almost certainly go to Chepstow.'

'I should think so,' Charlie agreed. 'He wouldn't want to draw attention to Padellic by going to Stratford, would you think?'

'No, I wouldn't.'

'Just what we wanted,' Charlie said with satisfaction. 'Jody going to Chepstow.'

'We thought he might.'

Charlie chuckled. '*You* thought he might.' He cleared his throat. 'See you tomorrow, in the trenches. And Steven . . .'

'Yes?'

'Good luck with turning the handle.'

Turning the handle . . .

I looked at my watch. Still only eight-thirty and too early for any action. I switched on the car's engine and let the heater warm me up.

All the little toys, revolving on their spindles, going through their programmed acts. Allie, Bert, Charlie and Owen. Felicity and Jody Leeds, Ganser Mays. Padellic and Energise and Black Fire. Rupert Ramsey and Pete Duveen.

And one little toy I knew nothing about.

I stirred, thinking of him uneasily.

A big man who wore sunglasses. Who had muscles, and knew how to fight.

What else?

Who had bought Padellic at Doncaster Sales?

I didn't know if he had bought the horse after Jody had found it, or if he knew Energise well enough to look for a double himself; and there was no way of finding out.

I'd left no slot for him in today's plan. If he turned up like a joker, he might entirely disrupt the game.

I picked up my raceglasses which were lying on the seat beside me and started watching the traffic crossing the top of the opposite distant hill. From two miles away, even with strong magnification, it was difficult to identify particular vehicles, and in the valley and climbing the hill straight towards me they were head-on and foreshortened.

What looked like car and trailer came over the horizon. I glanced at my watch. If it was Allie, she was dead on time.

I focused on the little group. Watched it down into the valley. Definitely a Land-Rover and animal trailer. I got out of the car and watched it crawling up the hill, until finally I could make out the number plate. Definitely Allie.

Stepping a pace on to the road, I flagged her down. She pulled into the lay-by, opened her window, and looked worried.

'Is something wrong?'

'Not a thing.' I kissed her. 'I got here too early, so I thought I'd say good morning.'

'You louse. When I saw you standing there waving I thought the whole darned works were all fouled up.'

'You found the way, then.'

'No problem.'

'Sleep well?'

She wrinkled her nose. 'I guess so. But oh boy, that's some crazy house. Nothing works. If you want to flush the john you have to get Miss Johnston. No one else has the touch. I guess they're really sweet, though, the poor old ducks.'

'Shades of days gone by,' I said.

'Yeah, that's exactly right. They showed me their scrap books. They were big in the horse world thirty-forty years ago. Won things at shows all over. Now they're struggling on a fixed income and I guess they'll soon be starving.'

'Did they say so?'

'Of course not. You can see it, though.'

'Is Black Fire all right?'

'Oh sure. They helped me load him up, which was lucky because I sure would have been hopeless on my own.'

'Was he any trouble?'

'Quiet as a little lamb.'

I walked round to the back of the trailer and looked in over the three-quarter door. Black Fire occupied the left-hand stall. A full hay net lay in the right. The ladies might starve, but their horses wouldn't.

I went back to Allie. 'Well . . .' I said. 'Good luck.'

'To you too.'

She gave me the brilliant smile, shut the window and with care pulled out of the lay-by into the stream of northbound traffic.

Time and timing, the two essentials.

I sat in the car metaphorically chewing my nails and literally looking at my watch every half minute.

Padellic's race was the last of the day, the sixth race, the slot often allotted to that least crowd-pulling of events, the novice hurdle. Because of the short January afternoon, the last race was scheduled for three-thirty.

Jody's horses, like those of most other trainers, customarily arrived at a racecourse about two hours before they were due to run. Not often later, but quite often sooner.

The journey by horsebox from Jody's stable to Stratford on Avon racecourse took two hours. The very latest, therefore, that Jody's horsebox would set out would be eleven-thirty.

I thought it probable it would start much sooner than that. The latest time allowed little margin for delays on the journey or snags on arrival and I knew that if I were Jody and Ganser Mays and had so much at stake, I would add a good hour for contingencies.

Ten-thirty . . . But suppose it was earlier . . .

I swallowed. I had had to guess.

If for any reason Jody had sent the horse very early and it had already gone, all our plans were for nothing.

If he had sent it the day before . . If he had sent it with another trainer's horses, sharing the cost . . . If for some unimaginable reason the driver took a different route . . .

The ifs multiplied like stinging ants.

Nine-fifteen.

I got out of the car and extended the aerial of a large efficient walkie-talkie. No matter that British civilians were supposed to have permission in triple triplicate before operating them: in this case we would be cluttering the air for seconds only, and lighting flaming beacons on hill-tops would have caused a lot more fuss.

'Charlie?' I said, transmitting.

'All fine here.'

'Great.' I paused for five seconds, and transmitted again. 'Owen?'

'Here, sir.'

'Great.'

Owen and Charlie could both hear me but they couldn't hear each other, owing to the height of the Downs where I sat. I left the aerial extended and the switches to 'receive', and put the gadget back in the car.

The faint drizzle persisted, but my mouth was dry.

I thought about the five of us, sitting and waiting. I wondered if the others like me were having trouble with their nerves.

The walkie-talkie crackled suddenly. I picked it up.

'Sir?'

'Owen?'

'Pete Duveen just passed me.'

'Fine.'

I could hear the escaping tension in my own voice and the excitement in his. The on-time arrival of Pete Duveen signalled the real beginning. I put the walkie-talkie down and was disgusted to see my hand shaking.

Pete Duveen in his horsebox drove into the lay-by nine and a half minutes after he had passed Owen, who was stationed in sight of the road to Jody's stable. Pete owned a pale blue horse-box with his name, address and telephone number painted in large black and red letters on the front and back. I had seen the box and its owner at race meetings and it was he, in fact, whom I had engaged at Sandown on my abortive attempt to prevent Jody taking Energise home.

Pete Duveen shut down his engine and jumped from the cab.

'Morning, Mr Scott.'

'Morning,' I said, shaking hands. 'Glad to see you.'

'Anything to oblige.' He grinned cheerfully, letting me know both that he thought I was barmy and also that I had every right to be, as long as I was harmless and, moreover, paying him.

1082

He was well-built and fair, with weatherbeaten skin and a threadbare moustache. Open-natured, sensible and honest. A one-man transport firm, and making a go of it.

'You brought my horse?' I said.

'Sure thing.'

'And how has he travelled?'

'Not a peep out of him the whole way.'

'Mind if I take a look at him?' I said.

'Sure thing,' he said again. 'But honest, he didn't act up when we loaded him and I wouldn't say he cared a jimmy riddle one way or another.'

I unclipped and opened the part of the side of the horse-box which formed the entrance ramp for the horses. It was a bigger box than Jody's but otherwise much the same. The horse stood in the front row of stalls in the one furthest across from the ramp, and he looked totally uninterested in the day's proceedings.

'You never know,' I said, closing the box again. 'He might be all the better for the change of routine.'

'Maybe,' Pete said, meaning he didn't think so.

I smiled. 'Like some coffee?'

'Sure would.'

I opened the boot of my car, took out a thermos, and poured us each a cup.

'Sandwich?' I offered.

Sandwich accepted. He ate beef-and-chutney with relish. 'Early start,' he said, explaining his hunger. 'You said to get here soon after nine-thirty.'

'That's right,' I agreed.

'Er . . . why so early?'

'Because,' I said reasonably, 'I've other things to do all the rest of the day.'

He thought me even nuttier, but the sandwich plugged the opinion in his throat.

The sky began to brighten and the tiny-dropped drizzle dried away. I talked about racing in general and Stratford on Avon in particular, and wondered how on earth I was to keep him entertained if Jody's box should after all not leave home until the last possible minute.

By ten-fifteen we had drunk two cups of coffee each and he had run out of energy for sandwiches. He began to move restively and make ready-for-departure signs of which I blandly took no notice. I chatted on about the pleasures of owning racehorses and my stomach bunched itself into anxious knots.

Ten-twenty. Ten-twenty-five. Ten-thirty. Nothing.

It had all gone wrong, I thought. One of the things which could have sent everything awry had done so.

Ten-thirty-five.

'Look,' Pete said persuasively. 'You said you had a great deal to do today, and honestly, I don't think . . .'

The walkie-talkie crackled.

I practically leapt towards the front of the car and reached in for it.

'Sir?'

'Yes, Owen.'

'A blue horsebox just came out of his road and turned south.'

'Right.'

I stifled my disappointment. Jody's two runners setting off to Chepstow, no doubt.

'What's that?' Pete Duveen said, his face appearing at my shoulder full of innocent enquiry.

'Just a radio.'

'Sounded like a police car.'

I smiled and moved away back to the rear of the car, but I had hardly got Pete engaged again in useless conversation when the crackle was repeated.

'Sir?'

'Go ahead.'

'A fawn coloured box with a red slash, sir. Just turned north.'

His voice trembled with excitement.

'That's it, Owen.'

'I'm on my way.'

I felt suddenly sick. Took three deep breaths. Pressed the transmit button.

'Charlie?'

'Yes.'

'The box is on its way.'

'Halle-bloody-lujah.'

Pete was again looking mystified and inquisitive. I ignored his face and took a travelling bag out of the boot of my car.

'Time to go,' I said pleasantly. 'I think, if you don't

mind, I'd like to see how my horse behaves while going along, so could you start the box now and take me up the road a little way?'

He looked very surprised, but then he had found the whole expedition incomprehensible.

'If you like,' he said helplessly. 'You're the boss.'

I made encouraging signs to him to get into his cab and start the engine and while he was doing it I stowed my bag on the passenger side. The diesel engine whirred and coughed and came to thunderous life, and I went back to the Cortina.

Locked the boot, shut the windows, took the keys, locked the doors, and stood leaning against the wing holding binoculars in one hand and walkie-talkie in the other.

Pete Duveen had taken nine and a half minutes from Jody's road to my lay-by and Jody's box took exactly the same. Watching the far hill through raceglasses I saw the big dark blue van which contained Owen come over the horizon, followed almost immediately by an oblong of fawn.

Watched them down into the valley and on to the beginning of the hill.

I pressed the transmit button.

'Charlie?'

'Go ahead.'

'Seven minutes. Owen's in front.'

'Right.'

I pushed down the aerial of the walkie-talkie and

took it and myself along to the passenger door of Pete's box. He looked across and down at me enquiringly, wondering why on earth I was still delaying.

'Just a moment,' I said, giving no explanation, and he waited patiently, as if humouring a lunatic.

Owen came up the hill, changed gears abreast of the lay-by, and slowly accelerated away. Jody's horsebox followed, doing exactly the same. The scrunched near-side front had been hammered out, I saw, but respraying lay in the future. I had a quick glimpse into the cab: two men, neither of them Jody, both unknown to me; a box driver who had replaced Andy-Fred and the lad with the horse. Couldn't be better.

I hopped briskly up into Pete's box.

'Off we go, then.'

My sudden haste looked just as crazy as the former dawdling, but again he made no comment and merely did what I wanted. When he had found a gap in the traffic and pulled out on to the road there were four or five vehicles between Jody's box and ourselves, and this seemed to me a reasonable number.

I spent the next four miles trying to look as if nothing in particular was happening while listening to my heart beat like a discotheque. Owen's van went over the traffic lights at the big crossroads a half second before they changed to amber and Jody's box came to a halt as they showed red. The back of Owen's van disappeared round a bend in the road.

Between Jody's box and Pete's there were three

private cars and one small van belonging to an electrical firm. When the lights turned green one of the cars pceled off to the left and I began to worry that we were getting too close.

'Slow down just a fraction,' I suggested.

'If you like ... but there's not a squeak from the horse.' He glanced over his shoulder to where the black head looked patiently forward through a small observation hatch, as nervous as a suet pudding.

A couple of private cars passed us. We motored sedately onwards and came to the bottom of the next hill. Pete changed his gears smoothly and we lumbered noisily up. Near the top, his eye took in a notice board on a tripod at the side of the road.

'Damn,' he said.

'What is it?' I asked.

'Did you see that?' he said. 'Census point ahead.'

'Never mind, we're not in a hurry.'

'I suppose not.'

We breasted the hill. The fruit stall lay ahead on our left, with the sweep of car park beside it. Down the centre of the road stood a row of red and white cones used for marking road obstructions and in the north-bound lane, directing the traffic, stood a large man in navy blue police uniform with a black and white checked band round his cap.

As we approached he waved the private cars past and then directed Pete into the fruit stall car park, walking in beside the horsebox and talking to him through the window.

'We'll keep you only a few minutes, sir. Now, will you pull right round in a circle and park facing me just here, sir?'

'All right,' Pete said resignedly and followed the instructions. When he pulled the brake on we were facing the road. On our left, about ten feet away, stood Jody's box, but facing in the opposite direction. On the far side of Jody's box was Owen's van. And beyond Owen's van, across about twenty yards of cindery park, lay the caravan, its long flat windowless side towards us.

The Land-Rover and trailer which Allie had brought stood near the front of Jody's box. There was also the car hitched to the caravan and the car Bert had hired, and all in all the whole area looked populated, official, and busy.

A second large notice on a tripod faced the car park from just outside the caravan.

DEPARTMENT OF THE ENVIRONMENT
CENSUS POINT

and near a door at one end of the caravan a further notice on a stand said 'Way In'.

Jody's horsebox driver and Jody's lad were following its directions, climbing the two steps up to the caravan and disappearing within.

'Over there, please sir.' A finger pointed

authoritatively. 'And take your driving licence and log book, please.'

Pete shrugged, picked up his papers, and went. I jumped out and watched him go.

The second he was inside Bert slapped me on the back in a most unpolicemanlike way and said, 'Easy as Blackpool tarts.'

We zipped into action. Four minutes maximum, and a dozen things to do.

I unclipped the ramp of Jody's horsebox and let it down quietly. The one thing which would bring any horsebox driver running, census or no census, was the sound of someone tampering with his cargo; and noise, all along, had been one of the biggest problems.

Opened Pete Duveen's ramp. Also the one on Allie's trailer.

While I did that, Bert brought several huge rolls of three-inch thick latex from Owen's van and unrolled them down all the ramps, and across the bare patches of car park in between the boxes. I fetched the head collar bought for the purpose from my bag and stepped into Jody's box. The black horse looked at me incuriously, standing there quietly in his travelling rug and four leg-guards. I checked his ear for the tiny nick and his shoulder for the bald pennyworth, and wasted a moment in patting him.

I knew all too well that success depended on my being able to persuade this strange four-footed creature to go with me gently and without fuss, and wished passionately for more expertise. All I had were nimble hands and sympathy, and they would have to be enough.

I unbuckled his rug at high speed and thanked the gods that the leg-guards Jody habitually used for travelling his horses were not laboriously wound-on bandages but lengths of plastic-backed foam rubber fastened by strips of velcro.

I had all four off before Bert had finished the sound-proofing. Put the new head collar over his neck; unbuckled and removed his own and left it swinging, still tied to the stall. Fitted and fastened the new one, and gave the rope a tentative tug. Energise took one step, then another, then with more assurance followed me sweetly down the ramp. It felt miraculous, but nothing like fast enough.

Hurry. Get the other horses, and hurry.

They didn't seem to mind walking on the soft spongy surface, but they wouldn't go fast. I tried to take them calmly, to keep my urgency to myself, to stop them taking fright and skittering away and crashing those metal-capped feet on to the car park.

Hurry. Hurry.

I had to get Energise's substitute into his place, wearing the right rug, the right bandages, and the right collar, before the box driver and the lad came out of the caravan.

Also his hooves . . . Racing plates were sometimes put on by the blacksmith at home, who then rubbed on oil to obliterate the rasp marks of the file and give the feet a well-groomed appearance. I had brought hoof oil in my bag in case Energise had already had his shoes changed and he had.

'Hurry for gawd's sake,' said Bert, seeing me fetch the oil. He was running back to the van with relays of re-rolled latex and grinning like a Pools winner.

I painted the hooves a glossy dark. Buckled on the swinging head collar without disturbing the tethering knot, as the lad would notice if it were tied differently. Buckled the rug round the chest and under the belly. Fastened the velcro strips on all four leg-guards. Shut the folding gates to his stall exactly as they had been before, and briefly looked back before closing the ramp. The black head was turned incuriously towards me, the liquid eye patient and unmoved. I smiled at him involuntarily, jumped out of the box, and with Bert's help eased shut the clips on the ramp.

Owen came out of the caravan, ran across, and fastened the ramp on the trailer. I jumped in with the horse in Pete's box. Bert lifted the ramp and did another silent job on the clips.

Through the windscreen of Pete's box the car park looked quiet and tidy.

Owen returned to the driving seat of his van and Bert walked back towards the road.

At the same instant Jody's driver and lad hurried out of the caravan and trampled across to their horsebox. I ducked out of sight, but I could hear one of them say, as he re-embarked, 'Right lot of time-wasting cobblers, that was.'

Then the engine throbbed to life, the box moved off, and Bert considerately held up a car or two so that it should have a clear passage back to its interrupted journey. If I hadn't had so much still to do I would have laughed.

I fastened the rug. Tied the head collar rope. Clipped on the leg guards. I'd never worked so fast in my life.

What else? I glanced over my beautiful black horse, seeking things undone. He looked steadfastly back. I smiled at him, too, and told him he was a great fellow. Then Pete came out of the caravan and I scrambled through to the cab, and tried to sit in the passenger seat as if bored with waiting instead of sweating with effort and with a heart racing like tappets.

Pete climbed into his side of the cab and threw his log book and licence disgustedly on to the glove shelf.

'They're always stopping us nowadays. Spot check on log books. Spot check on vehicles. Half an hour a time, those. And now a census.'

'Irritating,' I agreed, making my voice a lot slower than my pulse.

His usual good nature returned in a smile. 'Actually the checks are a good thing. Some lorries, in the old days, were death on wheels. And some drivers, I dare say.' He stretched his hand towards the ignition. 'Where to?' he said.

'Might as well go back. As you say, the horse is quiet. If you could take me back to my car?'

'Sure thing,' he said. 'You're the boss.'

Bert shepherded us solicitously on to the south-bound lane, holding up the traffic with a straight face and obvious enjoyment. Pete drove steadfastly back to the lay-by and pulled in behind the Cortina.

'I expect you think it a wasted day,' I said. 'But I assure you from my point of view it's been worth it.'

'That's all that matters,' he said cheerfully.

'Take good care of this fellow going home,' I said, looking back at the horse. 'And would you remind the lads in Mr Ramsey's yard that I've arranged for a security guard to patrol the stable at night for a while? He should be arriving there later this afternoon.'

'Sure,' he said, nodding.

'That's all then, I guess.' I took my bag and jumped down from the cab. He gave me a final wave through the window and set off southwards along the A34.

I leaned against the Cortina, watching him go down the hill, across the valley, and up over the horizon on the far side.

I wondered how Energise would like his new home.

CHAPTER THIRTEEN

Charlie, Allie, Bert and Owen were all in the caravan when I drove back there, drinking coffee and laughing like kids.

'Here,' Bert said, wheezing with joy. 'A bleeding police car came along a second after I'd picked up the census notices and all those cones. Just a bleeding second.'

'It didn't stop, I hope.'

'Not a bleeding chance. Mind you, I'd taken off the fancy clobber. First thing. The fuzz don't love you for impersonating them, even if your hatband is only a bit of bleeding ribbon painted in checks.'

Charlie said more soberly, 'It was the only police car we've seen.'

'The cones were only in the road for about ten minutes,' Allie said. 'It sure would have been unlucky if the police had driven by in that time.'

She was sitting by one of the desks looking neat but unremarkable in a plain skirt and jersey. On the desk stood my typewriter, uncovered, with piles of stationery

1095

alongside. Charlie, at the other desk, wore an elderly suit, faintly shabby and a size too small. He had parted his hair in the centre and brushed it flat with water, and had somehow contrived a look of middling bureaucracy instead of world finance. Before him, too, lay an impressive array of official forms and other literature and the walls of the caravan were drawing-pinned with exhortative Ministry posters.

'How did you get all this bleeding junk?' said Bert, waving his hand at it.

'Applied for it,' I said. 'It's not difficult to get government forms or information posters. All you do is ask.'

'Blimey.'

'They're not census forms, of course. Most of them are application forms for driving licences and passports and things like that. Owen and I just made up the census questions and typed them out for Charlie, and he pretended to put the answers on the forms.'

Owen drank his coffee with a happy smile and Charlie said, chuckling, 'You should have seen your man here putting on his obstructive act. Standing there in front of me like an idiot and either answering the questions wrong or arguing about answering them at all. The two men from the horsebox thought him quite funny and made practically no fuss about being kept waiting. It was the other man, Pete Duveen, who was getting tired of it, but as he was at the back of the queue he couldn't do much.'

'Four minutes,' Owen said. 'You said you needed a minimum of four. So we did our best.'

'You must have given me nearer five,' I said gratefully. 'Did you hear anything?'

Allie laughed. 'There was so much darned racket going on in here. Owen arguing, me banging away on the typewriter, the traffic outside, pop radio inside, and that heater . . . How did you fix that heater?'

We all looked at the calor gas heater which warmed the caravan. It clattered continually like a broken fan.

'Screwed a small swinging flap up at the top here, inside. The rising hot air makes it bang against the casing.'

'Switch it off,' Charlie said. 'It's driving me mad.'

I produced instead a screwdriver and undid the necessary screws. Peace returned to the gas and Charlie said he could see the value of a college education.

'Pete Duveen knew the other box driver,' Allie said conversationally. 'Seems they're all one big club.'

'See each other every bleeding day at the races,' Bert confirmed. 'Here, that box driver made a bit of a fuss when I said the lad had to go into the caravan too. Like you said, they aren't supposed to leave a racehorse unguarded. So I said I'd bleeding guard it for him. How's that for a laugh? He said he supposed it was okay, as I was the police. I said I'd got instructions that everyone had to go into the census, no exceptions.'

'People will do anything if it looks official enough,' Charlie said, happily nodding.

'Well . . .' I put down my much needed cup of coffee and stretched my spine. 'Time to be off, don't you think?'

'Right,' Charlie said. 'All this paper and stuff goes in Owen's van.'

They began moving slowly, the reminiscent smiles still in place, packing the phoney census into carrier bags. Allie came out with me when I left.

'We've had more fun . . .' she said. 'You can't imagine.'

I supposed that I felt the same way, now that the flurry was over. I gave her a hug and a kiss and told her to take care of herself, and she said you, too.

'I'll call you this evening,' I promised.

'I wish I was coming with you.'

'We can't leave that here all day,' I said, pointing to the Land-Rover and the trailer.

She smiled. 'I guess not. Charlie says we'd all best be gone before anyone starts asking what we're doing.'

'Charlie is a hundred per cent right.'

I went to Stratford upon Avon races.

Drove fast, thinking of the righting of wrongs without benefit of lawyers. Thinking of the ephemeral quality of racehorses and the snail pace of litigation. Thinking that the best years of a hurdler's life could be wasted in stagnation while the courts deliberated to whom he belonged. Wondering what Jody would do when he found out about the morning's work and hoping that I knew him well enough to have guessed right.

When I drew up in the racecourse car park just before the first race, I saw Jody's box standing among a row of others over by the entrance to the stables. The ramp was down and from the general stage of activity I gathered that the horse was still on board.

I sat in my car a hundred yards away, watching through race glasses. I wondered when the lad would realise he had the wrong horse. I wondered if he would realise at all, because he certainly wouldn't expect to set off with one and arrive with another, and he would quite likely shrug off the first stirring of doubt. He was new in the yard since I had left and with average luck, knowing Jody's rate of turnover, he would be neither experienced nor very bright.

Nothing appeared to be troubling him at that moment. He walked down the ramp carrying a bucket and a bundle of other equipment and went through the gate to the stables. He looked about twenty. Long curly hair. Slight in build. Wearing flashy red trousers. I hoped he was thinking more of his own appearance than his horse's. I put the glasses down and waited.

My eye was caught by a woman in a white coat striding across the car park towards the horseboxes, and it took about five seconds before I realised with a jolt who she was.

Felicity Leeds.

Jody might have taken his knowing eyes to Chepstow, but Felicity had brought hers right here.

I hopped out of the car as if stung and made speed in her direction.

The lad came out of the stable, went up the ramp and shortly reappeared, holding the horse's head. Felicity walked towards him as he began to persuade the horse to disembark.

'Felicity,' I called.

She turned, saw me, looked appalled, threw a quick glance over her shoulder at the descending horse and walked decisively towards me.

When she stopped I looked over her shoulder and said with the sort of puzzlement which takes little to tip into suspicion, 'What horse is that?'

She took another hurried look at the black hindquarters now disappearing towards the stable and visibly gathered her wits.

'Padellic. Novice hurdler. Not much good.'

'He reminds me . . .' I said slowly.

'First time out, today,' Felicity said hastily. 'Nothing much expected.'

'Oh,' I said, not sounding entirely reassured. 'Are you going into the stables to see him, because I . . .'

'No,' she said positively. 'No need. He's perfectly all right.' She gave me a sharp nod and walked briskly away to the main entrance to the course.

Without an accompanying trainer no one could go into the racecourse stables. She knew I would have to contain my curiosity until the horse came out for its race and until then, from her point of view, she was safe.

I, however, didn't want her visiting the stables herself. There was no particular reason why she should, as trainers mostly didn't when the journey from home to course was so short. All the same I thought I might as well fill up so much of her afternoon that she scarcely had time.

I came up with her again outside the weighing room, where she vibrated with tension from her patterned silk headscarf to her high-heeled boots. There were sharp patches of colour on her usually pale cheeks and the eyes which regarded me with angry apprehension were as hot as fever.

'Felicity,' I said. 'Do you know anything about a load of muck that was dumped in my front garden?'

'A what?' The blank look she gave me was not quite blank enough.

I described at some length the component parts and all-over consistency of the obstruction and remarked on their similarity to the discard pile at her own home.

'All muck heaps are alike,' she said. 'You couldn't tell where one particular load came from.'

'All you'd need is a sample for forensic analysis.'

'Did you take one?' she said sharply.

'No,' I admitted.

'Well, then.'

'You and Jody seem the most likely to have done it.'

She looked at me with active dislike. 'Everyone on the racecourse knows what a shit you've been to us. It doesn't surprise me at all that someone has expressed the same opinion in a concrete way.'

'It surprises me very much that anyone except you should bother.'

'I don't intend to talk about it,' she said flatly.

'Well I do,' I said, and did, at some length, repetitively.

The muck heap accounted for a good deal of the afternoon, and Quintus, in a way, for the rest.

Quintus brought his noble brow and empty mind on to the stands and gave Felicity a peck on the cheek, lifting his hat punctiliously. To me he donated what could only be called a scowl.

Felicity fell upon him as if he were a saviour.

'I didn't know you were coming!' She sounded gladder than glad that he had.

'Just thought I would, you know, my dear.'

She drew him away from me out of earshot and began talking to him earnestly. He nodded, smiling, agreeing with her. She talked some more. He nodded benignly and patted her shoulder.

I homed in again like an attacking wasp.

'Oh for God's sake, leave the bloody subject alone,' Felicity exploded.

'What's the fella talking about?' Quintus said.

'A muck heap on his doorstep.'

'Oh,' Quintus said. 'Ah . . .'

I described it all over again. I was getting quite attached to it, in retrospect.

Quintus was distinctly pleased. Chuckles quivered in his throat and his eyes twinkled with malice.

'Serves you right, what?' he said.

'Do you think so?'

'Shit to a shit,' he said, nodding with satisfaction.

'*What* did you say?'

'Er . . . nothing.'

Realisation dawned on me with a sense of fitness. 'You did it yourself,' I said with conviction.

'Don't be ridiculous.' He was still vastly amused.

'Lavatory humour would be just your mark.'

'You are insulting.' Less amusement, more arrogance.

'And the police took away the card you left to test it for fingerprints.'

His mouth opened and shut. He looked blank. 'The police?'

'Fellows in blue,' I said.

Felicity said furiously, 'Trust someone like you not to take a joke.'

'I'll take an apology,' I said mildly. 'In writing.'

Their objections, their grudging admissions and the eventual drafting of the apology took care of a lot of time. Quintus had hired a tip-up truck for his delivery and had required his gardener to do the actual work. Jody and Felicity had generously contributed the load.

Quintus had supervised its disposal and written his message.

He also, in his own hand and with bravado-ish flourishes, wrote the apology. I thanked him courteously and told him I would frame it, which didn't please him in the least.

By that time the fifth race was over and it was time to saddle the horses for the sixth.

Felicity, as the trainer's wife, was the natural person to supervise the saddling of their runner, and I knew that if she did she would know she had the wrong horse.

On the other hand if she did the saddling she couldn't stop me, as a member of the public, taking a very close look, and from her point of view that was a risk she didn't want to take.

She solved her dilemma by getting Quintus to see to the saddling.

She herself, with a superhuman effort, laid her hand on my arm in a conciliatory gesture and said, 'All right. Let bygones be bygones. Let's go and have a drink.'

'Sure,' I said, expressing just the right amount of surprise and agreement. 'Of course, if you'd like.'

So we went off to the bar where I bought her a large gin and tonic and myself a scotch and water, and we stood talking about nothing much while both busy with private thoughts. She was trembling slightly from the force of hers, and I too had trouble preventing mine from showing. There we were, both trying our darnedest to keep the other away from the horse, she because she thought it was Energise and I because I knew it wasn't. I could feel the irony breaking out in wrinkles round my eyes.

Felicity dawdled so long over her second drink that the horses were already leaving the parade ring and going out to the course when we finally made our way back to the heart of things. Quintus had understudied splendidly and was to be seen giving a parting slap to the horse's rump. Felicity let her breath out in a sigh and dropped most of the pretence of being nice to me. When she left me abruptly to rejoin Quintus for the race, I made no move to stop her.

The horse put up a good show, considering.

There were twenty-two runners, none of them more than moderate, and they delivered the sort of performance Energise would have left in the next parish. His substitute was running in his own class and finished undisgraced in sixth place, better than I would have expected. The crowd briefly cheered the winning favourite, and I thought it time to melt prudently and inconspicuously away.

I had gone to Stratford with more hope than certainty that the horse would actually run without the exchange being noticed. I had been prepared to do anything I reasonably could to achieve it, in order to give Ganser Mays the nasty shock of losing every penny he'd laid out on his squeezer.

What I hadn't actually bargained for was the effect the lost race would have on Felicity.

I saw her afterwards, though I hadn't meant to, when she went to meet her returning horse. The jockey, a well-known rider who had doubtless been told to win, was looking strained enough, but Felicity seemed on the point of collapse.

Her face was a frightening white, her whole body shook and her eyes looked as blank as marbles.

If I had ever wanted any personal revenge, I had it then, but I drove soberly away from the racecourse feeling sorry for her.

CHAPTER FOURTEEN

Rupert Ramsey met me with a stony face, not at all the expression one would normally expect from a successful trainer who had invited one of his owners to dinner.

'I'm glad you're early,' he said forbiddingly. 'Please come into the office.'

I followed him across the hall into the familiar room which was warm with a living log fire. He made no move to offer me a drink and I thought I might as well save him some trouble.

'You're going to tell me,' I said, 'that the horse which left here this morning is not the one which returned.'

He raised his eyebrows. 'So you don't deny it?'

'Of course not.' I smiled. 'I wouldn't have thought all that much of you if you hadn't noticed.'

'The lad noticed. Donny. He told the head lad, and the head lad told me, and I went to see for myself. And what I want is an explanation.'

'And it had better be good,' I added, imitating his schoolmasterly tone. He showed no amusement.

'This is no joke.'

'Maybe not. But it's no crime, either. If you'll calm down a fraction, I'll explain.'

'You have brought me a ringer. No trainer of any sense is going to stand for that.' His anger was cold and deep.

I said, 'The horse you thought was Energise was the ringer. And I didn't send him here, Jody did. The horse you have been trying to train for the Champion Hurdle and which left here this morning, is a fairly useless novice called Padellic.'

'I don't believe it.'

'As Energise,' I pointed out, 'you have found him unbelievably disappointing.'

'Well . . .' The first shade of doubt crept into his voice.

'When I discovered the wrong horse had been sent here, I asked you expressly not to run him in any races, because I certainly did not want you to be involved in running a ringer, nor myself for that matter.'

'But if you knew . . . why on earth didn't you immediately tell Jody he had made a mistake?'

'He didn't,' I said simply. 'He sent the wrong one on purpose.'

He walked twice round the room in silence and then still without a word poured us each a drink.

'Right,' he said, handing me a glass. 'Pray continue.'

I continued for quite a long while. He gestured to me

to sit down and sat opposite me himself, and listened attentively with a serious face.

'And this security firm . . .' he said at the end. 'Are you expecting Jody to try to get Energise back?'

I nodded. 'He's an extremely determined man. I made the mistake once of underestimating his vigour and his speed, and that's what lost me Energise in the first place. I think when he got home from Chepstow and heard what Felicity and the box driver and the lad had to say, he would have been violently angry and would decide to act at once. He's not the sort to spend a day or so thinking about it. He'll come tonight. I think and hope he will come tonight.'

'He will be sure Energise is here?'

'He certainly should be,' I said. 'He'll ask his box driver about the journey and his box driver will tell him about the census. Jody will question closely and find that Pete Duveen was there too. Jody will, I think, telephone to ask Pete Duveen if he saw anything unusual and Pete, who has nothing to hide, will tell him he brought a black horse from here. He'll tell him he took a black horse home again. And he'll tell him I was there at the census point. I didn't ask him not to tell and I am sure he will, because of his frank and open nature.'

Rupert's lips twitched into the first hint of a smile. He straightened it out immediately. 'I don't really approve of what you've done.'

'Broken no laws,' I said neutrally, neglecting to

mention the shadowy area of Bert's police-impression uniform.

'Perhaps not.' He thought it over. 'And the security firm is both to prevent the theft of Energise and to catch Jody redhanded?'

'Exactly so.'

'I saw them in the yard this evening. Two men. They said they were expecting instructions from you when you arrived, though frankly at that point I was so angry with you that I was paying little attention.'

'I talked to them on my way in,' I agreed. 'One will patrol the yard at regular intervals and the other is going to sit outside the horse's box. I told them both to allow themselves to be enticed from their posts by any diversion.'

'To *allow*?'

'Of course. You have to give the mouse a clear view of the cheese.'

'Good God.'

'And I wondered . . . whether you would consider staying handy, to act as a witness if Jody should come a-robbing.'

It seemed to strike him for the first time that he too was Jody's victim. He began to look almost as Charlie had done, and certainly as Bert had done, as if he found counter-measures attractive. The tugging smile reappeared.

'It depends of course on what time Jody comes . . . if he comes at all . . . but two of my guests tonight would be the best independent witnesses you could get. A lady magistrate and the local vicar.'

'Will they stay late?' I asked.

'We can try.' He thought for a bit. 'What about the police?'

'How quickly can they get here if called?'

'Um . . . Ten minutes. Quarter of an hour.'

'That should be all right.'

He nodded. A bell rang distantly in the house, signalling the arrival of more guests. He stood up, paused a moment, frowned and said, 'If the guard is to allow himself to be decoyed away why plant him outside the horse's door in the first place?'

I smiled. 'How else is Jody to know which box to rob?'

The dinner party seemed endless, though I couldn't afterwards remember a word or a mouthful. There were eight at table, all better value than myself, and the vicar particularly shone because of his brilliance as a mimic. I half-heard the string of imitated voices and saw everyone else falling about with hysterics and could think only of my men outside in the winter night and of the marauder I hoped to entice.

To groans from his audience the vicar played Cinderella at midnight and took himself off to shape up to Sunday, and three others shortly followed. Rupert pressed the last two to stay for nightcaps: the lady magistrate and her husband, a quiet young colonel with an active career and a bottomless capacity for port. He settled happily enough at the sight of a fresh decanter, and she with mock resignation continued a mild flirtation with Rupert.

The wheels inside my head whirred with the same doubts as in the morning. Suppose I had been wrong. Suppose Jody didn't come. Suppose he did come, but came unseen, and managed to steal the horse successfully.

Well . . . I'd planned for that, too. I checked for the hundredth time through the ifs. I tried to imagine what I hadn't already imagined, see what I hadn't seen, prepare for the unprepared. Rupert cast an amused glance or two at my abstracted expression and made no attempt to break it down.

The door bell rang sharply, three long insistent pushes.

I stood up faster than good manners.

'Go on,' Rupert said indulgently. 'We'll be right behind you, if you need us.'

I nodded and departed, and crossed the hall to open the front door. My man in a grey flannel suit stood outside, looking worried and holding a torch.

'What is it?'

'I'm not sure. The other two are patrolling the yard and I haven't seen them for some time. And I think we have visitors, but they haven't come in a horsebox.'

'Did you see them? The visitors?'

'No. Only their car. Hidden off the road in a patch of wild rhododendrons. At least . . . there is a car there which wasn't there half an hour ago. What do you think?'

'Better take a look,' I said.

He nodded. I left the door of Rupert's house ajar and we walked together towards the main gate. Just inside it stood the van which had brought the security guards, and outside, less than fifty yards along the road, we came to the car in the bushes, dimly seen even by torchlight.

'It isn't a car I recognise,' I said. 'Suppose it's just a couple of lovers?'

'They'd be inside it on a night like this, not out snogging in the freezing undergrowth.'

'You're right.'

'Let's take the rotor arm, to make sure.'

We lifted the bonnet and carefully removed the essential piece of electrics. Then, shining the torch as little as possible and going on grass whenever there was a choice, we hurried back towards the stable. The night was windy enough to swallow small sounds, dark enough to lose contact at five paces and cold enough to do structural damage to brass monkeys.

At the entrance to the yard we stopped to look and listen.

No lights. The dark heavy bulk of buildings was more sensed than seen against the heavily overcast sky.

No sounds except our own breath and the greater lungs of the wind. No sign of our other two guards.

'What now?'

'We'll go and check the horse,' I said.

We went into the main yard and skirted round its edges, which were paved with quieter concrete. The centre was an expanse of crunchy gravel, a giveaway even for cats.

Box fourteen had a chair outside it. A wooden kitchen chair planted prosaically with its back to the stable wall. No guard sat on it.

Quietly I slid back the bolts on the top half of the door and looked inside. There was a soft movement and the sound of a hoof rustling the straw. A second's flash of torch showed the superb shape patiently standing half-asleep in the dark, drowsing away the equine night.

I shut the door and made faint grating noises with the bolt.

'He's fine,' I said. 'Let's see if we can find the others.'

He nodded. We finished the circuit of the main yard and started along the various branches, moving with caution and trying not to use the torch. I couldn't stop the weird feeling growing that we were not the only couple groping about in the dark. I saw substance in shadows and reached out fearfully to touch objects which were not there, but only darker patches in the pervading black. We spent five or ten minutes feeling our way, listening, taking a few steps, listening, going on. We completed the tour of the outlying rows of boxes, and saw and heard nothing.

'This is no good,' I said quietly. 'There isn't a sign of them, and has it occurred to you that they are hiding from us, thinking we are the intruders?'

'Just beginning to wonder.'

'Let's go back to the main yard.'

We turned and retraced our steps, taking this time a short cut through a narrow alleyway between two sections of boxes. I was in front, so it was I who practically tripped over the huddled bundle on the ground.

I switched on the torch. Saw the neat navy uniform and the blood glistening red on the forehead. Saw the shut eyes and the lax limbs of the man who should have been sitting on the empty kitchen chair.

'Oh God,' I said desperately, and thought I would never ever forgive myself. I knelt beside him and fumbled for his pulse.

'He's alive,' said my friend in the grey flannel suit. He sounded reassuring and confident. 'Look at him breathing. He'll be all right, you'll see.'

All I could see was a man who was injured because I'd stationed him in the path of danger. 'I'll get a doctor,' I said, standing up.

'What about the horse?'

'Damn the horse. This is more important.'

'I'll stay here with him till you get back.'

I nodded and set off anxiously towards the house,
shining the torch now without reservations. If permanent harm came to that man because of me . . .

I ran.

Burst in through Rupert's front door and found him
standing there in the hall talking to the lady magistrate
and the colonel, who were apparently just about to
leave. She was pulling a cape around her shoulders and
Rupert was holding the colonel's coat. They turned
and stared at me like a frozen tableau.

'My guard's been attacked. Knocked out,' I said.
'Could you get him a doctor?'

'Sure,' Rupert said calmly. 'Who attacked him?'

'I didn't see.'

'Job for the police?'

'Yes, please.'

He turned to the telephone, dialling briskly. 'What
about the horse?'

'They didn't come in a horsebox.'

We both digested implications while he got the
rescue services on the move. The colonel and the magistrate stood immobile in the hall with their mouths half
open and Rupert, putting down the telephone, gave
them an authoritative glance.

'Come out into the yard with us, will you?' he said.
'Just in case we need witnesses?'

They weren't trained to disappear rapidly at the
thought. When Rupert hurried out of the door with me
at his heels they followed more slowly after.

Everything still looked entirely quiet outside.

'He's in a sort of alley between two blocks of boxes,' I said.

'I know where you mean,' Rupert nodded. 'But first we'll check on Energise.'

'Later.'

'No. Now. Why bash the guard if they weren't after the horse?'

He made straight for the main yard, switched on all six external lights, and set off across the brightly illuminated gravel.

The effect was like a flourish of trumpets. Noise, light and movement filled the space where silence and dark had been total.

Both halves of the door of box fourteen swung open about a foot, and two dark figures catapulted through the gap.

'Catch them!' Rupert shouted.

There was only one way out of the yard, the broad entrance through which we had come. The two figures ran in curving paths towards the exit, one to one side of Rupert and me, one to the other.

Rupert rushed to intercept the smaller who was suddenly, as he turned his head to the light, recognisable as Jody.

I ran for the larger. Stretched out. Touched him.

He swung a heavy arm and threw out a hip and I literally bounced off him, stumbling and falling.

The muscles were rock hard. The sunglasses glittered.

The joker was ripping through the pack.

Jody and Rupert rolled on the gravel, one clutching, one punching, both swearing. I tried again at Muscles with the same useless results. He seemed to hesitate over going to Jody's help, which was how I'd come to be able to reach him a second time, but finally decided on flight. By the time I was again staggering to my feet he was on his way to the exit with the throttle wide open.

A large figure in navy blue hurtled straight at him from the opposite direction and brought him down with a diving hug round the knees. The sunglasses flew off in a shiny arc and the two blue figures lay in a writhing entwined mass, the blue uniform uppermost and holding his own. I went to his help and sat on Muscles' ankles, crushing his feet sideways with no compunction at all. He screeched with pain and stopped struggling, but I fear I didn't immediately stand up.

Jody wrenched himself free from Rupert and ran past me. The colonel, who with his lady had been watching the proceedings with astonishment, decided it was time for some soldierly action and elegantly stuck out his foot.

Jody tripped over and fell sprawling. The colonel put more energy into it, leant down and took hold of the collar of Jody's coat. Rupert, rallying, came to his aid, and between them they too more or less sat on Jody, pinning him to the ground.

'What now?' Rupert panted.

'Wait for the police,' I said succinctly.

Muscles and Jody both heaved about a good deal at this plan but didn't succeed in freeing themselves. Muscles complained that I'd broken his ankle. Jody, under the colonel's professional ministrations, seemed to have difficulty saying anything at all. The colonel was in fact so single-handedly efficient that Rupert stood up and dusted himself down and looked at me speculatively.

I jerked my head in the direction of box fourteen, where the door still stood half open, showing only darkness within. He nodded slowly and went that way. Switched on the light. Stepped inside. He came back with a face of stone and three bitter words.

'Energise is dead.'

CHAPTER FIFTEEN

Rupert fetched some rope with which he ignominiously tied Jody's hands behind his back before he and the colonel let him get up, and the colonel held the free end of rope so that Jody was to all intents on a lead. Once up, Jody aimed a kick at the colonel and Rupert told him to stop unless he wanted his ankles tied as well.

Rupert and my man in blue uniform did a repeat job on Muscles, whose ankles were not in kicking shape and whose language raised eyebrows even on the lady magistrate, who had heard more than most.

The reason for Muscles' ubiquitous sunglasses was at once apparent, now that one could see his face. He stood glowering like a bull, seething with impotent rage, hopping on one foot and pulling against the tethering rope which led back from his wrists to my man in blue. His eyelids, especially the lower, were grossly distorted, and even in the outside lighting looked bright pink with inflammation. One could pity his plight, which was clearly horrid.

1120

'I know you,' Rupert said suddenly, looking at him closely. 'What's the matter with your eyes?'

'Mind your own effing business.'

'Macrahinish. That's what your name is, Macrahinish.'

Muscles didn't comment. Rupert turned to me. 'Don't you know him? Perhaps he was before your time. He's a vet. A struck-off vet. Struck off the vets' register and warned off the racecourse. And absolutely not allowed to set foot in a racing stable.'

Muscles-Macrahinish delivered himself of an unflattering opinion of racing in general and Rupert in particular.

Rupert said, 'He was convicted of doping and fraud and served a term in jail. He ran a big doping ring and supplied all the drugs. He looks older and there's something wrong with his eyes, but that's who this is, all right. Macrahinish.'

I turned away from the group and walked over to the brightly lit loosebox. Swung the door wide. Looked inside.

My beautiful black horse lay flat on his side, legs straight, head flaccid on the straw. The liquid eye was dull and opaque, mocking the sheen which still lay on his coat, and he still had pieces of unchewed hay half in and half out of his mouth. There was no blood, and no visible wound. I went in and squatted beside him, and patted him sadly with anger and regret.

Jody and Macrahinish had been unwillingly

propelled in my wake. I looked up to find them inside the box, with Rupert, the colonel, his wife and the man in blue effectively blocking the doorway behind them.

'How did you kill him?' I asked, the bitterness apparent in my voice.

Macrahinish's reply did not contain the relevant information.

I straightened up and in doing so caught sight of a flat brown attaché case half hidden in the straw by the horse's tail. I bent down again and picked it up. The sight of it brought a sound and a squirm from Macrahinish, and he began to swear in earnest when I balanced it on the manger and unfastened the clips.

The case contained regular veterinarian equipment, neatly stowed in compartments. I touched only one thing, lifting it carefully out.

A plastic bag containing a clear liquid. A bag plainly proclaiming the contents to be sterile saline solution.

I held it out towards Jody and said, 'You dripped alcohol straight into my veins.'

'You were unconscious,' he said disbelievingly.

'Shut up, you stupid fool,' Macrahinish screamed at him.

I smiled. 'Not all the time. I remember nearly everything about that night.'

'He said he didn't,' Jody said defensively to Macrahinish and was rewarded by a look from the swollen eyes which would have made a non-starter of Medusa.

'I went to see if you still had Energise,' I said. 'And I found you had.'

'You don't know one horse from another,' he sneered. 'You're just a mug. A blind greedy mug.'

'So are you,' I said. 'The horse you've killed is not Energise.'

'It is!'

'Shut up,' screamed Macrahinish in fury. 'Keep your stupid sodding mouth shut.'

'No,' I said to Jody. 'The horse you've killed is an American horse called Black Fire.'

Jody looked wildly down at the quiet body.

'It damn well is Energise,' he insisted. 'I'd know him anywhere.'

'Jesus,' Macrahinish shouted. 'I'll cut your tongue out.'

Rupert said doubtfully to me, 'Are you sure it's not Energise?'

'Positive.'

'He's just saying it to spite me,' said Jody furiously. 'I know it's Energise. See that tiny bald patch on his shoulder? That's Energise.'

Macrahinish, beyond speech, tried to attack him, tied hands and dicky ankle notwithstanding. Jody gave him a vague look, concentrating only on the horse.

'You are saying,' Rupert suggested, 'that you came to kill Energise and that you've done it.'

'Yes,' said Jody triumphantly.

The word hung in the air, vibrating. No one said

anything. Jody looked round at each watching face, at first with defiant angry pride, then with the first creeping of doubt, and finally with the realisation of what Macrahinish had been trying to tell him, that he should never have been drawn into admitting anything. The fire visibly died into glum and chilly embers.

'I didn't kill him,' he said suddenly. 'Macrahinish did. I didn't want to kill him at all, but Macrahinish insisted.'

A police car arrived with two young and persistent constables who seemed to find nothing particularly odd in being called to the murder of a horse.

They wrote in their notebooks that five witnesses, including a magistrate, had heard Jody Leeds admit that he and a disbarred veterinary surgeon had broken into a racing stable after midnight with the intention of putting to death one of the horses. They noted that a horse was dead. Cause of death, unknown until an autopsy could be arranged.

Hard on their heels came Rupert's doctor, an elderly man with a paternal manner. Yawning but uncomplaining, he accompanied me to find my security guard, who to my great relief was sitting on the ground with his head in his hands, awake and groaning healthily. We took him into Rupert's office, where the doctor stuck a plaster on the dried wound on his forehead, gave him some tablets and told him to lay off work for a couple of days. He smiled weakly and said it depended if his boss would let him.

One of the young policemen asked if he'd seen who had hit him.

'Big man with sunglasses. He was creeping along behind me, holding a ruddy great chunk of wood. I heard something . . . I turned and shone my torch, and there he was. He swung at my head. Gave me a right crack, he did. Next thing I knew, I was lying on the ground.'

Reassured by his revival I went outside again to see what was happening.

The magistrate and the colonel seemed to have gone home, and Rupert was down in the yard talking to some of his own stable staff who had been woken by the noise.

Macrahinish was hopping about on one leg, accusing me of having broken the other and swearing he'd have me prosecuted for using undue force to protect my property. The elderly doctor phlegmatically examined the limb in question and said that in his opinion it was a sprain.

The police had rashly untied the Macrahinish wrists and were obviously relying on the leg injury to prevent escape. At the milder word sprain they produced handcuffs and invited Macrahinish to stick his arms out. He refused and resisted and because they, as I had done, underestimated both his strength and his violence, it took a hectic few minutes for them to make him secure.

'Resisting arrest,' they panted, writing it in the note-books. 'Attacking police officers in the course of their duty.'

Macrahinish's sunglasses lay on the gravel in the main yard, where he had lost them in the first tackle. I walked down to where they shone in the light and picked them up. Then I took them slowly back to him and put them in his handcuffed hands.

He stared at me through the raw-looking eyelids. He said nothing. He put the sunglasses on, and his fingers were trembling.

'Ectropion,' said the doctor, as I walked away.

'What?' I said.

'The condition of his eyes. Ectropion. Poor fellow.'

The police made no mistakes with Jody. He sat beside Macrahinish in the back of the police car with handcuffs on his wrists and the Arctic in his face. When the police went to close the doors ready to leave, he leant forward and spoke to me through rigid lips.

'You *shit*,' he said.

Rupert invited the rest of my security firm indoors for warmth and coffee and in his office I introduced them to him.

'My friend in grey flannel,' I said, 'is Charlie Canter-field. My big man in blue is Bert Huggerneck. My injured friend with the dried blood on his face is Owen Idris.'

Rupert shook hands with each and they grinned at him. He sensed immediately that there was more in their smiles than he would have expected, and he turned his enquiring gaze on me.

'Which firm do they come from?' he asked.

'Charlie's a merchant banker, Bert's a bookies' clerk, and Owen helps in my workshop.'

Charlie chuckled and said in his fruitiest Eton, 'We also run a nice line in a census, if you should ever need one.'

Rupert shook his head helplessly and fetched brandy and glasses from a cupboard.

'If I ask questions,' he said, pouring lavishly, 'will you answer them?'

'If we can,' I said.

'That dead horse in the stable. Is it Energise?'

'No. Like I said, it's a horse I bought in the States called Black Fire.'

'But the bald patch . . . Jody was so certain.'

'I did that bald patch with a razor blade. The horses were extraordinarily alike, apart from that. Especially at night, because of being black. But there's one certain way of identifying Black Fire. He has his American racing number tattoed inside his lip.'

'Why did you bring him here?'

'I didn't want to risk the real Energise. Before I saw Black Fire in America I couldn't see how to entice Jody safely. Afterwards, it was easier.'

'But I didn't get the impression earlier this evening,'

Rupert said pensively, 'that you expected them to kill the horse.'

'No ... I didn't know about Macrahinish. I mean, I didn't know he was a vet, or that he could over-rule Jody. I expected Jody just to try to steal the horse and I wanted to catch him in the act. Catch him physically committing a positive criminal act which he couldn't possibly explain away. I wanted to force the racing authorities, more than the police, to see that Jody was not the innocent little underdog they believed.'

Rupert thought it over. 'Why didn't you think he would kill him?'

'Well ... it did cross my mind, but on balance I thought it unlikely, because Energise is such a good horse. I thought Jody would want to hide him away somewhere so that he could make a profit on him later, even if he sold him as a point-to-pointer. Energise represents money, and Jody has never missed a trick in that direction.'

'But Macrahinish wanted him dead,' Rupert said.

I sighed. 'I suppose he thought it safer.'

Rupert smiled. 'You had put them in a terrible fix. They couldn't risk you being satisfied with getting your horse back. They couldn't be sure you couldn't somehow prove they had stolen it originally. But if you no longer had it, you would have found it almost impossible to make allegations stick.'

'That's right,' Charlie agreed. 'That's exactly what Steven thought.'

'Also,' I said, 'Jody wouldn't have been able to bear the thought of me getting the better of him. Apart from safety and profit, he would have taken Energise back simply for revenge.'

'You know what?' Charlie said. 'It's my guess that he probably put his entire bank balance on Padellic at Stratford, thinking it was Energise, and when Padellic turned up sixth he lost the lot. And that in itself is a tidy little motive for revenge.'

'Here,' Bert said appreciatively. 'I wonder how much Ganser bleeding Mays is down the drain for! Makes you bleeding laugh, don't it? There they all were, thinking they were backing a ringer, and we'd gone and put the real Padellic back where he belonged.'

'Trained by Rupert,' I murmured, 'to do his best.'

Rupert looked at us one by one and shook his head. 'You're a lot of rogues.'

We drank our brandy and didn't dispute it.

'Where did the American horse come from?' Rupert asked.

'Miami.'

'No . . . This morning.'

'A quiet little stable in the country,' I said. 'We had him brought to the census point . . .'

'And you should have bleeding seen him,' Bert interrupted gleefully. 'Our capitalist here, I mean. Whizzing those three horses in and out of horseboxes faster than the three card trick.'

'I must say,' Rupert said thoughtfully, 'that I've wondered just how he managed it.'

'He took bleeding Energise out of Jody's box and put it in the empty stall of the trailer which brought Black Fire. Then he put Padellic where Energise had been, in Jody's box. Then he put bleeding Black Fire where Padellic had been, in your box, that is. All three of them buzzing in a circle like a bleeding merry-go-round.'

Charlie said, smiling, 'All change at the census. Padellic started from here and went to Stratford. Black Fire started from the country and came here. And Energise started from Jody's . . .' He stopped.

'And went to where?' Rupert asked.

I shook my head. 'He's safe, I promise you.' Safe with Allie at Hantsford Manor, with Miss Johnston and Mrs Fairchild-Smith. 'We'll leave him where he is for a week or two.'

'Yeah,' Bert said, explaining. 'Because, see, we've had Jody Leeds and that red-eyed hunk of muscle of his exploding all over us with temper-temper, but what about that other one? What about that other one we've kicked right where it hurts, eh? We don't want to risk Energise getting the chop after all from Mr Squeezer bleeding Ganser down the bleeding drain Mays.'

CHAPTER SIXTEEN

Owen and I went back to London. I drove, with him sitting beside me fitfully dozing and pretending in between times that he didn't have a headache.

'Don't be silly,' I said. 'I know what it feels like. You've got a proper thumper and notwithstanding that snide crack to the doctor about your boss not letting you take a couple of days off that's what you're going to get.'

He smiled.

'I'm sorry about your head,' I said.

'I know.'

'How?'

'Charlie said.'

I glanced across at him. His face in the glow from the dashboard looked peaceful and contented. 'It's been,' he said drowsily, 'a humdinger of a day.'

It was four in the morning when we reached the house and pulled into the driveway. He woke up slowly and shivered, his eyes fuzzy with fatigue.

'You're sleeping in my bed,' I said, 'and I'm taking the sofa.' He opened his mouth. 'Don't argue,' I added. 'All right.'

I locked the car and we walked to the front door, and that's where things went wrong.

The front door was not properly shut. Owen was too sleepy to realise at once, but my heart dropped to pavement level the instant I saw it.

Burglars, I thought dumbly. Today of all days.

I pushed the door open. Everything was quiet. There was little furniture in the hall and nothing looked disturbed. Upstairs, though, it would be like a blizzard ...

'What is it?' said Owen, realising that something was wrong.

'The workshop door,' I said, pointing.

'Oh no!'

That too was ajar, and there was no question of the intruder having used a key. The whole area was split, the raw wood showing in jagged layers up and down the jamb.

We walked along the carpeted passage, pushed the door wider, and took one step through on to concrete.

One step, and stopped dead.

The workshop was an area of complete devastation.

All the lights were on. All the cupboard doors and drawers were open, and everything which should have been in them was out and scattered and smashed. The work benches were overturned and the racks of tools were torn from their moorings and great chunks of plaster had been gouged out of the walls.

All my designs and drawings had been ripped to pieces. All the prototype toys seemed to have been stamped on.

Tins of oil and grease had been opened, and the contents emptied on to the mess, and the paint I'd used on the census notices was splashed on everything the oil had missed.

The machines themselves . . .

I swallowed. I was never going to make anything else on those machines. Not ever again.

Not burglars, I thought aridly.

Spite.

I felt too stunned to speak and I imagine it was the same with Owen because for an appreciable time we both just stood there, immobile and silent. The mess before us screamed out its message of viciousness and evil, and the intensity of the hate which had committed such havoc made me feel literally sick.

On feet which seemed disconnected from my legs I took a couple of steps forward.

There was a flicker of movement on the edge of my vision away behind the half-open door. I spun on my toe with every primeval instinct raising hairs in instant alarm, and what I saw allowed no reassurance whatsoever.

Ganser Mays stood there, waiting like a hawk. The long nose seemed a sharp beak, and his eyes behind the metal-rimmed spectacles glittered with mania. He was positioning his arms for a scything downward swing, which was the movement I'd seen, and in his hands he held a heavy long-handled axe.

I leapt sideways a thousandth of a second before the killing edge swept through the place where I'd been standing.

'Get help,' I shouted breathlessly to Owen. 'Get out and get help.'

I had a blurred impression of his strained face, mouth open, eyes huge, dried blood still dark on his cheek. For an instant he didn't move and I thought he wouldn't go, but when I next caught a glimpse of the doorway, it was empty.

Whether or not he'd been actively lying in wait for me, there was no doubt that now that I was there Ganser Mays was trying to do to me what he'd already done to my possessions. I learned a good deal from him in the next few minutes. I learned about mental terror. Learned about extreme physical fear. Learned that it was no fun at all facing unarmed and untrained a man with the will and the weapon for murder.

What was more, it was my own axe.

We played an obscene sort of hide and seek round the wrecked machines. It only needed one of the ferocious chops to connect, and I would be without arm or leg if not without life. He slashed whenever he could get near enough, and I hadn't enough faith in my speed or strength to try to tackle him within slicing range. I

dodged always and precariously just out of total disaster, circling the ruined lathe . . . the milling
machine . . . the hacksaw . . . back to the lathe . . .
putting the precious bulks of metal between me and
death.

Up and down the room, again and again.

There was never a rigid line between sense and
insanity and maybe by some definitions Ganser Mays
was sane. Certainly in all that obsessed destructive fury
he was aware enough that I might escape through the
door. From the moment I'd first stepped past him into
the workshop, he gave me no chance to reach safety
that way.

There were tools scattered on the floor from the
torn-down racks, but they were mostly small and in any
case not round the machines but on the opposite side
of the workshop. I could leave the shelter of the row of
machines and cross open space to arm myself . . . but
nothing compared in weight or usefulness with that
axe, and chisels and saws and drill bits weren't worth
the danger of exposure.

If Owen came back with help, maybe I could last
out . . .

Shortage of breath . . . I was averagely fit, but no
athlete . . . couldn't pull in enough oxygen for failing
muscles . . . felt fatal weaknesses slowing my
movements . . . knew I couldn't afford to slip on the oil
or stumble over the bolts mooring the base plates to

the floor or leave my hands holding on to anything for more than a second for fear of severed fingers.

He seemed tireless, both in body and intent. I kept my attention more on the axe than his face, but the fractional views I caught of his fixed, fanatical and curiously rigid expression gave no room for hope that he would stop before he had achieved his object. Trying to reason with him would have been like arguing with an avalanche. I didn't even try.

Breath sawed through my throat. Owen ... why didn't he bloody well hurry ... if he didn't hurry he might as well come back tomorrow for all the good it would do me ...

The axe crashed down so close to my shoulder that I shuddered from imagination and began to despair. He was going to kill me. I was going to feel the bite of that heavy steel ... to know the agony and see the blood spurt ... to be chopped and smashed like everything else.

I was up at one end, where the electric motor which worked all the machines was located. He was four feet away, swinging, looking merciless and savage. I was shaking, panting and still trying frantically to escape, and it was more to distract him for a precious second than from any devious plan that I took the time to kick the main switch from off to on.

The engine hummed and activated the main belt, which turned the big wheel near the ceiling and rotated the long shaft down the workshop. All the belts to the machines began slapping as usual, except that this time half of them had been cut right through and the free ends flapped in the air like streamers.

It took his eye off me for only a blink. I circled the electric motor which was much smaller than the machines and not good cover, and he brought his head back towards me with a snap.

He saw that I was exposed. A flash of triumph crossed his pale sweating face. He whipped the axe back and high and struck at me with all his strength.

I jumped sideways in desperation and slipped and fell, and thought as I went down that this was it . . . this was the end . . . he would be on me before I could get up.

I half saw the axe go up again. I lunged out with one foot in a desperate kick at his ankles. Connected. Threw him a fraction off balance. Only a matter of a few inches: and it didn't affect the weight of his downward swing, but only its direction. Instead of burying itself in me, the blade sank into the main belt driving the machines, and for one fatal moment Ganser Mays hung on to the shaft. Whether he thought I had somehow grasped the axe and was trying to tug it away from him, heaven knows. In any case he gripped tight, and the whirling belt swept him off his feet.

The belt moved at about ten feet a second. It took one second for Ganster Mays to reach the big wheel above. I dare say he let go of the shaft at about that point, but the wheel caught him and crushed him in the small space between itself and the ceiling.

He screamed . . . a short loud cry of extremity, chokingly cut off.

The wheel inexorably whirled him through and out the other side. It would have taken more than a soft human body to stop a motor which drove machine tools.

He fell from the high point and thumped sickeningly on to the concrete not far from where I was still scrambling to get up. It had happened at such immense speed that he had been up to the ceiling and down again before I could find my feet.

The axe had been dislodged and had fallen separately beside him. Near his hand, as if all he had to do was stretch out six inches and he would be back in business.

But Ganser Mays was never going to be back in business. I stood looking down at him while the engine hummed and the big killing wheel rotated impersonally as usual, and the remaining belts to the machines slapped quietly as they always did.

There was little blood. His face was white. The spectacles had gone and the eyes were half open. The sharp nose was angled grotesquely sideways. The neck was bent at an impossible angle; and whatever else had broken, that was enough.

I stood there for a while panting for breath and sweating and trembling from fatigue and the screwed tension of past fear. Then whatever strength I had left drained abruptly away and I sat on the floor beside the electric motor and drooped an arm over it for support like a wilted lily. Beyond thought. Beyond feeling. Just dumbly and excruciatingly exhausted.

It was at that moment that Owen returned. The help he'd brought wore authentic navy blue uniform and a real black and white checkered band on his cap. He took a long slow look and summoned reinforcements.

Hours later, when they had all gone, I went back downstairs to the workshop.

Upstairs nothing, miraculously, had been touched. Either our return had interrupted the programme before it had got that far, or the workshop had been the only intended target. In any case my first sight of the peaceful sitting-room had been a flooding relief.

Owen and I had flopped weakly around in armchairs while the routine police work ebbed and flowed, and after lengthy question-and-answer sessions and the departure of the late Mr Mays we had found ourselves finally alone.

It was already Sunday morning. The sun, with no sense of fitness, was brightly shining. Regent's Park sparkled with frost and the puddles were glazed with ice.

'Go to bed,' I said to Owen.

He shook his head. 'Think I'll go home.'

'Come back when you're ready.'

He smiled. 'Tomorrow,' he said. 'For a spot of sweeping up.'

When he'd gone I wandered aimlessly about, collecting coffee cups and emptying ashtrays and thinking disconnected thoughts. I felt both too tired and too unsettled for sleep, and it was then that I found myself going back to the devastation in the workshop.

The spirit of the dead man had gone. The place no longer vibrated with violent hate. In the morning light it looked a cold and sordid shambles, squalid debris of a spent orgy.

I walked slowly down the room, stirring things with my toe. The work of twenty years lay there in little pieces. Designs torn like confetti. Toys crushed flat. Nothing could be mended or saved.

I supposed I could get duplicates at least of the design drawings if I tried, because copies were lodged in the patents' office. But the originals, and all the hand-made prototype toys, were gone for good.

I came across the remains of the merry-go-round which I had made when I was fifteen. The first Rola; the beginning of everything. I squatted down and stirred the pieces, remembering that distant decisive summer when I'd spent day after day in my uncle's workshop with ideas gushing like newly-drilled oil out of a brain that was half child, half man.

I picked up one of the little horses. The blue one,

with a white mane and tail. The one I'd made last of the six.

The golden barley-sugar rod which had connected it to the revolving roof was snapped off jaggedly an inch above the horse's back. One of the front legs was missing, and one of the ears.

I turned it over regretfully in my hands and looked disconsolately around at the mess. Poor little toys. Poor beautiful little toys, broken and gone.

It had cost me a good deal, one way and another, to get Energise back.

Turn the handle, Charlie had said, and all the little toys would revolve on their spindles and do what they should. But people weren't toys, and Jody and Macrahinish and Ganser Mays had jumped violently off their spindles and stripped the game out of control.

If I hadn't decided to take justice into my own hands I wouldn't have been kicked or convicted of drunkenness. I would have saved myself the price of Black Fire and a host of other expenses. I wouldn't have put Owen at risk as a guard, and I wouldn't have felt responsible for the ruin of Jody and Felicity, the probable return to jail of Macrahinish, and the death of Ganser Mays.

Pointless to say that I hadn't meant them so much harm, or that their own violence had brought about their own doom. It was I who had given them the first push.

Should I have done it?

1141

Did I wish I hadn't?

I straightened to my feet and smiled ruefully at the shambles, and knew that the answer to both questions was no.

EPILOGUE

I gave Energise away.

Six weeks after his safe return to Rupert's stable he ran in the Champion Hurdle and I took a party to Cheltenham to cheer him on. A sick tycoon having generously lent his private box, we went in comfort, with lunch before and champagne after and a lot of smiling in between.

The four newly-registered joint-owners were having a ball and slapping each other on the back with glee: Bert, Allie, Owen and Charlie, as high in good spirits as they'd been at the census.

Charlie had brought the bridge-playing wife and Bert his fat old mum, and Owen had shyly and unexpectedly produced an unspoiled daughter of sixteen. The oddly mixed party proved a smash-hit success, my four conspirators carrying it along easily on the strength of liking each other a lot.

While they all went off to place bets and look at the horses in the parade ring, I stayed up in the box. I stayed there most of the afternoon. I had found it

impossible, as the weeks passed, to regain my old innocent enthusiasm for racing. There was still a massive
movement of support and sympathy for Jody, which I
supposed would never change. Letters to sporting
papers spoke of sympathy for his misfortunes and
disgust for the one who had brought them about.
Racing columnists, though reluctantly convinced of his
villainy, referred to him still as the 'unfortunate' Jody.
Quintus, implacably resentful, was ferreting away
against me in the Jockey Club and telling everyone it
was my fault his son had made 'misjudgements'. I had
asked him how it could possibly be my fault that Jody
had made the misjudgement of taking Macrahinish and
Ganser Mays for buddy-buddies, and had received no
answer.

I had heard unofficially the results of the autopsy
on Black Fire. He had been killed by a massive dose
of chloroform injected between the ribs straight into
the heart. Quick, painless, and positively the work of a
practised hand.

The veterinary bag found beside the dead horse had
contained a large hypodermic syringe with a sufficient
length of needle; traces of chloroform inside the syringe
and Macrahinish's fingerprints outside.

These interesting facts could not be generally broad-
cast on account of the forthcoming trial, and my high-
up police informant had made me promise not to repeat
them.

Jody and Macrahinish were out on bail, and the

racing authorities had postponed their own enquiry until the law's verdict should be known. Jody still technically held his trainer's licence.

The people who to my mind had shown most sense had been Jody's other owners. One by one they had melted apologetically away, reluctant to be had for mugs. They had judged without waiting around for a jury, and Jody had no horses left to train. And that in itself, in many eyes, was a further crying shame to be laid at my door.

I went out on the balcony of the kind tycoon's box and stared vacantly over Cheltenham racecourse. Moral victory over Jody was impossible, because too many people still saw him, despite everything, as the poor hardworking little man who had fallen foul of the rich robber baron.

Charlie came out on the balcony in my wake.

'Steven? What's the matter? You're too damned quiet.'

'What we did,' I said sighing, 'has changed nothing.'

'Of course it has,' he said robustly. 'You'll see. Public opinion works awful slowly. People don't like doing about-turns and admitting they were fooled. But you trust your Uncle Charlie, this time next year, when they've got over their red faces, a lot of people will quietly be finding you're one of their best friends.'

'Yeah,' I said.

'Quintus,' he said positively, 'is doing himself a lot of personal no good just now with the hierarchy. The *on dit* round the bazaars is that if Quintus can't see his son is a full-blown criminal he is even thicker than anyone thought. I tell you, the opinion where it matters is one hundred per cent for you, and our little private enterprise is the toast of the cigar circuit.'

I smiled. 'You make me feel better even if you do lie in your teeth.'

'As God's my judge,' he said, virtuously, and spoiled it by glancing a shade apprehensively skywards.

'I saw Jody,' I said. 'Did you know?'

'No!'

'In the City,' I nodded. 'Him and Felicity, coming out of some law offices.'

'What happened?'

'He spat,' I said.

'How like him.'

They had both looked pale and worried and had stared at me in disbelief. Jody's ball of mucus landed at my feet, punctuation mark of how he felt. If I'd known they were likely to be there I would have avoided the district by ten miles, but since we were accidentally face to face I asked him straight out the question I most wanted answered.

'Did you send Ganser Mays to smash my place up?'

'He told him how to make you suffer,' Felicity said spitefully. 'Serves you right.'

She cured in that one sentence the pangs of conscience I'd had about the final results of the Energise shuttle.

'You're a bloody fool, Jody,' I said. 'If you'd dealt straight with me I'd've bought you horses to train for the Classics. With your ability, if you'd been honest, you could have gone to the top. Instead, you'll be warned off for life. It is you, believe me, who is the mug.'

They had both stared at me sullenly, eyes full of frustrated rage. If either of them should have a chance in the future to do me further bad turns I had no doubt that they would. There was no one as vindictive as the man who'd done you wrong and been found out.

Charlie said beside me, 'Which do you think was the boss? Jody or Macrahinish or Ganser Mays?'

'I don't know,' I said. 'How does a triumvirate grab you?'

'Equal power?' He considered. 'Might well be, I suppose. Just three birds of a feather drawn to each other by natural evil, stirring it in unholy alliance.'

'Are all criminals so full of hate?'

'I dare say. I don't know all that many. Do you?'

'No.'

'I should think,' Charlie said, 'that the hate comes first. Some people are just natural haters. Some bully the weak, some become anarchists, some rape women, some steal with maximum mess . . . and all of them enjoy the idea of the victim's pain.'

'Then you can't cure a hater,' I said.

'With hardliners, not a chance.'

Charlie and I contemplated this sombre view and

the others came back waving Tote tickets and bubbling over with good humour.

'Here,' Bert said, slapping me on the back. 'Know what I just heard? Down in the ring, see. All those bleeding little bookies that we saved from going bust over Padellic, they're passing round the bleeding hat.'

'Just what, Bert,' said Allie, 'do you bleeding mean?'

'Here!' A huge grin spread across Bert's rugged features. 'You're a right smashing bit of goods, you are, Allie, and that's a fact. What I mean is, those little guys are making a bleeding collection all round the country, and every shop the smart alecs tried it on with, they're all putting a fiver in, and they're going to send it to the Injured Jockeys' bleeding Fund in honour of the firm of Scott, Canterfield, Ward, Idris and Huggerneck, what saved them all from disappearing down the bleeding plug-hole.'

We opened a bottle of champagne on the strength of it and Charlie said it was the eighth wonder of the world.

When the time came for the Champion Hurdle we all went down to see Energise saddled. Rupert, busy fastening buckles, looked at the ranks of shining eyes and smiled with the indulgence of the long-time professional. The horse himself could scarcely stand still, so full was he of oats and health and general excitement. I patted his elegant black neck and he tossed his head and sprayed me with a blow through his nostrils.

I said to Rupert, 'Do you think I'm too old to learn to ride?'

'Racehorses?' He pulled tight the second girth and fastened the buckle.

'Yes.'

He slapped the black rump. 'Come down Monday morning and make a start.'

'In front of all the lads?'

'Well?' He was amused, but it was an exceptional offer. Few trainers would bother.

'I'll be there,' I said.

Donny led Energise from the saddling boxes to the parade ring, closely followed by Rupert and the four new owners.

'But you're coming as well,' Allie said, protesting.

I shook my head. 'Four owners to one horse is enough.'

Bert and Charlie tugged her with them and they all stood in a little smiling group with happiness coming out of their ears. Bert's mum, Owen's daughter and Charlie's wife went off to plunder the Tote, and I, with the most reputable bookmaking firm in the business, bet five hundred pounds to three thousand that Energise would win.

We watched him from the balcony of the private box with hearts thumping like jungle drums. It was for this that we had gone to so much trouble, this few minutes ahead. For the incredible pleasure of seeing a superb creature do what he was bred, trained, endowed and eager for. For speed, for fun, for exhilaration, for love.

The tapes went up and they were away, the fourteen best hurdlers in Britain out to decide which was king.

Two miles of difficult undulating track. Nine flights of whippy hurdles. They crossed the first and the second and swept up the hill past the stands, with Energise lying sixth and moving easily, his jockey still wearing my distinctive bright blue colours because none of his new owners had any.

'Go on boyo,' Owen said, his face rapt. 'Slaughter the bloody lot of them.' Generations of fervent Welshmen echoed in his voice.

Round the top of the course. Downhill to the dip. More jumps, then the long climb on the far side. One horse fell, bringing a gasp like a gale from the stands and a moan from Allie that she couldn't bear to watch. Energise flowed over the hurdles with the economy of all great jumpers and at the top of the far hill he lay fourth.

'Get your bleeding skates on,' muttered Bert, whose knuckles showed white with clutching his raceglasses. 'Don't bleeding hang about.'

Energise obeyed the instructions. Down the leg-twisting slope he swooped like a black bird, racing level with the third horse, level with the second, pressing on the leader.

Over the next, three of them in a line like a wave. Round the last bend swept all three in a row, with

1150

nothing to choose and all to be fought for over the last of the hurdles and the taxing, tiring, pull-up to the winning post.

'I can't bear it,' Allie said. 'Oh come on, you great . . . gorgeous . . .'

'Slaughter them, boyo . . .'

'Shift, you bleeding . . .'

The voices shouted, the crowd yelled, and Charlie had tears in his eyes.

They came to the last flight all in a row, with Energise nearest the rails, furthest from the stands. He met it right, and jumped it cleanly and I had stopped breathing.

The horse in the middle hit the top of the hurdle, twisted in the air, stumbled on landing, and fell in a skidding, sliding, sprawling heap. He fell towards Energise, who had to dodge sideways to avoid him.

Such a little thing. A half-second's hesitation before he picked up his stride. But the third of the three, with a clear run, started away from the hurdle with a gain of two lengths.

Energise put his soul into winning that race. Stretched out and fought for every inch. Showed what gut and muscle could do on the green turf. Shortened the gap and closed it, and gained just a fraction at every stride.

Allie and Owen and Bert and Charlie were

screaming like maniacs, and the winning post was too near, too near.

Energise finished second, by a short head.

It's no good expecting fairytale endings, in racing.

DICK FRANCIS

Field of Thirteen

THE NEW BESTSELLER

There's a bomb scare at Kingdom Hill racecourse, where failed conman Tricksy Wilcox watches his dreams blown to kingdom come . . .

At Chelthenham's glittering National Hunt Festival, protocol is rocked as a love-struck owner falls madly in love with her jockey . . .

There is passion – and revenge – at the glorious Kentucky Derby . . .

. . . and then ten other tantalizing stories to hold you enthralled from the starting gates to the finish.

Award-winning Master of Crime Dick Francis tackles a new distance with thirteen nerve-tingling tales of politics, passion, horses and crime – each one of them tied to a milestone event in the international racing calendar.

The result is beyond question.

'At his best, Francis can make you feel the hot breath
of horses on the back of your neck'
Michael Dobbs, *Express On Sunday*

DICK FRANCIS

To the Hilt

'Another one for the winner's enclosure'
Daily Telegraph

Alexander Kinloch found solitude and a steady income painting in a bothy on a remote Scottish mountain. Until the morning the strangers arrived to rough him up, and Alexander was dragged reluctantly back into the real and violent world he thought he had left behind.

Millions of pounds are missing from his stepfather's business. A valuable racehorse is under threat. Then comes the first ugly death and the end of all Alexander's doubts. For the honour of the Kinlochs he will face the strangers . . . committed up to the hilt . . .

'The book is a cracker . . . the former champion jockey is still taking the jumps with consummate grace'
Sunday Telegraph

'Fast-moving, readable and beautifully constructed . . . a cracking yarn'
Country Life

DICK FRANCIS

For Kicks

Proprietor of a stud farm in the breathtaking region of Australia's Snowy Mountains? Or muck-raking stable boy in Yorkshire?

The Earl of October persuades young Australian Danny Roke to accept the English alternative. It's the change of scene and the challenge that pushes Danny undercover, on the scent of a suspect racehourse dope scandal.

But the pain involved, dealing with vicious swindlers and the Earl's two attractive daughters, could overturn all his pleasure in the chase . . .

DICK FRANCIS

Bonecrack

'Excitement and sheer readability'
The Daily Telegraph

It started with mistaken identify and a threat to his life.
And rapidly became a day-to-day nightmare with little
glimmer of escape.

For Neil Griffon, temporarily in charge of his father's
racing stables, blackmail is now a terrible reality. A reality
not only threatening valuable horses but testing his nerves
to the limit.

And proving just how brittle bones can be . . .

'A classic entry with a fine turn of speed'
Evening Standard